History of the Presbyterian Church in the United States of America

Vol. 2

SALZWASSER
VERLAG

E. H. Gillet

History of the Presbyterian Church in the United States of America

Vol. 2

Reprint of the original, first published in 1864.

1st Edition 2022 | ISBN: 978-3-75259-216-0

Verlag (Publisher): Salzwasser Verlag GmbH, Zeilweg 44, 60439 Frankfurt, Deutschland
Vertretungsberechtigt (Authorized to represent): E. Roepke, Zeilweg 44, 60439 Frankfurt, Deutschland
Druck (Print): Books on Demand GmbH, In de Tarpen 42, 22848 Norderstedt, Deutschland

HISTORY

OF THE

PRESBYTERIAN CHURCH

IN THE

UNITED STATES OF AMERICA.

BY THE

REV. E. H. GILLETT, D.D.

REVISED EDITION

VOL. II.

PHILADELPHIA

CONTENTS.

CHAPTER XXVIII.

OHIO, 1800–1815.

CHAPTER XXIX.

KENTUCKY, 1800–1815.

CHAPTER XL.

THE GENERAL ASSEMBLIES OF 1837 AND 1838.

CHAPTER XLI.

RESULTS OF THE DIVISION.

THE HISTORY

OF THE

PRESBYTERIAN CHURCH

IN THE

UNITED STATES.

CHAPTER XXIV.

DELAWARE.—NEW CASTLE AND LEWES PRESBYTERIES, 1787–1825.

At the commencement of the present century, the churches in the region between the Chesapeake and Delaware Bays were few, and, for the most part, feeble. There had been but little advance for several preceding years; and during the quarter of a century which followed, the progress was scarcely perceptible. Here, where were to be found some of the oldest congregations within the bounds of the Church, missionary effort was called for almost as urgently as in the new fields at the West. Year after year, missionary appointments for this region were made by the Assembly, and the pastors on the field were constrained to volunteer in this important work. Among the ministers employed in this service, from 1805, were Rev. Dr. Read, Messrs. B. Marcy, E. Glasgow, J. D. Perkins, Moderwell, Conklin, Ballantine, Scovil, Campbell, and Marshall. A portion of the means for their support was derived from the

General Assembly, and a portion from a local missionary society within the State of Delaware.

Emigration from the older States greatly retarded the growth of the Church in many places, but perhaps nowhere more seriously than in Delaware and Maryland. The population of the former State from 1800 to 1820 increased only twelve per cent. Some of the oldest churches dwindled away till they almost became extinct. It required no small effort to stay the tide of desolation and sustain what remained but was ready to die.

In 1789, the Presbytery of New Castle, extending into Pennsylvania, numbered sixteen ministers and twenty-five congregations, of which five were vacant. In 1800, it consisted of fifteen ministers, and had under its care thirty-four congregations, of which fifteen were vacant. In 1825, the number was still thirty-four.

The patriarch of the Presbytery, Dr. Robert Smith, who died in 1793, had been settled for forty-two years over the church of Pequa, Pa., with which that of Leacock was united till 1759. Under his instructions a large number of the ministers of the Church had been trained; and of his two sons, one was destined to become President of Union, and the other of Princeton, College. A thorough scholar, a devoted pastor, and a wise counsellor, his life was crowned with memories of goodness and usefulness. His successors at Pequa were William Arthur[1] (1796–1818) and Amzi Babbit. At Leacock, in conjunction with Lancaster

---

[1] William Arthur, a native of Scotland, and educated at the University of Edinburgh, was settled in Janunry, 1796. Distinguished for his common sense and firmness of purpose, and for the brevity, point, and effectiveness of his sermons, his ministry continued till 1818; although his life was continued in enfeebled health till 1827.

and Middle Octorara, Nathaniel W. Semple, a graduate of Princeton in 1776, was settled 1780–1821.

The pastorate of William McKennan over the churches of White Clay Creek and Red Clay Creek commenced in 1755, and continued till his death in 1809. For thirty-four years he had charge also of the First Church of Wilmington, where he was succeeded in 1796 by F. A. Latta, who left soon after 1803. The Christiana, popularly called "Second Presbyterian," Church was formed by a colony from the First in 1772, under Joseph Smith, whose pastorate continued to 1778. His successors were William R. Smith (1779–96), Thomas Read (1798–1817), E. W. Gilbert (1817–34 and 1849–41), William Hogarth (1841–46), J. E. Rockwell (1849–51), A. D. Pollock (1852–55), William Aikman (1857–68), Lafayette Marks (1869——). Under Dr. Gilbert's pastorate a new church edifice was erected, and the name changed to Hanover Street Presbyterian Church. The First Church, meanwhile, remained vacant for a long period after the dismission of Mr. Latta, and was temporarily supplied by Dr. Read after his dismission from the Second Church.[1]

At Fagg's Manor—associated with the name and labors of Samuel Blair—John E. Finley labored as pastor from 1777 till his removal to Kentucky in 1795. His successors were Patrick Davidson (1798–1807 ?), Robert White (1810–35), and A. Hamilton.

At Donegal, Pa., Colin McFarquhar had been long settled, but was succeeded about 1809 by William Kerr, —"highly esteemed by his brethren,"—who died in

---

[1] The Central Presbyterian Church of Wilmington was organized by the Presbytery of Wilmington, Dec. 6, 1855. The original membership numbered twenty-three. On Jan. 1, 1856, G. F. Wiswell was called as pastor. The church has been prosperous, and has enjoyed successive seasons of revival.—*Presbyterian Almanac*, 1860.

1823. His successor, who had charge also of Marietta was Orson Douglass.

At Chesnut Level, Pa., the pastorate of Dr. James Latta, which commenced in 1770, closed in 1800. It was several years before his son Francis A. Latta, whose ministry continued till 1834, was settled as his successor.

At Forks of Brandywine, where for twenty-five years previous John Carmichael had made proof of a faithful ministry, Nathan Grier was settled in 1787. Upon his death, in 1814, his son, Dr. John N. C. Grier, was chosen unanimously as his successor, and has retained the pastorate for nearly half a century.

Christiana and New Castle had long been vacant, when—Aug. 13, 1800—John E. Latta commenced his pastorate of the united congregations, closing it with his life in 1824.

White Clay and Head of Christiana had John McCreary probably from 1769 to 1799. Subsequently, for several years, the churches were vacant. About 1812, Andrew K. Russell succeeded McCreary, and remained for several years.

Upper Octorara and Doe Run, Pa., had Alexander Mitchel in 1789. He left in 1795–96, and the churches remained vacant until the settlement of James Latta, whose pastorate has extended down to a recent period.

At Middletown and Pencader, Thomas Smith was settled previous to 1789, but left before 1795. In 1809, Pencader was reported as forming a united charge with St. George's, where John Burton was laboring in 1789 and John Collins in 1803. In 1796–9, Pencader and Middletown were united under William Chealy; but in 1814 we find Pencader united with St. George's under Samuel Bell, who was still in charge in 1825, Middletown meanwhile disappearing from the roll of Presbytery.

At Center and Bethel, Md., George Lucky commenced, previous to 1786, a pastorate which continued for over a quarter of a century. At Slate Ridge, Dr. Samuel Martin was settled in 1793, taking charge shortly after of Chancetord, and, with an interval of a few months (1812), his pastorate of about fifty years was in connection with these two congregations. Of Middletown and Lower Brandywine Thomas Grier took charge about 1801–02, but left before 1809. Previous to 1814, Lower Brandywine formed a part of the charge of Samuel Henderson, in connection with Red Clay Creek and Doe Run, of which he had meanwhile taken charge. At West Nottingham, where James Munro was laboring in 1789, James Magraw was settled previous to 1809; and here he continued for many years. At New London, Pa., and the Rock,—reported vacant from 1789 to 1814,—Robert Graham was reported pastor at the latter date, and here remained for several years. At the same time (1814) William Finney was reported settled at Deer Creek, where he still remained in 1819. Of quite a number of vacant congregations more than one-half were unable to support a pastor.

Several of the names mentioned above are worthy of more specific notice. Among them we may mention especially those of Grier, Read, Gilbert, the two sons of Dr. Latta, and Dr. Martin. Grier was of Scotch-Irish descent, but a native of Bucks county, Pennsylvania. Devoted to God from his youth, and remarkable for piety from his early years, he intelligently devoted himself to the work of the ministry. His classical studies were pursued under his brother, Rev. James Grier, of Deep Run. In 1783 he was a graduate of the University of Pennsylvania, and in 1786 he was licensed to preach by the Presbytery of Philadelphia. In the following year he was settled at the Forks of the Brandywine, and there continued to labor for twenty-seven years. His successor was his son, John N. C. Grier.

In his devotion to his large and important charge, Mr. Grier was eminently blessed. Firm of purpose, faithful in duty, but dignified as well as affable in demeanor, his whole course secured respect and esteem. Many of the ministers of the Church, as well as his own sons, were trained for future usefulness under his direction. His reputation as a teacher and a preacher stood deservedly high; while "the quiet and order of his house, his example as a devoted Christian, pastor, and preacher, his pleasant manners, his kind and ready efforts to promote the piety, comfort, and knowledge of his students," rendered the memory of the times and circumstances with which his name was associated "pleasant and imperishable."

Dr. Thomas Read, from 1798 to 1817 the pastor of the Second Presbyterian Church of Wilmington, was of Irish descent, a native of Maryland, and a pupil of Dr. Francis Alison at the University of Pennsylvania. For some years he was engaged as tutor of the Classical Academy at Newark, not far from his native place. From 1772 to 1797 he was settled as pastor at Drawyer's Creek, in Delaware. He found his people a small and feeble band. They worshipped in "a log house in the midst of the wilderness;" but in 1773 they erected a capacious brick edifice for worship, and became ultimately one of the most flourishing congregations in the State.[1] While laboring in this connection, he performed much missionary labor, taking a circuit in the surrounding

---

[1] Drawyer's is reported vacant after Dr. Read left in 1797. In 1809 this was still the case. In 1814 and 1819, John Burton is reported as stated supply. In 1825, Joseph Wilson had charge of Drawyer's, Middletown, and Smyrna, or Duck Creek; but Smyrna was given up after one year.

region of from thirty to forty miles. Grave and dignified in manner, devoted to his work, impressive and earnest in speech, and consistent in life, his labors were remarkably blessed.

His successor was Eliphalet W. Gilbert, afterward President of Delaware College, and finally pastor of the Western Presbyterian Church of Philadelphia. Dr. Gilbert received his collegiate education at Union College and his theological at Princeton Seminary, and in 1817, after a missionary tour to the West, was settled at Wilmington. Self-forgetful, disinterested, and devoted, an independent thinker, fearless in utterance, but with a gentleness of demeanor that changed opponents to friends, he labored in this sphere of the pastorate, with a short intermission, until 1841.

Like his predecessor, he was in the habit of making missionary visits, sometimes in company with other brethren, to different towns and neighborhoods in the peninsula. The results of these were cheering. Great good was accomplished. New churches were established, feeble ones were strengthened, and some of the prominent men of the region, who had before been neglectful of religion, were thus brought to reflection and repentance.

Of John E. Latta and Francis A. Latta,—the two sons of Rev. Dr. James Latta, pastor of Deep Run and afterward of Chesnut Level congregation, in Lancaster county, Pa.,—the first was settled at New Castle and Christiana village, and the last at Wilmington. The first was for several years permanent clerk of the General Assembly, and for a number of years he had an academy at New Castle, in connection with which several men of high distinction in Church and State were educated. Intelligent, exemplary, and conscientious, with warm sympathies, enlarged views, and liberal feelings, he was honored with universal respect and esteem. He was "a faithful, clear, and instructive expounder of the word of God."

His brother Francis was an excellent classical scholar, a man of fine and well-cultivated mind, a poet, and an eloquent pulpit-orator. There were few, if any, in his day who could be accounted his superiors in scholarly pursuits and the graces of public speech. During a large part of his ministry he devoted himself to the work of a teacher, and in the latter part of his life to that exclusively.

At Chanceford, Pa., for nearly half a century Samuel Martin, a native of Chesnut Level and a theological pupil of Dr. James Latta and Dr. Smith of Pequa, lived and labored. His early life was that of a farmer's boy; and, though under the training of Christian parents, it was not until his conversion, in his twenty-second year, that his attention was drawn to a preparation for the ministry. By native energy he was enabled to overcome many obstacles, and in 1790 was graduated at the University of Pennsylvania. Licensed in 1793 by Baltimore Presbytery, he was soon after ordained and installed pastor of Slate Ridge, Pa., between which and the congregation of Chanceford—after serving the first exclusively for five years—he divided his labors. With the exception of about eighteen months during which he removed to Rockville, Md., this was the scene of his pastorate until his death in 1845.

Rarely has any people enjoyed the services of a pastor more worthy or beloved. In him the lofty characteristics of a noble mind were combined with the simplicity and playfulness of a child. Void of worldly ambition, he aimed simply to be useful. Sincere, generous, ardent, he was a guileless friend, and placed himself on a level with the humblest that approached him. Yet he was "a master in Israel," and in the higher ecclesiastical courts an able debater. His ministerial qualifications were of no common order The announcement—wherever he was known—that he was expected to preach, secured a crowded house. His sermons were seldom written, and his Sabbath preparations were embodied in a few brief notes. His Bible and Concordance constituted his authorities for reference. His delivery was energetic and animated, and his discourses at once convinced the mind and impressed the heart. An independent thinker, he dealt not so much with commonplace ideas draped in fine rhetoric, as in glowing thoughts adorned by their freshness and originality or arresting attention by their simple grandeur.

Before the commencement of the Revolutionary War, the Presbytery of Lewes, the bounds of which extended over Southern Delaware and the Eastern Shore of Maryland, had been reduced (1773) to but four members. These were John Miller[1] (1749–91), of Dover and Smyrna, Matthew Wilson (1756–90), of Lewestown, Cool Spring, and Indian River (1767–90), Jacob Ker (1764–95), who for about nine years had been in charge of the old congregations of Monokin and Wicomoco, and Alexander Huston, pastor (1764–85) till his death of Murderkill and Three Runs. The care of the feeble churches devolved upon these men a double duty at a time when their own congregations seemed to claim their entire attention. Throughout the period of the war, only on three occasions was a single member of Presbytery present at the meeting of Synod,—Ebenezer Brooks, whose connection with the body was but transient, in 1777, and John Miller, whose health was already greatly enfeebled, in 1780 and 1781.

The peculiar circumstances in which they were placed

---

[1] Father of Professor Miller, of Princeton.

fully sufficed to account for their absence.[1] The hazards to which their journey would expose them were too perilous to be encountered; and as to Dr. Wilson,[2] his decided preference for Congregationalism, in which he failed to secure the co-operative sympathy of Miller,—though the latter had been ordained in Boston by a council of which Sewall, Webb, and Byles were members,—would not incline him to any thing which could be construed into ecclesiastical martyrdom. These four men—Miller, an exemplary, self-denying, laborious, studious, and devoted pastor, Wilson, mild, instructive, persuasive, rather than animated or powerful, and with few superiors for talent, learning, or devoted piety, Ker, "a great and good man," "a bright luminary in the Church, who lived exemplarily, preached warmly, and prayed fervently," and Huston, over whose early decease the tears of many fell—had before them an extended but destitute field, which demanded of them a measure of culture which they were unable to bestow. The feeble health of both Miller and Wilson devolved upon Ker and Huston an increased burden. They could not comply "with half the calls made upon them to preach and to administer the ordinances." At this crisis it was resolved to petition the adjoining Presbytery of New Castle for aid. An urgent appeal was drawn up (Oct. 19, 1773), setting forth the fact that "here are numbers of starving souls crying to us for the bread of life, and we are unable to assist them. We therefore apply to you, our dear Christian fellow-laborers, who are not only concerned for your particular churches, but for the whole Church of Christ, and earnestly request you, as you regard the common

---

[1] For fifteen months the Tory agitation prevented the Presbytery from meeting.

[2] Father of Rev. Dr. James Patriot Wilson, of Philadelphia.

interest of our Lord Jesus, that you send us what supplies you possibly can."

Two noble-hearted young men caught the echo of this "Macedonian cry," and responded promptly to the appeal.[1] These were Samuel McMaster and John Rankin. The former found his field of labor at Snow Hill and Pitts Creek; the latter, who was as yet only a candidate, was not licensed until 1775. Supplying for a time the churches of Buckingham and Blackwater, yet extending his labors to the vacant churches of Fishing Creek and Vienna, he received from the former a call to settle with them, with which he complied in 1778.

For more than twenty years his ministry was efficient and successful. He had great difficulties to meet. The distractions of the times, political and martial strife, and the sufferings and hardships inflicted by the war, constituted but a portion of his obstacles. "Wicked men walked abroad in the unrestrained indulgence of every lust, infidelity was rife, strange sectarists were diffusing their erroneous and even poisonous sentiments over the length and breadth of the Peninsula," and at no time, perhaps, had the prospects of religion been more dark or dubious.

But Rankin devoted himself to his work; and his labors were not in vain. A well-trained[2] and able theologian, a fervid and zealous preacher, with a ready utterance and a manifest sincerity which commanded confidence, he was attentively listened to wherever he went. Few men have enjoyed greater popularity, and fewer still have turned it to better account. With unremitting energy he visited the waste places, and preached to the destitute wherever he could find them.

---

[1] Sprague, iii. 361.

[2] His theological instructor was Dr. Read, of Wilmington.

His own church was remarkably blessed. It was not long before the old frame building in which he entered upon his work had to be pulled down to accommodate his increasing congregation, and a stately and commodious brick edifice was erected, which, after withstanding the storms of more than seventy winters, was unroofed and dilapidated by the tempest of January, 1857.

Mr. Rankin left behind him a hallowed memory. The charm of his conversations, exhortations, and sermons long lingered in the minds of those that heard them, and in the traditions of his life and labors. His holy influence had its record in many a humble memorial, though the records of the Sessions of his churches have not been preserved. With his name is associated a character which combined cheerfulness, energy, piety, and usefulness. Not a traditionary reminiscence of an imprudence or indiscretion seems to have survived him. The obituary record of the Presbytery pronounced that in him "the Church had lost a zealous advocate, the Presbytery a worthy member, and his country a warm patriot." He died in 1798, and after several years Charles Wallace[1] was reported (1814–19) pastor of Blackwater, Buckingham, and Queponco.

Upon the death of Wilson, who had been settled at Lewes, in conjunction with Cool Spring, from 1756 to 1790, he was succeeded by Francis Hindman (who had charge also of Indian River), John Burton (so reported in 1799 and 1803), James P. Wilson (1804–06), and Joseph Copes (1809 and 1819). Benjamin Ogden was pastor at Lewes in 1825.

At Murderkill, Three Runs, and Johnstown,[2] McKee's

---

[1] In 1809 he was at "Queen Ann's." Stuart Williamson had charge of the churches in 1804.

[2] Sometimes written St. Johnston.

ministry closed before 1795; soon after which he was succeeded by John Johnson, who left before 1801, although he is again reported at Murderkill in 1803. Both churches were vacant in 1809, and neither appears on the roll of Presbytery in 1819. From 1795 Dover is reported vacant till 1819, when E. P. Swift was stated supply for Dover and Milford. In 1825, Robert M. Laird is reported as settled at Princess Ann.

Not long after the death of Jacob Ker, in 1795, the churches of Monokin and Wicomoco came under the pastoral charge of John B. Slemons, who continued with them for over twenty years. The pastorate of Samuel McMaster over the congregations of Snow Hill, Pitts Creek, and Rehoboth, which commenced about 1775, continued till after 1809; in 1814 he had been succeeded by Stuart Williamson, but in 1819 they were left vacant. In 1825, Thomas B. Balch was pastor.[1]

Thus the Presbytery of Lewes scarcely made good what it lost by deaths and removals. In 1802 it numbered but four ministers, the same as in 1773. In 1808 there had been no increase; and for several years—its feebleness had become such—it was conjoined (reports for 1814 and 1819) with the Presbytery of New Castle. In 1825, after the Presbytery of Lewes had been restored, it numbered eighteen churches, with six ministers and two licentiates. The Presbytery of New Castle at the same time had under its care thirty-four churches, and numbered twenty-one ministers. About two-thirds of its churches were in Pennsylvania, and several of them were quite large and flourishing.[2]

---

[1] At Columbia, Stephen Boyer was settled soon after 1814, and continued till about 1830. Queen Ann's was vacant in 1795; and, although Charles Wallace was reported there in 1809, it thencefor h disappears from the roll of Presbytery.

[2] The large membership of the several charges, averaging for

CHAPTER XXV.

MARYLAND AND VIRGINIA, 1800-1820.

BALTIMORE Presbytery, which had seven pastors in 1800, had but eight in 1818. The growth of the Church had been rather in the strengthening of congregations already established, than in the gathering of new organizations. At Baltimore, the church of which Dr. Allison was so long pastor—from 1763 until his death in 1802—could not agree on the choice of a successor. James Inglis and John Glendy were rival candidates, the former receiving a call by a bare majority. The friends of the latter, resolved to secure his services, withdrew, in order to form a new congregation; and in 1803 a house of worship was erected, and in due time Mr. Glendy was installed as pastor.

The first efforts to establish the Third Church date from 1819. In October of that year, Nicholas Patterson, a licentiate of the Presbytery of Philadelphia, on a visit to the city, found no evangelical church west of Eutaw Street. Happening to step into a school-

each over two hundred, indicated their general prosperity. The Fagg's Manor Church, under Robert White, reported four hundred and fourteen; the Upper Octorara, under James Latta, three hundred and seventy-three; Forks of Brandywine, under John N. C. Grier, three hundred and forty-eight; Leacock and Middle Octorara, under Joseph Barr, two hundred and thirty-two; while within the bounds of Delaware, the Second Church of Wilmington had three hundred and thirty-three, New Castle and Christiana one hundred and sixty-six, Head of Christiana and White Clay Creek two hundred and seventy-two, and St. George's and Pencader one hundred and eighty-seven.

house in Franklin Street, near the present Twelfth Presbyterian Church, he was invited to address the children. The effect was such that the teacher, Mr. Vallow, offered the room as a place for preaching and holding a school on the Sabbath. Meetings were held here, at which some of the most devoted Christians of different evangelical denominations in Baltimore frequently attended. A Sabbath-school of one hundred and sixty scholars was gathered, and the prospect was so encouraging that steps were soon taken to organize a church. Two thousand dollars were secured in Baltimore, and aid was solicited at the North. In May, 1822, the organization was effected, and in the following year W. C. Walton was installed as pastor. He left in the following year, and in 1827 the church was supplied by Truman Osborn, who remained for about two years. In 1830–31, George W. Musgrave was installed as pastor.[1]

At Georgetown the pastorate of Dr. Balch extended from 1782 to 1833, and his successor was John C. Smith. At Alexandria, Elias Harrison was called (1817) as assistant of Dr. Muir; and a Second Church was shortly afterward organized, under the pastoral care of Wells Andrews. The latter was succeeded in May, 1827, by

[1] The Fourth and Fifth Churches were organized about 1835–36. In 1837, the pastors of the city were—John C. Backus of the First Church, R. J. Breckenridge of the Second, G. W. Musgrave of the Third, and James G. Hamner of the Fifth, while Sheridan Guiteau was stated supply of the Fourth. In 1820, on the death of Dr. Inglis in that year, William Nevins was ordained and installed as his successor. Upon his death, in 1835, Dr. Backus was called to succeed him. In 1826, John Breckenridge was settled as colleague of Dr. Glendy in the Second Church. The former was called in 1831 to the Secretaryship of the Board of Education in Philadelphia, and Dr. Glendy died in 1832. In the course of the year (Nov. 1832), R. J. Breckenridge was called to succeed him (1832-45).

William C. Walton, who was dismissed in October, 1832. His successor in 1836 was Dr. William Hill, whose pastorate continued only for two years.

At Washington, the efforts of the Associate Reformed to establish a Presbyterian church delayed the measures taken for establishing one in connection with the Assembly. After a few years, however, Bladensburg and Washington were the joint charge of John Brackenridge. Meanwhile, Samuel Knox, of Fredericktown, had accepted the Presidency of Baltimore College. Enoch Matson still (1819) remained in the pastorate at (the Island of) Bermuda, and Joshua T. Russell had for a short time been settled at Cabin John, while Patrick Davidson had succeeded Samuel Knox at Fredericktown and Pipe Creek. The other members of the Presbytery in 1819 were Thomas L. Birch, William Maffit, James Carnahan, engaged as a teacher at Georgetown, Thomas C. Searle, Thomas B. Balch, and Andrew Hunter,—the last a chaplain in the service of the United States.[1]

---

[1] A letter from Rev. Dr. S. Martin, written March 20, 1839, published in the "Presbyterian Standard," April 16, 1863, says of another minister of Maryland, although a member of the Presbytery of New Castle,—

"The Rev. George Lucky, who labored and died at Bethel, Harford county, Md., and for a large part of his time also preached at Centre Church, about seven miles north of Bethel on the Maryland and Pennsylvania line, was born in Fagg's Manor, Chester county, Pa., and brought up under the ministry of Mr. Blair. He was a fine classical scholar, an intelligent preacher, in his manners plain, in labors unwearied; in his pastoral labors from house to house he excelled. Few, very few, had an equal acquaintance with the Scriptures; and he had an art, possessed by but few, of introducing religious duties when thrown into society who were ignorant of them and had an aversion from them. He was a Calvinist full grown."

Mr. Lucky's name first appears on the Minutes of Synod in 1785 It is last mentioned in 1819.

In 1823, the Presbytery of the District of Columbia was formed from that of Baltimore, leaving to the latter, beside the churches of the city, only those of Bethel, and Fredericktown and Pipe Creek. Of the first of these, George Morrison was pastor till after 1833; of Fredericktown, vacant for several years, James G. Hamner became pastor in 1831–32; but previous to 1837, both had been dismissed.

In 1825, the Presbytery of the District of Columbia consisted of thirteen ministers and nine churches,—Dr. Balch, and his colleague, John N. Campbell, at Georgetown, John Brackenridge at Bladensburg, John Mines at Cabin John and Bethesda, James Laurie, of the Associate Reformed Church of Washington, who in 1822 came into connection with the General Assembly, Reuben Post, of the First Church, Washington, Daniel Baker, of the Second Church, Elias Harrison and Wells Andrews, of the First and Second Churches of Alexandria, together with some other ministers without charge. No other churches, with the single exception of the Fourth Church of Washington, were organized in connection with the Presbytery previous to 1837.

Although the city of Washington was founded and the corner-stone of the Capitol laid in 1793, it was not till 1800 that it became the seat of government; and it was three years later before a successful effort was made to establish here a Presbyterian church.

The enterprise, in the form which it assumed, was due to the forethought of Dr. John M. Mason, of New York. On his visit to Scotland in 1802, he induced several young clergymen to accompany him on his return to this country, to seek in the new settlements fields of missionary labor.[1] One of these young men was James Laurie, a native of Edinburgh, a graduate

[1] Sprague, iv. 314.

of Edinburgh University, and a licentiate of the Associate Presbytery of Edinburgh. When the seat of the Federal Government was removed to Washington, it was deemed important that some clergyman of high standing and character should be located there; and Mr. Laurie was the person whom Dr. Mason designated for the field. In March, 1803, Mr. Laurie, who had been in this country but a few months, at the request of several gentlemen—among them the late venerable Joseph Nourse—visited Washington, with the view of endeavoring to gather there an Associate Reformed congregation. The city at that time existed only on paper and in the landmarks of the surveyor. It is said that Mr. Laurie, on what he supposed his way thither, inquired of the stage-driver how far it was to the city, and received for reply, "Sir, we have been driving through it for the last two miles."

A congregation was soon gathered, and in June, 1803, he was installed as pastor. For several years he preached in the old Treasury building burned by the British in 1814. Meanwhile, he was exerting himself to collect funds for the erection of a church-edifice. After travelling as far north as Boston and as far south as Savannah, securing such aid as he could, he had at length the satisfaction of seeing, early in 1807, a substantial and, for that day, elegant brick edifice opened for public worship. It is now known as the F Street Church; and it was the first place of Protestant worship erected in the national capital. In that building Mr. Laurie was spared to officiate for forty-six years. In 1822, in common with a considerable portion of the Associated Reformed Church in this country, his ecclesiastical relations and those of his church were transferred so as to bring him into connection with the churches under the care of the General Assembly.

The history of the Second Presbyterian Church of

the city—known as the First, because the first in connection with the General Assembly—dates from 1809. In May of that year, the General Assembly[1] authorized the Presbytery of Baltimore to employ a missionary at Bladensburg, and "in the city of Washington, near the navy-yard, to be compensated for not more than three months." In the following year they were authorized to employ one "in the city of Washington and at Bladensburg for six months." In 1811, John Brackenridge was appointed a missionary for three months in this field; and from this period he continued for several years in charge of the newly-organized church, leaving it, however, previous to 1819, and taking subsequently the pastoral charge of Bladensburg.[2]

After his withdrawal, Reuben Post,[3] a licentiate of Baltimore Presbytery in 1819, became the pastor of the church. This relation he continued to sustain for about twenty years; and his successors have been Charles Rich, William T. Sprole, and Byron Sunderland.

In 1820–21, it was felt by quite a number of individuals that there was a call for the organization of

---

[1] Minutes of Assembly

[2] From the Assembly's minutes, it appears that Mr. Brackenridge was a licentiate of Baltimore Presbytery in 1795, and that he soon after resided in Washington, which is reported in 1798 as his charge He probably supplied a congregation here for several years in connection with one at Bladensburg, although from 1801 to 1809 he is reported without charge. After 1801, Washington is reported unable to support a pastor. The organization of Dr. Laurie's church doubtless led to the abandonment for a time of the original enterprise.

[3] Reuben Post was a native of Vermont, and a graduate of Middlebury College and Princeton Seminary. He was ordained over the First Presbyterian Church in Washington in 1819. Here he remained till his removal to the pastorate of the Circular Church, Charleston, 1836, where he labored till his death, September 24, 1858. He was zealous and faithful in the discharge of his duty

another Presbyterian church. Proceeding immediately to the erection of a house of worship (near the Presidential mansion), the congregation met from Sabbath to Sabbath in the navy building, and invited Daniel Baker to supply the pulpit. He did so for a short time, and was subsequently elected pastor.[1] Declining a call to Savannah in the church made vacant by the death of Dr. Kollock, Mr. Baker entered upon his labors at Washington. The church numbered but thirty-nine members, and his salary was only six hundred dollars. A clerkship in the Land-Office, with a salary of eight hundred dollars, was secured for him; and thus, under burdensome exactions, he was enabled to sustain himself in his position. In the spring of 1828 he resigned his charge,—the number of the communicants having increased to one hundred and forty-two.

His successors in the pastorate were John N. Campbell and E. D. Smith. After the resignation of the former, an attempt was made to recall Mr. Baker, but in vain. The church continued feeble, and after the resignation of Mr. Smith in 1836 the membership had fallen to ninety-seven.

The Fourth Presbyterian Church of Washington—the F Street Church, by its uniting with the Presbytery, taking the place of the Third—was organized in 1827–28, and in 1829 its membership—thirty-six in the preceding year—had been doubled. Shortly after this, Joshua N. Danforth became stated supply, but after one or two years was succeeded by Mason Noble, who in 1832–33 became the pastor of the church. His successor, after his removal to New York, was John C. Smith.

Of those pastors who have labored in the field which at the commencement of the century was occupied by

---

[1] Life of Rev. D. Baker.

Baltimore Presbytery and who have been called to their reward, there are not a few well entitled to command the respect and affection of the Church. Inglis, Glendy, Nevins, and J. Breckenridge, of Baltimore, Laurie, Baker, and Post, of Washington, Walton, of Baltimore and Alexandria, Balch, of Georgetown, Muir and Harrison, of Alexandria, are the principal names which arrest our attention. Some of these have been briefly noticed already, or will be spoken of in another connection. Muir, Inglis, Glendy, and Balch for the first twenty years of the century were the leading men in this Presbytery.

At Alexandria, James Muir had been pastor of the Presbyterian church since 1789. He was a native of Scotland, a graduate of Glasgow University, and was licensed by the Scotch Presbytery in London in 1779.[1] Two years later he was ordained as an evangelist to Bermuda, where he remained, engaged in teaching and preaching, for nearly eight years. For some months after his arrival in this country he preached in New York, as a candidate for the post of colleague with Dr. Rodgers; but, as the congregation were divided between him and (Dr.) Jedediah Morse, both withdrew, and shortly after Mr. Muir was called to Alexandria.

A severe student, systematic in the discharge of pastoral duty, deeply impressed with the momentous responsibility of his charge, he might have sat for Cowper's well-drawn portrait of a "preacher like Paul." A United States Senator described him as "a short man, of short sermons and short sentences." This was strictly true. His discourses were carefully and elaborately prepared, and every thing redundant was expunged. He preached with his manuscript in his pocket and his sermon in his memory, while from

---

[1] Sprague, iii. 516.

a small Bible open before him he read the frequent passages of Scripture, which were as familiar to him as the alphabet. Although with a marked Scotch accent, and a defect in his utterance which interfered with his oratory, his discourses were clear, logical, concise, and rich with divine truth.

In March, 1818, Elias (now Dr.) Harrison was installed over the church as co-pastor, succeeding, on the death of Dr. Muir in 1820, to the sole pastorate, which he retained till a recent period.

During the closing period of Dr. Muir's ministry, the church was sadly divided,—although the character of Dr. Muir for gentleness and Christian forbearance could not be called in question.

The occasion of this exciting state of things was the necessity of calling a colleague pastor with Dr. Muir.[1] Two candidates were before the congregation,—one, Daniel Baker, of revival memory, and the other, Elias Harrison. The vote stood for the latter forty-five, for the former eighty-six; but Mr. Baker, feeling satisfied that Mr. Harrison was preferred to himself by Dr. Muir, respectfully declined the call, and Mr. Harrison was elected.

But a division and alienation of feeling had been occasioned which could not readily be healed. Three elders out of five, and about one-half of the congregation, withdrew, in order to organize another church. Of this—the Second Church—Mr. Baker was invited to become the pastor. Declining the invitation, he recommended Wells Andrews in his stead. Mr. Andrews was subsequently (1817)[2] settled, and, after a ministry of about ten years, was succeeded by William C. Walton

---

[1] Life of Daniel Baker, p. 102.

[2] The apparent discrepancy in the statements of the text is resolved by the fact that Dr. Harrison was chosen Dr. Muir's assistant a year before he was settled as college pastor.

In the circumstances of the case, it is not surprising that the new church should prefer to stand disconnected with the old (Baltimore) Presbytery; and, consequently, until the formation of the Presbytery of the District of Columbia, it was under the care of Winchester Presbytery.

The successor of Dr. Allison as pastor of the First Presbyterian Church of Baltimore was Rev. James Inglis. He was of Scotch descent, but a native of Philadelphia, and a graduate of Columbia College, N.Y. He studied law under the celebrated Alexander Hamilton, and for a time was in practice at the New York bar. While thus engaged, his mind became seriously impressed; and, abandoning his profession, he commenced the study of theology under the Rev. Dr. Rodgers, of New York. Soon after his licensure by the Presbytery of New York, he visited Baltimore, and for eighteen years continued his labors as pastor of the First Presbyterian Church. Kind and affable in private intercourse, with a ready utterance, ease of manner, and elegance of style, he added the charms of the most finished oratory to the attractions of his personal character, and was accounted, by competent judges, one of the most eminent lights of the American pulpit.[1] Yet he approached nearer the type of the Scottish Blair than the American Nevins, who, soon after his death, was called to succeed him as pastor of the church.

A rival candidate of Inglis at the time of his settlement was John Glendy, a refugee from Ireland in the stormy period of 1798. He had been settled for some years as pastor of a church in Londonderry; but his

---

[1] William Wirt says (Life, i. 339), writing from Georgetown, October 14, 1814, "Last night I went to church, and heard a Mr. Inglis, of Baltimore, deliver what I should call—not a sermon, but—a very elegant oration in a theatrical style. The composition was rich, but, I thought, out of place,—his manner still more so."

opposition to the policy pursued by the British Government toward Ireland rendered him obnoxious, and he was forced to flee. In an overcrowded emigrant-ship he embarked for this country, and landed at Norfolk, in 1799. For two years he supplied the congregations of Staunton and Bethel, in Augusta county, and, on a short visit to Baltimore, was invited to preach as a candidate in the pulpit of the First Presbyterian Church. When the choice of the congregation had fallen on the Rev. Mr. Inglis, a number of his friends were led to consider the project of organizing another church, in connection with which they wished to secure his services. In these plans they were successful; and, in 1803, Glendy took charge of the Second Presbyterian Church. For twenty-three years he remained sole pastor of the congregation; and in 1826 the Rev. John Breckenridge was chosen as his colleague. Graceful in the pulpit, with distinct voice, easy utterance, vivacity and elegance of style, he was to the last loved and admired as a preacher. Rarely profound, never *very* logical, he was clear in statement and earnest and impressive in manner. His Irish traits, some of which often betrayed themselves in the pulpit, made him most popular among his own countrymen, who were numerous in Baltimore; while his genial spirit and gentlemanly bearing *out* of the pulpit, as well as his eloquence *in* it, made him generally acceptable and admired.[1]

---

[1] John H. Smaltz, born in Philadelphia, 1793, a graduate of Rutgers College, was called in 1822 to the pastorate of the Third Church of Baltimore. He was subsequently settled at Germantown, Pa., Frederick, Md., Trenton, N.J., Harrisburg, Pa., spending his closing years in Philadelphia. A true man, a faithful, practical preacher, industrious, persevering, retiring and domestic in his habits, and with a heart devoted to every good cause, he was beloved. He died July 30, 1861.

The revival which commenced in Kentucky in 1800, and which was powerfully felt in the Carolinas, extended to the Baltimore and neighboring churches. But up to this period the organization of the churches had been greatly neglected. In 1802, means were taken to remedy this defect by the election of elders.[1] But "for fifty years there had been no regular Sessions in most, if not all, of the churches in this region."

William Nevins, the successor (1820) of Dr. Inglis in the pastorate of the First Presbyterian Church of Baltimore, was a native of Norwich, Conn., a graduate of Yale College in 1816, and of Princeton Theological Seminary in 1819. Quick of apprehension, thirsting for knowledge, of great natural vivacity, and with an irrepressible fondness for the ludicrous, his early years gave but little promise of the serious aims to which his life was to be devoted. Even in the seminary, in the weekly discussions of the theological society, his rising to speak was the signal to a large part of his audience to prepare for a hearty laugh. But under the effervescence of mirth, wit, and good-natured sarcasm was concealed a depth of warm devotion which constituted the real current of his life. One who had heard him pray could not but feel that, in spite of seeming levity, he had a heart not unused to self-communion and godly sorrow.

His first project on entering the ministry had been a mission to South America. Satisfied, however, that the time was not ripe for it, he travelled southward, and, in Richmond, made the wretched inmates of the penitentiary the objects of his evangelical effort. Called to Baltimore, he entered upon an arduous field. Its difficulties were aggravated by his resolve to innovate on the old usage of the Church which approved the

---

[1] Pres. Mag., March, 1858, p. 135.

baptism of infants whether their parents were members of the Church or not. He maintained his ground; and, after some years, his labors were rewarded by witnessing a powerful and genuine revival of religion in his congregation

Meanwhile, there had been a marked change in the tone of his pulpit-ministrations. His earliest efforts had been characterized by an exuberance of beautiful imagery which excited the hearer's admiration, and frequently, also, the apprehensions of the more serious and judicious. But a few years' experience effectually pruned the luxuriance of his rhetoric. His preaching became direct, pungent, and thrilling in its appeals. The earnestness of his convictions was felt where the affluence of his imagination had been once admired. Original as a thinker, perspicuous, concise, and striking as a writer, giving even to common thoughts a cast peculiarly his own, he soon rose to merited distinction; and his productions have won a permanent place in the religious literature of the land. Genial as a friend, faithful as a pastor, and attractive and impressive as a preacher, his untimely death at the age of thirty-eight years (1835) was the occasion not only of grief to his own congregation, but of wide-spread sorrow throughout the land.

In Virginia the progress of the Church for the first twenty years of the century was by no means rapid; and yet its increase was, proportionately, in advance of that of the population of the State. The latter amounted to but twenty *per cent.*, while the former was at least forty.[1]

The congregations, indeed, had not largely increased in number,—amounting in 1819 to only seventy, in place

---

[1] The estimate, in the lack of reports for 1800 and 1820, is made from those of 1799 and 1819, while the Presbytery of Abingdon, a portion of which was within the bounds of Tennessee, is omitted.

of the sixty-three of 1799. But the three Presbyteries, which jointly numbered in 1799 twenty-three members, of whom seventeen were pastors, had on their rolls in 1819 a membership of forty-three, of whom thirty-three were pastors. In place of twenty-eight congregations supplied at the earlier date, fifty were supplied at the latter, and, while in 1799 thirty-five congregations were vacant, only twenty were unsupplied in 1819.

In 1799, the Presbyteries of Hanover and Lexington numbered each nine ordained ministers. In Hanover Presbytery were James Waddel, William Irvine, and Archibald McRoberts, without charge; James Mitchel and James Turner, colleague pastors of the congregations of Bethel, Salem, and Pisgah; John D. Blair, pastor of Hanover and Henrico; Drury Lacy, of Cumberland; Archibald Alexander, of Briery; and Matthew Lyle, in conjunction with Alexander, of Briery and Buffalo. In Lexington Presbytery were William Graham, Benjamin Erwin, and John Montgomery, without charge; Archibald Scott, pastor of Bethel and Brown's Meeting-House; William Wilson, of Augusta; John McCue, of Staunton and Tinkling Spring; Samuel Houston, of Falling Water and High Bridge; Benjamin Grigsby, of Lewisburg and Concord; and Samuel Brown, of New Providence.

The Presbytery of Winchester, erected in 1794, had in 1799 five ordained ministers,—Moses Hoge, of Shepherdstown; Nash Le Grand, of Cedar Creek and Opekon; William Hill, of Charlestown and Hopewell; John Lyle, of Frankfort, Romney, and Springfield; and William Williamson, of South River and Flint Run.

In the twenty years that followed, the changes that took place left but nine of these twenty-three ministers on the field, and of these some were transferred to other settlements. Mitchel Turner, Blair, and Lyle (1819) retained their former posts in Hanover Presbytery. In Lexington, Samuel Houston was still at Falling Spring and High Bridge, where he remained till disabled by age, a few years before his death in 1839. William Wilson was without charge, and, in 1813, Conrad Speece was settled as his successor in Augusta; while in Winchester Presbytery William Hill was at Winchester, and William Williamson at Middleburg. Beside these, Moses Hoge, called from Shepherdstown in 1807 to succeed Archibald Alexander as President of Hampden-Sidney College, was a member of Hanover Presbytery, but died July 5, 1820.

All the other ministers of 1799 had died, or removed to other fields. James Waddel died September, 1805. Irvine had ceased to preach some years before his death. Drury Lacy, from 1789 to 1796 President of Hampden-Sidney College, and subsequently teacher of a classical school in the vicinity, died Dec. 6, 1815. Archibald Alexander, called to the Pine Street Church, Philadelphia, in 1806, had left this field also, to enter upon his charge as the first theological professor of Princeton Seminary (Aug. 12, 1812). William Graham died before the close (June) of 1799. Benjamin Erwin had been succeeded at Mossy Creek and Cook's Creek by Andrew B. Davidson, who had charge of Harrisonburg also, and previous to 1819 by John Hendren, Harrisonburg becoming in 1818 the charge of Daniel Baker. John Montgomery died previous to 1814. Archibald Scott died in 1799, and was succeeded in Bethel congregation by William McPheeters (1805–10) and Robert H. Chapman (1817–23). John McCue died Sept. 20, 1818, and, some years later, was succeeded at Tinkling Spring by James C. Willson, whose pastorate continued till his death, in 1840. John McElhenny succeeded Benjamin Grigsby at Lewisburg, which had long been vacant, previous to 1819, while a union congregation formed part of his charge. Samuel

Brown, of New Providence, died Oct. 13, 1818, and was succeeded a few months later by James Morrison.

In Winchester Presbytery, Nash Le Grand died in October, 1814, having left his charge, which still (1819) remained vacant, several years previous. In 1800, William Hill commenced his prolonged pastorate at Winchester. John Lyle was called from a sphere of great usefulness by death, in 1807, and his congregations, Springfield, Romney, and Frankfort, were left vacant for several years; though he was at length succeeded by James Black.

Meanwhile, the places of those who had died or removed had been supplied by others. James Robinson, before 1803, was settled at Cove and Rockfish, where he still remained. John H. Rice had been settled for some years at Cub Creek, where he was succeeded, on his removal to Richmond in 1812, by Clement Read. Benjamin H. Rice at about the same time (1812) commenced his labors at Petersburg. Joseph D. Logan was soon after settled at Bird and Providence, and previous to 1819, William S. Reid was at Lynchburg, John D. Porter at Norfolk, John McLean at Concord and Hat Creek, and Alexander McCowan at Blue Stone.

In Lexington Presbytery, George A. Baxter succeeded William Graham, upon his death in 1799, as Principal of Liberty Hall, taking charge also of the congregations of Lexington and New Monmouth, remaining in this post for about thirty years. Joseph Reid had been settled at Lebanon and Windy Cove, where he was succeeded previous to 1814 by John D. Ervin. Samuel McNutt had charge of New Dublin congregation; William Calhoon had been settled for nearly the whole period at Staunton and Brown's Meeting-House; while of the other members of the Presbytery,—as already mentioned,—Houston was at Falling Spring, Chapman at Bethel, Speece at Augusta, McElhenny at Lewisburg,

Hendren at Mossy Creek, Morrison at New Providence and Baker at Harrisonburg and New Erection.

In Winchester Presbytery, Dr. William Hill was (1819) at Winchester, William Williamson at Middleburg, John Matthews at Shepherdstown, where he had succeeded Dr. Hoge, called in 1807 to the Presidency of Hampden-Sidney, John Mines at Leesburg, S. B. Wilson at Fredericksburg, James Black at Mt. Bethel, John B. Hoge at Tuscarora and Falling Waters, where he remained from his settlement, Oct. 12, 1811, till called to Richmond in 1822, Samuel D. Hoge at Culpepper and Madison from his ordination in 1816 till his removal to Ohio in 1821, Wells Andrews at Alexandria, over the Second Church, and W. C. Walton at Hopewell.

In Lexington Presbytery, William Wilson, Robert Logan, Andrew B. Davidson, Robert H. Anderson, and Henry Buffner were without charge; while thirteen congregations were reported vacant. In Winchester Presbytery, Joseph Glass, Andrew A. Shannon, and William N. Scott were without charge; while only Middletown, Cedar Creek, and Opekon were reported vacant. In Hanover Presbytery there were nine vacancies; but the Presbytery had under its care nine licentiates.

The more important of the newly-organized congregations were those of Richmond, Petersburg, Fredericksburg, Leesburg, Lynchburg, and Norfolk. Winchester, perhaps, should be mentioned in the same connection; for though the congregation had formed a part of the same pastoral charge with Cedar Creek and Opekon for several preceding years, there had been difficulty in supplying it, and at length, in 1800, William Hill was called to the pastoral charge. Under his labors, protracted here for nearly a third of a century, it became a large and prosperous church.

At Richmond there were a few scattered Presbyterians previous to the time when the attention of Dr. Rice was called to the place. John D. Blair, of Henrico and Hanover, preached alternately with an Episcopal clergyman in the Capitol, each occupying it every other Sabbath. But the whole city was thrilled by the tragic event of the burning of the theatre, in which so many lives—embracing largely the flower and pride of the State—were lost, in December, 1811. A deep gloom pervaded the entire community, and, as if by a common impulse, a large number of the inhabitants of Capitol Hill were brought to the resolution of erecting a monumental church on the site of the late theatre.[1] In this enterprise, all the families, as well Presbyterian as Episcopal, who had been accustomed up to this time to worship in the Capitol, enlisted, without, as it would seem, any very definite understanding as to the ultimate destination of the edifice. Yet after its completion it was thought best that its use should be confined to a single denomination; and, as the Episcopal portion was in the majority, the exclusive use of the structure passed into their hands.

But the friends of John D. Blair,—a successor of Samuel Davies at Pole Green, in Hanover, and an alternate supply with the Episcopal clergyman at the Capitol during the preceding period, while engaged as a teacher at Richmond,—animated by a more liberal and energetic spirit than before, proceeded to erect a handsome church-edifice for themselves on Shockoe Hill. Here Mr. Blair officiated until his death, in 1823. His successor was John Blair Hoge.

At nearly the same time, Dr. John H. Rice commenced his labors at Richmond. For several years he had been settled at Cub Creek, and had at the same time discharged the duties of a tutor at Hampden-Sidney. At a meeting of Presbytery at Red Oak Church, on March

---

[1] Sprague, iii. 460.

12, 1812, "a call from a number of persons in Richmond and its vicinity attached to the Presbyterian Church" was presented to him, which he saw fit to accept, and on the second Sabbath in May he preached his first discourse to his new charge in Mason's Hall, Richmond. On the 17th of October he was installed pastor, retaining the office until June, 1823, soon after which he was succeeded by William J. Armstrong.

It was in December, 1812, that Benjamin H. Rice, a younger brother of John H. Rice, commenced his labors in Petersburg, then one of the most unpromising and difficult fields of labor which could have been selected. In a population of eight thousand, there were two, and only two, Presbyterians.[1] But the zeal of the youthful preacher, fresh from a missionary journey along the seaboard counties of North Carolina, was not to be daunted by difficulty. At first he preached in an unfinished storehouse. He soon succeeded in organizing a church of about twenty members, of which he was installed pastor in the spring of 1814. Here, in the discharge of the duties of an eminently successful ministry, he remained for the space of seventeen years, resigning his charge to accept the pastorate of the Pearl Street Church, New York (1829). He became, three years later, Associate Secretary of the Home Missionary Society, but in 1833 accepted a call to Princeton, New Jersey, where his pastorate continued till 1847. His closing years (1847–56) were devoted to the pastoral charge of the Hampden-Sidney College Church. His successor at Petersburg was E. C. Hutchinson.

At Leesburg, John Mines, a licentiate of Winchester Presbytery in 1803, commenced his labors previous to 1808, when he was reported pastor of the church. His ministry here continued for at least ten or twelve years.

---

[1] Obituary Sermon by W. E. Schenk. Life of Dr. J. H. Rice.

The church at Lynchburg dates from 1815. In 1808, William S. Reid commenced his labors here, opening a school for his own support, and at the same time endeavoring to establish, by regular Sabbath services which he performed, a Presbyterian church. It was seven years before an organization was effected, and seven more before he was installed pastor of the church. But during his pastorate, which continued till 1848, the church increased in numbers, strength, and efficiency, until it became "one of the most harmonious and well-disciplined bodies of Christians in the State."[1]

The church of Norfolk was gathered as a congregation probably about 1801. In 1803 the Committee of Missions were vested with discretionary power to send a missionary to the place.[2] Shortly after this, Rev. Mr. Grigsby was in charge of the church (1806), his death occurring Oct. 6, 1810. In 1812, John D. Paxton was ordained at the request of the church, and subsequently settled. His labors with the church closed previous to 1825, when Shepard K. Kollock, who had been for several years a professor in the University of North Carolina, became stated supply, and was soon after settled as pastor. In 1829, the membership of the church had risen to a little over two hundred.

The church in Fredericksburg is first reported in the

---

[1] Sprague, iv. 388. The Second Presbyterian Church of Lynchburg was organized with twenty-four members, all but three from the First Presbyterian Church, May 19, 1830. A new and enlarged house of worship was erected in 1852. The pastors have been D. L. Russell, 1830, J. D. Mitchell, 1830–35, J. L. Kirkpatrick, 1837–41, E. M. Cumpston, 1841–46, E. J. Newlin, 1847–52, and J. D. Mitchell, 1852.—*Presbyterian Almanac*, 1860.

[2] Assembly's Minutes, 1803. A Methodist church was gathered here as early as 1772. A powerful revival under the charge of Methodists prevailed at Norfolk and Portsmouth in 1802.—*Bangs's Methodism.* In 1810, Mr. Grigsby wanted a missionary to assist him in the neighboring region.—*Memoir of John H. Rice.*

minutes for 1809. At that time Samuel B. Wilson[1] was pastor, and here he remained for more than thirty years The church had in 1825 a membership of one hundred and eighty. The successor of Dr. Wilson was George Wilson McPhail.

With such institutions under their patronage as Hampden-Sidney College and Liberty Hall, afterward Washington College, the Synod of Virginia—after the revivals of 1787–89—had been enabled largely to supply their own destitutions; and among the ministers they sent forth into the field were some of the ablest and most effective within the bounds of the Church. It was natural, therefore, that the Presbyterians of Virginia should prefer to educate their own ministry within the bounds of the Synod. In the Assembly of 1809, when the subject of education for the ministry had been discussed, it was resolved to submit to the Presbyteries the three plans which had been suggested with reference to the establishment of seminaries. In the following year, a divided answer was returned, but the Presbyterians of Virginia determined in favor of Synodical seminaries. The Assembly, while adopting the policy of a single central institution, stated most explicitly that every Presbytery and Synod would, "of course, be left at full liberty to countenance the proposed plan, or not, at pleasure, and to send their students to the projected seminary or keep them as heretofore within their own bounds, as they think most conducive to the prosperity of the Church."[2]

In 1812, therefore, the Synod of Virginia resolved to establish a Theological Seminary within their bounds, and unanimously appointed Dr. Moses Hoge as professor. For the five preceding years he had occupied

---

[1] Since professor in Union Theological Seminary, Va.

[2] Assembly Minutes, 1810.

the post of President of Hampden-Sidney College, as the successor of Dr. Alexander, who in 1807 commenced his pastorate in Philadelphia. His acknowledged ability, his successful ministry at Shepherdstown, and the position which he so admirably filled as President of Hampden-Sidney, designated him as the fittest man for the responsible post; and, till his constitution began to give way under his multiplied and onerous labors (1819), he discharged the duties of President, and at the same time those of Professor of Divinity under the appointment of the Synod.[1]

With little that was prepossessing in person or manner, and ungraceful, if not uncouth, in his appearance in the pulpit, he was a man of thorough scholarship, profoundly read in theology, with great depth and originality of thought, affluence of illustration, and cogency of argument. As a teacher, he had not only great patience, but great skill. In unravelling difficulties, and exhibiting the harmony of the Christian system, he was perhaps unsurpassed. But he was as eminent for his piety as his learning, and his rare intellectual vigor was unreservedly devoted to his Master's cause. He was spared to see thirty of his pupils at Hampden-Sidney licensed and ordained ministers. In spite of his manner, John Randolph pronounced him "the most eloquent man in Virginia."[2]

His successor—after the operations of the seminary had been for some time suspended in consequence of his sickness and death—was John Holt Rice, who for more than ten years had been pastor of the church in Richmond. The state of the seminary at the time was such that an effort to increase its funds seemed absolutely necessary,[3] and Dr. Rice immediately devoted himself to the task. Shortly after resigning his pas-

[1] Sprague, iii. 429. [2] Ib. iv. 450. [3] Ib. iv. 329.

toral charge in June, 1823, he took a journey to the North, extending his applications for aid to the churches in New England, and everywhere met a cordial welcome both for himself and his object. Few men, indeed, possessed in an equal measure the graces and loveliness of the Christian character. "Tall, bony, and ungraceful" in person, with a countenance exceedingly grave in repose, yet occasionally breaking out into a jocund radiance and benignity altogether indescribable, with gestures confined, but under excitement powerful, and with a voice which, though strong, was unmusical, he owed nothing to the mere graces of oratory. Yet there were occasions when he was unquestionably eloquent, —when, kindling as he advanced, his reluctant frame seemed informed by an unwonted inspiration, while his whole soul glowed through his great, speaking eye. But his power resided in his thought and in his feeling. He was at once argumentative and earnest. Among the ministry of the day he had not, perhaps, his superior in the mastery of sound, free, vigorous English. Yet his ablest discourses were the product of the hour. If written down in the study, they were not allowed to enslave him in the pulpit. To his public ministry he brought the stores of an unusually varied learning. From his childhood, when he used to rise from his bed to read Horace by the light of the blazing pines on the hearth, until prostrated by his last illness, he was an eager devourer of books of various kinds. Yet his knowledge was well digested and ever ready for use.

But his intellectual eminence was crowned by his moral qualities and his Christian graces. His piety was deep and fervent, and none could be more devoted to the peace, unity, and prosperity of the Church. In every man he recognized a brother, and in the liberality of his views he overlooked none that bore the Christian name. Kind, genial, courteous, hospitable, he exemplified in daily life the spirit of his Master. No man could say more appropriately or effectively than he did, "The Church is not to be purified by controversy, but by holy love." His favorite adage was, "*Love is power.*" To him, more than to any one else, the Theological Seminary stands indebted. He needs no other monument to his memory. His labors in its behalf closed only with his life, in 1830.

A year before the death of Dr. Rice, Benjamin F. Stanton had accepted the charge of the Hanover Church; and his services were for a time called into requisition to lecture on theology in the place of Dr. Rice. Intellectually he was fully equal to his predecessor. A Calvin in theology,[1] he was a very Knox in the fearlessness of his pulpit-ministrations. Naturally inclined to be sarcastic, he was sometimes facetiously caustic, but "oftener solemn as the judgment, and terrible as retribution." For brainless arrogance and impudent folly he had no mercy. Above all artifice, he never disguised his sentiments, however unacceptable. A close thinker, a strong writer, and sometimes an impassioned speaker, his feeble health alone prevented him from taking rank among the princes of pulpit-oratory.

An efficient assistant of Dr. Rice in the management of the seminary, and one upon whom in his illness a large share of responsibility devolved, was Hiram P. Goodrich, employed to give instruction in languages. Mr. Goodrich was a native of Richmond, Mass. (1800), a graduate of Union College, a student of theology at Princeton, and in 1825 a licentiate of Albany Presbytery. In 1826 he was elected a professor in Union Seminary, and, while occupying this post, labored extensively as an evangelist. Dr. Rice reposed in him the

---

[1] Sprague, iv. 526.

utmost confidence; and his conduct justified it. Upon the division of the Church (1837–38) he resigned his professorship, and took the post of Professor and afterward of President of Marion College, Mo. On the failure of that institution, he labored as a missionary within the bounds of that State. His death occurred May 19, 1859.

But a permanent successor of Dr. Rice as Theological Professor, one well worthy to wear his mantle, was found within the bounds of the Synod, and inaugurated April 11, 1832.

At the head of Liberty Hall—Washington College—stood, at the time of Dr. Rice's death, a man who in the qualities of intellectual and moral greatness had scarcely a superior in his native State. This was George Addison Baxter, a graduate of the institution in 1796, and a theological pupil of the rector, William Graham.[1] After laboring as a missionary for some time, he took charge of New London Academy, from which in 1798 he was called to the Professorship of Mathematics at Liberty Hall. Upon the death of the principal, Mr. Graham, in the following year, he was chosen to succeed him; and in this post he continued—officiating at the same time as pastor of New Monmouth and Lexington Churches—until 1829.

Few men, for the same period of time, have undertaken so much; and fewer still have accomplished what he achieved. In seasons of revival he was known to spend five hours each day in his college duties, and to preach every night for weeks together. His desire to devote himself exclusively to pastoral labor led him to relinquish his connection with the college; and two years afterward, in the autumn of 1831, he was called as Theological Professor to succeed Dr. Rice.

---

[1] Sprague, iv 192.

The seminary at the time was in an embarrassed state, and the several vacations of the institution were devoted by Dr. Baxter to soliciting pecuniary aid on its behalf. Until his death, in 1841, he continued almost uninterruptedly to devote himself to the duties of his office.[1]

With a mind exceedingly well balanced, an understanding vast in its powers of comprehension and eminently profound, logical, and lucid, a judgment accurate and discriminating, and a memory remarkably retentive, he combined an amount of fervent emotion which in his pulpit-utterance "sent forth his great thoughts in burning and melting masses." Always clear, he was almost always convincing. He seemed to grasp a difficult subject and apprehend all its bearings almost by intuition. His power of condensation, moreover, was remarkable. Few ministers whose sermons, like his, extended to three-quarters of an hour,

---

[1] The successor of Dr. Baxter upon his death, in 1841, was Dr. Samuel B. Wilson, who for more than twenty years had been settled at Fredericksburg. In 1835, Stephen Taylor was elected to the Professorship of Ecclesiastical History. For nine years he had been settled at Richmond, and, to the regret of a warmly-attached congregation, he accepted the call to the seminary. In the division of the church, the majority of the Synod placed themselves on the basis of the Excision, and he felt it incumbent on him to resign his office. This he did in the spring of 1838. For a year or two, at about this period, Elisha Ballantine was employed as an assistant; and subsequently, for many years, the faculty consisted of Dr. S. B. Wilson, Professor of Theology, Dr. S. L. Graham, Professor of Oriental Literature, and Rev. F. S. Sampson as assistant instructor. In 1851 (Oct. 23), Dr. Graham tendered his resignation. Dr. R. J. Breckenridge was chosen to succeed him, but declined to serve. In 1854 (March 23), Dr. Robert L. Dabney was elected to the vacancy. The death of Dr. Sampson occurred April 9, 1854; his successor was Rev. B. M. Smith, elected June 14, 1854. At about this time arrangements were made for the endowment of a Fourth Professorship, to which W. J. Hoge was elected April 12, 1856.

have been requested, as he was by his hearers, to preach longer. His prayers were brief but comprehensive. He rarely used the pen, and wrote but few of his lectures. In the pulpit he scorned the aid of even the briefest outline. Yet his words were well chosen and weighty. Nor were they made less impressive as the hearer gazed upon his tall, manly frame, and the expanded, massive brow on which the very majesty of mind seemed enthroned. He had imagination, and he had pathos; and in his preaching he not rarely had to struggle powerfully to suppress his emotions. His mind was more rapid than his words, and his heart kept pace with his intellect.

His modesty was equal to his merit, and in a strange pulpit he was as easily embarrassed as the humblest and plainest student fresh from the seminary. Yet, while he seemed to shun notice, his abilities were equal to the highest position.[1]

During the period under review, Virginia could boast of some of the most eminent preachers within the bounds of the Presbyterian Church. Besides those already mentioned, there were—in Hanover Presbytery—Mitchel, at the Peaks, the fire of his youth still unquenched; his colleague James Turner, with his "soul-stirring, tear-drawing eloquence,"[2] and his power, unrivalled among his brethren, over the passions of men, now winning by the soft melody of his voice, and now startling by tones that made the hearer quake; Matthew Lyle, of Briery, for some time a colleague of Archibald Alexander, of whom the latter said, "I never knew a man who was more incapable of insincerity:" in Lexington Presbytery, William Calhoon, of Staun-

---

[1] For a sketch of the life and character of Jonathan P. Cushing, successor of Dr. M. Hoge in the Presidency of Hampden-Sidney, see American Quarterly Register for Nov. 1838.

[2] Sprague, iv 195.

ton, a son-in-law of Dr. Waddel, a man of vigorous intellect, great self-command, ready mind, fine conversational powers, and enlarged public spirit; Speece, of Augusta, "tall, large, and lubberly," a great reader, a charming conversationist, overflowing with droll humor, and, though steeped in Virginianism and Presbyterianism, still retaining a spice of the native sap of his German stock; Daniel Baker, who, after passing the ordeal of Presbyterial examination, and scarcely, after two days' discussion and doubt, obtaining his licensure, had commenced (1818) his pastorate at Harrisonburg, soon, however, to enter upon those extended and arduous labors which were to class him along with Nettleton as one of the most eminent "evangelists" of the age: in Winchester Presbytery, William Hill, of Winchester, a man of fine appearance and noble bearing, with a clear and vigorous intellect, a Roman firmness, ardent, fearless, and enthusiastic,—one who might have stood as a model of Paul before Felix, or of Luther at the Diet of Worms; William Williamson, of Middleburg, of powerful intellect, and a bold, exciting preacher; John Matthews, of Shepherdstown, no unworthy successor of Moses Hoge, but ere long to occupy a responsible post in the new seminary of the Northwest; William N. Scott, a missionary and an evangelist, eminent for sound sense, fervent piety, and extensive usefulness; John Blair Hoge, of graceful form, courteous manner, penetrating intellect, and torrent-like eloquence; along with others who in obscure spheres were content to toil on, often eking out their salary by teaching or labor on the farm, yet, in devotion to their great work, declining to yield to the attractions of more inviting spheres.[1]

[1] James Black, born at Millerstown, Pa., was licensed by Abingdon Presbytery in 1809. From 1810 to 1825 he was settled at

The Great Revival in Kentucky in 1801 exerted a powerful influence throughout portions of the Synod of Virginia within the bounds of the State. The testimony of Dr. Baxter in regard to this remarkable work—the scenes of which he visited and the features of which he carefully noted—was to the effect that it was "among the most extraordinary that had ever visited the Church of Christ, and, all things considered, peculiarly adapted to the circumstances of that country."

It is not strange that, entertaining such views, which he communicated in a lengthy letter to his friend Alexander, he should find others, more excitable than himself, prepared to welcome religious awakening even though accompanied with the "exercises." The excitement did, in fact, spread to a large extent through Western Virginia. It was first felt in the Presbyterian settlements along the head-waters of the Kanawha,[1] in Greenbrier county. Here were no settled ministers. Occasional visits were indeed made by missionaries to this region; but the work began at a prayer-meeting of private Christians.

In the latter part of 1801, the churches under the care of Messrs. Mitchel and Turner were greatly revived. There were numerous conversions. Many were subject to bodily agitations, and fell upon the ground as if smitten by a resistless power. In the succeeding spring the work was still more powerful. The Presbytery of Hanover met at Bethel. Crowds gathered to listen to the preaching of the ministers. There were some bodily exercises, but no noise or disorderly

---

Romney, removing afterward to Elk Branch. He subsequently labored in Ohio, but died at Shepherdstown, Va., 1860. Mild and gentle, he conciliated affection and respect. His successor at Romney for many years has been Dr. W. H. Foote.

[1] Foote's Sketches of Virginia, Second Series, p. 288.

manifestations of feeling. The work extended to the east of the Ridge. The congregations in Albemarle, in Prince Edward, and in Charlotte were greatly awakened. Baxter's congregations became deeply interested. The excitement spread through the length of the Valley. The bodily exercises were in some cases violent Were they a necessary part of the work? was the question asked by many. Samuel Brown, of New Providence, declared them a profane mixture,—a device of Satan to mar the work of God. Baxter and others were in doubt. They dared not denounce, even where they could not approve. The general sentiment, however, was against them; and at length they were rarely manifested.

For several years, however, the effects of the revival continued to be witnessed in different parts of the State.[1] There were conversions in places where there were no organized churches or stated ministry. The Presbyterian Church was not prepared fitly to occupy the field. She lacked the men needed to seek out the scattered sheep in the wilderness. This fact had its weight in impelling the Synod to prosecute more energetically their plans for theological education.

---

[1] The Synod of Virginia in 1816 and 1817 were able to speak of the encouraging prospects of their field. The Christian activity of the congregations of Norfolk, Petersburg, Winchester, Leesburg, Fredericksburg, and Richmond was commended. Revivals had prevailed at Winchester and Leesburg in 1816, and in the following year the church of Alexandria was perhaps saved from extinction by a revival.—*Christian Herald*, ii. 254, iii. 105.

CHAPTER XXVI.

THE CAROLINAS AND GEORGIA, 1800–1820.

In 1800, the strength of the Presbyterian Church south of Virginia was represented by four out of the six Presbyteries constituting the Synod of the Carolinas. These were the Presbyteries of Orange, South Carolina, Concord, and Hopewell. Concord had been formed by a division of Orange in 1795, and Hopewell by a division of South Carolina in 1796.

The Presbytery of Orange in 1800 numbered twelve ministers, of whom eight were pastors, and had under its care not far from forty congregations, of which nearly one-half were vacant. Henry Patillo, the pupil of Davies, cheerful in the hardest lot and unwearied in devotion to pastoral duty, was still at Grassy Creek and Nutbush, where he had been settled for twenty years. But his life, which had been a pattern of resignation, usefulness, and piety, was drawing near its close, and in 1801 he died, at the ripe age of seventy-five years. For quite a time the congregations were left without a pastor; but, previous to 1809, Ezekiel B. Currie—a pupil of Dr. Caldwell[1]—commenced his ministry with them, and here he remained for many years.[2] David Caldwell already had labored for nearly thirty-five years as pastor of Buffalo and Alamance congregations, and till 1820, when he had reached his ninety-fifth year, he continued to supply them both.[3] William Moore was at Upper and Lower Hico, which he left

[1] Sprague, iii. 65. [2] Succeeded by Samuel L. Graham.
[3] Succeeded by Eli W. Caruthers.

before 1803, and previous to 1809 The Red House and Rattlesnake congregations, to which he had hitherto ministered, were supplied by Hugh Shaw, who was succeeded in the latter within a few years by William B. Meroney, who was stated supply also at Greer's and Bethesda.[1] Samuel Stanford was at Black River and Brown Marsh,—though his subsequent charge was Grove and South River, and in his first charge he was succeeded by Robert Tate,[2] who (1819) had charge of Hopewell, Rockfish, and Keith, as well as Black River. Angus McDermot was at Barbacue Bluff and McCays;[3] James H. Bowman at Eno and Little River, where he was succeeded (1814–15) by Samuel Paisley, previously (1813) stated supply at Cedar Creek and Haw River; William Thompson at New Hope, which he left before 1803, and which continued vacant for a long period; John Gillespie at Center, Laurel Hill, and Raft Swamp, which he left before 1803, and in which he was, before 1809, succeeded by Malcolm McNair;[4] William D. Paisley at Union and Lower Buffalo,[5]—though he soon after removed to Hawfields and Cross-Roads; Samuel McAdow at Speedwell and Haw River, which he soon left, and which remained for some time vacant; and Robert Tate at South Washington and Rockfish.

The vacant congregations in 1809 were Salem, Mt.

---

[1] Mr. Meroney's successor, who took charge also of Haw River, was John H. Pickard, born in 1783, in Orange county, N.C. His early education was limited, and he never enjoyed the advantages of liberal studies. In 1816, he was licensed and installed over Stony Creek and Bethesda Churches. In his later years he preached, as health permitted, in divers localities. He was an energetic preacher and a humble and fervent Christian. His death occurred in his seventy-eighth year, Sept. 4, 1858.

[2] In 1803 and 1809 at South Washington and Rockfish.

[3] His successor in 1815–16 was Allan McDougal.

[4] He is reported as having Hopewell instead of Raft Swamp.

[5] Succeeded by Murdoch McMillan before 1809.

Hermon, Old Fork, Lumber Ridge, Philadelphia, Hico, Bethesda, Stony Creek, New Hope, Speedwell, Bairds, and Haw River.

The church at Raleigh dates from 1810. In that year William McPheeters, who had been called to preside over the Academy, acceded to the request to preach to the town congregation, then without a pastor. No church of any kind had as yet been organized for the place; but the people worshipped together in the hall of the House of Commons.[1] Dr. McPheeters continued his connection with the Academy until 1820, and with the congregation as stated supply for several years longer. It was some years after he left that the church was formally organized; and in 1836 he received an invitation to become its pastor. This, however, he saw fit to decline, and Drury Lacy was soon after called to the pastorate. His ministry here continued for many years.[2]

The church at Newbern was gathered but a short time previous to 1809, and in that year James K. Burch was its pastor.[3] For a long time subsequent it must have remained in a feeble state, even if it retained its organization.[4] In 1819, it was vacant; but previous to 1825, when its membership amounted to fifty-four, it had secured Lemuel D. Hatch as pastor.

The church at Chapel Hill dates from the accession of Robert H. Chapman to the Presidency of the State University in 1812. This institution was at the time in a depressed condition; but, with all his efforts in its behalf, Dr. Chapman did not neglect the spiritual destitutions around him. The wants of his own immediate

[1] Sprague, iv. 305. [2] His successor is J. M. Atkinson.

[3] Assembly's Minutes for that year. The report for 1825 gives twenty-five as the number of communicants,—which would indicate an organized church. This is at variance with Sprague.

[4] It is not mentioned in the report for 1814.

neighborhood engaged his special attention, and to him principally the establishment of the church at Chapel Hill is due. During his connection with the institution he served as stated supply of the congregation, and upon his resignation and removal the charge devolved upon Dr. Joseph Caldwell, who succeeded him in the Presidency.[1]

The church at Oxford is first reported in 1819. At that time Shepard K. Kollock united the charge of it with his duties as an officer in the State University. In 1821, the church, which was in a languishing state, became the charge, in connection with Grassy Creek, of Samuel Lyle Graham, afterward Professor in the Union Theological Seminary of Virginia. Under his ministry it continued to prosper, until, in 1828, he resigned it for Nutbush Church, which he served as pastor in conjunction with Grassy Creek.

At Hillsborough a church was formed previous to 1819, when John Witherspoon was reported as pastor. His connection with the church closed in 1835–36, when he was succeeded by Robert Burwell. For a period (1825) it formed a joint charge with Bethlehem.

The church of Fayetteville is first reported in the minutes of 1814; but it had been in existence for many years previous. Its first minister was a Mr. Kerr;[2] but in 1800 it was supplied by John Robinson, who, uniting with his pulpit-labors the occupation of teaching, remained for less than two years. His successor, in 1802, was Andrew Flinn, subsequently of Charleston, S.C.; but on the resignation of the latter, in 1806, he was induced to return to Fayetteville and resume his pastoral labors and his classical school. Of the Presbyterian church in the place he may be said to have

---

[1] His successor was Professor E. Mitchell, of the University.

[2] Memorial of Henry A. Rowland, D.D., 53.

been the father. He not only organized it, but received to its communion many who have been its pillars since.[1] His firmness, dignity, and courtesy enabled him to exert an influence in such a community, in favor of religion and good order, which few could have successfully attempted.

In 1809, William M. Turner, who had been for some years previous at Raleigh, removed to Fayetteville, engaging in the work of teaching, while he served also as stated supply of the congregation.[2] His term of service closed with his untimely death, in 1813; but his brief ministry—in which he had shown himself to be a man of marked talents and character, as well as of great promise—was eminently blessed. For several subsequent years the pulpit was successively occupied for brief periods by different ministers, until Henry A. Rowland was settled as pastor, in 1830. During his ministry the town itself was almost reduced to ashes, and the church-edifice (1831) was burned. Largely through his energy and efforts, it was speedily rebuilt. "Few churches in the Union can point to such a succession of able, faithful, and godly ministers as the pastors of the Fayetteville Church. Kerr, Robinson, Flinn, the three Turners, Morrison, Snodgrass, Hanmer, Kirkpatrick, Rowland, and Gilchrist,—this is the honored list whose names have graced her annals and to whose virtues she refers with grateful affection."[3]

The church at Wilmington was organized previous to 1819, and a congregation, supplied by Robert Tate, had been gathered there for many years; but it had no settled pastor, and for many years subsequent it had but a feeble existence. In 1831, it reported a membership of only twenty-eight.

---

[1] Sprague, iv. 114. [2] Ibid. iii. 582.

[3] Memorial of Rowland. Quotation from "North Carolina Presbyterian."

In 1812 the Presbytery of Fayetteville was formed by a division of the Presbytery of Orange, and in the following year consisted of eight ministers and had under its care eight congregations. The territory which it occupied had formed the eastern border of Orange Presbytery, but it steadily increased, till it numbered in connection with it some of the most able and influential churches of the State. In 1819 it consisted of eleven ministers and had under its care thirty-two congregations. It had thus outstripped in growth the original Presbytery, which in that year numbered only ten members and twenty-two congregations. The first twenty years of the century passed away and left but four of the original members still on the field. These were David Caldwell, already past his ninetieth year, Samuel Stanford, William Paisley, and Robert Tate. A large proportion of the ministry of the State had during this period been educated at the State University, which was officered by Presbyterians. At its head were, successively, Robert H. Chapman and Joseph H. Caldwell, both bearing honored names, and both men of sterling worth. Kollock and Mitchell likewise, while connected with the University, were active and efficient members of the Presbytery.[1]

The services of Dr. Chapman in connection with the University were limited to the period from 1812 to 1817; but the influence which he exerted was long felt. Tender and earnest in the pulpit, he shunned all affectation of style or learning, and presented the truth in a clear, simple, but convincing manner. With a mind well balanced, and characterized by sound sense rather than

[1] The Scotch-Irish lineage of the ministers is attested by their names. Of the eleven ministers of Fayetteville Presbytery in 1819, *seven* were *Mcs:* two McMillans, McFarland, McNair, McIver, McDougal, and McIntyre.

brilliancy, he was exemplary in the discharge of his duties in every relation. Under his Presidency a most salutary moral change, largely due to his instrumentality, was effected in the University; and not a few received through him the impressions which resulted finally in their conversion.[1]

His successor—who had for a brief time been his predecessor—in office, Dr. Caldwell, was one of the most eminent scholars of his day. Educated at Princeton largely through the liberal benefactions of Dr. Witherspoon, he repaid the kindness by his diligence, and throughout his college-course retained the first rank, and graduated with the highest honors. After teaching for a time, studying theology, and acting as tutor at Princeton, he was called in 1796 to the Professorship of Mathematics in North Carolina University. The institution had been established seven years previous (1789), but its condition yet was far from hopeful. It was in a feeble state, with no fixed course of study, without discipline, poorly officered, short of funds, and nearly destitute of buildings, library, and apparatus. The Board of Trustees were mostly uneducated men, who had little skill to organize or sustain the institution. Even its existence was repeatedly threatened; and to Dr. Caldwell is justly ascribed the merit of having saved it from ruin and secured it the rank which it has continued to hold. A spirit less determined than his might well have yielded to the difficulties with which he was called to struggle.[2]

His Presidency of the institution extended from 1804 to 1812, and again from 1817 to his death in 1835,—or over a space of more than twenty-five years. To its prosperity he devoted the strength and energies of his life, visiting Europe to procure books and apparatus.

---

[1] Sprague, iv. 91.   [2] Ibid. iv. 173.

Nobly did he express and fearlessly carry into practice his conviction that piety and learning should be closely allied, and that the most efficient security of literary institutions is a sound religious influence. Patient laborious, and exact, he was also possessed of warm social sympathies. His ascendency over the minds of youth, and his power to control the disobedient and refractory, were almost unrivalled. It is possible that with special devotion to the work of the preacher he might have attained distinction; but the pulpit was not his throne. His proper sphere was the one which he was called to fill; and his name, embalmed in usefulness, will long be fragrant among the sons of his adopted State.

John Robinson—to whose earlier years reference has been already made, and whose name is identified with Fayetteville (1800–18) and Poplar Tent (1818–36) Churches—was a man of mark among his brethren. With a generosity rarely equalled, a keen sensibility to want and distress, a liberality of spirit that overleaped denominational limits and bade God-speed to every humane, benevolent, and Christian enterprise, he seemed to rise above all merely selfish interests with an almost chivalrous enthusiasm. Humble, unassuming, and unostentatiously devout, he was yet as fearless as Knox or Luther in his rebuke of sin.

Few men have ever commanded at once a larger measure of affection and reverence. His life commended his profession, and his integrity and liberality were preeminent. A thorough classical scholar himself, he was the devoted friend of learning, and a zealous patron of it. When a college in the western part of the State was proposed, he was one of the most active supporters of the project. When the more recent and successful attempt was made by the Presbyterians of North Carolina to found Davidson College, he made great efforts and sacrifices in its behalf, and they were continued to the close of his life.

In the pulpit he gave place to no fine-spun speculation or ingenious theory. He presented the truth as he found it in the Bible, in its penetrating force and with majestic simplicity. His style was clear, direct, and perspicuous. His delivery was interesting, earnest, and at times highly eloquent. His voice, clear, strong, and melodious, was admirably modulated from the highest to the lowest key, and gave fitting expression to his deep convictions of truth, his elevated sentiments, and his warm emotions; nor is it strange that he should have been reckoned among the most popular preachers of his day.

Malcolm McNair (ordained 1802) was a native of Robeson county, and his studies were pursued first with Dr. McCorkle, and afterward at Dr. Caldwell's school.[1] For nearly twenty years he was pastor of Centre and Ashpole Churches in Robeson and Laurel Hill in Richmond county. His labors were remarkably blessed. Several revivals occurred under his ministry. His address was "so sweetly captivating, so irresistibly alluring," that he was always listened to with deep attention even by opposers. His eloquence was not of the vehement, but of the persuasive, kind. With all kindly and generous sympathies his nature overflowed

Murdoch McMillan, licensed, although not ordained, in the same year with McNair, was also a member of Orange Presbytery until the erection of that of Fayetteville. In some respects, he was a striking contrast to McNair. For the *suaviter in modo* he substituted the *fortiter in re.* Yet his name is worthy of honorable mention. Along with McNair, he was eminently useful in building up the churches of Fayetteville Presbytery.

---

[1] Foote North Carolina.

Ezekiel B. Currie (ordained 1802), a native of North Carolina, was educated in part by Dr. Caldwell, and in part by Mr. McGready. To the ministry of the latter he attributed his conversion. He was first awakened by a question put him by an old gentleman who had silently listened to his merriment for a whole evening:—"Young man, when will you turn to serious things?" The question troubled him, and he could not shake off the impression. Under the labors of Mr. McGready, he at length was led to entertain a Christian hope and direct his attention to the gospel ministry. He labored first at Bethany Church in Caswell, seven years later removing to Nutbush and Grassy Creek, and finally to Hawfields and Cross-Roads. Repeated revivals occurred under his ministry.

A more remarkable man in some respects was John McIntyre, a native of Scotland, and for some time an apprentice to a shoemaker in Glasgow.[1] From his early years he was the subject of serious impressions, and in his boyish days was nicknamed by his associates "preacher McIntyre." Leaving Glasgow, he engaged himself in the Highlands as shepherd to a wealthy land-owner. At the age of twenty, he made a public profession of his faith, and subsequently gave evidence of the strength of his principles in trying circumstances.

Soon after this he was married, and, in 1791, emigrated to North Carolina. On his voyage he buried his first-born child. Domestic afflictions, like successive waves, rolled over himself and his family, and, after remaining for some years in North Carolina, he removed to Chesterfield District in South Carolina. Here, in attending the camp-meetings of the Great Revival, he was led for a time to doubt the genuineness of his piety. This constituted an epoch in his life. Recovering his hope, he

---

[1] Sprague, iv. 418.

felt an anxious desire to preach. His advanced age, his limited education, and the advice of his friends were all against it. In his fifty-third year he commenced the study of the Latin grammar, and, after laborious application to the requisite studies, was licensed to preach. Sept. 25, 1807. For two years he labored as a missionary, subsequently settling in Robeson county, where for nearly thirty years he supplied the four congregations of Philadelphia, Bethel, Lumber Ridge, and St Paul. His active pastorate continued till 1838; but his life was spared till 1852, when he had reached the one hundred and third year of his age. Pre-eminently devout, prayerful, and vigilant of the interests and welfare of the Church, he shrank from no duty and was ready for every emergency. When McNair, more eminent as a preacher, had exhausted, on the occasion of a visitation of a church, his stock of written sermons, and resolved, if he must preach, to go and procure others, McIntyre opposed it. "Oh, man," said he, "that will never do: do you not see that a good and great work is begun, and is going on prosperously? You must not, you cannot, leave this great and interesting assembly of people." McNair insisted on his purpose. "But can't you take a new text, man," replied McIntyre, "and get along in that way?" The counsel was characteristic. He had no sensibility to be wounded by a lack of elegance or polish, and he could not see the interest of religion exposed to suffer from what he regarded as a matter of intellectual pride. He was ever prepared himself. He never forgot what he had learned while a shepherd, following the flocks over the hills of his native land and reading and meditating upon the Scriptures. His mind was stored, not with the skeleton of a doctrinal system, but with the vital truths of the word of God; and his heart, glowing with the fervor of devotion, supplied the lack of erudite expression. At communion-seasons he was truly in his element. By participation in such privileges he seemed always to be refreshed and strengthened. "Of the palms of victory, the crowns of glory, the white robes of righteousness and salvation, the joyful and eternal rest,—all that pertains to the idea of heaven,—he would speak in strains of love and sweetness well becoming those immortal themes." Lingering on enfeebled, and incapable of active service, till after he had passed his hundredth year, it was a profound mystery to him why his Master should delay so long to call him home.

The Presbytery of Orange, until it was divided to form that of Concord, covered the entire State. Concord was erected in 1795, Fayetteville in 1812, and Roanoke in 1835. The first embraced the western portion, the second the southeastern, and the third the northeastern, of the territory of the original Presbytery. The membership of the Presbyteries in 1836 was sixty-six in place of the twenty-eight in 1800; and the churches under their care numbered one hundred and sixteen, where a little more than half the number had existed in 1800.

But to make up the aggregate, Concord Presbytery must be taken into account. In 1800, its members were Dr. S. E. McCorkle at Thyatira, James Hall at Bethany, James McRee at Centre, David Barr at Philadelphia, William Davis at Olney, Samuel Caldwell at Sugar Creek and Hopewell, James Wallis at Providence, Joseph D. Kilpatrick at Third Creek and Unity, Lewis F. Wilson at Concord and Fourth Creek, Humphrey Hunter at Goshen and Unity, John M. Wilson at Quaker Meadows and Morgantown, John Carrigan at Ramah and Bethphage, John Andrews at Little Britain, Samuel Davis at Mamre, and George Newton at Swananoa and Rimm's Creek. The churches of Steel Creek, Poplar Tent, Rocky River, Smyrna, Knob Creek, Mineral Spring,

Chesnut Spring, Mt. Pleasant, Mountain Creek, and Long Creek were vacant.

In 1809, McCorkle, Hall, McRee, Caldwell, Wallis, Kilpatrick, Hunter, J. M. Wilson, Carrigan, Newton, and S. Davis—eleven out of the fifteen—were still members of the Presbytery, and the places vacated by the others had been filled by John Brown, Thomas Hall, and Andrew S. Morrison, all without charge. Ten years later, only Hall, McRee, Caldwell, Wallis, Hunter, Kilpatrick, Wilson, Carrigan, and S. Davis remained, while John Robinson, removed from Orange Presbytery, was at Poplar Tent and Ramah, Robert B. Walker at Bethesda and Ebenezer, James S. Adams at Bethel and Beersheba, John B. Davies at Fishing Creek and Richardson, John Williamson at Hopewell and Paw Creek, Henry M. Kerr at Olney, Long Creek, and New Hope, and Francis H. Porter at Ashville, Rimm's Creek, and Swananoa. The vacant congregations were Bullock's Creek and Salem; Bethany, Concord, and Fourth Creek; Little Britain and Hebron; Duncan's Creek and Morgantown; Jersey, Joppa, and Quaker Meadows; Smyrna and Muddy Creek; Lincolnton, Unity, Concordtown, Salem, Mamre, Lane Creek, Buffalo, Amity, Purity, Edwards, Shiloh, Yorkville, Hopewell, S.C., and Waxhaw.

The fifteen ministers of 1800 had increased but one in nineteen years; while the congregations had risen from thirty-two to fifty-eight. One of the most painful features of the history of Presbyterianism in this region, including Georgia at a subsequent period, was the inability of the Presbyteries to secure men trained under their care for the work of the ministry. Nearly all that could be accomplished was to make good the places of those who removed to other fields or were cut off by death.

And yet the fault could be scarcely due to any defect

in the character or policy of the ministry in the field. Among them were to be found men not only foremost in Christian enterprise, but commanding the respect and confidence of the community for their practical wisdom, and in some cases for their statesmanship. In the scenes of the Revolutionary conflict, and subsequently in assisting to lay firm the foundations of established government, or making provision by schools and colleges for the cause of popular education, they were entitled to high honor. Men like the Caldwells and Wilsons, or of the stamp of Robinson, McCorkle, McRee, and Hall, could not fail to leave behind them a bright and noble record.

But perhaps no member of the North Carolina Presbyteries was, on the whole, more meritorious or effective in his labors to extend the bounds of the Church than James Hall, of whose earlier years mention has already been made.

At first (1778) he took charge of Bethany, Fourth Creek, and Concord congregations, ere long, however, resigning the two latter in order to devote himself personally to missionary labor under the care of the Synod. A more devoted, self-denying, sagacious, and energetic laborer was probably not to be found within the limits of the Church. His itinerant ministry extended far and near,—to central Georgia on the south, and to the settlements on the Mississippi at the west. His frame seemed to know no weariness or exhaustion. Unencumbered by domestic cares, he gave himself up with his whole soul to labors as pastor, evangelist, and missionary.

Of the powerful and impressive eloquence of Dr. Hall we have the most conclusive testimony from those that heard him. The Rev. Dr. Morrison (Sprague's Annals, iii. 386) says, speaking of a period previous to his own conversion, "When other ministers preached, I succeeded in preserving a good degree of indifference; but when Dr. Hall rose to speak, his looks and voice and solemn manner filled me with an indescribable awe and the most painful apprehensions. . . . His solemn and fervid manner generally awakened the bodily exercises incident to that day. It was no uncommon thing for persons to cry out in distress and plead aloud for mercy, or give thanks to God for their feelings of joy and offer audible supplication for their families and friends."

Dr. Charles Caldwell, in his Autobiography (p. 82), speaks of Dr. Hall's aspect as "more venerable and apostolic" than that of any other man he had ever seen. "In the power and majesty of pulpit eloquence he had no superior." He relates the circumstances of a discourse on a sacramental occasion in Poplar Tent congregation, at which so powerful was the impression that, when he concluded one of his descriptions, "a scream was uttered by several women, two or three were stricken down by their emotion, and a large portion of the assembled multitude made an involuntary start."

"Never," says Dr. Caldwell, "did I in any other instance, except one, witness an effort of oratory so powerful and bewitching." He speaks also of Dr. Hall's course during the war. He solicited and obtained the captaincy of a regiment of volunteer dragoons, on conditions—prescribed by himself—of raising his own company, and serving as their chaplain without pay. "An excellent rider, personally almost Herculean, possessed of a very long and flexible arm, and taking, as he did, daily lessons from a skilful teacher of the art, he became in a short time one of the best swordsmen in the cavalry of the South. Being found, moreover, as judicious in council as he was formidable in action, he received the *sobriquet* of the 'Ulysses of his regiment.'"

"Notwithstanding his stern and formidable qualities

as a soldier, he was one of the mildest and meekest of men." Somewhere about 1819, Dr. Caldwell met him for the last time at the General Assembly in Philadelphia. He speaks of him at that time in the following language :—"From the superior size of his person, the form and grandeur of his head and countenance, the snowy whiteness of his hair, of but little of which he had been shorn by the hand of time, and from the surpassing venerableness of his whole appearance, he was by far the most attractive and admired personage in the reverend body of which he was a member. He was instinctively regarded by all who beheld him as the rightful Nestor and ornament of the Assembly." "Never, as I verily believe, was he surpassed in moral rectitude, pure, fervent, and practical piety, and usefulness in the wide sphere of his diversified labors in the Christian ministry, by any individual our country has produced."

Among the ministers of the State were not a few who were in full sympathy with Dr. Hall, and who nobly sustained him in his zeal for missions. Wallis, pastor of New Providence (1792–1819), a warm friend of learning, and for several years at the head of a classical school, and also a trustee of the State University;[1] Kilpatrick, of Third Creek, a zealous friend of revivals, and less scrupulous than McCorkle in excepting to their irregularities;[2] the Caldwells, a trio memorable in the history of the State; Robinson, perhaps better entitled than any other to be regarded as the father of Fayetteville Presbytery; the two Paisleys, of revival memory; the three Turners, one of them at Raleigh giving promise in his early ministry, so untimely closed, of eminent service in the cause of Christ; together with McPheeters, Tate, and, at a later period, Kollock and

---

[1] Sprague, iv. 60. [2] Ib. iv. 601

Mitchell, Kerr and Porter,—these constituted the nucleus of a band which nobly sustained for many years under great discouragements, the cause of religion and learning.

In 1799, South Carolina Presbytery, representing the strength of the Presbyterian Church within the bounds of South Carolina and Georgia, numbered eighteen ministers, and had under its care fifty-one congregations, of which nearly one-half were vacant. Of the others, in most cases two, and sometimes three, were united under the charge of a single pastor.

At Bullock's Creek, teaching a school of a high order, while he supplied the church, was Joseph Alexander, a man of fine talents and accomplishments, and an uncommonly animated and popular preacher.[1] In 1805, he was succeeded by the gifted but erratic William C. Davis, subsequently (1811) deposed from the ministry for unsoundness of doctrine, but drawing off others into connection with him, and becoming the founder of a sect.

At Broadaway was James Gilliland, modest, diffident, and self-distrustful, but fearless in the utterance of his sentiments, and shrinking from no conclusion to which he was forced by his convictions. His anti-slavery sentiments as early as the date of his settlement (1796) were offensive to a portion of his congregation.[2] The

[1] Sprague, iii. 331.

[2] Ib. iv. 138. The subject of slavery had been discussed at Charleston, and violent results had followed, as early as 1802. Two Methodist preachers, John Harper and George Dougherty, were stationed at the time in that city. Hearing that Mr. Harper had received documents from the North containing resolutions to memorialize the Legislature against slavery,—though the documents were burned in presence of the Mayor,—a lawless mob resolved to avenge themselves on Mr. Harper. He escaped them, however; but Mr. Dougherty was seized, dragged through the streets to the pump, and would have been suffocated by the water pumped on him, if he had not been rescued. See Bangs's Methodism, ii 125.

dissolution of his pastoral relation, in 1805, followed upon the difficulties and differences of sentiment and feeling upon this subject, and he removed, to spend the residue of his life and ministry among the churches of the Northwest, where freer utterance might be allowed him.

At Goodhope and Roberts congregations was John Simpson, whose pastorate closed previous to 1808, and who was succeeded, after an interval of several years, by Richard B. Cater, who took charge, soon after his licensure in 1814, of the two congregations, together with that of Broadaway, which had been left vacant by the resignation of Mr. Baird, Gilliland's successor. At Nazareth was James Templeton, succeeded previous to 1808 by James Gilliland, Jr., whose pastoral charge of the congregation closed previous to 1819, when it was reported vacant. At Rocky River, although but for a short time, was Dr. Francis Cummins; but soon after 1804 he was succeeded by Moses Waddel, who, on establishing his classical school at Willington, supplied Hopewell and Rocky River, till elected President of Georgia University in 1819.[1] In charge of Catholic and Purity congregations was Robert McCulloch, whose pastorate at Purity closed previous to 1803, where he was succeeded (before 1808) by Thomas Neely, who also had charge of Edmonds congregation; while Mr. McCulloch had (1814) Catholic and Concord, which he retained for many years. James Stephenson had charge of Bethel congregation in Williamsburg and Indiantown, which he retained till 1808. His successors, previous to 1814, were Andrew Flinn, for a brief period, and Daniel Brown.[2] The pastor of Waxhaw congregation was John Brown, whose pastorate

[1] His successor was R. B. Cater, at Willington.

[2] In 1819, Robert W. James had charge of Bethel and Indiantown.

here closed with his acceptance of the post of Professor of Logic and Moral Philosophy in the University of South Carolina, in 1809. At Long Canes was Robert Wilson, whose pastorate closed previous to 1808, but who previous to 1814 was succeeded at Lower Long Cane by Henry Reid. At Fair Forest was William Williamson, whose pastorate continued till after 1803, and who was succeeded previous to 1808 by Daniel Gray, who took charge also of Union and Grassy Spring, which had long been vacant, but who was succeeded by Joseph Hillhouse previous to 1819.

At Bethesda was Robert B. Walker, whose pastorate continued as late as 1808.[1] At Columbia was David E. Dunlap, whose successors were Benjamin R. Montgomery (previous to 1814) and Thomas C. Henry (Nov. 1818–24). At Lebanon and Wateree was Samuel W. Yongue, whose charge in subsequent years till 1819 is reported as Lebanon and Mt. Olivet. At Salem was John Foster, succeeded previous to 1803 by George G. McWhorter, whose pastorate closed previous to 1808, the church subsequently remaining vacant for many years. At Duncan's Creek and Little River was John B. Kennedy, whose pastorate extended over more than a quarter of a century. At Bethel and Beersheba was George G. McWhorter, who shortly after removed to Salem and Witherspoon, and whose successor for a brief period was Thomas Neely. Mr. McWhorter's subsequent charge, assumed previous to 1814, was that of Beaver Creek and Concord congregations, which had long been vacant. At Bethel[2] and Cane Creek was Andrew Brown, whose charge of the latter was demitted previous to 1819, while he still retained the former. John B. Davis was at Fishing Creek and

---

[1] Subsequently of Concord Presbytery.

[2] Written Bethlehem in the report for 1800.

Richardson, where his pastorate continued as late as 1809.

The vacant churches in 1800 were Hopewell, Carmel, Greenville, Rocky Creek, Smyrna, Coffeetown, Hopewell on Pee Dee, Beaver Creek, Hanging Rock, Mt. Olivet, Zion, Aimwell, Concord, Ebenezer, Fish Dam, Grassy Spring, Union, Newton, Milford, North Pacolate, Fairview, Liberty Spring, Calvary, Bethany, and Unity.

Hopewell and Carmel long remained destitute of a pastor; but previous to 1819, James Hillhouse had them as a joint charge. Previous to 1803, Smyrna was supplied by Hugh Dixon, whose charge subsequently included Greenville, and whose pastorate extended over more than a quarter of a century. At about the same time, James Gilliland, Jr., took charge of Nazareth and Fairview, resigning the latter before 1814 and the former previous to 1819, when he had removed to Pearl River, Mississippi, leaving both churches vacant. Before 1808, Mt. Olivet was united with Lebanon under the charge of S. W. Yongue. Before 1803, William G. Rosborough had taken the charge of Concord (with Horeb), where his successor, before 1814, was G. G. McWhorter, who had Beaver Creek as a joint charge.[1] Before 1808, Aimwell and Hopewell had become the joint charge of Duncan Brown, who was succeeded previous to 1814 by Daniel Smith.

Besides these, Thomas D. Baird, for two or three years, as a successor of James Gilliland at Broadaway, had charge of Goodhope and Roberts (1812-15). In 1809, William H. Barr commenced a pastorate of thirty-four years over the Upper Long Cane congregation, Abbeville District. The church at Camden dates from 1806, when Andrew Flinn commenced his labors here and succeeded in organizing and building up a respect-

---

[1] Mt. Zion is reported with these in 1814.

able congregation. His successor was George Reid, whose pastorate, commencing previous to 1814, closed before 1819, when the church was reported vacant. Previous to 1808, John Cousar had charge of New Hope; but before 1814 his charge was Midway and Bruington, which he retained for many years.

The church of Augusta, though in existence previous to 1792, when Dr. William McWhirr declined the invitation to take charge of it in conjunction with the academy, on account of the affairs of both being complicated by the movements of political parties, is not reported in the minutes of Assembly until 1814, when John R. Thompson had the pastoral charge. Dr. McWhirr, however, soon after declining the call of the Augusta church, commenced his labors at Sunbury and Springfield, Ga., and in 1809 commenced preaching at the court-house in McIntosh county, where he succeeded in organizing a church, subsequently transferred to Darien.

The first pastor reported at Waynesborough was E. B. Caldwell (1819). This church, as well as that of Winnsborough, was organized previous to 1814, when it is first found on the minutes of Assembly. At Charleston a Second Presbyterian Church was formed, through the desire felt to secure the services of Andrew Flinn, then laboring at Bethel and Indiantown. On occasion of visiting Charleston, he had preached several times in the Scotch Presbyterian Church. Such was the impression made by his fervid eloquence that the project was immediately formed to build a new and elegant Presbyterian church in the upper part of the city, with the express intention of calling him as pastor. Such was the enthusiasm in his favor that a large subscription was raised, and the foundations laid of an edifice which cost not less than one hundred thousand dollars. While the edifice was in process of erection, he commenced his ministry among the new congregation, who had secured the use of an unoccupied Methodist house of worship. His installation took place April 4, 1811; and under his pastorate the church and congregation had a rapid and healthful growth.[1]

Two years after the settlement of Dr. Flinn, A. W. Leland was called to the pastorate of the First Presbyterian Church of Charleston. The death of Dr. Buist, one of the finest scholars of his day, had occurred, after a pastorate of fourteen years, in 1808; and during the closing period of his ministry he had been at the same time Principal of the Charleston College and pastor of the church. The Third Church was not organized till about the year 1820; and three years later Dr. William A. McDowell was called to take its pastoral charge.

At the commencement of the century, quite a number of churches within the State were Congregational or, as reported to the Assembly at a later period, Independent Presbyterian. Among them were Circular Church, Charleston,—of which William Hollingshead and Isaac S. Keith, both educated as Presbyterians, were collegiate pastors,—Edisto, Walterborough, Wiltown, Stony Creek, and one or two others on the "maritime islands." At what time the pastors of these churches united to form a Congregational Association is uncertain; but the Association itself continued to exist till 1822, when it was dissolved and its members were united with the Presbytery of Harmony. The churches, however, still retained their previous ecclesiastical character, at least for many years. The majority of the Presbytery promptly rejected the new "basis of 1837 and 1838."[2]

---

[1] Dr. Flinn's death occurred Feb. 24, 1820. His successors were Artemas Boies (1820–23), Thomas Charlton Henry (1823–27), William Ashmead (1829), and Thomas Smyth (1832).

[2] The facts are given in a publication from the pen of Dr. Smyth.

In 1799, the First Presbytery of South Carolina was divided in order to form the Second Presbytery. The name of each was (1809–10) subsequently changed,—the first to that of Harmony, and the last to that of South Carolina. In 1813, the Synod of the Carolinas was divided, and the Synod of South Carolina and Georgia constituted from the Presbyteries of Harmony, South Carolina, and Hopewell. But in 1821, such had been the growth of these that from the latter the Presbytery of Georgia was constituted, and from the two former the Presbytery of Alabama in the same year.

In 1822, upon a proposal from the Presbytery of Harmony, the Congregational Association of Charleston dissolved itself, and its members were received (Nov. 19) into the Presbytery.[1] A few days later (Nov. 23), these, with some other members of Harmony

---

When the division took place, he was one of the minority of the Presbytery who withdrew, and who still, as recognized by the Synod, claimed to constitute the Presbytery. The Synod was largely in favor of the "New Basis," and required the Presbytery to conform to their order. By refusing to do this, it was claimed that the majority ceased to constitute the Presbytery.

[1] Its principal churches were the Circular Church of Charleston, those of Dorchester and James Island, probably those of Midway and Savannah in Georgia, besides which it may have had a few others.

Simms, the historian of South Carolina, says, "In 1696, a colony of Congregationalists, from Dorchester in Massachusetts, ascended the Ashley River nearly to its head, and there founded a town, to which they gave the name of that which they had left. Dorchester became a town of some importance, having a moderately large population and considerable trade. It is now deserted; the habitations and inhabitants have alike vanished; but the reverend spire, rising through the forest-trees that surround it, still attests (1840) the place of their worship, and where so many of them yet repose."—*History of South Carolina*, p. 52.

Presbytery, residing in and around Charleston, were erected into the Presbytery of Charleston Union.[1]

During this period, Dr. Flinn (1810–20), of Charleston, was perhaps the most eminent among the Presbyterian ministers of the State. A graduate of North Carolina University, and a licentiate of Orange Presbytery (1800), his first efforts in the pulpit excited great attention and secured him reputation as one of the most popular candidates of the day. At Hillsborough, Fayetteville, and Camden, S.C., he had given full proof of his ministry before he was called to the charge of the Second Presbyterian Church of Charleston. As a preacher, he was distinguished by earnestness, solemnity, and pathos.[2] Fully devoted to his work, and faithful alike in the pulpit and in pastoral duty, he gathered around him a large congregation, who regarded him with warm affection and the highest respect. The kindness of his manner and the charm of his social intercourse won the hearts of all with whom he came in contact; while his faithful presentations of gospel-truth were delivered in tones of affection and in a style which commended them to the acceptance even of opposers.

Joseph Alexander, of Bullock's Creek,[3] of fine talents and accomplishments, and popular as a preacher, George Reid, an intimate friend of Dr. Flinn, and an able thinker, Dr. A. W. Leland, whose pastorate of the First Church of Charleston commenced in 1813, Thomas C. Henry, of Columbia (1818), and afterward (1824) of Charleston, graceful and polished in manner, exemplary as a pastor, and rarely surpassed as a pulpit-orator,—these, and quite a number of others, might be mentioned as holding a high rank among the ministers

---

[1] Baird's Digest, 850. [2] Sprague, iv. 277

[3] Sprague, iii. 331. He died in 1808.

of the State. Several, whose sphere of labor was some times within the bounds of South Carolina and sometimes within that of Georgia, might be claimed perhaps by the former; but the closing period of their labors was devoted to the interests of the latter State.

The Presbytery of Hopewell was erected, by a division of the Presbytery of South Carolina, in 1796.[1] It was taken off from the extreme western part of the old Presbytery, and extended over Northern Georgia It had at first but five members, and for many years its growth was far from rapid. In 1803, only four members are recorded as in connection with it,—Robert M. Cunningham, William Montgomery, Thomas Newton, and Edward Pharr,—the last a licentiate of Orange Presbytery in 1800.

Ebenezer Church, in Hancock (Green county), was organized in the autumn of 1792 by R. M. Cunningham. The church at Bethany was of older date. As early as 1788[2] it had been for some time a missionary station of the North Carolina (Orange) Presbytery. Several other churches were soon after organized,—some of them by Francis Cummins, who began his ministry at Bethel Church, York District, S.C., in 1782, and fifty years afterward closed his course at Greensborough, Ga. In the latter State twenty-five years of his life were spent. But he was not limited in his labors to a single parish. A score of churches in North Carolina and Georgia considered him as in some sense their pastor, during nearly the whole period of his ministry.

Thomas Goulding, a native of Midway, Ga., commenced his ministry at White Bluffs soon after his

[1] Duly constituted March, 1797.

[2] It was in that year that Moses Waddel, subsequently (1819) President of the University of Georgia, received at this place his first permanent religious impressions. He was at the time engaged in teaching, but immediately began to study for the ministry.

licensure by Harmony Presbytery in 1813. Here he remained till 1822, when he removed to Lexington, Oglethorpe county, completing at the latter place a pastorate of eight years. His later years were spent first at Columbia as Theological Professor, and subsequently at Columbus as pastor of the church.

At Alcovia, Edward Pharr[1] was settled for a long period. He was one of the early, but not original, members of the Presbytery, and was licensed to preach by Orange Presbytery in 1800. The church of Athens originated in the labors of Dr. Robert Finley, who in 1817 accepted the invitation to the Presidency of the University of Georgia. The zeal and energy with which he devoted himself to collect funds for an institution "at its last gasp" proved too much for his already debilitated frame; and he sank under the attack of disease, Oct. 3, 1817.

Augusta, which has been mentioned in connection with the Presbytery of South Carolina, was subsequently transferred to the care of Hopewell Presbytery, and in 1820 this Presbytery numbered under its care some twenty churches, mostly in the northeastern portion of the State.[2]

Although the Presbytery of Georgia was not formed till 1821, several of the churches which constituted it had been in existence for several years. In 1823, these were six in number,—Augusta, St. Mary's, Mt. Zion, Darien, Louisville, Clinton. Within a short time after, the churches of Savannah and of St. Augustine, as well as of

---

[1] Sometimes written Farr.

[2] There is no report of the churches in the minutes of the Assembly until 1825. At that time they were Greensborough and Bethany, Mt. Zion and Eatonton, Athens, Alcovia, Madison Second and Third, Gwinnet Court-House, Sandy Creek, Washington and Salem, Lincolnton, Lexington and Cherokee Corner, Augusta, Thyatira, Hall Court-House, Hebron, Louisville, Mulberry, and Newhope.

Midway, were received under the care of the Presbytery. The last was Congregational in its form of government, and derived its existence from Puritan immigration at a very early date.

In October, 1695, a church was organized in Dorchester, Mass., "with a design to remove to Carolina, to encourage the settlement of churches and the promotion of religion in the Southern plantations." Embarking, after solemn religious services, the church arrived, with its pastor, in Carolina on the 20th of December, and formed a settlement on the Ashley River, eighteen miles from Charleston. To this, in memory of their former home, they gave the name of Dorchester. But the settlement proved unhealthy, and the quantity of land too small; and on May 11, 1752, three persons were sent to Georgia to select a place to which the church, or a portion of it, might remove. The place selected was called Midway, from its supposed equal distance between the Ogeechee and Altamaha. From the Council of Georgia a grant of thirty-one thousand nine hundred and fifty acres of ground was secured, and, after many misfortunes by land and sea, the colony, in March, 1754, located in their new home. The name of the pastor was John Osgood, a graduate of Harvard in 1733, and he removed with them. A log church was immediately built, which, three years later, was replaced by one larger and more commodious. Mr. Osgood died in 1773, and in 1776, Moses Allen, of Northampton, Mass., succeeded to the pastoral charge.[1] In November, 1778, the society was entirely broken up and dispersed by the British army from Florida, under General Provost, and the house of worship, as well as nearly every dwelling-house in the settlement, was burned. On the return of peace the scattered inhabitants re-collected in Mid-

[1] Sprague's Annals, ii. 240.

way, and became again established in their former rights and privileges. The pastoral services of Abiel Holmes[1] were secured in 1784, and on the failure of his health, two years later, his place was supplied for a time by Jedediah Morse. A constant succession of pastors was kept up, and an academy was established and sustained to promote the cause of learning. Years before the church came under the care of Presbytery, it had furnished from its own membership several pastors for Presbyterian churches within the State.

The church of Savannah had been long in existence. It dates probably from the time of Whitefield. In 1760, J. J. Zubly commenced his pastorate, which extended to 1778, when, on account of his political sentiments, he was exiled from the State. In 1801, Robert Smith, who had previously been settled at Schenectady, N.Y., was its pastor,[2] and was succeeded in 1806 by the gifted Henry Kollock, whose pastorate continued till his death, in 1819.

The church of St. Augustine was organized in 1824, and owed its existence to the labors of Dr. William McWhirr, the father and founder of the church of Darien (1809).

Several of the churches in the central portion of the eastern part of the State remained still in connection with Harmony Presbytery of South Carolina, so that at the time of the erection of Georgia Presbytery the Presbyterian strength of the State was divided between the three Presbyteries of Hopewell, Harmony, and Georgia. In 1820, the number of Presbyterian churches within the State limits could not have been far from twenty-five or thirty.

But already several distinguished ministers had devoted themselves to extend in this field the bounds of

---

[1] Author of "American Annals." [2] Dwight's Travels, ii. 490.

the Church. McWhirr at the south, performing no small share of missionary labor, and for the most part with scant remuneration, Francis Cummins at the north, the patriarch of Hopewell Presbytery, Goulding, a native Georgian, and a man of great sagacity and energy, fully devoted to the cause of religion and learning, and mourning over the apathy which he met around him, Moses Waddel, ultimately President of the State University, and proving himself fully equal to every emergency which he was called to meet, a man of shrewd insight, scrupulous conscientiousness, unwearied application, and devoted piety, John Brown, his predecessor as President (1811–19), a model teacher, loving and beloved of his pupils, while known among his friends as "Our Apostle John,"—such were some of the men who grace the early history of the Presbyterian Church within the State, and to whom its subsequent prosperity is largely due.

While at the North and in portions of the West the missionary work of the Church was largely in the hands of the Assembly,—more especially after the erection of the Synod of Kentucky,—it was left at the South and Southwest in the hands of the Synod of the Carolinas. At the sessions of this body in 1800, missionaries were appointed to visit the Western country as far as Natchez on the Mississippi; and, when their report was made in the following year, the Synod were "happy to find that, by the blessing of Divine Providence, the good consequences of that mission appear to have exceeded their most sanguine anticipations." Encouraged by the result, the Synod took measures to bring the subject before all their congregations and to obtain collections for the support of missionaries. William Montgomery, the father of the Mississippi Presbytery, but at this time a member of Hopewell Presbytery, and John Matthews, subsequently of Indiana, were appointed missionaries to the Mississippi Territory; and Thomas Hall, a licentiate of Concord Presbytery, was directed to itinerate through the Carolinas and Georgia for eight months.[1]

In the following year Mr. Matthews was appointed a missionary to Natchez, and with him was associated Hugh Shaw, a licentiate of Orange Presbytery. The missionary work of the Synod received increased attention, and in 1802 a commission of the Synod was appointed to whom it was given in charge. In the following year, eight missionaries were appointed to itinerate within the bounds of the Synod, one of whom, William C. Davis, was to act until the next meeting of Synod as missionary to the Catawba Indians.

The increasing demand for missionaries drew attention to the claims of ministerial education. It was, therefore (1802), enjoined upon each Presbytery to establish within its bounds one or more grammar-schools, except where such schools had been already established; and each minister was to make it his business to select and encourage youths of promising piety and talent, who might be expected to turn their attention to the ministry.

New members were from time to time added to the list of the members of Synod, but the supply of laborers was quite insufficient to meet the demand. In 1802, the year of the great revival, the accession was most remarkable. Leonard Prather was received by the Presbytery of Orange from the Methodist Church, and Daniel Brown,[2] Andrew Flinn, Malcolm McNair, Ezekiel B. Currie, and John Matthews were likewise ordained. John Cousar, George Reid, and Thomas Neely were reported as licentiates of the First Presbytery of South Carolina, Thomas Hall a licentiate of Concord, Edward Pharr of Hopewell, and Hugh Dickson of the Second South

---

[1] Foote's North Carolina. [2] Report for 1803 says *Duncan* Brown.

Carolina. Other licentiates of this period were Hugh Shaw, Murdoch Murphy, Murdoch McMillan, Robert Dobbins, and Benjamin Montgomery. At a still later period,[1] the licentiates within the bounds of the Synod were Andrew and Joseph Caldwell, Samuel Paisley, W. B. Meroney, John McIntyre, Allen McDougal, Davis Parks, William Barr, John Gloucester, and others.

As a general thing, immediately after their licensure, they were sent forth as missionaries. A meagre salary was given them; for the churches from which the necessary funds were raised were few and feeble. But it sufficed to furnish them with "scrip and staff;" and, thus equipped, they were commissioned to take practical lessons in preaching, by itinerating in the wilderness, looking after the scattered sheep, supplying the vacant congregations, and addressing such assemblies as they could draw together. It was a rough experience. It required men of energy and vigor, mental and physical, as well as no small measure of self-denying love for souls, to meet it. But the training in such a school was worth the price of tuition; and it brought into the field some of the most efficient and successful ministers of the day.

From year to year the Synod continued or renewed their missionary appointments. Its field extended westward to the banks of the Mississippi, and the men who were most eminent in the service were Hall, Smylie, McNair, Brown, Barr, Currie, and Flinn. In 1811, the Synod arranged to resign the charge of the missionary business into the hands of the Assembly, with the appointments and measures of which the Presbyteries might individually co-operate. The lack of candidates of which the Southern churches found reason to complain, operated against the prosecution

---

[1] 1807–08.

by the Synod of the missionary work.[1] In spite of all the efforts of the Synod, the cause of ministerial education was in a languishing state.

In no part of the land, during the period under review, were the most unexceptionable features of the great Kentucky revival more largely reproduced than in portions of the field occupied by the Synod of the Carolinas, and especially within the bounds of Orange and Concord Presbyteries, in the central and western parts of North Carolina. It was here that McGready, before his removal to Kentucky, had lived and labored; and the memory of his presence and words, as well as the fruits of his ministry, still remained. The report of what had taken place in the Cumberland region was brought back across the mountains, and excited everywhere the deepest interest.

There had been already—subsequent to the close of the war—two marked seasons of revival in this region. The first began in Iredell county; the second commenced at a period when the prospects of religion were exceedingly dark, and when immorality and vice had come in like a flood. The leading instrument in the work was McGready himself, who on his return from Pennsylvania passed through the scenes of the great revival in Virginia. His glowing spirit quickly caught, and was ready to communicate, the flame. Wherever he went, he preached with a fervor and pungency peculiar to himself. Among his congregations there were close searchings of heart and solemn attention. At Hawfields and Cross-Roads (Orange county) the revival broke out under his preaching in 1791, extending, and continuing

[1] In 1822, Dr. Goulding, of Georgia, said, "There are but two native Georgians in the Presbyterian ministry of this State." The two were Goulding himself and Quartermann, of Midway. Dr. Goulding thus informed the author of this note. F.

for several years, in what is now the upper part of Orange Presbytery.

In 1796, McGready removed to Kentucky, lingering on his way to preach for a few months in Eastern Tennessee. At length, in 1799–1800, the great Western revival commenced. The fame of it spread over the whole land; but nowhere did it command more attention or excite deeper interest than in the region where McGready had previously labored, and where, as a Boanerges, his stern denunciations of sin were yet vividly remembered. At Hawfields and Cross-Roads, William Paisley had succeeded McGready, and under his ministrations a communion-season was held at Cross-Roads in August, 1801. Dr. Caldwell and Messrs. Prather, Shaw, and Currie, the two last recent licentiates of Orange Presbytery, assisted upon the occasion. On the days preceding the Sabbath,—for the meetings uniformly commenced on Friday,—and during the administration of the ordinance, nothing unusual or remarkable occurred. There was deep solemnity, as well as earnest prayerfulness, but nothing more to indicate that a blessing was at hand.

But on the next day, as the pastor arose to dismiss the large congregation which had gathered to the scene, —many of them from a great distance,—it was his purpose first to say a few words expressive of his grief that no advance apparently had been made in bringing sinners to God. But, overcome by his emotions, he found himself unable to speak, and sat down. A solemn silence pervaded the assembly. In a few moments he rose again, but, before he had uttered a word, a young man just from the scenes of revival in Tennessee, who during the meetings had had much to say to others of what he had witnessed of the work of God in that State, raised up his hands, and exclaimed, "Stand still and see the salvation of God." In a few moments the silence was broken by sobs, groans, and cries, which rose commingled from all parts of the house. There was no longer any thought of dismissing the congregation. The remainder of the day was spent in prayer, exhortation, singing, and personal conversation; and it was midnight before the people could be persuaded to return to their homes. The awakening continued to extend, and the converts were quite numerous.

This was in August. In October the sacrament was administered at Hawfields, the other congregation under Mr. Paisley's charge. From the first, there were manifestations of deep feeling. The report of the previous communion-season had been widely spread, and had drawn together an unusual number. The people from Cross-Roads were present, in the fervor of excited expectation. The meeting continued for five consecutive days. Persons from a distance, who had come in their wagons, remained over-night on the ground. With the exception of short intervals for refreshment during the day, and a few hours of sleep at night, the various religious exercises were continued without interruption. The assemblage had become, in fact, a camp-meeting. It was the first in the whole region. But the impression made was deep and lasting, and its apparent results encouraged other appointments. These were successively made until the camp-meeting became a kind of established institution in connection with the still extending revival.

The excitement spread rapidly over the upper part of Orange Presbytery. At the close of 1801, and at the commencement of 1802, its influence began to be felt west of the Yadkin, and within the bounds of Concord Presbytery, as well as in the eastern portion of the State around Fayetteville. Early in January, Dr. Caldwell, of Guilford, appointed a meeting near Bell's Mills, on Deep River, in Randolph county, and invited the ministers west of the Yadkin to attend. But they had doubts and fears in regard to the work, from their distrust of the unusual bodily exercises by which already to some extent it was characterized. Yet four ministers and about one hundred of their people accepted the invitation. They came to witness and to scrutinize the work. Dr. McCorkle, strongly prejudiced against the "exercises," took some of his congregation with him, designing merely to be a spectator of the proceedings. L. F. Wilson, from Iredell county, Kilpatrick, of Third Creek, and James Hall, of Bethany, each accompanied by members of his congregation, were present. On Friday evening the preachers reached the ground. On Saturday morning the people in their wagons came pouring in. The meeting proved to be one of great excitement. All the companies, one after another, were more or less affected. The doubts of all the ministers but Dr. McCorkle, in regard to the genuineness of the work, were dispelled. He still held out,—when a message reached him, with a request from his son, who had been struck down, to come and pray for him. He went, knelt by his side, and began to pray; but, as he prayed, his soul seemed melted within him, his heart glowed with longing desires for the conversion of the whole world, his doubts and scruples gave place to conviction, and, notwithstanding the bodily exercises, he confessed his sympathy with the revival, and gave in his adhesion to it as a genuine work of the Spirit of God.

The ministers and people from the other side of the Yadkin who had attended the meeting had travelled from fifty to eighty miles. They carried back with them the spirit of the scenes in which they had mingled. They had witnessed what they dared ascribe only to a divine power. "Impressions ran through the assembly like fire along a train of powder." The greater portion of the young people were "religiously exercised," and at times during the meeting nothing was to be heard but cries for mercy. Nor was the influence of the occasion confined to those who were present. As these returned to their homes, "the work broke out like fire" in different places. Opposition was silenced. Some of the most obstinate were brought to submission. From this time the revival continued to spread rapidly in all directions, and "general meetings," as they were called, began to be held, at which thousands were present.[1]

On Friday, January 22, 1802, one of these was appointed within the bounds of Concord Presbytery, at a place eight miles south of Bethany, the residence of Dr. James Hall. It was attended by eight Presbyterian, one Baptist, and three Methodist clergymen. More than one hundred wagons, besides chairs and carriages, were on the ground, while many came to the meeting on horseback. The number of persons present was probably from one thousand five hundred to two thousand. The place selected for the meeting was a solitary grove, remote from any house. The weather was quite unfavorable. A moderate rain continued from the commencement of the exercises until Saturday morning, when it greatly increased and was followed by sleet and snow and a still greater fall of rain. It was expected that the assembly would disperse; for, although most were provided with tents, the rain and cold rendered the weather exceedingly inclement. At this juncture, one of the ministers took his stand in a large tent and began to preach. Dr. Hall, at a convenient distance, followed his example. Crowds immediately collected, and when the ministers had concluded their discourses they were followed by other speakers. The exercises continued till near dark, and the number of those who had been previously affected was largely

---

[1] New York Miss. Magazine, iii. 176.

increased. Quite a number fell. Not less than a dozen might be seen at a time lying in one tent,—some speechless and motionless, others with every breath crying for mercy, and some rising with acclamations of joy and praise.

On Sabbath the Lord's Supper was to be celebrated. But about the time that service was to begin, "such a torrent of cries burst forth" that it was found vain to attempt the administration of the ordinance. The ministers mingled with the multitude, who divided into parties convenient for hearing a single speaker. The exhortations were continued till twilight, and, even after they had withdrawn from their tents, religious exercises were continued till after midnight. Monday presented a repetition of the scenes of the preceding day; but on Monday night the number affected was greater than ever before. On Tuesday morning, the provisions and forage having been consumed, the assembly was dismissed.

On the 5th of February another meeting was commenced at Morgantown, sixty miles west. At this, six Presbyterian, one Baptist, and six Methodist preachers were present. The region around was near the mountains, thinly inhabited, and scantily supplied with religious privileges. But here the scenes of the former meeting were repeated. The first to be visibly affected were three men, one nearly sixty years of age, and all of them conspicuous characters. Others fell in considerable numbers,—some of them not under the preaching, but while sitting in their tents or listening to the singing of hymns. For many months previous, there had appeared in the public mind a tenderness and susceptibility which had rarely been witnessed before, and which seemed to prepare the way for this remarkable outburst of religious feeling.

On the 12th of March the third general meeting

was held. It was attended by fourteen Presbyterian, two Baptist, five Methodist, two Dutch Calvinist, and two Episcopal clergymen. Dr. Hall pronounced the assembly by far the most numerous and solemn that he had ever beheld. On the first day the proportion of persons affected was much greater than ever before. More than two hundred wagons, besides carriages, were on the ground. The communicants numbered about six hundred, and the entire assembly must have been four times as numerous. Three stands were occupied for preaching, and were surrounded by assemblies "vastly large." The work continued steadily to increase in power till two o'clock on Tuesday morning, and, "moderately speaking, there must have been several hundreds" who were affected.

The fourth general meeting was appointed on Friday, March 27, and was held at New Providence Church, under the charge of Mr. Wallis, in Mecklenburg county, about twelve miles southeast of Charlotte, and somewhat more than seventy miles north of Camden. The encampment was on a beautiful mount, easy of ascent from every direction, and more than half surrounded by a little crystal stream, which afforded water sufficient for the people and horses. It was clothed with a thick growth of giant oaks, with very little undergrowth. By three o'clock in the afternoon it was swept clear of timber, the tents were pitched, the fuel was gathered, and thousands, with their covered wagons and stretched canvas arranged in regular lines of encampment, covered the summit.

The services then commenced. A holy fervor glowed on the faces of the ministers, and a grave solemnity rested on the countenances of the people. A loud and lofty song of praise,—like "the sound of many waters," —swelled by the united voices of the great assembly, and waking the echoes of the neighboring hills, rose to heaven. Prayer was then offered; and as the words of the text, "This is the house of God, this is the gate of heaven," were uttered, it seemed but the instinctive expression of the feelings of every heart.

During the evening, and throughout the greater part of the night, there were exercises of singing, prayer, and exhortation in the several tents. The novelty of the scene, the fervor of devotion, and the depth of feeling so affected the multitude that few closed their eyes in sleep to the dawn of day. Before the services commenced on Saturday morning, three persons were struck down. At the close of the forenoon sermons several more were similarly affected; and the number continued to increase until the close of the meetings. Seventeen ministers were present, and about five hundred communicants participated in the sacrament of the Lord's Supper, which was administered in the midst of the camp without noise or disturbance. At the same time preaching was going forward at three different stations. At the close of the services on Monday, continuing as they did till midnight, there were about one hundred persons prostrate on the ground, the greater part of whom were shouting aloud, and many of them in the most earnest manner entreating for mercy. While Dr. Hall was at prayer, about forty fell at the same instant. It was estimated that the whole assemblage amounted to at least five thousand persons. How large a number were "stricken" could not be ascertained. Besides those affected at the preaching-stations, many were taken in their tents, many more in their wagons, and a great many in the woods while at prayer or on their return to their homes.

Still other meetings were held; but their general features were substantially the same with those already described. The scenes they presented were pronounced "truly august and solemn," especially in the night-season. When the fires were lighted up, the whole camp was illuminated, and revealed the canvas tents, the overhanging boughs of the trees left for shelter, and the eager listening groups, while the air was laden with solemn sounds which seemed more impressive amid the strangeness of the scene. Lofty songs of praise, pathetic prayers, thrilling appeals, stirring exhortations, groans or sighs of keen mental anguish, loud cries for mercy, or rapturous shouts of "glory" and thanksgiving from those who had found relief, were heard from every quarter of the encampment, and yet "with as little confusion and disturbance as the people of a city pursue their various occupations in the busy scenes of life."[1] Every object, every utterance, seemed to conspire to deepen the solemnity. All that might interfere to distract attention was shrouded in darkness. The devout spirit seemed to realize the immediate presence of Jehovah, the presence of Him whose temple is all space, and beneath its dome of stars, with fellow-worshippers around him, bowed with reverence and awe appropriate to a "house not made with hands."

The impression made upon those who had been drawn thither by curiosity was one which they could not shake off. It was almost impossible for them to sneer at what they witnessed. Those who came to mock often "remained to pray." The most hardened cases were the very ones whose "exercises" were most marked. In some instances not more than one in five, in others not more than one in ten, of those who were

---

[1] Letter of Dr. John Brown, New York Miss. Mag., iii. 182. The fullest account of the revival which I have met with is in a pamphlet of thirty-six pages 16mo, entitled "A Narrative of a most extraordinary Work of Religion in North Carolina. By Rev. James Hall. Also a Collection of Interesting Letters from Rev. J. McCorkle." Elizabethtown, 1803.

supposed to have been converted, were in the least physically affected. But where a person had been noted for his opposition or his incredulity, he was one of the most probable candidates for the "exercises."

And yet there was no stereotyped formula of experience. While all seemed to be awed and impressed, those who fell did not always find peace. Some persons were struck down successively as many as five or six times before they obtained relief, while others even then did not attain it. In numerous instances the effect of the stroke was to take away the power of speech and motion, and frequently it was not recovered for several hours. Toward the last, however, persons would pray in whispers and then rise in triumph. In other instances the control of the body seemed lost, while the power of speech was retained. Persons thus affected would cry out, "Oh, the hardness of my heart!" "Oh, my unbelief!" As hope gleamed upon them from the gospel, or they gained clearer views of the Saviour, they poured their souls forth in pathetic pleadings, exclaiming, "Oh for one grain of faith!" or, "Blessed Jesus, what a Saviour art thou!" sometimes varying these for similar expressions. When the soul at length could feel that it had obtained relief, its joy found utterance first in whisperings, and then in shouts, or even in raptures of praise and irrepressible ecstasies of "Glory, glory to God!"

Yet relief was not always obtained. In many instances those who were affected gradually recovered their strength, but still walked in darkness. Some even went back to their former ways, whilst others, after weeks or even months of darkness, or after repeated "strokes," at last found peace. As a general thing, the loss and the recovery of power over the limbs were gradual. During the state of helplessness the person ceased to weep, the features of his face grew calm and composed, his pulse became less rapid, his extremities cold, his voice more and more feeble till it ceased, and the eyes were nearly closed. After an interval sometimes of less than an hour, sometimes of far more than that period, speech and motion would return. The countenance would beam with pleasure as peace entered the soul. The ecstasy that usually followed was of but brief duration. Yet, calm, mild, sedate, the subject of this experience showed for days the evidence in his features of his inward joy, and in some cases manifested "a sweet mixture of love and joy, which no tongue or pen can describe."

Theories to explain these strange phenomena were abundant. But those who were most sanguine in their confident ability to discover a solution were soon forced to confess that their ingenuity was baffled. Bodily imbecility, fear, nervous weakness, sympathy, ministerial oratory, demoniac delusions,—these were the causes severally or successively assigned, but subsequently abandoned. It was felt that in the work there was, with all its peculiarities, something inexplicable, something divine. Its results were such as to commend it. It was a vine that bore "figs" rather than "thorns." A permanent and salutary change was wrought in the morals of the community. Infidelity, rampant before, received a blow from which it never recovered. The order and tone of social life were modified for the better, and of the reformation effected none could stand in doubt. The exercises themselves disappeared, and were at length almost forgotten, but the substantial results of the revival remained to attest its genuineness. No extravagance or fanaticism, as in Kentucky, kindled its torch from its embers, and then pleaded the precedent of its excesses to justify its own.

A more sagacious, discriminating, and judicious observer of the work than Dr. Moses Hoge, of Virginia, could not easily have been named. He visited the scenes of the revival and acquainted himself with the experience of its subjects. He confessed, indeed, that "it would be more to his taste could we get the world reformed in a manner more conformable to his ideas of order and propriety;" yet he pronounced the work "very extraordinary," and freely expressed his conviction that it was "a work of God." He remarked that it was not merely the ignorant, the weak, and the timid that were its subjects. In that case it might be ascribed to the measures employed to carry it on; but when men of information, of strong nerves and vigorous understandings, were overcome,—especially when Deists of this description, who had fortified themselves against every religious impression, from the writings of Bolingbroke, Hume, Voltaire, and Paine,—when such men fell, Deists themselves should be ashamed of the solution that would ascribe this to the word of a weak mortal. No natural cause with which he was acquainted seemed to him adequate to so astonishing an effect; nor, he adds, "have I so learned the Scriptures as to ascribe such a work as this to the finger of the devil."

In the intelligent convictions of the subjects of the work, in their clear and vivid apprehensions of the evil of sin and the justice of their condemnation, in their lamentations over their hardened hearts, in their piercing cries for mercy, and in their joyful acceptance of Christ as a Saviour able, suitable, and willing to save, Dr. Hoge felt satisfied that he had before him the evidences of the operation of divine truth and of the Spirit of God. What he witnessed could not have been affected. "A Garrick could not have acted the character of a convinced sinner and of an exulting young convert" as he saw it manifested by ignorant youth. Nor was there any thing specially remarkable in the discourses preached. "I have heard," he says, "in Virginia, sermons and exhortations more powerful and impressive, as it appears to me, than any I have heard in this State." The sermons were generally listened to with decorous and devout attention, and with but slight disturbance; and at their close, when one and another conceived it their duty to rise and exhort their friends and neighbors to flee from the wrath to come, he could see no just reason why they should be altogether prohibited. To him, moreover, it was singularly remarkable that the most inveterate opposers were sometimes made subjects of the work, even when the exercises were conducted in a manner that seemed more likely to strengthen than to overcome their prejudice. "Is not this," he asked, "the doing of the Lord?"[1]

The movement which had thus commenced in North Carolina extended southward, and several meetings of a similar description to those held within the bounds of Concord Presbytery were held in South Carolina. The first of which we have any account occurred in connection with Fair Forest congregation, under the care of William Williamson.[2] The church had long been in a cold and lifeless state. Formalism within and profanity without seemed to threaten the dissolution of all religious society. On the 21st of March (1802), "the first praying society" ever held in the congregation met for social worship. For two or three meetings there were few members who would venture to pray. But as the meetings were continued, the attendance increased; a growing "attention to the word" appeared, and the spirit of prayer began to manifest itself. Quite a number were awakened, but

---

[1] Letter of Dr. Hoge. New York Miss. Mag., iii. 307.

[2] New York Miss. Mag., iii. 276.

few, if any, for several weeks, gave expression to hope in Christ. Fear was mingled with hope, lest the signs of promise should vanish away and leave no fruits behind.

But on the last day of April—the Friday preceding the season for the administration of the sacrament—a meeting was appointed, at which Messrs. Joseph Alexander, William C. Davis, and John B. Kennedy, co-presbyters of William Williamson, were present. On Saturday, under a sermon by Mr. Davis, five persons were "struck to the earth under the sense of their guilt and danger." After its close, several others, and some after they had withdrawn to their tents, were similarly affected. From this time the power of the work continued steadily to increase till Monday noon, when it was estimated that as many as forty or fifty had fallen. The fruits of the work continued to manifest themselves even after the public means to promote it had ceased.

No undue attempt was made by the speakers to work upon the passions of the audience. No scenes of confusion were to be witnessed. Decorum and good order were observed; and in the cases of those who were affected, there was seen little that could be noted as weak or imprudent. Not an irrational or unscriptural expression was to be heard. Yet the distress of the convicted was "awful," and the joys of those who had found relief were not wild or extravagant, but often ecstatic. Every one present felt that it was a mighty display of the power and grace of God. Among the subjects of the work who were peculiarly affected were quite a number of young men who seemed least likely to be brought under its power.

Another "general meeting" was held within the bounds of Broadaway congregation (Pendleton District), under the charge of James Gilliland, on the 25th of

July. On this occasion, Methodist and Baptist as well as Presbyterian ministers were present, and the assembled multitude was estimated as high as five thousand. Some came from a distance of from twenty to forty miles. Here the features of the former meeting were reproduced. Persons of all ages, from ten to seventy years of age, were stricken down. Some recovered in two, and some not for thirty, hours. Those who fell were as likely to be affected while passing through the encampment, or after having withdrawn to their tents, as during the sermons. Those were exercised "with the greater apparent severity" who had led the most immoral lives; while persons whose conduct had been upright and moral, though deeply impressed, rarely lost the control of their speech or limbs, and sooner recovered serenity of mind.[1]

The subsequent history of the Southern churches affords no parallel for the revival of 1802. It stands alone with its marked and peculiar features. Its influence was powerful and extended, and its results were such as to justify the hopes it excited. The entire community felt its influence. Each meeting was a radiating point for a region from fifty to one hundred miles in diameter. In many distinct congregations where none of the meetings were held, the cause of piety received a new impulse; and those who had visited them bore back to their own neighborhoods a revived zeal in the cause of religion. Nor was this all. The moral tone and religious life of the community were invigorated. Social and civil welfare were promoted. The churches were greatly strengthened, and the prevalent vice and infidelity received a check that was permanently felt. Continuing as it did to a greater or less extent for several years,—indeed, scarcely ceasing before the ex-

[1] New York Miss. Mag., iii. 312

citing influences and commotions of the last war with England began to operate,—the revival wrought a powerful change in the tone of religious sentiment throughout the State. Many young men, numbered among its subjects, were led to consider their duty to preach the gospel, and eventually entered upon the work of the ministry. Peacock and McIntyre, who had reached mature years, left their occupations, prepared themselves for the pulpit, and became eminently useful.

The growth of the Church during this period was largely due to the results of the revival. But for these, the destitution, which was great, would have been far greater. For the entire period, from fifty to sixty of the congregations were vacant and unable to sustain pastors. The field occupied by the Synod was so far of a missionary character that Dr. Hall finally urged the surrender of all outside its bounds to the care of the Assembly, that the Synod might concentrate all its energies within its own limits.

The cause of learning found in the Carolinas no more efficient friends than the pastors of the Presbyterian churches. A large number of these, for longer or shorter periods, were actively engaged in the work of instruction. The University of North Carolina,[1] established in 1789, had, as successive Principals, Rev. David Kerr and Drs. Chapman and Caldwell, and among its instructors Kollock, Mitchell, and others who performed service in the cause of the Church.[2] The

---

[1] For a sketch of the history of the University of North Carolina, see Am. Quar. Reg., Nov. 1842.

[2] Davidson College was founded by the Presbyteries of Concord and Morgantown in North Carolina, and Bethel in South Carolina. It was located in the upper part of Mecklenburg county, N.C., and within the bounds of Concord Presbytery. Before 1837, subscriptions and donations amounting to nearly forty thousand dollars had been secured. It was proposed to connect manual labor with the

names of Brown and Waddel, Turner, McPheeters, and McWhirr, not to mention others who united pastoral duty with devotion to the cause of classical and liberal education, are worthy of special honor; and when the College of South Carolina was rescued mainly by Presbyterian influence from the blighting effects of infidel control, the cause of sound learning as well as of piety was a debtor to those by whom it was exerted.

In 1785, three colleges were constituted by the Legislature of South Carolina on the same day, and by a single charter common to them all. One was located at Charleston, another at Winnsborough, and another at Cambridge in the northwestern part of the State.

In 1791, a new charter was granted for the College of Charleston. The original endowment of the college by the Legislature consisted of eight and seven-eighths acres of land in Charleston, and was comprised between Boundary, Philip, Corning, and George Streets. The college square was one-fourth of the tract. Legacies and donations to the amount of several thousand pounds were made to the institution,—some as early as 1772 and 1776 "to the college to be established in Charleston."[1]

In 1789, Robert Smith, afterward Bishop of South Carolina, was elected Principal, and transferred his school of sixty pupils to the buildings that had been used as soldiers' barracks in the War of the Revolution. The institution, however, was little more than a gram-

---

institution, and a valuable farm was procured. The Rev. R. H. Morrison, of Mecklenburg, was elected President and Professor of Mental and Moral Philosophy and the Evidences of Christianity Rev. R. J. Sparrow, of Salisbury, was chosen Professor of Lan guages, and Mortimer Johnson, Tutor. The original plan was to have three departments,—a normal school for teachers, a preparatory department, and the college proper.—*Am. Quar. Reg.*, May, 1837.

[1] Am. Quar. Reg., Nov. 1839.

mar-school during his administration. He sent his two sons to the North to be educated. The institution was running more and more deeply into debt, until all the land, except College Square, was sold (1806) to meet the liabilities. Thomas Bee (1797) and Rev. Dr. George Buist (1805) were Bishop Smith's successors. Under Dr. Buist there were no graduates. From 1807 to 1811 "the whole college was a dreadful nuisance to the neighborhood. It was a cage of every unclean bird. . . . The teachers paid no regard whatever to the morals of the boys."

In 1823, an attempt was made to revive the institution. Under Jasper Adams, previously of Brown University, it promised to be successful. But the State institution at Columbia proved a formidable rival; and from 1835, Charleston College began rapidly to decline.

The feebleness of the Presbyterian Church in the Carolinas and Georgia prevented their undertaking those enterprises in behalf of ministerial education which attained a more rapid success in the Northern States. North Carolina extended her patronage to the Union Theological Seminary in Virginia, while South Carolina and Georgia combined their efforts at a subsequent period to establish an institution of their own.[1]

---

[1] In 1827, the General Assembly was requested to denominate the seminary in Virginia the "Union Seminary of the General Assembly, under the care of the Synods of Virginia and North Carolina." In the previous year the Synod of North Carolina had been induced by the influence of Dr. John H. Rice to unite with that of Virginia in support of the institution.

From this time the Synod of South Carolina and Georgia cherished the purpose of establishing a seminary within their own bounds. As early, at least, as 1824, there had been a design to establish a literary as well as theological seminary,—the State institution at Columbia being under infidel auspices; but the former part of the design was soon abandoned, and, within a few months after the North Carolina churches had decided to extend their patronage tc

During the most of this period the opportunities for a good common education in North Carolina came far short of those which were enjoyed in some of the other States. The school-accommodations consisted of a rude structure of logs, without windows save the spacious openings between the logs, with the earth for a floor, rude pine benches for seats, and a stick chimney. Yet occasionally in such scenes as these the higher branches of an English education, mathematics, and the Latin and Greek languages, were taught; and sometimes to these advantages the future eminence of distinguished men was largely due. The name of Angus Currie McNeill is one well known in certain parts of North Carolina and Alabama as that of a man who deserves well of the Presbyterian Church, to the interests of which his life, as teacher and pastor, was devoted. In his early years he manifested a strong love for learning. Left by his father's death in humble circumstances, he was carefully trained by his pious

---

the Union Seminary in Virginia, the Synod of South Carolina and Georgia took active measures to found the Southern Theological Seminary. In 1833 they applied for active aid in New England, and in 1836 the institution numbered sixteen students. From the bounds of the Synod, there were only six students in other seminaries.

The professors in Columbia Theological Seminary have been Drs. T. Goulding (1828), G. Howe (1831), A. W. Leland (1833), C. C. Jones (1836), A. T. McGill (1852), B. M. Palmer (1854), J. H. Thornwell (1856), J. B. Adger (1857), A. W. Leland, re-elected (1856), and B. E. Lanneau and James Cohen successively teachers of Hebrew.

To aid in securing an endowment for the Southern Theological Seminary, application was made by the agent of the Synod to the General Association of Massachusetts; in response to which the churches were recommended "to render such pecuniary assistance as they may feel able to do in the establishment of a Professorship of Christian Theology in that seminary."—*Am. Quar. Reg.*, Nov. 1838.

mother. When too young to attend school, he stealthily left home and in his morning slip wended his way to the school-house. "Whose wee bit of a bairn is that?" demanded the good old Gaelic teacher. "I am called Angus McNeill," was the reply; "I ran away from mamma, and come here to learn books like the other boys. Will you learn me books?" was the prompt question of the little truant. "I certainly will," said the teacher, taking him in his arms, pressing him fondly to his bosom, and shedding tears of delight over the noble Scotch-Irish boy, whom for a time he carried to and from school each day on his back. Here McNeill learned to read and spell, memorized the Catechism, and became fond of his Bible. We are not surprised that he subsequently won the first honor in the university of his native State.

During the period under review (1800–1820), the population of North Carolina had increased from four hundred and seventy-eight thousand one hundred and three to six hundred and thirty-eight thousand eight hundred and twenty-nine, or at the rate of about thirty-three per cent. The Presbyterian ministers of the State at the same time had increased from twenty-nine in 1800 to thirty-eight in 1819, or at the rate of about twenty-five per cent. The churches had advanced from seventy-three, of which thirty-one were vacant, to one hundred and twelve, of which about forty were vacant; thus indicating that, while there had been a comparative falling off in the ministry, the increase in the congregations had kept pace with the growth of the State.[1]

---

[1] In the "Christian Herald" for 1818, p. 614, it is stated that the population of Georgia and North and South Carolina amounted to one million two hundred and twenty-three thousand and forty-eight, among whom were only one hundred and ten competent ministers, thus leaving nine-tenths of the people destitute of proper religious instruction. A respectable native citizen of South Carolina stated

During the same period, the population of South Carolina had advanced from three hundred and forty-five thousand five hundred and ninety-one in 1800 to five hundred and two thousand seven hundred and forty-one in 1820, or at the rate of about forty-five per cent. Meanwhile the Presbyterian ministers of the State had increased from eighteen to thirty-four, and the congregations from about fifty, of which just one-half were vacant, to nearly sixty, of which little more than one-fourth were vacant.

In Georgia the population had increased at the rate of over one hundred per cent., from one hundred and sixty-two thousand one hundred and one in 1800, to three hundred and forty thousand nine hundred and seventy-eight in 1820. But, from the lack of full reports, we are unable to determine the proportionate advance of the Church in the same period,—although it must have kept pace, at least, with that of the population of the State.

CHAPTER XXVII.

NEW YORK, 1800-1815.

IN 1800, the Presbytery of Long Island—the name of which had been changed in 1790 from that of Suffolk—consisted of fifteen ministers, twelve of them with, and three without, charges. Benjamin Goldsmith was at Aquabogue and Mattituck (1764-1810), where he was

---

that in an ancient district of that State, embracing nine hundred square miles contiguous to the sea-coast, there was but one place of worship, and that not used, and not one Christian church or minister of any denomination.

succeeded in 1811 by Benjamin Bailey (Nov. 6, 1811–May 18, 1816) and Nathaniel Reeve (1817–23).[1] William Schenk was at Huntington (1793–1817), where he was succeeded by Samuel Robertson (1816–23) and Nehemiah Brown (1824–32).[2] George Faitoute was at Jamaica (1789–1815), where he was succeeded by Henry R. Weed (1816–22).[3] Nathan Woodhull was at Newtown (1789–1810), where he was succeeded by William Boardman (1811–18) and John Goldsmith. Zachariah Green was at Brookhaven (Setauket), where his ministry extended from 1797 down to a recent period. Aaron Woolworth was at Bridgehampton (1787–1821), where he was succeeded by Amzi Francis (1823–45). Luther Gleson was at Smithtown and Islip (1797–1807), where he was succeeded by Bradford Marcy (1811–15), Henry Fuller (1816–21), Richard F. Nicoll (1823–27), Ithamar Pillsbury (1827 to 1833), and James C. Edwards at Smithtown. Joseph Hazard was at Southold (1797–1806), where he was succeeded by Jonathan Hunting[4] (1807–28). Daniel Hall was at Sag Harbor (1797–1806), where he was succeeded—after an interval, during which the church was supplied by N. S. Prime, Stephen Porter, and a Mr. Gaylord—by John D. Gardner (1812–32). David S. Bogart was at Southampton (1798–1806 and 1807–13), where he was succeeded by John M. Babbit (1817–21).[5] Lyman Beecher was at Easthamp-

[1] The successors of Mr. Reeve were Jonathan Hunting, a Mr. Gilbert, and Abraham Luce. The two congregations were known as Union Parish.

[2] His successors were S. F. Halliday (1833–36) and James McDougal.

[3] His successors were S. P. Funck (1823–25), Elias W. Crane (1826–40), J. M. McDonald, and Peter D. Oakey.

[4] His successors were, Ralph Smith (1836–38), George F. Wiswell (1845–50), and Epher Whitaker (1851—).

His successors were, Peter B. Shaw (1821–29), Daniel Beers (1830–35), and Hugh N. Wilson.

ton (1799–1810), where he was succeeded by Ebenezer Phillips (1811–30).[1] Southhaven (or Fireplace), vacant in 1800, had subsequently as pastors Herman Daggett (1801–07), Ezra King, and Abijah Tomlinson. Hempstead, vacant till 1805, had William P. Kuypers (1805 to 1811), Samuel Robertson (1812–17), and Charles Webster (1818–37).[2] Middletown (Middle Island) was vacant till united with Southhaven under Ezra King (1814–39). Shelter Island,—Whitefield's "Patmos,"—where William Adams—here in 1764—continued for more than thirty years as stated supply, was in charge of Daniel Hall from 1806 to 1812, and was subsequently supplied by Ezra Youngs, Jonathan Hunting, Daniel M. Lord, and others. Brookfield, for some time after 1807, was under the care of Jonathan Robinson. Fresh Pond, previously vacant, was united with Smithtown, under the pastoral care of Henry Fuller, in 1816.

The first twenty years of this century added but little to the numbers or strength of Long Island Presbytery. In 1825,—including the churches of Newtown, Hempstead, and Jamaica, whose relations had been transferred to the Presbytery of New York, the First Church of Brooklyn, organized in the same connection, and the church of Huntington, transferred to the care of the Second New York Presbytery,—all the Presbyterian churches on the island amounted to but twenty, with nineteen ministers residing within their bounds, of whom two were without charge. The increase, therefore, for a quarter of a century had been only about thirty per cent.

The patriarch among the pastors of the island was for many years Zachariah Green, of Setauket. He was born at Stafford, Conn., in 1760. In the Revolutionary

[1] His successors were Joseph B. Condit (1830–35) and Samuel R. Ely, stated supply.

[2] His successors were Sylvester Woodbridge and N. C. Locke.

War he joined the army, and was present on Dorchester Heights when the British landed at Throgg's Neck. He was also engaged at the battle of White Plains, and at the battle of Whitemarsh, Pa., he was wounded by a ball in the shoulder. On his recovery he entered Dartmouth College (1782). His health failed, and he did not remain to graduate. His theological course was completed under Dr. Jacob Green, of Hanover, N.J., and in 1785 he was licensed by the Morris County Associated Presbytery, and by them, in 1787, ordained pastor of the church of Cutchogue. Ten years later he was settled at Setauket, where he remained for fifty-one years.[1] His death occurred June 20, 1858, in his ninety-ninth year

In New York City several new churches were founded during this period. In 1808, Duane Street (first known as Cedar Street) Church was organized, and John B. Romeyn (1808–25), of Albany, was installed (November 9) as pastor. In 1809, the Canal Street Church was organized; and in the following year John McNeice (1810-15) was called to the pastorate of this, which, from its membership, was commonly called the "Irish Presbyterian Church." In 1811, the Laight Street Church was organized, and Matthew La Rue Perrine was installed pastor. In the same year, Elizabeth Street Church, upon its reorganization, was received by the Presbytery, although it had but a brief existence. No further efforts for church-extension were made for several years, until Elihu W. Baldwin, in 1816, laid the foundations of the "Seventh Presbyterian Church."

Along the line of the Hudson the older churches had

---

[1] I met him about the year 1854, and in conversation with him found him in full possession of his faculties, and delighting to repeat the reminiscences of earlier days. He spoke of the founding of Rutgers College as due to a suggestion made by himself to Colonel Rutgers.

been strengthened, and several new churches had been organized. Andrew King (till 1815), the father of the Presbytery of Hudson, was still settled at Wallkill. Goshen had Isaac Lewis for its pastor from 1806 to 1811; and in 1813, Ezra Fisk began there his ministry of twenty years. Daniel Crane had for some time been settled at Fishkill. John Johnston had commenced in 1807, at Newburgh, his pastorate which was to extend to nearly half a century. Ebenezer Grant was settled at Bedford, and John Ely at Salem. At Catskill, where the congregation was yet feeble and worshipped in the court-house, David Porter had commenced his labors in 1803, on his removal from Spencertown, and in part through his efforts a church had been organized at Cairo, which was supplied for some years by Herman Daggett. John Chester, soon to be removed to Albany, had succeeded Reuben Sears at Hudson (1810), where a church had been gathered about the year 1790. Jonas Coe, pastor for eleven years (1793–1804) of Troy and Lansingburg, continued in charge of the former till 1822; while at Lansingburg, thenceforth united with Waterford, he was succeeded by Samuel Blatchford (1804–28). The Presbytery of Columbia had been erected, by a division of the Presbytery of Albany, in 1802, and, besides Coe, Blatchford, and Chester, had upon its list of members R. H. Chapman at Cambridge (1801–12), F. Halsey at Plattsburg, and S. Tomb at Salem. Its congregations numbered fifteen, of which several were unable singly to support a pastor. The Presbytery of Albany had the same number of churches under its care, nearly half of which were vacant. In 1813, the Second Church of Albany was formed, and soon after Dr. William Neill was settled as its pastor. Several other churches were organized within the bounds of the Presbytery at about the same period, and in 1820 the Synod of Albany numbered eight Presbyteries. The original Presbytery of Albany was successively divided; and in 1802 the Presbyteries of Oneida and Columbia were formed, in 1814 that of Champlain, in 1818 those of St. Lawrence and Otsego, and in 1820 that of Troy. Meanwhile, with the Synod of Albany, as most accessible, the Presbyterian churches of New England (Londonderry Presbytery) became connected.

In 1809, the Presbytery of Londonderry, afterward subdivided to form the Presbytery of Newburyport, came under the care of the General Assembly. Here in New Hampshire, as in South Carolina, the Presbyterian Church had taken root independent of any connection with the Synod or Assembly. At the period of the large Irish immigration to this country in 1719, quite a number of Presbyterians directed their course to New England. They were to be found in Maine, Massachusetts, and New Hampshire, as well as in New York, New Jersey, and Pennsylvania.

The early churches of New England were largely leavened with Presbyterian tendencies. The church at Leyden declared that their form of order was identical with that of the French Presbyterian churches, except that the latter chose their ruling elders for a limited period instead of for life. Leyden furnished Plymouth its model, and the constitution of the latter was copied by others.[1] In the Eastern colonies, however, the State had usurped the place of Presbyteries and Synods in the supervision of the welfare and purity of the churches.[2] The theory of the New England settlers conceded this ecclesiastical care to the magis-

---

[1] Morton's New England Memorial, Appendix; and Life of Bradford.

[2] No town could be incorporated until a church was gathered, a house of worship built, a minister settled who had been approved by the General Court, and provision made for his support F

trate, and the result was that Synods were rarely held, although strenuous efforts were made to revive them after they had fallen into disuse, and to secure their regular observance, until the king, at the instigation of New England Episcopalians, expressly forbade their convocation without his consent.

But just before this took place, the Irish immigration had commenced. The Presbyterians were heartily received. Cotton Mather wrote to Principal Stirling, of Glasgow, expressing the hope that, "as great numbers are like to come to us from the North of Ireland, the bond between the churches of Scotland and New England will every day grow stronger and stronger." This was in 1713. Five years later, he says, "We are comforted with great numbers of the oppressed brethren coming from the North of Ireland. The glorious providence of God, in the removal of so many of a desirable character from the North of Ireland, hath doubtless very great intentions in it."

A church of Presbyterians was established at Londonderry, under James McGregor.[1] A company with Edward Fitzgerald at their head located at Worcester. Robert Abercrombie, with a number of families, settled at Pelham. Others located at Casco Bay, Macosquin, and other places. With comparatively little increase or change, the churches thus early founded, with the few others soon connected with them, continued through the century. Dependent often upon Congregational pastors, isolated from the great body of the Presbyterian Church, and feeble in themselves, it would not have been strange if they had been absorbed in other bodies. But for the most part, except in Maine, they maintained their position and their distinctive character until in 1809 they united with the Synod of

---

[1] See History of Londonderry.

Albany and came into connection with the General Assembly.

They had indeed, at an earlier period, attempted to occupy an independent position and maintain a rank co-ordinate with that of the old Synod. But the times were unpropitious, and the attempt proved vain. It was at the most critical moment—at the opening of the Revolutionary War, May 31, 1775, shortly after the battle of Lexington—that the churches and ministers were so divided into the three Presbyteries of Londonderry, Salem, and Palmer as to constitute a Synod.[1]

---

[1] The following statement, from Dr. Dana, is given in Dr. Hill's History:—

The First Presbytery in New England was constituted in Londonderry, N.H., April 16, 1745, and consisted of Messrs. Moorhead, of Boston, McGregor, of Londonderry, and Abercrombie, of Pelham, with the elders of their churches. Three years after, the church of Newburyport (Jonathan Parsons, pastor) came under its care. In 1770, it had grown so as to embrace twelve ministers and as many congregations. The Synod (1775) consisted of three Presbyteries,—Salem, which, with the churches of Newburyport, Boston, Salem, Seabrook, (N.H.), Bristol (Me.), and several vacancies, had as ministers Parsons, Whitaker (Salem), Paley, and McLean. Londonderry had McGregor, Mitchell, of Pembroke, Williams, of Windham, Strickland, of Oakham; while Peterborough and other vacancies were under its care. Palmer had Hueston, of Bedford, Baldwin, of Kingston, and Messrs. Hutchinson, Merritt, Gilmore, and Patrick, with the vacancies of Blandford, Pelham, and Coleraine. These, constituting the Synod of New England, met Sept. 4, 1775. See Webster, 666; also Dr. Dana, as quoted by Dr. Hill, pp. 56, 57.

But before this a Presbytery had been formed in Maine. Mr. Murray, previously of Philadelphia, but then of Boothbay, was the leading minister. This body was styled the Presbytery of the Eastward, and never connected itself with the Synod of New England.—*Dr. Hill.* For other facts concerning the earliest Presbytery, see Webster, 119. I suspect there were two Presbyteries before that of Londonderry, one in Maine, the other "Boston" Presbytery. See also Greenleaf's "Churches of Maine."

At the best, each Presbytery had little more than a quorum, and the disastrous influence of the war materially weakened what was weak before. In 1782, the Synod was dissolved, and the ministers and churches were united in the Presbytery of Salem. Yet even this could boast barely of a quorum.

In 1789, negotiations were commenced with a view to the union of New England Presbyterians with the Associate Presbytery of New York. The object was accomplished in 1793, and the new body took the name of the Presbytery of Londonderry. With the beginning of the present century it grew more rapidly, and in 1809, having withdrawn from the Associate Church, it became connected with the Synod of Albany. In 1821, this Presbytery of Londonderry, afterward (1826) divided to form that of Newburyport, reported twenty-seven ministers and thirteen churches, with a membership of eleven hundred and eighty-five. Thus, in the first twenty years of the present century, the Presbytery of Albany had grown to a Synod, embracing, apart from Central and Western New York, eight Presbyteries, with more than one hundred ministers, a still larger number of churches, and a membership of not far from ten thousand.

In the central and western portions of the State the progress of the Church during the early years of the present century was much more rapid than at the east. From 1800 to 1810, nearly fifty churches were organized in this region, most of them destined to permanence. In 1801, the churches of Homer and Skaneateles were gathered; in 1803, those of Pompey, Otisco, Hopewell, Trumansburg, and Newark. Before 1806, those of Ithaca, Romulus, Lansing, and Penfield had been added to the list. Before 1810, there had been formed within the bounds of each of the Presbyteries of Onondaga, Cayuga, Geneva, Cortland, Bath, and Ontario, as now constituted, from four to ten churches. This ratio of progress continued through the ten following years. From 1810 to 1815, more than twenty churches were organized in this region, including Manlius, Auburn Second, Clyde, Mount Morris, Angelica, Buffalo First, Corning, and Rochester First.

In 1800, Rev. Jedediah Chapman, a member of the Presbytery of New York, was stationed at Geneva by the General Assembly. His appointment was for four years, and his sphere of labor was throughout all the surrounding region. He was a kind of missionary bishop, and his duty was to direct the routes of the ministers sent abroad by the Assembly, give them advice in executing their commissions, and look after the interests and welfare of the churches generally.

Among those who were sent out with him for shorter periods were his own son, Robert H. Chapman, who had just commenced his ministry, Robert Logan, who had already traversed the region the year previous, Rev. John Lindsley, who subsequently settled at Ovid, Rev. William Boyd, of Lamington, N.J., a trustee of Princeton College, and the late Dr. Perrine, of Auburn Seminary, then a licentiate under the care of the New Brunswick Presbytery. The report of their labors was encouraging, and inspired to renewed effort.

In January, 1805, James Carnahan was settled as pastor over the United Society of Whitesborough and Utica, having previously declined a much more inviting call from the Dutch Church in Albany. He was of Scotch-Irish descent, and was born in Cumberland county, Pa., in 1775. His early years were spent in labor on the farm. At the age of twelve years he was deprived by death of a father's care. In 179[illegible] he commenced his classical studies at Canonsburg, and in 1800 was graduated at Princeton. In the following year he was elected a tutor in the college, and in 1804 was licensed to preach the gospel.

In 1811, on account of the failure of his health, he was compelled to relinquish his charge, in which he was succeeded by Henry Dwight, and subsequently engaged as a teacher at Princeton, N.J., and at Georgetown, D.C. In 1823, he was elected as the successor of Dr. Green to the Presidency of New Jersey College, and in a successful administration of more than thirty years retained this responsible position, resigning it in 1854, but surviving till 1859, when he had attained to his eighty-fourth year.

With few of the gifts of genius, he was possessed of strong good sense and a remarkably sound judgment. His early life had been one, if not of hardship, yet far removed from the comforts of affluence. He had to struggle with great difficulty to obtain an education, and was enabled to prosecute his purpose of studying at Princeton by a timely loan from Dr. McMillan. In company with Jacob Lindsley, who generously allowed him to share his travelling-equipments,—one riding the horse, which Lindsley owned, for five or ten miles, and then tying him by the roadside for the other to mount, while he proceeded on foot,—he accomplished his journey across the mountains from a point thirty miles west of the Monongahela River to Princeton. Here upon his graduation he received the highest honor, and ever after maintained his rank as a thorough scholar. With such training he not only attained literary distinction, but acquired a practical acquaintance with the common affairs of life. A great student of books, he was a greater student of men and things. He was equally at home whether consulted on a question of philosophy or agriculture, the construction of a sentence or a house, the discipline of the mind, or the ventilation of a dwelling.

To a stranger somewhat stiff and formal in manner, he was yet, when social familiarity had overcome his self-distrust and reserve, a genial and cheerful companion. Just, generous, meek, unassuming, yet fearless at the call of duty, with a mind stored with information and anecdote, a somewhat slow and cautious but accurate perception, a perfect independence in the formation of his opinions, yet with a large liberality for minor differences and a scorn for every thing petty or mean, he was no unworthy successor of the noble list of Presidents,—Burr, Edwards, Davies, Finley, Witherspoon, Smith, and Green.[1]

In 1801, James H. Hotchkin, a licentiate of the Northern Associated Presbytery, took up his permanent residence as pastor at West Bloomfield. At about the same time, Seth Williston, who for some time had been engaged in the employ of the Connecticut Society as a missionary, and had travelled extensively in the new settlements of the State, commenced his pastorate, extending to 1809, at Lisle,[2] devoting a portion of his time to the destitute places around him. In the following year, David Higgins, who had performed missionary service in the region under a commission from the Connecticut Society, began his labors at Aurelius. He was the first settled Presbyterian minister in the region known as the Military Tract, embracing the counties of Cayuga and Onondaga,—seventy miles in length by fifty in breadth, and in 1803 containing a population of about thirty thousand. He was a native of Haddam, Conn., a graduate of Yale College (1785), a theological pupil of Dr. Lyman, Mass., and pastor of the church in North Lyme, Conn., from 1787 to 1801. In 1802, he accepted a call from

[1] Macdonald's discourse at the funeral of Dr. Carnahan.

[2] Hotchkin's Western New York, 65.

Aurelius, where he had become well known by his labors as a missionary of the Connecticut Society. On the 6th of October he was installed by a council of Congregational and Presbyterian ministers. On the 5th of January following, Hugh Wallis was installed over the church on the West Hill of Pompey; and on the 2d of February, Nathan B. Darrow was settled over the church in Homer.

For several years previous to the settlement of these ministers, this region had enjoyed the transient labors of missionaries from the Connecticut Society, especially of Williston and Bushnell. Revivals had prevailed here, more or less, since as early as 1797. Several churches were at that time, or shortly after, organized. Among these were Genoa, Scipio, Locke, Aurelius, Camillus (Elbridge), Skaneateles, Pompey, Homer, and Nine-Mile Creek. All of these were established as Congregational churches.

In 1803 an association was formed, denominated "The Middle Association on the Military Tract and its Vicinity." It maintained its existence with steadily increasing numbers till 1811, when it was merged into the Presbyteries of Cayuga and Onondaga. Its constitution was modelled after that of the elder association, by which ministers and churches were held amenable both as respected doctrine and practice. It thus approximated to the Presbyterian system; and some of its members, as Mr. Chapman, of Geneva, were at the same time members of Presbytery.

In August, 1804, Rev. William Allen, subsequently President of Bowdoin College, visited the field.[1] As "a solitary horseman," he made a journey of eight hundred miles from Massachusetts to Niagara Falls, preaching as he passed through "the Western Wilderness," when

[1] From his letters in the New York Evangelist, Nov. 5, 1863.

opportunity offered, at various new settlements. The ministers east of the Genesee River were Mr. Chapman, at Charlestown, Mr. Hotchkin, at West Bloomfield, Mr. Parmele, at North Bloomfield, Mr. Collins, at Bloomfield, Mr. Joseph Grover, at North Bristol, Mr. Warren, at South Bristol, Mr. Solomon Allen, at Middletown, Mr. Field, at Canandaigua, Mr. Chapman, at Geneva, Mr. Higgins, at Aurelius, Mr. Woodruff, at Scipio, Mr. Chadwick, at Milton. And this was the entire supply of ministers for a region of country equal to many of the petty kingdoms of the Old World.

West of the Genesee River to Lake Erie, and from Lake Ontario to the Pennsylvania line, there was no meeting-house, no settled minister, or any known preacher except Mr. Allen himself. On his return from his journey he published a brief "Plea for the Genesee Country." In this he stated,—

"There is a small church in Batavia, the county town, in which is a large court-house, which may be employed as a house of worship. The town contains two or three hundred inhabitants, who seldom have any religious instruction, and who with thankfulness and joy would receive a preacher of the gospel.

"Ganson's Settlement is twelve miles east of Batavia, and in connection with it would be able to support a preacher. But none is to be found who will consent to penetrate into the wilderness and encounter the difficulties of a new settlement. Ought not their situation to be regarded by missionary societies?

"Besides Ganson's Settlement and Batavia, there is another suitable station for a missionary in Buffalo, forty-five miles west of Batavia, lying on Lake Erie. Here are twenty or thirty families, in a very pleasant situation, and a missionary might do much good among them."

While the progress east of the Genesee had been

comparatively rapid, so that in 1812 the Synod of Geneva, embracing the Presbyteries of Cayuga, Onondaga, and Geneva, was constituted by the Assembly, the region west of the river was left comparatively neglected. For several years after the commencement of the present century its prospects were dark indeed. Joseph Ellicott, agent of the Holland Land Company, exerted a very pernicious and disastrous influence. He disregarded the Sabbath, and was opposed to all religious institutions. The whole surrounding region was long noted for its irreligion. It was a common remark that the Sabbath had not found its way across the Genesee River. An infidel club was early formed, and by them a circulating library containing the works of Voltaire, Volney, Hume, and Paine was established. One or two Dutch churches, composed of settlers from Pennsylvania, had been organized, but lingered out a feeble and sickly existence. At Caledonia a colony of Scotchmen was settled, and a church was there organized by Rev. Mr. Chapman in 1805. It was almost the only point where religious institutions could be said to be established. Ministers sent out by the missionary societies visited the region for several weeks during each year, yet but little was accomplished. The most distinguished laborer in the field was "Father" Spencer, at first a deacon in the Congregational church of Worcester, in Otsego county. In mature years, with only such learning as an ordinary school education and his own reading and observation afforded, he entered the ministry. Licensed by the Northern Associated Presbytery, he was employed as a missionary on the Holland Purchase by the Connecticut Society, and his labors were highly useful in forming and sustaining churches. Of these, in 1812, some six or eight had been organized west of the Genesee River, among which were the First Presbyterian of Buffalo (1812), and those of Attica, Fredonia, Warsaw, and Hamburg.

The labors of the missionaries of the Berkshire, Hampshire, and Massachusetts Societies were for the most part confined to other fields. Few of them penetrated into the neighborhood of Lake Erie. Those who did so—and some were sent out by the Connecticut Society—came back despondent. "In many of the settlements,"[1] says Rev. R. Phelps, "the state of society is truly deplorable. Scarcely is the form of godliness visible. The Sabbath is awfully profaned, and God's name is dishonored in various ways. Great carelessness and stupidity prevail. . . . Infidelity abounds to an alarming degree, and in various shapes. Self-styled preachers of the gospel, also, are very numerous. Missionary aid is greatly needed here." In a similar tone wrote the indefatigable "Father" Spencer. "I find," says he (December, 1808), "no special seriousness on any minds." A later communication is in the same tone. The Connecticut Society's Missionary Narrative of 1811 justly pronounces this region bordering on Lake Erie "among the most destitute in the United States."

But already there was promise of a change. Rev. Mr. Ayer, in 1811 and 1812, and Rev. Orange Lyman, in 1814, visited the Holland Purchase under commission from the Connecticut Society. Their reports were more favorable. "I have been kindly received as a missionary," writes Mr. Lyman. "My encouragement with respect to Zion's cause in this wilderness is increasing," says "Father" Spencer. He was now beginning to see the fruit of his labors. His perilous journeys, exposures, and self-denial had not been in vain. The people at different places on his route as itinerant claimed so much of his time at their own expense that

---

[1] Conn. Evan. Mag.

he had but seven weeks left for the Society. Already the hope was warranted that the Holland Purchase would be redeemed for Christ.

During this period, the churches planted in the more central counties of the State continued to prosper, and new organizations were of frequent occurrence. The tide of immigration continued to pour in, for the most part strengthening the institutions already established. The different missionary societies sent each year such of their pastors or licentiates as were designated, to travel and preach through this extensive region, some of them visiting Luzerne county in Pennsylvania. The Berkshire and Hampshire Societies sent annually one or two of their ministers, the Connecticut Society repeatedly as many as four or six. In 1808, David Harrower was in the counties of Broome and Chenango, Silas Hubbard in Madison, Ebenezer Kingsbury in Otsego, Delaware, and Chenango, and Daniel Waldo in Wayne and Luzerne. In 1809, Messrs. Avery, Brainerd, Loomis, Waterman, Lockwood, and Frost traversed the same field. In the following year the appointments were Messrs. Benedict, Avery, Kingsbury, Colton, Brainerd, and Frost. Messrs. Wright, Kingsbury, Benedict, Mason, Hyde, and Brainerd were commissioned the next year. The labors of these men, though generally limited to a few weeks, were abundantly blessed.

In harmonious co-operation with these, the General Assembly prosecuted its missionary work, and very much on the same plan Pastors were found willing to leave their own churches for a few months to itinerate among the destitute settlements. But, as its own boundaries were extended, it was found necessary to depute the charge of the missionary work largely to the Synods. By these it was prosecuted with com mendable zeal. The large region of Northern Penn sylvania and Central and Western New York fell to the care of the Synods of Pittsburg, Albany, and the recently-organized Synod of Geneva. The most perfect harmony of co-operation prevailed. Among the numerous churches of the Congregational order there was a strong leaning toward a stricter usage than had hitherto prevailed. The Unitarian defection among the Massachusetts churches had already commenced. In many quarters it was felt that a more orderly and reliable system of discipline, which should extend to the relations of pastors and churches, was demanded. This necessity had already been met in the constitution of the two Associations which had been formed in Central and Western New York. A favorable and fraternal spirit was manifested by these toward the Presbyterian system; and when the Middle Association, with the sanction of the General Assembly, became connected with the Synod of Albany, the question as to any State Congregational Association was virtually decided.

The Synod of Albany at first extended over all Northern and Western New York. But it was too large for the convenient attendance of ministers. It was considered desirable, therefore, that a new Synod should be formed embracing the Western churches. To prepare the way for it, the Synod of Albany, in October, 1810, by request, formed the Presbytery of Geneva and the Middle Association into three Presbyteries, distinguished by territorial limits. These were consequently the Presbyteries of Cayuga, Onondaga, and Geneva. In this manner Congregational and Presbyterian churches were brought into harmonious co-operation. In one case, the session consisted of the body of the brethren of competent age; in the other, of a bench of elders elected by the church. Ministers were in all cases installed in accordance with the orders prescribed by the Book of Discipline, and, in case they came from other than Presbyterian bodies, were required to adopt the Confession of Faith and form of government and discipline of the Presbyterian Church. The principles thus adopted were acted upon elsewhere. The Presbyteries of Albany, Columbia, Newark, Susquehanna, and others pursued a similar course. The appeal from a church congregationally constituted was received in the same way with an appeal from a session. The pastor was a member of Presbytery, and the church, either by delegate or ruling elder, was represented in the body.

The course pursued by the Middle Association of the Military Tract exerted a decisive influence over the action of the other Associations of Central and Western New York. While the plan of union with the Synod was yet under discussion, the Ontario Association (June 13, 1810) met at Richmond, and appointed delegates to attend a convention of delegates from other Congregational bodies in the State, to take into consideration the project of forming a State Association. The convention met at Clinton, in July; but it was found that great diversity of opinion prevailed as to the expediency of forming a General Association. The Middle Association had sent no delegates, and it was thought by many that the terms of union with the Synod, which it had concluded to accept, were such as might generally be adopted, and thus lay a foundation for a general union of all the Congregational and Presbyterian churches within the State. In the judgment of some, the Associations should seek a union with the Synod on the same terms with the Middle Association, while others preferred their dissolution, and a union with the Presbyteries within their bounds. No steps were taken, therefore, toward the formation of a State Association. The idea of such an organization was entirely relinquished. The general interests of religion were felt to be paramount to any indulgence of preferences which might result in collision; and "many of the Congregational brethren, especially among the ministry, thought that the general principles of Presbyterian government were better calculated to preserve unity of action and purity of doctrine while in a forming state and to a great extent destitute of a State ministry, than the Congregational form." The result was that the next year the Ontario Association was dissolved, the ministers and churches united with the Presbytery of Geneva, and from 1811 no Congregational organization of ministers and churches existed for many years in the State of New York west of the east line of the Military Tract.

The reasons for this union were strong and decisive, and its influence was felt to be most happy. Between the missionaries and ministers of both denominations there was substantial unity in doctrine. In those of either body were to be found subordinate diversities of sentiment as great as between members of both bodies. The missionaries of the Connecticut Society and of the General Assembly alike were for the most part settled pastors, and were selected for their missionary tours with discreet reference to their fitness for the work. Great care was exercised in the organization of the churches, and the forms of admission and confession were generally copied from those already adopted by pastors in the older States. One of the first acts of the short-lived Association of Susquehanna was to examine the Confessions of Faith and Covenants of a number of churches, to see if they could agree to walk in fellowship with one another. As early as 1800, Williston wrote to the New York Missionary Magazine, in reference to the revival of the previous year, "The doctrines which God makes use of to awaken and convince sinners among us are those which are commonly distinguished as Calvinistic." His own well-known views of doctrine are a sufficient commentary upon the significance of his words.

The revival of 1800, extending over several counties, "particularly the counties of Otsego and Delaware," which "comprehended a tract of country almost as large as the State of Connecticut," commenced at Delhi. "This place," says Rev. Mr. Bushnell (Conn. Ev. Mag., 1801), "had been remarkable for stupidity. Religion was treated with contempt, and the little church, consisting of three or four male members, concluded that they must soon become extinct. The revival began in the month of March, 1800." The work slowly but steadily increased. About the last of May it was powerful in the part of the town called Little Delaware. At the same time, amid much opposition, it commenced in the southern part of the town. For many months the revival continued, and about fifty persons were added to the church.

The awakening next extended to Franklin, seventeen miles west, where the Rev. David Harrower was preaching half of his time. At Stamford, ten miles north, the revival was marked with much power.

Contemporaneous with these events in Delaware county, revivals commenced in Otsego county, at Union (Lisle), Metcalf Settlement, and at length at Springfield, and subsequently at Worcester. The meetings for public worship were crowded, and the services were characterized by great solemnity. At Cooperstown a large and respectable society had been organized in the summer of 1800, and a church formed by Rev. Isaac Lewis, who was soon after installed as pastor.

In Cayuga, Onondaga, and Oneida counties there were also powerful revivals. Milton, Scipio, and Homer were especially favored. Paris and Clinton shared to a large extent in the blessing. The academy at Clinton, under the care of Rev. Mr. Niles, was also "considerably favored." In Genesee and Ontario counties several of the churches were greatly revived.

"These awakenings," says Mr. Bushnell, "in the new settlements have been regular and free from enthusiasm. Persons have, at the beginning of their convictions, been solemn, and have manifested a great eagerness to hear the word. As their convictions increased, they have complained much of the stubbornness of their hearts and of their helpless state by nature. . . . As far as we can judge, since the commencement of the awakening, the fruits have been the effect of that wisdom from above which is first 'pure, then peaceable,' &c."

Yet, he says, "notwithstanding the great revivals of religion in the new settlements for two years past, a great part of the wilderness remain stupid in their sins. The tract of country through which missionaries from the United States travel is several hundred miles square. This tract has but partially experienced the influences of the Holy Spirit."

In subsequent years revivals more or less extensive prevailed, but none, probably, of such power and extent as occurred some two or three years subsequent to the period under review. The minutes of the Assembly, however, make grateful mention of the special outpouring of the Spirit within the bounds of Long Island and Albany Presbyteries in 1805, of Long Island, Albany, and Hudson in 1809, Long Island, New York, and Hudson in 1810, Onondaga, Albany, and Hudson in 1813, and Onondaga and Oneida in 1814.

CHAPTER XXVIII.

OHIO, 1800-1815.

WHILE Western New York was inviting immigration, the broader regions of the farther West were not without their attractions to the hardy emigrant. The commencement of measures for their settlement dates from the passage by Congress of the ordinance for the government of the Northwestern Territory.[1] Even before this, portions of this Territory lying upon the Ohio had been carefully surveyed, and the New England Ohio Company, through whose exertions the earliest band of settlers was sent out, was formed March 1, 1786. General Tupper, an officer of the Revolution, a friend of General Rufus Putnam, and an assistant surveyor of Hutchins, who had been appointed to survey the Territory by the Congress of 1785, was a leader in the movement. In concert with his friend Putnam, the plan of a company was devised, and by the aid of Rev. Dr. Manasseh Cutler, a clergyman of Massachusetts, and one or two others, Congress was induced to grant lands on favorable terms.

In conference with Hutchins, Dr. Cutler was led to decide in favor of the region embracing the Muskingum Valley for the proposed settlement. The agent of the company, General S. H. Parsons, after fuller examination, approved this selection, for which General Tupper had originally expressed his preference.[2] The territory which the company expected to secure ex-

---

[1] North American Review, July, 1838, p. 12.

[2] Ibid., Oct. 1841, p. 329; also July, 1838.

tended so as to embrace the eastern valley of the Scioto. Among its attractions were not only the soil of inexhaustible richness and the beautiful scenery which greeted the eye along the banks of the rivers, but the mineral wealth of salt, iron, and coal with which the region was supplied, and especially the comparative neighborhood of the Virginia settlements, which in time of need could furnish alike food and men.[1]

By a vote of the company, one hundred settlers were to set forth at once for the land of promise. They were to be furnished with provisions for their journey, and, from the time of their arrival at Pittsburg until the ensuing May, to be paid at the rate of four dollars per month. Each man was to provide himself with "a good musket, bayonet, and cartridge-box;" and if he had besides these an axe and hoe, or, if a mechanic, the needful tools, he was to be transported free of cost. At Danvers, Mass., the first party assembled December, 1787, and a second detachment left Hartford Jan. 1, 1788. Their route was the old road by which Braddock's army took up its march to Pittsburg. But their progress was slow, and it was April before the united parties left the Youghiogheny and began to drift with the river's current toward the spot destined to be their first settlement.

It was on the third day of the month that the *Mayflower*,—a name significant to the New England emigrant,—bearing the small party, reached Pittsburg. They had embarked at Simrall's Ferry, or Robbstown, where West Newton now stands. Here they had laid in their stock of provisions and made the necessary preparations for their voyage. Merrily did they push out into the "Yoh," and, compared with their previous

---

[1] Wheeling was settled as early as 1770.

experience, their progress toward their destination was rapid. Sometimes they grazed on the shallows, and at others grounded on the sand-bars. But by dint of rowing and pushing they pressed on till they struck the stronger current of the Monongahela. Mooring their uncouth and unwieldy water-craft by making it fast to a stake on the bank, they landed at the point where the Ohio takes its name, and, after purchasing articles necessary for the comfort of their families, continued their voyage.

On the 7th of April, 1788, this little band of forty-seven persons, instead of one hundred as at first proposed, reached the mouth of the Muskingum, and landed and encamped on the spot where Marietta now stands. This was the original place of their destination. On the black canvas coverings of the settlers' wagons, as they left their native State, was to be read, in large white capital letters, "To Marietta on the Ohio."[1] Washington augured favorably of the prospects of the new settlement which had thus been commenced. "No colony," he said,[2] "in America was ever settled under such favorable auspices as that which has just commenced at the Muskingum. Information, property, and strength will be its characteristics. I know many of the settlers personally; and there never were men better calculated to promote the welfare of such a community."

The progress of the settlements for the first year was rapid. The first explorers of the region had sent or borne back to the East surprising reports of the wonders of this new land of promise. The beauty of the rich river-bottoms was suggestive of Eden scenes.

---

[1] This was the case with the second emigration. Flint's Indian Wars. North American Rev., Oct. 1841.

[2] Sparks's Washington, ix. 384.

The soil was fabulously productive and apparently inexhaustible. The lofty sugar-tree, the graceful elm, the black and white walnut, the massive oak, the spice-wood with its fragrance, the papaw with its luscious fruit, the wild plum, and, besides these, the luxuriant vines with their bounteous clusters of grapes festooning the forest, while, beneath, the wild rye, green as a wheat-field, mixed with the prairie- and buffalo-clover, all conspired to present to the beholder a scene which needed but the sparkling rivulet, rippling along its pebbly bottom or garlanded by flowers, to give the last finishing touch to this enchanting picture. The memory of it lingered in the mind like some bright vision of the Golden Age.[1]

It is not surprising that the unparalleled fertility of the soil and the luxuriance of its uncultured vegetation excited in Eastern homes a strange enthusiasm. Immigration was for a short time at flood-tide. The commandant at Fort Harmar reported four thousand five hundred persons as having passed that post between February and June, 1788. At Marietta the settlers were busy in erecting new dwellings; and, had the company been prepared to receive and accommodate the multitude of emigrants, the progress of the colony would have been still more rapid. As it was, Marietta continued to have a steady and healthy increase, until the Indian depredations from stealing horses and sinking boats broke out into open war. From 1790 to 1795, the colony was constantly on the brink of ruin from the pressure of famine and the hostilities of the Indian tribes.

The unfavorable report of this new state of affairs reached the East and gave a check to emigration. The colony, moreover, had its enemies, some from jealousy

---

[1] Autobiography of Rev. J. B. Finley, 107.

of its progress, or a desire to encourage the settlement of other regions. Horrible accounts of hoop-snakes of deadly malignity, caricatures of prairie luxuriance, such as springs of brandy, and stalks of flax bearing cloth on their stems, together with stories of Indian barbarities and massacres and the unhealthiness of the region, were widely circulated.

But with the close of the Indian wars, through the victory of General Wayne in 1794, Marietta began again to prosper. Vessels were built at its wharves to navigate the Ohio and Mississippi as far as New Orleans. By the commencement of the century it had become a thriving town. It was a centre of business, a scene of industry. The first minister who entered this field was Daniel Story,[1] a native of Boston (1755) and a graduate of Dartmouth College (1780). In the summer of 1789 he supplied the congregations of Marietta, Waterford, and Belpre. At Waterford the people met for worship under the shadow of a huge tree; at Marietta, from 1791 to 1795, the Northwest block-house of Campus Martius served as a house of worship. No church was organized till 1796; and before Mr. Story left, in 1804, the missionaries of Pittsburg Synod had entered the field. In 1806, Samuel Prince Robbins, from Connecticut, commenced his pastorate of the church of Marietta. At the same time, Stephen Lindsley, a licentiate of the Presbytery of Ohio in 1803, had commenced his labors as pastor of a Presbyterian congregation, probably in another part of the town.

Some points on the line of the Ohio nearer to Pennsylvania had already been occupied. Rev. Thomas E. Hughes, previously settled in Beaver county, Pa., was the first minister of the gospel who was permanently located north of the Ohio River. He was a graduate

---

[1] Hildreth's "Pioneer Settlers of Ohio."

of Princeton in 1797, and, after studying theology with Dr. McMillan, was licensed by the Presbytery of Ohio, Oct. 17, 1798. In the following year he commenced his labors at Mt. Pleasant and New Salem,—in the first of which he continued for many years. As early as 1802, James Snodgrass began a pastorate, which extended through many years, at Steubenville and Island Creek. Within a short time after this, there was at Steubenville—in another part of the town, probably—a Congregational church, under the care of Lyman Potter.

Meanwhile, settlements had commenced in the south-western portion of the State. The region between the two Miamies had long enjoyed the reputation of being one of great fertility. Boone had taken note of it as early as 1778, during his captivity among the Shawanese. The hostility of these tribes to the whites, however, prevented any attempt at settlement previous to the Indian Treaty of 1786. In that year, Cleves Symmes, a Congressional representative from New Jersey, became interested in the accounts given of the beauty and fertility of the Miami country, and, after visiting it in person, determined to purchase and settle a large tract. In July, 1788, he succeeded in starting an emigrant company of thirty persons and eight four-horse wagons on their journey to this new country. By January, 1789, two settlements had been effected. One of these was at Columbia, where a few Baptist families united to sustain a meeting among themselves, which individuals conducted in turn.[1] The other was at Cincinnati (Dec. 28, 1788), then, and for several years subsequent, known as Losantiville.[2] On the 24th of December, Israel Ludlow and Colonel Patterson,

---

[1] Benedict's History of the Baptists, p. 877.

[2] The etymology of this word is curious:—*ville*, town, *anti*, opposite to, *os*, the mouth, *L*, of the Licking River.—*Cincinnati Directory*, 1819.

two of the proprietors, with fourteen other persons, left Maysville "to form a station and lay off a town opposite Licking." The river from shore to shore was filled with floating ice, but, by caution and perseverance, a successful landing was effected. A few log huts and block-houses were soon erected, and the settlers proceeded to lay out the town. In December, 1789, twelve months from the first arrival on the ground, the population numbered "eleven families and twenty-four bachelors," besides the garrison that had been sent out to defend this frontier-post and repel the incursions of the Indian tribes.

Several new stations were successively occupied in the surrounding region; but the defeat of General St. Clair, Nov. 4, 1791, sent dismay to the hearts of the settlers. Deserting their fields and dwellings, they rushed to places of security, and the fate of the colony seemed to be determined. Immigration ceased; and only with the victory of Wayne in August, 1794, did it recommence.

But the settlers, largely emigrants from New Jersey, did not wait the return of peace before making provision for the establishment of public worship.

When Cincinnati was laid out in 1789, certain lots were dedicated to church and school purposes. In the following year, "Father" Rice, of Kentucky, organized in the place the First Presbyterian Church, and the religious society proposed to occupy the premises thus set apart for religious uses. But they found themselves, with all the aid which they could obtain in the town, too feeble to carry out their project of building a church-edifice. The premises, therefore, were used only as a graveyard. Meetings for worship were held at a horse-mill on Vine Street, below where Third Street has since been opened, and also occasionally at private houses.[1]

[1] Cist's Cincinnati, 1859, p. 136.

For a time the church was dependent on occasional supplies. A Baptist preacher, subsequently implicated in Burr's conspiracy, sometimes occupied the pulpit In 1791, James Kemper consented to serve the church, and a number of the inhabitants formed themselves into a company to escort him from beyond the Kentucky River to Cincinnati. Upon his arrival, a subscription was set on foot to build a church-edifice. Meanwhile the people met for worship upon a portion of the church-lot—partially cleared—on the corner of Fourth and Main Streets, where, gathering in a small circle, they seated themselves upon the logs, with their rifles by their sides. The precaution of defence was not uncalled for. By sudden assaults upon the settlements, the Indians carried terror to every dwelling. No company could feel secure except when well armed; and sometimes the peaceful farmer was forced to flee while he followed the furrow, leaving his team behind.

In 1792, the house of worship was erected,[1] and the four lots devoted to church-purposes were enclosed. The timber for the building was taken from the spot upon which it was erected. More than one hundred persons subscribed to the object. Till 1804, when the church-edifice was removed to Vine below Fifth Street, and a large brick building erected in its place, it answered the purposes for which it had been built.

For many years after Mr. Kemper left (1795), the congregation had no settled pastor,[2] and its progress must have been inconsiderable. In 1796, Cincinnati was still "a small village of log cabins, including perhaps a dozen coarse frame houses with stone chimneys, most of them unfinished."[3] In 1800, it had but seven

---

[1] United States Gazetteer.

[2] Rev. P. Wilson supplied the church from the summer of 1797 till his death, July, 1799.

[3] Judge Burnet, in Ohio Hist. Soc. Transactions.

hundred and fifty inhabitants, and in 1805 less than one thousand. In 1802, Matthew G. Wallace was in charge of the church; but at length, in 1808, Joshua L. Wilson accepted a call to the pastorate, and from this time the growth of the church,[1] as well as of the city, was rapid.

Meanwhile, the region back from the city had received an immigration estimated in 1805 at twenty-five thousand. Dayton was laid out in 1799; but in 1810 it numbered only three hundred and eighty-three inhabitants. For some years preceding this it had enjoyed the stated, and finally the pastoral, labors of James Welsh, who for eight years (1796–1804) had been settled over the Lexington and Georgetown churches in Kentucky.

In 1799, the Presbytery of Washington, consisting of seven ministers, was erected by the transfer of pastors and churches from Transylvania Presbytery, Ky. The field it occupied embraced the region on both sides of the Ohio River, central to Cincinnati. In 1802, by the erection of the Synod of Kentucky, this, which in common with several other Presbyteries had been under the care of the Synod of Virginia, was transferred to the new Synod. In 1802, it had five pastors and thirty-two congregations. William Speer was at Chillicothe,[2] although he shortly after removed to Unity and Greenburg in Redstone Presbytery; John P. Campbell was at Fleming and Locust, Ky., John Dunlavy at Red Oak and Eagle Creek, Richard McNemar at Cabin Creek, Ky., and Matthew G. Wallace at Cincinnati. Orange-

---

[1] It is a noticeable fact that the church enrolled the names of the baptized children as members, and regarded them as subjects of discipline. The membership was thus enlarged, and in 1795 numbered two hundred and twenty-six.

[2] Settled there in 1798, as successor of R. W. Finley, one of the first settlers in 1796.—*Autobiography of J. B. Finley*, 109.

dale and Springfield had at that time called John Thomson. Johnson's Fall and Washington, New Market, Turtle Creek and Clear Creek, Dayton, Bulack, Mad River, and Post St. Vincent were vacant, but able to support a pastor. Those vacant and unable were Mouth of Fleming, Mouth of Big Sandy, Union, Brush Creek, Big Indian, Duck Creek, Williamstown, High Bank Prairie, Peeper, Darby, Old Chillicothe, Buckskin, Paint Creek, and Three Islands.

Previous to 1809, Honey Creek and Beulah had William Robinson as stated supply; James Gilliland, whose anti-slavery sentiments had virtually driven him from South Carolina, had commenced his pastoral labors at Red Oak[1] and Straight Creek; Matthew G. Wallace supplied Springfield and Hambleton; Robert Wilson was at Washington and Germantown.

At Chillicothe, in connection with the Union Church, Robert G. Wilson was settled in 1805, and here he remained until his acceptance of the Presidency of Ohio University in 1824.[2] At Columbus a church was organized in February, 1806, by Wilson, of Chillicothe, and consisted originally of thirteen members.[3] The church was located in Franklinton, on the opposite shore of the Scioto, then the county-town of Franklin

---

[1] The church of Red Oak "is one of the oldest, if not the very oldest, Presbyterian church in Ohio." This was the scene of the first public development of New-Lightism and of Shakerism in the West. Soon after Dunlavy began to preach as a licentiate, he settled with a small company of Presbyterians at Red Oak, but he soon became openly Unitarian. When detected and exposed, he established a Shaker community in the neighborhood, but afterward removed to near Lebanon. He was succeeded by "Father" Finley, who got into difficulty, was suspended from the ministry, and died here. He was succeeded by Father Gilliland.

[2] Sprague, iv. 122. At Chillicothe the first territorial land-office was opened in 1800.

[3] Statement of Dr. Hoge.

county. In October, 1807, James Hoge was called as pastor, and was ordained June 11, 1808. He was a native of Moorfield, Hardy county, Va., although most of his early years were spent at Shepherdstown, whither his father, Dr. Moses Hoge, removed in 1787. He was educated chiefly under his father's instructions, and was licensed in 1805 by the Presbytery of Lexington. Sent out to Ohio by the Assembly's Board of Missions, he was present at the organization of the church of Columbus. When he became its pastor, it numbered twenty members; and in 1809 the number was more than doubled.

At the time when this church was formed, there was no other north of it to Lake Erie, except on the Western Reserve. South of it in the Scioto Valley were the churches of Mt. Pleasant, Chillicothe, and Buckshire, now Salem, in Ross county. Within a few months, churches were established in Lancaster, Zanesville, London, Walnut Plains (near Chillicothe), Upper Liberty (now Milford Center), and Lower Liberty.

For the first eight years, the preaching to Columbus Church was at Franklinton. For the next four years one-half was in Columbus, and subsequently the name of the church was changed and public worship was held altogether in the latter place.

Within the original bounds of the church have been formed the churches of Liberty (on Whenstone River), Worthington, Blendon, Mifflin, Truro, and Hamilton. At Upper Liberty, William Woods, a native of Cumberland county, Pa., and a graduate of Dickinson College, was ordained as pastor June 14, 1808, but was removed by death in 1819. He was the first pastor of Upper and Lower Liberty, on Darby Creek. At Lancaster, John Wright, a native of Pennsylvania and a graduate of Dickinson College, was the first pastor. He was ordained and installed in 1806–07, and removed to

Indiana in 1835. At Mt. Pleasant, James Robinson, a graduate of Jefferson College, was ordained in 1808–09, and dismissed in 1820, when he was called to succeed Mr. Woods at Liberty. In Delaware county, the first pastor of the churches of Delaware, Radnor, and Liberty was Joseph S. Hughes, son of Rev. J. Hughes, a graduate of Jefferson College, and ordained in 1811. His death occurred in 1822.

In 1808, the Presbytery of Lancaster was erected, numbering five ministers,—Wright, of Lancaster, Robinson, of Mt. Pleasant and Rickaway, James Scott, of Ebenezer, Clinton, and Frederick, Stephen Lindsley, of Marietta, and Jacob Lindsley, without charge. The vacant congregations were Waterford, Zanesville, and Springfield, Delaware, to which Mr. Hughes was soon after called, Crooked Creek, Newark, Worthington, Berkshire, High Banks, Scioto Salt-Works, Leading Creek, Ohio, Athens, Federal Creek, and Salem. The churches of Chillicothe and Columbus, or Franklinton, as it was then called, remained as yet under the care of Washington Presbytery, in connection with the Synod of Kentucky.

By their locality, the churches thus gathered in the Miami region came properly into this connection. Several of the earliest missionaries and pastors in this field came from that State. The settlers were in part, doubtless, from New England, but more largely from New Jersey, Pennsylvania, and Virginia. Following the line of the Ohio, they distributed themselves along that river, or, ascending its tributaries, the Scioto and the two Miamies, located on their banks. From the close of the Indian war, in 1795, the immigration rapidly increased.

For many years after the tide of emigration had begun to populate Southern and Southwestern Ohio, the region of the Western Reserve had scarcely been explored by the foot of civilized man. This region, at first and for years embraced under the name of Trumbull[1] county, extended one hundred and twenty miles from east to west, and, upon an average, fifty-two from north to south. Its area embraces three million acres, to which, after the formation of the Federal Government, Connecticut, in virtue of her original charter, still laid claim. A compromise was at length effected, the jurisdiction being conceded to the General Government, while the State retained the proprietorship of the soil. The Reserve was then, and for many subsequent years, known as New Connecticut. It first began to attract public attention in 1799, when the population of what now constitutes the State was sufficient to entitle it to a Territorial government, with a representative body.

But access to it from the East was difficult. The emigrant to Southern Ohio could follow the route from Philadelphia to Pittsburg, and then float down the Ohio to his point of destination. But the New-Englander must take a tedious journey through the swamps and forests of Western New York, and then along the shores of Lake Erie, unless he was prepared to launch his frail craft on its treacherous waves, before he could set foot on what ere long was pronounced the El Dorado of the West. It is true, he too might take the Pittsburg route; but this still left him with a trackless wilderness intervening between him and the goal of his journey.

In 1800, three years after the first settlement was made on the Reserve, its population numbered just eleven hundred and forty-four white inhabitants. In the following years the immigration rapidly increased,

---

[1] In 1774, Rev. Dr. Trumbull, of Connecticut, issued an elaborate pamphlet vindicating the claims of the State in that region.

and by 1810 the population had exceeded sixteen thousand. A large number of these, though by no means the majority,[1] were from New England; and Connecticut was more largely represented than any other of the Eastern States.

From its position, the Reserve came naturally into most immediate connection with the churches of the Pittsburg Synod. This last body was the first, in its missionary zeal, to explore the field. The Ohio Presbytery was perhaps unsurpassed by any other in connection with the Assembly in the ability, enterprise, and devotion of its individual members, and the readiness with which they welcomed self-denial in order to extend the knowledge of the gospel. The task before them, stationed as they were on the very borders of civilization, with new settlements springing up still farther on in the wilderness which seemed assigned to them as their own peculiar field, was arduous indeed. But they spared no effort to meet the emergency, and the most intimate and friendly relations long continued

---

[1] The Connecticut Evangelical Magazine of August, 1813, says, "There has been no time in which the majority of the people of New Connecticut have been natives of New England." "Other parts of the State have had as great a proportion of New England settlers as that." The fact, indeed, is unquestionable. The Rev. Thomas Robbins, whose characteristic taste for statistics is well known, and who labored himself for several years in this field, says, under date of June, 1805, "Since the beginning of the present year, I have been taking pains to make an actual enumeration of the families in this county (Trumbull county, embracing all the region of the Western Reserve then settled). The work I have just completed. There are families in sixty-four towns. The number of families the 1st of January, 1804, was about eight hundred. The 1st of last January there were a little more than eleven hundred; of these, four hundred and fifty are from New England. There are twenty-four schools and seven churches, and more than twenty places where the worship of God is regularly administered."

to exist betwee. he ministers of the Synod and the churches on the Reserve.

In the year 1800, the first permanent laborer in the ministry entered the field. This was William Wick,[1] a native of Southampton, L.I., who, after spending his early years in the city of New York, removed with his father's family to Western Pennsylvania. He received his classical and scientific education at Canonsburg Academy, and studied theology with Dr. McMillan. He was licensed to preach, August 28, 1799, and in the course of a few months, probably as a missionary under the direction of Presbytery, he entered upon his labors on the Western Reserve. In the following year he was ordained and installed as pastor of the United (Presbyterian) Church of Youngstown and Hopewell. To this his time was mainly devoted, although he was still able to make missionary tours in the surrounding region. After nearly three years, a revival commenced at Youngstown, and among its first-fruits was a young man twenty-eight years of age, who was destined to be one of Mr. Wick's most efficient co-laborers. This was the Rev. Thomas Barr, a decided Presbyterian, the first pastor of the church at Euclid (1810), but whose missionary zeal extended far and near. At Newburgh, Cleveland, Painesville, and, indeed, in all parts of the Reserve, his labors were abundant.

Mr. Wick had labored but a few months at Youngstown when he was gladdened by the arrival of strange from the East, who on the last Sabbath o 1800 pr ached to the small congreg ion which M Wick had gathered. This was Joseph Badger, the first missionary sent out by the Connecticut Missionary Society to the Reserve. Among all the ministers of New England, no one, perhaps, could have been found

[1] Sprague's Annals, iv. 443. Hist. of Jefferson College.

better fitted by taste and education for the experience of a pioneer missionary. With David Brainerd his parents were intimately acquainted, and by him two or three of their children were baptized. Joseph was a native of Wilbraham, Mass., and was born in February, 1757. The family soon after removed to Berkshire county, and the only advantages for education which he had were those of the fireside.

Three weeks after the battle of Lexington, though less than twenty years of age, he entered the Revolutionary Army. He was at the battle of Bunker Hill, and accompanied the expedition designed for the capture of Quebec, sharing all its hardships and dangers. After serving two years in the army and sinking under disease almost to the borders of the grave, he received his discharge. But two days after arriving on his return at New Preston, he was called out to join in an attack upon the enemy, who had just destroyed Danbury. After an interval of a few weeks he again enlisted, and when the term of service expired found the two hundred dollars of Continental money which he had saved so depreciated that with the whole he could not procure cloth for an ordinary coat. After weaving sixteen hundred yards of cloth, in order to earn the means to clothe himself, he determined to devote his attention to study that he might be fitted to occupy a higher position in the army.

To carry out his purpose, he applied to Rev. Mr. Day, of New Preston, for the privilege of enjoying his instructions. Though twenty-two years of age, his education was so defective that he used the books fitted for children of eight or ten years. Possibly he may have shared the lessons of the venerable ex-President of Yale College, then a little child playing about the house. But truths more important than those of mere science now commanded his attention. He had often been serious before, but his impressions had worn off. Now, however, they proved more permanent, and his conversion was the first-fruit of a powerful revival.

His purpose to return to the army was abandoned, and he resolved to prepare for the ministry. It was the struggle of indomitable energy with almost overwhelming difficulty. His progress was slow. Sometimes he resorted to the loom, and sometimes taught school, to eke out his scanty means. "Yet still," he says, "I dug away, like a miner after gold."[1] Health and strength gave way under the pressure, and his hopes seemed destined to defeat. He gave up the idea of entering college. But, visiting New Haven with Mr. Day at commencement, he offered himself for examination, and was admitted. Still, he had no means to prosecute his studies. Teaching a singing-school for six weeks, he secured enough for one term, and then applied to President Stiles for dismission. "Oh, no, Badger," was the reply; "you must not leave; you may go and teach; study, and earn, and pay your bills as well as you can." He did so. By teaching, sometimes at a distance, sometimes in New Haven, or by waiting in the hall and ringing the bell, he contrived to secure the means to prosecute his design. By constructing a *Planetarium* for the college he received an order on the steward for one hundred dollars. In 1785 he was graduated, and, after studying theology with the venerable Mark Leavenworth, was settled as pastor of the church in Blanford, Mass., Oct. 24, 1787. Here he labored in the ministry for thirteen years, and was dismissed Oct. 24, 1800, in order to accept the commission of the Connecticut Society for the Western field.

On the 15th of November he started on his journey. Sometimes he was detained for days by storms of rain

[1] Am. Quar. Reg., xiii. 321.

and snow, and his progress was often hindered by the badness of the roads, which, as he approached his destination, were merely a bridle-path, and for nearly two hundred miles he had to lead his horse. The Mahoning, though swollen, he was forced to swim; but, after all vicissitudes, he at length found hospitable shelter with the Presbyterian brother at Youngstown.

Spending the winter and spring in the southern part of the Reserve, Mr. Badger visited nearly all the settlements and families, preaching in every place as he found opportunity. His work was difficult and sometimes dangerous, for there were no regular roads from one place to another, and "the marks of intercourse were not very plain." In June, as soon as the waters were fordable, he visited the more interior settlements. The 4th of July he spent at Hudson. Thence he proceeded to Cleveland, extending his tour through the northern settlements. By the request of the Ohio Presbytery, he went in company with the Rev. Thomas Hughes to visit the Indians at Detroit. On the way, he preached through an interpreter to the Delawares on the Huron River. After accomplishing his mission he set out to return; but exposure and hardship had reduced him to such a condition that he could scarcely cling to his horse. Taking calomel one day, and an emetic the next, for five days in succession, he was brought so low that he could not mount without help. Through the unexplored forest he directed his way to Hudson, subsisting for two days on chestnuts. After a brief respite he went to Austinburg, and on the 24th of October, 1801, organized in that place a church of eight male and six female members.

Nearly a year of service had now expired, and Mr. Badger returned to Connecticut to report to the society and to bring back his family for a permanent location in the region of the Reserve. With a four-horse wagon, which contained all his movables and afforded transport for himself, his wife, and six children, he set out for his new Western home. Through deep drifts of snow, he made slow progress across the mountains of Massachusetts till he arrived at Schodack, on the Hudson. The snow now was two feet deep, and, placing his wagon-box on a long horse-sled, he proceeded on his journey. Crossing the river at Troy, he soon found the mud had replaced the snow, and, in attempting to work his way, one accident after another obstructed his progress. His forward axletree broke, and, without help, he had to mend it with such tools as he had. Four miles from Batavia his wagon-bolt broke, and he had to pay two dollars for a new one. At length, after a journey of over two months, he reached his destination at Austinburg.

In two weeks he had reared his humble cabin. It had flooring enough on which to spread the beds of the family, but neither a table nor a chair. No door was hung, nor were the chinks stopped. Yet in these circumstances he left his family to plant their garden, and set out himself on a missionary tour which continued till the middle of June. In an open sail-boat he started for Buffalo to procure conveniences for his family, and, after a voyage not without hazard, safely returned. Three weeks were devoted to rendering his cabin more comfortable and to preaching in the surrounding region, when he commenced another tour, in which he visited the settlements in the southern part of the Reserve. Next he directed his steps toward the lake-settlements, and in December, 1802, commenced his winter's tour. The streams were impassable in some places and dangerous in others. Grand River was full of floating ice; but he had to cross it. His horse seemed to share his own enterprise, and in April, 1803. he returned again in safety to his family.

Here a letter from the Missionary Society informed him that his salary was reduced to six dollars per week. This seemed to him unreasonable, and he wrote repeatedly to remonstrate against a policy which he denominated "injudicious and oppressive." But a remarkable revival had been in progress for months in his congregation, and, though his family were suffering for want of clothing, he would not leave the field. At length, when patience was exhausted, he resigned his commission from the Connecticut Society, and accepted an appointment as missionary to the Indians from the Western Missionary Society of the Synod of Pittsburg.

A decided Congregationalist in sentiment, he readily enlisted under the Presbyterian banner. The treatment he received from the Connecticut Society might possibly have effected some change in the direction of his sympathies. But at an early period—indeed, soon after he came into the region of the Reserve—he united with the Erie Presbytery. There were only three Presbyterian ministers besides himself settled west of the Ohio: of these Jacob Lindley was at Marietta, Mr. Hughes at Mount Pleasant, and Mr. Wick at Youngstown. Knowing his Congregational sentiments, they expressed their surprise that he could join the Presbytery. "I believe," he replied, "that you are ministers of the gospel; and, as I am alone, I need your watch and counsel."

In 1802, the Synod of Pittsburg constituted itself the Western Missionary Society, and Mr. Badger, as a member of the Presbytery of Erie, participated in the measure. To this society, in conjunction with that of Connecticut, the new settlements of the Reserve looked for aid. Both of them sent out missionaries to the region for longer or shorter periods. The Connecticut Society had the more ample pecuniary means, but it could not procure the men who were willing to undertake the long and arduous journey. Many a pastor might be willing for a few weeks to visit the destitute regions of Vermont, or even of Western New York; but it was a more appalling task to pass to the region of the Ohio and the Lakes. The consequence was, that for many years the Connecticut Society could accomplish but little for the Western Reserve. During successive seasons, its missionaries in this field did not average at most more than two or three. In fact, it was forced, meanwhile (1805–06), to apply to the Pittsburg Synod for men.

Until this period, its missionaries west of New York were David Bacon,[1] Ezekiel J. Chapman, Thomas Robbins, and Calvin Chapin.[2] But the original destination of Mr. Bacon was to the Indians south and southwest of Lake Erie. He entered upon his work with energy and zeal. Part of his westward journey was prosecuted on foot, at the comfortable rate of twenty-five miles a day. After repeated conferences with the Indians, and after exhausting all his tact and eloquence in appeals which he admitted were sometimes too long, he could make no real progress in carrying out what had been a favorite project with the Connecticut Society. The Indians wanted no missionaries. They would like, indeed, some of the arts and comforts of civilized life, but on the whole, through the influence of their medicine-men, they preferred to take nothing of the white man but his brandy. The zeal and logic of the missionary were unavailing to overcome their repugnance to the gospel; and, after repeatedly seeming to himself on the verge of success, but with the experience also of repeated failure, Mr. Bacon abandoned his undertaking. The society reluctantly, but with the thorough con-

---

[1] Father of Dr. Leonard Bacon, of New Haven.

[2] The late Dr. Chapin, of Rocky Hill, Conn.

viction that future effort would be vain, acquiesced in his decision. Early in 1805, after a visit to Connecticut, he returned to Ohio to labor for a portion of his time at Hudson, while during the other he itinerated among the new and destitute settlements. He declined, however, to accept his appointment from the Connecticut Society.[1]

Ezekiel J. Chapman left Connecticut in November, 1801, and for two or three years, for the most part sustained by the Connecticut Society, labored on the Reserve; returning, however, to settle in Western New York. Thomas Robbins remained in Ohio for three or four years, leaving in May, 1806, and Calvin Chapin remained but a single season.

The Connecticut Society, as we have seen, found itself better able to furnish the means than the men for the work. After six years of effort, it had but a single missionary in the field under its patronage. Quite a number of churches had been gathered, and the needs of the new settlements were urgent. An ecclesiastical convention[2] was formed, which in April, 1806, represented the churches of Richfield, Hudson, Vernon, Canfield, Vienna, and Warren, with an aggregate membership of one hundred and sixty.[3] Quite a number of other places demanded missionary attention. Thousands each year were flocking hither from the East, and it was utterly impossible for the society,

---

[1] Ev. Mag., vii. 282.

[2] Conn. Ev. Mag., xii. 284.

[3] The early churches were formed at the following dates:—Austinburg, 1801; Hudson and Poland, 1802; Vernon and Warren, 1803; Canfield, 1804; Vienna, 1805; Euclid, 1807; Tallmadge and Springfield, 1809.—*Am. Quar. Reg.*, viii. 219.

The church at Hudson was organized by Mr. Badger in September, 1802, and consisted of fourteen members,—some of them from Goshen, Conn. In the following year Thomas Robbins commenced his labors at Canfield.

unless furnished with the men, to meet the applications made to it through the convention and other channels.

In these circumstances, it was most fortunate that the Pittsburg Synod, although to an inadequate extent, was able to furnish the men. Canonsburg Academy in 1802, the same year with the formation of the Western Missionary Society, was transformed—out of compliment to the newly-elected President, or to procure from the Democratic majority of the State Legislature the necessary charter—into Jefferson College. Quite a large proportion of its graduates, both before and after the transformation, entered the ministry,—not a few of them amid the scenes of the great revival of that region soon after the commencement of the century.

These men were trained amid scenes kindred to those in which they were expected to labor. They had a pioneer education, and were content to share the settler's lot. William Wick at Youngstown was aided by the Connecticut Society for one or two years, and performed missionary labor under their patronage for a part of the time. Abraham Scott, Jonathan Leslie, Joshua Beer, and James Boyd, who entered upon their work in 1808-09, were men furnished by the Synod but sustained by the society. Scott became pastor in Jefferson county. Leslie labored first at Harpersfield and subsequently at Westfield. Beer was settled at Suffield and Springfield, and Boyd at Warren and Newton. Thomas Barr, converted under the ministry of Mr. Wick at Youngstown, was settled at Euclid in August, 1810; and within a year or two after, three ministers were sent out from New England, viz.: Giles H. Cowles (previously pastor in Bristol, Conn.), who settled at Austinburg, John Seward, who settled at Aurora, and John Field, who became pastor of Burton.

Besides these, Nathan B. Derrow, originally from New England, but who had been settled for several years at Homer, N.Y., where his labors had been blessed with successive revivals, removed to the Reserve, and was settled at Vienna in 1807. He lingered here, however, only for a few years, till the impulse of the wave of emigration bore him on to Western Ohio and Indiana, where we shall meet him again.

Through the labors of these men mainly, and their coadjutors,—missionaries sent out by the Synod of Pittsburg and the General Assembly,—the wilderness began to show signs of culture. By 1808, at least from fifteen to twenty churches had been organized. The missionaries reported "a growing respect for the institutions of heaven." "People in general here," writes Rev. Abraham Scott[1] (September, 1809), "profess a desire for the gospel. They appear in some measure to dread the consequences of being without it, and that both in respect to themselves and their posterity." "It is to be lamented," says Mr. Derrow, "that there are not more clergymen in the country." "In New Connecticut," writes Rev. J. Leslie[2] (1808), "prospects are flattering. Preaching has been very general in it this summer, and many, I hope, are bowing to the conquering Jesus."[3]

The people generally were "anxious for schools, far beyond their circumstances." This was a pleasing fact to the missionaries. Wisely enough, they were "especially mindful of children and youth." They visited the schools and catechized the pupils. The prospects of religion were, on the whole, regarded as promising.

It is true, there were deplorable exceptions. In some towns of from twelve to fifteen families not a praying

---

[1] Ordained by Ohio Presbytery July 12, 1808.

[2] Reports to the Connecticut Society. [3] Ibid.

person could be found. In others, "it seemed to be forgotten that the Lord had a Sabbath." And elsewhere, again, "open infidelity was notorious and insolent, lifting up in affected scorn its brow of brass and its neck of iron." But "the number of praying societies increased. Pious characters were more engaged and fervent. The Sabbath was more seriously respected. The ungodly in many places were more attentive, at least to the externals of religion."

Nor had the churches been without special evidences of the presence and power of the Spirit. Even in their feeble and destitute condition they were repeatedly visited by revivals. These commenced, indeed, almost contemporaneously with the settlement of the region. The powerful influence of the great awakening within the bounds of Pittsburg Synod in 1802-03, extended to the Reserve. The earliest ministers of this region, Messrs. Badger and Robbins,—to say nothing of ministers of the Synod who labored alike in the revival and on the missionary field,—had visited the churches in which the revival prevailed, on their westward journey, or had personally participated in its remarkable scenes. Having witnessed there the "falling exercises," they were not altogether surprised when they occurred under their own labors on the Reserve. Numbers, however, were converted. Solemn and privileged seasons were enjoyed, and the churches were refreshed, before any thing more marked transpired. At length persons began to "fall." This was the case more especially under the preaching of Mr. Badger. Those affected belonged to no single class, although they were generally the more youthful part of the congregation. At length these features of the revival disappeared, and do not seem to have been witnessed at any subsequent period. The churches, however, still enjoyed the special outpouring of the Spirit. From 1807 to

1809, there was "more or less of an awakening in many towns."

In the autumn of 1808, the Synod of Pittsburg erected the Presbytery of Hartford. It was formed largely from the ministers of Erie Presbytery, some of whom were settled on the Reserve, while its bounds were extended, at the request of the Ecclesiastical Convention already mentioned, so as to include the churches in its connection. The members of the Presbytery were Thomas E. Hughes at Mt. Pleasant, Pa. (1799–1831), William Wick at Youngstown and Hopewell (1800–15), Joseph Badger, James Satterfield at Moorfield (1801–34) and Neshanock (1801–12), Benjamin Boyd at Beulah, Trumbull, and Pymatuning (1806–09), Nicholas Pittenger at Westfield (1805–09) and Poland (1805–10), Clement Valandingham at New Lisbon (1807–39) and Long's Run (1807–17), and Johnston Eaton (1808) at Springfield and Fairview.[1]

The accessions to the Presbytery were James Boyd at Newton and Warren (1808–13), John Bruce at Ellsworth (1810–15), Thomas Barr at Euclid (1810–20), Joshua Beer at Springfield (1810–15), Robert Semple at New Castle (1811–37) and Slippery Rock (1811–34), Giles H. Cowles at Austinburg (1812–35) and Morgan (1812–18), Ezekiel Glasgow at Beavertown and New Salem (1813–15), Jonathan Leslie at Harpersfield (1814–20), William Matthews at Neshanock (1814–15), and James Wright at Poland (1815–32) and Westfield (1815–41).

In 1810, the ministers of the Presbytery numbered thirteen; two of whom, Alexander Cook and Jonathan Leslie, were without charge. But the demands of the field required at least twice or thrice the number of laborers. The Connecticut Society exerted itself to

[1] Transferred to Erie Presbytery in 1812.

send out more; but John Field and John Seward were the only names added to the missionary list in 1811. By the Synod of Pittsburg and the General Assembly quite a large number of men were, during successive years, sent into the field, but these remained often but a few weeks or, at most, months. Yet there was steady progress, and revivals were not infrequent. Mr. Seward, too, traversing extensively the entire region of the Reserve to enlarge his knowledge of the country, found—notwithstanding great destitution of religious principles—"some in many places who are uncommonly engaged about religion," while "some places were favored with the influences of the Spirit in a great degree."

In 1810, Alexander Cook, a missionary of the Assembly, made an extensive tour throughout the State. From his own residence—Slippery Rock and New Castle were his pastoral charge—he took a westerly course to the Scioto. This extensive region was rapidly filling up with "emigrants from every State." Their manners and habits, as might have been expected, were "not a little discordant." Yet he says, "In every neighborhood through which I passed, some of God's dear children are to be found." In many places, in the lack of preaching, they had established prayer-meetings, and the effect had been happy. A restraining influence was thus exerted over the community, and "the dissolute part" were kept "from hunting on the Sabbath."

"Near the Tuscarora River," he writes, "I formed several congregations, and was the first who preached the gospel among them. In some instances we had moving and melting scenes." Passing near the forks of the Sandy, where he preached, Mr. Cook took thence a northerly course to Lake Erie. In the Connecticut Reserve there was "ample field for labor." He preached every day and made many visits to families. Amid his exhaustion, his mind "was much comforted by discovering a prevailing taste for divine things." From the Reserve he travelled westward along the lake. He met the Presbytery of Hartford at Euclid, and received an appointment to preach at Cleveland. He went thither, but the field was a hard one. "Here," he wrote, "Satan keeps his strongholds." Infidelity here walked "in brazen front." Remonstrance, tears, and entreaties were vain to stop the mouths of the scoffers.

Rev. Samuel Tait labored in the region between Alleghany and Lake Erie in the summer and fall of 1810. He travelled six hundred and thirty miles and preached fifty-seven sermons. His reception was hospitable and his labors were blessed. "In every congregation," he says, "there was earnest pressing for more preaching. It is with pain I look over our wilderness and see some hardened in sin, some beginning to ask what they shall do to be saved, and some mourning when they think on ancient days, when they used to go to the house of God, and none to go forth to warn, to guide, or to comfort them. . . . The vacant congregations are looking up to the Assembly to extend their benevolence to them as in years past."

In the course of 1811, several new churches were organized by Mr. Derrow. Mr. Leslie, on his missionary tour, found "the people making exertions to form themselves into Ecclesiastical Societies, and, according to their ability, to furnish themselves with the gospel ministry." Mr. Boyd's experience was similar. Mr. Scott reported that, "in general, there is great apparent attention under preaching. In some places there is considerable solemnity. . . . In almost every place I have visited, the people have solicited me to visit them as much as possible."

At Euclid, under the labors of Mr. Barr, a people

who had been "deplorably sunk in ignorance and error" had become "solemn and engaged about religion." Many were inquiring, and conversions were frequent. "The change in that part of the wilderness is so great, and the attention to religion so earnest, that Christians feel themselves called to acknowledge the hand of God with gratitude, and praise him for his wonderful works. God carries on his work although errors and enmities oppose."

During the year closing October, 1812, the Connecticut Society had been the means of procuring for the Reserve the amount of two hundred weeks of missionary labor. A considerable portion of this was from the missionary tours of settled pastors, for a portion of the year. They found much encouragement, and generally received a hearty welcome wherever they went. Many societies were asking for preachers, at least a part of the time. Missionary labor was "thankfully received" by the greater part of the population. It was not mere compliment. "Many, with tears," says Mr. Boyd, "will speak of their destitute situation, not having a sermon on the Sabbath more than twice or thrice in the year, and urgently solicit us to visit them again." Mr. Barr speaks of his cordial reception in almost every place, and "the anxiety of the people to hear the gospel." In the northern part of the Reserve, in the neighborhood of Vienna, where Mr. Derrow was settled, a number of towns were "visited by the effusions of the Spirit," and "the wilderness became vocal with the praises of God." This was the case also in a part of the region around Austinburg, where Mr. Cowles was laboring.

Meanwhile, the tide of immigration continued to pour in. "Assemblies for public worship," says Mr. Scott, "are considerably more numerous than formerly, owing principally to our growing population." Revivals prevailed in many places. This was the case especially in Portage county, and in the vicinity of Aurora, where the Rev. John Seward was settled in August (5), 1812. From a state of stupidity, the people were "quickened," and became "zealously engaged in the great concern." Bold opposers were humbled and deeply impressed. Quite a number of the aged were converted, and many heads of families began "the practice of worshipping God with their households." In the extent of the change wrought, the town of Tallmadge was specially mentioned. Yet in this and five other places in the same neighborhood, the people, though desirous of pastoral labor, could not procure it.

Up to this period, there had been almost uninterrupted religious progress throughout the Reserve. But the prospects of the churches were now darkened from divers causes. The war with England had commenced. Some of the settlers were drafted for the army. Interest in religious truth was displaced by patriotic anxiety or military alarm. A false report that the enemy had landed at Cleveland led Mr. Barr with all his flock to a hasty retreat. They took what goods they could pack up with them, and fled many miles before they were apprized of their mistake. Other communities suffered, but not to the same extent. Still, "the effects of the war," says Mr. Boyd, "are sensibly felt in consequence of so many of our inhabitants being called forth in our defence."

This, however, was not the only cause of anxiety. In consequence of the lack of educated ministers, ignorant ranters and teachers of error found an open field. They crowded into places where seriousness prevailed, to turn the people away from the truth. In some instances they did great mischief.

But the general character of the population had already received a permanent impression. The future was evidently promising. The intervention of the war prevented for a time the movement which resulted in the formation of the First Presbytery of Northern Ohio,—that of Grand River, in 1814. Yet, as the sounds of conflict died away, and the blessings of peace were restored, the Presbyteries entered with fresh hope upon the broad and inviting field.

Outside of the Reserve, the Connecticut Society had but a single missionary in their employ, within the bounds of the State. This was the Rev. Timothy Harris,[1] in the counties of Muskingum and Delaware. He was appointed to itinerate as a missionary in the settlements around the town of Granville, where he was located as pastor of the church. This body had emigrated from the town of Granville, Mass., where it had been organized in 1804 with twenty-seven members. Three years after this, Mr. Harris arrived and entered upon his labors in connection with the church. He was the only pastor in the region, and he willingly accepted a commission from the Connecticut Society for such a portion of his time as he could be spared from the people of his stated charge. His labors were not in vain. He writes (Oct. 14, 1809), "I have reason to believe that God in some measure smiled on my labors. Prospects where I have been are encouraging." The following year he devoted more time to the mission-field around him, and speaks of it with more confident hope. Visiting from house to house through the week, his efforts were blessed to the conversion of many, while "Sabbath assemblies were invariably full and solemn." In many places, he found some to welcome him at times even with tears. "Like Mary, they were ready to sit at the feet of Jesus and catch in-

---

[1] His predecessor in this field for a short time was Rev. James Scott.

struction, blessing God for the opportunity;" or, "like Lot in Sodom, they were preserved to bear witness for the truth." At the same time, irreligion and vice were fearfully prevalent. In some settlements he found that year after year had passed without witnessing a worshipping assembly. The people did not know how to behave themselves decently when they were called together. Urgent was the necessity for more laborers. The Connecticut Society made a single appointment; but even that was not fulfilled.

On the southern border of the State the prospect was far less encouraging. From Steubenville to Marietta—one hundred and ten miles—there was no minister. Mr. Schermerhorn, who accompanied Samuel J. Mills on his Southwestern tour in the autumn of 1812, proposed to the people bordering on the Ohio the establishment of a missionary route. The proposal was kindly received, but the difficulty was to procure a preacher. Many counties of the State were altogether destitute of a Presbyterian or Congregational ministry. Many others had but one, whose charge extended over two, and often over three, churches. In all, there were twenty-four clergymen in the State, exclusive of the Western Reserve. Three of these were Congregationalists; although one of the number was without charge. The names of the three, as given by Mr. Mills, were Potter, Robbins, and Harris. Potter was at Steubenville, Robbins at Marietta, and Harris at Granville.

In 1814, the Synod of Ohio was erected. It consisted of the Presbyteries of Lancaster, Washington, and Miami. Of these, the two last had been connected with the Synod of Kentucky, as the first had been with the Synod of Pittsburg.

Lancaster Presbytery had been erected in 1808, and consisted, as already stated, of five ministers. At the time of its transfer to form the Ohio Synod, six of its twenty-four vacancies had been supplied. Five new laborers, James Cunningham (Salem and Fearing), George Vanneman, William Jones (Circleville and Walnut Plains), Joseph S. Hughes (Delaware and Liberty), and James Culbertson (Zanesville and Springfield), had entered the field.

The erection of the Presbytery of Washington by the Synod of Kentucky was one of its first acts after it had been constituted in 1802. The list of its original membership has been already given. At the time of its transfer to form Ohio Synod, its list of members had been greatly enlarged. In 1805, Robert G. Wilson, a native of North Carolina and a graduate of Dickinson College, had accepted the call of the small church just gathered at Chillicothe, dividing his labors for several years between it and Union Church, five miles distant. With an insufficient maintenance,[1] but with a cheerful self-denial, he prosecuted his labors. In conjunction with Dr. James Hoge,[2] sent out shortly after by the General Assembly as a missionary in Ohio, he

[1] So scant was his support that, in order to procure the means of subsistence, he reluctantly accepted the office of postmaster of the town. One of the Assembly's missionaries who visited him found him "living in a cabin of a single apartment, prosecuting his studies and performing his ministerial duties with as great assiduity and cheerfulness as if he had been favored with all the advantages of a comfortable home and refined society." With great force of character, untiring energy, and devotion to his work, he continued to discharge the laborious duties of his pastorate, till called to the Presidency of the Ohio University at Athens.

[2] In the year 1805, James Hoge performed, by appointment of the General Assembly, a six-months missionary tour in the State, and during the time assisted in organizing the church of Columbus, of which he was two years later ordained and installed as pastor. Here for a long series of years he was permitted to remain, the missionary patriarch of an extended region, which he lived to see covered with churches, many of which he assisted to organize.

organized the first church of Columbus, over which Dr. Hoge was subsequently ordained pastor. Opposed, on principle, to any connection with slavery, his sympathies removed him from North Carolina, his native State, to the northern banks of the Ohio; and here, as pastor of a church, and subsequently President of Ohio University, he completed a long and useful life.

More decided in his anti-slavery feeling was another member of the Presbytery, who united with it, like Wilson, from the Carolinas. This was James Gilliland, also a graduate of Dickinson College, and a licentiate of the Presbytery of South Carolina. His zeal on the subject of emancipation in his native State subjected him to embarrassment, and the matter was brought to the attention of Synod. The Presbytery had enjoined upon him silence in the pulpit on this subject, and the Synod declared itself of opinion that "to preach publicly against slavery in present circumstances, and to lay down as the duty of every one to liberate those who are under their care, is that which would lead the way to disorder and open the way to great confusion."

For nearly eight years Gilliland labored in the Southern field. But his anti-slavery views at last ultimated in differences that led to the dissolution of the pastoral relation. At about the same time with his copresbyter Wilson, he turned to a Northern field. On the 3d of April, 1805, he was dismissed to Washington Presbytery, and soon after was settled at Red Oak, Brown county, Ohio, where for nearly forty years he continued his labors. Besides these, the Presbytery in 1814 had upon its list of newly-arrived ministers the names of William Williamson, pastor of West Union, Manchester, and Cabin Creek; Nicholas Pittenger at Nazareth, Rocky Spring, and New Market; Robert B. Dobbins at Smyrna and Williamsburg; James H. Dickey at Buckskin, Concord, and Pisgah; as well as several others, unsettled ministers or stated supplies. Its membership was thirteen, and its congregations had increased to twenty-eight.

Miami Presbytery was erected in 1810 (from Washington) by the Kentucky Synod. In 1814 it embraced six ministers and twenty congregations. James Welch was settled at Dayton; Matthew G. Wallace had charge of the churches at Hamilton, Seven-Mile, and Dick's Creek; Daniel Heyden was pastor at Hopewell and Duck Creek, John Thompson at Springfield and Unity, Joshua L. Wilson at Cincinnati; and William Robinson was without charge. There were vacant churches organized at Bath, Lebanon, Yellow Spring, Honey Creek, Mackacheck, Washington, Troy, New Lexington, New Jersey, Brookville, and White-Water.

Most of the laborers had but recently arrived upon the field. Wilson, better known subsequently as the prosecutor of Dr. L. Beecher, was the most distinguished of the little band. In 1781, he removed with his father's family from Virginia to Kentucky. Here, at Harrod's Station, he heard from "Father" Rice the first sermon preached beyond the mountains. In 1802 he was licensed to preach at Spring Hill, Tenn., and in 1804 was ordained pastor of the churches of Bardstown and Big Spring. In 1808 he removed to Cincinnati, where he remained for thirty-eight years pastor of the First Presbyterian Church.

Thus the Synod of Ohio, consisting of the three Presbyteries of Lancaster, Washington, and Miami, was constituted in 1814 on the petition of the Presbytery of Lancaster. It covered Central and Southern Ohio, and was composed of twenty-nine ministers and eighty-one congregations. In 1815, on a petition from the Synod of Ohio, the Ohio River was by the Assembly made the dividing line between the Synods of Kentucky and Ohio,—the congregation of Cabin

Creek alone being excepted from the application of the act.

The cause of education within the bounds of Ohio received the early attention of the settlers. The General Government, however, had already made wise provision for the promotion of its interests. In the ordinance of 1785 for the sale of Western lands, No. 16 of every township was reserved "for the maintenance of public schools within the said township." The ordinance of 1787 provided that, "religion, morality, and knowledge being necessary to good government and the happiness of mankind, schools and the means of education shall be forever encouraged."

The inhabitants of this State proved themselves capable of appreciating this excellent provision. The Constitution, framed in 1802, approved the wisdom and adopted the very language of the ordinance. The value of land at the time was indeed a mere trifle; and it seems like romance to read that the entire plain on which the city of Cincinnati is built was sold only seventy years ago for less than fifty silver dollars. But with the progress of settlement the lands rose in value; and the wisdom of the fathers of the Constitution is fully reflected in those measures of the General Government which at the same time consecrated the Northwest Territory to freedom and made provision that it should be occupied by an intelligent and enlightened population.

The settlers themselves displayed, not only on the Reserve but in the southern portions of the State, a commendable disposition to establish schools and colleges. We may smile at the pedagogic features of the nomenclature of Marietta, with its square fronting on its block-houses called *Campus Martius*, and other squares known as *Cecilia* and *Capitolinum*, while the great road through the covert way was known as *Via*

Sacra;[1] but even these indicate that among its inhabitants were men who possessed a taste for classic lore. One of the first acts of the Territorial Legislature was to take measures for the establishment of the Ohio University. The provision for this was found in the two townships given by Congress in the Ohio Company's purchase for this express object. The place of its location, selected by General Rufus Putnam, was called Athens,—as if to revive the memories and associations of ancient learning. It was not, however, till 1810 that effectual measures were taken to furnish the means of public instruction by the organization of an academy. It was not till 1815 that the institution exercised the full prerogatives of a college. In that year the first literary degree conferred northwest of the Ohio was received by Hon. Thomas Ewing, subsequently a Senator of the United States from Ohio.

In the Miami region a similar provision was made for the encouragement of learning. In the Symmes Contract for the purchase of one million acres of land, an entire township was appropriated for the support of a literary institution. It is still doubtful whether the suggestion which led to the introduction of this appropriation proceeded from Symmes himself or from members of Congress.

The "College Township" was first located at or near the mouth of Little Miami River, a few miles above Cincinnati. But for some reason it was found advisable to change it, and Congress, in 1803, authorized the State to locate in lieu of it a township west of the Great Miami River. Accordingly, three commissioners —one of whom was Jeremiah Morrow, long a ruling elder in the Associate Reformed Church, subsequently Governor of Ohio and member of Congress—proceeded

[1] North American Review, July, 1838, p. 15.

to locate and enter, for the purpose specified, the township now known as Oxford, in Butler county. The first meeting of the Board of Trustees was held in 1809; but it was several years before the institution commenced operations.[1]

But even as late as 1815 the means and energies of the people of the State were so greatly absorbed in their struggle with the difficulties of new settlements and provision for comfortable homes, as to preclude any large outlay for more than the means of a common-school education. In subsequent years, we shall perceive that as their means increased they proved themselves not unworthy representatives of the regions from which they had gone forth.

CHAPTER XXIX.

KENTUCKY, 1800-1815.

BEFORE the close of the last century, Transylvania Presbytery had become so extended as to call for a division. With the consent of the Synod of Virginia, it was broken up (March 27, 1799)[2] into three Presbyteries,—Transylvania, West Lexington, and Washington. The first of these, bounded northeast by the Kentucky River, north and northwest by the Ohio River,

---

[1] For a sketch of the early history of Miami University, down to 1839, see American Quarterly Register for August, 1839.

[2] The Minutes of 1802 report that in 1798 there were two Presbyteries in Kentucky,—Transylvania and West Lexington,—and a list of the members of each is given. I have followed, however, the statements of Dr. R. Davidson in his "History of the Presbyterian Church in Kentucky."

and comprehending on the south the settlements on the Cumberland and its tributaries, comprised ten ministers:—David Rice, whose pastorate of the congregations of Concord at Danville, Cane Run, and Dick's River (1784–97) had closed, and who had removed to Green county; Thomas B. Craighead, subsequently (1805–08) pastor of Shiloh congregation, though he had been long in the field; Terah Templin, a faithful evangelist, supplying destitute congregations (Road's Run near Springfield, and Hardin's Creek, now Lebanon) in Washington county; James McGready, pastor of the congregations of Gaspar River, Red River, and Muddy River (1796–1814); Archibald Cameron at Simpson's Creek, Bullskin, and Achor congregations (1796–1803), and subsequently in charge of Shelbyville and Mulberry Churches (1804–36); Samuel Finley at Stanford (1797–1807); Matthew Houston, successor of Carey H. Allen as pastor of Paint Lick and Silver Creek Churches (1797–1802); William McGee, pastor of Beech Church; and John Howe, settled (1798) over Beaver Creek and Little Barren.

West Lexington Presbytery, bounded south and southwest by Kentucky River, north and northwest by the Ohio, and north and northeast by the Main Licking, comprised nine ministers:—James Crawford, till his death pastor of Walnut Hill Church (1785–1803), gathered by his own labors; Samuel Shannon at Bethel and Sinking Spring (1789–93), and subsequently (1794–1806) at Woodford; Isaac Tull at Green Creek and Pleasant Point (1796–98); Robert Marshall at Bethel (1793–1833) and Blue Spring (1793–1803?); James Blythe at Clear Creek and Pisgah (1793–95?), of the last of which he was stated supply for over forty years; Joseph P. Howe at Mt. Sterling and Springfield (1795–1830); James Welch at Lexington and Georgetown (1796–1804), and subsequently at Dayton, Ohio;

Samuel Rannels at Paris and Stonermouth (1796–1817); and William Robinson at Mt. Pleasant and Indian Creek (1796–1802).

Washington Presbytery, extending across the Ohio and comprising the remaining portion of Kentucky northeast of the Main Licking, consisted of seven ministers,—Peter Wilson, James Kemper, John P. Campbell, John E. Finley, William Speer, John Dunlavy, and Richard McNemar.

In 1802, the three Presbyteries were constituted the Synod of Kentucky, and their aggregate membership had risen from twenty-six to thirty-seven. In 1810, the Presbytery of Muhlenberg was erected from that of Transylvania; and in 1814, the three Presbyteries, Transylvania, West Lexington, and Muhlenberg, covering most of the State, reported an aggregate of thirty ministers and sixty-five congregations. At this time several new laborers, worthy of special mention, had entered the field. Among these were Thomas Cleland, of Union (1804–16), New Providence, and Cane Run (1813–52) congregations, Samuel K. Nelson (1809–27), of Danville, S. B. Robertson (1801–13), of Cane Run and New Providence, Nathan H. Hall, R. M. Cunningham, and others to whom reference will hereafter be made.

Among the ministers to whom, at the commencement of the century, the charge of the churches in Kentucky was committed, there were a few of devoted piety and a high order of talent. Rice and Marshall have already been mentioned. Crawford had studied at Princeton, and was a man of industry, zeal, and usefulness. Campbell was a genius, and at the same time a close student and a well-read theologian. He was a graceful speaker, an elegant writer, and a powerful controversialist. Dr. Alexander, who knew him well while he was studying with Graham and Hoge in Virginia, pronounced his talents fit for any station. Lyle was moderately gifted, but studious, cautious, and discreet. Rannels was pious and indefatigable, but unequal in his efforts, and by no means eminent. Stuart was unassuming, prudent, and considerate, but fearless in the discharge of duty. Cameron was a countryman of John Knox, whom in many respects he resembled. Robertson was much admired as a preacher, and was warm and ardent in his devotions.[1] Blythe was at once scholarly and practical, conservative and decided, commanding in person and magisterial in manner,—a man of little pliancy, but great decision. Many of the others, however, were either weak in intellect or inefficient as pastors. Howe (J. P.), though he could sing and pray well, was a tedious preacher. Houston, Dunlavy, and McNemar became New-Lights or Stoneites, and finally Shakers. Bowman (1810) was suspended for refusing to appear and answer charges against him. Mahon was deposed for drunkenness. Tull was a good but weak man, and an indifferent preacher. Taking the whole body together,[2] "a dull formality seems to have been their general characteristic." With two or three shining exceptions, the majority were of barely respectable abilities, a few hardly above mediocrity, and not a few, though sound in principle, "deficient in the spirit of the gospel." At one time or other, nearly half the preachers had been under ecclesiastical censure. Several were cut off for heresy or schism, two were deposed for intemperance, and several were rebuked for wrangling or improprieties.

With such facts as these established beyond question, we are not surprised at the statements of the historian

[1] Life of Cleland.

[2] Davidson, 129. See Cleland's Life, and Crisman's "Origin of the Cumberland Church"

of the Cumberland Presbyterians. "The ministry," he says, "aimed at little else than to enlighten the understanding." Craighead for fifteen years was never heard to speak "in favor of the new birth, evangelical repentance, or saving faith;" and his course was scarcely exceptional. The ministers spoke of the *elect*, the *predestinated*, the *preordained*, but little of individual accountability or spiritual regeneration. A stiff technical theology or a dry speculative orthodoxy left the heart and conscience unmoved. Members were received to the churches without professing a change of heart or being aware of its necessity.

Yet it was in these circumstances that the great Kentucky Revival of 1800—one of the memorable events in the history of the Church in this country—commenced. It was characterized, as it progressed, by great extravagances and indiscretions. Some of its results, indirectly at least, were deplorable. Yet it exerted a powerful and permanent influence, and wrought a marked change in the aspect and condition of society.[1] The most incredulous repeatedly became its subjects.

In January, 1799, the Rev. James McGready took charge of three congregations—Red River, Gaspar River, and Muddy River—in Logan county, Ky. Among the neighboring ministers in sympathy with him were John Rankin, William McGee, and William Hodge,—the latter one of his own converts, from North Carolina. His field was a most unpromising one. Spiritual life seemed almost everywhere extinct. But a few members were found by the pastor ready to unite with him one day in each month, and an hour in each week, in prayer for the conversion of sinners and the revival of

---

[1] For Dr. Baxter's favorable judgment of the revival as a genuine work of grace, see New York Miss. Mag. for 1802–03.

God's work. In the course of three or four months there were signs of change. A woman long connected with the church (Gaspar River) renounced her hope as false and delusive. Struck under deep conviction, she at length found peace. Immediately she visited her friends, warning them from house to house, in a most solemn manner, to attend to the interests of their souls. The congregation soon became interested, and some ten persons professed conversion.[1]

In July, 1798, the work, which had declined toward the close of the preceding year, recommenced. There was scarce a family in which there were not anxious souls. Within a few days, nearly all worldly business was laid aside. The work soon extended to McGready's other congregations. "The people seemed to hear for eternity. In every house, and in almost every company, the whole conversation of people was about the state of their souls." "The awakening work went on with power under every sermon." Unfortunately, at this juncture, Rev. James Balch visited the region. He spoke freely, if not bitterly, against the character of the work. The churches were "involved in confusion and disputation," and the revival ceased.

In July, 1799, again upon a sacramental occasion, it commenced anew. Several ministers (probably Rankin and the McGees) were present, and on Monday the large congregation was powerfully affected. "Many of the most bold, daring sinners in the county covered their heads and wept bitterly." Numbers lingered after the services were closed. Every countenance indicated seriousness, and not a few were bathed in tears. They were called back, a meeting of prayer was held, and the impressions were deepened. Christians were awakened to new life. "The dreadful state of sinners

---

[1] McGready's Letter in New York Miss. Mag., 1800.

out of Christ" seemed to impose upon them "a sensible, heartfelt burden."

In August, a similar scene occurred among the Gaspar River congregation,—now under the charge of Rankin. "The almighty power of God was displayed in the most striking manner." The next day the solemnity visibly increased. For the first time the features afterward regarded as peculiar to this work made their appearance. "Many persons were so struck with deep, heart-piercing convictions that their bodily strength was quite overcome, so that they fell to the ground, and could not refrain from bitter groans and outcries for mercy." These effects were limited to no class. "The work was general, with old and young, black and white." Large numbers were awakened, and quite a number of hopeful conversions followed.

On the following Sabbath, a similar scene occurred at Clay Lick,—another of Mr. McGready's congregations. On the fifth Sabbath of September, the sacrament was administered at Muddy River, and the occasion was more remarkable than any that had preceded. On the last Sabbath of October, the sacramental season was observed at the Ridge, a vacant congregation in the Cumberland settlements in Tennessee. A very general revival followed, and continued with great power for several months.

In the summer of 1800, still more extraordinary scenes were witnessed. The work began at Red River on the third Sabbath of June. The following day "was indeed the great day of the feast." At the close of the sermon, by Rev. Mr. Hodge, "a dreadful striking solemnity overspread the assembly. The vast multitude were all in tears. Awakened sinners were struck with such keen, piercing convictions that many of them fell to the ground, and roared out, in extreme anguish, 'What shall I do to be saved?'" Children "of nine, ten, and twelve years of age" might be seen "lying prostrate on the ground, weeping, praying, and crying for mercy."[1]

On the fourth Sabbath of July, the congregation at Gaspar River were similarly visited. "A surprising multitude of people" had collected, many from a distance of thirty, and some from a distance of sixty or even a hundred, miles. After the second day of the meeting, the impression became more deep and pervading. "The greater part of the ministers and several hundreds of the people remained at the meeting-house all night. The hours were spent in prayer and praise and conversation with inquiring souls." At the close of the next day's sermon, "the power of God seemed to shake the whole assembly." "The cries of the distressed," at times, almost drowned the voice of the speaker. After the congregation was dismissed, none seemed willing to depart. Careless professors were led to more searching self-examination, and to abandonment of their former hopes. "Awakening and converting work" went forward throughout the vast multitude. Many of the children were deeply affected, and gave evidence of genuine conversion. "The good language, the good sense, the clear ideas, and the rational scriptural light in which they spoke," says Mr. McGready, "amazed me. I felt mortified and mean before them. They spoke upon these subjects beyond what I could have done."

The next day (Monday) there was "a vast concourse of people." It was "another day of the Son of man." Two "powerful sermons" were preached by McGee and Hodge, and "a universal solemnity" was manifested. The congregation was dismissed, but none seemed willing to leave the place. Persons of all ages and colors

---

[1] McGready's Letters in the New York Miss. Mag.

were found to be under conviction, some of them "crying out for mercy in the most extreme distress" The assemblage remained together until Tuesday morning after sunrise, when "they broke up after they were dismissed by prayer."

This was the origin of CAMP-MEETINGS; and it initiated a new system of evangelical effort. There was not a little in the circumstances of it to attract and impress. A regular encampment was formed Some occupied tents, while others slept in covered wagons. The arrangement of these was such as to form a hollow square, the enclosure being fitted up for public worship. Parallel rows of roughly-hewn logs served as seats for the audience, while in the centre was the stand, a platform rudely constructed of logs, which served the purpose of a pulpit.[1]

The novelty of the scene, as well as the report of what had already occurred on similar occasions, brought large multitudes together Several preachers from the neighboring region were present to assist each other in the exercises. The scene itself, as one and another were struck under conviction and cried out in agony or fell from exhaustion, was well calculated to affect all but those of the strongest nerves.

The preachers themselves were roused, by the demand which seemed to be made upon them, to extraordinary effort. Nor were they lacking in just those gifts which enabled them to make the most of the occasion. McGready had left, but two or three years before, a congregation in Orange county, N.C., in consequence of the odium which his unsparing censures had brought upon him from those who could not endure his rebukes. He was indeed a Son of Thunder, a Boanerges in manner and matter. "The curses of the law lost none of their

---

[1] Davidson's Kentucky, 134.

severity in falling from his lips; and, like Mirabeau, the fierceness of his invectives derived additional terror from the hideousness of his visage and the thunder of his tones."[1] He was now in the early vigor of manhood, and gave full scope to the intense energy of his nature.

His associates—Rankin, Hodge, and the two McGees—were for the most part possessed of kindred sympathies. Rankin was a man of little stability, and repeatedly carried away by his own enthusiasm. He was one of the Revivalists who fell off first to the New Lights and afterward to the Shakers. From the outset, he was unsettled in his doctrinal views; but his very susceptibilities gave him for a time a peculiar and powerful influence. William McGee had been converted in North Carolina under McGready's preaching, and soon followed him to Kentucky. He was exceedingly animated and zealous in the pulpit, and, like McGready, wielded the curses of Sinai with great power. "He would sometimes exhort after sermon, standing on the floor, or sitting or lying in the dust, his eyes streaming, and his heart so full that he could only ejaculate, 'Jesus! Jesus!'" His first pastorate was the charge of the Shiloh congregation. His difference with his elders led to his removal, and he was succeeded by Mr. Hodge.

William Hodge, like McGee, was from North Carolina. He had entered the ministry at a somewhat advanced age, and had been preaching for ten years when he succeeded McGee in the pastorate of the Shiloh church. Although less stern than McGready, and rather a Son of Consolation, he was most efficient and zealous in promoting the revival. He was a powerful speaker, and under his preaching some of the most surprising

---

[1] Davidson's Kentucky.

scenes occurred. In his own congregation a division soon sprang up, and a new organization was the result.

The other McGee was a Methodist preacher. With all the warm feeling and quick susceptibility of his brother, he had the Methodist peculiarities. Some of the most objectionable features of the work are said to have been countenanced and promoted by him.

Encouraged by their past success in the new measures which they had adopted, these men prosecuted them with increased energy. The plan of camp-meetings spread like wildfire. They were held, one after another, in rapid succession. Crowds assembled from every direction. "The laborer quitted his task; age snatched his crutch; youth forgot his pastime; the plough was left in the furrow; business of all kinds was suspended." Young and old, the farmer and the hunter, white and black, flocked to the centre of attraction. The paths leading through the forest were alive with people, and the number reported in attendance upon these occasions is almost incredible.

The camp-meeting at Gaspar River was attended by a number of young people from Shiloh congregation, fifty miles distant. They came with "great curiosity to see the work," yet strongly prejudiced against it. Some of them on their return felt it their duty to warn their young associates. Quite a number were brought under conviction; and by the influence thus exerted religious meetings were commenced, even while without a minister, and a powerful revival was the result. It led to the settlement of William Hodge.

At this time a company of eighteen or twenty persons, in "a very wicked, thoughtless settlement," happened to meet together at a certain house. None had any particular errand, and they began to converse together on the concerns of their souls. At length they concluded to meet together in solemn prayer. Here again a revival of religion commenced.

Thus the work was continually extending. The camp-meetings were still kept up. A sacramental season was observed at Muddy River on the fifth Sabbath of August. Sunday night, says McGready, "was one of the most solemn nights I ever saw in the world." A large majority of the congregation remained with the ministers at the meeting-house all night. On Monday night the scene was repeated. None seemed to feel the want of food or sleep.

The second Sabbath of September was the sacrament-season at Ridge, Cumberland county; the third, at Shiloh. In October the scene was transferred to Mr. Craighead's congregations, in the same neighborhood, then successively to Clay Lick, Montgomery's Meeting-House, and Hopewell. At these various places large numbers of conversions are reported to have occurred. The work extended to many vacant congregations. McGready visited meanwhile the settlement of Red-Banks, one hundred miles distant on the Ohio. It was, according to his report, "a Satan's seat, a second hell." He went there twice, Mr. Rankin once, Mr. Hodge once. A powerful revival commenced. Several professed deists were converted, and "an orderly good congregation" might have been gathered there, if there had been "a faithful minister to take charge of them."

Many striking incidents and surprising conversions occurred in connection with these scenes. A strange gentleman from Georgia, who had come into the region to conduct the sale of lands which he possessed in Cumberland, was riding near the spot where one of the meetings were held. Attracted by the cries of the distressed, he turned aside from curiosity, but was converted, and at once changed his purpose, resolving to sell his Georgia rather than his Kentucky lands, and thus reside on the latter. Another stranger, from a distance, was about to leave. His foot was in the stirrup; but he was asked, "How can you go without Christ?" He "sank to the ground under the most pungent conviction," and only left the place when he had found peace in believing. Bitter opponents were strangely subdued. Scoffers and revilers were brought to cry out in agony for mercy.

During the following year (1801), the revival was still more powerful and extensive. Early in May "the flame began to spread." The scene at "Mr. Campbell's meeting-house" was extraordinary and affecting. On the third Sabbath of May, at Cabin Creek, "about sixty persons were struck down;" on the next Sabbath, at Fleming Creek, "about one hundred." During June and July, similar scenes occurred at Concord, Pleasant Point, Indian Creek, and other places. But the most remarkable of all was witnessed in August, at Cane Ridge. This was a beautiful spot in the vicinity of a country church of the same name, under the pastoral care of Mr. Stone, in the county of Bourbon, and seven miles from Paris. It was finely shaded and watered, and admirably adapted to the purpose of an encampment. A great central area was cleared and levelled, two or three hundred yards in length, over which was extended a spacious tent as a shelter from heat and rain. The adjoining ground was laid off in regular streets, along which the tents were pitched. The concourse was immense. A Revolutionary officer, accustomed to estimate encampments, computed it to amount to not less than twenty thousand souls. The number of communicants is variously stated at from eight hundred to eleven hundred.

All who have left us any account of the scene agree in confessing that language is inadequate to describe it.[1] It was sublime, grand, "awful." The noise was "like the roar of Niagara. The vast sea of human beings was agitated as if by a storm." The tide of emotion seemed to roll over them like tumultuous waves. Sometimes hundreds were swept down almost at once, "like the trees of the forest under the blast of the wild tornado." Seven ministers, some in wagons, others standing on stumps, might have been counted, all addressing the multitude at the same time. Of the people, some were singing, others praying, others crying aloud for mercy, others still "shouting most vociferously;" while hardened men, who with horrid imprecations rushed furiously into the praying circles, were smitten down as if by an invisible hand, and lay powerless, or racked by "fearful spasms, till their companions beholding them were palsied by terror." At times the scene was surpassingly terrible, and the boldest heart was unmanned. The infidel forgot his philosophy, and trembled till he sank to his knees or fell to the earth. "At one time," says a spectator,[2] "I saw at least five hundred swept down in a moment, as if a battery of a thousand guns had been opened upon them; and then immediately followed shrieks and shouts that rent the very heavens. My hair rose upon my head, my whole frame trembled, the blood ran cold in my veins, and I fled for the woods." Such is the testimony of one who "would not have fallen to the ground for the whole State of Kentucky," and who, when his feelings had become "intense and insupportable," sought to allay them by a dram of brandy.

As darkness settled down over the scene, it lost nothing of its impressiveness. The solemnity was rather deepened. New features of sublimity or terror presented themselves to the beholder. The camp-fires

---

[1] Autobiography of Rev. J. B. Finley, 364. [2] Ib. 167.

gleamed with a strange light. Hundreds of candles and lamps suspended from the overarching trees, with torches in every direction lighting up with strange brilliancy the motley groups beneath and the tremulous foliage above, gave to the whole panorama the aspect of wild enchantment; while chanted hymns, impassioned exhortations, and earnest prayers, interrupted by sobs and shrieks and shouts and startling cries for mercy, deepened the impression made upon the beholder. The feeling became intense, the excitement indescribable and beyond control. No wonder that multitudes drawn together by various motives should fall under the powerful spell of such an occasion. Yet to many it was attractive for those very features of it most open to exception.[1]

---

[1] [Such were the excitement and distress, the shrieks, prayers, and praises, that at times the preachers found it impossible to gain the attention of the people, and were compelled to desist from preaching, sometimes in the midst of a sermon. This I have from a witness who was present.—F.]

Dr. Thomas Cleland, of Kentucky, who had not yet entered the ministry, was present himself at the meeting of Cane Ridge. In his autobiography, speaking of it, he says, "A great and solemn one it was, sure enough. . . . As to myself, I had fancied that no sooner than I would reach the place and enter the religious atmosphere, I would enjoy quite a different feeling from that which I had so long experienced and lamented. I expected to fall quite soon, or experience some softening, pleasing, inward ecstasy,—something I could not tell what. But, to my great disappointment, I felt unmoved, cold, and hard as a stone. I went from tent to tent, witnessing many prostrate as though dead or dying,—persons all around singing and praying. Though fond of singing myself, I could not join with them. I retired to a tent to sleep, but could not. I thought of home, and wished myself there. . . . I had 'neither joy nor song.' Thus I continued until the hour of preaching next day, which was the Sabbath. The preacher was my old favorite, Rev. Robert Marshall. He occupied the stand, while another occupied the church. The congregation was immense. The text was Cant.

The question was now decided that such meetings must be held. The popular feeling in their favor amounted almost to a passion. All classes and all denominations thronged together where one was announced. Even the more sober and discreet of the Presbyterian ministers did not feel warranted to offer direct opposition. From Logan and Cumberland counties the excitement extended far and near throughout the State and across the Tennessee line, and even into Georgia. The question was no longer whether the meetings should be held, but how they should be conducted. "Father" Rice, Craighead, Lyle, Blythe, and others were the advocates of order. They fearlessly discountenanced the extravagances of the revival. Month after month, and year after year, these became more marked and objectionable. The Methodist preachers were generally welcome, and their peculiar fervor gave a new impulse to the excitement. There was a great variety of *exercises*, some of them almost too absurd for grave mention. And yet to the subjects

---

ii. 10: 'Rise up, my love, my fair one, and come away.' In the course of the sermon my case was described exactly. The preacher, if I may so say, '*struck the trail*' of my experience some distance back, and came on plainer and plainer, and at every step more sensibly and with more effect. At length he came right up with me: my religious state and feeling were depicted better than I could have possibly done it myself. I thought it was indeed the heavenly bridegroom calling and inviting. . . . My heart was melted; my bosom heaved; my eyes for the first time were a fountain of tears. I stood behind one of the benches, leaning forward against its back. I wept till my handkerchief was saturated with my tears. I felt like giving way. I felt an indescribable sensation, as when one strikes his elbow against a hard substance. I do not say that mine was the prevailing exercise, or that it did not arise from natural causes. So it was. My position was discovered by a friend near me." It was some hours before he recovered. "I greatly enjoyed the meeting," he says, "as long as I remained."

of them, and to most of the crowd assembled, they wore any thing but a ludicrous aspect. There was the *falling*, the *jerking*, the *rolling*, the *running*, the *dancing*, and the *barking* exercise. Individuals were seized by these, often in spite of studied resistance, and sometimes almost while the jest or open blasphemy was upon their lips. Dreams and visions, the holy laugh and the holy kiss, helped forward the enthusiasm of the occasion or the grotesqueness of the scene. The entranced must relate what had been revealed to them in their state of outward insensibility. They had seen the darkened sky, or light beyond the blazing of the sun. Nature, with her various objects, had become a treasury of spiritual types. A great highway of splendor stretching a thousand miles in the distance was seen traversed by messengers of glad tidings. Broad rivers were crossed, high mountains climbed, venomous serpents vanquished. Gross and fleshly pollutions were cleansed away in purgatorial fire, spiritual hunger was satisfied from the tree of life. A golden bridge spanning fearful chasms was seen reaching to the gates of heaven. There were "strange, curious caverns" beneath, and above a lofty mountain, "with silver-topped leaves," leading up "to God and heaven." Some professed to have been more highly favored than Paul in his unearthly vision. They brought back in their breasts the melodies of another sphere; they enjoyed the fragrance which still enfolded them from their visit to more than ambrosial scenes.

As the excitement extended, such things were by no means uncommon.[1] The extraordinary exercises were

[1] Dr. Thomas Cleland, while a youth attending a school occasionally visited by the Methodist preachers, was the witness of scenes which will afford some idea of the character of the excitement which was sometimes produced by their efforts. He boarded with a Methodist preacher by the name of Thomas Kyle, who kept the

accounted necessary, as well as supernatural and divine. Even the more discreet ministers could not explain them; while the most zealous interpreted them as the results and marks of the Spirit's influence.

But such encouragement was not needed. The tide of feeling which bore these strange things along with it was becoming almost irresistible. He who criticized or even questioned them was accounted an opposer of religion. But the proceedings had become extravagant, and it was necessary that some limit should be set to the excesses of this work. Only McGready, Crawford, Rankin, Stone, Hodge, Houston, Marshall, and McGee had allowed themselves to be swept by the tide of popular feeling beyond the limits of propriety. Most of the other Presbyterian ministers felt that the proper

---

school; and on a certain day in each month there came along the *circuit rider*, who, by request of the teacher, heard the pupils rehearse a small catechism at the close of the forenoon sessions. "He then proceeded to prayer and exhortation with great vehemence and effervescence, until nearly the whole female part of the school became in a perfect uproar, crying for mercy, exhorting careless brothers and some others of the male sex to repent and give up their hearts to God. The scene lasted perhaps for one hour, when all became still as ever. The preacher retired; our dinners were eaten; playtime was attended to in usual style, so that no one would have known that any thing unusual had occurred." Cleland's father disapproved the proceedings, and his request that his son might withdraw at such times was reluctantly granted. He spent the time in study, and on his return was hailed with the jocular, sportive language, "Here comes the lost sheep," "Here comes the prodigal," &c. "The girls, increasing in their zeal, held through the summer, in playtime, religious meetings in the woods, sometimes in one place and sometimes in another. You might hear them at the top of their voices nearly a mile. One or two led in prayer, until all joined in the outcry. . . . The autumn approaching, the novelty ceasing, the whole affair died away, leaving no trace of real piety, and not one to join the church by public profession."—*Life of Cleland*, p. 34.

tests of a genuine revival should be constantly applied. They—the majority, at least—did not presume to utter an unqualified condemnation of all that had taken place. They would not pronounce judgment even on the spasmodic convulsions, the fallings, and the strange raptures. Yet they felt that whatever permanent results for good were accomplished must be accomplished by the truth alone. They knew that "a work of God" should, as far as genuine, be such as to bear the test of his word.

The time had now come when that test should be applied. Doctrinal errors, it was already evident, were making head in some quarters, and there could be no question of their lamentable result if left unchecked. The extravagances of some of the meetings had become a stumbling-block in the way of religion. Reaction of some kind would be sure to follow. Infidelity, for a while checked and abashed, would be encouraged to assume a bolder front. As early as 1801, Mr. Lyle apprehended the threatened danger. He warned the people against that enthusiasm "which, like a worm, destroyed the beauty of a revival, and would ere long discredit it as the work of God." He reproved the strolling parties, and insisted on the observance of quiet and order. A few weeks later, "Father" Rice, at a conference on a sacramental occasion at Walnut Hill, proposed a plan for the regulation of the meetings. By several it was favored; but the majority of the ministers present opposed it. Some of them "vehemently dissented." At once the signs of a division became manifest. The more sober and discreet were now stigmatized as *Anti-Revival* men. They were denounced as "hindrances to the work," as "standing in the way," as deists at heart and having no religion. "Father" Rice was singled out as the chief offender: yet his views very nearly accorded with those of Lyle, Blythe, Cameron, and Craighead.

The *Revival* men, meanwhile, as the other party styled themselves, affected a kind of holy superiority. They were "forward and noisy" in their enthusiasm. The meetings became scenes of discord rather than harmony. The stand itself was sometimes changed into the arena of controversy. It was Blythe against Marshall, or Stone *versus* Lyle and Cameron. Harsh words were sometimes spoken, and private intercourse was sometimes marred by passion, if not rage.

In such scenes, it would have been difficult for the coolest to retain the exercise of a calm judgment. Every thing was carried to extremes. The more cautious ministers were charged with "coldness and deadness in religion." Yet among those approved by their opponents were some whose conduct should be severely reprehended. Some explained the strange phenomena as "manifestations of the Spirit." Some dropped the Spirit altogether out of account, and would not hear of his operations. Here one might be seen raving like a Pythoness, there another praying with "clenched fists," while yet another shouted "Glory to God!" with "wild and distracted eyes," and, speaking to sinners, "*looked like a fury*." Women and children exhorted. They pronounced judgment on ministers. Persons were addressed or prayed for by name. Falling, or other exercises, came to be a necessary stimulus to the interest of the meetings. It was a tame occasion when there was no such exhibition.

To add to the mischief, evil-minded persons seized the opportunity to ridicule religion, or mingle in the scene for the purpose of entertainment or even to gratify their lusts. Hucksters and traders crowded to the meetings to vend wares, or even liquors. Not a few gave practical evidence of their new belief, that crept in with other errors, of falling from grace. It was, indeed, time that a check should be put to the abuses of the meetings.

At its second meeting (1803) the attention of Synod was drawn to the erroneous doctrines promulgated by Messrs. McNemar and Thompson. The Synod entered upon their examination and trial; but, pending the discussion, these men, together with Marshall, Stone, and Dunlavy, entered their protest, and declared their withdrawal from the jurisdiction of Synod.

The five seceding members formed themselves into a Presbytery. The Synod, roused by this act of seeming defiance, proceeded, perhaps too precipitately, to suspend them from the ministry, and directed that their pulpits should be declared vacant. Matters were thus brought to a crisis. The suspended ministers, some of them at least Arminian in their views, were highly popular, and exerted themselves to gain the sympathy of the multitude on the ground of persecution. For a time they seemed to carry all before them. The whole land was deluged with enthusiasm. New societies were formed on "completely democratic principles," within the space of two years, at seven places in Ohio, eight in Kentucky, besides several others in regions more distant. All the varieties of *exercises* were to be witnessed in connection with their meetings, including "dreaming, prophesying, and looking as through a glass at the infinite glories of Mount Zion, just about to break open upon the world."

The Springfield Presbytery, formed by the seceding members, now issued their "Apology." They distinctly rejected all creeds and confessions. They denied the doctrines of the Decrees, Atonement, and the influence of the Spirit in producing faith. The Bible alone was to be the bond of Christian fellowship. But, as they progressed in knowledge, they perceived, as they thought, the unscripturalness of their own organization. They consequently dissolved it, and informed the world of the fact in a strange document, oddly entitled, "*The Last Will and Testament of the Springfield Presbytery.*" The new body had lasted (June 28, 1804) only nine months.

Consistently enough, they renounced the title of "Reverend," and affirmed the independence of each individual congregation and its prerogative for the exercise of all ecclesiastical power, including discipline, licensure, and ordination. All sectarianism they denounced, and assumed for themselves the title of "The Christian Church." Infant baptism, soon to be denied also, was yet an open question. Exhorters and preachers, some of them of the wildest notions, were approved and sent out upon their mission.

Meanwhile the Synod (in 1804), by the advice of a committee of the General Assembly, entered upon the consideration of a plan of conciliation, with a view to healing the disorders which had prevailed.[1] The plan, however, proved abortive. The seceding members repudiated the standards of the Church, both for doctrine and discipline.

No other course remained but to meet the evil in detail. In 1805 and 1806, Messrs. Campbell and Stuart were directed by the Assembly to itinerate through Northern, and Stuart and Rice through Southern, Kentucky, with a view to regulating disorders, restoring harmony, and reviving the spirit of the scattered and despondent flocks.

Just at this crisis (1805), Matthew Houston, boisterous and jovial except when in the pulpit, added his name to the list of seceders. He informed the Presbytery that he relinquished the faith of the Church and

---

[1] The Cumberland schism was at the same time considered.

declined the authority of her judicatories. He was first suspended, and finally deposed from the ministry. It was but a few months before he found the New-Lights too unprogressive, and went over to the Shakers.

But the radical error of some of the New-Lights was now discovering itself. Stone's letters on the Atonement were exposed by Dr. Campbell, and shown to be full of the rankest Unitarianism. Stone felt himself forced to retract language in which he had unwittingly adopted almost the very words of an eminent deist. To add to his confusion, his two associates, McNemar and Dunlavy, followed Houston to the Shakers. Quite a large number, controlled by their influence, swelled the accession to the Shaker ranks. Rankin was not long in finding his way there also.

This was mortifying indeed. The New-Lights had hoped to turn successfully against those whom they had regarded as their persecutors; but a fearful defection was now manifest among themselves. In spite of their objections to ecclesiastical prerogative, they enjoined silence upon quite a number of their own seceding preachers, including McNemar and Dunlavy. The bold Unitarianism of Stone likewise forced Marshall and Thompson to seek a reunion with the Synod. The mongrel elements of the comprehensive union had no bond of sympathy but their latitudinarian affinities. There was no order or system. Every one pursued his own course, independent of all others. "I see," wrote Stone to Marshall, in regard to his churches, that they are "wrong in many things. They are not careful to support preachers; they encourage too many trifling preachers, are led away too much by noise," &c.

Such a confession did not help matters. Marshall and Thompson issued a pamphlet in their joint names, frankly confessing and unequivocally retracting their errors. This was a severe blow to the body. Stone was now left almost alone, a Pelagian and Socinian in his sentiments; and from him, as their patriarch, his followers were known as *Stoneites.* The tide had now turned. The views of the more discreet members of Presbytery were fully in the ascendant. Eight years of experience had justified all their predictions and their fears. They had manfully stood forward in the crisis. The great battle had been fought and won, and pamphlet skirmishes of no great consequence followed at successive periods. At length the death of Stone left his followers without a head; and when their principles became better known to the Campbellite sect, a fraternal union took place between them (1831). The dwindling ranks of the Stoneites merely served to swell the growth of another body which had, strangely enough, come to occupy the same ground.[1]

Meanwhile a new schism had sprung up,—one far more important in its character and results. In consequence of the revival, there was an unprecedented demand for preachers. The lack of educated men led even "Father" Rice to consider whether laymen might not be found adapted and qualified to be useful in the pressing emergency. Accordingly, at a meeting of Transylvania Presbytery in October, 1801, four men, Alexander Anderson, Finis Ewing, Samuel King, and Ephraim McLain, by the advice of the revival ministers,

---

[1] The influence and historical importance of the Stoneites were thus perpetuated. In 1845, the Campbellites, by whom they, as well as many of the regular Baptist and some Methodist churches were absorbed, numbered in Kentucky three hundred and eighty churches and more than thirty-three thousand communicants. Intellectual faith and baptism by immersion were their cardinal and distinctive doctrines. Stone came from North Carolina at about the same time with McGready. Never settled in doctrine, he is said early to have embraced Arminian views, ripening, however, into an Arian at last.

offered themselves for the service of the Church. They were somewhat advanced in life (one was an elder), and were spoken of as intelligent, zealous, and anxious to preach. After some discussion and opposition, they were allowed to read the discourses, which they had prepared for the occasion, privately to "Father" Rice. Upon his favorable report, they were appointed to the duty of catechizing and exhortation in vacant congregations.

At the meeting of Presbytery the ensuing April, Anderson was received as a candidate for the ministry, but the others were rejected. At the fall meeting, by the necessary absence of some of the members in order to attend the meeting of Synod, the others, largely composed of the lay element, were enabled to manage things in their own way. Petitions were presented from different societies urgently praying for the licensure of the four catechists. Notwithstanding their lack of education, and their objection that the doctrine of fatalism was embodied by the Confession of Faith in the articles on Election and Reprobation,[1] the Presbytery, by a vote of seventeen to five, voted to proceed to the licensure of all but McLain. At the same time, two others were licensed to preach, and three others to exhort.

The members opposed to the measure, under the lead

---

[1] It is but justice to those who took exceptions to the Confession of Faith to say that the historian of the Cumberland Presbyterians claims that "it had been the practice of the Presbyterian Church in North Carolina to ordain men to the ministry who adopted the Confession with the exception of the idea of fatality taught therein. The Transylvania Presbytery, in whose bounds the revival of 1800 took place, had adopted the same plan, and permitted ministers in their ordination-vows to make the exception if they chose to do so. And it is worthy of notice, also, that most of the ministers who promoted the revival were men who made this exception in the doctrine of the Presbyterian Church."—*Crisman*, p. 33.

of Craighead, entered their dissent. Meanwhile, in ignorance of what had been done, the Synod had divided the Transylvania Presbytery and formed the new Presbytery of Cumberland. It was composed of most incongruous elements. In the main there were two parties, nearly equally balanced. On one side were James McGready, William Hodge, William McGee, John Rankin, Samuel McAdow, known as the revival party. On the other were Thomas B. Craighead, Terah Templin, John Bowman, Samuel Donnell, and James Balch, known by the name given them by their opponents as the Anti-Revival party.

There was little or no sympathy between them. They met only when brought together in Presbytery. McGready considered Balch as an opponent, who in his own neighborhood and among his own congregations had headed a party against him. There was not a little of mutual exasperation. Yet neither party was strictly homogeneous in itself. McGready and Hodge professed to be Calvinists. Rankin and McGee, with their associates among the exhorters, made no secret of their Arminian leanings. On the other side, Craighead had, with all his brilliant talents and love of order, Pelagian sympathies; while Bowman leaned to the Stoneites, and McAdow, Templin, and Donnell were men of little note either by nature or education.

At the first meeting of the new Presbytery, four additional catechists were licensed. Soon after, Finis Ewing, already licensed, on the petition of several congregations, was ordained. Exhorters whose doctrinal views were indefinite, if not directly opposed to the Confession, were multiplied till they numbered seventeen. Some of these were received as candidates upon very insufficient grounds. They were merely directed to show the sermon which they had prepared to the nearest or most accessible minister. They were required to receive the Confession of Faith *so far only* as they believed it to agree with the word of God. The exhorters travelled on their "circuits," and the congregations were directed to contribute to their support. Their labors were reported as wonderfully successful. New societies were organized and furnished with elders. It was obvious that, if this state of things was to continue, the ascendency of the lay element representing the churches would soon reduce the influence of the more orderly ministers to a mere cipher.

The aspect of affairs now began to excite apprehension. "Father" Rice, by direction of the Presbytery of Transylvania, from which that of Cumberland had been set off by the Synod, addressed a letter to the General Assembly, asking advice in regard to the course to be pursued in licensing men to preach without a liberal education. The reply urged caution, in the selection of *prudent* and *sound* men, yet admitted that catechists like those of the primitive times might be useful assistants. They were not, however, to be considered as standing officers in the church. Yet if they proved diligent and promised usefulness they might in time be admitted to the ministry.

In 1803, the records of Cumberland Presbytery were not before Synod. But in the following year a protest and complaint against the doings of the majority, signed by Craighead, Donnell, and Bowman, brought up the subject. The difficulties presented by the case forced them to lay it over to another year. All that could be done at the time was to enjoin particular attention to the constitutional rules and the advice contained in the Assembly's letter. A committee, consisting of Rice, Blythe, Lyle, Cameron, and Rannels, was appointed to attend the meeting of Cumberland Presbytery and report the facts of the case.

None of the committee attended but Cameron. He

declined to sit as a corresponding member, and was regarded in the light of a spy. The young men refused to read their trial-pieces before him; and the very appointment of the committee was held up to odium as an inquisitorial proceeding.

In 1805, the whole case came before Synod upon the review of the Cumberland records, which were at last forthcoming. Only two members of the Cumberland Presbytery, Donnell and Dickey, were present. The committee on the records were Cameron, Lyle, and Henderson. They reported them extremely defective, discordant, and obscure. They noticed the reception of a Methodist preacher, the licensing of the seventeen exhorters, sometimes called licentiates, the establishment of "circuits," and other points of a kindred character. The Synod were embarrassed in regard to the course to be pursued. For immediate action they were not prepared. No one was present to defend the Presbytery; and they could not be sure of all the facts necessary to form a judgment. The adoption of the Confession with reservations was not mentioned in the records. Of the degree of disqualification on the part of the licentiates, they were not authoritatively informed. Cameron, the only member of the committee of inquiry who had attended the meeting of Presbytery, declined to make any report.

Something, it was felt, must be done. The Synod, however, adopted a questionable expedient. A commission was appointed, *vested with full synodical powers*, to investigate and adjudicate the case. It consisted of ten ministers and six elders,—seven of the former, with as many elders as should be present, to form a quorum. They were to meet within six weeks at Gaspar River Meeting-House, and the Stated Clerk was charged to cite all parties to attend. The day of their meeting was appointed to be observed by the churches of the

Synod as a day of fasting and prayer for the divine blessing upon the proceedings of the commission.

On Tuesday, Dec. 3, 1805, the commission met. Lyle was moderator, and in a sermon three hours long he dilated on the call and qualifications necessary to the exercise of the gospel ministry. There was profound attention to the close. Some seemed pleased and edified; but most of the members of Cumberland Presbytery were ill at ease. The policy of the commission was foreshadowed by the sermon.

The members of the Cumberland Presbytery, so far as implicated, were all present,—McGready, Hodge, Rankin, McGee, McAdow, Hawe, and the four licentiates, Ewing, King, Nelson, and Hodge; as also Kirkpatrick, Porter, Bell, Foster, and Calhoun, licentiates, and Guthrie, Blythe, and Donnell, candidates.

The commission soon found that their task was to be no light one. Their office was represented to be merely to cut off the young preachers and circuit-riders and stop the revival. Each of them was designated by some opprobrious nickname. Only one man in the whole region would extend them hospitality, and he lived three or four miles from the church. Rankin, the pastor, who afterward joined the Shakers, was an avowed Arminian; and, preaching after adjournment, in the presence of the commission, he employed the most inflammatory language, "well calculated," says Davidson,[1] "to provoke mobbing and personal violence."

The commission, however, proceeded to their work. The case of the Methodist, Hawe, was first taken up; but he prudently refused to be examined, on the plea that he could not be reached except by a regular trial for heresy. The subject of the licensures and ordina-

---

[1] History of Presbyterian Church in Kentucky, p. 235.

tions was then considered. Of these cases there were no less than twenty-seven. In regard to them it was clearly ascertained that the candidates had been permitted to adopt the Confession with the reservation, "so far as they deemed it agreeable to the word of God." Yet nothing of the kind appeared on the records.

The Presbytery justified their course. Most of them were delinquent themselves, and the cause of the licentiates was also their own. The Confession, they said, was a human composition, and of course fallible, and they could not in conscience feel bound by it any further than it agreed with the Scriptures. They freely avowed that they did not believe all its contents, nor could they consistently require such belief of others. For their conduct in regard to the licensing of uneducated men, they pleaded the exception in the fourteenth chapter of the Form of Government, as well as numerous precedents in the history of the Church.

In these circumstances, the commissioners determined to examine for themselves and judge of the young men's qualifications. But the majority of the Presbytery here interposed, claiming for themselves the exclusive right to examine and license their own candidates. "I stand," said Mr. Hodge, "between these young men and your bar." The commissioners addressed them, urging compliance. The moderator, Howe, solemnly adjured both the majority and the young men to submit, pledging himself that no injustice should be done, and that those who were found fitted should receive a license. The parties proposed to withdraw for deliberation. This was assented to. As they were about to leave, Stuart, one of the commissioners, rose under the impulse of the moment, entreating them seriously to weigh the consequences of their decision. Under the earnest pathos of his appeal, all present, including the young men, were melted into tears. It was felt on all sides to be a solemn and critical moment. In the interval of the absence of the parties, the commission, with the Assembly, engaged in prayer.

On the return of the parties, the major part of the Presbytery—McGready, Hodge, McAdow, Rankin, and McGee—collectively and individually answered the question, "Do you submit?" in the negative. The young men were next called upon. They gave individually the same reply. They declared themselves amenable to the Presbytery alone, which they considered a regular church judicatory and the proper tribunal.

The commission, whether wisely or not, adopted decisive measures. The recusants, twenty-four in number, were accounted by their contumacy to have virtually renounced the jurisdiction of the Presbyterian Church, and were solemnly prohibited, until they should submit themselves, from preaching or administering ordinances by any Presbyterial authority. As to McGready, Hodge, McGee, Rankin, and McAdow, the commission waived its right to proceed against them for error or contumacy, and remanded them to Synod, at whose next meeting they were cited to appear.

Hodge, Rankin, and McGee handed in a written refusal to obey the citation, on the ground that it was unconstitutional. But the commission reaffirmed the citation. There existed, according to their view, an imperative necessity for taking the case out of the hands of the Presbytery. To obviate the objection to a general charge of heresy against the three members, they specified the errors held by them,—"the denial of the doctrine of election, and the holding that there is a certain sufficiency of grace given to every man, which if he improve, he shall receive more until he arrive at true conversion."

At the same time the case of the Shiloh Church was considered, and the judgment of the Presbytery in regard to it reversed. The pastor of the church was Mr. Hodge; but his extravagances disaffected the more orderly portion, who withdrew, organized a new church, and called Thomas B. Craighead to be their pastor. The commission, avoiding all interference with the civil aspects of the case, permitted the appellants to continue as a church, excepting only to the name (Shiloh), which they retained from the old congregation.

The commission had discharged its task,—responsible, arduous, and odious. Its members were able, devoted, and generally discreet men. They were called to act in a crisis without precedent, and in which they had to rely largely upon their own good judgment. In the midst of opposition, ridicule, and invective, they aimed to discharge their duty; and if they erred, they were unquestionably conscientious in their error. The Synod by appointing them had assumed beforehand the responsibility for their acts.

Their report was published, and the commission dissolved. The Cumberland Presbytery formed itself into a *council* composed of ministers, elders, and representatives of vacant churches. All the congregations connected with the party remained faithful to it, with few exceptions. The preachers, in spite of the prohibition by the Synod's commission, continued their labors. The revival still progressed, and numbers were added to the churches.

The next meeting of Synod was at Lexington, Oct. 21, 1806. From the Cumberland Presbytery, Craighead, Templin, Hodge, Rankin, Donnell, and Dickey were present. Hodge and Rankin came, not in obedience to the citation, but by the advice of their brethren, for the purpose of effecting a reconciliation. Being called upon, they professed themselves willing to submit to an examination; but they could not assent to the silencing of the young men. They disavowed all heterodox opinions, but would not yield on this point to the authority of Synod. The result was that, after considerable delay and much effort by private conference, sentence of suspension was pronounced upon them. They refused to appeal to any earthly tribunal, yet soon joined with the *council* of their brethren in sending up a letter of remonstrance to the next General Assembly.

This step was doubtless felt by them to be the more imperative from the fact that the Synod, despairing of all prospect of change in the policy of the Cumberland Presbytery as then constituted, reannexed the members to the Presbytery of Transylvania.

In May, 1807, the matter was brought, by the remonstrance of the members of the Cumberland Presbytery, to the attention of the General Assembly. Here diverse views were taken of it. From the Synod of Kentucky were Cameron, Kemper, and McCalla, an elder. Cameron alone sustained the Synod. In the Assembly, Dr. Green, Messrs. Janeway, Cathcart, and Linn, agreed with him, while Drs. Miller, Woodhull, James P. Wilson, and Speece were strenuous in opposition. The debate was keen and spirited. The prevalent opinion was that the Presbytery had erred, but that the Synod had been too rigorous. It was argued that a Synod could not proceed against individual members of a Presbytery except in case of appeal; that only a Presbytery could examine licentiates, or call its members to account; that for Synod to suspend ordained ministers, especially by a commission, was a transcending of its powers. The reannexing of the Cumberland to the Transylvania Presbytery was fully justified, but on the other points the measures of the Synod were represented as harsh and unwarranted.

The defenders of the Synod were not silent. They contended strenuously for the necessity of strict discipline, and insisted on the rights and authority of Synod and General Assembly. The case seemed as difficult at the East as it had appeared at Lexington. The result was that the Assembly addressed two letters, one to the Synod, and one to members of the Presbytery.

In the first, the Assembly commended the Synod's zeal, at the same time suggesting that the commission's insisting upon a re-examination of the candidates was "at least of questionable regularity," and advising them to review their proceedings and adopt milder methods.[1] "Without implying that the demands of our standards should be regarded otherwise than inviolable and indispensable, yet there must be supposed the right and duty of exercising a sound discretion, which will consult the spirit as well as the letter of the law; which will sometimes forbid the exercise of legitimate power; which will endeavor, with equal caution, to avoid the extremes of rigor and laxness; which will yield something, yet not concede every thing, to circumstances; which, in a word, will recollect that power is given for edification and not for destruction, and endeavor to be guided by this rule." They closed by expressing the hope that Synod might be able to reestablish the Presbytery of Cumberland, restoring some of its former members to their place, without sacrificing either the doctrines or the government of the Church.

In their other letter they express their regret in

[1] Davidson, p. 247.

view of the difficulties which existed, and their apprehension that they had been caused by the improper course of the Presbytery in licensing unqualified persons, and in allowing them to adopt the Confession of Faith in a form not sufficiently explicit. This conduct the Assembly decidedly disapproved, as *highly irregular and unconstitutional.* As the complainants had made no regular appeal, there was no call for a judicial decision, and they were referred back to the Synod, now advised to review their proceedings. The letter closed with an exhortation to a strict and steady adherence to the Constitution of the Presbyterian Church, and endeavors to promote the peace and the best interests of the Redeemer's kingdom.

The Synod reviewed their proceedings, including the measures of the commission. But they saw nothing to retract. They denied that the irregularly-ordained preachers had been suspended at all in a technical sense, or that the commission had dealt with them without process. A committee was appointed to answer the Assembly's letter; but their communication did not reach its destination until 1809, a year after the time when it should have been received.

The recusant members were now in the hands of Transylvania Presbytery. They were invited by it to a friendly interview; but only Mr. Hodge was present. After protracted deliberation, they concluded to insist on the necessity of acknowledgment and submission from the contumacious members, and a re-examination and new and more explicit adoption of the Confession of Faith on the part of the young men.

The *Council* refused to submit to the terms imposed. They again made application to the Assembly (1808), and petitioned for relief. But they were again referred back to the Synod as the only body competent to redress their grievances. Yet there were in the Assembly many who strongly sympathized with them. After its adjournment, Dr. Wilson wrote to Mr. Hodge a letter, in which he expressed his own judgment and feelings. He regarded the commission as unconstitutional, assured Mr. Hodge of the favorable sentiments of the Assembly, urged him to return and appeal regularly,—although a disagreeable condescension,—recommended the establishment of a grammar-school, and gently advised adherence to the standards.

The Synod learned that their letter had not been received. They drew up another of similar tenor, but more condensed. It was laid before the Assembly of 1809, at which Messrs. Lyle and Stuart appeared also to defend the Synod. At first the case wore a dark aspect; but in the light of the facts elicited, and through the impression made by the speech of Mr. Lyle, the prospect changed. Dr. Green and Dr. Dwight, that year a delegate from the General Association of Connecticut, warmly supported the cause of the Synod, and their proceedings were sustained without a dissenting voice. The decision was final. The *Council* had no more to hope from the action of the General Assembly.

Yet they resolved on one further effort for reconciliation. A committee was appointed to propose their terms to the Synod. These were, a willingness to be examined by the Synod, Presbytery, or a committee, on doctrinal points, provided that they were received or rejected as a connected body, and that all the ordained ministers or licentiates retain their former authority derived from the Cumberland Presbytery. As to the Confession, they were willing to adopt it, if required, except only that portion which seemed to them to teach the doctrine of fatality.

The Synod refused to accept the terms, but directed the Presbytery of Transylvania to meet for the special purpose of restoring such individuals as should be found qualified, and submissive to the authority of Synod. The meeting was held at Greentown, Dec. 6, 1809. William Hodge, his nephew Samuel Hodge, and Thomas Nelson, were present. The first, after profession of sorrow for past irregularities, and avowing his full subscription to the Confession of Faith and submission to the discipline of the Church, was restored to his former standing. The others were examined and approved, and their former license and ordination unanimously confirmed. They were recognized and welcomed, and took their seats as members of the Presbytery. McGready, decidedly Calvinistic in his sentiments, had for some time felt a decreasing sympathy with the Council. On Oct. 3, 1810, he followed up a letter of submission to the Presbytery, which he had previously written, by full acknowledgments in person, and was likewise restored. McGee was so undecided between Arminianism and the Confession that he ceased to preach. McAdow was in too feeble health to continue his functions. Rankin apostatized to the Shakers, and was deposed. So that Ewing and King were the only ordained ministers left, and they were under the ban of the Synod. Thus the *Council* that had resolved to form itself into a Presbytery found itself without a necessary quorum.

The only resource left was to apply to McAdow.[1]

[1] Peter Cartwright, in his Autobiography, states (p. 47) that the Cumberland Presbyterians sought at one time to effect a union with the Methodist Church. "While in this amputated condition, they called a general meeting of all their licentiates. They met our presiding elder, J. Page, and a number of Methodist ministers, at a quarterly meeting in Logan county, and proposed to join the Methodist Episcopal Church as a body; but our ministers declined this offer, and persuaded them to rise up and embody themselves together and constitute a Church. They reluctantly yielded to this advice, and in due time and form constituted themselves the Cumberland Presbyterian Church."

After some hesitation, light at last dawned upon his mind. He consented to co-operate with Ewing and King in the formation of a Presbytery by the old name of Cumberland. The first act of the new body was to ordain the licentiate McLean. A brief constitution, stating their grievances and their patient waiting through four years for redress, and justifying their procedure, was adopted. They recognized as their standards the Confession and discipline of the Presbyterian Church, but made provision for the relief of those who objected that the doctrine of fatality was taught in the articles. Candidates were to be examined for licensure, but acquaintance with languages was not required.

The Presbytery of Transylvania suspended McAdow for his proceedings in the matter. McGee was dealt with in a similar manner, though on other grounds, by the Presbytery of Muhlenburg, set off (1810) from the Presbytery of Transylvania. The breach was thus widened. Some subsequent efforts for union proved futile, and intercommunion between the Cumberland Presbyterians and those who adhered to the General Assembly (1811) thenceforth ceased.

No longer trammelled by its former connections, the progress of the new Presbytery was rapid. In three years it grew into a Synod numbering sixty congregations. It was composed of three Presbyteries,—Cumberland, afterward changed to Nashville, Logan, and Elk. Its first meeting was Oct. 5, 1813, when it presented to the world a summary of its tenets.

In the following year it took a bolder step. The Confession of the Presbyterian Church was "modelled, expunged, and added to," to suit its views. It aimed to steer a middle course between Arminianism and the Confession, rejecting the articles charged with teaching the doctrine of fatality. Most appropriately in the same year the Assembly decided that those constituting the Synod were to be viewed as deriving no authority from the Presbyterian Church; and in 1825 their relation to it was declared to be the same with that "of other denominations, not connected with our body."

From the period of its formation, the new denomination continued to make a steady advance. In 1827, so obvious had become the importance among them of increased attention to ministerial education, that a chartered manual-labor institution was opened at Princeton, Caldwell county, Ky. It bore the title of the Cumberland Presbyterian College, under the Presidency of Rev. Dr. Cossit, and to it was annexed a theological department. In 1829, the one Synod had multiplied to four,—Missouri, Green River, Franklin, and Cumberland. A General Assembly comprising them was now convened; and thus the new denomination took the name, place, and rank which it still holds among the Presbyterian bodies of the land.

The Cumberland schism—we use the term in no harsh sense, for it in fact rent in sunder the churches of Kentucky—originated in part in the necessity created by the revival for an increase in the number of ministers, and in part in the crude doctrinal views promulgated in a time of excitement by men more intent in their zeal to produce excitement than to instruct the ignorant or present gospel truth in its proper and relative proportions. The first difficulty was one which had been experienced for the whole period of the preceding century, as the bounds of the Church were extended and new congregations were multiplied, although in connection with the Kentucky Revival it assumed a graver aspect. The supply of ministers fell far short of the demand. This was not disputed in any quarter. It was at the suggestion of Father Rice himself that laymen were selected to serve, as occasion required, in the capacity of catechists or exhorters.[1] The General Assembly sanctioned this plan as far as prudence would warrant. But, as the result of the introduction of what was virtually the lay element into

[1] As an illustration of the liberality, not to say laxness of views, which prevailed among even the more conservative Presbyterians in regard to introducing uneducated men into the ministry, it will suffice to state the circumstances in which Thomas Cleland was licensed and ordained. Although he had obtained the rudiments of a classical education, the death of his father and mother threw upon him the entire responsibility of a family unprovided for; and his necessary labors for their support and his subsequent marriage seemed to preclude the hope of his entering the ministry. But on one or two occasions, under the pressure of circumstances which seemed to demand a religious address, he had ventured to exhort, and had done so with great acceptance. This fact had come to the knowledge of the Presbytery. During its session at New Providence Church his marriage took place. Of the Presbytery only three members were present,—a bare quorum. These, on invitation, adjourned to the place of marriage. After supper, about ten or eleven o'clock, he was conducted by one of the members, Mr. Cameron, before the body, with a view, as he supposed, to obtain a license to exhort. He was examined on experimental religion, and his views of what constituted a call to the ministry,—all which he regarded as necessary to his preparation for licensure as exhorter. After some other inquiries, he was asked if he could not be induced to consent to be a candidate for the ministry. He replied in the negative. Again and again they endeavored to remove his difficulties. He was assured of a lenient consideration of his case; but all in vain. Still the Presbytery persisted, and gave him a text to write upon, "Woe is me if I preach not the gospel," requesting him to be ready at the spring-meeting of Presbytery. He wrote his sermon, dismissed the subject from his thoughts, gave up the idea of meeting the Presbytery again, but by peculiar circumstances was induced, contrary to his expectations, to attend its spring sessions. He found that on the records of Presbytery he was a candidate, had been examined, &c., greatly to his surprise. Happily, his sermon was with him: he preached it, and received his licensure, and few men ever made better proof of their ministry.—*Life of Cleland.*

the Presbytery, as well as in consequence of the party-zeal of those who assumed the title of "Revival Men," a controlling influence in Cumberland Presbytery was secured by those by whom the authority of the Synod was regarded with jealousy and distrust. Some of the teachers, moreover, who were now admitted to the charge of churches were quite incompetent; and their unsoundness is perhaps full as chargeable to their deficient education as to any proper aversion to the doctrines of the Confession. These were evidently misinterpreted and misunderstood. If a kindly feeling could but have been maintained between the Presbytery and the Synod, misconceptions and misapprehensions might in time have been removed. But the extraordinary and extrajudicial measure of the Synod,—however it might seem to have been necessitated by the occasion,—and the fixed resolve to revoke the licenses already granted, produced a degree of alienation and exasperation which forbade the hope of reconciliation.

Reviewing the whole matter at this distance of time and with the coolness of historical impartiality, we find much on both sides which we can palliate and excuse, as well as some things which we must condemn. The Synod—considering its own antecedents, or, at least, the acts of some of its own members—might well have exercised lenity toward those who *at first* erred simply in slightly improving upon its own example. Not a few of its ministers had been introduced to their work with but little more preparation than the Cumberland candidates. And as to the act of the Presbytery in dispensing with strict subscription to the standards, although a dangerous and unwarranted measure, more healing methods of correction might have been devised, and probably, if applied in the spirit which evidently prevailed when the matter was first brought before the Assembly, would have proved successful. The more summary method which was adopted—and adopted, too, by those who had themselves established precedents which might almost justify the action of the aggrieved party—only hastened events which kindness and wisdom, with the aid of time, might have prevented. The Cumberland Presbytery offered to submit, provided the men already licensed and ordained were allowed to hold their position. If the commission of Synod or the Presbytery had consented to this compromise, there is no doubt that it would have been sanctioned by the General Assembly; and, as a result, a vast number thenceforth alienated would have been brought under the influence of, and in all probability have been led to full conformity to, our orthodox standards.[1] It was with manifest reluctance, and, we apprehend, under as strong and clear a sense of justice as that evinced by the commission, that they finally withdrew. It is impossible, from a candid review of the attitude of parties, and the heat evinced by some of the "Anti-Revival" men who exerted a powerful influence in the Synod, to avoid the conviction that to their strenuousness, if not their exaggeration of the errors charged on the opposite party, the extent at least of the secession was largely due.

The revival had swept almost like a tornado over

---

[1] To one who lived among the scenes where the Cumberland secession began, and who had the opportunity of freely and often conversing with the ministers and members of that Church, it would be plain that an unhappy persistency and severity of spirit at the wrong time forced those into schism who were willing to accept almost any concession which would allow those still to remain ministers who had been licensed and ordained. It is a fault to stickle on unnecessary points, and by an obstinate adherence to them force schisms in what ought to be, and might be, our great undivided Church.—W.

the field, and its effects were alike manifest in the refreshing influence it exerted and the desolation it wrought.[1] Looking at either of these alone, we might fail to do justice to the other. Infidelity was laid prostrate; but churches were rent in sunder. The deadness and lethargy of religion were broken up; but Stoneites, Shakers, and the Cumberland schism sprang up out of the chaos.

The bewildered were drifted on with the current that swept them into fanatical excess; while the sanguine were plunged by excitement into error and folly. The Shakers drew off hundreds with them. The Stoneites prepared the way for Campbell. Elder Holmes gathered a band of pilgrims and started in quest of the Holy Land, only, however, to wander into the wilderness

---

[1] In order to do full justice to the merits of the revival, the state of society in the region where it commenced should be taken into consideration. One of McGready's congregations was only three miles from the residence of Peter Cartwright's father; and the son had ample opportunities to observe the facts which he has narrated in his Autobiography. He says, "Logan county (Ky.), when my father moved to it (1793), was called 'Rogues' Harbor.' Here many refugees from almost all parts of the Union fled to escape punishment or justice; for, although there was law, yet it could not be executed, and it was a desperate state of society. Murderers, horse-thieves, highway-robbers, and counterfeiters fled here, until they combined and actually formed a majority." A battle with guns, pistols, dirks, knives, and clubs took place between the "Rogues" and the "Regulators," and the latter were defeated. One of the "Rogues" who fled thither was an apostate Methodist minister from Georgia. He "fell from grace," broke the laws, shot the sheriff, and fled to "Rogues' Harbor."

Cartwright also confirms the statement of the historian of the Cumberland Presbyterians. "These [Presbyterian] old preachers licensed a great many young men to preach, contrary to their Confession of Faith. In the revival, almost to a man, they gave up these points of High Calvinism, and preached a free salvation to all mankind."

and to die—to the dismay of his deluded followers—on an island of the Mississippi. Elder Farnum, pretending to immediate inspiration, headed the sect of the "Screaming Children." Other *isms*, strange as human fantasy could devise, sprang up to mislead and dupe the ignorant, till even the grossest denial of fundamental truth was covered by the claim to a divine sanction. Some of those who had been led astray from the Presbyterian Church at last, like Thompson and Marshall, saw their error, and returned. Others, like McNemar, Dunlavy, Houston, and Rankin, were only dazzled by the "clearer light" into which they believed they had emerged, and became thenceforth identified with the errorists whom they aspired to lead or defend.

Meanwhile, the Synod of Kentucky, in spite of all the embarrassments and conflicts through which it had been called to pass, was making steady progress. In 1812, the Presbytery of West Tennessee was formed. In 1814, three new Presbyteries—Louisville, Mississippi, and Shiloh—were erected. The first was formed by a division of Transylvania; the second covered a portion of Western Tennessee; while the last was composed in part of churches set off from the Presbytery of Muhlenburg. Upon the erection of the Synod of Tennessee, in 1817, Shiloh and Mississippi were united with it. Of the three, the Presbytery of Louisville alone remained in connection with the Synod of Kentucky. At the same time, the dividing line between the Synod of Ohio and Kentucky was changed by the Assembly so as to include within the bounds of the latter so much of the former as lay within the State of Indiana, west of a line drawn due north from the mouth of Kentucky River.

Through great difficulties and opposition this progress had been attained. The defection of Thomas B. Craighead to Pelagian, if not rationalistic, views was sorely felt. The earliest publication of his sentiments was a sermon before the Synod in 1806. But previously to this he had been arraigned before Synod for suspicion of unsoundness in doctrine. His answers, although not perfectly satisfactory, had screened him from censure; but in his sermon he took positions flatly opposed to the Confession of Faith. He railed at some of its distinctive doctrines, held that the Spirit in the word is the sole cause of faith and sanctification, that believing is an intellectual and not a moral act, that the testimony and not the disposition to believe is supplied from heaven; nor did he fail to heap ridicule on the idea of praying for faith, introducing in the appendix to his sermon the prayer of a Necessitarian, intended to caricature the views of Edwards on the Will, and of Miller, as presented in his "Retrospect of the Eighteenth Century."

Thus boldly were his positions taken. The Synod could not ignore the errors which were thus broached, and for several years the agitation which they produced was kept up. Dr. J. P. Campbell took up his pen to controvert them, and not without effect. He admitted Craighead's eloquence, but unsparingly exposed his errors. "You are no Locke," said he; "you are no Edwards; you are no Butler; but you are capable of being, what I should covet a thousand times more, a Massillon or a Bridaine. No, sir! You have too much fire, too much velocity, too much impatience, for metaphysics. You can manage a metaphor infinitely better than a syllogism. Oh, what might you not be, under such circumstances as I could wish!"

Dr. Campbell's pamphlet had a prodigious effect. It was attractive in style, clear and vigorous in logic, and extensively circulated. Craighead attempted a reply, but its feebleness scarcely challenged the annihilating blow which was again dealt out by Dr. Campbell. In 1810, Craighead was suspended by Synod, and, as he continued to preach, he was in the following year deposed. Successive attempts were made to secure his restoration, but they failed until in 1824, only a short time previous to his decease. We may trace, doubtless, to his influence something of the evils which were felt by the churches when, a few years subsequently, the Rev. Dr. Holley, with his Unitarian sympathies, was elevated to the Presidency of Transylvania University.

Upon the disorders of the revival, the enthusiasm of the New-Lights or Stoneites, the success of the Shakers, the Cumberland schism, and the errors of Craighead, supervened the troubles and excitements of the second war with England. Kentucky was rent and torn by the strife of parties. The popular mind was convulsed by political dissension. The people, with the exception of a small minority, were enthusiastically in favor of the war. Kentucky eagerly contributed volunteers for Harrison in the West and Jackson in the South. The adjoining territories were richly saturated with her noblest blood.

In the dreadful strife Kentucky bore her full share. All along her frontiers echoed the terrific war-whoop. The darkness of the night was illuminated by the flames of burning cabins. The horrors of Indian warfare were brought in fearful proximity to the border settlements. Many were called to mourn sad bereavements as well as other bitter calamities. A son of Dr. Blythe was tomahawked, standing and unresisting, by a savage that had taken him a prisoner. Scarcely less merciless was the fate of hundreds of others.

The unsettling, disorganizing, and demoralizing effects of the war were sadly felt throughout the entire region. Nor did they at once pass away with the return of peace. Mutual estrangements and recriminations divided pastors and people, churches and congregations. A minister who was known to maintain the expediency or the inexpediency of the war was unacceptable—even though silent on the subject in the pulpit—to those whose views were known to differ from his own. The alienation that occurred between William L. McCalla and Dr. Blythe is an illustration of the sad prevalence of political feeling. The peace of 1815 did not bring peace to the troublous elements of the Kentucky churches.

CHAPTER XXX.

TENNESSEE, 1800–1815.

At the commencement of the present century, Eastern Tennessee was divided between the two Presbyteries of Abingdon and Union, both connected with the Synod of the Carolinas. The Presbytery of Abingdon had been erected at the time of the formation of the General Assembly, and consisted of seven members. In 1796, the Hopkinsian views of one of its number, Hezekiah Balch, combined with his own indiscretions, had given great offence, and produced no little excitement within the bounds of the Presbytery. In consequence of this dissatisfaction, a majority of the members withdrew and formed the Independent Presbytery of Abingdon. This action was condemned by the Synod; and upon the submission of the withdrawing members, the old Presbytery of Abingdon was constituted as before. But in 1797 the Presbytery petitioned for a division, and Union Presbytery was erected out of it by setting off as members of the new body Hezekiah Balch, John Cossan, Samuel Carrick, Robert Henderson, and Gideon Blackburn. The members of the old Presbytery who still continued in connection with it were Charles Cummings, Samuel Doak, Jacob Lake, and James Balch.

In 1799, the Presbytery of Greenville began its brief existence. It numbered but three ministers,—Hezekiah Balch, John Cossan, and George Newton. It was afterward joined by Samuel Davis and Stephen Bovelle; but in 1804, at the request of its members, the Presbytery was dissolved,—George Newton and Samuel Davis uniting with the Presbytery of Concord, Hezekiah Balch and John Cossan with the Presbytery of Union, and Stephen Bovelle with the Presbytery of West Lexington in Kentucky.

In 1800, Samuel Doak, at Little Limestone in Washington county, was preaching to the "Salem Congregation," and conducting under promising auspices his feeble institution now known as Washington College. Hezekiah Balch, preaching at Harmony, was indefatigable in promoting the interests of Greenville College, in whose behalf, in 1805, he secured the services of Rev. Charles Coffin. George Newton was laboring at Swananoa and Rimm's Creek. Robert Henderson had charge of the churches of Westminster and Hopewell. Gideon Blackburn was laboring at Maryville, performing much itinerant missionary labor and devising a plan for carrying the gospel to the Cherokee Indians. Samuel G. Ramsey, whose incessant efforts mainly in connection with Grassy Valley congregation had exhausted his strength, was laid by from active service. Samuel Carrick, elected to the Presidency of Blount College, was discharging the duties of this station and preaching statedly to the church at Knoxville.

The revival at the beginning of the present century, which commenced and was most remarkable in Kentucky, and which extended largely over the entire country, was felt also to some extent in Eastern Tennessee. The labors of Blackburn and Henderson were greatly blessed. The influence of these men was extensively and powerfully felt, and the social and moral condition of the people was greatly and beneficently changed.

Blackburn had labored in connection with the congregations of New Providence (Maryville) and Eusebia since April, 1794.[1] Something of a revival prevailed shortly after his settlement; but in 1798 and 1799 his labors were attended with the least success. No wave of the Kentucky revival had yet reached his congregations. Christians were cold and indifferent; few serious impressions seemed to be made; the youth became more dissolute, and levity and dissipation were alarmingly prevalent. But in April, 1800, a striking change took place. A general seriousness seemed to overspread the community. The Sabbath assemblies, large before, were now crowded. Several persons seemed to be deeply impressed. In May, the semi-annual administration of the sacrament took place, and impressions were deepened. A society for prayer and religious conversation was instituted, and was followed by happy results. A monthly lecture for children was appointed, which was signally blessed. At this juncture the first number of the "New York Missionary Magazine" came into the hands of the pastor. He read to his people the revival and missionary intelligence, and continued to do so as successive numbers arrived.[2] It proved "a great means of awakening the thoughtless and animating and reviving the pious." The revival continued with a steady progress, free from enthusiasm or extravagance, till the pastor's house "was almost constantly crowded" with anxious inquirers. The next season of communion was a memorable one. A large number were received to the church, and more than

[1] New York Miss. Mag., ii. 238.

[2] He subscribed for fifty copies of it.

three hundred and fifty participated in the ordinance. "It appeared," says Blackburn, "like the gate of heaven. The assembly was melted into tears; solemnity, weeping, and joy appeared in the audience."

In 1799, Joseph Bullen was sent out by the New York Missionary Society to labor among the Indians of the Southwest, and, in his journeys to and from his field of labor, passed through the place where Blackburn was settled. We can readily believe that the two men, congenial in spirit, conversed together in regard to the missionary work in which one was engaged, and we know that shortly after, Blackburn's purpose was formed to establish a mission among the Cherokees.

Yet the subject was one already familiar to him. The tinder was ready for the kindling spark of Bullen's zeal. Blackburn had accompanied the hostile expeditions sent out against the Cherokees, and, while he sought to guard the youth of his flock from the vices of military life, was led to inquire into the causes of their savage and wretched state. "Some cheering rays of hope would flash" on his mind when he "reflected that they were of the same race with ourselves."[1] More and more the subject took possession of his mind. He prayed over it. He asked what could be done. At this juncture, the tide of missionary feeling which had been felt at the East had crossed the Alleghanies; and in 1799 he introduced the subject to the Presbytery of Union, of which he was a member. The Presbytery could only find "embarrassing difficulties" in the way. The scarcity of money and the poverty of the people seemed to present insuperable barriers to effort. But Blackburn would not thus be disheartened. In 1803 he was chosen commissioner to the General Assembly. He went to it with a paper in his pocket, containing

[1] Blackburn's Letters to Dr. Morse, in the "Panoplist," 1803–07.

the outlines of a plan for the education of heathen children. A petition for supplies for frontier settlements came before the body, in which the Cherokee nation was presented as a field for missionary service. Blackburn appeared before the committee to which it was referred, and secured an appropriation of two hundred dollars for the support of a mission and his own employment on the service for two months. The Assembly recommended the object; and he collected more than four hundred dollars more toward it on his return to Tennessee.

This was not all. Indefatigable in his purpose, he enlisted the interest of the Indian agents of the General Government in the prosecution of his plan. The President and Secretary of War expressed their concurrence in his design, and directed Colonel Meigs to facilitate it. In October, a council of two thousand Indians was assembled, and the missionary explained to them his purpose. After some delay on their part, it was approved, and early in 1804 the mission was commenced. By unwearied exertion and self-denial, and by encroaching severely upon his own scanty means, Blackburn was able to continue his operations till the spring of 1806. He then on a Southern tour collected fifteen hundred dollars for his enterprise, and in the succeeding year, on a journey to the North, secured more than four thousand dollars. This effort is the more remarkable as the foundation of the Cherokee mission, and as conducted under the auspices of no society,--an instance of individual enterprise, except as sanctioned and commended by the General Assembly.

Of the new laborers who soon commenced their career in this field, the most eminent were Coffin, Anderson, and Stephenson. Charles Coffin was a native of Newburyport, Mass. Precocious in intellect, ardent in his thirst for knowledge, and from his earliest years unexceptionable in moral conduct, he gave promise of the eminence to which he afterward attained. At the age of fourteen (1789) he entered Harvard College, where he gained a high reputation for scholarship and deportment. His theological teachers were Dr. Dana, of Ipswich, and afterward his own pastor, Dr. Samuel Spring. In 1799 he was licensed to preach by the Essex Middle Association, and, on account of his health, engaged in a Southern tour, preaching for a time to the feeble Presbyterian congregation at Norfolk, which met in the town-hall. He travelled on horseback through Virginia and North Carolina to Greenville, Tenn. In this region he preached for several months, and became deeply interested in the prosperity of Greenville College. Returning to the East, he engaged in collecting funds for the more ample endowment of the institution, and in 1804 set out for his distant and future home. All his energies were devoted to the building up of the institution of which Hezekiah Balch was President, and of which Coffin himself, who was in full sympathy with the new Hopkinsian system that Balch embraced, became Vice-President. This post he held for five years, and upon the death of the President in 1810 was elected as his successor. He continued to discharge the duties of his station till 1827, when he accepted a call to the Presidency of East Tennessee College at Knoxville. This post he held till failing health compelled him to resign it in 1833.

Yet, though mainly devoted to the cause of education, President Coffin performed much labor in the pulpit. For many years he supplied the Rogersville and New Providence churches, and was also instrumental in building up the church of Jonesborough, with which he continued to labor to some extent till 1820. For the larger part of the time that he resided in Greenville he had charge of the Harmony Church in that place.

Cheerful, sociable, generous, with a great flow of animal spirits, and the most amiable and gentlemanly qualities, he was by no means lacking in decision and independence of character. He commanded respect while he conciliated affection. His invariable cheerfulness spread sunshine all around him. His benignant countenance, clear judgment, willing hand, and devoted piety, combined to give efficiency to efforts that by speech or act were as kindly directed as they were well timed. His eloquence was more pathetic than commanding. Yet, even to old age, his intellectual energies were fresh and his activity scarcely abated. Long will his memory live in the region in which he was known and loved, and in which he scattered seed for harvests that succeeding centuries will reap. His death occurred in 1853.

Another minister of Tennessee whose influence was widely and deeply felt was Isaac Anderson, associated early with Blackburn, Henderson, and Ramsey in the Presbytery of Union. He was of Scotch-Irish descent, but a native of Rockbridge county, Va. His ancestors had fought at the siege of Derry, and he retained all their strong Protestant and Presbyterian sympathies. At the age of nineteen he emigrated (1799) with his father, a Virginia farmer, to Grassy Valley, Knox county, Tenn. But already he had consecrated himself to the work of the ministry. For several years he had studied with Rev. William Graham at Liberty Hall. Here his progress was rapid, and at the age of eighteen he made a public profession of religion. For some time he hesitated in regard to the choice of a profession. The bar presented great attractions; but the views with which he proposed to enter upon it could not bear the searching scrutiny of his own conscience. Surrendering its inviting prospects, he cheerfully gave himself to a preparation for the ministry of the gospel.

Samuel Carrick was his first theological instructor. But Carrick found his pupil an overmatch for him on some controverted points of divinity, and was by no means reluctant to hand the young *heretic* over to Gideon Blackburn, who had charge of the church at Maryville. Till midnight Blackburn and Anderson sat discussing together the New Divinity, till the latter felt, as he afterward confessed, his "head empty as a barrel," and his "whole system of theology," which he had regarded as incontrovertible, "completely set aside and utterly demolished." After much study and prayer, and after a considerable period had elapsed, his mind settled down into an approval of Blackburn's system, as "sound, scriptural, and true."

In April, 1802, he was licensed by Union Presbytery, and a few months afterward was installed pastor of Washington Church. With a scant support from his people he labored upon his farm, and extended his missionary tours throughout the surrounding counties. Strange, oftentimes, and not unfrequently disheartening, were the scenes of his experience; but his energy was not to be overcome nor his self-denial exhausted.

In 1811, he succeeded Blackburn at Maryville. Here, more deeply than ever, he was impressed with a sense of the wide-spread spiritual desolation around him. One strong desire took possession of his heart. "Oh that I could get hundreds of young men, to educate them for the ministry!" "We want more preachers." So he spake and so he felt, and he labored with redoubled energy to supply the want. He wrote to the missionary societies, representing to them the condition of East Tennessee, beseechingly sending forth the Macedonian cry. But there came back no satisfactory response. Not discouraged, he resolved to see what could be accomplished by himself and by those around him, whose aid and sympathy he could enlist in the cause. He consulted his friends, and, after mature deliberation and much prayer, he resolved to establish a school of the prophets. A class of five young men was gathered, and he entered upon his work. This was the commencement of the Southern and Western Theological Seminary, known now, under the act of incorporation, as Maryville College.

To facilitate his plans, he established a boarding-house, employing a man to take charge of it, and becoming himself responsible for supplies. Board was to be a gratuity to needy students. With feeble resources of his own, the devoted man found none at first prepared to help or to endow the enterprise. But he put his trust in God; for he believed that he was doing God's work. Sometimes as many as fifteen or twenty young men were to be provided for, and he knew not what to do. Yet repeatedly at the critical moment help came. Unknown donors sent repeatedly sums of money. Friends came and brought, one from his farm, and another from his merchandise, timely contributions. His faith was animated, and his trust in God strengthened. Sometimes weary and disheartened, sometimes opposed, often forced to endure great self-denial, he yet prosecuted his noble work. One hundred ministers, at least, were educated and given to the Church through his instrumentality. Some still labor in the region whose destitution excited his commiseration. Others are scattered in distant States; and thousands, through their ministry, have been brought into the Christian fold.

His appearance in the pulpit was conciliatory, but dignified and commanding. His lofty purpose was stamped upon his calm and placid brow. The broad expanse of his noble forehead made no false impression of the strength and depth of his intellect, while his sparkling eye, with its quick glance, betrayed at once his keen perception and his warm sympathies.

As a teacher he was patient, devoted, and as accurate and thorough as his multiform and arduous duties would allow. An independent thinker himself, he asked none to be his blind followers. His pupils regarded him with respect and veneration as a teacher, while they loved him as a friend. A decided Calvinist, he taught "the doctrines held by Edwards, Dwight, and Spring," with some of the peculiarities of Hopkins's system. But the word of God was with him final and supreme. "Truth was his object, and he sought to attain it in the love of it, by a simple, manly, prayerful searching of the Scriptures."

As a preacher, pastor, theologian, and teacher, he was alike eminent and above reproach. But the pulpit was "his joy and throne." "I have been in Philadelphia, New York, and Boston," said the late Dr. Allan, of Huntsville, "and have heard their greatest speakers; I have been in London, Liverpool, and Manchester, and have listened to the preaching of their most distinguished ministers; but Dr. Anderson is the greatest man I ever heard." His labors were continued down to 1857.[1]

James White Stephenson, of Scotch-Irish extraction, was a native of Virginia; but his early years were spent in the neighborhood of Waxhaw Church, in Lancaster District, South Carolina. Little is known of his childhood; but his education was probably conducted under the direction of Dr. McCaule at Mt. Zion College, Winnsborough, S.C. For some years subsequent, he had charge

---

[1] See a biographical sketch of Anderson in the "Presbyterian Quarterly Review." In Dr. Ely's "Quarterly Theological Review" of 1818 will be found an article by the editor controverting the Hopkinsianism of Anderson, and replying to his attack on the "Contrast."

of a classical school in the same neighborhood, and Andrew Jackson was one of his pupils. In the scenes of the Revolutionary conflict he took an active part, and, after the close of the war, commenced his preparation for the ministry. In 1789, he was licensed by the Presbytery of South Carolina, and shortly after accepted a call to the pastoral charge of Bethel and Indiantown Churches, in Williamsburg District. Here, in difficult and trying circumstances, he was remarkably blessed in his ministry. In every department of ministerial labor he was especially diligent, and his churches grew proportionally in numbers and in spirituality. But at length his attention, as well as that of a portion of his people, was directed to the favorable openings in the great field beyond the mountains, and they determined together to carry the gospel into the almost unbroken wilderness. Accompanied by about twenty families, Stephenson migrated to Maury county, Tennessee, and the company jointly purchased a large tract of land, belonging to the heirs of General Greene, of Revolutionary fame.

In March, 1808, the company set out upon their journey. They reached the place of their destination, and began the foundation of the "Frierson Settlement." As years passed by, the kind and degree of influence exerted by Mr. Stephenson upon the young community became more distinctly marked. His preaching was solid and instructive, and sometimes highly impressive. His good sense, consistent life, gravity of deportment, and devoted piety, were reflected in the manners and character of the people. Few churches in the State maintained thenceforth so enviable a reputation, particularly for the faithful public and private instruction of the blacks. The pastor possessed in a high degree the missionary spirit, and was especially intent upon evangelical labors among the Indian tribes. Under his training a Christian colony was established, and the tree he planted was known by its fruits. To the ripe age of seventy-six years he continued his labors among a people a portion of whom had been his parochial charge for forty-two years. He died in 1832, in the hope and triumph of a Christian faith.

In 1810, Duncan Brown,[1] who for eight years had been settled over the churches of Hopewell and Aimwell in South Carolina, followed Stephenson to Maury county, within the bounds of which, although in charge of different churches, he continued to reside until his death in 1861. For a time he labored at Bethesda and New Hope, afterward at Bethesda, Newport, and Bethany, and subsequently at Columbia; although his missionary excursions extended through Middle Tennessee and Northern Alabama. Shortly before his arrival in the field, Matthew Donald took charge of Mt. Tabor, Joseph B. Lapsley of Tennessee and Gallaher's Creek, and John McCampbell of Shunem, with which Washington subsequently formed a joint charge. A few years later (1814) we find David Weir pastor of Hopewell and Westminster, and Thomas H. Nelson of Knoxville. At this time the Presbytery of Union consisted, besides Donald, Nelson, McCampbell, and Weir, of Ramsey at Grassy Valley, Anderson at New Providence, and Coffin at Harmony.

Meanwhile (1810) the Presbytery of West Tennessee was erected, and consisted shortly after its organization of Stephenson, in charge of Zion congregation, with which Cathie's Creek was subsequently united, Blackburn in Maury county, whither he removed in 1810, although in the following year he took charge of Nash-

[1] Dr. Duncan Brown was born in Robeson county, N.C., in 1771, and studied theology with Dr. David Caldwell. He labored in Maury county as a missionary and stated supply for many years.

ville and Franklin, Henderson at Columbia, Salem, and Ebenezer, Samuel Donnell at Spring Creek, Stone's River, and Round Lick, George Newton, John Gillaspie at Fayetteville and Providence, and Duncan Brown. Previous to 1814, Thomas J. Hall at Murfreesborough and Jefferson, Andrew S. Morrison at Bethsaida, and Samuel Hodge at Smith's Fork, Penuel and Liberty, had become members of the Presbytery. The vacant churches were Elk Ridge, Mars' Hill, Rocky Mount, Double Spring, Elkton, Pulaski, Snow Creek, Purity, Cripple Creek, Winchester, Hopkinsville, Vernon, Yellow Creek, Bethberei, and Piedmont.

The Presbytery of Abingdon, reduced by the erection of other Presbyteries out of it, numbered in 1803 but six ministers, not one of whom was a settled pastor. Dr. Doak, the patriarch of the body, while discharging his duties as President of Washington College, labored also in the ministry; and the congregations of Bethel and Timber Ridge, in Green county, as well as several in the county where he resided, were organized through his efforts. For a short time previous to 1809, his son, John W. Doak, was settled as pastor of Bethel and Providence Churches. Several years passed away before John N. Bovelle was settled at Jonesborough, James Gallaher at Rogersville, and Samuel W. Doak at Greenville. The other pastors of the Presbytery, previous to 1825, were Stephen Bovelle, Alexander M'Ewen, A. S. Morrison, James Gallaher, and Robert Glenn,—all but the last within the bounds of Virginia.

The Presbytery of Union, till 1808 connected with the Synod of the Carolinas, was in that year, at its own request, transferred to the Synod of Virginia. The Presbytery of Abingdon had been in like manner transferred a short time previous. The Presbytery of West Tennessee stood connected with the Synod of Kentucky. In 1815, the three Presbyteries numbered within the bounds of Tennessee, as nearly as can be estimated, about twenty-five ministers and not far from sixty congregations, of which one-half, at least, were without pastoral care.

CHAPTER XXXI.

THE GENERAL ASSEMBLY, 1816-1825.

THE growth of the Church from 1816 to 1825 is sufficiently indicated by the summary of the statistical reports made to the Assembly during this period. The minutes of 1816—which give us the strength of the Church at the commencement of that year—report in connection with the Assembly forty-three Presbyteries. In 1826, the number had exactly doubled. Those erected during the period were Shiloh (1816); Niagara, Ontario, Bath, Richland, Newton (1817); Portage, St. Lawrence (name changed to Watertown in 1828), Missouri, Otsego, Genesee, Rochester, Steubenville (1818); Washington, North River (1819); Troy, Allegheny, Ebenezer (1820); Susquehanna, Alabama (changed to South Alabama in 1826), Georgia, Cincinnati, Ogdensburg (changed to St. Lawrence in 1829), (1821); New York Second, Philadelphia Second, Charleston Union, Athens (1822); Buffalo, Oswego, District of Columbia, Huron, Salem (1823); Newark, Elizabethtown,[1] North Alabama, Mecklenburg, Bethel (1824); Cortland, French Broad, Madison, Wabash (changed in 1830 to Vincennes), and Newburyport (1825).

The increase of the Presbyteries, however, fell short of the growth of the Church in other respects. The five

---

[1] Newark and Elizabethtown were formed by a division of Jersey

hundred and forty[1] ministers of 1816 had become more than eleven hundred and forty previous to 1826; while the churches during the same period had risen from about nine hundred and twenty to over two thousand. The increase in the membership was much more marked. In 1816 it had fallen something short of forty thousand. In 1825[2] it had reached an aggregate of over one hundred and twenty-two thousand,—an increase in less than ten years of over three hundred per cent.

To explain this remarkable and altogether unprecedented growth of the Church, several co-operative and powerful influences must be taken into account. Notwithstanding some local conflicts, and a growing jealousy, in some quarters, of what was regarded as Hopkinsian error, there was throughout the period a general harmony of spirit and effort. The cause of ministerial education was vigorously promoted. A deeper interest was felt in behalf of home as well as foreign missions. The tide of New England emigration flowed with almost unbroken volume into the channels of the Presbyterian Church. Accessions from other ecclesiastical bodies—especially from the Associate Reformed Church—were by no means inconsiderable; while powerful revivals had extensively prevailed in nearly every portion of the Church.

A mere glance at the list of the new Presbyteries noted above will show that nearly five-sixths of the whole number were at the North and West. The sympathies of the New England emigrants, scattering abroad over Central and Western New York, Ohio, Indiana, and other States, scarcely needed, in many cases, the co-operative influence of the Plan of Union to bring them into connection with Presbyterian organizations. Till

---

[1] An approximate estimate, from imperfect reports.

[2] The reports of 1826 give no summary.

toward the close of the period no jealousy of their influence was manifest, even if it was felt.

But the revivals of the period produced a powerful influence, and resulted in large accessions. The report of 1816 made special mention of those which had prevailed in Philadelphia, Bound Brook, Baskingridge, Norristown, New York, Albany, and Troy, and among the churches of the Presbyteries of Long Island, Hudson, Oneida, Onondaga, Champlain, Geneva, and Cayuga, as well as of Winchester, Virginia. In 1817, the report was still more cheering. The Presbytery of Jersey speak of "wonders of mercy." Fifteen hundred conversions were reckoned to have occurred within its bounds. In the city of Troy above five hundred had been added to the different churches. The Presbyteries of Columbia, Champlain, Cayuga, Onondaga, Geneva, Grand River, and Northumberland had experienced remarkable visitations. In 1818, the Assembly received cheering intelligence from the Presbyteries of Cayuga, Champlain, Columbia, Jersey, West Lexington, and Concord. In Cayuga Presbytery seventeen of its twenty-six congregations had been visited by the outpouring of the Spirit. Six or eight of the congregations of Jersey Presbytery had gathered in the harvest of revivals; and the character of all these revivals had been "such as to prove them divine."

In 1819, revivals were reported as having prevailed to a considerable extent in Northern, Central, and Western New York, and within the bounds of Grand River Presbytery in Ohio, as well as in Northern New Jersey and Eastern Tennessee. In 1820, between seventy and eighty churches were found to have been visited by special seasons of refreshing,—fifteen of these in contiguous congregations under the care of Grand River Presbytery, a large number in Central and Northern New York, and in the northern part of New Jersey.

In 1821, reports of revivals were received from the Presbyteries of Rochester, Ontario, Cayuga, Onondaga, Troy, Albany, Columbia, Hudson, New York, Jersey, Newton, Philadelphia, Grand River, Portage, Lexington, and Lancaster. The accession to the churches of the Presbytery of Albany had been nearly fourteen hundred, to those of Hudson over one thousand; while the aggregate within the bounds of the Church had been over nine thousand.

In 1822, the Assembly made grateful mention of revivals not only in Central and Northern New York, but in the Presbyteries of Troy, New York, Abingdon, Orange, Fayetteville, Concord, Philadelphia, Richmond, and Wilmington, as well as those of the Synod of Pittsburg. In 1823, nearly thirty Presbyteries reported revivals within their bounds,—a larger proportion than before in Virginia, North Carolina, and Georgia. In 1824, the list of revivals was much reduced; but in 1825 more than twenty Presbyteries had been specially favored by the outpouring of the Spirit, all of them—with the exception of Lexington and Abingdon in Virginia, Redstone in Western Pennsylvania, Grand River and Portage in Ohio—within the bounds of New York or Northern New Jersey. During the period of ten years, not less than fifty thousand must have been added to the Church, as the fruits of the revivals which had been enjoyed.

In 1816, the style of the Assembly's missionary committee was changed to that of the "Board of Missions," while its membership was increased and its powers were enlarged. The persons constituting it were to be annually elected by the Assembly, but they were authorized to appoint and remunerate missionaries at their discretion. A project for enlisting the Church, as an ecclesiastical body, in the cause of foreign missions, was laid aside in anticipation of the formation of a society so organized as to draw into sympathy with it the Reformed Dutch and Associate Reformed Churches. The outlines of a constitution for this society were considered at a meeting composed of committees from two of the three bodies whom it was sought to ally together, at New York, in October, 1816. In May, 1817, the constitution was approved by the committees of the three bodies, and soon after received the sanction of their highest judicatories.

The society, which was formed July 28, 1817, took the name of the United Foreign Missionary Society. To it were transferred the funds and stations of the New York Missionary Society, while the Northern Missionary Society, as well as other organizations and individual congregations, became its auxiliaries. Its receipts for the first year were two thousand five hundred and seventy-eight dollars, for the second nearly three thousand four hundred dollars, and in 1821 they amounted to over fifteen thousand dollars. Its missionaries—mainly among the Indian tribes of our own country—were largely from the Presbyterian Church; and among them we meet the names of Chapman, Vaill, Requa, Pixley, Jones, Sprague, Newton, Crane, Harris, Kingsbury, Goodall, Williams, and Wright.

The formation of this society and the co-operation of the Presbyterian Church in its support were fully in accordance with the spirit of the Assembly. The formation of the American Bible Society—which occurred but a few days before the Assembly (1816) met—was hailed "with gratification and heartfelt pleasure." The cause of tract-distribution as well as of Sunday-schools continued year after year to receive favorable notice and commendation. The pastoral letter of the Assembly (1817) sufficiently indicates the attitude which it was disposed to assume toward voluntary missionary organizations. "Embrace every opportunity, to the extent of the ability which God has given you, to form and vigorously support *missionary associations*, Bible societies, plans for the distribution of religious tracts, and exertions for extending the benefits of knowledge, and especially of spiritual knowledge, to all ages and classes of persons around you. . . . In these hallowed labors let none refuse to join. . . . Let your plans of co-operation . . . embrace every class and age. . . . We are persuaded that all those periods and Churches which have been favored with special revivals of religion have been also distinguished by visible union and concert in prayer. We entreat you, brethren, to cherish this union and concert." While urging a spirit of harmony with all denominations of Christians, the Assembly does not fail to commend the standards of the Church; yet, while holding fast the form of sound words, it warns against the indulgence of a pernicious spirit of controversy. "It is never necessary to sacrifice charity in order to maintain faith and hope. That differences of opinion, acknowledged on all hands to be of a minor class, may and ought to be tolerated among those who are agreed in great and leading views of divine truth, is a principle on which the godly have so long and so generally acted[1]

[1] The disposition and views of the Assembly during this period are further evinced by the utterance in reply to an application made in 1824, from the Tammany Street Church of Baltimore. The application, while inadvertently mentioning names connected with serious charges,—a method disapproved by the Assembly unless prosecution was intended,—was merely designed to obtain an expression on the importance and binding force of the Confession of Faith. In reply, the Assembly pronounced confessions of faith "necessary and expedient," and "absolutely requisite to the settled peace of the Church and to the happy and orderly existence of Christian communion." While disclaiming for the Confession and standards any "original authority independent of the Scriptures," they say, "we regard them as a summary of those divine truths which are diffused

that it seems unnecessary, at the present day, to seek arguments for its support. Our fathers, in early periods of the history of our Church, had their peculiarities and diversities of opinion, which yet, however, did not prevent them from loving one another and cordially acting together."

Some of the sentences of the closing paragraph of the pastoral letter had, undoubtedly, reference to the internal affairs of the Church. In New York and Philadelphia, "Hopkinsian" views had become matters of controversy. No little warmth of feeling had been already elicited. There was truly some occasion for the admonition, "Surely those who can come together on the great principles of our public standards, however they may differ on non-essential points, ought not to separate, or to indulge bitterness and prejudice against each other."

The alienations and prejudices to which reference is here made were, in their origin, nearly contemporary with the settlement of Rev. (Dr.) G. Spring as pastor of the Brick Church, New York. His father was reputed a leading "Hopkinsian" of New England, and a volume of his, soon after published, had been regarded in certain quarters as peculiarly objectionable. To Dr. John M. Mason, of the Associate Reformed Church, (Dr.) J. B. Romeyn, Dr. McLeod, and Dr. Milledoler, the "New Divinity" was especially odious. To such an extent did party feeling prevail, that the Young Men's Missionary Society (1816), by a vote of one hundred and sixty to ninety, refused to employ Rev. (Dr.) S. H. Cox as a city missionary, on the ground of his theological views. The significance of the rejection was the more marked that Mr. Spring—who opposed the project of

throughout the sacred volume," nor could they, as "a system of doctrine," "be abandoned in our communion without an abandonment of the word of God."

subjecting Mr. Cox to a theological examination—chose rather to assume the place of the objectionable missionary, and that on examination, as his representative, he was pronounced unsound in the faith.

Meanwhile, the alienation had developed itself in another form. Four or five years previous, an attempt was made to brand the "New Divinity" as heresy, by the publication of a volume entitled "The Contrast." The work was prepared by Rev. (Dr.) Ezra Stiles Ely, himself a native of Connecticut, but at the time a resident and laboring as a missionary in the city of New York. In parallel columns it arrayed the sentiments of different authors or systems on a variety of theological topics, to the evident disparagement of "Hopkinsianism." It was regarded as a challenge by those who disclaimed the title yet had incurred the odium of the "Hopkinsians;" nor was the man wanting who stood prepared to accept it. Samuel Whelpley, a Presbyterian clergyman, who had taught school at Norristown and Newark, and who at about this juncture removed to New York, was not indisposed to vindicate the character of those who were held up to theological odium for adhering to what he regarded as sound doctrine and vital truth. Feeble in health, and already brought by disease to the borders of the grave, from which he felt that he had but a brief respite, he was possessed of some of the rarest gifts of genius, and of a chivalric fearlessness in the utterance of his convictions. In a series of successive numbers, subsequently published under the title of the "Triangle," he turned upon those whom he regarded as assailants, and, by a singular combination of wit, rhetoric, allegory, and satire, endeavored to expose their inconsistencies, while he presented what he regarded as the leading features of the evangelical system. The *ad captandum* style of the work, and its splendid declamation, sometimes too high-wrought for good taste, as well as the boldness of its utterance and the earnestness of its tone, commanded for it general attention, and made it manifest that, however "Hopkinsianism" might be defined, the "Triangular Theology" was not likely to prevail without a spirited and vigorous opposition.

In Philadelphia, the prejudice against the "New Divinity," already strong, was not allayed by the transfer of Mr. Ely (1813) to the charge of the church from which Dr. Alexander had been recently dismissed. A portion of the congregation were strongly opposed to the author of "The Contrast;" and the result of his settlement was the division of the church, and the organization of a new congregation. By leading members of the Presbytery of Philadelphia it was resolved not to license students who were found to hold "Hopkinsian" tenets;[1] and Mr. T. H. Skinner, colleague pastor of the Second Church, whose "Edwardian" views had subjected him to suspicion, was pronounced by a theological friend and associate the victim of the "Old Side" prejudices which for more than fifty years had survived the union of the two Synods.

In 1817, the subject of "Hopkinsian" doctrine was brought to the notice of the Assembly by a report of the committee appointed to examine the records of the Synod of Philadelphia. Exception was taken in the report to certain parts of the Synod's pastoral letter, in which the several Presbyteries were enjoined to call to account all such ministers as were suspected of embracing "any of the opinions usually called Hopkinsian." The Synod had classed together "Arian, Socinian, Arminian, and Hopkinsian heresies," as among "the means by which the enemy of souls would, if pos-

[1] Reference is made to the cases of Dr. S. H. Cox, and of Dr. Howe, of South Carolina.

sible, deceive the very elect." They had said, "May the time never come in which our ecclesiastical courts shall determine that Hopkinsianism and the doctrines of our Confession of Faith are the same thing!" In a subsequent paragraph, also, they had employed language which seemed depreciatory of revivals, remarking that, "if the thunder-storm in summer excites the most attention, it is the continued blessing from the clouds which replenishes the springs and makes glad the harvest of the husbandman."

On these portions of the letter the Assembly, adopting the report of the committee, remarked "that while they commend the zeal of the Synod in endeavoring to promote a strict conformity to our public standards,—a conformity which cannot but be viewed as of vital importance to the purity and prosperity of the Church,—the Assembly regret that zeal on this subject should be manifested in such a manner as to be offensive to other denominations, and especially to introduce a spirit of jealousy and suspicion against ministers in good standing, which is calculated to disturb the peace and harmony of our ecclesiastical judicatories. And whereas a passage in the pastoral letter above referred to appears capable of being construed as expressing an opinion unfavorable to revivals of religion, the Assembly would only observe that they cannot believe that that venerable Synod could have intended to express such an opinion."[1]

[1] The Anti-Hopkinsian zeal of this period, rebuked by the Assembly, does not appear to have found much sympathy outside of the Presbytery of New York and the Synod of Philadelphia. "Princeton orthodoxy" at this time could not have savored of a "rigid Calvinism." Dr. Samuel Stanhope Smith, who was Theological Professor before the seminary was established, says (1815) of the volume which contained his lectures to the theological students, "The principles of this system, though a *moderate Calvinism* reigns

Against this action of the Assembly two several protests were presented by members of the Synod,—the first signed by seven and the second by five members. The signers of the first, among other things, protest against the resolution of the Assembly, because, say they, "We do not believe that the doctrines called Hopkinsian are innocent, or that they are so trivial as not to require the interference of the Synod in the manner adopted in their records to prevent their propagation." They protested against it, also, for its apparent contradiction to previous decisions of the Assembly in the cases of the Rev. Messrs. Davis and Balch.

The second protest was substantially the same with the first. It objected to the resolution of the Assembly as assuming "that the distinguishing doctrines of the Hopkinsian system are either consonant with our public standards, or are of so trivial a nature that their departure from strict conformity ought not to be re-

---

in two or three chapters, are such, I persuade myself, as will meet the approbation of those gentlemen who accord with the 'Christian Observer.'" It was after Dr. Green had removed to Princeton that Dr. Smith said, "Dr. Green has entirely disused my lectures on the Evidences of Religion and on Moral Philosophy, on the plea that they are not exactly conformed to his notions on the subject of divine grace." Shortly before Dr. Kollock was settled as pastor at Princeton and Professor of Theology in the College (1803), he wrote to (Bishop) Hobart, "I have found myself obliged to renounce the sentiments of the rigid Calvinists. The doctrine of imputation, as held by them, appears to me inconsistent with the justice of God. My mind revolts from the idea, &c." When Dr. Spring, in 1810, was received by the Presbytery of New York, he read a sermon "as strong on natural ability" as Hopkins or Smalley could have preached. It excited among some members suspicions of his theology; but Dr Miller, of Wall Street,—removed to Princeton in 1813,—rose, and said, "Gentlemen, you may condemn the views of that young man; but in condemning him you condemn me."

garded as matter of censure; whereas we suppose them to be essentially contradictory to sound orthodox doctrines, and, consequently, the preaching of them to be a violation of ordination-vows."

The language of the Synod and of the protestants manifests a considerable degree of feeling in reference to the imputed errors. In Philadelphia, especially, a strong prejudice existed against what were regarded as New England innovations or perversions of orthodox doctrine. The Presbytery was, in fact, divided within itself; and but for the influence of Dr. Wilson, of the First Church, the old prejudices of the previous century might have been so kindled as to work out kindred results on the field they had once ravaged.[1] The wisdom of the Assembly, calmly but firmly imposing a check, at least retarded their mischievous development.

The cause of ministerial education received during this period a fair share of the attention of the Church. The annual reports made by the Presbyteries to the Assembly showed, for a considerable portion of the period, a steadily increasing and healthful interest in the selection and training of young men for the ministry. In 1816 the number of licentiates reported was sixty; in 1825 it was one hundred and seventy-six, while the number of candidates was one hundred and ninety-six. Education societies had been formed for several years previous, both in New England and within the bounds of the Presbyterian Church. Their formation was hastened by the imperative necessity of providing pastors for the churches which were rapidly springing up on the Western field. From every portion of the newly-settled regions the great demand was for ministers and missionaries. In 1822, the Presbytery

---

[1] For a full account of the matter, see Patterson's Pamphlet, 1836

of Niagara, with twenty-six congregations, had but four pastors; Genesee, with nineteen, had but two; Bath was equally destitute; while there were but six ministers in as many adjoining counties. In the bounds of Champlain Presbytery many towns were destitute of any religious service on the Sabbath. Of the twenty-nine congregations of Erie Presbytery, twenty-one were without a stated ministry. The Presbytery of West Tennessee, with a population of three hundred thousand inhabitants within its bounds, had but fourteen ministers. Missouri and Mississippi were equally destitute. Hopewell Presbytery, covering half of Georgia, had but eight ministers. Till 1824, there was not a Presbyterian minister in East or West Florida. The whole Territory of Michigan was almost unbroken missionary ground.

Facts like these, spread abroad not only in the reports of the Assembly, but through the public journals and by published appeals, excited a deep and general interest throughout the community. They were not overlooked by thoughtful men, who discerned the importance of the crisis. New Territories were forming and springing up to the dimensions of States, while the tide of immigration was pouring westward with accelerated rapidity and increased volume. The Assembly of 1825 was not premature in urging the churches to "consider very seriously the case of the destitute parts of our country, and especially of the many thousands of families in the new States in the West and in the South which are growing up almost entirely destitute of the preaching of the gospel and of all religious instruction." They were exhorted by increased liberality to supply the means for the solution of the great problem of the nation's future, and furnish the Board of Missions with means not only to send out missionaries, but to assist when necessary in the support of settled pastors, especially where there was the prospect of a permanent establishment of the means of grace.

But an equal necessity demanded that the men as well as the means should be provided; and in 1819 the Board of Education was established. At this time fifty young men, preparing for the ministry, were supported by the different Presbyteries. The contributions of Albany Presbytery in 1823 amounted to twelve hundred dollars. To secure concert and efficiency of action, a General Board was established, and the committee by whom the Constitution of it was drawn up consisted of Drs. Hill, Richards, and Blatchford, and the Rev. Messrs. Martin and Herron. The voluntary societies, however, had largely anticipated the necessity for this organization, and absorbed the funds which would otherwise have flowed through this channel.

The prospects of the Church, however, in connection with its theological and literary institutions, continued to be more and more cheering. Throughout the entire period the colleges of the land were remarkably favored with revivals. In 1821, the number of pious young men in Union, Hamilton, and Princeton Colleges was estimated at more than one hundred and ten.[1] The seminary at Princeton continued to prosper, and funds continued still to be collected for its endowment. In 1816 it numbered forty-seven students, in 1820 seventy, and in 1823 eighty-five. In 1818 the Presbyteries of Central New York proposed to the Assembly the establishment of another theological seminary within their bounds. Unwilling to assume the responsibility of the undertaking, the Assembly left to the Presbyteries the consideration and prosecution of the project. The result was that, by a vigorous and persevering effort, Au-

---

[1] In 1822 the number in Union alone was seventy.

burn Seminary was established. At nearly the same time the churches of Pittsburg, Ohio, and Kentucky Synods projected the founding of a seminary convenient for themselves. But local differences intervened, and the Western Theological Seminary at Alleghany was not founded till 1826. The germ of the Union Theological Seminary in connection with Hampden-Sidney College in Virginia, which had long existed, began to attract more attention, and to give promise of enlarged influence and success.

The cause of domestic missions failed to receive from the Assembly during this period that measure of attention to which it was entitled. Although there had been an absolute advance, it had by no means kept pace with the growth of the Church or the demands of the mission-field. The number of missionaries annually sent out by Board continued, indeed, steadily to increase,—rising in the course of ten years from about fifty to more than eighty. The method of missionary operations was also made more systematic; and, before the close of the period, measures were taken to extend aid to feeble churches in support of pastors. Some of the Synods also, as those of Pittsburg and Ohio, were prosecuting missionary labor at their own expense within their bounds; but the aggregate fell short of what was demanded by the needs of the churches. The deficiency was, no doubt, largely due to the fact that the interests and sympathies of the churches were largely drawn off by local missionary societies, prosecuting, in fact, the same work with the Board of Missions.

In 1822 the United Domestic Missionary Society of New York commenced its operations. It was formed by a convention of delegates from different missionary organizations within the bounds of the State. Rev. Dr. Proudfit represented the Northern Missionary

Society; Rev. Dr. David Porter, the missionary society of the Middle District; Rev. Messrs. W. R. Weeks, James Southworth, Dirck C. Lansing, Benjamin Stockton, and Stephen Porter, the Eastern, Middle, and Western divisions of the missionary society of the Western District; Rev. Elihu Baldwin and Eleazar Lord, the New York Evangelical Society; Rev. James M. Matthews and John D. Keese, the Young Men's Missionary Society of New York; Rev. Messrs. Elisha Yale and William Chester, the Presbytery of Albany; Rev. Henry Dwight and Abraham B. Hall, the Genesee Missionary Society; and Rev. Messrs. John Smith and John Truair, the Union Society for Domestic and Foreign Missions.

Upon the assembling of the delegates, it was resolved that it was expedient to form a domestic missionary society, and Drs. Proudfit and Porter and Rev. Mr. Lansing were appointed a committee to draught, in the form of a Constitution, the articles of agreement. The Young Men's Missionary Society and the Evangelical Missionary Society of New York City, which had stood toward each other somewhat in the attitude of rivals, were merged in the new organization which was to assume their obligations.

An address to the Christian public gave the reasons for the measure that had now been inaugurated. The different missionary societies which had hitherto been organized had sent out many faithful laborers into the field. But their efforts had been desultory. They had been able to survey but a limited region and provide for limited demands. "Some destitute regions had been regularly visited by missionaries of different societies; others, equally in need of missionary aid, had been passed by and suffered to remain unexplored. Nor was it reasonable to expect that a complete survey should be made even of the moral wastes in a single

State, except under the auspices of a general missionary society."

To remedy this defect, and "to excite a fresh and more extensive interest in the cause of domestic missions," the "United Domestic Missionary Society" was formed. Each auxiliary might co-operate in the most efficient manner as a branch of the society; while "every privilege in regard to the application of its funds" was fully secured to it.

On the 26th of June, a general and public meeting of the society was held in Murray Street Church. The two missionary societies which had previously existed in the city were declared incorporated with the new organization. By this union the United Domestic Missionary Society had twenty-nine missionaries already in the field committed to its charge. Although for the most part composed of Presbyterians, the society numbered among its Vice-Presidents Dr. Livingston and Colonel Rutgers, of the Reformed Dutch Church, while Hon. Stephen Van Rensselaer was President of this society and at the same time of "The Missionary Society of the Reformed Dutch Church," formed a few months anterior to the United Domestic Missionary Society, and for kindred objects.

On March 17, 1823, the Young Men's Missionary Society of New York was formed as an auxiliary, and one object of the formation of the General Society seemed attained,—viz., to excite a fresh and deeper interest in the cause of home missions. Its first report showed that within twelve months of its formation it had in its employ sixty missionaries, mainly within the bounds of the State. Its policy differed in a marked manner from that pursued by most of the other societies. It distinctly referred to the advantages attendant upon a permanent location of missionaries over the plan of itinerating. By aiding infant churches to support and settle pastors, the church and the society shared the burden, which thus fell more lightly on each, while the institutions of the gospel in destitute regions were placed on a more permanent basis.

This policy was distinctly announced and advocated in the first report of the society; and it shows the enlarged views of its founders that they had thus perceived the point in which, from the necessary lack of means, the plan of operations of the General Assembly, excellent as it was in some respects, was defective.

The field opened before the society was one which demanded all its resources. These amounted for the year to nearly six thousand dollars: yet "there exist," say the directors, "within our knowledge, more than a hundred stations where, with partial aid from our funds, young men might be immediately settled."

From the six societies which had become auxiliary during the year, and from others that were to become so, additional contributions were confidently expected; and, to secure co-operation on the most satisfactory terms to all concerned, it was distinctly stated that auxiliaries were "entitled to designate the stations where the funds they contribute are to be employed in supporting missionaries."

The Young Men's Missionary Society proved an efficient auxiliary. Its funds were managed and disbursed by itself, the parent society appointing the missionaries and designating the stations which were to be under the superintendence of the auxiliary. It employed ten missionaries in the counties of Delaware, Genesee, Schoharie, Herkimer, Essex, Warren, Rensselaer, &c., in the State of New York. The congregation at Esperance was gathered through its aid; a church was formed in a neighboring village, while at Andes, where for nine years pastoral labor had not been enjoyed, the services of a minister were secured, and the members of the church were doubled. Such was the specimen given of its operations.

For several years these and other local societies were in active and successful operation within the bounds of the Presbyterian Church. Beneficent in aims and results, they labored in perfect harmony with one another and with the Assembly's Board. The magnitude of their plans and success was not yet such as to make their patronage, concentrated in a single society, dangerous to the peace or calculated to excite the jealousy of large portions of the Church, and come at least into seeming conflict with the plans and methods of the Assembly's operations.

The rapid growth of the Presbyterian Church warranted the Assembly in renewing to the Synods of the Associate Reformed and Dutch Reformed Churches[1] the overtures for mutual correspondence which had been rejected (1798) some twenty years previous. Measures were therefore taken by the Assembly of 1819 with a view to this object. A plan of correspondence with the Reformed Dutch Church was not adopted until 1823; but one with the Associate Reformed was carried into effect in 1820. In the following year, a committee was appointed by the Assembly to confer with a similar committee[2] from the Associate Reformed Synod, then in session in Philadelphia, with a view to concert measures for union between the two bodies, and to report the result as soon as convenient. The proposal was met in a fraternal spirit, and the result of the conference was in favor of the projected union. The Presbyteries of the Synod might retain their dis-

---

[1] Minutes of 1819.

[2] The committee of the Assembly consisted of Drs. Green, Blatchford, and McDowell, and Messrs. B. Strong and H. Southard; that of the Synod, of Dr John M. Mason, Rev. Messrs. E. Dickey, John Lind, William Wilson, and Mr. Joseph Cushing.

tinct organization,—a concession to the *elective affinity* principle,—or be amalgamated with those of the Assembly at their own choice. The Theological Library and funds of the Synod were to be transferred to the seminary at Princeton, and the churches of the Synod were to raise funds for the partial endowment of a Professorship of Biblical Literature.

These articles of union were readily accepted by the Assembly. But the Synod, while approving the plan, referred it back to the Presbyteries for their adoption. The project for providing a new psalmody for the Church had already been taken up by the Assembly, but seems to have had no prejudicial effect upon the disposition in favor of union between the two bodies. In 1822 the proposed measure was carried into effect,—not, however, by a majority of the Synod, nor without strenuous opposition from some of its Southern and Western Presbyteries.[1]

---

[1] The Rev. Dr. Forsyth states that when the question of union was submitted to the Associate Reformed Synod the vote stood—*for* union, seven; *against* it, six; and silent, four. "The majority immediately declared the Synod dissolved, and, in palpable violation of the Constitution of the Presbyterian Church, they were at once admitted as members of the Assembly, to which they had never been chosen. Within a week after this secession from the Associate Reformed Church, her valuable library was, with singular expedition, removed from New York to Princeton." A full attendance of members, on their way to the Synod when the vote was taken, would have prevented the measure. Three Presbyteries were brought into connection with the Presbyterian Church by this measure,—New York Second, Philadelphia, and Big Spring,—the last two becoming, on their dissolution, amalgamated with other Presbyteries. New York Second had Cedar Street Church (Dr. McLeod, soon after succeeded by Dr. McElroy), Pearl Street Church (W. W. Phillips, pastor), and Murray Street Church (W. D. Snodgrass, pastor). In Philadelphia were Dr. Dickey, Dr. Duncan, of Baltimore, Mr. McLean, of Gettysburg, Dr. Grey, and a few others. Among others

The Associate Reformed Church in this country originated in a union, formed June 13, 1782, between the Reformed and a portion of the Associate Church. The Associate body in Scotland commenced its existence in 1747, on the basis of opposition to the Burgess oath, by means of which the seceders were divided into two bodies,—the Anti-Burgher Synod assuming the name of Associate. Three years later, the grounds of the division were so well understood and approved by emigrants from Scotland who had settled in Pennsylvania, that a petition for ministerial aid was addressed by them to the Associate Synod of Scotland.[1]

It was not till 1753 that the Synod found themselves so situated as to grant the request. In that year Alexander Gellatly and Andrew Arnot were sent out to this country as missionaries. They were authorized to organize congregations, ordain elders, and, if judged proper, constitute themselves with ruling elders into a Presbytery. In the exercise of their authority they formed themselves, soon after their arrival in 1754, into the "Associate Presbytery of Pennsylvania, subordinate to the Associate Synod of Edinburgh."

The field which this body assumed to occupy was within the bounds of the "Old-Side" Synod of Philadelphia, but more especially within the territory covered by the Presbytery of New Castle. By the latter—who had learned, from their experience in connection with the Tennents, Whitefield, and their sympathizers, to look with a jealous eye on those who assumed to dispense the ordinances of the gospel within their bounds —the Scottish Associate ministers were regarded as

who thus came into connection with the Church were Drs. Junkin and Engles. See Presbyterian Quarterly Review, 1854, p. 151.

[1] Miller's Biographical Sketches and Sermons of some of the first ministers of the Associate Church in America, with a historical introduction, p. 10.

intruders, and were represented as seceders from the Presbyterian Church in America as well as in Scotland. A "warning" was issued against them, in which they were not only denounced as schismatics and separatists, but, in connection with the Associate Church, as holding and teaching error concerning the gospel offer, the nature of faith, and the obligation of the religious covenant engagements of the forefathers of the Scotch Reformation on their posterity. To this "warning" Mr. Gellatly replied; and the controversy was carried on for some time with a considerable degree of spirit, and not without the use of sharp language.

The Associate Presbytery, however, in spite of opposition, continued to increase. Mr. Gellatly was settled at Octorara and Oxford, in Lancaster county, and soon after several other ministers were sent over to this country,—among them, James Proudfit, Matthew Henderson, and John Mason, the latter the first pastor of the Associate Church which was gathered by his labors in the city of New York.

In the course of ten years, applications to the Presbytery for preaching were received from various parts of New York, Pennsylvania, Virginia, and the Carolinas. Several of the Burgher brethren had, meanwhile, been received into the body,—a measure which was regarded with disfavor by the Associate body in Scotland, and one which the Presbytery was required to annul before other ministers could be sent over at their earnest request. In 1770 and 1771, a correspondence took place between the Presbytery and the Synod of New York and Philadelphia respecting a union between the two bodies; but the project was at length abandoned as hopeless.

In 1776, the Presbytery numbered thirteen ministers in New York and Pennsylvania. An unwise division was made of the body into two Presbyteries, and the reunion was not effected till 1782. Meanwhile, repeated efforts were made to effect a union with the Reformed Presbytery, commonly called Covenanters. This Presbytery had been constituted in 1774, and was connected ecclesiastically with the Reformed Presbyterians of Scotland. It consisted of three ministers,—John Cuthbertson, William Linn, and Alexander Dobbin, who preached mostly in Pennsylvania. From 1777, repeated conferences were held, and the points of difference freely discussed. The project for union appears to have been successively reviewed and abandoned,—a large minority, and sometimes a majority, of the Associate body opposing it, until at last it was carried in the Presbytery by the casting vote of James Proudfit, the moderator.

The minority refused to acquiesce in the decision, and still maintained their organization. They protested that the powers of the Presbytery were still vested in themselves, who adhered to its true principles and constitution. Continuing to increase, they were at length organized into a Synod, in May, 1801, at Philadelphia, and assumed the name of the Associate Synod of North America.

The united body, adopting the style of "The Associate Reformed," became, in fact, a new denomination. It was not, however, till 1804 that they attained strength sufficient to warrant their organization as a Synod. In May (30th) of that year this body was constituted at Greencastle, Pa., and the opening sermon was preached by Dr. John M. Mason, of New York.[1] More, perhaps, than any other man he contributed to the influences by which the body was brought, in 1821, to entertain proposals for a union with the General Assembly. His own superiority to the narrowness of

---

[1] Wilson's Presbyterian Almanac, 1859, p 185.

view which could make dividing lines of non-essentials, and the extent to which in the missionary co-operation of the times he and his brethren were brought into contact with other branches of the Church, prepared the way for the measures by which the Associate Reformed body became a part of the Presbyterian Church under the care of the Assembly. The Southern and Western Synods, however, still declined to be included in the union, and reclaimed for themselves the property which the General Synod had made over to the Assembly.

No exception was taken to any irregularity by which the delegates of the Synod were conceded seats in a body to which they had never been elected, or to their anomalous position as representatives of Presbyteries which at the time were not—and, perhaps, never would become—constituent parts of the Presbyterian Church. Formalities, however, were laid aside, and the delegates to the Synod were cordially invited to take their seats as members of the Assembly. The invitation was accepted, and the occasion was described as "deeply interesting and affecting." The union thus brought about introduced an element which hitherto had stood aloof on grounds which, in this country, had for the most part lost the significance which had seemed to justify separation in Scotland. It really brought together those whose unity was essential and whose differences were mainly technical, and thenceforth we find prominent in the history of our Church names that had become already conspicuous in another connection.

In this same year, moreover,—as if to afford contemporaneous illustration of the broad and liberal spirit of the Church, another accession was received, of a somewhat diverse character. The Charleston Congregational Association (S.C.), which had been in existence many years, upon the report of a committee appointed to examine the distinctive features of the Presbyterian Church and lay the results of the examination before the Association, voted (1822) its own dissolution in case a union could be effected with the Presbytery of Harmony. The plan of union was carried out; and in 1823 Charleston Union Presbytery, consisting of the ministers of the Association and the members of Harmony Presbytery, was erected.

Among matters of a more miscellaneous character which during this period claimed the attention of the Assembly, there are several which require at least a passing notice. In 1818 steps were taken for the preparation of a digest of the most important acts of the Synod of New York and Philadelphia, and of the General Assembly which issued in the publication of the volume of 1820. In 1819 the first steps were taken for providing an authorized Psalmody adapted to the wants of the Church, and which resulted in the publication adopted and published eleven years later by order of the Assembly. The subjects of colonization, intemperance, and Sabbath-observance came up repeatedly for notice, and received due attention. From 1812 to 1819, the Assembly was repeatedly engaged in discussions concerning measures to promote the proper observance of the Lord's day, and petitions were again and again drawn up and sent down to the congregations to be signed and forwarded to Congress, praying for the repeal of the law which required the conveyance of the mail on the Sabbath. The interest of the Assembly in behalf of the monthly concert of prayer, and the cause of Sabbath-schools, tract, Bible, and missionary societies, was repeatedly evinced by its utterances. It was stated in 1820, as a matter for gratulation, that at that time there were nine thousand children in attendance on Sabbath-schools in New York, fourteen thousand in Philadelphia, eight thousand in Baltimore, and a proportionate number in other cities. In 1821, the subject of Free Masonry was brought before the Assembly; but no decisive action was taken upon it.

In 1816, Drs. Romeyn, Alexander, and Miller were appointed a committee to re-examine our forms of process, and to prepare and report such additions and explanations as might appear needful and expedient. Their report, made in 1819, was sent down to the Presbyteries for their suggestions. The report of the following year was sent down to the Presbyteries for their adoption; and by a large majority the amendments, which reduce the book of Discipline to its present form, were approved, and by the Assembly of 1821 were declared to be adopted. The rules for the government of judicatories which were adopted by the Assembly of the same year, having never been ratified by the Presbyteries, form no part of the constitution of the Church.

This was the case also with the notes which in 1794 had been printed in connection with the standards of the Church. Having never been submitted to the Presbyteries, their authority was simply that of the approval of the Assembly. In 1816, attention was called to this subject by an overture of the Presbytery of Philadelphia, and, in consequence of objections urged, the Assembly decided to omit those which referred to the subject of man-stealing in connection with the question, "What is forbidden in the eighth commandment?" The Assembly, however, took occasion to declare that in directing the omission they were "influenced by far other motives than any desire to favor slavery, or to retard the extinction of that mournful evil as speedily as may consist with the happiness of all concerned." At the same time, the question whether masters who were members of the Church were in duty bound to present the children of parents in servitude for the ordinance of baptism, provided they were in a situation to give them a religious education and training, was considered, and answered in the affirmative.

But here the subject was not permitted to rest. In 1818, the sale of a slave—a member of the Church—was brought to the attention of the Assembly,[1] and a committee, of which Dr. Ashbel Green was chairman,[2] made a report which was unanimously adopted. It shows the decided stand which the Assembly, without a dissentient voice, was prepared to take on the subject of slavery. It declares, "We consider the voluntary enslaving of one part of the human race by another, as a gross violation of the most precious and sacred rights of human nature, as utterly inconsistent with the law of God, which requires us to love our neighbor as ourselves, and as totally irreconcilable with the spirit and principles of the gospel of Christ, which enjoin that 'all things whatsoever ye would that men should do to you, do ye even so to them.' Slavery creates a paradox in the moral system: it exhibits rational, accountable, and immortal beings in such circumstances as scarcely to leave them the power of moral action. It exhibits them as dependent on the will of others whether they shall receive religious instruction; whether they shall know and worship the true God; whether they shall enjoy

[1] It was done by submitting to the Assembly the following resolution:—"That a person who shall sell as a slave a member of the Church, who shall be at the time of sale in good standing in the Church, and unwilling to be sold, acts inconsistently with the spirit of Christianity, and ought to be debarred from the communion of the Church."

[2] It was "after considerable discussion" that the subject was put into the hands of a committee consisting of Dr. Green, Dr. Baxter, of Virginia, and Rev. Dyer Burgess, of Southern Ohio (Miami Presbytery), who were to prepare a report "embracing the object of the above resolution, and also expressing the opinion of the Assembly in general as to slavery."

the ordinances of the gospel; whether they shall perform the duties and cherish the endearments of husbands and wives, parents and children, neighbors and friends; whether they shall preserve their chastity and purity, or regard the dictates of justice and humanity. Such are some of the consequences of slavery,—consequences not imaginary, but which connect themselves with its very existence. The evils to which the slave is *always* exposed often take place in fact, and in their very worst degree and form; and when all of them do not take place, as we rejoice to say that in many instances, through the influence of the principles of humanity and religion on the minds of masters, they do not,—still the slave is deprived of his natural right, degraded as a human being, and exposed to the danger of passing into the hands of a master who may inflict upon him all the hardships and injuries which inhumanity and avarice may suggest.

"From this view of the consequences resulting from the practice into which Christian people have most inconsistently fallen, of enslaving a portion of their *brethren* of mankind,—for God hath made of one blood all nations of men to dwell on the face of the earth,—it is manifestly the duty of all Christians who enjoy the light of the present day, when the inconsistency of slavery, both with the dictates of humanity and religion, has been demonstrated and is generally seen and acknowledged, to use their honest, earnest, and unwearied endeavors to correct the errors of former times, and as speedily as possible to efface this blot on our holy religion, and to obtain the complete abolition of slavery throughout Christendom, and, if possible, throughout the world."

While rejoicing that the Presbyterian Church had early devoted attention and effort to the work of putting an end to slavery, and that many of its members subsequently had proved to be among the most efficient, active, and vigorous laborers in this work, the Assembly expressed its sympathy for those portions of the Church upon which the evils of slavery had been entailed, "where a *great* and the *most virtuous part of the community* abhor slavery, and wish its extermination as sincerely as any others," but where the number, ignorance, and vicious habits generally of the slaves forbade, out of regard to master and slave alike, immediate emancipation. Yet they are exhorted to increase their exertions for "a total abolition of slavery," suffering no greater delay than regard for the public welfare "truly and *indispensably* demands."

The necessity of this delay the Assembly fully admits. Immediate emancipation might only "add a second injury to the first." Yet this delay should not be made "a cover for the love or practice of slavery, or a pretence for not using efforts that are lawful and practicable to extinguish the evil." Exhorting all to forbearance from "harsh censures and uncharitable reflections upon their brethren," the Assembly takes occasion to commend the Colonization Society, recently organized, to recommend increased attention to the religious instruction of slaves, and to enjoin upon church Sessions and Presbyteries the prevention of all cruelty in the treatment of slaves, subjecting those who should presume to sell slaves, members of the Church, against their will, to the discipline of the proper church judicatories, by whom the offender, until his repentance, was to be suspended from all the privileges of the Church.

In 1825, the Assembly embodied in its "narrative" a reference to the claims of the African race. "We notice," they remark, "with pleasure the enlightened attention which had been paid to the *religious instruction and evangelizing of the unhappy slaves and free people of color* of our country in some regions of our Church. We would especially commend the prudence and zeal combined in this work of mercy by the Presbyteries of Charleston Union, Georgia, Concord, South Alabama, and Mississippi. The millions of this unhappy people in our country, from their singular condition as brought to the gospel by a peculiar providence, constitute at home a mission field of infinite importance and of a most inviting character. No more honored name can be conferred on a minister of Jesus Christ than that of *Apostle to the American slaves;* and no service can be more pleasing to the God of heaven or more useful to our beloved country than that which this title designates."

During the period under review three new Synods had been erected,—the Synod of Tennessee in 1817, the Synod of Genesee in 1821, and the Synod of New Jersey, formed by a division of the Synod of New York and New Jersey, in 1823. Never had the progress of the Church been more rapid, and at no time had the promise for the future been more cheering. And yet at the close of the period under review the Assembly was constrained to speak of the sad destitution of portions of its mission field. Missouri and Illinois, with a population of one hundred and sixty thousand, had but eighteen Presbyterian churches and seven ordained ministers. Mississippi and Louisiana, with a population of two hundred and thirty thousand, had but eleven ministers of the gospel in the field; and these facts were cited as "specimens of this wide and melancholy waste."

CHAPTER XXXII.

NEW YORK, 1816-1830.

In the period from 1816 to 1830, the churches within the State of New York were largely increased in numbers and in strength. Besides several church organizations which had but a temporary existence, there were gathered in the city of New York the Allen Street (1819), the Colored (1822), the Bleecker Street (1825), the Central, Broome Street (1821), the Spring Street (1825), and the North, afterward Carmine Street (1829), Presbyterian Churches. Along the line of the Hudson there were few new church organizations, but those already existing were increased in strength. At Albany a Third Presbyterian Church was organized in 1817, and the Fourth Church was gathered by E. N. Kirk in 1829. To the Presbyteries of Troy and Albany quite a large number of churches were added, insomuch that the aggregate fell little short of sixty. Among these were the church of Saratoga Springs, organized in 1817, and the Second and Third Churches[1] of Troy. The four Presbyteries of Champlain, Troy, Albany, and Columbia embraced, in 1830, seventy-six ministers and eighty-six churches, of nearly ten thousand members. The report from the Presbyteries of Londonderry and Newburyport, in New England, indicated a rapid growth. The membership of the churches had increased in fifteen years something like fifty per cent., numbering in 1830 nearly two thousand members.

At the close of the period there were in New York

[1] The Third may have been in 1831.

City alone nineteen Presbyterian churches. In the Wall Street Church, Philip M. Whelpley had succeeded Dr. Miller in 1815. With a fine intellectual countenance, dark eye, perfectly symmetrical form, and altogether of most attractive appearance, his clear, rich, and perfectly melodious voice and faultless rhetoric secured him the reputation of a perfect elocutionist. Although but twenty-one years of age when called to occupy his eminent and highly responsible position, he immediately took rank as one of the most gifted and eloquent pulpit-orators of the age. He had early cherished the hope of bearing the standard of the Cross as a missionary to foreign lands. From the narrative of Brainerd's life he had caught an enthusiasm which could only be damped by insuperable obstacles; but he carried with him to the sacred desk, with the graces of the orator, the fervor of an evangelist. The charms of his voice, manner, and rhetoric were consecrated to the work of commending the gospel of Christ to dying men. But his physical frame, unequal to the task imposed, sank under its burdens, and in the thirtieth year of his age and the tenth of his ministry his earthly labors were brought to their close. His successor in 1826 was Dr. W. W. Phillips.

In the Brick Church the successor of Dr. Rodgers in 1810 was Gardiner Spring, whose pastorate of more than half a century has been crowned by memories of usefulness, scenes of revival, and the abundant success of philanthropic efforts which, reaching in their results across the continent and around the world, have enshrined the name of the Brick Church and that of its pastor in the fond affections of thousands.

In the Rutgers Street Church Dr. Milledoler[1] was suc-

---

[1] Dr. Milledoler's excellence as a pastor and his warmly sympathetic nature rendered him greatly beloved. His gifts in prayer, in

ceeded by Dr. McClelland in 1815, and by Dr. Thomas McAuley in 1822. Rarely has any one had more occasion to rejoice over a successful pastorate than Dr. McAuley while in charge of this church. By no means remarkably eloquent or profound, he was a man of ready utterance, and from a mind richly stored with scriptural knowledge, and far from lacking in the lore of the scholar, he poured forth with the freshness and fervor of pastoral fidelity those expositions of truth which were at once instructive and edifying. The charm of his genial spirit, racy humor, conversational tact, and warm sympathy almost idolized him in the hearts of his people. Succeeded by John W. Krebs in 1827, he removed to Philadelphia, only, however, to be recalled a few years later to the charge of the Murray Street Church.

In the Scotch Presbyterian Church the successors of John M. Mason (who resigned in 1810) were Robert B. E. McLeod and Joseph McElroy (1824). Dr. Mason himself undertook the task of collecting a new congregation, and the Murray Street Church was the result. He was still, until 1822, in connection with the Associate Reformed body; but he chafed against the narrow restrictions which the prejudices of some who belonged to it assumed to impose. His own catholicity of spirit led him heartily to unite with his Presbyterian brethren in missionary and charitable effort. Worshipping in the edifice of the Cedar Street Church while his own was building, he felt free to unite with Dr. Romeyn's people in the communion of the Lord's Supper, and even, in seeming contempt of Rouse, to use their psalmody. His work, published four years later, on "Catholic Communion," was in reality his protest against the prejudices of some of his own denomination, as well as a

which he seemed to identify himself with the object of it, are spoken of as most remarkable.

vindication of his views and practice. Before the union of the Associate Reformed Synod with the churches of the General Assembly was consummated, he was one in spirit and sentiment with the American Presbyterian Church.

As a pulpit-orator, he held the very foremost rank among his contemporaries. He had no superior; and none has yet ventured to name his peer. Nature had lavished upon him her princeliest gifts. His physical frame was magnificent in its proportions; while its perfect symmetry was the admiration of the beholder. His majestic mien and commanding presence inspired awe and respect. His gesture was dignity, and his look eloquence. Nor did the exterior belie the inner man. His mind was proportioned to his frame. In the admirable balance of his faculties, it would be difficult to say which predominated. His rhetoric was but the grace with which he wielded his logic. His argumentation was splendid, but his declamation overwhelming. His controversy with Bishop Hobart would alone have sufficed for his fame as a polemic; and his "Messiah's Throne" would have established his claim to rank among the princes of the pulpit.

His rare gifts had been diligently and carefully cultivated. His father, Dr. John Mason, the first pastor of the Scotch Church (1761–92), whom he was called to succeed, was a man of eminent abilities and superior education. Under his direction until 1791, when he crossed the ocean in order to complete his theological course at the University of Edinburgh, the son received his training. Recalled by his father's death, he had no sooner fairly entered upon his pastorate in New York than his reputation was established. Although only about twenty-two years of age, he proved himself fully equal to the responsible duties of his position. Not content even with these, he labored to secure for the

Associate Reformed Church the advantages of a more liberal provision for ministerial education. The plan of a theological seminary was projected by him, and carried into effect in 1804. Meanwhile, he visited Great Britain for the purpose of procuring a library for the institution, of which he was himself the very life and soul. He succeeded in obtaining about three thousand volumes, and on his return induced several young men—theological students or graduates—to return with him, to seek in this country fields of usefulness. Of the institution he was appointed the first professor, and, in connection with his various other duties, continued to bear the responsibilities of the office till failing health admonished him to retire.

As if the duties of pastor and theological professor, and the demands made upon his time by other public engagements, were not enough to task his herculean energies, he accepted, in 1811, the office of provost of Columbia College. For several years subsequent, the amount of labor which he performed is almost incredible. Of the college he was really the acting and responsible head, and by the splendor of his talents and the energy of his administration gave it a character which it never had before. But even his gigantic frame was unequal to the burdens imposed upon it. In 1817 his health began to fail, and, though greatly benefited by a voyage to England, it was never fully restored. In the autumn of 1821 he resigned the pastorate of the church, and for three years assumed the Presidency of Dickinson College, to which he had been urgently invited. He relinquished it, however, in 1824, and in the gradual decay of his strength and faculties awaited the close of life. His death occurred in 1829, and his successors in the Murray Street Church were William D. Snodgrass (1823) and Thomas McAuley (1833).

The vigor of his active powers was exhausted before

he had reached his fiftieth, and his life closed before he had completed his sixtieth, year. His personal disability was felt as a public loss. If rigidly orthodox, he was of a noble, enlarged, and catholic spirit; and, from the formation of the New York Missionary Society in 1796, the cause of missions found in him one of its most ardent, devoted, and effective champions. While unrelenting in his opposition to error,—on one occasion, when a portion of his audience was composed of Unitarians, embodying in the benediction the formula of the Trinity, and adding, "Blistered be the tongue that will not say *Amen*,"—his whole soul was enlisted in the work of Christian evangelization. Some of his most powerful and eloquent utterances in the pulpit were in vindication of the truths or doctrines of the Bible which had been subjected to the assaults of the skeptic or the errorist. In pouring these forth he seemed resistless as a river's torrent. In their sublimity and impressiveness they might perhaps be pronounced not only unapproached, but unapproachable. Sir James Mackintosh once observed that no man could comprehend why all Greece went to hear Demosthenes, until he had listened to Robert Hall. Yet Robert Hall, on hearing Dr. Mason preach in London his magnificent discourse on "Messiah's Throne," was so overwhelmed by the impression of his power as to declare for himself, despondent in the attempt to rival such a model, that he could never preach again.

Such eminence as this, however, was due to no oratorical *clap-trap*. None could have abhorred more deeply than Dr. Mason any resort to methods of speech or manner unbecoming the character of the pulpit. The mannerism of his sentences—usually short, direct, and remarkably forcible—was but the shaping which they naturally received from the channel of his own clear but majestic conceptions. Few men have ever paid less attention to the mere polish of style.[1] The aid of manuscript in the pulpit he scorned. His thoughts were marshalled with such order and system, and presented in language so pertinent and appropriate, as to leave the impression due to the order, precision, and force of the most elaborate preparation. Yet only a small number of his discourses were ever written; and of those which have been preserved, a few only are complete, or retain the precise form in which they were delivered. His reputation, however, rests on a broader base than his published writings. Nearly half a century after he preached in London, the tradition of his wonderful power was still fresh; and there are a few yet left amid the scenes of his labors in this country, whose memory kindles to enthusiasm at the mention of his name.[2]

In the Pearl Street Church, organized in 1797 as the Second Associate Reformed, and forming for a few years (till 1804) a collegiate charge with the Scotch Church in Cedar Street, John X. Clark, who succeeded Robert Forrest (the first pastor) in 1810, continued his labors

---

[1] It is but justice to the truth of history to say that his discourses were not unfrequently quite unworthy of his fame. The *published* testimonies to his eloquence are all sufficiently accordant and flattering; but, by persons who at different times were privileged to hear him, I have been informed that he sometimes fell far short of the ordinary standard.

[2] Dr. McVickar, in his "Professional Years of Hobart," says of Dr. Mason, "Powerful with his pen, he was still more powerful in debate, . . . while at the same time his truly great powers, both of argument and sarcasm, seemed to justify him in that disdainful self-confidence of tone and manner with which he was apt to put to silence opponents of whom he stood not in awe."—P. 121. He speaks of him afterward as "joining a Warburtonian coarseness of manner to unquestioned learning and overbearing talent" (p. 134), and as "leaving behind him" in the Presbyterian Church "neither equal nor second."

for about seven years. He was succeeded in 1818 by W. W. Phillips,—called to Wall Street in 1826,—Walter Monteith (1826), Benjamin H. Rice (1829), Henry A. Rowland (1834), and Charles H. Read (1843), at the close of whose ministry the church was absorbed in the Broome Street (Central) Church.

In the Canal Street Church, of which John McNeice was the first pastor (1809–15), Henry Blatchford labored from 1815 to 1819. His successors were John Alburtis (1819), Robert McCartee (1821), John Anderson (1839), Richard W. Dickinson (1840), and Hugh Carpenter, after whose dismission the church was dissolved.

In the Duane Street Church, organized in 1808, but occupying for several years a house of worship on Cedar Street between William and Nassau, John B. Romeyn commenced his labors with the organization of the church. He was the son of Dr. Romeyn, pastor of the Reformed Dutch Church of Schenectady, and, after completing his classical studies at Columbia College and his theological with Dr. Livingston and his own father, received a call to the Reformed Dutch Church of Rhinebeck, where he labored for four years, after which he was invited to the charge of the Presbyterian Church of Schenectady. He remained here but a single year, when (1804) he accepted a call to the First Presbyterian Church of Albany. Here he remained until called to New York in 1808. Both at Schenectady and Albany he well sustained the high expectations which his first appearance in the pulpit awakened, and in his new sphere of labor he soon gathered around him one of the largest and most respectable congregations in the city. An apt scholar, a great reader, of quick perception and exquisite taste, of ardent feelings and great frankness of manner, he was a man to conciliate affection as well as command respect. Of compact and well-proportioned frame, though of spare habit, his nervous temperament, expressive countenance, ready utterance, graceful but rapid motions, as well as the animation which beamed from his fine, intelligent eye, sufficiently indicated the peculiar characteristics of his genius. There was nothing uncertain or vacillating in his manner,[1] nothing sluggish or slow in his composition. His opinions were clearly conceived and boldly expressed. His purposes were promptly formed and vigorously executed. Whatever he did, he did with his might. His devotion to his ministerial duties was unremitted. As a social companion he was cheerful and genial, without the aid of jest or witticism, and, though neither a rhetorician nor logician, neither a metaphysician nor a profound thinker, the ardor of his thought glowed with the enthusiasm of his feelings. His printed discourses will scarcely sustain his pulpit-reputation.[2] To his impassioned, rapid, earnest, and impressive utterance their popularity was largely due. No subtle processes of reasoning, no delicate touches of fancy or flights of imagination, no splendid diction or elaborate rhetoric, lent them their charm, but rather the vivacity, energy, pathos, naturalness, and sincerity of his manner,—his very soul speaking through the body that trembled with emotion or erected itself in the attitude of authority, while every line of his face was instinct with passion, and his eye, kindled or tearful, seemed by its look to thrill the hearer with responding emotion. For years his house of worship overflowed. Accessions to the church—which while under his charge might be considered a model church—were numerous and frequent.

After his death (1825), at the age of fifty-two years,

---

[1] Sprague, iv. 222. [2] Two octavo volumes were published in 1816.

he was succeeded by Cyrus Mason in 1826. The pastors of the church subsequent to the resignation (1835) of the latter have been Dr. George Potts (1836), and Dr. James W. Alexander (1844–49).

In 1811 the Laight Street Church was organized, and Dr. M. L. R. Perrine was installed its pastor. In 1820 he was succeeded by Dr. S. H. Cox, and in 1835 by Flavel S. Mines, whose pastorate closed in 1840. In 1843, owing mainly to pecuniary embarrassments and difficulties, the church was dissolved.

The Seventh Presbyterian Church, in a destitute portion of the city, was gathered by the unwearied energy and devotion of Elihu W. Baldwin, and in 1820 he was installed its pastor. Few men have ever more fully exemplified the virtues or the graces of an apostolic ministry. With scarcely one of the gifts of genius, with an exterior pleasing and winning indeed, but far from commanding, he had yet that excellence ascribed by a political foe to Sir Walter Raleigh when he said of him, "He can toil terribly." Possessed of a calm and even temper, and a spirit cheerful and hopeful in the most discouraging scenes, and, while struggling against obstacles seemingly insuperable, "bating no jot of heart or hope," and never entertaining the thought of deserting his post for the difficulties which bound him to it, he accomplished a work which would have conferred fame upon abilities and endowments far superior to his own. But his good sense, unwavering firmness of purpose, steady loyalty to duty, practical tact, and ready sympathy conspired to render him "the right man in the right place." His piety was unostentatious, but deep and fervent; and no showy exterior gave a counterfeit promise of his real worth. "None knew him but to love" him, or could come in contact with him without feeling that he was a man in whom they could confide. Dr. Dwight—whom he served for a short time as an amanuensis—declared him fully entitled to the epithet of "the beloved disciple;" and the confidence and respect of his co-presbyters—grounded on his well-tried qualities of sound judgment, tact, perseverance, and energy, as well as his learning and piety—are sufficiently attested by their recommendation of him in 1835 to the post of first President of Wabash College. Duty alone extorted his consent to the resignation of his charge. Like the tree rooted deeper by the blasts, his attachment to his people had been strengthened by their common experience of hardship and self-denial. A rare success had also crowned his labors. In a single year of his ministry his church received an accession of nearly two hundred members; and before the close of his pastorate it had become, in spite of its locality and the discouraging nature of much of the surrounding population, large and flourishing. His death occurred during his Presidency of Wabash College, in 1840. His successors were Edwin F. Hatfield[1] (1835–55) and T. Ralston Smith.

The Allen Street Church owed its existence largely to the efforts of Rev. Ward Stafford and Samuel J. Mills, who in the summer of 1816 explored a large and forbidding portion of the city and succeeded in gathering a small congregation. The church was organized in 1819, with twenty-five members, and was supplied till 1827 by William Gray, a city missionary. His successors were Henry White,—called in 1837 to the professorship of Theology in Union Theological Seminary, where he remained until his death in 1852,—William Bradley (1837–39), George B. Cheever (1839–44), D. B. Coe, George Thatcher, and Dr. W. W. Newell.

The Eighth Presbyterian Church, gathered by Dr.

[1] After a twenty years' ministry, called to the pastorate of the North Presbyterian Church.

Stephen Rowan in 1819, had some grave difficulties to contend with, and subsequent to the pastorate of Dr. Rowan's successor, Henry Hunter (1831–35), was merged into the new organization known as Chelsea Church, of which Edward D. Smith (1843) was installed pastor.

Of the Central Presbyterian Church, gathered by the persevering labors of Rev. William Patton in 1819, he was installed pastor in 1822, resigning his charge in 1834. His successors were William Adams (1834–52), A. A. Wood, and —— Dunn. The other churches were—Bowery, subsequently disbanded, but memorable as the scene of the labors of the lamented Christmas, whose successors were Woodbridge and Dickinson; the Spring Street Church, a new organization formed out of the old congregation in 1825, and under the pastorate of H. G. Ludlow (1828–37), who was succeeded in 1837 by W. W. Patton; Union Church, organized 1829[1] under the pastorate of Herman Norton (1830–35); the West Church, organized in 1829, of which David R. Downer (1832–41), Edwin Holt (1842–46), Thomas H. Skinner, Jr., and Thomas S. Hastings, have been successively pastors; the Bleecker Street Church, organized in 1825, of which the pastors have been Matthias Bruen (1825–29), Erskine Mason (1830–51), Joel Parker, and Howard Crosby; and the First Free Presbyterian Church, organized 1830, and under the charge of Joel Parker (1830–33), and E. P. Barrow (1835–37), but in 1838 absorbed in the Tabernacle Church.

The first pastor of the Bleecker Street Church, under whose labors it was gathered in 1825, was Matthias Bruen. Of Puritan ancestry, he was born at Newark, N.J., April 11, 1793. Trained in a pious home, he was hopefully converted in his eighteenth year. From his

[1] Dissolved 1838.

childhood he evinced an uncommon fondness for books, and at the age of fifteen entered Columbia College. Graduated with high honor in 1812, he soon after commenced his theological studies under Dr. John M. Mason, and in 1816 was licensed to preach by the Classis of New York. In 1822, after his return from a voyage to Europe, he commenced his labors as a city missionary. The result was the organization of the church of which he continued the pastor till his early death in 1829. A ripe scholar, a chaste and elegant writer, and fully devoted to his work, his defects as a speaker interfered with his popularity. Yet few have ever commanded greater respect, or more thoroughly secured the esteem, confidence, and affection of their brethren.[1]

His successor, Erskine Mason, was the youngest child of the distinguished John M. Mason, and was born in New York, April 16, 1805. While a student in Dickinson College, the sudden death of an older brother produced a deep impression upon his mind, which led to his conversion. Graduated in 1823, he pursued his theological studies, first under the direction of his cousin, Dr. Duncan, of Baltimore, and subsequently at Princeton Theological Seminary. In 1827, he was installed pastor of the Presbyterian Church at Schenectady, and three years later accepted a call to New York. From 1836 till 1842 he discharged the duties of Professor of Ecclesiastical History in Union Theological Seminary. His pastorate closed with his life, in the meridian of manhood, May 14, 1851.

Dignified, courteous, kind, Dr. Mason was the model of the Christian gentleman. He was frank and unassuming. Yet his intellectual gifts were of a high order. His discourses were perhaps too metaphysical, too much devoted to arguments addressed to the reason. Yet some

---

[1] Sprague, iv. 543.

of his appeals at the close of his sermons were overwhelmingly powerful. Still, he was rather an instructive than a moving preacher. His discourses were all written, and in his later years he abandoned his early *memoriter* method of delivery, and was even closely confined to his manuscript. His style, while elegant, was vigorous and chaste; nor was he lacking in earnestness of utterance. "A masculine imagination gave a glow and warmth to his appeals. His demonstrations were tremulous with emotion, and his proofs were with power, because they were so earnest and sincere."[1]

Joseph Stibbs Christmas, for only a few months (Oct. 1829–March, 1830) pastor of the Bowery Church, was born at Georgetown, Beaver county, Pa., in 1803. In 1819,—when he had already resolved to devote himself to the ministry,—he was graduated at Washington College, with the highest honors. Difficulties interfered with his pursuit of a theological course till 1821, when he became a member of Princeton Seminary. Licensed in 1824 by the Presbytery of Philadelphia, he was immediately invited to the charge of a church just organized in Montreal. After a few years' pastorate his health failed, and he removed to New York. After visiting New Orleans as agent of the Bible Society, and laboring for a time at Bolton, Mass., he accepted the call to the Bowery Church. Here he fell at his post in his twenty-seventh year. Beautiful in person, courteous in manner, meek and unambitious, his social qualities endeared him to all who enjoyed his acquaintance, while his retentive memory, clear, sound, and penetrating understanding, and manliness of intellect and sentiment gave high promise of future eminence. Studious, earnest, and devoted, his sermons glow with the fervor of a Christian spirit and the appeal of ministerial fidelity.

---

[1] Sprague, iv. 708.

The Colored Presbyterian Church was organized January 13, 1822, and numbered twenty-four members. For several years it maintained, under the charge of its pastor, Samuel E. Cornish, a feeble existence. Its house of worship, erected on Elm Street near Canal at a cost of fourteen thousand dollars, passed out of its hands; and the failure of Mr. Cornish's health led to his dismissal in 1828. His successor (1829) was a man of education and culture, a former student at Princeton, and a licentiate of Albany Presbytery,—Theodore S. Wright. Under his ministrations the structure of the German Lutheran Church on the corner of Frankfort and William Streets was secured, and for several years the church enjoyed a large measure of prosperity.

The Synod of Albany at its meeting at Utica in October, 1818, set off from the Presbytery of Oneida that of St. Lawrence.[1] The Rev. Messrs. Jones, Murdock, Isaac Clinton, S. F. Snowden, Judath Highby, and David Banks, with the congregations of Martinsburg and Ogdensburg, composed the new body, embracing the counties of Jefferson, Lewis, and most of St. Lawrence. The first meeting of this body was at Martinsburg, Oct. 31, 1816. In the same year the Presbytery of Otsego was set off from that of Oneida, and numbered seven ministers. In January, 1822,[2] the Ogdensburg—afterward (1828) St. Lawrence—Presbytery, with six ministers, was set off from that of Champlain, and the name of the original St. Lawrence Presbytery was changed (1828) to that of Watertown. Oswego Presbytery, with five ministers, was set off from that of Oneida in 1823; and in 1829, when the Synod of Utica was erected, it consisted of the Presbyteries of Oneida, Watertown, Otsego, St. Lawrence, and Oswego.

At that time[3] Oneida had forty-three ministers and

[1] The Revivalist, 116.
[2] Baird's Digest gives the date 1818.
[3] The Report for 1831.

licentiates and thirty-eight churches; Watertown, fifteen ministers and twenty-six churches; Otsego, eight ministers and fifteen churches; St. Lawrence, ten ministers and nine churches; and Oswego, ten ministers and twenty-two churches: making a total, in connection with the Synod, of eighty-six ministers and one hundred and ten churches.[1]

---

[1] As the necessary limits of this work forbid the insertion of extended details of local interest, I have omitted in this chapter much in reference to the individual churches, which may be found *in extenso* in Hotchkin's "Western New York," and have felt it necessary to reduce to the form of a note what is stated of the churches in the neighborhood of Albany. A large number of these are passed over without notice, as many of them were indebted to missionary labor which was not devoted to this field to any considerable extent before 1822.

The pastors of Albany Presbytery up to 1830 were, at Albany (First Church), Eliphalet Nott (Oct. 3, 1798–Aug. 4, 1804), John B. Romeyn (1804–08), William Neill (1809–16), A. J. Stansbury (1817–21), Henry R. Weed (1822–29), and J. N. Campbell (1830–64); at the Second Church, John Chester (1815–29), and William B. Sprague (1829–); in the Third Church, Hooper Cumming (1817–23), Joseph Hurlbut (1823–24), John Alburtis (1825–28), and William H. Williams (1828–30); at Charlton, Joseph Sweetman (1800–17), Isaac W. Platt (1820–25), and John Clancy (1825–45); at Kingsborough, Elisha Yale (1804–52); at Schenectady, Robert Smith, Jonathan Edwards, s.s. (1801), John B. Romeyn (1803–04), Nathaniel Todd (1805–06), John Joyce, s.s., Alexander Monteith (1809–15), Hooper Cumming (1815–17), Walter Monteith (1820–26), Erskine Mason (1826–30), and Jonathan T. Backus (Dec. 6, 1832–); at Ballston, Joel Bradley (1802–12), Stephen Porter (1812–15), Reuben Smith (1816–25), and James V. Henry (1826–29); at Galway, John J. Christie (1803–12), Joseph Farrar (also in charge of Edinburgh, 1818–21), Adams W. Platt (1829–33); at East Galway, Sylvanus Haight (1808–10), N. W. Wells (1811–18?), William Chester (1820–23), S. Nott (1823–29), Rufus R. Deming (1829–32); at New Scotland, Thomas Holliday (1807–30); at Princetown (formerly Currie's Bush) and Duanesburg, William Boardman, Thomas Holliday (in charge also of New Scotland) (1816–26), and T. Frazier, s.s. (1830–34?); at Amsterdam (and Veddersburg), Halsey A. Wood

The Narrative of the Synod of Albany for 1820 speaks of revivals in Potsdam and Loraine, Clinton, New Hartford, Whitesborough, Utica, Westmoreland, Mt. Vernon, Litchfield and Union, Cooperstown and Sherburne,—the converts in the latter numbering two hundred,—Saratoga Springs, Malta, Stillwater, Ballston, Galway, East Galway, Amsterdam and Schenectady,—in all which the work had been overwhelming, —Schaghticoke, North Pittstown, Nassau, Lansingburg, and other places. But these revivals were but the earnest of far more extended and powerful awakenings which took place in this field some eight or ten years subsequently, and of which mention is elsewhere made.[1]

(1816–25), succeeded by James Wood in 1826; at Stillwater, Mark Tucker (1818–24) and John Blatchford (1825–29); at Saratoga Springs, organized in 1817, Darius O. Griswold (1822–23), and S. H. Whelpley (1825–26); at Esperance, organized in February, 1818, Luke Lyons (1824–27); at Carlisle, organized in 1803, Joel N. Austin (1818–22), and Lyman S. Rexford; at Hadley and Lucerne, received in 1823, Adams W. Platt (1823–28?): at Westerlo, Marcus Smith (1823–26); at Knox and Hamilton Union, J. Judson Buck (1825–28); at Johnstown, Simon Hosack (1790–1832), and Gilbert Morgan (1826–28); at Onesquithaw, Thomas Halliday (1827–29); at Albany (Fourth), E. N. Kirk (1829–38?); at Northampton, and for a time at Edinburgh, Lebbeus Armstrong. Previous to 1830 the churches of Mayfield First (1823) and Second, Greenbush, Rensselaerville, Malta, Moreau, Stratford, and Ephratah had come under the care of Albany Presbytery. Greenfield was for a time united with Milton, of which the pastors were Jonathan Hovey (1816–20), Joseph Bracket (1821–24), James B. Ambler, and Aaron Garrison (1827–29).

[1] In 1816, a minister who had visited the region of which he writes, speaks of the destitution of the field in Northeastern New York. "To the north," he says, "as far as the St. Lawrence, and east to Champlain, there are probably not six gospel ministers,—an extent of territory including the quarter of the State of New York, with a population of seventy or eighty thousand souls, sitting comparatively in a state of darkness and death." Western, Lee, Flo-

Although in the eastern portion of the State the growth of the Church had been steady and even rapid, its increase in the central and western parts had been far more remarkable. The most signal advance was indeed in that region which at the commencement of the century had invited the combined missionary energies of the State societies and the General Assembly.

In 1815, there were not far from one hundred churches in what was then known as Western New York, under the care of Presbyteries. In the fifteen years which followed, the number was multiplied not far from threefold. In 1815, the First Presbyterian Church at Rochester was organized, and the church at Le Roy at about the same time. In 1816 and 1817, those of Cicero, Camillus, West Groton, Clarkson, Orville, Lysander, Genoa Second, Palmyra, Waterloo, Ludlowville, Newfield, Owego, Pulteney, Lewiston, Clarence, Alden, Hamburg, Portland, and Pembroke had been organized, and most of them were received under the care of Presbyteries. To this list of new churches there were added previous to 1820, as near as can be ascertained, those of Wolcott, Scott, Reading, Sweden, East Aurora, Evans, Concord, Sheridan, Jamestown, Byron, Batavia, Sheldon First, China, and Moscow in 1818; those of Cayuga Village, Chili, Wilson, Lancaster, West Aurora, Alexander, Gainesville, Pike, Groveland, and Sparta First in 1819; and in 1820 those of Liverpool, Peruville,

---

rence, Camden, Bengal, Ellisburg, Richland, Rotterdam, and Oswego, some of them "populous towns," and "all of them able to support the gospel," were wholly destitute of a regular ministry.—*Christian Herald*, March, 1816.

A little later a missionary writes, "We could not find one minister settled in the counties of Warren or Essex; in Clinton, only two; in Franklin, two; in St. Lawrence, we could not hear of any; there are very few on the Black River." To a population of one hundred thousand he estimated that there were but ten or twelve regularly ordained ministers.—*Christian Herald*, April, 1816.

South Dansville, Royalton, Knowlesville, Barre Center, Wales, Eden, Ripley, Portage, and others.

From 1820 to 1825 the increase of new churches was equally rapid. During this period more than fifty were organized. Among those most worthy of mention are the Brick Presbyterian Church of Rochester, the churches of Lockport (1823), Preston, Salina, Scipio Second, Penn Yan (1823), Wolcott, Newark, Union, Conklin, Mead's Creek, Southport, Wheeler, Murray, Wheatland, Mendon, Somerset, Porter, Gaines, Niagara Falls, Ellicottsville, Stockton, Westfield, Napoli, Connewango, Mayville, Attica, Wyoming, Sheldon Second, Ossian, Centerville, Black Creek, Olean, Andover, &c.

In the five years which followed, from 1825 to 1830, from thirty to fifty new churches are reported as organized; among them, those of Syracuse, Albion, Cuba, Lodi, Rochester Third, Havanna, Otselic, Portageville, Allen, Dunkirk, West Otto, Ellington, Covington, York Second, Parma, North Bergen, Big Flats, Jasper, Burdet, Jordan, Auburn Second, and Weedsport.

Western New York furnished the chief field for the operations of the United Domestic Missionary Society from the time of its formation, in 1822, until 1826, when it was merged in the American Home Missionary Society. Of its eighty missionaries, at the latter date, nearly all were scattered among the new churches and destitute settlements of this region. Yet, as the churches increased in strength and numbers, they joined in repaying, for the benefit of other fields, what they had so liberally received for their own. The missionary societies which sprang up in the East were not left to stand alone. Churches, counties, and Presbyteries co-operated in behalf of the great interests of the cause of Christ. Missionary and education societies were formed, whose funds—the gifts of poverty—steadily increased. A variety of educational institutions were founded and fostered,—conspicuous among them, Hamilton College and Auburn Seminary.

In 1815, and for several succeeding years, the Connecticut Missionary Society had in its employ from three to five laborers annually in the western portion of the State. They devoted, however, only a portion of their time to itinerant labor. "Father" Spencer exercised a general supervision over the field. In 1818, there were in connection with him three other missionaries employed. David M. Smith, pastor at Lewiston on the Niagara, David Dudley Field, for twenty weeks in the region bordering on Lake Ontario, and Eleazar Fairbanks, on the Holland Purchase, were his co-laborers. At this time, in the tract extending from Oswego to Niagara River, and from the Great Western Road to Lake Ontario,—a tract forty miles wide by one hundred and fifty long,—there were forty Presbyterian and Congregational churches, one-half of which had been formed during the preceding three years. In connection with all upon this field there were but fifteen pastors (or stated supplies), many of them having charge of at least two churches.

In 1815, Batavia had become "a flourishing village." There was a small Congregational church in the town, although but a single professing Christian in the village. Rochester, which in 1812 could boast but fifteen inhabitants, had attained in 1815 to three hundred and thirty-one; and in that year the First Presbyterian Church was organized, with sixteen members. But neither they nor any other denomination had a place of worship. Buffalo was likewise a mere village, and had no church-edifice within its bounds. Yet a congregation had been gathered, to which Miles P. Squier, at the urgent and almost authoritative advice of Dr. Backus, of Hamilton College, had commenced his ministrations a few months previous. The court-house, although in an unfinished state, with temporary benches for seats and the floor as yet unlaid, was used for public worship.

The fifteen years which followed wrought a striking change. At Rochester, Comfort Williams was installed January 17, 1816, although the services were performed in an unfinished store. In the following year a house of worship, forty feet by fifty, was erected, which was replaced in 1824 by the present one, eighty-four by sixty-five feet. Meanwhile the original church had dismissed (1817) nine members to form the nucleus of Brighton Church, and in 1825 the Second (Brick) Presbyterian Church was organized by a colony of twenty members from the First, and shortly after the same number were dismissed with a view to form a Third Church. Yet in 1830 the original church, over which Joseph Penny (1822-32) had been settled as successor of Mr. Williams, numbered over four hundred members, while the Third fell but little short, and the Second reported over two hundred.[1]

A strong church, meanwhile, had been gathered at Buffalo,[2] where Mr. Squier had been succeeded by Sylvester Eaton. But it was not till the completion of the Erie Canal in 1825 that the place received the impulse to which it had been indebted for its subsequent prosperity. In about 1834-35 the Pearl Street Church was organized, and John C. Lord was called to the pastorate.[3]

---

[1] In 1836, Bethel Free Church—now Central Presbyterian—was organized; in December, 1853, St. Peter's Church; and in 1855, Plymouth Congregational Church.

[2] Buffalo was laid out originally in 1801, but gave little promise of its future until 1825, when the opening of the Erie Canal made it the gateway from the Great Valley to the Atlantic States.—*Eighty Years' Progress*, i. 176.

[3] The Free Church was formed at about the same time, and in 1837 George R. Rudd was stated supply. The Park Church, or-

The Narrative of the Synod of Geneva for 1819 was of a most cheering character.[1] Revivals, some of them

ganized about 1839, with Luther H. Angier for pastor, numbered in 1840 a membership of sixty-six, and in 1843, of two hundred and twenty-one. In 1845-46, La Fayette Street Church was formed, Dr. G. W. Heacock, pastor. In 1849, the North Church reported a membership of one hundred and sixty-three, while during the preceding year twenty-three had been received on examination and one hundred and forty-eight by certificate. Rev. Dr. A. T. Chester became during the year the pastor of this church. Dr. A. T. Hopkins, in the First Church (1835-47), was succeeded (1848) by M. L. P. Thompson, who after a pastorate of about eleven years removed to Cincinnati.

[1] In 1817 there were powerful revivals within the bounds of the Synod of Geneva. In Homer there were reported one hundred and fifty-five conversions, and one hundred and five additions to the Church; in Locke, one hundred and seventy conversions, and sixty additions; in Palmyra, one hundred and twenty-six conversions, and one hundred and six additions; while similar revivals to a greater or less extent prevailed in Cazenovia, Pompey Hill, Otisco, Ithaca, Romulus, Lyons, Wolcott, Victor, Livonia, and Middlesex. Something of a work of grace prevailed also in Pompey, Onondaga, Geneva, Gainesville, Bloomfield, Rochester, Buffalo, Hamburg, Eden, Willinck, and Pomfret. Many new congregations were organized during the year, and the demand was urgent for more ministers.—*Christian Herald*, iii. 104.

Ithaca Church, with twenty members in 1816, received in the course of the year ninety additions. Genoa reported forty-four, Lansing, sixty, Aurelius, sixty-nine, and Auburn, two hundred and ten.

At Camillus, as the result of a revival, a church was constituted of about one hundred members.—*Ibid.* v. 21, 29.

It was in immediate connection with these revivals that Auburn Theological Seminary originated. In June, 1818, the committee appointed to consider the matter met at Auburn and appointed a meeting of the Synod at that place in the ensuing autumn. One hundred and ten persons were present, including the President of Hamilton College, and Dr. McAuley, then of Schenectady. The resolution—with the conditions provided—in favor of the institution and its location, were passed with a single dissenting vote.—*Ibid.* 383.

of remarkable power, had been enjoyed in many of the churches of nearly every Presbytery. In connection with the Synod were ninety-two ordained ministers and eleven licentiates. It had under its care one hundred and forty-three churches, embracing more than seven thousand communicants.

The increase in the number of its churches and ministers was pronounced to be almost "without a parallel." In the autumn of 1805 the Presbytery of Geneva —then covering the entire field of the Synod with its eight Presbyteries—was formed, consisting of only three ministers and perhaps eight or ten small Presbyterian churches. In a little over thirteen years its ministers had been multiplied thirty and its churches fifteen fold.

By 1821, the Synod of Geneva had become so large as to render a division expedient, and the Synod of Genesee was erected out of a portion of it. The churches numbered not far from one hundred and fifty, while their membership had increased to nearly ten thousand. The Presbyteries of Niagara, Genesee, Rochester, and Ontario composed the new Synod, with between forty and fifty ministers, seventy-five churches, and in connection with them a membership of over two thousand. In 1823, the Presbytery of Buffalo, with six ministers and twenty-three churches, was formed by a division of Niagara; and in 1825, the churches under the care of the two Synods numbered over two hundred. Such had been the remarkable increase during a single quarter of a century in a region which in 1800 numbered scarcely more than a half-dozen feeble churches.

In 1818 the Synod of Geneva, embracing Central and Western New York, reported six Presbyteries, eighty-two ministers, and one hundred and sixteen churches. Twenty ministers and seventeen hundred and ninety-one communicants had been added during the preceding year.—*Ibid.* 29.

In 1825, the Presbytery of Cortland was erected; in 1826, that of Chenango; in 1828, that of Angelica; and in 1829, that of Tioga. In the same year the Synod of Utica was formed, embracing, as has been stated, the Presbyteries of St. Lawrence, Watertown, Oswego, Oneida, and Otsego, in connection with which were ninety ministers and one hundred and five churches, with a membership of nearly eleven thousand. At this period the Synod of Geneva, with the Presbyteries of Chenango, Cortland, Onondaga, Cayuga, Tioga, Geneva, Bath, and Angelica, embraced one hundred and thirty-four ministers and more than one hundred and sixty churches, with a membership of not far from thirteen thousand five hundred. The Synod of Genesee, with its five Presbyteries already mentioned, embraced seventy-six ministers and one hundred and eleven churches, with a membership of about five thousand three hundred. Thus, in 1830, Central and Western New York contained three Synods, eighteen Presbyteries, three hundred ministers, and more than three hundred and seventy-five churches, with a membership of about thirty thousand. In this field alone, in less than the lifetime of a single generation, the Presbyterian churches had increased in numbers and strength till they nearly equalled the entire Church in 1801,—as represented by the Assembly by which the Plan of Union was formed.

Previous to the period now under review, the churches of Central New York had given evidence of their deep interest in the cause of learning. Hamilton Oneida Academy was incorporated by the Regents, January 31, 1793, mainly through the exertions of Rev Samuel Kirkland, for more than forty years a missionary among the Oneida Indians. By him the trustees of the infant institution were generously presented with the title-deed to several hundred acres of land In 1794, a commodious building was erected, the corner-stone of which was laid by Baron Steuben. The school was opened the same year under Rev. John Niles, whose successors were Rev. Robert Porter, Seth Norton, and Rev. James Robbins, all of them, as well as Kirkland, graduates of Yale College, and, it is believed, well fitted to foster the interests of sound learning and Christian morals.[1]

For eighteen years the academy existed, and attained to a high degree of prosperity. But with the growth of the neighboring settlements, and the rapid development of Western New York, the necessity was felt for an institution which should afford more ample facilities for instruction and a more extended course of study. Clinton and Fairfield became competitors for its location, and college charters of similar character and conditions were granted to each. By a compromise between the friends of the rival locations, Clinton secured to itself the coveted honor. The institution, bearing the name of Hamilton College, was chartered May 26, 1812, and Dr. Azel Backus, eminent as a preacher and a scholar, as well as the successor of Dr. Bellamy at Bethlem, Conn.,

---

[1] In 1793, Samuel Kirkland, missionary to the Indians, devoted a large share of his property towards "laying the foundation and supporting an academy contiguous to the Oneida nation for the mutual benefit of the early settlers of the country, and the various tribes of confederate Indians." After consultation with General Washington, who was at that time an owner of lands in this vicinity, and with other patriotic men of his acquaintance, he granted by deed to Alexander Hamilton and fifteen others about three hundred acres of land in trust for the purpose of building Hamilton Oneida Academy. Soon after, the corner-stone of the academy building was laid by Baron Steuben, with fitting ceremonies. In 1812 the academy was incorporated by the Regents of the University, as Hamilton College.—*Exercises at the Inauguration of President Fisher*, p. 7. In December of the same year Dr. Azel Backus was inaugurated the first President of the institution.

was chosen the first President. Upon his death in December, 1817, Dr. Henry Davis,[1] President for the previous eight years of Middlebury College, was elected his successor, and occupied the post until his resignation in 1833.[2]

---

[1] President Davis was a native of East Hampton, Long Island, and his parents were members of Dr. Buell's church. He was a graduate of Yale College in the class of 1796, and immediately after his graduation was elected tutor in Williams College. Two years later, after being licensed to preach by the Tolland Association, he was chosen tutor in Yale College, and in 1801 was appointed to the Professorship of Divinity in the same institution. This, the state of his health forced him to decline, and in 1806 he accepted a call to the Professorship of the Greek Language in Union College. In 1809 he entered upon the Presidency of Middlebury College, where he remained till 1817. His death occurred at Clinton in 1852.

[2] The successors of President Davis have been Sereno E. Dwight in 1833, Joseph Penny in 1835, Simeon North in 1839, and Samuel Ware Fisher in 1858. The lack of a sufficient endowment has been a serious obstruction to the full success and efficiency of the institution. Its prosperity was, moreover, seriously affected by dissensions between the trustees and the Presidents, from 1819 to 1832, and during the same period insubordination among the students was not infrequent. From 1838 to 1846, the college received three thousand dollars annually from the State: but the present constitution, upon going into effect, cut it off from the balance previously appropriated, and the grant has since been discontinued. By a free admission of students unable to pay tuition-fees, the funds of the institution were seriously affected, and the receipts from this source reduced to one-fourth of their former amount. The financial affairs of the college, consequently, became greatly embarrassed. To the relief demanded, and to secure which special efforts, with flattering prospects of success, have been made, the institution is well entitled. Many of the ministers of Central New York have here received their academical education.

The sum of fifty thousand dollars was granted by the State, June 19, 1812, to aid in the founding of the college. William H. Maynard, of Utica, in 1832, gave twenty thousand dollars to endow a Professorship of Law, and S. Newton Dexter, of Whitesborough, in 1826, gave his personal obligations for fifteen thousand dollars to

Outside of the city of New York, some of the leading Presbyterian ministers of the State during this period were Ezra Fisk, of Goshen (1810–33), John Johnston, of Newburgh (1806–55), David Porter, of Catskill (1803–47), Seth Williston, of Durham, Gideon N. Judd, of Montgomery, N. S. Prime, of Cambridge, Samuel Blatchford, of Lansingburg, N. S. S. Beman, of Troy, John Chester, of Albany, Elisha Yale, of Kingsborough, President Nott, of Union College, Simon Hosack, of Johnstown, D. C. Lansing, of Auburn, William Wisner, of Ithaca, David Higgins, of Bath, President Davis, of Hamilton College, Henry Axtell, of Geneva, John W. Adams, of Syracuse, Caleb Alexander, of Onondaga, Ebenezer Fitch, of West Bloomfield, Miles P. Squier, of Buffalo, and Joseph Penny, of Rochester, together with Professors Richards, Perrine, and Mills, of Auburn Seminary.[1]

In 1801, Dr. Alexander attended the commencement at Dartmouth College, and there became acquainted with Dr. Packard, of Shelburne, Mass. By his invitation, Dr. Alexander was induced to spend a few weeks with him, while an interesting work of grace was going forward in his parish. As the two men were walking past a house, Dr. P. said to his companion, "There! I wish you would go and talk with that *chunk* of a boy who stands by the fence yonder." Dr. Alexander did so, as faithfully as he could, never expecting to see or hear of him again. A number of years passed, and a stranger passing through Princeton called at Dr. Alexander's study. He said, "You are Dr. Alexander: do you remember that you spent a few weeks in Shelburne,

endow a Professorship of the Greek and Latin Languages. The observatory was built in 1854, at a cost of five thousand dollars.

[1] For the sketches which follow, as well as for those of the clergy of New York City, I have been very much indebted to Sprague's Annals.

Mass., many years ago?" "I do," was the reply. "Do you remember that Dr. Packard asked you one morning to talk with a *chunk* of a boy that stood by the fence?" "The circumstance," replied Dr. Alexander, "had long been forgotten, but I now recall it to mind." "That chunk of a boy," said the stranger, "was myself. The words you spoke to me were blessed to my spiritual good. I date my conversion to that time. My name is Ezra Fisk. I am pastor of a church in Goshen, N.Y."

Young Fisk pursued his studies preparatory to entering college with Dr. Packard, and in 1809—after associating as a kindred spirit with Mills and Richards, in a sense the originators of the American Board of Missions—was graduated at Williams College. In 1813, he commenced a pastorate of upwards of twenty years at Goshen. Elected to the Professorship of Ecclesiastical History in the Western Theological Seminary, he resigned his charge (1833), set out for his new field of labor, but died upon his journey.

With a fine person, a pleasant voice, accurate and distinct utterance, varied and enlivened by special emphasis, he was an acceptable and graceful speaker. In the pulpit, his air was solemn, and at times earnest and tender. A careful student, he presented the truth in its clearest outline to the understanding, rarely rising to any flights of imagination, and never sinking to any thing commonplace. As a friend he was kind-hearted and affectionate, as a critic keen and discriminating, as a counsellor eminently judicious, and as a pastor scrupulously faithful in the discharge of his duties.

Somewhere about the year 1798, a youth, with an ardent desire to secure himself an education, had engaged, in order to procure funds,—on his father's death and with his mother's consent,—to sell a portion of the stock on the farm where he had labored as a boy for several years. Having driven the cattle into the counties of Dutchess and Westchester, he stopped on his way home at Yorktown to spend the night. Before light in the morning, he was waked by two little boys in a trundle-bed near him, talking about God, and asking whether he could see them,—whether he could see them in the dark, could see them if they covered their heads with a blanket, &c. The conversation arrested his attention, and upon his mind, then oppressed by a sense of his solitude as a stranger, as well as perhaps by the death of his father, a deep and enduring impression was made. His character and purpose were decided by the trivial incident. He became a minister of the gospel, and forty years afterward narrated the incident as illustrative of the important influence of seemingly unimportant events. Among his hearers—for it was at a dinner-party during the meeting of the Synod of New York—there was present a gentleman who, on inquiring when and where the circumstances occurred, said, with quivering lips and eyes filled with tears, "I am one of those two little boys, and am here as a ruling elder in the Presbyterian Church." The minister was Dr. Johnston, of Newburgh.

After his graduation at Princeton, he commenced his theological studies with President Smith, and, on the burning of the college edifice and library, crossed the Alleghanies, and spent nearly two years with Dr. McMillan in completing his theological course. In 1807, after having been engaged as a teacher, and spending some time in the supply of vacant churches in the bounds of the Presbytery, he was settled at New Windsor and Newburgh,—in and after 1810 confining his labors to the latter place. At the time of his settlement, the town was the hotbed of infidelity. The leading politicians, lawyers, and physicians were avowed disciples of Tom Paine. That wretched apostate and apostle of infidelity, "Blind Palmer,"[1] received here a cordial welcome from "The Society of the Ancient Druids." Religion, it need hardly be said, was in an exceedingly languishing condition, and the Church was in any thing but a promising state. Yet Dr. Johnston lived to see the barren waste bloom like a garden of the Lord, and again and again was he permitted to witness large and blessed harvests. Five successive revivals prevailed during the period from 1812 to 1831, and added largely to the strength and efficiency of the Church. The transformation wrought was largely due to the fidelity of his labors.

With nothing that could be denominated eloquence or profound learning, and discarding, moreover, all the arts of the polemic, he devoted himself, in a plain, simple, earnest way, to the preaching of the gospel,—which he thoroughly understood. He never affected a show of logic or metaphysical refinement, but dealt rather in pungent appeal and tender entreaty. Out of the pulpit, he was the model of dignified affability; and, with his warm heart, genial temper, quick sympathies, and a liveliness of conversation enriched sometimes by playful anecdote and at others by pious remark, he was everywhere welcome, and by the bedside of the sick, or amid the sorrows of the poor and afflicted, or in the innocent social gathering, his presence was sure of a cordial greeting. With a rare antiquarian taste, he had accumulated, through a long course of years, a mass of biographical and historical facts, of local or of general interest; and his memory must have been a rare thesaurus of biographical incident and studious observation. His reverence for ecclesiastical courts was extreme. He seemed to regard the General Assembly as the most august convention of men in the

---

[1] Who figures in Grant Thorburn's Reminiscences.

wide world; and when he was informed of his election as a Director of the Princeton Seminary, the perturbing flutter which it occasioned was not a little amusing, when narrated by himself. Perhaps beyond most of his contemporaries he might have sat for Goldsmith's limning of the Village Pastor,—

> "Who ne'er had changed nor wished to change his place."

A far different man was Dr. David Porter, of Catskill, a man of real genius, of great intellectual power, and of most unquestionable piety. A graduate of Dartmouth College in 1784, the pastor at Spencertown from 1787 to 1803 and at Catskill from 1803 to 1831, he survived the demission of his pastorate twenty years, and died at the ripe age of fourscore years and ten. A Congregationalist by education, he became a Presbyterian from choice and conviction, feeling the importance of a Session for the administration of discipline. As a pastor he was eminently faithful, ever realizing the solemn responsibility of his office. His discernment was quick and keen, his discrimination accurate, his judgment sound, and his reasoning faculties of a high order. In dealing with cases of conscience or practical difficulties, his course was eminently judicious. In the pulpit he gave ample proof of his vigorous intellect, and his style and manner of speaking were characteristic of his strong, original mind, and adapted to make a deep impression. He scorned the ornaments of a flowery rhetoric or fascinating imagery. All was clear, concise, forcible, perspicuous. His earnestness and sincerity were transparent.

Few men were ever more revered or loved. The children regarded him as a superior being. One speaks of having always associated him with the highest peak of the Catskills. Another had confused and very interchangeable ideas of Dr. Porter and the Saviour.

But, with years, reverence ripened into affection, though his presence never lost its impressiveness. With a head like the First Napoleon's, a short neck, a body large and fleshy, and legs unusually small, his uniform practice was to carry a large cane; and it is not strange that, as he walked abroad, his very appearance, as well as his quick, nervous, and even awkward motions, tended to arrest attention. If asked to describe him, those who knew him well would reply that he could not be described. "You cannot put him into words. He is the oddest man you ever saw." His peculiarities and eccentricities were numberless. He had an inexhaustible fund of wit and humor, but he never poured it out in malice. He was a shrewd reader of men's hearts, yet he never sported with their foibles. His treasures of thought and learning were almost unrivalled, yet they were never used for display; and no one could have a more thorough contempt for mere verbiage. He often had occasion to say to others,—especially in prayer,—"Be short;" and his own practice conformed to his precept. His *power of silence* was remarkable. He could bear an impertinence, and gaze into vacancy till it had evaporated into a folly that needed no reply. Few men ever manifested greater disinterestedness or devotion to the cause of Christ. Each of the benevolent societies—tract, Bible, missions—found in him an early and a steadfast friend. His sympathies were as broad as the gospel he preached. When he retired from his pastoral charge, he did not retire from active service in his Master's cause. For this "to beg" he was not ashamed, and he did it with a tact, energy, and success rarely surpassed.

And yet, though conscious of his power, he had the simplicity and guilelessness of a child. His heart was unusually kind, gentle, and affectionate. His eccentricities were unstudied, the natural expression of the man. Yet he was characterized ever by a deep humility. He adored with his whole heart the gospel of his salvation. No one that ever heard him exclaim, with his own peculiar intonation and emphasis, "I'm a miracle of grace, sir: I'm a miracle of grace," could doubt—whatever might be thought of his Hopkinsian leanings—that he had sat with Paul at the Master's feet. In speaking of personal piety, he dwelt, to the end of his life, on his great sinfulness. Of the divine grace he would say, "It is an ocean without a shore." "My transgressions are like mountains piled on mountains." "I *hope* to be saved, sir," he once said to Dr. Dickinson, "but I'm an awful sinner, sir,—an awful sinner. If I am seen in heaven, sir, it will astonish the universe." The benedictions of hundreds of grateful and loving hearts followed him to the grave.

Quite unlike him, and yet with the same downright sturdy energy of purpose and consecration to his work, was that veteran, Seth Williston, of Durham. A hardy pioneer in Central and Western New York at the commencement of the century, a large though scarcely voluminous writer, with more of strength than grace in his utterance, and with a hand and heart alike ready for every good word and work, his name deserves the honor ever due to those who, in the lack of brilliant gifts, consecrate their lives to aims of highest usefulness. His untiring energy, perseverance, and fidelity were crowned with results such as a sanctified ambition might well covet. His rigid adherence to some of the Hopkinsian tenets never interfered with his spirituality of conversation, or the benevolent spirit of his life. He had reached his eighty-first year when he died in 1851.

Gideon N. Judd was the successor of Dr. Porter at Catskill, although some of his earlier years were devoted to the pastorate of the Bloomfield Church, New Jersey.

He was not specially eminent as a preacher, nor had he the character or faculties which inspire awe or impress the hearer with a sense of hidden power. Yet he was well read, a good scholar, a judicious counsellor, an affectionate preacher, and a lovely man. In his gentleness and meekness was the secret of his success. If he did not command the homage of greatness, he won the confidence due to goodness. His spirit was eminently conciliatory. He could not quarrel. In him, nature and grace alike forbade it. In a clear, chaste, and graceful style he presented the truths which to his own heart had evinced their cheering, consoling, and sustaining power.

John Chester, of Albany, had been settled at Hudson for five years before he commenced his pastorate of the Second Presbyterian Church, gathered (1815) in the capital of the State. A native of Wethersfield, Conn., he had been graduated at Yale in 1804, and his theological studies had been pursued with Dr. Lyman, of Massachusetts. At Hudson he was eminently successful in regathering the scattered congregation and stirring them up to active effort. In Albany he had the satisfaction of seeing the new enterprise in which he had engaged a complete success; and before his decease, in 1829, its membership had risen to over three hundred. With untiring assiduity he devoted himself to the best interests of his own flock, and, indeed, to all the temporal and spiritual interests of humanity within his reach.

In all his deportment, he was the model of a Christian gentleman. Graceful in manner, genial in spirit, and with a ready tact to adapt himself to every occasion, he readily secured the affection and strong and lasting attachment of his people. In the pulpit, his commanding person and somewhat florid style favorably impressed the great mass of those that heard him; and, though he could scarcely lay claim to remarkable eloquence or profound learning, he exerted, wherever he went, a powerful influence. With quick and kindly sympathies, and a heart alive to every claim of a true philanthropy, it was not strange that at times his hearers should have been melted under the pathos of his tender appeals. Toward the close of his ministry, the "new measures" dispensation opened upon the churches of the region; but from him it received no countenance. He regarded it with distrust, and felt assured that its results could not fail to be disastrous. His successor in the pastorate of the church was (Dr.) William B. Sprague.

At Troy, the pastorate of Dr. Coe continued until his death in 1822. His successor was (Dr.) Nathan S. S. Beman, who, after having been settled at Portland, Me., and after laboring for some ten years in the destitute regions of Georgia, was called to the charge of what had now become a large and flourishing church, numbering soon after his accession nearly five hundred members. In the full maturity of his powers, with an energy of will and purpose equal to his abilities, and in charge of the largest and almost the wealthiest church in the northern portion of the State, it was inevitable that he should wield a powerful and commanding influence. Zealous in the cause of revivals, with a liberality almost fierce in the construction of the "new measures," and with a chivalry that not only knew no fear, but stood ready to challenge whatever wore the aspect of illiberality or bigotry, he was a man whom few could safely meet in controversy, and whom none could regard with indifference. By nature fitted to lead and unfitted to follow, he assumed a prominent position in the controversies with which the Church was agitated. His *sobriquet* of "The War-Horse," while it did injustice perhaps to his kindlier sensibilities, paid only a just tribute to the adventurous daring with which he rushed forward, against all odds, to encounter what he regarded as the hostility of error. For such a service nature had richly endowed him. With a clear purpose, a resolute energy, a seeming unconsciousness of fear, a ready utterance, and a perfect command of appropriate and forcible language, he was an antagonist whom no man could afford to despise.

In President Nott of Union College were united some of the rarest qualities that are to be found combined in a single individual. A clear and sagacious thinker, yet an eloquent declaimer, wise in general administration, and yet capable of noting in detail every practical subject, commanding respect, yet conciliating affection, of unwavering firmness, yet judicious in resorting to expedients when the emergency demanded, his name is associated not only with the interests of the institution over which he presided, but with the interests and welfare of the Church throughout the region, for more than half a century. Sent out by the Connecticut Society in 1796 as a missionary, and with decided preferences for the Congregational system, under which he had been educated, his intercourse with John Blair Smith, of Union College, early led to a change in his views, and of the Plan of Union he became a warm and steadfast champion. Henceforth his name was identified with the interests and growth of the Presbyterian Church. He labored as a pastor successively at Cherry Valley and at Albany, and with such reputation that on the death of the President of Union College he was elected in 1804 to the vacant office.

His early experience had led him to philosophical reflection on the methods of training youth, and dispensing largely with the harsh measures of a stern authority. The conclusions which he reached were practically embodied in his successful administration of one of the most important collegiate institutions in the land. Calm, sagacious, judicious, but decided. governed by cool reason rather than passion or enthusiasm, he was fitted by nature to hold an even balance between opposing parties, and to set forth his own views in a clear and convincing light. While tenacious of his own convictions, he was capable of making a just allowance for those of persons who differed with him; and if he failed to convince, he never allowed himself to exasperate. In the councils of the Church his suggestions always commanded respect, and, while eschewing the asceticism of religious duty, his aims were governed by a liberal and enlightened piety.

Samuel Blatchford, of Lansingburg, was a native of England, and was educated at the Dissenting College of Homerton. After laboring successively at Kingsbridge and Topsham, near Exeter, he emigrated to this country in 1795, and preached successively at Bedford. Greenfield, and Bridgeport, until, in 1804, he was called to the charge of the churches of Lansingburg and Waterford. Here he remained until his death in 1828.

Of dignified manner, well-balanced mind, no slight dexterity in argument, and a thorough devotion to the work of the ministry, Dr. Blatchford was a sober and well-read theologian, and an "able minister of the New Testament." With an enlarged Christian philanthropy he hailed with gratulation the formation of the various benevolent societies designed to evangelize the country and the world. Generous and hospitable, his heart overflowed with kindness and charity. In the social circle he gave full evidence of his vigorous powers and his treasures of thought. In the pulpit, where his manner was easy and natural, he was always instructive. never tame or commonplace, and occasionally rising to a manly eloquence.

Dr. Elisha Yale, of Kingsborough, was a native of Lee, Mass. He never enjoyed the advantages of a collegiate education; but his studies—academic and theological—were pursued at first under his own pastor, Dr. Shepard, and subsequently under Dr. Perkins, of West Hartford, Conn. In 1803 he was licensed by the North Association of Hartford county, and in 1804 took charge of the church of Kingsborough, continuing in the pastorate for a period of nearly fifty years, and nearly to the time of his death in 1853. Although till a recent period his church continued Congregational, he was a Presbyterian from choice and conviction. With little that was prepossessing in his appearance and manner, none that knew him could doubt his sterling integrity or firmness of purpose. Never remarkably popular as a preacher, neither ornate in style nor elegant and graceful in delivery, his sermons were rich in sound thought, combining in judicious proportion the doctrinal, practical, and experimental, and characterized by a lucid arrangement. His devotion to his pastoral charge was exemplary, and his zeal for missions untiring. He trained his church to share his own sympathies and respond to the claims of Christian evangelization throughout the world.

The church of Johnstown, under the pastorate of Dr. Hosack, which, commencing in 1799, extended through a period of more than forty years, was one of the largest and most prosperous in the northern part of the State. By him the church of Carlisle was organized in 1803, and for a long period he was the patriarch of the Presbytery, by his long and tried service commanding universal respect and confidence.

Passing westward, we meet at Auburn Dirck C. Lansing, a graduate of Yale College in 1804, a theological pupil of Dr. Blatchford, the founder in 1806 of the Onondaga Church, and from 1816 to 1829 the pastor of the First Presbyterian Church at Auburn, where more than one thousand persons were gathered into the Church under his ministry of twelve years. An earnest friend of "protracted meetings" and revival measures, he labored here, and subsequently, though in enfeebled health, with great zeal at Utica, in Central and Western New York, and at length as a Congregational pastor in New York and Brooklyn. His life, eminently laborious, useful, and successful, closed in 1857, at the age of seventy-two.

In connection with the Theological Seminary at Auburn were several whose names should not be passed unnoticed. This institution, projected by the Synod of Geneva in 1818, was incorporated in 1820, and went into operation in October of the following year. Dr. James Richards, of Newark, N.J., was elected Professor of Theology; Dr. M. L. R. Perrine, of New York City, Professor of Ecclesiastical History and Church Polity; and Henry Mills, of Woodbridge, N.J., Professor of Biblical Criticism and Oriental Languages. Dr. Richards declined his appointment, and the duties of his professorship were discharged by Dr. Perrine until the founding of the Richards Professorship in 1823.[1]

Dr. Perrine was "an Israelite indeed," a man of lovely spirit, and, though lacking perhaps in executive talents, of fair ability, clear perceptions, and devoted piety. His sincerity was transparent, and his Christian character inspired confidence and respect. In 1836 he fell at his post, honored and lamented. Of Dr. Richards mention has already been made. Dr. Mills has

---

[1] The professors of the seminary have been Dr. Richards (1823-43), Henry Mills, Dirck C. Lansing (temporarily), Dr. Perrine (1821-36), Dr. S. H. Cox (1834-38), Dr. Luther Halsey (1836-44), Dr. Baxter Dickinson (1839-47), Dr. Laurens P Hickok (1845-), Samuel M. Hopkins, John Few Smith, Ezra Huntington, and Edwin Hall.

been spared to perform the duties of a protracted period of useful service in the cause of Christian learning.

From 1812 to 1849, Henry Axtell was the pastor of the Presbyterian Church of Geneva. The revivals of 1819 and 1825 resulted each in adding to it nearly one hundred communicants; and in successive years his labors were crowned with the Divine blessing. With nothing of polish in speech or manner, he thoroughly understood his work, and was master of the method of accomplishing it.[1]

The name of Caleb Alexander, of Onondaga, is more intimately associated with the general interests of the Church than with any local sphere of labor. For twenty years he had been settled as a pastor in New England before his removal as missionary of the Massachusetts Society, in 1801, to Central New York. The founding of Fairfield Academy was due to his efforts; and Hamilton College and Auburn Seminary—the Presidency of the former of which he saw fit to decline—were largely indebted to his sagacity and his exertions in their behalf.

Azel Backus, the first President of Hamilton College, was born at Norwich, Conn., Oct. 13, 1765. In 1787 he was graduated at Yale College, and in 1791 was settled at Bethlem, Conn., as the successor of Dr. Bellamy. Here he remained till his acceptance of the

---

[1] B. B. Stockton was a native of Hackettstown, N.J., where he was born in 1790. A graduate of Middlebury College and Andover Seminary, he was ordained by Utica Presbytery in 1812, and travelled subsequently extensively in the United States, everywhere finding acceptance as an earnest and popular preacher. His life-work was mostly performed in Western New York. He was a member of Rochester Presbytery from its organization till 1858. He labored at different periods in connection with the churches of Skaneateles, Palmyra, Pompey, Camillus, Le Roy, Brockport, Montgomery, Geneseo, and Phelps. His death occurred at Brooklyn, Jan. 10, 1861.

Presidency, the duties of which he was spared to discharge for only about five years. With keen discernment of character, scholarly attainments, ready tact, and warm sympathies, he excelled as a teacher, while in the pulpit his peculiar, though natural, eloquence was often deeply impressive. He was master of a style which—in spite of an imagination vivid and powerful, but too unchastened—was simple, clear, concise, and remarkably energetic. His illustrations were admirable, his thoughts striking, and his wit not only keen but exuberant. As a pastor he was beloved, and as a teacher respected.

CHAPTER XXXIII.

OHIO, 1816-1830.

In 1818, the region of the Western Reserve in Ohio was occupied by the three Presbyteries of Hartford, formed from Erie in 1808, Grand River, formed from Hartford in 1814, and Portage, formed from Grand River in 1818. Huron was erected from Portage in 1823; and in 1825, Grand River, Portage, and Huron were constituted the Synod of the Western Reserve. In 1826, the Presbytery of Detroit, with five ministers, was erected. In 1827, Trumbull, formed from Grand River, with eleven members, was likewise connected with the Synod. To these was added, in 1830, the Presbytery of Cleveland, formed from that of Huron, and consisting of fourteen members.

The Presbytery of Hartford, remaining in connection with the Synod of Pittsburg, consisted in 1814 of fifteen ministers, and had under its care thirty-four congregations on the eastern border and in the northeastern part of the State. In 1830, it had but thirteen ministers and thirty-one congregations. During nearly the entire period, Thomas E. Hughes continued at Mt. Pleasant. The pastorates of James Satterfield at Moorfield and Hubbard, Clement Valandingham at New Lisbon, and Robert Semple at New Castle and Slippery Rock, remained unchanged. William Woods had succeeded William Matthews at Neshanock, Ward Stafford had succeeded William Wick at Youngstown, Joshua Beer had removed from Springfield and Canton to Middle Sandy and Bethesda, James Wright had become pastor of Poland and Westfield, William Reed had succeeded Ezekiel Glasgow at New Salem in conjunction with Long's Run, while William McLean had succeeded him at Beavertown, Robert Dilworth was settled at Pleasant Valley, and was stated supply of Middle Beaver, William O. Stratton had succeeded John Bruce at Ellsworth, and had charge also of Canfield, and William Nesbit was pastor of Hopewell. The other churches of the Presbytery, eleven in number, were vacant.

In 1814, when the Synod of Ohio was erected, it consisted of the three Presbyteries of Lancaster, Washington, and Miami. In 1817, Richland was formed from Lancaster, and consisted of six ministers and about twenty congregations. In 1821, Columbus and Cincinnati were erected, the latter from Miami. Athens was formed from Lancaster in 1822, and Oxford from Cincinnati in 1829.

In 1829, the Synod of Cincinnati was erected. It consisted of the Presbyteries of Chillicothe, Miami, Cincinnati, and Oxford; while the Synod of Ohio was composed of the central Presbyteries of Columbus, Richland, Lancaster, Athens, and Cleveland. The Presbyteries of Hartford and Steubenville (1818), both for the most part within the bounds of the State of Ohio, were connected with the Synod of Pittsburg.

Thus, in little more than fifteen years, the Presbyteries had increased from four to fifteen, the ministers from about forty-four to two hundred and sixteen, and the congregations from less than one hundred and fifteen to more than three hundred and sixty. The increase had been at the rate of more than three hundred per cent. during the period.

On the Western Reserve the number of churches under the care of the Presbyteries rapidly increased from 1816 to 1830. Those of Bricksville, Harrisville, Bristol, Brookfield, Ellsworth, and Farmington were organized in 1816; Strongsville, Lyme, and Fowler in 1817; Vermillion, Sheffield, Atwater, Shalersville, Andover First, Huntsburg, Milan, and Peru in 1818; Fitchville, Brunswick, Granger, Greene, Richfield, Wadsworth, Conneaut, Morgan, Rome, Brooklyn, Bainbridge, Kirtland, Sandusky, Brownhelm, and Medina in 1819; Cleveland Village Church, Chester, Thompson, and Bozetta in 1820; Ashtabula and Bloomfield in 1821; Clarksfield, Greenfield, Wakeman, Carlisle, Ridgeville, Ravenna, Turinsburg, and Hartford in 1822; Pierpont, Berlin, New Haven, Columbia, Bath, Edenburg, and Franklin in 1823; Windsor, Parkman, and Elyria in 1824; Gustavus, Hubbard, and Southington in 1825; Claridon, Ruggles, Austintown, and Weathersfield in 1827; Hinckley and Freedom in 1828; Monroe and Batavia in 1829; Madison Second, Montville, Norwalk, Penfield, and Westfield in 1830.[1]

In the five years that followed, the increase of the churches was yet more rapid. Colebrook and Orwell, Russell, Ridgefield and Monroe, Jefferson, Newbury, Guilford, Western Reserve College Church, Middlebury, and Kinsman were organized in 1831; Lenox, Florence, Sharon, Brimfield, Millsford, Liberty, Mecca, Mesopotamia, Milton, and Newton in 1832; Willoughby, Troy,

---

[1] American Quarterly Register, vol. viii.

York, Akron, Northfield, Sheffield, Williamsfield and Wayne, Newburg, Litchfield, and Streetsborough in 1833; Solon, Chardon, Concord, Unionville, Munson, Richmond, Ripley, Grafton, Legrange, Oberlin, Cheatham, La Fayette, Cuyahoga Falls, Deerfield, Garrettsville, and West Farmington in 1834; and New Lyme, Rockport, Le Roy, Bronson, Huron, Amherst, Avon, Olmstead, Wellington, Brighton, Weymouth, and Canfield First in 1835.

Thus on this field alone, from 1816 to 1830, nearly seventy-five new churches were organized, and from 1830 to 1835, sixty more, or something over one hundred and thirty in all. Many of these were Congregational in their form of government, but were, for the most part, under the care of Presbyteries. By far the larger portion of them were quite feeble, and unable, unless by missionary aid or in conjunction with others, to sustain a pastor. Several were destitute, for long periods, not only of pastoral aid, but of stated supply.

In 1825, quite a large number of the early ministers of the region were still laboring within its bounds, although only a few remained in their first places of settlement. Joseph Badger was at Gustavus, Dr. Cowles at Austinburg, E J. Woodruff at Wayne, N. B. Derrow at Vienna, Jonathan Leslie without charge at Harpersfield, Harvey Coe at Vernon, Luther Humphrey at Burton, J W. Curtis at Warren, Caleb Pitkin[1] at Charlestown, John Field at Atwater, John Seward at Aurora, William Hanford at Hudson, Joseph Treat at Windham, and Simeon Woodruff at Richfield. Five years later, Cowles, Woodruff. Leslie, Pitkin, Seward, Hanford. Treat, Badger, and Coe were nearly all that remained of the pioneer ministers of the region. At this time,

[1] Born at New Hartford, Conn , 1781, settled at Milford (1807-16) and Charlestown (1817-28), resided subsequently at Hudson till his death, Feb. 5, 1864.

only nine churches on the entire field numbered a membership of over one hundred. These were Wayne, Harpersfield and Geneva, Kingsville, Austinburg, Tallmadge, Hudson, Warren, Kinsman and Vernon, and Euclid.

The results secured during the period from 1815 to 1830 had not been achieved without earnest and persevering effort. The rush of immigration threatened to defeat the efforts to establish religious institutions adequate to the wants of the region. The constant demand, especially from the region of the Reserve, where religious privileges were best appreciated, was for a supply of ministers for the gathering congregations or newly-organized churches.

In 1815, when Luther Humphrey was settled at Burton, he was the only minister in a county adjoining which were a number of destitute settlements. There was a greater demand for preaching than the ministers could supply. Many places seemed desirous of settling pastors if they could be obtained. Numerous settlements could scarcely obtain "a Sabbath's preaching in the year." "More missionaries," writes Mr. Cowles, "are greatly needed here." "The state of the Church appears in this country," says Mr. Leslie, "to be progressive. In every part of the Reserve, an increasing attention to worship on the Sabbath appears observable. We need more ministers. Throughout the extensive bounds of this Synod there is a general cry,—*Give us ministers:* but we have them not."[1]

---

[1] The report of the Synod of Ohio for 1819 showed that it consisted of the four Presbyteries of Washington, Lancaster, Miami, and Richland. In connection with these were forty-eight ordained ministers, of whom forty-one were settled, three candidates, and two licentiates. The congregations numbered one hundred and twenty-six, of which sixty-one were statedly supplied, while sixty-five were vacant. Of the latter, sixteen were able and forty-nine unable to support a minister. The reports of fifty-nine congrega-

The Connecticut Society had in its employ at this time, in the region of the Reserve, twelve missionaries, most of them settled pastors who devoted a portion of their time to itinerant labor in the region around them. Of these, Rev. John Seward was settled at Aurora, Rev. Abraham Scott at Steubenville, Simeon Woodruff at Tallmadge, William Hanford at Hudson, and Luther Humphrey at Burton and Canton. The Synod of Pittsburg heartily welcomed the laborers sent out and sustained by the Connecticut Society. "The harmony which prevailed," says Rev. William Hanford, "and the conciliatory spirit which was manifested towards the New England divines, was not only pleasant, but really delightful." The missionaries of the society and the members of the Synod realized that they were brethren engaged in a common cause. All felt alike the greatness of this work. "Churches" were "forming in different places, and the cry" was "everywhere, *Come over and help us.*" The ministers often felt themselves overtasked. Rev. Luther Humphrey, by no means preeminent above his brethren, says, "During twenty-five weeks of missionary labor, I preached one hundred and seventy-six times." "Multitudes," writes Mr. Scott, "are perishing for lack of knowledge."

In the neighborhood of Granville, the state of things was much the same as in the bounds of the Reserve. Rev. Timothy Harris performed efficient service in this region. "Many," he writes, "are the calls around me for preaching; and it is truly affecting to know the wants of many and hear their calls, and not be able to go to them with the bread of life. I hope the God of

---

tions showed the number of communicants to be five thousand one hundred and sixty-seven. Reports from others would probably have swelled the number to near seven thousand.—*Christian Herald,* vi. 600.

mercy will soon multiply faithful ministers in this widely-extended field of usefulness."

In 1815, Rev. William R. Gould commenced his labors at Gallipolis, already "a county-seat and a flourishing town," but without a minister.[1] Here he gathered a congregation, formed a church, and was invited to the pastorate. His tours through the surrounding region were extensive. "There are now," he writes, "some truly religious people scattered through every part of the State. Missionaries have, therefore, a home in almost every place, and appointments are expeditiously circulated."

Cleveland was settled by a single family in 1799, and for many years gave but feeble promise of the rank which it was destined to assume among the cities of the West.[2] In 1825, when the Erie Canal, which gave the first impulse to its prosperity, was opened, it did not number a population of over seven hundred. In 1820, the First Presbyterian Church was organized, and, until the settlement of Dr. S. C. Aiken as pastor in 1835, was successively supplied by Messrs. Stone, McLean, Bradstreet, Hutchings, and Keep.[3] In 1830 there were but three or four male members of the church in the town, while the whole number of communicants was less than forty. In 1836 the membership had increased to nearly two hundred; and in 1834 the "Village Church," on the west side of the river, was gathered, under the labors of John Keep.

---

[1] This town was originally settled by *French infidels*, and neither the *place* nor church enjoyed much prosperity.—F.

[2] In June, 1801, when Mr. Badger visited Cleveland, he found there but two families. In 1803 he writes of it, "Infidelity and profaning the Sabbath are general in this place. They bid fair to grow into a hardened, corrupt society."—*Memoir*, p. 46. See also "Eighty Years' Progress."

[3] Report of U. D. M. S. for 1825, p. 62.

In the Presbytery of Cleveland (in 1830), Stephen Peet had succeeded Thomas Barr (1820) at Euclid, Stephen V. Barnes was at Medina and Brunswick, the former numbering but fourteen and the latter sixteen members, John Jay Shipherd was at Elyria, Alfred H. Betts at Brownhelm, Simeon Woodruff at Strongsville, Joel Talcott at Wellington, while nine churches were vacant, and the others had stated supplies.

In the Presbytery of Columbus, Dr. Hoge was settled at Columbus, William Burton at Circleville, Henry Van Deman at Delaware, Radnor, and Liberty, Abner Leonard at Truro, while he was also stated supply of Middletown. Fourteen of the churches had stated supplies, and eight were vacant. Columbus had a membership of two hundred and twenty-two, Circleville of one hundred and twenty, Mt. Pleasant of seventy-five, and Wellington of seventy.

In Richland Presbytery, James Snodgrass was settled at Sugar Creek and Pigeon Run, James Scott at Mt. Vernon, William Matthews at Hopewell, Archibald Hanna at Paintville and Unity, James Rowland at Mansfield, Richard Brown at Jeromeville, Jacob Wolfe at Blooming Grove and Bethel, Samuel Cleland at Newman's Creek, John McKinney at Frederick, and Henry Harvey at Martinsburg. Fifteen churches had stated supplies, and nine were vacant. Of the latter were Apple Creek, with a membership of one hundred and thirty-seven, Wooster, with a membership of one hundred and sixty-eight, Springfield, with twenty-nine, Plymouth, with twenty-eight, and Sandusky, which made no report. Mt. Vernon Church had a membership of one hundred and sixteen, and Mansfield of one hundred and eighty-six.

In Lancaster Presbytery, Jacob Little was at Granville, William Wallace at Cambridge and Buffalo, John Wright at Lancaster and Rush Creek, Thomas B. Clark at Washington and Seneca, James Culbertson at Zanesville and Putnam, Solomon S. Miles at Newark, John Hunt at McConnellsville, Deerfield, and Windsor, and Samuel W. Rose at Burlington and Hartford. Unity was supplied by the veteran from Western Pennsylvania, Thomas Moore; while sixteen of the thirty-three churches of the Presbytery were vacant.

In the Presbytery of Athens, Robert G. Wilson was President of the University, Ebenezer Hebard was settled at Alexander, Luther G. Bingham at Marietta,[1] John Spaulding at Athens, Addison Kingsbury at Belpre and Warren; while five of the ministers of the Presbytery labored as missionaries, and eleven of the churches were without pastors.

In the Presbytery of Chillicothe, James Gilliland, after his pastorate in South Carolina, had been settled at Red Oak for a quarter of a century; William Dickey was settled at Bloomingburg, Samuel Crothers at Greenfield, James H. Dickey at Salem, John Rankin at Ripley, William Graham at Chillicothe, Samuel D. Blythe at Hillsborough, John P. Van Dyke at West Union, while Nicholas Pittenger was stated supply at Pisgah. Thirteen of the churches were without pastors; although three of these had stated supplies.

In the Presbytery of Miami, Joseph Stephenson was pastor of the churches of Bellfontaine, Cherokee Run, and Stony Creek; Andrew W. Poage, of Yellow Spring and Muddy Run; John N. Belville, of Washington;[2]

[1] Congregational Church. S. P. Robbins died in 1823.

[2] Mr. Belville, commissioned in 1827 to labor in connection with Dayton and Union congregations in Montgomery county, organized two congregations,—one in Montgomery, and the other in the southern part of Miami, within three-fourths of a mile from Montgomery,—and succeeded in procuring for them a minister. He accepted, himself, a call from Miamisburg and Washington, and during the year Franklin Putnam commenced his labors as stated supply at Dayton.

while ten churches had stated supplies, and eight were vacant.

In the Presbytery of Cincinnati, Joshua L. Wilson was pastor of the First Church in the city,[1] David Root of the Second, James Gallaher of the Third, while the Fourth had a stated supply, and the Fifth and Sixth were vacant, the former with a membership of only ten. The other pastors of the Presbytery were James Kemper at Walnut Hills, John Thompson at Springfield, Daniel Hayden at Pleasant Ridge, Francis Montfort at Hamilton and Seven-Mile, Ludwell G. Gaines at Hopewell and Somerset, and Benjamin Graves at Reading. Eight of the churches of the Presbytery were vacant, and five or six had stated supplies.

In the Presbytery of Oxford, Robert H. Bishop was President of the University, Adam B. Gilliland was settled at Bethel, Adrian Aton at New Jersey, Archibald Craig at Mount Carmel, Samuel Miller at New Lexington and New Providence, Sylvester Scovill at Lawrenceburg, Elizabeth, Berea, and Harrison, and Thomas E. Hughes, the veteran pioneer across the Ohio, at Dunlapsville. Seven churches were vacant, and three had stated supplies.

Passing now to the southeastern portion of the State, in the Presbytery of Steubenville we find John Rhea settled over Beech Spring Church (Cadiz), James Robertson at Richmond and Annapolis, Thomas Hunt at Two Ridges, Charles C. Beatty at Steubenville, William Wallace at Nottingham, John C. Tidball at Island Creek, John McArthur at Ridge and Cadiz, Benjamin Mitchell

---

[1] Five years before the death of J. L. Wilson (which occurred August, 1846), his son, Samuel R. Wilson, was called as his colleague.

The Second Presbyterian Church was organized 1817, David Root pastor. The other churches had been gathered from 1828 to 1830, during the period of revival, and were the fruits of it.

at Bloomfield, and Jacob Coon at Crab Apple. Four churches were vacant, and nine had stated supplies.

The reported membership of the churches of the several Presbyteries in 1831[1] was as follows:—churches of Hartford Presbytery, two thousand nine hundred and twenty-one, of Grand River, twelve hundred and eighty-five, of Portage, eleven hundred and thirty-five, of Huron, four hundred and sixty-seven, of Trumbull, six hundred and ninety, of Cleveland, six hundred and sixty-eight, of Columbus, sixteen hundred and thirty-six, of Richland, two thousand four hundred and sixty-six, of Lancaster, seventeen hundred and fifty-seven, of Athens, eight hundred and ninety-four, of Chillicothe, two thousand and ninety-eight, of Miami, seventeen hundred and seventy-nine, of Cincinnati, three thousand one hundred and ninety-four, of Oxford, eleven hundred and forty, and of Steubenville, two thousand two hundred and twenty-eight; making a total of twenty-six thousand five hundred and six.

Such had been the growth of the Church on a field where but about a quarter of a century previous there was only here and there an opening in the forest or a solitary settlement of a few log cabins. The labor that had been performed, the energy that had been evoked in the conflict with rude nature, planting a ripe civilization in the heart of the wilderness which for uncounted centuries had been the hunting-ground of the savage, should not be denied due honor; but no record, even were it possible that it should exist or be preserved, could do justice to the Christian enterprise and indefatigable energy of the men who traversed the new State, planting along their way the institutions of the gospel, or lighting up their missionary-route by the rekindled flames of piety and devotion.

---

[1] Virtually, at the close of 1830.

The influences that gave shape and training to the churches of Ohio came from diverse sources. The Western Reserve only was largely affected by New England immigration. Yet here up to 1815 the majority of the settlers were not from New England. The remoteness of the field forced the Connecticut Society—as already noted—to call upon the Synod of Pittsburg for the men to employ in the field; and for many years but a small number of Congregational ministers were sent out. Till after 1812, less than one-third, probably, of the missionaries of the Western Reserve had been educated in New England. In 1836, of the one hundred and sixty ministers who had labored in connection with the churches, twenty-nine had been educated at Andover, eight at New Haven, fifteen at Princeton, seventeen at Auburn, and seventy-three without seminary training.[1]

The southeastern portion of the State came, from the first, almost exclusively under the influence of the Pittsburg Synod. Its ministers were largely educated at Canonsburg Academy (Jefferson College) or at Washington College. Pittsburg was itself the gateway of emigration to this portion of the State. The region at the Southwest around Cincinnati and along the Miamies came from the first under the influence and ecclesiastical jurisdiction of the Synod of Kentucky. All the early churches belonged to this Synod, and nearly the entire immigration in Southern Ohio for the first fifteen years of the century was from Kentucky, Virginia, New Jersey, Central and Western Pennsylvania, and New York.

Among the ministers on this field to whom the Church and State are alike indebted, there are not a few whose worth is quite disproportioned to the brief

---

[1] American Quarterly Register, viii. 32?.

record which we must make of their career. Connected by the scenes of their labor with the Reserve were Joseph Badger, more than forty years old when he entered the field, but full of energy and enterprise, equally ready to organize a church or establish a mission, to frame a barn or supervise schools, and who was spared till his ninetieth year (1846) to witness the ingathering of harvests from seed he had sown almost half a century before; Jonathan Leslie, long a laborious missionary, and carrying with him from Jefferson College the spirit of those among whom he had been trained; John Seward, of Aurora, retaining to the last his sturdy New England sympathies and attachment to sound doctrine; Caleb Pitkin, William Hanford, and Joseph Treat, kindred with him in spirit and effort; Charles Backus Storrs, Theological Professor and at length (1831) President of Western Reserve College, modest but resolute, indefatigable in study, single in his aims, and ever blending dignity with gentleness; Alvan Coe, whose energy was ever seeking missionary channels through which to pour itself forth; Giles H. Cowles, Alfred H. Betts, Harvey Coe, and not a few others whose memory still lives amid the scenes of their cheerful self-denial and toil.

Some of these were veterans when they entered the field. Dr. Cowles, a graduate of Yale in 1789, a theological pupil of the younger Edwards, and a licentiate of a Connecticut Association, had been settled for eighteen years at Bristol, Conn. In 1811, after having first visited the Reserve as a missionary, he set out on his journey to the far West, accompanied by his family, consisting of a wife and eight children. It was five weeks before he reached his destination. For twenty-two years he spent half his time as a missionary of the Connecticut Society, forming new churches or supplying the destitute, while Austinburg and Morgan congregations formed his stated charge. A man of the true Puritan stamp, with common sense rather than genius, but resolutely toiling on and refusing to submit to indolent repose, his gravity of manner in keeping with his devotion to principle and the serious purpose of his life, he never failed of fulfilling an appointment but in a single instance; and this was on the occasion of the death of a beloved son. His Congregational sympathies were undisguised; but his attachment to sound doctrine was not inferior to that of the foremost members of the Pittsburg Synod.[1]

Alfred H. Betts was born at Norwalk, Conn., in 1786. Having studied medicine, he removed to Florence, Ohio, where at a private house he established a meeting which was attended with a blessing. Feeling that his call to the ministry was clear, he studied theology with Dr. Hanford, of Hudson, and for four years labored in the neighborhood of Florence. In 1821 he was installed pastor of Brownhelm Church. After some years he extended his labors to Vermillion and Wakeman Churches. Sincere, self-denying, liberal and devoted, direct, simple, and earnest as a preacher, he was the model of a guileless New England Puritan. In 1835, he was forced from ill health to resign his charge; but he labored more or less till his death in 1860.

William Hanford was a native of Norwalk, Conn., a graduate of Yale College in 1808, and of Andover Seminary in 1813. Upon his licensure, soon after, he removed to Ohio, taking charge for many years of the church of Hudson, and subsequently of those of Wind-

---

[1] In 1816, a powerful revival prevailed under the ministry of Dr. Cowles at Austinburg and Morgan. It extended to some of the adjoining towns, and among the fruits of it about one hundred persons were added to the church of Austinburg alone.

ham and Middlebury. He died at Tallmadge, May 31, 1861. Wise, faithful, and laborious as a pastor, his ministry was largely blessed. His integrity and uprightness commanded implicit confidence.

Harvey Coe was born at Granville, Mass., Oct. 6, 1785. He was graduated at Williams College in 1811, and studied theology under President Fitch and Drs. Woodbridge and Cooley. Removing to the West, he was settled in 1814 over the united congregations of Hartford, Vernon, and Kinsman, and for some years was the only settled pastor in that part of the country. His labors were crowned with a powerful revival, in connection with which nearly two hundred persons were hopefully converted. He was a zealous friend of Western Reserve College, and in 1833 became agent for the American Board of Commissioners for Foreign Missions. His death occurred in March, 1860.

At Steubenville, successively pastors of the church were Obadiah Jennings and C. C. Beatty,—the last no unworthy descendant of Dr. Beatty of ante-Revolutionary and missionary memory, and the former an able lawyer before he entered upon the ministry, and ever after eminent as a reasoner and a disputant, while exemplary in the discharge of pastoral duty.[1] Memorable also are Dr. Hoge, of Columbus, devout, self-denying, the patriarch of the Presbytery, if not its Nestor, for many years; Thomas Barr, till 1820 at Euclid, but with his Presbyterian sympathies removing to Wooster and Apple Creek Churches, and here exemplifying the virtues of the discreet and devoted pastor; Thomas Moore, zealous in the cause of Calvinism and revivals, and transferring his missionary experience in Ohio Presbytery to regions still farther west; "Father" Gilliland, of Red Oak, Matthew G. Wallace, the patriarch

[1] He died, while pastor of the church in Nashville, in 1828.

of Miami Presbytery, Dr. Robert H. Bishop, at the head of the University at Oxford, and Dr. Joshua L. Wilson, at Cincinnati.

The interests of collegiate as well as common-school education had not been overlooked during the period that has been passed in review. As early as 1804, the University of Ohio was established at Athens, and among the ministers of the Presbyterian Church whose names grace its history at this period (1825) were Samuel D. Hoge,—brother of Dr. Hoge, of Columbus, but already the subject of that disease which was to cut him off in the strength and promise of early manhood,—Jacob Lindsley, for several years a professor in the institution, and Robert G. Wilson, the pioneer missionary and pastor at Chillicothe, who in 1824 accepted the Presidency of the university.

Miami University was established in 1824, at Oxford; and already the project was agitated which issued in the establishment of Western Reserve College in 1826. Of the first-mentioned institution, Rev. Dr. Robert H. Bishop had just accepted the post of President. He was a native of Scotland, a graduate of the University of Edinburgh, and a pupil of Finlayson and Dugald Stewart. His earliest ecclesiastical connection was with the Associate Synod, and through the representations of Dr. John M. Mason he was led, with other Scottish ministers, to emigrate to this country. For nearly two years he itinerated as a missionary in Kentucky and in Miami Valley. He finally settled at Lexington, and soon after accepted a professorship in Transylvania University. Here he remained for several years; but between him and President Holley, with the views which they respectively entertained on subjects of religious doctrine, there could be little sympathy. When the State of Ohio, therefore, established Miami University, he readily accepted the office of President to which he was invited. "The diligence, self-denial, unabated interest, and prayerfulness, with which he prosecuted his work, were seen and known of all, and were repaid by the increasing confidence of the community and an extended career of usefulness, the results of which it is impossible to estimate." For seventeen years he administered his trust with discretion, beneficence, and success.

In 1826 the Western Reserve College was established at Hudson, and, according to the intention of its founders, a Theological department was connected with it. The latter in 1840 was in charge of three professors, Dr. Pierce occupying the Theological chair. The number of students was, however, only fourteen.

CHAPTER XXXIV.

KENTUCKY, 1816–1830.

THE close of the war left the Presbyterian Church in Kentucky in a distracted and prostrate condition. But another effect of it had been to revive sympathy with France, and give a new impulse to the spread of infidel sentiments. Many who were regarded as intellectual and influential, especially among professional men, were avowed unbelievers. In many places with a large population, there was no trace of public religious worship. Samuel J. Mills, on his Southwestern tour, spent one Sabbath in Kentucky in a town of two to three thousand inhabitants, without being able to collect a congregation to listen to the word of God. Negroes stood in groups in the street, laughing and swearing, boys played and hallooed, while the men on the outskirts of the place were engaged in shooting pigeons, or, if of the more respectable class, were riding abroad for amusement. The Sabbath was distinguished from other days only by greater noise, amusement, profanity, and dissipation. This was by no means a solitary instance. The change that took place in the ten years subsequent may be judged from the fact that this same town then contained three large and flourishing churches.[1]

The adverse influences which prevailed, and against which the Presbyterian Church had to contend, culminated in the act of the Legislature of 1818, by which, on the motion of some of its members, the Board of Trustees of Transylvania University were suddenly and summarily ejected, and thirteen new trustees, of whom not one was a professor of religion of any denomination, substituted in their place. The act was a gross violation of the charter of the university, a usurpation of its legal and moral rights. It wrested the institution from Presbyterian control. Those who had nurtured it in its weakness, and labored and prayed for its success, saw it suddenly transferred to the hands of men who could feel little sympathy with evangelical religion. From an ally it was perverted into an instrument of bitter antagonism.

This strange episode in the history of the Presbyterian

---

[1] Some interesting facts in the history of the Presbyterian churches of Kentucky about the year 1818 may be gathered from Isaac Reed's "Christian Traveller." In that year Danville, with a population of twelve hundred, had not a male member in the Presbyterian Church; and the only other house of worship besides that in which Nelson preached was a Romish chapel. There were many Deists in the place.—P. 61.

The church in Frankfort was gathered about the year 1816. In 1818, Winchester Church had a membership of fifteen. There was but one male member living in the town. At Springfield, under the ministry of N. H. Hall, a female Praying-Society existed, the only one in the State. More than thirty counties in Kentucky had not a single Presbyterian minister.

Church of Kentucky is deserving of more than a passing notice. In 1788 the institution had been removed to Lexington. But the tone of sentiment which prevailed among the leading men of the place was deeply tinctured with French infidelity. It was the head-quarters of one of the Jacobin clubs, and the violent sympathy with every thing French which prevailed there was especially antagonistic to a pure Christianity. The results of the change of location were soon seen to be disastrous. In 1794 the Presbyterian teacher was ejected, and a disciple of Priestley appointed to succeed him.

The new principal was a zealous politician, and a sycophantic satellite of Thomas Jefferson. He was popular with the Deistical clubs. But the Presbyterians felt that an institution over which he presided was no longer of any value to them. In 1794 they issued proposals for a new institution,—a grammar-school that should be subject to their control. In the course of the same year they secured a charter for "The Kentucky Academy." This measure was followed up by vigorous efforts to secure an endowment. "Father" Rice and Dr. Blythe made collections for it in the Atlantic cities, having secured the recommendation of the General Assembly; and in the fall of 1797 the institution was opened at Pisgah.

It speedily outstripped the institution at Lexington, and by its success excited alarm among the friends of the university. An attempt was now made to conciliate the Presbyterians, who had been alienated by the policy hitherto pursued. Provision was made for their ascendency, by which it was supposed to be secured against all future vicissitudes. The new Board of twenty-one members was to comprise a majority of Presbyterians, and the charter was not to be altered or repealed except on petition of a majority. In consequence of this concession, and by act of the Legislature, the two institutions were amalgamated into one in December, 1798.

Under flattering auspices the new institution commenced its career. Three professorships were founded, and they were filled by Presbyterians,—Blythe, Stuart, and Welch. For several years it enjoyed a moderate degree of prosperity. But the Board was divided into two hostile parties, and a worldly policy led to the election of prominent political characters to fill the vacancies which occurred. At length a crisis arrived, and it was found that only seven of the twenty-one members of the Board were Presbyterians.

To fill the office of President, several eminent and excellent men were successively elected, but chose to decline. In this state of things, the name of Rev. Horace Holley, of Boston, was mentioned. He was unanimously chosen, but he also saw fit to decline. He was re-elected (1817), but with less unanimity. His Socinian views were more than suspected, and Dr. Dwight, who was written to on the subject, was no longer disposed to endorse his own pupil. But the majority were resolute in their purpose, and the minority, outvoted, retired from the Board. To complete the mischief, the Legislature, by an arbitrary and uncalled-for interference, violated the charter by appointing a new Board, not a member of which made any pretence to religion. The Presbyterians were thus dispossessed at a stroke of their property and interest in an institution largely endowed and built up by themselves.

Dr. Holley visited Kentucky in the spring of 1818.[1] Flattered by the attention paid him, and charmed with his hospitable reception and the seeming promise of an institution which, under his control, he imagined might become the most distinguished in the Great Western

---

[1] See Life of Dr. Holley.

Valley, his decision did not long remain doubtful. He accepted the post to which he had been elected, and removed from Boston to Lexington.

The new President entered upon the duties of his office with great *éclat*. At first he studied conciliation. Some of the Presbyterians even felt encouraged to hope that the institution might again begin to answer the design of its founders. Dr. Holley was a man of brilliant talents, of pleasing person and manners, and of great eloquence. Nature and education alike had done much for him. He was eulogized and idolized by his friends. He boasted a large and catholic spirit, and a contempt for sectarian prejudice. He fondly hoped to rally around him the popular sympathy and engage all denominations in the support of the institution.

But his proclivities soon discovered themselves. With all his boasts of liberality, he was a bitter opponent of evangelical religion. In the very writings which were put forth subsequently in his own defence, the hand of affection could not suppress the decisive evidence that he was in full sympathy with a *no-creed* Unitarianism. Such was not the man to conciliate the friends of sound religion among the Baptists and Methodists, any more than among the Presbyterians. But the latter first took the alarm. They petitioned the Legislature (1818) for a charter of a new college, to be erected at Danville.[1]

---

[1] The Synod of Kentucky in 1818 resolved to establish Centre College at Danville. They were, doubtless, encouraged in this measure by the revivals of the preceding year. There had been "a glorious accession" to the Church, especially in West Lexington Presbytery In Concord, Mt. Pleasant, and Paris, the work had been "particularly conspicuous." Fleming, Smyrna, Point Pleasant, Sugar Ridge, Springfield, and Augusta congregations had also been visited.—*Christian Herald*, v. 596.

At Lexington a powerful revival prevailed in 1817. A writer in the "Christian Herald" during that year says, "More than one hun-

The charter was granted, but so modified as to place the control of the institution and its funds in the hands of the Legislature instead of the Synod. In this shape it was unhesitatingly refused. Twice already the Legislature had betrayed its trust, and the Synod had learned not to put its "trust in princes."

The work of excluding the Presbyterians from their posts in Transylvania University now proceeded. Dr. Bishop was forced to leave, and Dr. Blythe and Mr. Sharpe felt constrained to resign. Meanwhile Dr. Holley, in his instructions from the pulpit and the chair, justified the worst apprehensions excited by his antecedents. Popular dissatisfaction was manifested, and the Board felt itself compelled to retrace its steps. Dr. Blythe was recalled, and for several years matters went on smoothly. The President enjoyed an almost unbounded popularity. The Presbyterians were reduced to silence, and the country rang with praises of the university and its brilliant President. The success of the law and medical schools connected with the university contributed not a little to this result.

The personal attractions of Dr. Holley, his gay and genial spirit, his social parties, with music, cards, and dancing, his frequent and sumptuous entertainments, accompanied by all that could charm the tasteful and refined, united to give new lustre to his fame. The Legislature were won by his tact, and extended their liberality to the university. But the friends of reli-

---

dred and twenty-three have already been baptized in the name of the Lord. Great seriousness continues to be manifested. Hundreds are, with broken hearts, inquiring the way to Zion." The surrounding region, previously given up to desperate iniquity, was powerfully affected, and four or five hundred were added to the churches. —*Christian Herald*, iii. 302.

The address of the Synod on the project of the establishment of the college at Danville is to be found in the Christian Herald, v. 597.

gion were more dissatisfied than ever. Dr. Holley's sermons were little better than eloquent Deism with the gilding of Christian phraseology. Public opinion began to be freely expressed. It found new provocation in the publication of the "Transylvania Theses," or Latin exercises of the students, which showed only too plainly that the rationalistic views of the President were bearing fruit in the minds of his pupils. In October, 1823, the Synod renewed the proposal of a college at Danville. A conference was had with the Trustees of Centre College to effect a reorganization. It was successful in its object. Arrangements were made to secure in behalf of the Presbyterian Church an institution of which they might have the control It was a step to which they were impelled by an obvious necessity. The views of Dr. Holley had now become too obviously antagonistic to evangelical religion to allow any longer delay. He ridiculed the doctrines of human depravity, the efficacy of prayer, and atonement through "Christ crucified." His lessons in morals may be judged from his address to the students:—"Young gentlemen, whatever you find within you, cherish it, for it is a part of your nature: restrain it not."

The attempt at conciliation was alike foolish and vain. It proposed to have divine service performed in the chapel by each of the clergymen of Lexington, including the Episcopalian and Roman Catholic. The two Presbyterian pastors, N. H. Hall and John Breckenridge, refused to have any thing to do with the plan. Even Dr. Fishback, a Baptist clergyman, found himself at one of the public examinations brought into collision with the President on points connected with divine revelation, and resigned his post as preacher and trustee. The plan proposed brought out a multitude of pamphlets in opposition to it, replete with irony and satire.

The fortunes of Dr. Holley and of the university were

decidedly on the wane. A Roman Catholic college was started at Bardstown, and the amended charter of Centre College answered the desires of the Presbyterians.[1]

---

[1] The circumstances in which the charter was secured are worthy to be narrated. Its grant was violently opposed by the friends of Transylvania University and other rival institutions. There was danger of its being denied; and Rev. S. K. Nelson went to Frankfort to use his personal influence in favor of the application. Dr. Cleland was sent for, for the same purpose. The two men met on the way. They conversed of the business in hand. Cleland related an amusing anecdote, appropriate as illustrating the folly of the opposition in making a bugbear of sectarianism. "Go to Frankfort," said Mr. Nelson, "and tell that story, and you will get your charter."

Dr. Cleland knew his man, and gave him the story to use. The opponent of the charter, a Baptist, and a friend of the university, entered the hall of the Legislature with an armfull of books, and a servant with a wheelbarrow-load behind him. In a violent philippic of several hours, he endeavored to excite indignation against Presbyterian lust of domination and desire to unite Church and State. When he had ended, Colonel James Davidson, a man of much dry humor and a deep sonorous voice, gravely told a simple anecdote by way of illustrating the terrors which had been so awfully presented. "An Irish Redemptioner lost himself in the woods one evening. He had heard a great deal of the Indians; and the novel sights and sounds around him inspired him with such alarm that he climbed a tree for safety and spent a sleepless night. When found the next day, he narrated his perils. The fireflies he mistook for savages in quest of him. The screams of the whippoorwills were mistaken by him for menaces of destruction. 'Whip him well! whip him well! cut and slash! cut and slash! and the fire flew all the time,' said he, 'like the de'il! In short, he did not know what would become of him, had it not been for the swate heavenly bairds,'—meaning the bull-frogs,—'who kept calling out, "Motheration! motheration!"'

"Now," said Colonel Davidson, "when I heard the honorable member conjuring up all those dreadful hobgoblins, they appeared to me of the same imaginary character as the poor Irishman's terrors, and I felt an irresistible impulse to rise up in my place and call out, 'Motheration! motheration!'" The ludicrous anecdote, related in the dryest manner and with his gravest intonations, convulsed the house with laughter. It is needless to say that advantage was taken

Meanwhile, the mismanagement of the funds of the university which had been brought to light exposed it to new odium. The Baptists had been alienated by the resignation of Dr. Fishback, the recriminations heaped upon him for it, and the statement of facts which he felt himself constrained to issue in his defence. Matters were verging to a crisis. It was useless to stem the tide. The experiment of Dr. Holley was a failure. He was chagrined at the decreasing number of the students and the uprising of rival institutions. Politically he had incurred the odium of one of the parties of the day, and, despairing of further aid from the Legislature, he resigned his post. Lexington had idolized him as her brightest ornament. His pupils, many of them, regarded him not only with the highest respect, but the warmest affection. But the magnificent vision which nine years before, at his entrance upon his task, rose to his view, was slowly but surely melting away. He turned with despondency and sad regrets to another field, a disappointed man. An untimely death a few months later closed his brief but brilliant career.

With his departure the university received a blow only less ruinous than that which his own mistaken policy had inflicted. Rival after rival started up in successful competition with it. Trusted by no denomination, the course of President Holley had alienated all. The Presbyterians struggled on with a half-endowed college at Danville, while the Roman Catholics at Bardstown, the Cumberland Presbyterians at Princeton, the Methodists at Augusta, the Baptists at Georgetown, and the Campbellites at Harrodsburg, had a somewhat kindred experience.

The successors of Dr. Holley were eminent men.

---

of the good humor thus induced to secure the charter.—*Life of Cleland*, and *Davidson's Kentucky*.

Among them were Drs. Coit and Bascom. But they could not restore the institution to the position it had lost. It has steadily continued to languish. Centre College had to labor under grave and manifold embarrassments, but it at length gave promise of independence and prosperity. Its successive Presidents were Jeremiah Chamberlain,[1] David C. Procter, Gideon Blackburn, and John C. Young In 1828 a Theological department was attached to it, modelled after that of Princeton. The difficulty of raising the necessary funds led to its abandonment in 1831. This, however, was to be but a temporary relinquishment of the project. The college was still in successful operation. In 1840 an effort, in part successful, was made to raise the endowment to one hundred thousand dollars. Subsequent efforts have greatly enlarged its resources, and nearly two thousand students have issued from its halls. Probably two-thirds of the Presbyterian clergy of the State are included in the number. The necessity of denominational education demanded in the circumstances the taking of a step the results of which have justified its wisdom.[2]

---

[1] The principal founder of the college was Samuel Kelsey Nelson, pastor of the Danville Church The terms of the charter required that twenty thousand dollars should be paid into the treasury before a Board of Trustees could be elected by the Synod. Mr. Nelson headed the subscription by a note of eight hundred dollars, and ministers of the Synod gave their individual bonds for the balance.—*Sprague*, iv. 416.

The original charter of the college was secured in 1819. Jeremiah Chamberlain, the first President, went into office in 1823. After a temporary occupancy of the office by David C. Procter, he was succeeded by Dr. Gideon Blackburn in 1827, and in 1830 by John C. Young, D.D., whose death occurred June 23, 1857. On the 1st of January, 1858, Rev. L. W. Green was inaugurated his successor.—*Presbyterian Herald*, July 14, 1861.

[2] Davidson's Kentucky.

From 1826 to 1829, the Church in Kentucky was signally blessed by revivals. The Spirit was copiously poured out on Centre College. More than thirty prominent towns or cities were the scenes of remarkable displays of divine grace. The additions to the churches in 1828 and 1829 were reported to be upward of four thousand.

The most marked instance of the power of the revival over a whole community was at Lexington. Five hundred persons were added to the Church. Infidelity and Unitarianism, which had so long and extensively prevailed, lost their ascendency. Evangelical truth regained the ground that had been lost by the adverse influences which had been so sadly dominant.

Indeed, it was at Lexington that the revival may be said fairly to have commenced. The Rev. Nathan H. Hall, pastor of the First Presbyterian Church,[1] with the approbation of his brethren, held a protracted meeting for four days, the first of the kind which had been held in that region since the revival at the commencement of the century. The meeting of Synod was held the same week, and its members returned to their respective charges with hearts kindled and impressed by the scenes which they had witnessed. Thus the spirit of the revival was spread abroad. Rev. Frederick A. Ross and Rev. James Gallaher acted a conspicuous part as itinerant evangelists or revival preachers. They travelled extensively in Kentucky and Ohio, and their

---

[1] In 1796, James Welsh was settled as pastor of Lexington and Georgetown Churches. Soon after, James Blythe was elected his colleague, and subsequently succeeded him at Lexington. In 1807, Robert M. Cunningham was settled as colleague of Dr. Blythe. His pastorate extended to 1822, and his successor was Nathan H. Hall. The Second Church was gathered by James McChord in 1814. He died in 1820, having left Lexington in the preceding year. His successor was John Breckinridge.

labors were successful in producing great religious awakening. The old system of camp-meetings was revived, and the occasions for them were sometimes unnecessarily multiplied. The "anxious seat" and other methods of testing and strengthening the religious excitement were extensively adopted. At length disorders began to creep in. Something of the previous experience of the revival of 1800 was renewed, and the camp-meetings, discountenanced by the more judicious, fell into disuse.

Among the eminent names which grace this period of the history of the Presbyterian Church of Kentucky, those of Hall, Breckinridge, the Nelsons, Cunningham, Stuart, and Cleland deserve notice.

Of Stuart and Cleland mention has already been made. Robert M. Cunningham was a native of Pennsylvania, a resident for some years of North Carolina, and a graduate of Dickinson College. On completing his education, he connected himself with the First Presbytery of South Carolina, and was licensed to preach in 1792. He labored for several years within its bounds, organized one church and helped to build up several others. He was one of the five ministers set off from the Presbytery of South Carolina in 1796 to form the new Presbytery of Hopewell.

In 1807 he removed to Lexington and was installed as colleague of Dr. Blythe. He was "a kind of Whitefield in his zeal and pathos, and untiring appeals to dying men in his public discourses." Although "not a great preacher," he uttered the truth with a tenderness rarely equalled. Commanding in person, distinct in utterance, clear in thought, and attractive by his earnestness, his goodness of heart was manifest to all. His influence was extensive, healthful, and blessed. His closing years were spent in a more Southern field.

John Breckinridge was born at Cabell's Dale, on

North Elkhorn, Ky., in 1797. His father was Jefferson's Attorney-General. He was educated at Princeton, graduating with high honor in 1818. After serving as tutor for some years, and pursuing at the same time his theological studies, he was licensed to preach in 1822. For a few months he was chaplain of the House of Representatives, and then transferred his relations to the West Lexington Presbytery. As pastor of the McChord Church at Lexington, and editor of the "Western Luminary," he came into direct antagonism with the plans and policy of Dr. Holley, and contributed in no small measure to the impulse which secured for the Presbyterian Church a college at Danville. Although soon removed to other and in some respects more distinguished spheres of labor at the East, he left behind him a deep and permanent impression. Courteous, hospitable, kindly in manner and feeling, he was bold, intrepid, and zealous in defence of what he regarded as just and true. On a memorable occasion, when he had employed expressions that were hissed as objectionable, he paused a moment, and then, drawing himself up to his full height, while a smile of conscious strength played about his mouth, he exclaimed, with undaunted firmness, "I am not to be put down by hisses or by threats. I was cradled where the Indian war-whoop yet mingled with the infant's lullaby, and trained by a mother whose earliest lessons taught me, next to the fear of God, not to be afraid of man." The effect of this utterance, delivered in an appropriate manner, was electric. There was no further interruption, and he closed his address amid enthusiastic applause.[1]

Kentucky might well be proud of such a son. He occupied the foremost rank among the pulpit-orators of the nation. All classes were alike captivated by his

---

[1] Sprague's Annals.

earnest, thrilling eloquence. The enthusiasm of his nature glowed, when he spoke, in every feature, and communicated itself to all who heard him. No popular odium could deter him from duty. He was a "Christian gentleman;" but he was "a Kentuckian;" nor was he the man to shrink from controversy when fairly challenged. In his discussion of Romanism with Bishop Hughes, he proved himself no contemptible antagonist. Incessantly active, he closed a life too short for the service of the Church. Yet, short as it was, it was characterized beyond most others by high and large achievements.

The course of his predecessor in the pastorate of the church at Lexington was somewhat similar to his own, —brief but brilliant. From his early years, James McChord had shown a remarkable taste and passion for studious pursuits. He studied law with Henry Clay; but his religious training would not allow him to rest satisfied with the arrangement by which his recitations were heard on the Sabbath,—the statesman's only day of leisure. As his serious impressions deepened and issued in his conversion, he was led to abandon the study of law and direct his attention to the ministry. Along with Duncan, of Baltimore, and (Dr.) John M. Matthews, he studied theology under Dr. John M. Mason, and labored a while in connection with the Associate Reformed Church. But his liberal views of Christian communion were obnoxious to that body,[1] and, on an appeal from the Presbytery to the Synod, the case was decided against him. In consequence of this, he renounced the jurisdiction of the Presbytery and abandoned the connection. Yet such was his popularity and the enthusiasm he inspired that the young men of Lexington resolved to build him a church. The edifice

---

[1] For a fuller, but adverse, statement, see Ely's Review, 1818. Mr. McChord was condemned by his Presbytery for doctrinal errors.

was completed in 1815, and a large congregation was soon gathered around the young and talented preacher He united with the Presbytery of West Lexington, and his church was placed under its care. His extreme sensitiveness injured his usefulness and shortened his days; but for several years he occupied a prominent position among the Presbyterian ministers of the State.

Both the Nelsons were remarkable men. Samuel Kelsey was by six years the senior of his brother David. He was born in 1787, and at the early age of sixteen was graduated at Washington College, Tennessee, under Dr. Doak. He commenced the study of law, but had not long pursued it before his purposes of life were changed. Relinquishing the fair prospect of fame and success which opened before him, and in disregard of the remonstrances of friends, he returned to Tennessee and prosecuted the study of theology under his old preceptor, Dr. Doak. He was licensed in 1807 by the Holston Presbytery, and for some time engaged in missionary labors in South Carolina and Tennessee. Of benign aspect, easy and graceful in his movements, with a shrewdness in discerning character that seemed almost intuitive, and a strong common sense that was rarely if ever at fault, he was more the man of counsel than of action. Governor Shelby's estimate of the man is expressed in a remark which he uttered, to the effect that Nelson would have made a capital lawyer. In the pulpit, every sentence was level to the comprehension of the humblest hearer. If not dazzling, he was eminently instructive, searching, and edifying.

In 1809 he received a unanimous call to the pastoral charge of the church in Danville, and for nearly twenty years he filled this important field with usefulness and efficiency. To him belongs the honor of having been the principal founder of Centre College. For this he labored with consummate skill and untiring assiduity.

It was through his efforts, ably seconded, indeed, by others, that the Act was obtained from the Legislature by which the institution was placed under the control of a Board of Trustees appointed by the Synod.

Cut down in the midst of his usefulness, he was succeeded in the pastorate of the church by his brother David. For several years the future author of "Cause and Cure of Infidelity" had been himself an infidel. For some years he was a surgeon in the army. He served in the expedition to Canada, and in Alabama and Florida. Dissatisfied with the sophistry of infidel writers and their dishonesty in dealing with the Bible, he determined to read for himself on both sides of the question. The result was that his skepticism gave way. He embraced Christianity not only as of divine authority, but as the only foundation of his personal hopes. Religion now became with him the all-engrossing subject. In spite of constitutional diffidence, he was unremitting in his exertions to do good to the souls of men, and by gradual advances at last became competent to conduct the devotions of public congregations.

His prospects as a physician were all that he could have asked. He was popular as a man; his practice was extensive and lucrative, not falling short of three thousand dollars a year. But his heart glowed with the desire to preach the gospel, and, relinquishing his profession, he placed himself under the care of Abingdon Presbytery.

For nearly three years he preached in various places in Tennessee, and at the same time was associated with Ross and Gallaher in conducting the "Calvinistic Magazine." In 1828 he was called to succeed his brother in the pastorate of the church at Danville. Here he labored, however, but two years. His subsequent career is identified with Marion College in Missouri, and Quincy Institute in Illinois.

His intimate acquaintance and friend Dr. Ross pronounced him one of the most lovely of human characters, and "the most fascinating preacher" he had ever heard. "His simple train of argument, his combination of thought, so original, his exquisite illustrations, inexhaustible, his strange unearthly voice, his noble face, his sweet smile, which made you feel the light and love of heaven, made him the object of undying affection in every heart that knew him." His eccentricities, his unique absorbed appearance, his odd but unaffected manners, his coarse attire, always careless and sometimes untidy, could not detract from his real power and merit. Under his wool hat was hidden a brain of immense power, and beneath his linsey-woolsey garb there beat a heart that glowed with the most fervent love and devotion to God and the warmest sympathy with all that was human. He freed his own slaves, and was undisguised in his hostility to a system which in his judgment was an offence to God as well as a gross wrong to his creatures. His missionary and revival labors were abundant and remarkably blessed. At the East and West, in the wilds of Missouri and in the Atlantic cities, among the sparse settlements of Tennessee, Kentucky, Ohio, and Illinois, and in the homes of civilization and refinement, he accomplished great results; and even yet "his works do follow him." In the midst of his plans of usefulness he was suddenly struck down. Yet to the last he cherished the hope that God would restore him to the work he loved so well.

Dr. John T. Edgar was a native of Delaware, but in 1793, when he was but three years of age, his father removed to Kentucky. The latter, although but a humble farmer, gave his son the best education that could be afforded in his adopted State. After studying at Transylvania University, he entered the seminary at Princeton, where he was graduated in 1816. In the following year he was installed by Ebenezer Presbytery over the church of Flemingsburg, from which, after acquiring high reputation as one of the most promising preachers and pastors of his day, he was called to Maysville, and subsequently (1827) to Frankfort, where his eloquence soon gathered around him the leading men of the capital of the State. "If you want to hear eloquence," said Henry Clay, "listen to the young Presbyterian preacher at Frankfort, named John Todd Edgar." In his manners he was a fine specimen of a courtly Christian gentleman, and as a pastor he was social, winning, and catholic. The poor as well as the wealthy secured his sympathies and were the objects of the same absorbing care.

In 1833 he was called to Nashville, Tenn.; and here the promise of his earlier years was fulfilled. For more than twenty-seven years this was the post which he continued to occupy, and where he exerted a commanding influence. In person he was a fine specimen of manly beauty. His address and bearing were simple, cordial, and refined. Habitually respectful to all, sympathizing deeply with the wretched and the wronged, with a settled aversion to all that was mean, cruel, or base, he was thoroughly unselfish, and was sustained by a personal and moral courage of the highest order. For his oratorical powers he was deservedly eminent. His personal appearance, exquisite voice and intonation, fervor and unction of spirit, and pathos of utterance placed him in the front rank of pulpit-celebrity. His death occurred Nov. 13, 1860.

Nathan H. Hall was born in 1783, in Franklin county, Va. When he was sixteen years of age, his father, a Baptist minister, removed to Garrard county, Ky. Converted in the revival of 1801, he studied theology with Dr. Wilson of Cincinnati, and in 1805 was licensed by Transylvania Presbytery. In 1807 he was settled over

Springfield, Hardin's Creek, and Lebanon Churches. In 1822 he was called to the First Presbyterian Church of Lexington. In 1847 he resigned his charge and became an Evangelist. As a revival preacher he was rarely excelled. In 1849 he removed to Missouri, and, after preaching some time for the Central Church of St. Louis, was installed pastor of Columbia Church, where he remained till shortly before his death. He sunk under the infirmities of age, June 22, 1858.

These names by no means exhaust the list of the clergy of the Presbyterian Church of Kentucky during this period, worthy of honorable mention. Death has removed many whose memories will long survive in the grateful mention and anecdotes of their usefulness, devotion, or eloquence. Chamberlain, Hall, Edgar, Crowe, Bishop, the Breckinridges, Harrison,[1] Young, Davidson, and Rice, as well as others of equal merit, were laborers in this field during the period under review, and some of them yet survive, attesting the efficiency of past by the success of present labors.

CHAPTER XXXV.

TENNESSEE, 1816-1830.

As we enter upon the period of the history of the Presbyterian Church in Tennessee from 1816 to 1830, we find the three Presbyteries of Abingdon, Union,

[1] In 1826, Joseph Cabell Harrison, just ordained by West Lexington Presbytery, commenced his labors as a missionary under their direction in the Green River country. He subsequently (1833) organized the churches of Burlington, Richwood, and Mt. Horeb, which for some time he supplied, and afterward was successful in resuscitating several feeble churches in Boone county.

and West Tennessee occupying the field, the two first connected with the Synod of Virginia and the last with the Synod of Kentucky. Anderson, in charge of New Providence Church and of his theological school, was laboring at Maryville. Dr. Coffin occupied the post of President of Greenville College, to which he had succeeded on the death of Balch. Stephenson, at Zion and Cathie's Creek, was impressing his own grave and noble character upon the region which, with a colony from his Carolina church, he had helped to settle. Blackburn was at Franklin,—where he remained till his removal to Louisville in 1823,—teaching, preaching, organizing and supplying new churches. James H. Bowman was laboring at Bethsaida and Mars' Hill, Duncan Brown at Bethesda and New Hope, Thomas J. Hall at Bethberei and Rock Spring, David Weir at Columbia and Lower Elk Ridge, Samuel W. Doak at Mt. Bethel and Providence, James Gallaher at Rogersville and New Providence, Alexander McEwen at Glade Springs and Rock Springs; while the venerable Dr. Doak still retained the Presidency of Washington College.

But already the necessity of a new connection of the Presbyteries, by which they might unitedly operate upon their common field within the bounds of the State, began to be felt. In 1817, upon the petition of the Synod of Kentucky, that body was divided, and the Presbyteries of Union, Shiloh (1816), West Tennessee, and Mississippi (1815) were constituted the Synod of Tennessee.

In 1818 the Presbytery of Missouri was erected; in 1824 that of North Alabama, and in 1826 that of Holston, erected by a division of Abingdon, were added to the list, all coming by their locality in connection with the Synod of Tennessee. By a division of the body, the Synod of West Tennessee was formed in 1826.

Thus a broad and extended region was placed under

the care of the Synod. The imperative necessities of this field were deeply felt,[1] and the Missionary Society of Tennessee was formed to co-operate with the Assembly's Board of Missions In successive years missionaries were sent out by the latter, but sustained in part by the former, by whom in many cases their route was prescribed. In 1817, William McFarland was sent to labor in Missouri, and Richard King in the Mississippi Territory. In the following year James C. Barnes was appointed to labor in the southern part of Kentucky and the adjacent parts of Tennessee. George M. Erskine (a colored preacher) was to spend four months under the direction of the Missionary Society of East Tennessee. In 1819 he was reappointed in like manner, and half his compensation was to be from the society. At the same time, Andrew Morrison was to labor for three months in the region lying between the rivers Hiawassee and Tennessee; while Jeremiah Chamberlain was sent out to the Missouri field. In the following year he was followed by Francis McFarland, and the commission of Erskine to act under the direction of the Missionary Society of Tennessee was renewed.

Meanwhile, in this new field opened to Christian enterprise, the Connecticut Society sent its missionaries, few, indeed, but cordially co-operating with the Assembly's Board as well as the Tennessee Society. Larned, Cornelius, and Royce, in Mississippi, acted in conjunction with the two denominations, as did also Giddings and Flint in Missouri. Two or three of the missionaries of the Connecticut Society were appointed to visit and

[1] The project for a Southwestern Theological Seminary originated within the bounds of the Synod of Tennessee in 1819. Early in the following year a circular address was issued, and invitations were sent to the adjoining Synods to appoint delegates to meet with the Synod of Tennessee at its session at Franklin on the second Wednesday of October, 1820.—*Christian Herald*, vi. 666.

labor within the States of Kentucky and Tennessee, and were cordially and hospitably entertained.

One of these was Cyrus Kingsbury, afterward a missionary to the Cherokees under the direction of the American Board of Commissioners for Foreign Missions. In 1816 he had been sent out by the Connecticut Society to visit the destitute portions of Tennessee. After spending some months in discharging his commission, he repaired to the Cherokee country. At a full council of the Cherokees and Creeks, at which Colonel Meigs, the Indian agent, and General Andrew Jackson, in behalf of the United States Government, were present, he proposed to the Indians his plan of missions. It was favorably entertained. The chiefs invited the establishment of mission-schools, and Mr. Kingsbury, in conjunction with a representative of the tribes, was directed to seek out a fit location. The result was the selection of the mission-station known thenceforth by the name of the devoted missionary "Brainerd." The project which Blackburn had so zealously prosecuted, and in which Stephenson and other ministers of Tennessee had taken such deep interest, had been frustrated by the adverse influences of the war (1812–15) and the removal of Blackburn to Nashville. It was now revived under better auspices. In 1817 the hands of Kingsbury were strengthened by a reinforcement of laborers, —among them the Rev. Ard Hoyt, who had been pastor for some years of the Presbyterian church in Wilksbarre, Pa., William Chamberlain, a member of his family, who for some time had been preparing himself for missionary labor, and Daniel S. Butrick, from Massachusetts.

In the following year the mission to the Choctaws was commenced, of which Mr. Kingsbury was invited to take charge. The laborers among the Cherokees were increased in number by the accession of the laymen Abijah Conger, John Vaill, and John Talmage, with their families, from New Jersey. The removal of the tribes to the region beyond the Mississippi, though sorely opposed to their own desires, had already commenced; and in the latter part of November, 1817, Alfred Finney and Cephas Washburn set out on their journey, through a wilderness rendered almost impassable by flooded swamps and overflowing creeks, from Brainerd to Eliot in Arkansas.

The laborers in the mission-field at Brainerd were for the most part connected with the Presbytery of Union, in East Tennessee. Robert Glenn was a licentiate, Christopher Bradshaw a candidate, and "Father" Hoyt a member of it. The meetings of the Presbytery were to them "refreshing seasons." Especially was this the case at the present juncture. "The Lord had recently poured out his Spirit in many parts of this Presbytery, and the friends of Zion" were "looking up with rejoicing." The Presbytery had six young men under its care as candidates for the ministry, most of them, doubtless, the pupils of Anderson.

The missionaries were visited and cheered, among others, by members of the Presbytery and missionaries sent out by the Assembly. Saunders and Moderwell visited them on their tour. Erastus Root from Georgia, and Vinal and Chapman, sent out by the United Foreign Mission Society at New York on an exploring-tour among the Indians west of the Mississippi, called upon them. Numerous and refreshing were these repeated visits from members or ministers of Presbyterian churches throughout the land. But a special interest was taken in the progress of the mission by the churches of Tennessee. In 1819, Isaac Anderson, Matthew Donald, and William Eagleton (of Kingston) were the visiting committee of the Presbytery, and signed the report of the examination of the mission-schools.

From year to year the reports were generally favorable. In 1822 the large establishment at Brainerd was divided, and its members distributed abroad throughout the bounds of the tribe. In the following year nearly one hundred persons gave evidence of hopeful conversion, and at Willstown a church "on the Presbyterian model," consisting of nine converted Cherokees, was organized (October 10), and connected with Union Presbytery. Already in September of the same year the churches at Brainerd, Carmel, and Hightower had been received: so that on the list of the Presbytery were four churches within the limits of the Cherokee mission. The number was increased by the organization of another church at Candy's Creek in the following year.

But already the plan was formed which was to result in disaster to the mission by the removal of the Cherokees beyond the Mississippi. Georgia took the lead in the harsh and cruel measures by which this plan was carried out. The missionaries were indignant and disheartened at the perfidy which violated repeated and most solemn treaties. They saw their own labors interrupted; they saw those whom they had been encouraged to hope would soon be brought to embrace the gospel, outraged and alienated by an injustice which found no excuse but in the sophistry of unscrupulous avarice, while the prospects of future success for the mission were becoming more dark and gloomy continually.

Still, they did not remit their efforts. Amid sad discouragements they labored on. Portions of the tribe were from time to time despairingly forsaking their old hunting-grounds and their fathers' graves for new homes in the distant wilderness. Yet, till actual violence was offered, and by the arrest of their persons the resolute purpose to effect a forcible removal of the Cherokees became too obvious to be longer questioned, they remained faithful to their work. But from 1829 to 1835 the odious project was pushed forward to its disastrous results. Yet for nearly twenty years the Cherokee mission, largely sustained by the sympathy of the Presbyterian Church in Tennessee, presented a noble example of self-denying Christian effort,—the more striking when contrasted with the greed and injustice of men who viewed the native tribes only in the light of their own mercenary projects.

It was doubtless through the interest excited by the missions to the Creeks and Cherokees that the attention of the United Foreign Missionary Society was directed to the Indian tribes west of the Mississippi. In 1821, the enterprise of sending out missionaries to the Osage Indians, five hundred miles west of the "Father of Waters," was undertaken. A very general sympathy throughout the Church was awakened in its behalf. A mission family, collected from nine different States, and consisting of twenty-five grown persons, male and female, and sixteen children, were set apart by the society in New York to spend their days in this remote field. The occasion was one of extraordinary interest. The exercises took place in Dr. Mason's church, and the farewell meeting was held at the Middle Dutch Church,—throngs crowding to the scene, but unable to gain admittance. Thousands of people, as the boat left the wharf, were present to witness their departure. At Elizabethtown, New Brunswick, and other places on their route they were received with cordial greetings and assisted on their way. The cause of missions received a new impulse, and an enthusiasm in its behalf was kindled throughout the Church by their initiation of an enterprise hitherto unprecedented in magnitude, at least in this country.

The cause of education in Tennessee made some progress during this period. The Southwestern Theological Seminary at Maryville, established in 1821, at the cost of no small effort and self-denial, will again claim our notice. The history of its origin and progress is the best and highest eulogy of those by whose efforts it was established. The University of Nashville, founded as Cumberland College in 1806, secured in 1824 the services of Dr. Philip Lindsley, Vice-President of New Jersey College, as President of the institution.[1] Admirably was he fitted for the post, and great was the necessity for such a man in the field he was called to occupy. A great State was just emerging from the wilderness and calling for the equipments of a Christian civilization. School-houses and churches were to be built, works of internal improvement were to be constructed; the literary, moral, and religious character of hundreds of communities was plastic now, but was taking shape for coming generations. The acquisition of such a man as Dr. Lindsley in such circumstances might well be hailed with satisfaction and gratulation by the Presbyterian Church. He was Princeton's favorite son,—a pupil of Samuel Stanhope Smith, an intimate friend of Drs. Alexander and Miller, and he was himself, withal, a master-workman. The Church in Tennessee was strengthened and cheered by his presence, sympathy, and co-operation, not only in the cause of learning, but of every "good word and work."

In 1830, the Presbytery of Union numbered twenty-

---

[1] The University of Nashville, known till 1826 as Cumberland College, was incorporated in 1806. It was opened for the reception of students in the autumn of 1809. The Faculty were James Priestly, President, William Hume, Professor of Languages, and George Martin, teacher of the grammar-school. In October, 1816, its doors were closed for sheer want of funds. In 1824 the operations of the institution were recommenced under Dr. Lindsley, who had been induced to accept the Presidency of the institution. From 1826 to 1839 the graduates numbered two hundred.—*Am. Quar. Reg.*, Feb. 1840.

five ministers and twenty-nine churches, and that of Holston (erected from Abingdon in 1826) about thirteen ministers and fourteen churches, forming an aggregate of thirty-eight ministers and forty-three churches in Eastern Tennessee. In twelve years the increase upon the field had been, of ministers more than fourfold, and of churches nearly threefold. The Second Presbyterian Church was formed at Knoxville about the year 1819; and seventeen new churches were reported as under the care of the Presbytery during the period from 1819 to 1825.[1]

The Presbytery of French Broad (erected from Union in 1825) numbered in 1830 eight ministers and ten churches, and that of West Tennessee, erected in 1810 with four ministers, had increased so as to be formed (1826) into a Synod consisting of the Presbyteries of West Tennessee, Shiloh, and North Alabama; while one of its earlier offshoots, the Presbytery of Mississippi (1815), had grown to the dimensions of a Synod. The Presbytery of West Tennessee numbered fifteen ministers and eighteen churches, and that of Shiloh (erected 1816) ten ministers and twenty-five churches. Thus the aggregate of the five Presbyteries, Union, Holston, French Broad, West Tennessee, and Shiloh,—representing the strength of the Presbyterian Church within the bounds of the State,—was ninety-six churches and seventy-one ministers, including, however, in this number, fourteen licentiates under the care of the Presbyteries.

In the field occupied by the West Tennessee Presbytery were to be found some of the most efficient and

---

[1] The church at Kingsport was formed about the year 1820, and was subsequently for nearly thirty years under the pastoral care of Dr. F. A. Ross. The Report of 1831 is the one which properly represents the churches of the preceding year, and this is the one referred to above.

laborious ministers within the bounds of the Church. The venerable Dr. Stephenson, who had removed to Maury county in 1808, was still, after more than twenty years of service in this field, in charge of Zion congregation. Gideon Blackburn, who had left Maryville in 1810 and who for a few months labored in Maury county, removed in the following year to Franklin, the capital of Williamson county, eighteen miles south of Nashville, taking charge of Harpeth Academy, and preaching in rotation at five different places within a range of fifty miles. At each of these, within a short period, he organized churches; and at his first communion-season three thousand persons were present and forty-five members were received to the Church. In 1823 he removed to Louisville, to take the pastoral charge of the church in that place.[1] His successor at Franklin was his son John N. Blackburn.

The successors of Dr. Blackburn at Nashville were Allan D. Campbell and Obadiah Jennings. The pastorate of the latter commenced here in April, 1828. His father, Jacob Jennings, was an early member of "Old Redstone" Presbytery, and the son was educated for the legal profession. After practising at the bar for several years at Steubenville, Ohio, his attention was drawn to the claims of religion, and in 1811 he united with the Church. Five years later, during a severe attack of disease, he was led to form the purpose of devoting himself to the work of the ministry. For six years he had charge of the church of Steubenville, and for five years of the church in Washington, Pa. Of earnest but unostentatious piety, a humble spirit, quick perception, and great eminence as a debater, Dr. Jennings commanded respect and confidence, and exerted a powerful influence in his new sphere of

[1] Sprague, iv. 46.

effort, where in a celebrated debate with Alexander Campbell he distinguished himself by his argumentative skill and irresistible logic.[1] His pastorate closed with his life in 1832.

Dr. Jennings's immediate predecessor at Nashville, Dr. A. D. Campbell, was a native of Lancashire, England (1791), but at an early age removed with his father's family to this country. He was educated in connection with the Associate Reformed Church, in which his father was an elder. A graduate of the University of Pennsylvania and a theological pupil of Dr. John M. Mason, he was licensed by the Philadelphia Presbytery in connection with the Associate Reformed Church, and sent to preach in the vacant churches in the neighborhood of Pittsburg. In 1818 he was settled over the congregations of Meadville and Sugar Creek, and soon after united with the Presbytery of Redstone. From 1820 to 1827, Nashville was his field of labor; but soon after this he became connected with the Allegheny Theological Seminary, in which he remained a professor till 1840. His mind was quick and active, and in extemporaneous debate he was often eloquent and irresistible. Largely perceptive and keenly sensitive, he was prompt to discern the traces of error in doctrine or morals. Outspoken and impulsive, he sometimes gave offence, and by some was regarded—especially in the crisis of 1837—as largely responsible for the division of the Church. Yet he was generous, tender, and humane, faithful as a minister, and in "pastoral aptitudes" rarely surpassed. Whatever estimate may be formed of the practical wisdom of his course in some of the emergencies of the Church, his ready self-denial, overflowing liberality, and promptitude in meeting the

[1] Sprague, iv. 554.

demands of duty entitle him to the highest respect. His death occurred Sept. 20, 1861.

The First Church of Memphis was established through the instrumentality of Samuel McCulloch Williamson. He was a native of North Carolina, and graduated at Yale College in 1823; he removed in 1826 to Tennessee with a view to enter upon the practice of the legal profession. In listening to a sermon by John W. Hall, of Murfreesborough, and through the perusal of Doddridge's "Rise and Progress," his attention was drawn to his religious duty, and he was led to devote himself to the service of Christ. Sacrificing his worldly prospects, he placed himself under the tuition of Dr. Blackburn, and in 1829 was licensed to preach by Shiloh Presbytery.

After travelling as a missionary in Western Tennessee, and laboring for a brief period among the Chickasaw and Choctaw Indians, he settled in the fall of 1830 at Memphis, where he soon succeeded in gathering a prosperous congregation. When he commenced his labors, there were but few dwellings, and not a single church-edifice, in the town; nor was the state of public morals such as to promise support or sympathy for the pastor who should be faithful in the discharge of his duty. But, with a constancy that never wavered and a firmness that never faltered, he addressed himself to his work. The consequence was that vice and impiety quailed before him, and his labors were soon crowned with the divine blessing.

In connection with his charge at Memphis, which he retained for three years, he preached at two other stations,—one ten, and the other twenty-four, miles distant. It was not uncommon for him to preach five times a week; and in order to meet his appointments he was often obliged to make his horse swim the swollen streams which abounded in that region at certain seasons of the year. His labors as an evangelist were particularly successful, and his career furnishes a parallel to that of the early ministers of Eastern Tennessee. On removing from Memphis he labored first with the Mountain and Covington congregations, and subsequently at Lagrange and Bethany, until his death in 1846.

Unsparing in his devotion to the great work of his life, he accomplished much during his short ministry. Ardent, unselfish, and steadfast, he sought the good of others while neglectful perhaps of his own. Brilliant in the social circle, he was pre-eminent in the pulpit. Although not a learned theologian nor even a profound thinker, yet for activity and energy of mind, clearness of thought, impressiveness and earnestness of manner, and fervid unaffected eloquence, he had not his superior, either in the pulpit or at the bar, in the whole Western District.[1]

The early ministry of Dr. Frederick A. Ross was in connection with the church of Kingsport, under the care of the Presbytery of Holston. A native of Eastern Virginia, he was upon the death of his father required to attend to the settlement of his estate, a portion of which lay in Hawkins county, East Tennessee. Here he came under the influence of James Gallaher, one of whose sermons he regarded as the means of his conversion. From this time he resolved to devote himself to the ministry. Licensed in 1825, his labors as a pastor and evangelist were thenceforth abundant and largely blessed, and for several years his name is associated in revival efforts with that of his former pastor.

This man—James Gallaher—was, during the period under review, one of the most efficient and popular preachers within the bounds of the State. He was of

[1] Sprague, iv. 766.

Scotch-Irish descent, and was born in Washington county, Tenn., in 1792. Upon his father's removal to Blount county, the family were exposed to constant annoyance and danger from the Creek and especially the Cherokee Indians. The home of his boyhood was a rude block-house, and his early years, when not posted as a sentinel to give the alarm against hostile attack, were devoted to labor on the farm. His advantages for education were limited, and the Bible may be said to have been almost his only text-book. With this he was remarkably familiar, and his scriptural knowledge proved his best preparation for the work of the ministry.

In 1811 he entered Washington College, then under the Presidency of Dr. Doak. But, though hopefully pious, he had not yet fully determined to devote himself to the work of the ministry. Graduated in the fall of 1813, he opened in the spring of the following year a high-school in Knoxville, which he continued for several months. While thus engaged, he formed an intimate acquaintance with members of the bar, and through their influence was for a while disposed to devote his attention to the study of the law. Upon more deliberate reflection, however, and in accordance with the expressed wishes of his pious father, he abandoned the project, and formed the definite resolve—which he never regretted—to preach the gospel.

His theological studies were prosecuted under the direction of Rev. Edward Crawford, and subsequently of Dr. Stephen Bovelle. Upon their completion he was licensed by the Presbytery of Abingdon, in December, 1815. Almost immediately he was invited by the church of New Providence and by the people of Rogersville to become their pastor.

The church-accommodations at New Providence were merely a small brick school-house that would seat about one hundred and fifty persons.[1] In a short time, under his labors, the congregation increased until it numbered four hundred church-members, and sometimes a thousand hearers.

"Lazy in every thing but thought and utterance," careless in dress, sometimes with neither hat nor coat that seemed made for him, of tall, spare frame, and with a forehead unusually low, one needed only to look into his splendid eyes, or listen to a voice whose every tone was the richest music, to feel that before him stood no ordinary man. His opportunities had not been the best, and they had not been very studiously improved. His scholarly attainments were, indeed, quite meagre. He was a stranger to the "nice points" of theology, and not much at home in theological discussion; but his imagination was fervid, his oratory wellnigh perfect, and his piety ardent and sincere. In manner, from good sense and native tact, he was free and easy, a genial companion and a warm friend. Taking in his sermons the broadest, plainest, most common-sense views of the Bible, he carried the convictions of his hearers with him, and, whether pathetic, violent, vociferous, earnest, or pointed, he uniformly secured their sympathy. Life, vivacity, excitement, seemed to overflow in his nature. In a word, he was the man for the sphere in which Providence had cast his lot. Wherever he went, he was sure to attract crowds around him, and to communicate to them the moods of his own mind; while his glowing zeal and ardent piety left no doubtful or transient impression. For fourteen years his field of labor was mainly among the churches over which he was first settled, and in the missionary field around him. In 1830, he removed to Cincinnati, to take charge of the Third Church. We meet him also in

[1] Sprague, iv. 533.

other fields; for his labors extended to Kentucky, Ohio, and Missouri.

The Presbyterian ministers of Tennessee were, in 1830—in Union Presbytery, Dr. Anderson, in charge of New Providence and the Second Church of Knoxville, Thomas H. Nelson, stated supply of the First Church, D. S. Butrick and S. A. Worcester, missionaries to the Cherokees, Elijah M. Eagleton, stated supply of Washington and Lebanon in the Fork, William A. McCampbell, stated supply of Grassy Valley, Fielding Pope, stated supply of Mars' Hill, Columbiana, and Shiloh, Thomas Brown, stated supply of Bethel and Mt. Zion, Darius Hoyt, stated supply of Eusebia and Pleasant Grove, Andrew Vance, stated supply of Baker's Creek, while Alexander McGhee, Abel Pearson, Sumner Mandeville, Michael A. Remley, A. G. McNutt, A. M. Keith, and Gideon S. White were without charge, and from twelve to fifteen churches were vacant; in the Presbytery of French Broad, President Coffin, John McCampbell, at Strawberry Plains, Hopewell, and New Market, William Minnis, at Westminster, St. Paul's, and New Salem, Francis A. McCorkle, at Mt. Zion, Harmony, and Timber Ridge, Nathaniel Hood, stated supply at Pisgah and Tazewell, and Stephen Foster, without charge; in Holston Presbytery, Dr. Doak, James Gallaher, F. A. Ross, S W. Doak, pastor at Mt. Bethel and Providence, L. G. Bell, pastor of Hebron and supply of New Bethel, A. S. Morrison, stated supply of Blountville and Paperville, and Robert Glenn and William Quillin, without charge, while five churches were vacant; in West Tennessee Presbytery, Dr. Stephenson, stated supply at Zion, Dr. Henderson, at Franklin, Dr. D. Brown, at Ebenezer and Salem, Thomas J. Hall, at Bethberei, Dr. Robert Hardin, at Columbia and Bethesda, Dr. Jennings, pastor at Nashville, William Hume, at Harpeth and Communion, Hugh Shaw, stated supply at Cathie's Creek,

James Hall Brooks, at Pulaski and Bethany, Samuel W. Calvert, at Elk Ridge and Mars' Hill, while President Lindsley, S. C. McConnell, Edmund Lanier, Lewis McLeod, and James H. Shields were without charge, and three or four churches were vacant; in Shiloh Presbytery, George Newton, stated supply at Shelbyville, Beth-Salem, and New Providence, Jesse Alexander, at Stone's River, Hopewell, Cripple Creek, and Mt. Vernon, James Macklin, at Fayetteville and Unity, William Eagleton, at Murfreesborough, John W. Hall, pastor of Gallatin and Shiloh, Ebenezer McEwen, stated supply of Eldad, Salem, and Jehoshaphat, Amzi Bradshaw, of Smyrna and Spring Creek, John L. Sloane, of Peyton's Creek, while seven churches were vacant.[1]

The progress of the Church in Tennessee for the first thirty years of the century had been healthful and steady, although far less rapid than in some other portions of the country. The five or six ministers of 1800 had been multiplied nearly tenfold. The churches, if not proportionally increased in numbers, had advanced in strength, and not a little had been accomplished in the cause of literary and theological education. We shall be led hereafter to note the urgent demand which was still made for more laborers.

---

[1] It is a noteworthy fact that in 1830 the Presbyteries of Union and Shiloh had each but one settled pastor, West Tennessee had two pastors, and Holston and French Broad had three each, making in the five Presbyteries and within the bounds of the State only ten settled pastors.

CHAPTER XXXVI.

THE CHURCH AT LARGE—GENERAL SURVEY, MISSIONS, THEOLOGICAL EDUCATION, AND REVIVALS—1825-1830.

In the period which elapsed from 1825 to 1835, the numbers and strength of the Presbyterian Church throughout the country advanced more than fifty per cent. The Synods increased from fourteen to twenty-three, and the Presbyteries from eighty-one to about one hundred and twenty-five. At the commencement of this period the number of ministers connected with them was ten hundred and eighty; at its close they amounted to about two thousand. The churches had increased from seventeen hundred and seventy-two to nearly two thousand eight hundred; while the membership had more than doubled, amounting in 1835 to a little more than two hundred and fifty thousand.

A portion of the period—to which our attention is more especially called in this chapter—was characterized by powerful and extensive revivals. They were limited to no section, but were especially prevalent in Western New York, Ohio, and South Carolina. An extraordinary energy seemed to pervade the Church. Union measures for evangelical effort were adopted with great readiness, and even fervor. Plans were entertained for establishing Sunday-schools extensively throughout the Mississippi Valley, for placing a Bible in each family throughout the land, for disseminating tracts and religious books in connection with the American Tract Society then recently established at New York, and for the general causes of ministerial education and home missionary enterprise. The report of the Postmaster-General (1829) in favor of Sunday mails aroused a strong feeling of indignation, and excited the churches to measures for vindicating the Lord's day from profanation. Many of the churches and Presbyteries co-operated effectively with the "Sabbath Union." The cause of temperance, in connection with the labors of Drs. Beecher and Hewitt, was successfully promoted. The monthly concert came to be more generally and extensively observed; and by the General Assembly of 1830 its claims were recommended to the attention not only of its own churches, but of the various religious denominations throughout the land.

Throughout the bounds of the Church a new religious life seemed to be powerfully at work. In the midst of great destitutions, there was a missionary zeal awakened which aimed zealously at some effectual means for their supply. Independent of the Assembly's Board of Missions, there were several local societies which had gone into operation. The First Presbyterian Church of Philadelphia had its Missionary Association. The Western Missionary Society of Utica was organized in 1826, and within the first year of its existence sent into the field thirty ministers, whose labors extended to fifty towns and villages, in eight of which no church had yet been organized. The Monroe County Missionary Society was organized at about the same time, and both were auxiliary to the American Home Missionary Society, which was established the same year.

In its organization this society absorbed in itself the Young Men's Missionary Society of New York, which had sent missionaries to Illinois and Missouri as well as Western New York, and also the United Domestic Missionary Society, whose responsibilities it assumed, thus receiving upon its list from this source alone more than three-fourths of the missionaries whom it employed.[1]

This society had been formed after long and extended correspondence with prominent members of the different co-operative denominations in 1826. At the time of the May anniversaries of that year, a convention, embracing friends of missions from every part of the country, met in the city of New York and resolved upon its formation. If the United Domestic Missionary Society should see fit to adopt the constitution framed by the convention, it was resolved that it should become the American Home Missionary Society. The recommendation was adopted, and on the list of the officers consequently elected were to be found the names of prominent members of the Presbyterian, Reformed Dutch, and Congregational Churches,—Drs. Alexander, Rice, Richards, Hillyer, Davis, De Witt, Griffin, Miller, Porter, Wilson, Taylor, Tyler, Beman, Payson, Day, Carnahan, Neill, McDowell, Fish, and others scarcely less distinguished for eminence and piety. The formation of the society was hailed almost by acclamation from all parts of the Union. From Kentucky, Mississippi, and the Carolinas, as well as from the States west of New York, there came back a cheerful response to a project which placed another on the list of *national* societies and which promised to be not less beneficent than any of the others. The first address of the executive committee dwelt with great emphasis upon its *national* character. It was to be national in its *object*, *plan*, *dependence*, and *location*. It designed "no interference with the benevolent exertions of those who might deem it their duty to act apart from its advice." On these broad grounds

---

[1] One hundred and one missionaries, eighty-one of whom were in the State of New York, were in the service of the United Domestic Missionary Society.

it claimed to be exempt from the charge of presumption in assuming "the style of a national institution."

With scarcely so much as a single dissenting voice, it received the suffrage and sympathy of the Presbyterian Church. No jealousy was felt in its feebleness of an organization which in full maturity of strength might wield almost the power of a distinct denomination. Its missionaries went forth to the West and South to receive from every quarter a cordial welcome. There was a broad field opened before it, more than justifying its organization. Taking the whole West into view, with its six Synods (1828), the missionary field which it presented was one which might well excite alarm and yet inspire to effort. Its condition urgently demanded the most serious attention of Eastern Christians and the concentration of all their missionary energies. The number of organized congregations was not far from six hundred and fifty, while the places which were yet unoccupied and open to Presbyterian organization might be counted not by scores, but by hundreds. Yet in the entire field there were but little more than three hundred ministers. Five hundred, at least, were immediately needed to supply its urgent necessities.

In the South and Southwest—in Virginia and North Carolina, as well as in Louisiana and Mississippi—the demand for additional laborers was equally urgent. Even the oldest-settled portions of the Church were but scantily supplied, and many congregations were entirely destitute of regular preaching. Yet the Atlantic States were highly favored when compared with those beyond the mountains. It is not surprising, when the state of the entire country is taken into view, that the great mass of the Presbyterian Church should hail with joy the inauguration of a national institution which promised to supply a national want. It may not be amiss to review—not only with reference to the circumstances which gave birth to the American Home Missionary Society, but with respect also to the condition and prospects of the Church—the religious state of the country as related to Presbyterian progress at the time when the American Home Missionary Society was instituted. In the State of New York, where missionary operations had been vigorously conducted for more than twenty years, and in which the United Domestic Missionary Society had about eighty commissioned ministers in its employ, the population was more liberally supplied with the means of grace than in almost any other part of the Presbyterian Church. Yet even here the field was far from fully occupied. Even as late as 1830 the demand was urgent for more ministers and the means to support them. The Presbytery of Troy at this period had under its care twenty-six churches, and only eleven or twelve ministers engaged in pastoral duty. Nine or ten of the churches were without preaching, except through an occasional supply from the Presbytery or from some travelling minister.

In many of the western parts of the State there was even greater destitution. Of the twenty-two churches of Oswego Presbytery, only two were fully supplied with preaching. Eight were partially supplied, and twelve were entirely destitute. In what was called "the Western District" of the State, there were fifty congregations vacant, and a call for the organization of fifty more in fields as yet unoccupied. In 1825–26 there was but one self-supporting church within the bounds of Niagara Presbytery.

In Northern Pennsylvania the state of things was much the same as in Western New York.[1] In New

[1] Some estimate of its character at a later period may be derived from Prime's Life of Dr. Murray.

Jersey there was a loud call for missionary effort. Some portions of the State might almost be denominated heathen ground. On the Eastern Shore from Shrewsbury to Cape May there was but a single Presbyterian Church.[1] A missionary who traversed nearly the whole southern part of the State said, "On the whole, the country through which I travelled presents a very gloomy aspect to the eye of Christian philanthropy."

Passing onward to the regions farther West, we find that in Geauga county, on Lake Erie, in the northeast of Ohio, there was but a single Presbyterian pastor in 1827. The moral and religious condition of the region was represented as most deplorable. In connection with the Synod of the Western Reserve, there were eighty-seven churches, and within its limits forty-two Presbyterian ministers; but of the churches forty-one consisted of not over twenty members each, and of the ministers three only preached their whole time to single congregations. To the north of Granville, when the revivals of 1828 commenced, the church at Hartford, consisting of fifteen members, had not enjoyed the privilege of the communion for seven years. Bennington and Burlington, where the work extended with great power, had never enjoyed the stated ministrations of the gospel. A large number of the churches throughout the State were altogether unsupplied with ministers, and many of them were in such a feeble state that even if two or three had united in their efforts they would have been utterly unable to support a pastor without aid from abroad. The northwestern portion of the State could not, indeed, be said to be settled. Here and there an opening had been made; but there was scarcely as yet an organized church in this region, which was soon destined to receive a large accession of population.

---

[1] Report of U. D. M. S., 1826.

Into Indiana (1827) a tide of immigration was pouring with unexampled rapidity. Farms were "everywhere opening in the wilderness." Already "every twenty or thirty miles the spire of a handsome courthouse of brick" rose "amidst the deadened trunks" of the veterans of the forest. The tract of country bordering on the Wabash was fast becoming "the garden-spot" of the State. Population was augmenting at a most rapid rate. It was estimated already at between two and three hundred thousand within the State limits. Yet there were but twelve resident Presbyterian ministers. The field of the Presbytery which included Indianapolis was two hundred miles long by eighty broad, and, although numbering nineteen congregations, it had but four members with pastoral charges. The resident pastor at Indianapolis, George Bush, had to travel one hundred and forty miles to the meeting of Presbytery; and his nearest clerical neighbor was from forty to fifty miles distant from him. Two years later there had been a great advance; but the religious destitution was still lamentable. In 1826–27, five churches within the bounds of one of the Presbyteries had become extinct through want of ministers. Within the State there were estimated to be sixty Presbyterian churches, with only twenty-five ministers; and in thirty counties there was not a single minister.

In Illinois there were but six or seven ministers settled as pastors. The labors devolved upon them were overwhelming. All that they could accomplish seemed lost in the broad waste which stretched around them on every side. This was the case also in Missouri There were but five or six missionaries in the whole State in connection with the Presbyterian Church, while many places stood in pressing need of aid.[1]

---

[1] The population of Illinois and Missouri together amounted, in

Michigan, with a population of thirty thousand, had in 1830 but seven Presbyterian ministers, members of the Presbytery of Detroit. Two others were on the way to the field; but they could scarcely keep good the proportion to the immigrant population at the same time entering the Territory.

In Kentucky there were in 1827 only three points, in the extensive portion of it bordering on the Ohio River, where the ministry was supported. These were Maysville, Augusta, and Louisville. In the bounds of Muhlenburg Presbytery there were sixteen vacancies. In one portion of the State, with a population of one hundred thousand, there was not a Presbyterian minister. In the whole State, with a population of nearly six hundred thousand, there were but forty Presbyterian pastors.

In East Tennessee, no society that had yet been formed had been hailed with greater joy by the friends of the Presbyterian Church than the American Home Missionary Society. The number of ministers in the region was very small, compared with the population; yet there were many congregations ready and anxious to do something, if they could be assisted in the support of a minister.[1] West Tennessee was even less favored. Its destitutions were greater, and its means of supply were far more limited. So pressing were its necessities that the Synod in 1827 determined to establish a theological seminary in connection with the university re-

---

1824, to one hundred and sixty thousand; but in this field there were at this time only eighteen organized churches, nearly every one of them exceedingly feeble, and only seven ordained ministers.

[1] A missionary having charge of four churches in Rutherford county, in the central part of the State, writes, Aug. 28, 1830, "There is not another Presbyterian preacher between me and the Cumberland Mountain,—a region of ten counties, and most of them thickly populated."—*Chris. Adv.*, 1830, p. 560.

cently incorporated at Nashville, for the training of young men for the ministry.

At New Orleans there was the single Presbyterian church gathered by Cornelius and Larned, and of which Theodore Clapp was now pastor. The population of the city was nearly fifty thousand, and in the busy season not far short of seventy thousand. Its position gave it an important influence over the entire valley of the Mississippi. Yet several years passed while its appeals were unheeded save by the few friends who in 1826–27 aided J. L. de Fernex in his attempt to build up a French Protestant church.

In the rest of the State there were but two Presbyterian ministers. West of the Mississippi there was not one. South of Tennessee and west of Alabama there were but six, including the two at Natchez and New Orleans. The two States of Mississippi and Louisiana were within the bounds of the Mississippi Presbytery, and among a population of nearly three hundred thousand the Presbytery numbered but twelve members, only nine of whom were engaged in ministerial labors upon the field. Yet Memphis, Port Gibson, The New Purchase, Liberty, and Pisgah were importunate for supplies. Five or six new churches were organized during the year,—one at Baton Rouge,—and were urgent in their demands for pastors. East of Pearl River every church was destitute of regular preaching. The only aid which they had received was from three missionaries sent out by the Assembly, and from De Fernex at New Orleans.

In the bounds of the Presbytery of Alabama there were numerous settlements which invited aid, and where by missionary and pastoral labor churches might be organized. This was especially the case in the southeastern section of the State, on the borders of Florida. At Pensacola, in the country west of Black

Warrior River, in the region north and northeast of Tuscaloosa, there were fields which urgently claimed attention. The table of the Presbytery "was literally covered with the petitions of these people for supplies." In 1827 the recently organized church at Mobile, consisting of one hundred and twelve members and supplied but once a month by Rev. Mr. Kennedy, commenced the erection of a church-edifice which was to serve as church, academy, Sunday-school room, and Bible and tract depository. At about the same time a church of sixty members was organized in Pike county; but for these and other churches it was impossible to procure regular preaching. In Georgia the Presbytery of Hopewell, extending over nearly the entire State, had numerous vacant churches applying for aid; but, after making appointment of settled pastors as temporary supplies as far as they felt warranted, they could not meet the demand which was made upon them. With seventeen ordained ministers, they needed at least, and at once, more than twice as many. The number of churches was rapidly multiplying, at a rate fivefold the increase of the members of Presbytery. The earnestness of the applications for ministerial aid was deeply affecting,—"to the Presbytery, heart-melting." It was most trying to be compelled, from want of men and means, to deny them aid.

In East Florida there was a single Protestant church in a population numbering six thousand, one-third of which was at St. Augustine. Mr. Eleazar Lathrop, seconding McWhir in his efforts, had labored to build up a Presbyterian congregation at this place; but in 1826, on the failure of his health, he was succeeded by Mr. Snowden. In West Florida, D. R. Preston, sent out by the Assembly's Board of Missions to labor in Pensacola and places adjacent, found but a single Protestant minister,—a Methodist. Prior to his visit, only one sermon had ever been preached in the region by a Presbyterian minister. Throughout the Territory the state of morals was sad indeed. At St. Augustine especially this was the case. Gambling-houses and billiard-tables were licensed by law.

South Carolina Presbytery, embracing the western part of the State, had (1827) thirty-five churches and but twelve members. Not a single congregation enjoyed the undivided labors of a pastor. Some of the ministers supplied three, and even four, congregations. Yet twelve churches were vacant, and there was no prospect of supply unless laborers were sent from abroad. Three of the oldest and, at one time, most flourishing churches of the Presbytery were sinking to decay from the want of pastors. The edifices in which they worshipped were unoccupied and crumbling to ruins.

The destitution in North Carolina was extreme. A home missionary on his way to his field in Davidson county said, "I travelled over the space of about two hundred and forty miles from Newbern, and found a region of country between Greensborough, in Guilford county, and Salisbury, in Rowan county, fifty miles in extent, entirely destitute of that kind of influence exerted by a well qualified ministry." As a general thing, throughout the State, ministers with two or three congregations from six to fifteen and twenty miles apart were obliged to obtain no small part of their support from secular employments.

In Northwestern Virginia and the extensive bordering regions in Ohio and Kentucky, the religious destitution which prevailed was extreme. A home missionary found himself here in a tract one hundred miles in diameter in which there was not another Presbyterian minister, and in which there were only the two small churches of Burlington and Bethesda. In the bounds of Winchester Presbytery, embracing twelve counties on the east and seven on the west of the Blue Ridge, there were but fourteen ministers; and it was estimated that at least a population of one hundred and thirty thousand were without the regular ministrations of the gospel.

In Maryland and Eastern Virginia many of the Presbyterian churches were in a very decayed state. Some that were once flourishing had but a name to live. The church at Drummondstown, where Makemie once preached, had totally disappeared. In Vienna, on the banks of the Nanticoke, not a vestige was left of the building in which the Presbyterians once worshipped. Eight miles from Snow Hill, a congregation, which within fifteen years previous was large and flourishing, was entirely scattered. In Cambridge there had been a Presbyterian church; but now, said the report, "*Ichabod* may be written amidst its ruins." Other churches had met with a similar experience, while others still gave feeble warrant of a protracted existence. Only with great difficulty could many of them be sustained. In the Presbytery of Lewes there were about eight hundred members and but four ordained ministers. Yet the peninsula which it occupied opened "a wide and inviting field for ministerial enterprise." There were large towns where, without intruding on ground occupied by others, new congregations might be formed.

In such circumstances as these, it is not surprising that among all classes and in all sections the Home Missionary Society should appear to be just the agency demanded by the emergency. It had a noble field, and it speedily rallied around it the sympathies of the friends of evangelical religion throughout the land. Various influences concurred to secure it a favorable prestige and popular sympathy. The old method of sending out itinerants to organize churches in fields which in some cases were not revisited for years, would no longer answer. In many instances the remoteness of the field, except for ministers already settled, was such that more time was consumed on the journey than in the duties of the mission. It not unfrequently happened that the transient labors of a Presbyterian missionary merely laid the foundation upon which other denominations, or perhaps errorists, might build. The tour of Messrs. Mills and Schermerhorn in 1812–13 enabled them to see the impolicy of such efforts to sustain missions; and in their report they gave full expression to their convictions. The Eastern Societies, the United Domestic Missionary Society, and its successor the American Home Missionary Society, endeavored to improve on these suggestions. They sent out men for the most part not already settled as pastors, but who might locate themselves on the field. The reports of such men, known at the East, excited interest there; while the Western churches looked more hopefully to the societies which met their wants, than to the Assembly's Board, which failed to do it. This fact is attested by the transfer of popular sympathy, by which the missionary resources of the Assembly's Board fell, several years previous to 1826–27, from five thousand to four thousand dollars; and even in this latter sum was included the interest of the permanent fund, then amounting to nearly twenty-one thousand dollars.

In connection with the work of home missions there was an increasing and more urgent demand for ministers of the gospel. To meet this demand, extraordinary efforts were made. Until 1818, Princeton Seminary was the only public institution for the special education of ministers of the gospel within the bounds of the Presbyterian Church; although Hampden-Sidney had enjoyed the labors of a Theological professor. In that year the Synod of Geneva, convened at Rochester, resolved, after a protracted discussion, on the establishment of a seminary in Western New York. In the following spring the project was laid before the General Assembly. Although this body did not feel warranted to promise its support or extend aid, it threw no obstacle in the way of the Synod. Measures were therefore taken for the endowment of the institution. More than sixteen thousand dollars were almost immediately subscribed, and Auburn was selected as the site for the seminary. An act of incorporation was secured in 1820, by which the general supervision and direction of the institution were taken from the Synod and placed in the hands of a Board of Commissioners, to be annually selected from the Presbyteries. Messrs. Mills and Lansing and Dr. M. L. Perrine were elected professors, and on the second Wednesday of October, 1821, the course of instruction in the seminary commenced. The students the first year numbered eleven. Seven years later, they amounted to seventy-six.

Perhaps in no portion of the Church was the need of enlarged means of liberal education more deeply felt than within the bounds of the Western Reserve. The necessities of the region have been already stated. Miami College, under Dr. Bishop, had been established in 1824, but the local demands of the Reserve led to the establishment of the college founded two years later at Hudson. At a subsequent period a Theological department was connected with it. For many years it struggled for existence. It was without a presiding officer, and its endowments were quite limited; but in three years the number of its students rose from four or five to forty. Two additional buildings were erected, and accommodations provided for eighty students. The citizens of New York, in 1830, contributed liberally toward the necessities of the institution.

In 1826 the American Home Missionary Society applied to Andover and Princeton Seminaries for Western missionaries. Nowhere were they in greater demand than in Illinois and Missouri. In the former State it was felt unwise to wait for the tardy operations of Eastern benevolence. Immediate provision should be made for training up men on the mission-field. In 1826 measures were taken for the establishment of a Theological Seminary at Rock Spring; and before the close of the following year the institution numbered two theological, and fifty other, students, while applications were numerous beyond the means of accommodation.

In 1828 the Presbytery of Illinois deputed one of its members, J. M. Ellis, to apply at the East for aid for the more ample endowment of a seminary of learning, which they hoped would grow into a college. This was the first important step toward securing the funds necessary to found Illinois College. Mr. Ellis visited New Haven and New York. In the latter city he was warmly received by members of the Presbyterian and Reformed Dutch Churches. At a meeting of several gentlemen interested in the cause, two thousand dollars were subscribed in its behalf, and the subscription was afterward considerably increased. Before the close of 1829 the walls of the college-building were up, and it was ready soon after for the reception of students.

Already the Presbyterians of Indiana had commenced their labors in the cause of education. Hanover Academy, at South Hanover, in Jefferson county, had been established, the germ of South Hanover College; and the cheering fact was announced that fourteen of its twenty students were hopefully pious. In 1829 measures were taken by the Synod to establish a Theological Seminary in connection with the institution. The trustees tendered their charter to the Synod, and it was accepted. A Theological department was instituted, and Dr. John Matthews was unanimously elected Theological Professor. In 1830, at the meeting of Synod, the constitution of the "Indiana Theological Seminary" was adopted, directors were appointed, and another professor (John F. Crowe) chosen.

Kentucky was urgent for the establishment of a Theological Seminary on the plan of Princeton; and the subject was brought to the attention of the Assembly of 1825. But other portions of the Church at the West were interested in the project, and the question of the location of the seminary was one of no little perplexity. The report of a committee to whom the subject was given in charge, and which was made to the Assembly of 1826, designated Alleghany Town, in Western Pennsylvania, as the site of the proposed institution. This was too far East to suit the great majority of the Western members. It was finally resolved that the institution be located either at Alleghany Town, or at Walnut Hills, near Cincinnati, or at Charleston, Indiana, as the General Assembly of 1827 should direct. Against this resolution deferring action Rev. Dr. J. L. Wilson entered his protest. The Western Synods, he said, had too long languished for the want of such an institution. The action of the Assembly was, moreover, objectionable as setting up the site of the seminary to the highest bidder, and might have the effect of locating it on a spot which would not meet the wishes or wants of the Western churches. The decision of the Assembly was also, in his view, calculated to divide the attention, distract the counsels, and cut off the hopes of those sections of the Western country which most needed such an institution, while it would effectually deter Cincinnati—the neighborhood of which was most favorable for the site—from earnest effort in its behalf.

In spite, however, of all the objections that were

urged, Alleghany City was finally chosen, in 1827, as the site of the Western Theological Seminary. The institution was opened in the fall of the same year. For some time its prospects were far from cheering. The professors chosen to fill its chairs declined their appointments. Its funds had been mismanaged, and each year for quite a period the Assembly was under the necessity of making large appropriations not merely for the support of the instructors, but the erection of buildings.

The establishment of this seminary in Western Pennsylvania was not regarded by the more Western Synods with entire satisfaction. It was almost immediately after the decision of the Assembly was announced that the Indiana Synod commenced its independent operations; and the attention of the Kentucky Synod already began to be drawn to the project which resulted in the establishment of its own institution at Danville. They went so far as to appoint a Theological Professor in connection with the college.

Meanwhile, Southwestern Ohio felt that its claims had been overlooked, and there was here also a disposition to proceed independently of the Assembly. The means only were wanting for carrying out the project; but these were soon, in part at least, to be supplied. Walnut Hills had been the rival of Alleghany Town in its claim as the site of the seminary which the Assembly was to establish. This claim the Western Synods were not yet prepared to relinquish. They felt that the Assembly's choice was unfortunate; and, though compelled to acquiesce in the decision which was carried by a bare majority, they were disposed to improve whatever occasion might offer to secure the advantages of a seminary of their own.

The seminary at Alleghany Town promised in 1829

to be little better than a failure.[1] The Synods of Kentucky, Ohio, and Indiana had very decidedly refused to co-operate with it, as, indeed, its remoteness in great measure precluded co-operation. The way was now opened for carrying out the project of a literary and theological institution at Walnut Hills, two miles from Cincinnati, the place selected by the committee of the Assembly in 1827. Some time after the revival of 1828, the two Messrs Lane, of Boston, having been convinced from personal observation on their way to New Orleans of the demand which existed for the establishment of a theological institution, resolved to found it themselves. They were Baptists, but men of liberal and comprehensive views. They presented the project first to their own denomination, but, finding them indisposed to co-operate, they resolved to make their munificent offer to the Presbyterians. Lane Seminary was accordingly founded, after conference with the professors at Princeton, and with Dr. Wilson at Cincinnati and Dr. Nelson at Danville. At first only a literary department was established, which was afterward transferred to the Miami University under the care of Dr. Bishop. When the Theological department was established, Arthur Tappan, of New York, offered to found a professorship, on condition that Dr. Lyman Beecher should be the incumbent. The condition was accepted. Dr. Wilson was consulted in the matter, and is said to have been instrumental in inviting to the Presidency of the institution the man whom only a few months subsequently he prosecuted for heresy.[2]

The Southern and Western Theological Seminary at Maryville in East Tennessee, and under the care of the

[1] For a description of the location of the seminary, see Assembly's Minutes for 1828, p. 251.

[2] Davidson's Kentucky. Dr. Wilson himself, however, denied this.

Synod, was, amid great discouragement, doing a good work for the supply of the churches. No institution kindred to it was to be found within the distance of five hundred miles. It was located in a position central to a population of two millions, large numbers of whom were altogether destitute of the stated privileges of the gospel, and while many churches of the region, once flourishing, were going to decay. It may serve to give some idea of the primitive simplicity of the arrangements of the institution, as well as of the difficulties which it had to encounter, to state that while many of its members were charity-students, twelve hundred bushels of corn were credited to their labor in a single year, and the expense of the institution for their board was thus reduced to *one dollar per month.* Effort was made to give greater efficiency to the operations of the seminary and enlarge its resources, and urgent appeals were made in its behalf to the Christian public. But it was less fortunate at this period than some other kindred institutions its juniors in age, but not its superiors in merit.

Western Tennessee was also dissatisfied with the location of the Assembly's seminary, and in 1827 the Synod resolved to devise and mature a plan for a Theological Seminary within its bounds. Nashville College had gone into operation in 1825, and it was considered wisest by some to appoint a Theological Professor in connection with it.

Even Mississippi, feeble in Presbyterian resources, felt at this juncture the common impulse in favor of the cause of education. In 1829, Jeremiah Chamberlain presented to the Presbytery of Mississippi the plan, which for several months he had been maturing, of an institution to be under the care of the Presbyterian Church and to be located somewhere in the Southern country. This was the germ of Oakland College, of which Dr. Chamberlain was chosen the first President. He entered upon his duties in 1830.

In the bounds of Virginia, the Union Theological Seminary had been engaged for two or three years with fair prospects in the work of ministerial education; but its endowment was insufficient, and in 1826 it was received, at the request of its trustees, under the care of the General Assembly. Measures were taken, however, at this period to enlarge its resources. Dr. John H. Rice was appointed a professor, and with great energy labored to secure the amount necessary for the endowment of the institution. By his efforts in New York the means (thirty thousand dollars) were secured for one professorship. Philadelphia gave ten thousand dollars, Virginia about twenty thousand dollars, and with the Synod of Virginia the Synod of North Carolina heartily co-operated. In the course of four years from the appointment of Dr. Rice, the number of theological students in connection with the seminary was thirty-five. A plan for a similar institution in South Carolina was consequently, for the time, deferred.

While the cause of theological and collegiate institutions was thus receiving an attention and exciting an interest unprecedented in the history of the Presbyterian Church, corresponding effort was likewise necessary for the aid of candidates for the gospel ministry. This was not a new subject. More than seventy years before, the Synod of New York had felt the necessity of making provision for the education of indigent candidates, and at successive periods their plan for an annual collection toward the object had been revived. In 1806 the claims of ministerial education were earnestly pressed by the Assembly upon the attention of the Presbyteries; but it was not till 1819 that a Board of Education was established.

But already there were several voluntary and local

societies in the field. In 1815 one had been formed at Boston. Eight years previously one had been organized at Dorset in Vermont. Soon after the action of the Assembly in creating its own Board, education societies sprang up extensively throughout the bounds of the Church. Some of these were auxiliary to the Board, and some to the American Education Society.

This last institution was located at Boston. The one formed at New York was auxiliary to it. This was their mutual relation till it was reversed by the removal of the society to New York in 1830. The appointment of Elias Cornelius as secretary of the society, in 1826, gave a new impulse to the cause. His labors in New York City were eminently successful. He infused into other minds the enthusiasm and energy of his own. In 1828 the Laight Street Church resolved to educate thirty, and the Central Church ten, young men for the ministry. To more distant parts of the country this reawakened interest in the cause of ministerial education was extended. Numerous auxiliaries were formed in different States, and extensively throughout the bounds of the Church. The resources of the society, as well as the applications made to it, were doubled within a few months, and the removal of its location to New York seemed to give it rank and standing by the side of the other societies which had assumed to themselves a national character.

The union of the American and Presbyterian Education Societies was effected in 1827. The latter society had at the time about one hundred young men under its patronage. The sphere of its operations, which had previously been more extended, was now confined to the Middle States. The two denominations were united thus in the same organization. Dr. Rice, of Virginia, approved the plan. "I am very greatly pleased with it," he wrote. "I do delight greatly in witnessing the union and co-operation of Christians in building up the kingdom of our common Lord." "My heart rejoices," said Cornelius, "in the smile of Heaven upon this holy alliance." This was the feeling which prevailed with great unanimity throughout the bounds of the Church.

The success of the society thus organized occasioned joyful surprise. At the close of the year (in 1827) there had been thirty-five who had been taken under the society's patronage. In 1829, only two years later, the number amounted to over two hundred.

But its very success sowed in some quarters the seeds of jealousy. The Assembly's Board had accomplished little. The energies and resources by which it should have been sustained were drawn off to the national society. While this counted its beneficiaries by hundreds, the Board had but nineteen upon its list. In estimating the influences that bound one portion of the Presbyterian Church in sympathy with the national societies and repelled another from them, thus contributing to the division, this fact is not to be overlooked.

To the New York Missionary Society of New York the United Foreign Missionary Society had succeeded in 1817. But the American Board of Commissioners for Foreign Missions had been instituted several years previous, and its labors in foreign lands had drawn largely to it the sympathies of the Presbyterian Church. The reports of its missionaries were read throughout the country, and in various quarters secured for it active co-operation. Even the missionary society of South Carolina and Georgia became an auxiliary. In these circumstances, a plan of union was proposed between the New York Society and the American Board. It was presented to the Assembly of 1826, and was received with general favor. Although there were some who were very decidedly opposed to it, and the members of the Assembly and the Church generally were far from unanimous in their approval of the project, it was enforced by weighty reasons. The United Foreign Missionary Society was not under the Assembly's control, although largely sustained by its churches. The American Board already received a large proportion of its funds from within the bounds of the Presbyterian Church. The society at New York was consequently crippled for the want of means, and the magnitude of the foreign missionary work was not yet such as to require two distinct organizations for denominations so kindred in doctrine and effort as the Congregationalists of New England and the supporters of the society at New York. The result was the consent of the Assembly to the amalgamation of the two societies, and its recommendation of the Board to the favorable notice and Christian support of the Church and people under their care.

Thus the tendency of things seemed to be decidedly in favor of voluntary societies. The jealousy which they were destined to excite had as yet scarcely begun to be developed. In connection, moreover, with their inauguration, and unquestionably due in part to their influence, a new religious life seemed to pervade the churches of the land. An unwonted activity was manifest in all quarters, and, with the single exception of the comparative failure of Presbyterian organizations as such,—although the explanation was not difficult,—the future seemed full of promise.

Within the bounds of the Synod of New York the prospects of the Church were, on the whole, cheering. In the Presbyteries of New York, Hudson, and North River there were, in 1827, powerful revivals. In New York City, Rutgers Street, Cedar Street, Laight Street, and Spring Street Churches were greatly blessed. The following year was less marked in this respect; but in

1829 more than one thousand members, mostly upon examination, were added to the churches. In 1830 the number was not so great; but in the following years the revival was still more extensive and powerful than it had been at any previous period.

Within the bounds of the Synod of Albany, especially in the Presbytery of Troy, there were during a portion of this period extensive revivals. In many of the Western churches, indeed in nearly all of them, there was a new and unprecedented development of spiritual life. The journals of the day spoke of revivals among them by tens and scores. In some cases there was doubtless a zeal not always according to knowledge, and questionable methods were sometimes employed in conducting the meetings; but for several successive years the work of grace among the churches of Western New York was characterized by great power, and the number added to their communion was unprecedented in their previous history. In the larger towns and cities, as well as in the villages, there was a prevalent religious tone of feeling, which powerfully modified the character of the entire community.

Of more than one hundred churches under the care of the Synod of New Jersey in 1828, only four reported revivals among them. But in the following winter among many of them the Spirit of God was manifestly at work. Fourteen congregations in East Jersey were visited by seasons of refreshing At Morristown, Paterson, and Mendham the work was especially powerful.

In Pennsylvania there were revivals (during the period of 1827–30) in a large number of places, although less marked than in some other portions of the Church. In Philadelphia, the congregations of Messrs. Hoover and Patterson were specially favored.[1] During a part

[1] In 1831–32, two hundred were added on examination to the church under the care of Dr. T. H. Skinner.

of the time Mr. Finney labored with them; and during the few years which had elapsed since the church of which Rev. James Patterson was pastor had been organized, twelve hundred members had been received to its communion. At Mercer, York, Milford, and several places within the bounds of the Synod of Pittsburg there were seasons of spiritual refreshing.

Revivals occurred in Ohio at numerous places. In 1827 there were extensive awakenings at Lebanon, Canaan, Portage, &c.; but at the close of the year a remarkable work of grace commenced in the First Presbyterian Church at Cincinnati. The pastor, Dr. Wilson, had visited, a short time previous, the scenes of the Kentucky revival. Here, at the close of a communion-season at New Providence, he heard Rev. Joseph C. Barnes[1] read a number of appointments for the Rev. James Gallaher and Rev. Frederick Ross, who had itinerated extensively as evangelists throughout the State. Impressed with the desirableness of their labors in his own region, he besought them to visit Cincinnati. They complied with the invitation; and almost immediately a work of grace commenced. It continued with great power for several months. Dr. Wilson himself pronounced Messrs. Gallaher and Ross "most admirably qualified" for their work. Within the year revivals were enjoyed in ten of the neighboring churches, —among them, those of Pleasant Ridge, Springfield, Reading, and Hopewell; and the number added to the First Church in Cincinnati on examination amounted to three hundred and sixty-four.

In the more central parts of the State revivals extensively prevailed. At Granville, Burlington, Bennington, Hartford, Jersey, McKane, St. Albans, Berlin, Berkshire, Harrison, Worthington, Zoar, Hillborough,

---

[1] New York Observer: account of the revival.

Franklin, and other places, there were powerful awakenings. At Burlington and Bennington churches were formed. At Granville thirty-six families for the first time "set up the family altar." At Claridon, Hamden, Huntsburg, and Burton, to the northeast, there were also revivals of great power. In Delaware county this was likewise the case. In Berlin, Kingston, Berkshire, Sunbury, Genoa, and Orange, not less than three hundred were numbered among the converts. In Canaan, Marion county, Mifflin, Franklin county, Gallipolis, and quite a number of the smaller churches, revivals were reported as in progress.

In 1830, several Presbyterian camp-meetings were held in Ohio, the first at the time and place of meeting of the Cincinnati Presbytery near Williamsburg. Others soon followed, at Sharon and Montgomery. They were regarded as most successful, and were favored by the presence of Mr. Gallaher, who had been blessed in his labors in similar scenes in Kentucky and Tennessee. Some questionable methods were pursued, which were afterward brought to the attention of the General Assembly. Individuals who were led to entertain hope during the progress of the meetings were received to communion on examination before their close. But the meetings themselves were conducted with great decorum; and among the prominent conductors or speakers present were Drs. Wilson and Morrison, of Cincinnati. The revival in this city, where they labored, still continued to progress. More than two hundred were received during the year by the Third Church, which had but recently been organized.

In this period of general revival even the feeble congregations of Indiana and Illinois were not left unvisited. In the course of the summer of 1828 sixty-two were added to the church at Vincennes. Quite a number of the churches were refreshed; but amid the scattered population and among the feeble churches, although the advance might be proportionally greater than in other parts of the country, it was yet almost imperceptible, so far as any report of revivals was concerned.

This was the case also, to a great extent, with Illinois. Several of the churches were highly favored, but the united membership of all within the State was but about the same with that of a single church in Cincinnati. At Salem a revival commenced under the labors of B. C. Cressy. At Golconda, Carmi, and Sharon there were numerous conversions.

Michigan at this period had scarcely begun to be settled. Yet even here, in villages just springing up in the wilderness, there were not wanting signs of spiritual progress. In 1830 there were blessed seasons of revival in several localities, especially in Ypsilanti and Dexter.

In Missouri there were revivals in Cooper's county, and to the church at New Lebanon, and one contiguous, forty members were added; while several other congregations had been refreshed.

During this period Kentucky was especially favored with revivals. A work of grace commenced, in connection with the temporary labors of Gideon Blackburn, at Danville, early in 1828. At Springfield, Harrodsburg, Nicholasville, Lexington, Mt. Pleasant, Pisgah, New Providence, Flemingsburg, and several other places, revivals had commenced several months before, and during the following winter and spring they became more extensive. A correspondent at Paris, where one hundred members had just been added to the Presbyterian Church, said,—doubtless with some exaggeration,—"This place, and indeed the whole State, for the last two or three months has been a scene of the most astonishing revivals of religion ever witnessed in this country." At Lexington it was estimated that there were at least one thousand hopeful converts. The whole aspect of society was changed. Vices before prevalent and unblushing almost entirely disappeared. At Danville the revival continued to progress with remarkable power. Within the course of four months antecedent to May, 1828, the churches of Ebenezer Presbytery were strengthened by the accession of nearly five hundred members on profession of their faith. Some of the other Presbyteries were equally, if not more highly, favored.

The work continued with great power at Louisville and Danville. In 1830 it was felt in Greenup county. Places which had not been visited before were visited now. The labors of Messrs. Ross and Gallaher were attended with large and blessed results. They went from place to place as evangelists; and in almost every region which they visited there were signal manifestations of divine grace.

The work had commenced in Tennessee somewhat earlier than in Kentucky. In 1827 the Synod of West Tennessee remarked, in their Narrative, "Never before has there been in the same length of time so much attention to the means of grace, or so many additions to the Church, as during the last year." Before the close of 1828, the revival, in promoting which the labors of Messrs. Ross and Gallaher were eminent, had extended far and wide. Within the region embracing Murfreesborough and its vicinity, more than six hundred, in the course of a few weeks, professed conversion. East Tennessee shared also largely in the revival.

In Mississippi, Louisiana, and Alabama the churches were few and feeble. Yet some among them experienced the blessings of revival. At Greensborough in Alabama the work was powerful, and in other places was largely felt.

In Georgia there was an almost unprecedented display of divine grace throughout this period. The laborers were few, but they were earnest and devoted to their work.

The college at Athens—in which it is not known that there had ever been a pious student prior to 1822, but which in that year had seven who commenced Sabbath-schools and meetings for prayer, most of them afterward entering the ministry—was visited by a revival in 1827. From other portions of the State there were cheering reports. When the Presbytery met at Decatur, at least two thousand persons were in attendance, and large numbers were deeply impressed. Presbyterian camp-meetings were repeatedly held, and many of the churches received large accessions. Twenty were added at one time to the church in Butts county, thirty to the one in Crawford, and equal or larger numbers to other churches. A writer, dating from Knoxville, Ga., April 1, 1828, says, "Such attention to religion among the people has not been known or recorded since the day of Pentecost. I hear daily of hundreds being added to the churches and of thousands inquiring for the bread of life." In July, at a single season of communion, fifty-eight were received by the church of Hebron, Green county, and the work was still in progress. In September, Hopewell Presbytery met at McDonough, Henry county, and nearly two thousand were present at the communion.

In 1825 the Presbytery had formed a domestic missionary society, and secured the services of as many missionaries as they could obtain in their field of labor. The results were most cheering. Quite a number of new churches were organized, and the missionary spirit received a new and powerful impulse.[1]

---

[1] The same year an education society was formed within the Pres-

South Carolina shared with Georgia the divine blessing. Early in 1826 a revival commenced at Augusta. It extended, through the labors of those engaged in it, to Beach Island, where shortly afterward a Presbyterian church was organized, of thirty or forty members. In Anderson district in 1828 there was a powerful revival. At Brewington a camp-meeting was held, which was regarded as a scene of thrilling interest. Yet there was no departure from the strictest decorum. For more than two years previous the churches in the region had enjoyed seasons of refreshing. In 1829 a four-days meeting was held at Varennes, and forty or fifty tents were pitched upon the ground. This was the case also in York district at the same time, and at each place from twenty to thirty were received to the communion. Similar scenes occurred at Bullock's Creek Church, Westminster Church, Fairview, and other places. For two years revivals prevailed extensively throughout the bounds of the Synod which embraced South Carolina and Georgia. The churches received new accessions of strength and gave evidence of unexampled prosperity. In by far the greater portion of them the special influences of the Spirit had been enjoyed, and the Synod were able to say that, so far as their knowledge extended, there was not a single church in its connection which was in a declining state.

While other portions of the country were favored to a remarkable extent, North Carolina remained still like Gideon's fleece amid the surrounding dews. This was the case, however, only till 1828. The Synod in that year was enabled to report an accession of four hundred to the membership of the churches, as well as an increase in the number of preachers. One hundred and nineteen

---

bytery on the same principles with the American Society, but in the following year it became a Presbyterian education society.

new members were added to the church under Mr. Kerr at Little Britain; while a revival had also commenced at Morgantown, and the first signs of awakening were manifest at Fayetteville, where a work of marked power soon afterward commenced.

Virginia, with her vast destitutions, and several of her churches without pastors and in a declining state, was highly favored. In 1827 a powerful revival of religion, commencing at Portsmouth, extended to Norfolk, Williamsburg, Suffolk, and Gosport. The church at Richmond under William J. Armstrong enjoyed a season of refreshing. In the following year the church at Alexandria received large accessions as the result of a quiet but powerful work of grace. In the bounds of Hanover Presbytery the indications of the special presence of the Spirit were manifest in quite a number of the congregations. From Alexandria the revival extended to Washington, and quite a number were added to the Church. In the early part of 1828, Mr. Nettleton, at the urgent request of Dr. Rice, visited Prince Edward county, and in a short time, in connection with his labors, a most interesting revival commenced, which extended to the surrounding congregations, and the influence of which was felt far and near throughout the State.

Of some of the proceedings of the General Assembly during this period, notice may be taken more appropriately hereafter. In 1826 the ratio of representation in the General Assembly was so modified that each Presbytery of less than twelve ministers should be entitled to send one minister and one elder as delegates; if over twelve, two ministers and two elders, who were to be styled commissioners. The Colonization Society also was commended to the patronage of the churches, and the first Sabbath in July was designated as the day for collections in its behalf. In 1827 the practice which allowed commissioners to the Assembly to hold their seats for a time and then resign them to their alternates was disapproved, and it was resolved that it be discontinued. The subject of intemperance received appropriate notice, and the object of the American Society for its suppression was approved.

In 1828 the constitution of the General Union to promote the observance of the Christian Sabbath was laid before the Assembly and "highly approved," while the duty of discipline in cases of the violation of the day was enjoined upon Presbyteries and churches. In 1829 the American Peace Society received the sanction of the Assembly, and the cause of seamen was commended to the affection, charities, and prayers of all its churches. In 1830 an overture from the Presbytery of Cincinnati "for the organization of a General Assembly in the Western country" was dismissed, and the proposal of a change in the mode or ratio of representation was rejected. The subject of lotteries was also taken up, and it was decided that they must be viewed in no other light—though sanctioned by legislative acts—than legalized gambling. The arrangements for providing a Psalmody of the Church, which had engaged the attention of the Assembly annually during this period, were at length perfected, and measures were taken for its publication.

The Presbyteries erected from 1826 to 1830 were—Chenango, Detroit, Holston, and Trumbull in 1826, Trumbull in 1827, Angelica, Centre of Illinois, and Tombigbee in 1828, Bedford, Tioga, Oxford, Crawfordsville, East and West Hanover, and Western District in 1829, and New York Third, Blairsville, Cleveland, Indianapolis, Illinois, Kaskaskia, and Sangamon in 1830.

The Synods formed were—West Tennessee and Indiana in 1826, and Utica, Mississippi, and Cincinnati in 1829.

The membership of the Church had increased during

the period from about one hundred and thirty thousand in 1826 to about one hundred and eighty thousand at the close of 1830, or at an average of about ten thousand a year. In 1826 the additions reported from seven hundred and twenty congregations were nine thousand five hundred and fifty-seven. In 1827 the entire number from all the churches which made reports was twelve thousand nine hundred and thirty-eight; in 1828 they amounted to fifteen thousand and ninety-five; in 1829 they were fourteen thousand eight hundred and forty-six; in 1830 the number was but eleven thousand seven hundred and forty-eight.

CHAPTER XXXVII.

THE MISSION-FIELD AT THE SOUTH AND SOUTHWEST, 1810–1830.

The domestic mission-field of the American Presbyterian Church embraced, in rapid succession, during the first quarter of the present century, New York, Tennessee and Kentucky, the Carolinas and Georgia, Ohio, Indiana, Missouri, Mississippi Territory, Illinois, and Michigan. Of these several portions of the field, New York, Ohio, Tennessee, Kentucky, and the Carolinas have already been surveyed. Without following out the history of each of the others with the same distinctness, a general review may be taken of the efforts that were designed to bear upon them all.[1]

---

[1] In 1818, Indiana, Mississippi, and Louisiana, with the Territories of Alabama, Illinois, Michigan, and Missouri, contained a population of three hundred and fifty thousand, with not more than seventeen competent or stated ministers,—or but one to twenty thousand. Mo-

In 1804 the Synod of Carolina directed the Presbytery of Orange to ordain James Smylie, who had been laboring at Natchez in the Louisiana Territory, with a view to his returning thither to engage in missionary labor. This region of the Southwest, rapidly filling up after the Louisiana purchase, was for the most part under the supervision of the Synods of Virginia and Carolina.

The way had been prepared for the labors of Mr. Smylie by that veteran in the cause of Presbyterianism at the South, Rev. James Hall, of North Carolina. In the autumn of 1800, under a commission of the General Assembly, he commenced a mission to Natchez. Two other brethren whom the Synod appointed accompanied him. This was the first in the series of Protestant missionary efforts in the lower valley of the Mississippi. The report of the mission was made to Synod in 1801, and, as published in the papers of the day, excited a very general interest throughout the Southern country. The Presbytery of West Tennessee, erected in 1810, had this field under its care; but it was not till 1815 that, by a division of it, the Presbytery of Mississippi was formed.

In 1817 this body consisted of five ministers and had under its care eight congregations. At the head of its list stood the name of the venerable Joseph Bullen, verging upon his threescore years and ten, a pioneer in the cause of Indian missions. Soon after the formation of the New York Missionary Society, it was determined to attempt the establishment of a mission among the Chickasaws of "West Georgia," and Mr. Bullen was selected as the man to conduct it. He was

---

bile, Blakely, Fort Claibourne, Huntsville, Madisonville, Baton Rouge, and Natchez had no Christian ministers of any kind.—*Christian Herald*, v. 614.

a native of Vermont, and had already reached his forty-seventh year when he commenced the undertaking. At New York he received his public charge from the venerable Dr. Rodgers, and set out March 26, 1799, on his journey to the Southwest.[1] He was accompanied by his son, a youth of seventeen years, who it was thought might render important aid in acquiring the language and giving instruction as a teacher of Indian children.

His route led him through Philadelphia, where he received the friendly attentions not only of Dr. Green, but of Mr. Pickering, Secretary of State, and other distinguished persons. Thence he proceeded westward, by way of Lexington, Va., to Knoxville and Nashville, Tennessee. Here he was two hundred and seventy miles distant from his point of destination, and his friends urged him to delay his journey for several weeks, in order to secure company. Such were the dangers of the way that it was quite unadvisable to attempt the journey without guides. But the zeal of the missionary would not allow him to pause. He had already had experience of hardship, exposure to storms, and perils from swollen streams, sometimes crossing "waters almost to the horse's back." Unappalled by the representations made to him, he resolved to press on. "Trusting in divine goodness to direct" their way, the travellers set out for the Indian country. Their horses were encumbered with baggage, and their movements were slow. But, provided with food, blankets, an axe, and a gun, they made such progress as they were able. Their lonesome way was occasionally cheered by meeting traders from Natchez and New Orleans, returning to Kentucky. Sometimes they were impeded by the rains and the swollen streams. The waters of the Tennessee were high, and places of entertainment were few

[1] New York Missionary Magazine, i. 262.

and far between. The food which they could procure was not of the best kind,—sometimes hominy or damaged meal. A bed of bear-skin was a luxury for the night's lodging.

At length Mr. Bullen reached his destination, worn, weary, and almost an invalid. The Chickasaws he found "without any kind of religious observance, and without temple and priest," except that a few of their enchanters had images, the use of which was little understood among the people. He preached and conversed as he had opportunity, witnessed their frolics and their "mysteries," their "singing, yelling, and running," gained their confidence, and, with alternate experience of encouragement and disappointment, prosecuted his work. From one town he journeyed to another, distributing his labors among Indians and whites, and coming in frequent contact with the hundreds of traders who, after their trip down the Mississippi, returned by land to their homes. His greatest success was among the slaves, five of whom he baptized on one occasion. Daunted by no difficulties or hardships, wet, hungry, shelterless oftentimes, he labored at all seasons to prosecute the missionary work in which all the sympathies of his soul were enlisted.

Worn out with labors, he returned to the North in the fall of 1800. On his way he stopped at Maryville, where Gideon Blackburn ministered to a church of over three hundred communicants. The two men, kindred in missionary zeal and devotion, conferred together; and, though we have no record of the themes upon which they conversed, we can scarcely doubt, from our knowledge of the men, that the subject nearest to Mr. Bullen's heart claimed their attention. This, at least, we know, that within a few months of that meeting Mr. Blackburn threw his whole soul into the work of Indian missions, and pleaded their cause with a glowing eloquence in the Eastern cities, both North and South.

Mr. Bullen soon returned to his field of labor, accompanied by his family, resolved thenceforth to make his home in the Southwest. Deacon Rice, who was employed as his assistant, proved unacceptable to the Indians, who forced him to leave the country. But Mr. Bullen remained; and ere long we find him disconnected with the Indian mission, and one of the original members of the Presbytery of Mississippi,—indeed, the patriarch of the body.

William Montgomery took charge of the Scotch congregations of Ebenezer and Salem in 1808–09. A fine scholar,[1] a well-read theologian, a fluent, animated, and effective speaker, he would have taken a high rank among the preachers in the Eastern cities. To the close of life he retained his early taste for classical studies, and many of the odes of his favorite Latin author, *his friend Horace*, he could repeat from memory. Without looking into the book, he could hear a recitation from Virgil. The friend of sound learning, a punctual attendant of school-examinations, a fast friend of Oakland College after it was established, the cause of sound education in the Southwest is deeply indebted to him. But theological investigation was his chosen pursuit; and in his old age few things delighted him so much as choice books on systematic divinity. On the great doctrines of grace he loved to dwell. In his last illness he declared—and it was one of the last remarks which his failing speech permitted him to utter—that these doctrines, which he had delighted to preach, then loomed up before his mind with greater brilliancy and power than ever.

In the pulpit he was a ready and earnest speaker.

[1] The True Witness, March 31, 1860.

He never wrote his sermons or made use of notes, but his discourses were prepared by careful study, arranging not only the heads and thoughts, but the language also. In his younger days his voice was unusually musical, and his enunciation clear and distinct. His animation he never lost. His sincerity was manifest in tone, look, and gesture. His method was expository and argumentative, rarely hortatory, and his sermons were instructive and edifying. In his best days he enjoyed a high popularity, and crowds flocked to his ministry. His deportment was marked with the unaffected simplicity of childhood: it was singularly free from all appearance of eccentricity, yet cheerful and sociable, while his large fund of anecdote made him the charm of every circle, and his genial laugh communicated its own delight.

No man gave clearer evidence of single-minded devotion to the work of the ministry. The highest salary he ever received was about three hundred dollars. Yet, while receiving but one hundred dollars at Union for half his time, he declined a call to Pine Ridge for eight hundred dollars for the same amount of service. Still he was a poor man, and at some periods in great straits for the support of his family. His attachment to his own people was strong, and his sense of duty was stronger than his desire even for a competence.

For forty years Mr. Montgomery was spared,—the venerated pastor of the two churches of Ebenezer and Union. He was the first permanent missionary from the Carolinas to the Territory of Mississippi. The original log church in which he first preached the gospel in the wilderness has long since vanished; but his name will be ever memorable as that of one of the fathers of the Presbyterian Church in the Southwest, and the apostle of a pure and primitive Christianity.

But already James Smylie, missionary of the Synod

of the Carolinas, had entered the field. At a later period he was followed by Jacob Rickhow,[1] who settled at Bayou Pierre, while Mr. Smylie, after his itinerations, located at Bethany and Amity. These, together with Mr. Montgomery, were members of the West Tennessee Presbytery previous to the erection of the Presbytery of Mississippi. At their instance, the Presbytery of West Tennessee petitioned the Synod of Kentucky at their session in Danville, Oct. 6, 1815, that a new Presbytery might be formed, having for its boundary eastwardly the Perdido River, thence a direct line to Fort Jackson at the junction of the Coosa and Tallapoosa Rivers, thence to the line of division between the Choctaw and Chickasaw Indians, and along that line indefinitely, forming a division between the contemplated Presbytery and the Presbytery of West Tennessee. Bullen, Montgomery, Rickhow, and Smylie were to constitute the Presbytery. The petition was granted; and the first meeting of the Mississippi Presbytery was

---

[1] "In 1808, Jacob Rickhow, a native of Staten Island, arrived at Natchez, and in the fall of that year preached for a short time in the structure belonging to the Methodists. In the absence of a preacher, many of the Presbyterian families were accustomed to worship at Pine Ridge Church, eight miles north of Natchez. In 1810 a subscription was opened with a view to secure means to erect a house of worship. Although it was not dedicated till February, 1815, a congregation was collected in 1811, and Mr. Montgomery, of Pine Ridge, supplied them a part of the time. Daniel Smith began his labors here April 1, 1816, and continued as supply till 1819, when he left for lack of support. The church, meanwhile, had been organized (1817), with eight members. In May, 1820, William Weir accepted a call to the pastorate; but his death occurred in November, 1822. In May of the following year, George Potts commenced his labors here. In June he was called, and in December installed. His pastorate closed in 1836, and in 1837 he was succeeded by Samuel G. Winchester."—*Pres. Mag.*, April, 1852, p. 177.

held, according to appointment, at Pine Ridge Church, March 16, 1816.

In the preceding year the General Assembly authorized the Committee of Missions to appoint a missionary to Natchez—if the funds should prove sufficient—for the space of six months.[1] The missionary appointed was Daniel Smith,[2] who, after laboring for some months, succeeded, in 1817, in forming the First Presbyterian Church in that place. He had already commenced his labors when the Mississippi Presbytery held its first meeting, and was present as a corresponding member.[3] He subsequently united with the body, although he did not long continue in the field.[4]

The oldest church under the care of the Presbytery was that of Bethel, organized by Mr. Bullen in 1804. Union Church was organized by him in 1811; and in the same year Ebenezer Church was organized by Mr. Rickhow. Salem, or Pine Ridge, Church was organized by Mr. Smylie in 1807. Amity, Bethany, and Florida Churches—the last subsequently removed to Jackson, La.—were also probably organized by Mr. Smylie.

The visit of Messrs. Samuel J. Mills and Schermerhorn to this region of the country in 1814 gave a new impulse to evangelical and missionary effort. They explored and reported its destitutions. Mr. Schermerhorn, during his short stay at New Orleans, gathered a small congregation, who were urgent that he should remain and settle as their pastor. In 1815, Daniel Smith left Natchez to visit the little band, who were still united and earnest in desiring the privileges of the gospel. He found them, without a pastor, sustaining a weekly prayer-meeting, and labored with them

---

[1] Minutes for 1815.

[2] Probably a graduate of Yale College in 1791.

[3] New Orleans "True Witness," March 31, 1860.

[4] He died about the year 1822, in Kentucky.

for two months. The Assembly of the same year commissioned Ezra Fisk, the well-known pastor of the Presbyterian church of Goshen, N.Y., a kindred spirit and intimate companion of Samuel J. Mills and his early missionary associates, to labor with this feeble band in the city of New Orleans for four months.

In the following year Elias Cornelius was appointed by the trustees of the Connecticut Missionary Society to a missionary tour, like that which Mills had already performed, through the Southwestern States, and more especially to visit New Orleans, which already contained a population of nearly thirty thousand and but a single Protestant minister.[1] He was directed to examine its moral condition, and, while preaching the gospel to many who seldom heard it, to invite the friends of the Congregational or Presbyterian communion to establish a church and secure an able and faithful pastor. His journey was a missionary-route. He preached one hundred and fifteen times on his way, spending considerable time among the Cherokees. While at Princeton, N.J., arrangements were made by which he was to be followed or assisted at New Orleans by that eminent preacher Sylvester Larned, whose brilliant prospects, after a short career of usefulness, were too suddenly clouded, and who at this time was pursuing his theological studies at Princeton.

Cornelius did not reach New Orleans till the last of December, 1816. Fisk had left, and he labored alone. Larned was unexpectedly delayed, and pursued his journey from Niagara to Detroit, thence by land through Ohio and a part of Kentucky to Louisville, and by steamboat to New Orleans. It was not till the 22d of January, 1818, after a passage of thirty-five days from

[1] In 1804 the population of New Orleans was eight thousand and fifty-six. In 1820 it had increased to twenty-seven thousand one hundred and seventy-six.—*Eighty Years' Progress*, i. 181.

Kentucky, that he reached his destination. But he was received "by many with open arms."[1] In "a population of thirty-four thousand" he found but a single Protestant (Episcopal) church. After preaching three Sabbaths, there seemed to be a settled purpose to retain him in the city. A subscription for the erection of a church-edifice was immediately commenced. It quickly reached the sum of fifteen thousand dollars, and seemed to warrant a loan that would secure the forty thousand dollars required. Larned was animated to the greatest energy by the field before him; and few could be found better fitted for the post. "The moral state of things," he says, "is terrible, but not so bad as is thought in the Northern States." His heart was fully set upon his work. Alluding to the possibility of a call from the Presbyterian church of Baltimore, he declared, "Were I offered the bishopric of creation, I would not at this time leave New Orleans."[2]

Cornelius remained in the city, diligent in his missionary labors, until April, 1818.[3] The two missionaries labored heartily together, and the foundation of a Presbyterian church was firmly laid. There was no lack of liberality on the part of the congregation. The subscriptions rapidly advanced to an amount which warranted the erection of the contemplated edifice. On the 8th of January, 1819, the corner-stone was laid.

Meanwhile, other parts of the Mississippi Valley were visited by the Assembly's missionaries. In 1817, Jeremiah Chamberlain, afterward President of Danville College, but who had just been licensed to preach by

---

[1] Life of Larned.

[2] The circumstances of Larned and the facts in regard to the effort to establish the church are noted in the Christian Herald for 1818, vol. v. p. 228.

[3] Life of Cornelius.

the Presbytery of Carlisle, accepted the Assembly's commission to descend the Ohio to St. Louis, there join Larned on his way to New Orleans, "and then visit the destitute towns on the Mississippi below Natchez, and, if practicable, visit the settlements on the Mobile."

At the same time, Larned was commissioned for six months in New Orleans, and Richard King for the same period in Mississippi Territory. The latter was to descend the Tombigbee to Fort Stoddart, thence across to Fort Jackson, up the Alabama, and through the lower parts of Tennessee and Kentucky. In the following year he was followed by Robert Gibson, commissioned for four months.

The labors of Cornelius at New Orleans, previous to the arrival of Larned, were arduous and self-denying. His eye ranged over an extended field of misery and of sin. No part of it escaped his notice. The various scenes through which he passed in the discharge of his duties were of the most affecting kind. He supplied on the Sabbath the pulpit of the congregation who were awaiting Larned's arrival, and during the week he explored the sad field of iniquity and wretchedness around him. He visited the hospitals, directed attention to the neglected condition of the sufferers there, and through his influence a great improvement was visible. He boarded the vessels in the harbor and conversed with the sailors. He secured the cabin of a ship, and made of it a floating Bethel. It was filled with sea-captains, to whom he preached; and the assembly was "attentive, solemn, and affected."

Nor was this all. He was not content merely to care for the inmate of the hospital or the neglected seaman. He gathered a congregation of two hundred Africans, who were powerfully affected under the preaching of this devoted man. Thus no scene repelled and no difficulty disheartened him. In the wards of the hospital.

among the sick, in the cells of the jails among the criminals, in the streets and lanes of the city, and in cabin and forecastle, he labored with a zeal and devotedness which nothing could check or tire.

Nor should the name of his fellow-missionary, Rev. Samuel Royce,—received as a licentiate by the Presbytery of Mississippi,—be forgotten. He was a kindred spirit of Cornelius, sent out like him by the Connecticut Society to the valley of the Mississippi. His journey was a missionary-route. He preached on his way to destitute congregations. He crossed the Mississippi at Baton Rouge, and thenceforth occupied ground "never trodden before by a Protestant minister," except by a few who were very illiterate. Accepting an invitation to settle at Alexandria, on Red River, he yet made the whole surrounding region his parish. There was scarcely a brother minister within a hundred miles. Many of his hearers, before his arrival, had never heard a sermon except from Roman Catholic priests. Here infidelity had spread abroad its baneful influence. The evil was aggravated by the fact that the few who assumed the exercise of the gospel ministry in the region were so illiterate as only to bring it into contempt. Yet even here pious persons were now and then to be met with. As the missionary fell in with them, "their countenances and tears, more than words, expressed emotions easier to imagine than describe." "A woman brought up in New England, when she heard of the arrival of Mr. Royce, sprang from her seat, clasped her hands, and said she had not heard so good news since she had been in the country.'[1]

[1] A report of a religious convention held at Washington, Miss., Nov. 19, 1818, and composed of members of different denominations, is given in the Christian Herald, vol. v. p. 655. It reveals the necessity which all good men felt for co-operative evangelical effort.

Mr. Royce found a field which tasked all his energies. He felt himself unequal to it, but he engaged with alacrity in his work. He extended his excursions on all sides, visiting Natchitoches, eighty miles above Alexandria. The population was a curious conglomerate of various tongues and creeds,—Americans, French, Spaniards, Indians, and negroes,—Roman Catholics, Protestants of different kinds, deists, infidels, and heathen. In 1819 his missionary labors were mainly devoted to the counties of Jefferson and Wilkinson.

The founder of the church of Port Gibson was Dr. Zebulon Butler. A grandson of Colonel Zebulon Butler, famous as the leader of the little band of patriots in 1778 at the time of the disastrous conflict and bloody massacre of Wyoming Valley, he was graduated at Nassau Hall, and in 1826, after completing his theological course at Princeton, was commissioned for six months by the Assembly's Board of Missions to labor at the Southwest. On reaching Vicksburg, he met a cordial reception. The people for a year assumed his entire support; and during this time he instituted a prayer-meeting and a Sabbath-school. On the expiration of his engagement, he accepted a call to Port Gibson, where he organized a church. Gathering the few professing believers together, and visiting from house to house, he pressed the truth upon the attention of an unevangelized population. A house of worship was at length erected, and a flourishing congregation was collected, to which, through many trials and bodily infirmities, Dr. Butler ministered, with a blessing upon his labors, for nearly thirty-four years. Buoyant in spirit, generous, self-denying, and genially social, he became the object of warm and enduring affection to a large circle who knew his worth. Through his widely-extended influence he became virtually a diocesan bishop, establishing churches and confirming the disciples in many localities. Young men preparing for the ministry found in him a steadfast and sympathizing friend. The spiritual welfare of the slaves was an object that lay very near to his heart. To his closing days it was a cherished desire to erect an "African Presbyterian church," for which he went so far as to purchase the site and gather the materials. It was his last request to his friends that the project might be executed. Earnest, solemn, fluent in speech and fervent in spirit, overflowing with love to God and man, he was a preacher of rare excellence, and his praise is in all the churches of the Southwest. He died Dec. 23, 1860.

One of the first—if not the first—to labor as pastor at Baton Rouge, was Dr. John Dorrance, a native of Pennsylvania, and a graduate of Nassau Hall and of Princeton Seminary. On the completion of his studies, in 1826, he was sent to the South under a commission from the Board of Missions, and his field of labor was Baton Rouge and vicinity. This had been, and still was, a place of great immorality. Its population, numbering about twelve hundred, had been collected from every State of the Union and every part of Europe. It is not strange that infidelity should have been common and openly avowed. Yet, in view of the temporal benefits of Christian institutions, the people invited the missionary to remain, and contributed to his support. He was ordained and installed, by the Mississippi Presbytery, pastor of the church at Baton Rouge in 1827; and during a pastorate of four years his labors were eminently successful.

Although the future scene of his ministry was in a Northern State (Wilkesbarre, Pa.), he left behind him the testimony that he had not labored in vain. Possessed of rare intellectual endowments, his mind was not brilliant, but admirably balanced, and capable of a prodigious grasp. If he did not shine as a student, he was wise and prudent as a man. He died in the triumph of a Christian faith, April 18, 1861.

Although the population of this entire region was rapidly increasing, yet the number of Presbyterian ministers in Mississippi and Louisiana amounted at the close of 1822 to only eight or ten. The missionaries sent out by the Assembly were few in number:—in 1821, Salmon Cowles; in 1822, one or two who were to receive compensation from the Presbytery of Mississippi; in 1823, Isaac Burd and Edmond Lanier; and in 1824, Benjamin Chase.

In 1825 the Presbytery of Mississippi, extending over the region of Louisiana and Mississippi, which embraced a population of two hundred and fifty thousand, consisted of but thirteen ministers, of whom eight—for the most part missionaries of the Assembly's Board—were without charge. These were Joseph Bullen, James Smylie, Jacob Rickhow, James Gilliland, Hiland Hulburt, Thomas Savage, Benjamin Chase, and J. H. Van Court. Theodore Clapp, although soon to abandon the Presbyterian Church, still occupied the post vacated by the death of Larned at New Orleans; George Potts was pastor of the church at Natchez, Samuel Hunter was settled at Salem and Bayou Pierre, John Patterson at Bethany and Friendship, and William Montgomery at Union and Ebenezer. Benjamin Woodbury was the single licentiate of the Presbytery. The number of churches, including one at New Orleans, one at Natchez, and those at Pisgah, Salem, Bethany, Carmel, Rock Spring, Bayou Pierre, Bethel, Friendship, Harmony, Ebenezer, and Union, amounted only to thirteen.

The project for the establishment of Oakland College originated with Jeremiah Chamberlain, who became the first President of the institution. A graduate of Dickinson College and Princeton Seminary, he set out, upon the completion of his studies in 1817, under a commission from the Board of Missions, on a missionary tour to the Southwest. He visited Natchez, New Orleans, and Mobile, and although settled for some years afterward at Bedford, Pa., and subsequently President for some five or six years of Danville College, Ky., yet his thoughts were still directed toward the region in which he had commenced his ministerial career. During the summer and autumn of 1828 he matured a plan for the establishment of a literary institution to be located at the Southwest; and—with the sad experience of Transylvania University before him—he provided that it should be subject to Presbyterian control and supervision. Presenting his views fully to the Presbytery of Mississippi, that body adopted his plans and took the proposed institution under their care. The establishment of Oakland College in Claiborne county, Miss., was the result. Dr. Chamberlain was by the Presbytery elected President, and in 1830 removed to the college grounds. A charter was secured, and Dr. Chamberlain spared no expense and shrank from no sacrifice to promote the interests of the institution. Funds, buildings, and friends were continually added, until Oakland College became a noble monument of the untiring zeal and Christian philanthropy of its President.

Among the early friends of the institution were Dr. Butler, of Port Gibson, and John Dorrance, of Baton Rouge, while Montgomery, Smylie, and other members of the Presbytery regarded it with the deepest interest. In 1837, Rev. Samuel Vance Marshall, Professor of Languages in Transylvania University, was called to occupy a similar post in Oakland College; and his subsequent life is largely identified with the history of the college. Another of the professors was Rev. O. S. Hinkley.

In 1828 the Presbytery of Tombigbee was formed from the Indian mission, and embraced as members Messrs. T. Archibald, Kingsbury, A. Wright, C. Byington, D. Wright, H. Patrick, H. Allen, L. S. Williams, and H. Caldwell. By 1830 the Presbytery of Mississippi numbered sixteen ministers and three licentiates, and the membership of its churches amounted to eight hundred and fifty-three.

In 1831[1] the Presbytery of Clinton was erected from that of Mississippi, and in 1835 that of Amity (name changed to Louisiana in 1836) was set off from the same body. In 1837 the latter numbered ten ministers, two licentiates, and eight candidates, with a membership in its thirteen churches of five hundred and sixty-four. The Presbytery of Clinton had nine ministers, one licentiate, and thirteen churches, with a membership of two hundred and seventeen; while the Presbytery of Louisiana had ten ministers, four licentiates, and thirteen churches, with two hundred and twenty-eight members. William Montgomery was still at Ebenezer and Union, Natchez had been left vacant by the removal of Dr. Potts to New York, Dr. Butler was at Port Gibson, Dr. Chamberlain at Oakland College, and Dr. Joel Parker at New Orleans. In the three Presbyteries there were but three settled pastors,—Montgomery, Butler, and Parker. Fifteen of the twenty-nine ministers were stated supplies, and six were without charge.

The field embraced within the limits of the State of Georgia came properly under the care of the Synod of South Carolina, and by members of that body had been extensively visited. But the Synod, unequal to the supply of its own destitutions, made application to the Assembly for aid. In 1820, Mr. R. Chamberlain, a recent graduate of Princeton, was sent thither, and labored in all the towns of the upper country of Georgia, preaching at Waynesborough, Louisville, Mt. Zion, Bethany, Green-

[1] For a report of the state of society at the Southwest in 1831, see Missionary Reporter for November of that year.

borough, Madison, Athens, Lexington, Washington, Sparta, Milledgeville, Clinton, &c. At about the same time Azariah G. Orton and Charles J. Hinsdale,[1] recommended for the service by one of the professors at Princeton, were sent into the same field.

Previous to this, little labor had been bestowed upon it, except at Midway and Savannah and their vicinity. The Assembly had, indeed, repeatedly sent out missionaries, whose labors were to be extended to places within the borders of the State. In 1816, John Covert was commissioned to labor for six months in South Carolina and Georgia, his route to be prescribed by Dr. Flinn, of Charleston. His labors were continued during a portion of the following year in the same field. In 1818, William Moderwell[2] was commissioned for four months in the upper part of Georgia, and in 1819, Moses Waddel was elected to the Presidency of the University of Georgia. Thomas Alexander had for some time been laboring as pastor of the Salem and Mt. Zion[3] Churches, in Clark county, Thomas Goulding at White Bluff,[4] and E. B. Caldwell at Waynesborough. There were, doubtless, other missionaries laboring in other parts of the State; but, with the exception of the churches of Savannah and Midway, all the others were feeble and for the most part unable to sustain a pastor. The church at Savannah was the oldest in the State. It had been formed previous to 1760, when John J. Zubly, a native of Switzerland and an emigrant to this country, assumed the pastoral charge. An able, learned, and devoted minister of the gospel, he labored at his post

---

[1] Mr. Hinsdale organized a church at Clinton, Jones county.—F.

[2] Settled at Augusta. Afterward deposed. Died a sot.—F.

[3] Mt. Zion Church is not in Clark, but in Hancock county, sixty miles distant from Clark county.—F.

[4] Goulding settled at Cherokee Corner and Lexington, Oglethorpe county, Ga.—F.

till for his political views he was exiled from the State. His death occurred in 1781, somewhere in South Carolina; although his remains were brought to Savannah for interment. How long after his death the church remained vacant does not appear. In 1801, Robert Smith, who had been laboring for some time as pastor of the church of Schenectady, was forced by the failure of his health to seek a milder climate, and in that year he was called to the charge of the church of Savannah.[1]

In the autumn of 1806 the church secured the pastoral services of the gifted and devoted Henry Kollock. As yet but thirty-four years of age, Kollock had already acquired a reputation coextensive with the bounds of the Church. A full match for Bishop Hobart when the two were intimate associates at Nassau Hall, and already, previous to his call to Savannah, Professor of Theology and pastor of the congregation at Princeton for three years, he entered upon his work at the South in the fulness of his fame and with prospects of usefulness which were not belied by the experience of his pastorate.[2] With a voice in no wise remarkable for compass, flexibility, or even harmony, with nothing marked in gesture and without artifice of manner, he was yet a man of powerful eloquence and ranked among the first pulpit-orators of the land. His countenance was—under the excitement of the occasion—remarkably expressive. His eye sparkled with joy, or kindled with indignation, according to the promptings of his theme. Yet "his eloquence was not at one time a mountain-torrent, dashing and foaming, and anon a meandering river, pursuing its unruffled course through an extended plain: it was a strong, uniform, and noble stream, acquiring velocity and beauty and power as it advanced." With

---

[1] See Dwight's Travels, notice of Schenectady, ii. 488.

[2] Sprague's Annals.

no ostentation of learning, nothing of metaphysical discussion, little of rhetorical verbiage, his discourses were plain and simple, yet rich with imagery and glowing with feeling. He brought the truth in an intelligible and impressive manner into direct contact with the heart. His success was what might have been anticipated. At his first communion-season after he entered upon his labors at Savannah, twenty publicly professed their faith in Christ; and at the second the number was eighteen.

Such was the reputation that he here acquired that in 1810 he was called to the Presidency of the University of Georgia, the post afterward accepted by Dr. Waddel; but his attachment to the ministry led him to decline the appointment. For fourteen years—although for a brief time his reputation was clouded by his failings—he remained in connection with the church at Savannah.[1]

A neighbor and fellow-laborer of Kollock was William McWhir, who for several years before his arrival had taken charge of the church at Sunbury and a school at Springfield in Liberty county, some twenty miles south of Savannah. The labors of the school at length became such that he was forced to abandon it, while the great destitution of the means of grace in the surrounding region impressed him with the obligation still to preach as he had opportunity. He organized the McIntosh Church, afterward removed to Darien, and labored till 1820 at various places in the counties of Bryan, Liberty, and McIntosh. In 1827 he resumed his labors in this region, and continued them for ten years.

Another pioneer laborer of the Presbyterian Church in Georgia was Rev. (Dr.) John Brown, whose career has already been briefly traced. For several years—

---

[1] For a time he seems to have withdrawn from the Presbytery.

subsequent to 1811—he discharged the duties of his office as President of Georgia University, after which he was chosen pastor of Mt. Zion Church in Hancock county. This station he held for twelve years, at the same time laboring extensively as an evangelist.

In 1820, Hinsdale and Orton, who have been already mentioned as the Assembly's missionaries, entered the field. Following the advice of the Synod of South Carolina, they selected as the sphere of their itinerancy the region embraced by the then seven western counties of Georgia,—Baldwin, Jones, Twiggs, Pulaski, Laurens, and Wilkinson, lying between the Oconee and Ocmulgee, and the southern part of Washington county between Oconee and Ogeechee Rivers.

The whole region had been purchased of the Indians only fourteen years previous, and all the settlements were of recent date. The vices of a new population were extensively prevalent. The want of an enlightened and faithful ministry was deplorable. Before the arrival of the missionaries there was no Presbyterian preaching whatever. Religion was lightly esteemed, and the "walk of many professors was inconsistent and ungodly." Yet, before the period of their service was complete, the missionaries were able to report a prospect that several Presbyterian congregations might be organized.

In 1821 the Presbytery of Georgia, which had recently been formed, and which covered more than half the State, contained but eight ministers. They were still aided, but to a feeble extent, by the missionaries sent out by the Assembly. The burden of their support fell mainly upon the Synod. Horace S. Pratt and Charles K. Hinsdale were commissioned in 1821 to labor in this region. In 1822,[1] John H. Vancourt was appointed for

---

[1] William F. Curry, a native of Paris, Ky., a graduate of Transyl-

six months. The supervision of this field devolved mainly upon the Synod of South Carolina and Georgia; and the destitutions of other portions of the region under its care were such that it could give but little attention to the wants of the Presbyterian Church in Georgia.

In 1825 the Presbytery had but six ministers and one licentiate. Of the six, four, viz.: William McWhir, S. J. Davis, Murdock Murphy, and G. G. McWhorter, were without charge, although not less efficient and energetic in missionary labor than their brethren Horace S. Pratt and Robert Quarterman, the first pastor at St. Mary's and the last at Midway. Prior to this period, Rev. N. S. S. Beman (Dr. Beman, of Troy) had preached with great acceptance at Mt. Zion, Eatonton, and other places for several years, and his brother Carlisle Beman—afterward President of Midway College—had been licensed to preach the gospel. Besides these, there were within the State, though connected mainly with the Presbytery of Hopewell, Dr. Francis Cummins, at Shady Grove, Greene county, Dr. Waddel, President of the State University, at Athens, Dr. Alonzo Church,[1] a native of Vermont, and associated with Waddel as a teacher in the university from 1819, William Moderwell, at Augusta, Remembrance Chamberlain, at Madison, in Morgan county, John S. Wilson, at Laurensville, Alexander H. Webster,[2] at Washington, Wilkes county, Joseph Y. Alexander, at Lincolnton,

---

vania University and Princeton Seminary, on completing his studies (1822) accepted an appointment as a missionary to Northern Georgia, where his labors were blessed in the formation of several Presbyterian churches. He subsequently labored at Pittsford, Lockport, and Geneva, N.Y.

[1] Now President of Franklin College, at Athens.

[2] A graduate of Union College, and tutor in the University of Georgia.—F.

and Thomas Goulding, at Lexington, Oglethorpe county. In 1825, Rev. George Foot, a licentiate of the Presbytery of Hopewell, was ordained and located at Monticello, Hillsborough, and Clinton, and (Dr.) Joseph C. Stiles was licensed. But all these, besides licentiates and ministers without charge, numbered only about twelve: so that the entire number of Presbyterian ministers within the bounds of the State scarcely exceeded twenty. Yet this (1825) was the date of the revival of the system of four-days meetings in Hopewell Presbytery,[1] with which a great improvement in the state of religion commenced.

In 1830 the number of ministers had been but slightly increased. The churches numbered from thirty to forty, and their membership was but little more than twelve hundred.

In 1837 the Presbyterian Church in Georgia was represented by the three Presbyteries of Hopewell, Georgia, and Flint River, the first with eighteen ministers and forty churches, with a membership of ten hundred and nine, the second with ten ministers, nine churches, and a membership of three hundred and forty-five, and the last, set off as "Good Hope" from Hopewell in 1833, and numbering eleven ministers. The pastors of the State were Robert Quarterman, of the Congregational Church, Midway, N. A. Pratt, of Darien, Washington Baird, of Waynesville, Joseph L. Jones, of Savannah, Nathan Hoyt, of Athens, George James, of Monticello, and John W. Baker, of Milledgeville. More than twenty of the churches had stated supplies, and about the same number were vacant. Among the members of the Presbytery were President Church, of Athens, President Beman, of Milledgeville, Professor Jones, of Columbia, Francis R. Goulding, stated supply of Wash-

---

[1] This was the origin of protracted meetings.—F.

ington Church, and Theodore M. Dwight, of Burke County Church.

One of the earliest missionaries to Alabama was J. W. Platt, sent out by the Young Men's Evangelical Missionary Society of New York. He arrived at Huntsville on the 26th of November, 1819.[1] Of this place he remarked, "Its inhabitants will suffer nothing by a comparison of those of most other towns in our country as it respects intelligence, refinement, and wealth." Yet there was in the place no organized church, or stated ministry, or house of worship, although many were anxious for gospel ordinances. Through his influence, steps were taken to erect "a handsome brick church."

From Huntsville, where he was urgently pressed to remain, Mr. Platt proceeded to Tuscaloosa, St. Stephens, Blakely, and Mobile. Everywhere he was kindly and hospitably received. "It was pleasant," he says, "to be among these people,—to feed those sheep in the wilderness."

In the successive years from 1817 to 1820, Francis H. Porter was commissioned by the Assembly to labor as a missionary in Alabama Territory. In 1819 Lucas Kennedy was appointed with him to the same field. In 1819 we find James L. Sloss and Hiland Hulburt, members of the Presbytery of South Carolina, laboring in connection with the congregations respectively of Jackson and of Claiborne.

Of these names, that of James Long Sloss is deserving of special mention. He was a native of Ireland, but came to this country at an early age. It was the earnest desire of his pious parents that he should be devoted to the work of the ministry; and one of his earliest recollections was that his father placed his hand upon his head, and said, "My son, I would rather see you a faith-

---

[1] Christian Herald, 1819-20, p. 760.

ful minister of the gospel than a crowned monarch." Under the care of Dr. Waddel, he completed his preparatory theological course, and, notwithstanding the solicitations of some of his friends who urged him to devote himself to the legal profession, was licensed to preach, by the Presbytery of South Carolina, in November, 1817.

The next day after his licensure, he was commissioned by the Presbytery to labor as a missionary through portions of Georgia and the newly-formed settlements of what was then called the Alabama Territory. In less than a year he was ordained an itinerant on the Southwestern frontier, and soon after accepted a call from St. Stephens, Clark county, Ala., where he remained for three years, preaching successfully and at the same time taking charge of an academy. In 1821 he removed to Selma, in Dallas county, and took charge of the three churches of Selma, Pleasant Valley, and Cahawba. He subsequently labored at Somerville and New Providence, and finally at Florence, in Lauderdale county, where the closing years of his life were spent. Nearly his whole career was passed in Alabama. "It was characterized by great activity and devotedness, and much of it by great self-denial." With a logical mind, a fine imagination, a ready extemporaneous address, a natural gesticulation, a voice somewhat harsh, but of ample compass, a cultivated taste, extensive general as well as scientific knowledge, and a high spirit, delightfully softened and controlled by the influence of a consistent and enlightened piety, he stood eminent among his brethren, and his whole manner, by its fervor and boldness as well as propriety, was fitted to make a deep impression. He labored in connection with quite a number of churches during the period of his ministry; and in the camp-meetings which were annually held not many miles from his residence, he took an active part. From these occasions, when, as was usually the case, thousands were assembled,—some coming a distance of more than thirty miles,—hundreds dated their first religious impressions, and often their conversion.

Another efficient pioneer laborer in this region has been already mentioned,—Francis H. Porter. For several successive years he had itinerated largely throughout the northern portions of the State. In 1820 he visited Pleasant Valley, where "the assemblies were large, attentive, and serious," White's and Story's settlement in Green county,—where he organized the church of New Hope,—and the adjacent region.[1]

In 1821, Joseph P. Cunningham and Salmon Cowles were appointed by the Assembly missionaries to Alabama, the latter to labor in the northern part. In the following year the former was reappointed to the same field. James B. Stafford was directed also to labor within the bounds of the State. In 1823 the name of Francis H. Porter appears alone on the list of missionary appointments for this field, and in the two following years Samuel Taylor is the only laborer for Alabama and West Florida commissioned by the Board. The Presbytery of Alabama, however, was authorized to employ one or more missionaries, on the condition of bearing half the expense.

In 1825 the two Presbyteries of Alabama and North Alabama, covering the whole State, contained jointly seventeen ministers, of whom five—Thomas Newton, Neil McMillan, Henry White, Alexander A. Campbell, and Thomas C. Stewart—were without charge, but for the most part engaged in missionary labor. Besides these, James Hillhouse was pastor at Greensborough,

---

[1] In 1819, James Hillhouse, James L. Sloss, and Hiland Hulburt, to be mentioned hereafter, were laboring, the first at Hopewell and Carmel, the second at Jackson, and the last at Claiborne. They were connected with South Carolina Presbytery.

J. P. Cunningham at Concord, Green county, Thomas Alexander at Selma, Isaac Haden at Prairie Bluff, and John B. Warren at Mobile.

In North Alabama Presbytery, William Potter was pastor at Huntsville, A. K. Davis and John Allan labored in the same region, Joseph Wood at Tuscumbia, Hugh Barr at Courtland, and Robert M. Cunningham —who had recently resigned his charge at Lexington, Ky.—at Moulton, in the neighborhood of which his efforts were crowned with large success. He became instrumental subsequently in raising up the church at Tuscaloosa, and another in the neighboring town of Carthage. Joseph Parks Cunningham, already mentioned as a member of the Presbytery of Alabama, was his son.

At this period the churches connected with both Presbyteries, although two or three were within the bounds of Mississippi, numbered only twenty-eight. Of these nearly all were feeble and unable to support a pastor. The average number of members belonging to each was about thirty.

In 1830 the two Presbyteries of North and South Alabama numbered conjointly twenty-nine ministers and forty-one churches, with a membership of seventeen hundred and thirteen. In 1834 the Presbytery of Tuscaloosa was formed from that of South Alabama. In 1837 the Presbytery of North Alabama—connected with the Synod of West Tennessee—had eight ministers and sixteen churches, numbering five hundred and fourteen members. South Alabama had thirteen ministers, five licentiates, and thirty-one churches, with a membership of sixteen hundred and ninety-three. The Presbytery of Tuscaloosa had ten ministers and fifteen churches, with a membership of seven hundred and thirty-nine. In the northern part of the State the only pastors were James L. Sloss at Florence and Dr.

John Allan at Huntsville. The stated supplies were S. H. Morrison at Moulton, James Weatherby at Tuscumbia, and James H. Gillespie at Somerville. In Southern Alabama, William T. Hamilton was settled over the Government Street Church, Mobile,[1] Robert Nall at Marion, Elon O. Martin at Hopewell and Sandy Ridge, and James B. Adams at Hebron and New Hope. Thirty-three of the churches, or more than one-half, had stated supplies; while seventeen were vacant.

The First Presbyterian Church in East Florida was organized by William McWhir, in 1824, at St. Augustine. He had for many years been laboring in Georgia in the counties to the south of Savannah, but, in consequence of a representation of the destitution of the means of grace in this field, was induced to visit it. He accordingly constituted a Presbyterian church, ordained elders, and engaged in collecting the requisite funds for building a church-edifice, and in due time had the pleasure of seeing his object accomplished.

At the time he visited this recently-acquired territory there was not a Protestant minister within its bounds. A missionary of the Methodist Church had been laboring there, but had left. Rev. Eleazar Lathrop preached for some time in St. Augustine, and with encouraging success. On his way to New York, in the spring of 1824, to collect funds, he laid the condition of the Presbyterian society to which he had ministered before the Synod of South Carolina and Georgia, by whom his agency was endorsed; and it seems probable that the mission of McWhir was occasioned by the representations of Mr. Lathrop. The importance of aid for the erection of a place of worship was obvious, and both McWhir and Lathrop were active and energetic in their applications for help. The last

---

[1] James R. Johnston was stated supply at Mobile in 1833.

was appointed, previous to his return from his collecting tour, by the Missionary Board of the Assembly, to labor in the field in which he had become so deeply interested. He spent four months of labor in 1824 at St. Augustine, and two in Pensacola.

The church of St. Augustine was for several years the only one in East Florida. It stood connected with Charleston Union Presbytery, and, consequently, with the Synod of South Carolina and Georgia. After Mr. Lathrop left on account of ill health, it was supplied by E. H. Snowden, sent out and sustained by the American Home Missionary Society. He commenced his labors in 1831.[1] The Sabbath after his arrival, the Presbyterian congregation convened for the first time, in the new building which for years they had been engaged in erecting, and which afforded them "very pleasant accommodations." For almost ten years they "had been in the wilderness, without rest or shelter;" and it was cheering to them at last to be permitted to worship in their own tabernacle.

The Sabbath-school, previously languishing, was revived. An advance was manifest in morals and religion. In the surrounding country other Sunday-schools were instituted; and Mr. Snowden wrote, "I hope you will send on missionaries to Florida; but I would advise none to come who cannot endure hardness as good soldiers of Jesus Christ."

In 1837 a church of seven members was reported at Mandarin, and one of fifty-one members at Tallahassee.[2]

---

[1] Missionary Reporter, November, 1831. He had been laboring here temporarily before. In 1827 he was commissioned by the Assembly's Board for three months' labor at St. Augustine.

[2] Francis H. Porter was commissioned by the Assembly's Board in 1827 for three months at Tallahassee.

CHAPTER XXXVIII.

THE MISSION-FIELD AT THE WEST AND NORTHWEST, 1810-1830.

AT an early period the attention of the Presbyterian Church was directed to the mission-field embraced in Indiana Territory. In 1805, Thomas Williamson, a licentiate of the Second Presbytery of South Carolina, was appointed by the Assembly to three months' service, "in the lower parts of the State of Ohio, and in the Indiana Territory as low as Kaskaskias." In 1806, Samuel Holt, of the Presbytery of West Lexington, was appointed for three months "in the Indiana Territory, and especially at Vincennes." The First Presbyterian Church in the Territory was constituted at this place (Vincennes) in the same year by Rev. Samuel B. Robertson, and was called "Indiana Church." In the following year Rev. Samuel Thornton Scott, from Kentucky, took up his residence in the vicinity and preached to this church. He was the first resident minister. After one or two years he returned to Kentucky, but after about the same interval he came back to the neighborhood of Vincennes, where he continued till his death in 1827.

In 1809 and 1810, James H. Dickey was in the employ of the Assembly in this and the surrounding region In 1811, we find the names of Stephen Bovelle and James McGready on the list of missionary appointments for the field, and their commissions were renewed for the following year.

In 1814 the number of laborers was enlarged Toward the close of the year John M Dickey, a licentiate of Muhlenberg Presbytery,[1] better known afterward as "Father" Dickey, visited the field. He was of Irish descent, but a native of South Carolina. He came to the Forks of White River in December, and removed with his family in May, 1815. When he crossed the river (White), the charge for ferriage exceeded by fifty cents the money in his possession. He was settled over White River Church, at the forks of White River, near what is now Washington, Davis county. In 1817 he was ordained by Muhlenburg Presbytery, and dismissed to unite with others in forming Salem Presbytery.[2] Till 1819 he preached half the time at White River Church on a salary of fifty dollars a year, occupying a field sixteen miles long by ten broad. The other half of his time was spent as a volunteer missionary in various destitute places, from which he received barely enough to meet his travelling-expenses. To support his family he had to resort to manual labor and giving instruction in sacred music. In 1819 he removed to the vicinity of Lexington, Scott county, and took charge of three small churches,—Pisgah, Lexington, and Graham,—laboring

---

[1] See pamphlet, "A Brief History of the Presbyterian Church in Indiana," by J. M. Dickey, p. 12.

[2] Salem Presbytery, however, did not hold its first meeting until April, 1824. In October, 1823, the Synod of Kentucky divided Louisville Presbytery and constituted the Presbytery of Salem, embracing all of Indiana west of a line running due north from the mouth of Kentucky River.

The name *Salem* was suggested by Rev. Isaac Reed, with reference to its scriptural signification. See "Christian Traveller."

The first meeting was held in the town of Salem, April 1, 1824, and was opened with a sermon by Rev. Samuel T. Scott, from Eph. iv. 3, 4.

finally at Pisgah and Washington, near the Ohio. Here he was installed: yet he continued his labors as a missionary with untiring zeal and incessant diligence. A large number of churches were gathered and organized by his instrumentality, and, although two other Presbyterian ministers had been settled before him within the bounds of the State, his name will stand deservedly conspicuous as the father of the Presbyterian Church in Indiana. He entered the field when it contained less than half a dozen laborers, but lived to see Presbyteries and Synods spring up around him. Till 1847 he continued his pastoral and pulpit labors; and nothing but increasing infirmity prevented him from still pursuing the missionary work.

In 1815, Joseph Anderson and James Welch were employed, and the Pittsburg Society was authorized to engage others in the same field. In the following year Samuel T. Scott returned to Vincennes, and James McGready, William Wylie, Samuel Brown, Joseph B. Lapsley, and Thomas Cleland were to labor for longer or shorter periods within the Territory. This field fell properly within the bounds of the Synod of Kentucky, as the one to which it was most accessible; and by far the largest number of its missionaries were selected from that body. Already congregations had been gathered at several places, but none of them were able to sustain a pastor.

In 1816, Charles Robinson, sent out by one of the New York missionary societies to labor in Missouri, passed through this region. He found in the Territories of Indiana and Illinois but one settled pastor and five or six missionaries. In June of the same year, Rev. Nathan B. Derrow, for seven years an efficient missionary of the Connecticut Society in the Western Reserve, left that field to accept a missionary appointment to Indiana and Illinois. He passed through Ohio by a circuitous route to Jeffersonville.[1] Here he spent a few weeks, thence proceeding north to Fort Harrison, then down the Wabash on his tour of exploration.

He found the field at once destitute and inviting. Although the country was yet but thinly settled, "additions to the population were continual and great." Illiterate and enthusiastic preachers were numerous. He was deeply affected and distressed by the extreme ignorance which prevailed, especially among the first settlers and their children. "In every direction, many whole families were to be found without a book of any sort." The population was extremely heterogeneous. Many belonged to "the hunting class." In a large number of instances, extreme indigence was connected with extreme ignorance. When tracts were presented by the missionary, he was asked to read them by those who declared they could not read themselves. The state of general intelligence was humiliatingly low. The people were just in a condition to become the prey of false teachers.

Mr. Derrow commenced his labors with energy, and was instrumental in organizing four Bible-societies,—three in Indiana and one in Illinois. As immigration increased, the more unsettled and nomadic classes removed to more distant regions. Orderly government began to be established and recognized. The Legislature enacted laws frowning upon vice and immorality.

New laborers, for longer or shorter periods, were now continually arriving. Mr. Giddings, from St. Louis, sometimes crossed the Mississippi, extending his explorations into Indiana and Illinois. William Dickey and James McGready were appointed by the General Assembly of 1817 to spend each three months in the bounds of the State, the former at "discretion," the

---

[1] On the Ohio, opposite Louisville.

last in Clark, Harrison, Gibson, and Huron counties. John F. Crowe was also to labor three months in Illinois Territory. In the following year their places were taken, by appointment of the Assembly, by R. K. Rodgers, Samuel Graham, and Benjamin Low,—the former commissioned for Indiana and the two last for Illinois.

In the same year Orin Fowler was sent out by the Connecticut Society as a missionary to Indiana for six months. His circuit included ten counties in the middle and eastern parts of the State, and the region extending from this toward the Wabash. In every direction "the people were anxious to hear the word preached." The missionary, although addressing congregations almost daily, was able to meet but few of the pressing invitations extended to him. Many came eight, ten, fifteen, and some twenty, miles to hear a sermon. At one time he had appointments "for seven weeks forward" in nearly as many different counties. Within this period, also, he had appointments to administer the sacrament three times and organize two churches. Not an hour's leisure could he find for study.

In 1818, although quite a number of churches had been organized within the bounds of Indiana, not one of them[1] enjoyed the labors of a settled pastor. A small church had recently been formed at Madison, and was temporarily supplied by a minister who soon left. The membership was only seventeen. Pisgah Church, a few miles down the Ohio, had been organized not long before by James McGready, while performing service as a missionary by appointment of the General Assembly. At Charlestown, the county-seat of Clarke county, was a small church, with Mr. Todd as resident minister. At New Albany was a church of twelve

---

[1] Reed's Christian Traveller, 218.

members, recently organized by the Rev. D. C. Banks.[1] From this down the Ohio to the State line at the mouth of the Wabash, there was no church and no minister. In the direction of Vincennes there were two churches,—one at Blue River, and one at Livonia, —both formed by Mr. McGready; and these, in connection with the church of Salem, were supplied by Rev. William W. Martin. At Washington, Davis county, a feeble church existed, which for a short time had been supplied by the Rev. J. M. Dickey. In Knox county, and near Vincennes, was a small church,—already mentioned,—supplied by Rev. T. S. Scott. Thirty miles higher up the Wabash River a small church was supplied by Rev. J. Balch, already enfeebled by age. Three missionaries of the Connecticut Society were at the time laboring within the bounds of the State. One of these was N. B. Derrow, by whom one church was formed in Jennings and another in Jackson county. Another was Orin Fowler, by whom three churches were organized.

In September, Isaac Reed, a native of Granville, N.Y., and a graduate of Middlebury College, commenced his labors for a year at New Albany. In 1813, when the town was laid out, its site was thickly covered with heavy timber. In five years the population had increased to seven hundred, and a church had been formed, consisting of thirteen members. Before the close of the year (1819) the number had increased to thirty-five. The moral aspect of the place had been greatly changed.

---

[1] Another statement represents it to have been organized by Mr. McGready, Feb. 16, 1816. It was first known as Union Church of Jeffersonville. Six of the ten original members were from the latter place. The Second Church of New Albany was organized in November, 1837, with one hundred and three members. Causes of division in the original congregation had preceded the division in the Presbyterian Church at large.

The stores, which had been kept open on the Sabbath, were now closed. A Sunday-school of sixty scholars—the first organized within the bounds of the State—had been established; but, without missionary aid, the church was unable to retain Mr. Reed as stated supply, and he removed to Kentucky. His successor, Ezra H. Day, who commenced his labors in the summer of 1822, closed his life in the autumn of the following year.

In 1813 the seat of government was removed from Vincennes to Corydon, and at the latter place a church was organized by John F. Crowe, missionary from Kentucky, in 1818. In the spring of 1814 the town of Rising Sun was laid out. Two years later a church was organized by Mr. Derrow; but it was not till 1828 that a pastor was secured. In that year Lucius Alden, who for some time had preached in Aurora and Cæsar Creek township, was installed; but till 1831, when he was succeeded by William Lewis, the congregation depended for a place of worship on school-houses, shops, private houses, the shady woods, or the loan of the Methodist chapel. In 1819 a church was organized at Bloomington by Isaac Reed, and John M. Dickey was installed at New Lexington. Soon after, churches were gathered at Terre Haute (laid out in 1816) and Paris, and a stone meeting-house was erected at Dunn and Logan's Settlement, seven miles below Madison, while at the latter place Thomas C. Searle, sent out by the Young Men's Missionary Society of New York, had commenced (July 21, 1818) his labors, which were closed by death in 1821. In 1820, Hanover Church was formed and united with the Madison Church; and in the same year W. W. Martin was installed at Livonia.

In 1819, Stephen Bovelle was sent out by the Assembly to labor for a portion of the year in this field. For Illinois, which had now become a State, two missionaries were appointed, who were to labor at Edwardsville, Shawanee, and the adjoining settlements, and were to be in part sustained by the local missionary societies on the frontier. In 1820 the Connecticut Society sent out Ahab Jenks, and the Assembly, John Vancourt and George S. Boardman. Henry Perkins and Andrew O. Patterson were likewise to labor in Illinois, consulting in regard to their route with the auxiliary missionary societies. Isaac Reed also at this time commenced his labors under the commission of the Connecticut Society, but soon removed to Kentucky, returning two years later to Indiana and taking charge of Bethany Church, which was organized in Owen county in 1820 by John M. Dickey.[1]

At this period (1820) the population of the State had increased to one hundred and forty thousand, mostly bordering on the Ohio and the east line of the State, and extending up the Wabash for some two hundred miles. The emigrants were "mainly from the south of the Ohio River," and were "a mixture from almost every quarter." "Interest had drawn most; to be in new countries had induced others; while to get away from negro slavery had influenced not a few in their removals from slaveholding States. Many also were from the Ohio, and some—although few—from the Northern States."[2] In the bounds of the State there were only seven ministers, and but two of these settled pastors. In 1822, Isaac Reed commenced his labors in connection with Bethany Church in Owen county, and was installed in the following year. About the time of Mr. Reed's arrival, David C. Proctor became stated supply for a year of the congregation at Indianapolis. This was now made the permanent seat of the State Government. In the autumn of 1821 its first sale of lots took place.

[1] Reed's Christian Traveller, 121. [2] Ibid. 218.

But already—a few weeks previous—the place had been visited by a Presbyterian minister, O. P. Gaines, who preached the first Presbyterian sermon to a small congregation. In May of the following year, Mr. Proctor, missionary of the Connecticut Society, preached four or five sermons, and in October returned to commence his labors for the year. In July (5), 1823, he had the gratification of seeing a church organized with fifteen members. The day previous, Mr. Reed had preached to the little handful of hearers in a cabinet-maker's shop. On the close of Mr. Proctor's year of service, Indianapolis and Bloomington were left virtually to the care of Mr. Reed till the arrival of George Bush in 1824.

It may afford some idea of the hardships of the early ministers to state the circumstances of the laborers in this field. The nearest churches were those of Bethany in Owen county, and of Bloomington. The former was under the charge of Mr. Reed, and the latter, though seventy miles distant from Indianapolis, had one-fourth of Mr. Proctor's time. At Bethany Mr. Reed was forced to labor in erecting his own rude log dwelling; for his people were too busied with their own to afford him the necessary aid. With all his efforts, much was still lacking. His building progressed slowly, and the winter commenced early. The week before Christmas he took possession of it with his family; but it was without a loft, and there was "no plastering of the chinking between the logs, above the joist-plates." A large wooden chimney-place was cut out of the end of the house and built up a little above the mantel-piece. And yet this was the tenement which the self-denying missionary loved to style, in his correspondence, "the cottage of peace."[1] When forced to seek, some

[1] Christian Traveller, 139.

years later, a new settlement, he gave among his reasons for asking a dissolution of his pastoral relation the fact that for two years he had not received one dollar in money toward his salary from his people.[1]

The church at Evansville was organized in 1821, under the direction of D. C. Banks, then pastor of the Presbyterian Church of Henderson, Ky.[2] The original membership was but ten or twelve, and for several years there was but a small increase. The congregation had no house of worship, and the church was as "sheep without a shepherd." An old log school-house on the lower side of Locust Street, nearly midway between First and Second Streets, was a frequent place of meeting, until the old court-house was at length occupied. The scene when the congregation met was indeed primitive. There was no flooring. "Puncheon seats" were placed on the bare ground. The fire in winter was against the wall in a poorly-formed fire-place, and the smoke sometimes found in the numerous accommodating chinks and crannies of the building a more feasible method of escape than the chimney offered. Till 1832, the nearest Presbyterian church was that of Princeton, under the pastoral care of Calvin Butler. By his exertions, a house of worship was erected in that year. Removing to the place, he labored as pastor till 1834. His successors were Mr. McAfee and (1837) J. R. Barnes.

In 1824 the Presbytery of Salem,[3] embracing most of the churches of the State, was erected, and congregations began to be more rapidly formed. Bethlehem

---

[1] Christian Traveller, 158. [2] McCarer's memorial sermon.

[3] Salem Church was organized by Samuel Shannon, Aug. 15, 1817, with thirty members, and was first called Union Church. Its name was changed to Salem in 1821. Mr. Shannon was its first supply, and William M. Martin its first pastor (1818–29). Franklin Church was formed from it.

Church, in the southern part of Washington county, was formed early in the year; that in Crawfordsville in June, and New Hope Church, on the Illinois line, shortly after. Paris Church secured the services of John Young, a man of much promise, whose untimely death in the following year (1825) was felt as a public calamity. Shortly after this (December) Greenfield Church, in Johnson county, was organized, a little more than two years after the arrival of the first two families in the settlement.

By 1825 the population of the State had increased to not far from two hundred thousand, and the churches within its bounds numbered only forty-three, and the ministers but ten, of whom five were pastors, two of the others being ordained. Yet there was evident progress. The results of missionary labor began to be manifest, although the destitution which still continued and was extended by the increasing tide of immigration almost swallowed them up.

Retracing our course, we note the labors of the missionaries sent out into this field. Those of Mr. Flint during his short stay in Indiana were quite effective. Notwithstanding the prevalent profanity, the deplorable ignorance, and the fearful Sabbath-breaking which prevailed, he gathered large and attentive audiences. General Harrison threw open his house to the preachers. The first congregation numbered but thirty; the second amounted to two hundred. "The serious," wrote Mr. Flint, "everywhere beg me to represent the deplorable destitution of religious instruction."

Mr. Derrow's labors were not in vain. In the course of two years he organized several churches and performed a great amount of itinerant labor. In every instance he was received with kindness and respect. There was a growing attention to the institutions of the gospel, and, although there were few awakenings that could be termed revivals, he frequently met individuals who seemed to be the subjects of genuine religious experience.

In 1820, George S. Boardman was commissioned for six months to preach at Madison and the adjoining settlements. But, finding this field preoccupied by Thomas C. Searle, sent out to Indiana by the Young Men's Missionary Society of New York and settled at Madison with very favorable prospects of usefulness, he very properly directed his course to places more destitute of the means of grace. He itinerated chiefly in the settlements on White River and in those on Indian Kentucky River. On White River he found the towns new and flourishing. A church had been organized at Bloomington, a county-seat; and near it was the place selected for the University of Indiana. At Washington, situated at the junction of the forks of the river, he found a Presbyterian settlement. Yet the region had been visited by few missionaries. There were no settled pastors. The land was overspread with wickedness and with "the gross errors of the New-Lights and Dunkards." It claimed the special attention of missionaries, while a portion of its inhabitants, aware of its condition, earnestly entreated that some effort might be made to stay the progress of error and provide them with a few at least of the privileges of the gospel.

In the settlement on Indian Kentucky the prospect was more hopeful. Solemn attention was given, and tears attested the depth of feeling with which the word was heard. Yet the whole State was represented as claiming special attention from its present situation and future prospects. Intemperance prevailed to an alarming extent. Profanity, frauds, and gaming were common. The Sabbath was desecrated,—made a day of idleness and pleasure.

Nor was this all. The country was alike "fertile in the productions of the earth and of error." The Methodists, "with a variety of contradictory errors in opinion and practice," were the prevailing sect. The Baptists were lax in the observance of the Sabbath, the support of the gospel, and regard for a learned ministry,—some of them submerging all their religion in immersion. New-Lightism—"the moral monster of the West," a composite of all various errors—was common. The Dunkards, who were numerous, were Universalists or fanatics. Yet there were many who longed for the appearance of the missionary. Tears of joy and gratitude were seen upon his arrival, and tears of sorrow attended his departure. It was obvious that, with a rich soil and a healthiness superior to Illinois, Indiana was destined soon to "become rich and powerful."

In 1821, Adam W. Platt was commissioned by the Assembly to labor for six months in Indiana, and William B. Barton was appointed for the same period to occupy the place of Mr. Vancourt, who had returned his commission. Half of Mr. Barton's time was devoted to Jefferson Church, in which a revival was in progress: the rest was spent in tours, some within the limits of Ohio. Ludwell G. Gaines, D. C. Banks, and Thompson S. Harris were likewise appointed at the same time with Platt and Barton for this field.

In 1822 the appointments of the Assembly's Board were John Ross in Western Ohio and Eastern Indiana, James L. Marshall in the region previously visited by Messrs. Barton and Platt, Alexander McCandless for four months in the neighborhood of Indianapolis, and Thomas C. Kennedy for the same period on the line between Indiana and Illinois. Abraham Williamson and William H. Stewart were to labor in the latter State.

In the following year the Board commissioned Rev. N Pittinger to labor in the upper part of Indiana, John

M Dickey, who was to receive half his compensation from societies in that region, on the White and Wabash Rivers, while John Ross and Alexander McCandless were to occupy their fields of labor of the previous year.

Few and scant are the glimpses which we obtain of these heroic pioneers of Christian civilization,—these heralds of the gospel to the few feeble settlements scattered over the broad wilderness. But sometimes a journal like that of Joseph Badger, or some historical discourse like that of Fort Wayne,[1] falls in our way, and we are enabled to trace some of the hardships to which they were subjected. John Ross—better known as "Father" Ross—discharged his mission with zeal and fidelity. Only his own pen could fitly describe the peril and exposure of his first missionary journey,—how the first night's encampment in the woods a few miles north of Dayton was made memorable by the howling of wolves on every side; how the snow-storm afterwards met them in the wilderness with intense cold which froze the wheels of their wagon fast in the mud; how, failing to strike fire from the flint, the woodsman's last hope, they were compelled to leave their conveyance under the guard of a faithful dog; how, by walking and leading their horses when the intense cold forbade their riding, they at length reached Fort Wayne at a late hour of the wintry night and received a cordial welcome.

The next day—Sunday—there was preaching at the fort; for no other convenient place could be found. For five successive years,—from 1822 to 1826,—sometimes sent out by the Assembly and sometimes by the Synod of Ohio, "Father" Ross visited Fort Wayne and the surrounding region. He preached in St. Mary's, Shane's

[1] J. L. Williams's Historical Sketch of the First Presbyterian Church of Fort Wayne.

Prairie, and Willshire, scattering religious tracts and Bibles on his way. Fort Wayne was the most unpromising part of the field. Few there were who paid any regard to the Sabbath. It was not till 1831 that a church was organized, of eleven members.

In 1824, George Bush was appointed for Indianapolis, where he soon after was settled, remaining several years; McCandless for the counties of Wayne, Union, and Fayette, and T. Scott for Sullivan, Davis, and the adjoining counties; John Young, a recent graduate of Princeton Seminary, took the place of Mr. Searle in Indiana,[1] and, together with Benjamin F. Spilman and Charles Philips, was to devote a portion of his time to the destitutions of Illinois. The church at Crawfordsville was organized the same year by Rev. Isaac Reed. Rev. James Thompson was the first pastor.

In 1825, Isaac A. Ogden and John Ross were commissioned to labor on the line between Ohio and Indiana. James Stuart was to visit Urbana in Ohio, and thence proceed to labor in Rush, Decatur, Fayette, Hardenburg, and Posey counties. J. M. Dickey was to visit the East Fork of White River. Samuel Gregg was to labor in the counties of Bartholomew and Johnson, and William Nesbit in those of Perry and Spence. Samuel Taylor was to spend three months on the White River, on both sides, in Morgan county. In the southern part of Illinois, James Kerr was commissioned for five months;

---

[1] Mr. John Young, a licentiate under the care of the General Assembly, came to the State in 1824, and spent two months at Madison. He then spent six months on the west of the Wabash, and died on the 15th of August, 1825, at Vincennes, whither he had gone to attend the meeting of the Indiana Missionary Society. Mr. James H. Johnston, under the patronage of the Domestic Missionary Society of New York, came to the State in company with Mr Young, and succeeded him at Madison, where he remained until 1843, then removed to Crawfordsville, where he still resides. He is one of the veterans.

in the eastern part, Jesse Townsend for three; while at Shoal Creek and vicinity William Wallace was to devote six months.

The churches of Indiana and Illinois were at this period connected with the Synod of Kentucky. The members of Salem Presbytery,[1] within the bounds of the former State, were William Robinson, Samuel T. Scott, John M. Dickey, William W. Martin, John F. Crowe, Isaac Reed, George Bush, Baynard R. Hall, and

---

[1] The original members of Salem Presbytery (April 1, 1824) were Samuel T. Scott, installed at Vincennes, Aug. 5, 1825, died Dec. 20, 1827; John Todd, dismissed to West Lexington Presbytery, April 5, 1827; John M. Dickey, installed pastor of Pisgah and New Lexington Churches, Aug. 1819, set off to Madison Presbytery, 1825; William W. Martin, of Livonia; Isaac Reed, of Bethany Church, set off to Wabash Presbytery in 1825; John F. Crowe, installed over Hanover Church, Aug. 1823, and set off to Madison Presbytery, Oct. 1825; and William Robinson, who died March, 1827.

The subsequent members have been Joseph Trimble, died Aug. 11, 1824; T. H. Brown, ordained and installed June 25, 1825, over Bethlehem and Blue River Churches; George Bush, March 5, 1825; Baynard R. Hall, settled at Bloomington, April 13, 1825; Alexander Williamson, settled at Charlestown, July 3, 1825; Stephen Bliss, ordained at Vincennes, Aug. 5, 1825; J. H. Johnston, settled at Madison, Oct. 20, 1825; John T. Hamilton, Oct. 8, 1825; Samuel E. Blackburn, ordained at Jeffersonville, Dec. 1, 1826, dismissed 1828; Calvin Butler, ordained at Princeton, May, 1828; Leander Cobb, Ashbel S. Wells, settled at New Albany, Dec. 18, 1828; Benjamin C. Cressy, James A. Carnahan, Samuel K. Sneed, 1831; Michael A. Rawley, April 7, 1831; Moody Chase, settled at Orleans, June 7, 1833; S. Kittredge, ordained at Bedford, June 19, 1834; E. P. Humphrey, ordained at Jeffersonville, Nov. 20, 1834; Simeon Salisbury, Oct. 9, 1835; P. S. Cleland, ordained at Jeffersonville, Nov. 16, 1836; Daniel L. Russell, Oct. 6, 1836; James W. Phillips, Nov. 16, 1836; John L. Martin, ordained at Livonia, Nov. 25, 1837; W. C. Anderson, April 5, 1838; E. R. Martin, ordained at Salem, Oct. 5, 1838; Calvin N. Ransom, Oct. 4, 1838; Charles R. Fisk, Oct. 4; J. R. Barnes, Oct. 11; W. C. Rankin, Oct. 11; Alexander McPherson, ordained at Brownstown, April 3, 1840.—*J. M. B., in Indiana Christian Herald.*

John Todd. In Illinois, Charles Philips was settled as pastor at Shawneetown, and B. F. Spilman at Carmi, both in connection with the Presbytery of Muhlenburg.

Although several churches were often under the care of one pastor, the vacancies outnumbered the places which enjoyed pastors in the ratio of four to one. Of the thirty-seven Presbyterian churches under the care of Salem Presbytery, thirty were vacant. Most of these had been organized within the preceding five years. Only four at this period consisted of more than fifty members. These were the churches at Madison, Jefferson, Charleston, and Sand Creek. Columbus and Wabash numbered but fifteen each, New Providence but thirteen, and Crawfordsville but nine. All the others ranged variously between these extremes,—Indianapolis and Rushville each numbering twenty-five, Bloomington thirty, Dartmouth thirty-three, Hopewell thirty-three, Washington forty-seven, New Hope forty-nine, Graham forty-six, and Shiloh forty-two. Most of the eight or ten churches in Illinois, connected either with the Presbytery of Muhlenburg or that of Missouri, were feeble and destitute of pastoral labor. The one at Alton numbered but seven, and the one at Kaskaskia but thirteen, members.

But from that period the growth of the churches was more rapid; although it could scarcely be said to keep pace with the population. The Home Missionary Society sent out quite a number of missionaries into the region. The missionaries of the Assembly were, in 1826, S. G. Lowry in Delaware and Rush counties, Isaac A. Ogden in Union, Franklin, and Fayette counties, Joseph Robinson in Bartholomew and Shelby counties, and John Ross in the eastern part of the State; in 1827, Messrs. Ogden, Lowry, and James Thompson,—the latter of whom, at the earnest request of Judge Dunn, elder of Crawfordsville Church, deviated from his instructions to visit that place, where he was soon after settled for half his time, devoting the rest to feeble congregations, —while William J. Frazer was commissioned for Illinois; in 1828, Messrs. Lowry, Gaines, Ogden, Ross, and P. Montford for Indiana, and Benjamin F. Spilman for Southeastern Illinois.

In 1825 the Presbytery of Salem was divided to erect those of Madison and Wabash; and in 1826 the Synod of Indiana was erected. In 1828 the Presbytery of Centre of Illinois was erected by setting off a portion of Wabash; and in 1829 the Synod consisted of five Presbyteries, including the Presbytery of Missouri. In that year the Presbytery of Crawfordsville was erected from a portion of Wabash, and in 1830 Indianapolis from Madison and Crawfordsville. In 1830 the ministers within the State numbered about thirty-four, and the churches about eighty-four, with a membership not far short of three thousand.

In 1837 the strength of the Presbyterian Church within the State was represented by the Presbyteries of Salem, Vincennes,[1] Madison, Crawfordsville, Indianapolis, Logansport,[2] and a portion of Oxford. The first had eight ministers and twenty churches, the second nine ministers and nineteen churches, the third fourteen ministers and sixteen churches, the fourth fourteen ministers and nineteen churches, the fifth ten ministers and twenty-two churches, the sixth seven ministers and sixteen churches; while in connection with Oxford Presbytery were some seven Indiana ministers and ten churches, making an aggregate of sixty-nine ministers and one hundred and twenty-two churches, of which the aggregate membership was not far short of five thousand.

---

[1] Name changed from Wabash in 1830.

[2] Erected from Crawfordsville, 1835.

The principal ministers in the field were—W. W. Martin, stated supply of Livonia; Samuel K. Sneed, stated supply of New Albany; Leander Cobb, stated supply at Charlestown; Solomon Kittredge, at Bedford; James W. Phillips, at Corydon; Philip S. Cleland, pastor at Jeffersonville; Thomas Alexander, stated supply of Vincennes; Samuel R. Alexander, pastor of Indiana Church; Calvin Butler, stated supply of Washington; Ransom Hawley, of Bloomington; Matthew G. Wallace, of Terre Haute; Andrew Wylie, President of the institution at Bloomington; Drs. James Blythe, John Matthews, John F. Crowe,[1] and Professors George Bishop and M. H. H. Niles, all at South Hanover; John M. Dickey, pastor at Pisgah; Daniel Lattimore, of Paris and Graham; William C. Matthews, of the First, and James H. Johnson, of the Second, Church of Madison; James Humner, of Jefferson; William J. Monteith, of Port William; President Baldwin and Professor Hovey, of Wabash College, Crawfordsville; S. H. McNutt, pastor of Rockville; James Thompson, of Crawfordsville; James H. Shields, of Poplar Spring; John Crawford, of Coal Creek; John Todd, of Eagle Creek and South Marion; David Montfort,[2] of Franklin; John S. Weaver, of Sand Creek;

---

[1] Dr. John F. Crowe was a native of Tennessee, where he was born in 1787. His studies were pursued at Transylvania University and at Princeton. He was ordained by Louisville Presbytery, and preached at Shelbyville from 1816 till 1823, when he settled at Hanover, Indiana. At the request of Salem Presbytery, he opened a grammar-school, which was the nucleus of Hanover College. This institution was greatly indebted to him. He was judicious, discriminating, patient, and persevering. He was eminent as a teacher and beloved as a pastor. His death occurred Jan. 17, 1860.

[2] Dr. David Montfort, a native of Pennsylvania, a Huguenot by descent, was born in 1790. In 1817 he completed his theological course at Princeton, and in the following year was settled over Bethel Church in Oxford Presbytery. In 1829 he joined Wabash Presbytery and supplied the church at Terre Haute. The next year

Eliphalet Kent, of Greenfield; James W. McKennan,[1] of Indianapolis; David M. Stewart, of Rushville; David V. Smock, of Knightstown; M. M. Post, of Logansport; Michael Humner, of La Fayette; James A. Carnahan, of Dayton; Samuel Newbury, of Peru; and John Stocker, of Monticello.

The earliest notice taken of Illinois as a missionary field occurs in 1816. For several years most of those who were sent into this region were directed to itinerate also in Indiana. The names of several of these have been already mentioned in connection with the latter field. In 1816, Backus Wilbur was commissioned to itinerate for two months from the mouth of the Wabash to Kaskaskia, where he was principally to labor. Samuel Brown also, on his way to Missouri, was to pass through Indiana and Illinois Territories, laboring at discrĕtion. William Wylie received similar directions. In 1817, John F. Crowe was commissioned to devote three months to Illinois Territory, and Eliphalet W. Gilbert was to devote six months to Shawneetown, Kaskaskia, and adjacent places. Sylvester Larned, on his way to his chosen field in New Orleans, was directed to pass through Vincennes and Kaskaskia.

---

he supplied Sharon Church, Ohio, and in 1830 commenced a pastorate of twenty years at Franklin, Indiana. His death occurred in 1860.

Samuel Baldridge, a native of North Carolina, a compeer of Gideon Blackburn, licensed by Abington Presbytery in 1802, was one of the most worthy pioneers of the West. He practised medicine to support his family, preaching on the frontier, organizing churches in Ohio and Indiana. In 1830 he had a stroke of paralysis, but survived till 1860.

[1] In 1835, James Wilson McKennan, a native of Washington, Pa., was called to the pastorate of the church of Indianapolis. He was here, however, but a few years before his health failed. Simple, direct, devoted, meek, humble, faithful, and fervent, he was worthy of love and respect. His death occurred July 16, 1861.

Mr. Crowe, on his return to Kentucky, published a short account of his journey. He found the inhabitants very destitute of moral and religious instruction, and the state of society in many instances very deplorable. The population of the twelve counties of the Territory was about fifty thousand, among whom were a few Baptist and, in connection with circuits in some of the principal settlements, some Methodist preachers, but not a single Presbyterian minister. The Dunkards had a society on the Mississippi, and the "Christians" were organizing churches on the Wabash. At Kaskaskia the desire was expressed by several respectable citizens that they might have a clergyman settled among them.[1]

In 1818, Samuel Graham and Benjamin Low were sent to Illinois, each to labor mainly on the line of the Ohio and its tributaries for six months. The latter was a graduate of Princeton College in 1814, and, after completing his theological course, had visited the Western field. In January, 1818,[2] he was at Edwardsville, having performed a tour of labor in portions of the State. After a favorable journey of thirty-nine days, he reached Shawneetown, eight miles below the mouth of the Wabash, Nov. 20, 1817. Among its two or three hundred inhabitants there was not a single soul that "made any pretensions to religion." "Their shocking profaneness was enough to make one afraid to walk the street; and those who on the Sabbath were not fighting and drinking at the taverns and grog-shops were either hunting in the woods or trading behind their counters." A small audience gathered to hear the missionary preach; but even a laborer who could devote his whole time to the field "might almost as soon expect to hear the stones cry out" as to effect a revolution in the morals of the place. The lower part

---

[1] Christian Herald, iv. 329. [2] Ibid. v. 753.

of the State was settled chiefly by emigrants from Kentucky and Tennessee and the northern parts of Georgia and Carolina. The upper part contained a much larger proportion of people from the Eastern and Middle States.[1] Of the five hundred inhabitants of Kaskaskia, one-half were French and Roman Catholics. Among the other half were six professors of religion,—two Presbyterians, two Methodists, one Congregationalist, and one Seceder. The Sabbath was scarcely recognized: yet many families in the town were anxious for the gospel.

At Edwardsville, eighty miles north of Kaskaskia, was a population of about three hundred. Within a radius from this point of from twelve to thirty miles were Shoal Creek, Sugar Creek, Belleville, Silver Creek, Cahokia, Alton, and Mouth of Illinois, at each of which places an audience of from thirty to fifty could be collected. For the winter, Mr. Low devoted himself to this field.

In 1819 the appointments of the Board of Missions for Illinois were Samuel Graham, who was to labor chiefly at Edwardsville, and two other missionaries in the neighborhood of Edwardsville and Shawneetown. The New York Evangelical Missionary Society had also sent out the Rev. David Tenny, who was the first of those appointed to reach the field. In a State "of not less than seventy thousand inhabitants," while the influx of settlers into it was "perhaps without a parallel," he was for a while the only Presbyterian minister on the ground, and a portion of his time was devoted to the wants of Missouri. It was in the early summer of 1819 that he began his labors in the region of Kaskaskia, and in the latter part of October of the same

[1] The report of Mr. Tenny in the ensuing year speaks of large numbers of emigrants from New York State.—*Chris. Herald*, vol. vi.

year his course was brought to a close by his early death. A graduate of Harvard in 1815, he devoted himself with a glowing zeal to the cause of missions, and the promise of usefulness which he had already given aggravated the sorrow felt for his loss.[1]

In 1820, Abraham Williamson was commissioned to labor for six months at Kaskaskia, Edwardsville, and adjacent places. The next year he was reappointed for the same period, his field to be selected at his own discretion, and William H. Stuart was appointed for two months. In 1823 no appointments were made for Illinois; but in 1824 Benjamin F. Spilman and Charles Philips were sent out. In Green county was a single church, which offered a clergyman one hundred and fifty dollars for half his time. In the county north there was a call for the formation of three churches. In Bond county was a church which offered two hundred dollars to secure a pastor. In Madison county were four churches, in St. Clair county one, and in Randolph county one; while in the eastern part of the State were two churches connected with Presbyteries outside its bounds.

In 1825 the only Presbyterian ministers in Illinois who sustained the pastoral relation were Benjamin F. Spilman at Carmi and Charles Philips at Shawneetown. The first of these was born in Garrard county, Ky., in 1796, and the scenes of his early life were adapted to foster the training essential to the energy and success of a pioneer missionary. In 1822 he was graduated at Jefferson College, Pa., and in the following year, after studying theology with Dr. Wilson, of Chillicothe, he was licensed to preach by Chillicothe Presbytery. In 1824 he was ordained and installed pastor of Sharon Church, Ill., and, on commencing

---

[1] Christian Herald, vi. 351.

here his missionary labors, became an itinerant in Middle and Southern Illinois, devoting his time mainly to the counties bordering on the Ohio and Wabash Rivers.[1] In 1826 he organized the church of Shawneetown, where some eighteen years afterward he was settled as pastor. Till 1832, when the "Old Log" Church was erected, the congregation was forced to occupy warehouses and private dwellings.

In 1826, John M. Ellis, sent out by the American Home Missionary Society, commenced his labors within the bounds of the State. He found Madison and Montgomery counties on the northern frontier of settlement.[2] The "Sangamon" county had been but just explored. Although combining on a magnificent scale "the beauties of the alluvial meadow, the aristocratic park, and the most gorgeous flower-garden," it was yet waiting the advent of civilized and Christian enterprise. At this time there were within the State but three Presbyterian ministers beside himself,—one of these, John Brich, English by birth and education, who was quite advanced in years, but resided on a farm near Jacksonsonville and labored merely as stated supply; another, Stephen Bliss, a licentiate of Salem Presbytery, Indiana, and who, laboring in Wabash county, was connected with the Presbytery of Wabash; and the third, Mr. Spilman, who was in the same connection.

Mr. Ellis first commenced his labors at Kaskaskia, where a feeble Presbyterian church had been in existence for several years. But in 1827 John Matthews, who had been for some time settled in Missouri, removed to this place,[3] where he remained, serving the church and at the same time itinerating as a missionary, for

---

[1] Wilson's Presb. Hist. Almanac, 1860, p. 78.

[2] President Sturtevant's Quarter-Century Celebration of Illinois College, p. 8.

[3] Wilson's Presb. Hist. Almanac, 1862, p. 102.

some eight or ten years. To eke out a meagre support, he sometimes engaged in teaching, and at other times labored on the farm.

Meanwhile, three small churches had been organized along the line of Shoal Creek,[1]—Bethel, Shoal Creek, and Greenville. To Jacksonville—where a feeble congregation worshipped ordinarily in Judge Leeper's barn—Mr. Ellis removed in 1828, his mind already teeming with the project which eventuated in the founding of Illinois College at Jacksonville. But, while he was meditating upon this favorite plan, the providence of God had directed the thoughts of several young men in the theological department of Yale College into a similar channel. A correspondence was opened with Mr. Ellis, and the result was that, early in 1829, seven young men of the Theological Seminary at New Haven were found prepared to subscribe their names to a solemn pledge to one another and to God to devote themselves to the cause of Christ in the then little-known, distant, and wild State of Illinois. These men were Mason Grosvenor, Theron Baldwin, John F. Brooks, Elisha Jenney, William Kirby, Asa Turner, and J. M. Sturtevant, all of whom—except the first, detained by ill health—migrated to Illinois on the completion of their theological course.[2]

---

[1] Solomon Hardy, sent out by the United Domestic Missionary Society, commenced his labors at Shoal Creek about January, 1828.

[2] The plan of founding a college in the far West had, several years before this, been conceived by one of these young men (Mason Grosvenor, now of Ohio). Before entering the Theological Seminary, and while engaged as a teacher, he had projected such an institution, with which a seminary for theological students was to be connected. Soon after he entered upon his studies at New Haven, the project was revived by hearing an essay "On forming and executing high and noble plans of usefulness," read by a fellow-student (Theron Baldwin) before the missionary association. In reading

Mr. Baldwin commenced his labors at Vandalia as stated supply, with a church of some eight or ten members. John F. Brooks located at Belleville, where (1832) a church was organized of twelve members. Asa Turner (1832) became stated supply at Quincy, where a church was gathered of thirty-four members. J. M. Sturtevant became professor of the newly-founded Illinois College, over which Edward Beecher, from Boston, had been called to preside. William Kirby

---

the "Home Missionary Journal," with a view of fixing upon a location for the college, he fell upon a letter of Mr. Ellis respecting a contemplated seminary at Jacksonville. He wrote to him immediately, drawing out his plan of a college, mentioning it at the same time to his brother (David A. Grosvenor), who was a fellow-student and room-mate. It was resolved between them that while they had a mother and sister dependent on them one must remain at home, while the other might engage in the mission-work. The brother who had conceived the plan, on studying the map, satisfied himself that Jacksonville was the proper site for the institution, and resolved to engage in it. He unfolded his plan to members of the senior class in the seminary, and enlisted them in his project. The result was that the seven young men above named were found prepared to subscribe their names to a solemn pledge to one another and to God to engage in missionary labor in the new State of Illinois. These, with three men already on the ground, were in the charter of the college at Jacksonville named as the first trustees; and all of the seven except the first-named—detained by ill health, but subsequently connected with the college—went to Illinois.

Dr. Taylor, their theological teacher, warmly sympathized with the project of the young men; although his gratification at the promise of usefulness which it afforded was clouded by the regret that the churches of New England would be deprived of their services. From him they received encouragement, and from President Day they derived, especially, suggestions of practical wisdom which were embodied in the basis of their proposed institution. In the course of three months, with the aid of Mr. Ellis, the sum of ten thousand dollars was raised to execute the project.

likewise was called to occupy the post of professor in the same institution.

In 1829, when the graduates of New Haven reached Illinois, they found themselves preceded by several laborers, who had followed Mr. Ellis. John G. Bergen was stated supply at Sangamon and Edwardsville, each with a church of between thirty and forty members. Solomon Hardy had been settled as pastor of the churches of Shoal Creek and Greenville,—the former with fifty and the latter with twenty-nine members. Thomas A. Spilman[1] had charge of the churches of Hillsborough and Bethel,—the former with six and the latter with fifty-four members,—while the churches of Golconda, Vandalia, Collinsville, Paris, Fulton, Carrolton, Franklin, Fairfield, and perhaps a few others, were vacant.

In the course of the year, Thomas Lippencott, a licentiate of the Presbytery, became stated supply of Edwardsville, Collinsville, and Sugar Creek; and Cyrus L. Watson, another licentiate, became stated supply of Rushville Church, with twelve members. In the following year (1830–31), Horace Smith became stated supply of Fulton Church, with from fifteen to twenty members, John McDonald commenced his labors at Union Grove, Benoni Y. Messenger took charge of Edwardsville and Sugar Creek (part of Mr. Lippencott's field), William J. Frazer became stated supply of the recently-formed Providence Church, and Henry Herrick supplied the church of Carrolton, then numbering but twelve members.

In the next year (1831–32), Aratus Kent commenced laboring as stated supply at Galena, the church then numbering six members, Lucian Farnum at Fulton,

[1] Ordained in 1827, died 1858, aged sixty; at the time of his death a member of Sangamon Presbytery.

where forty-two out of the fifty-eight members were added during the year, and Albert Hale at Bethel (Greenville post-office), where the church, with one hundred and eleven members, had become the largest in the State. Romulus Barnes, Calvin W. Babbit, and John Montgomery had also—although not permanently located—entered the field; while Mr. Frazer had removed to the charge of Union Church, near Jacksonville, and Theron Baldwin, who had become a missionary agent, had been succeeded at Vandalia by William R. Stewart

The four years from 1833 to 1837 were to the churches in Illinois a season of rapid growth. The Presbyteries, numbering eight, had under their care nearly one hundred churches, while the ministers, many of them sent out by the Home Missionary Society, numbered not far from sixty. The church of Hillsborough numbered one hundred and ten; the First and Second of Springfield, each a little more than sixty; the church of Ottawa, R. W. Gridley pastor, sixty-one; Galesburg, G. W. Gale stated supply, eighty-three; Macomb, William K. Stewart stated supply, ninety-nine; Canton, Robert Stewart stated supply, one hundred and eighty-seven.

Among those who during this period entered the field to strengthen the hands of the pioneer missionaries were Roswell Brooks; Dewey Whitney, Second Church, Springfield; Alexander Ewing, Irish Grove; Flavel Bascom, Tazewell; Lemuel Foster, Bloomington; Thomas Galt, Farmington; Nahum Gould, Union Grove; Nathaniel C. Clark, Big and Little Woods; Heman S. Colton, Elisha H. Hazard; Jeremiah Porter, Chicago;[1] John H. Prentiss; Jonathan G. Porter; Warren Nichols, Robert B. Dobbins, Bennington; Cyrus Riggs; L. G. Bell; Solomon S. Miles; George G. Sill; Samuel Wilson;

---

[1] In 1812, Chicago was the place of an abandoned garrison. As an Indian trading-post, it collected some sixty or seventy persons in 1823.—*Eighty Years' Progress*, i. 177.

Solomon Hovey; Reuben K. McKay; Isaac Keller, First Church, Peoria;[1] Ephraim P. Noel, and some few others connected with Presbyteries which made no reports to the Assembly. The entire membership of all the Presbyterian churches within the State was (1837) not far from two thousand five hundred, averaging about twenty-five to each church.

The first missionary labors in Missouri are due to the influence exerted by the Southwestern tours of Samuel J. Mills, and his associates, Schermerhorn and Smith. With the former of these, Salmon Giddings at this period (1815) had formed an intimate acquaintance. He was a tutor in Williams College, and had just been licensed to preach. In repeated conversations with Mills, he had been brought to the determination to follow his track into the valley of the Mississippi and make St. Louis a point in his evangelical labors. The Trustees of the Connecticut Missionary Society, learning his intentions, sent him a commission to labor in the "Western country." In December, 1815, he commenced his journey on horseback to visit it, preaching Sabbaths, and often weekdays, on his way. His experience on the route was but the anticipation of what he was to meet on reaching his destination. He slept in log cabins, shared the humble fare of their inmates, conversed with them as opportunity offered on religious subjects, and, like a man of good common sense as he was, made himself at home everywhere, taking care of his own horse. On April 6, 1816, he reached St. Louis.

The field upon which he had entered was by no means an inviting one. The population was largely French and Roman Catholic. There were but two or three professed Presbyterians in the place. Protestant ministers

---

[1] Then with eleven members. The Main Street Church numbered thirty-five.

were rarely seen and Protestant preachers rarely heard. An itinerant Methodist "perhaps once a month" officiated at the court-house. It was not till 1814 that Messrs. S. J. Mills and Daniel Smith, sent out by the Philadelphia Bible and Missionary Societies, had visited the place.[1] Their presence awakened much interest. The people were pleased, and urged Mr. Smith to remain among them. This he was unable to do; but the visit was fruitful in good results. It cheered the heart and strengthened the hands of one faithful and devoted layman whose name is forever identified with the early history of the Presbyterian Church in Missouri. This was Stephen Hempstead, a native of New London, Conn., and at this time sixty years of age. He had served in the war of the Revolution, and for more than a quarter of a century had been engaged, as his secular affairs permitted, in the service of the church of Christ. Four of his sons had removed to Missouri, and in 1811 he followed them to St. Louis. For seven months he was in the country without hearing a Protestant sermon, and for three years never saw a Presbyterian minister.

But he was not disheartened. Although almost alone, his light shone forth steadily. "I made it," he says, "my daily business to converse with the prominent and leading heads of families on the necessity there was of having stated and regular religious worship in the place." All conceded the desirableness of such a measure; but the difficulty was to procure a suitable minister. After the visit of Messrs. Smith and Mills, he wrote to one of the Boston ministers, asking him to send one. "I do believe," he writes, "there is no place more in need of missionary aid than the Territory of Missouri."

---

[1] Presbyterian Quarterly Review, July, 1861. Rev. T. Hill's Historical Discourse.

He estimated that there were a thousand Presbyterian families within its bounds, while there was not a single church or society of their order. If two men could be sent, one might open a school in St. Louis, and the other itinerate and be there occasionally. Such was his project; but he sought in vain to have it executed.

A year or two passed away, and in February, 1816, Gideon Blackburn visited St. Louis, preached several times, and awakened great interest among the people. Some of the Roman Catholics were drawn to hear him. Among them was a French lady who attended regularly and often wept freely. Her priest heard of it, and called her to account for it, asking her why she never cried when he preached. Her reply was, "If you will preach like Mr. Blackburn, I will cry all the time."

Blackburn's stay, however, was short. The people were still left as sheep without a shepherd. There were twelve or fifteen Baptist elders, eight Methodist circuit-preachers, and four or five Cumberland Presbyterian preachers, but none whom Mr. Hempstead, or those who sympathized with him, could look to for help. All that he could do was to distribute the Bibles and tracts which Messrs. Mills and Smith exerted themselves to forward to him for distribution. These he scattered abroad; and it was at this juncture, shortly after Mr. Blackburn's visit, that Mr. Giddings arrived.

By nature and by grace he was well fitted for the post he was called to occupy. He was a man of excellent common sense, great resolution and self-reliance; calm, earnest, and possessed of indomitable perseverance; and, although grave and somewhat stiff in his manners, exceedingly kind-hearted. His physical constitution was capable of great endurance, and his demeanor was such as became a minister of Christ. Such a man was not to be disheartened by any ordinary difficulty. He stood prepared to endure hardness as a good soldier of Jesus Christ.

At St. Louis,[1] although there were a few warm hearts to welcome him, he was not as yet acquainted with them, nor they with him. "He walked lonely from house to house, and finally succeeded in securing a lodging-place." While resting, he took up a small printed sheet, and found it to be a St. Louis newspaper. On opening it, the first article which met his eye was headed "Caution," and, as he read it, he found that it warned the people against himself. The paper gravely informed the people of the place that a society had been recently formed in New England for sending out missionaries to the Western country, but it declared that this was done with a political object in view, growing out of the famous Hartford Convention. Such was the grossness of prejudice which met and confronted him at the very outset of his work.

The first year and a half was spent by Mr. Giddings in itinerant labors. He sought out the scattered Presbyterians and endeavored to gather them in congregations. The first church he organized was in Bellevue settlement, Washington county, about eighty miles southwest from St. Louis, and consisted of thirty members. This was Aug. 2, 1816. A much deeper interest is connected with this church—the earliest organized in the Territory—than with many another located at some more important point. As early as 1807, four Presbyterian elders, all from the same church in North Carolina, located here. Nor did they hide the light which they bore with them to their new homes. Their practice was to meet each Sabbath and hold a prayer-

[1] St. Louis was occupied as a French trading-post in 1763, and the town was laid out in the following year. In 1822 the population was four thousand five hundred and ninety-eight.—*Eighty Years' Progress*, i. 181.

meeting, and read a sermon, generally one of President Davies; and thus they continued until the Methodists came, when they worshipped with them. The next church organized was, in the same autumn, at Bonhommie settlement, thirty miles west of St. Louis. It at first numbered only sixteen members. Hitherto he had labored alone. But on December 8 of the same year, Charles S. Robinson, a native of Granville, Miss., sent out by the New York Evangelical Missionary Society, reached the field. He located at St. Charles River.

At about the same time—at least within the space of a few weeks—the Rev. Timothy Flint, sent out by the Connecticut Missionary Society, crossed the Missouri. He found opened before him "a boundless field." Declining any pastoral charge, he labored as an itinerant. His tours extended from the Forks to settlements more than one hundred miles up the Missouri River. To him it appeared as if no missionary station in the United States could be more interesting. The soil and climate were inviting. Beyond example, the inhabitants were multiplying by constant arrivals from almost every section of the Union. An average of one hundred emigrants a day passed through the town of St. Charles; but the missionary sadly reported, "not one family in fifty carries a Bible." Within a short time he had distributed among them five hundred copies of the word of God. Multitudes were "indisposed and careless;" but "a prevailing desire was manifested, in a number of places, for the Bible and preaching."

The labors of Messrs. Flint and Giddings were widely extended. They collected congregations, organized churches, and labored generally as itinerants. Mr. Giddings, eminently fitted for the task, taught a school in St. Louis for a portion of the year, extending his missionary excursions during the other portions of it in Missouri and in Illinois, and likewise supplying, as he was able, the feeble congregation of St. Louis, organized as a church Nov. 23, 1817. It was constituted of only nine members, and it was eight years before the little band were able to complete a house of worship. At that time it was considered "the finest and best-built church in the West;" and in the following year Mr. Giddings was installed as pastor,—a relation which he sustained till his death in 1828.

But while awaiting the organization of the church, and preaching often to a very small auditory,—sometimes only four or five hearers,—he extended his influence over the city. He was diligent in the circulation of the Scriptures, especially of French Bibles and Testaments. In many settlements he was gratified to observe a decided reformation. New churches were continually springing up in the wilderness. Mr. Flint, stationed at St. Charles on the Missouri, labored extensively in the adjoining towns. Green's Bottom, ten miles above St. Charles, was added to his missionary stations. But his tours were numerous and distant. He ascended the Mississippi and the Missouri, frequently crossing the rivers and preaching everywhere as opportunity was afforded. Many of his tours were performed on foot. He travelled eighty miles a week. In an excursion of seven weeks, he crossed the Missouri sixteen times, and on some occasions the attempt was hazardous. But no difficulty of this kind was allowed to withstand his persevering energy.

He was deeply affected by the moral wastes around him. The situation of the people where he travelled, he represents as being generally deplorable. "Many of them live and die without any thought of eternity. So engaged are they in making new settlements in the woods that they seem to regard nothing besides." There were, however, some marked exceptions. Repeatedly he met those to whom he had before preached or distributed Bibles, and listened with a joyous heart to their cordial expressions of gratitude. "I could give," he observes, "a thousand details of the evident good resulting from this blessed charity."

Other laborers now came to join and encourage the feeble band. Rev. Thomas Donnell was installed pastor of the church at Bellevue, April 25, 1818. Messrs. Giddings and Flint, and probably Robinson, were present. Mr. Giddings preached the sermon,—"the power of God unto salvation." It was printed at St. Louis, and was the first sermon ever printed west of the Mississippi.

In 1817 the General Assembly sent William McFarland to St. Louis for six months, or, in case that place was found to be supplied, he was to visit the destitute places in Missouri Territory. In 1819 the Connecticut Society commissioned John Matthews and the Assembly Jeremiah Chamberlain, each for six months, in the Territory of Missouri. The last was followed in the succeeding year by Francis McFarland, who was commissioned also for six months, "pursuing the course of the Missouri till he reach Charleston," and spending some time "in Franklin and its vicinity."

Mr. Matthews was of Scotch-Irish descent, a native of Beaver county, Pa., a graduate of Jefferson College, and a theological pupil of Dr. McMillan. For seven years he had been pastor of Gravel Run and Waterford Churches in Erie Presbytery, when, in 1817, he resigned his charge to become an itinerating missionary. He started on his journey West, going down the Ohio in a flatboat as far as Louisville, then on horseback across Indiana as far as Vincennes, then through the Territory of Illinois to St. Louis, where he met Mr. Giddings. Ascending the Missouri to the neighborhood of St. Charles, he took charge of the church of Louisiana, in Pike county, where he continued preaching and itinerating till 1825, when he removed to Apple Creek Church, Cape Girardeau county, two years subsequently leaving it for Kaskaskia, Ill.

The results of missionary labor now (January, 1819) began to be plainly visible. "People in the country," writes Mr. Giddings, "are surprised at the alteration in St. Louis within two years; and alterations for the better are visible in almost every place where missionary labors have been bestowed."

A church was organized by the name of Union at Richwood's settlement, in April, 1819; but it was feeble, seldom visited by a Presbyterian minister, and probably long since has become extinct. The Buffalo Church was organized a year or two earlier, by John Matthews; Shoal Creek Church, in Bond county, was organized, with thirty-three members, by Mr. Giddings, March 10, 1819; St. Charles Church, of nine members, by Giddings and Matthews, Aug. 19, 1818; Dardenne Church, of seven members, by Robinson, Sept. 19, 1819; and these, with the churches of Bellevue, Bonhommie, St. Louis, and perhaps one or two others, constituted all the Presbyterian churches in Missouri previous to 1820. The ministers up to this time were Giddings, Robinson, Flint, Matthews, Donnell, and David Tenny. The three first were from New England, Matthews was from Pennsylvania, and Donnell from North Carolina. Robinson was a faithful and devoted man, possessed of true missionary zeal. Flint was a scholar of no mean pretensions, distinguished subsequently as a writer, the master of an elegant and perspicuous style, and, after "ten years in the Mississippi Valley," recounted what he had seen in descriptions of the West and its scenery, which charmed and elicited the praise of English reviewers Matthews was a workman that needed not to be ashamed, in labors most abundant, and, with all his itinerancy, a thorough student of theology, leaving behind him a written system. Donnell was respectable as a preacher and eminent as a Christian; and a clerical brother who knew him well declared that "some of the most powerful appeals to sinful man to be reconciled to God which he ever heard, were from Father Donnell."

The labors of most of these men were of a most arduous kind. For several years after Mr. Giddings's arrival, and till seven churches had been formed, there was but a single settled pastor within the Territory. The burden devolved upon Messrs. Giddings, Matthews, and Flint was almost crushing. But the calm, resolute energy and self-possession of the first, and the untiring energy of the others, did not give way. "These destitute churches," wrote Mr. Giddings, "are calling on me for preaching, and consider themselves as under my pastoral care. I can feel for them and pray for them; and that, for some of them, is the most that I can do." Well it might be. The distance of some of the churches from one another was not less than one hundred and forty miles.

The morals of the people of the Territory were, as a general thing, far from commendable. Little respect was paid to the Sabbath. Stores were open on that as on other days, and the sacred hours were given up to mirth and pleasure. Flint says of St. Charles, "There was not a professor of our form of religion in St. Charles when I went there. The first Sabbath that I preached, before the morning service began, directly opposite the house where the service was to take place, there was a horse-race. The horses received the signal to start just as I rode to the door." Education was grossly neglected. Giddings says, "In most of the principal settlements Methodist or Baptist churches had been formed, some of which were in a flourishing condition: yet the state of moral feeling and the tone of piety was low throughout the country. Little attention has been paid to education, and not more than one in five can read."

In 1818 the Presbytery of Missouri was erected and united with the Synod of Tennessee. Its opening sermon was preached by John Matthews. For several years it numbered only from six to eight members. In 1823 some of the churches enjoyed a season of revival. A letter from Rev. J. M. Peck stated that in the county of Boon's Lick an extensive revival had been in progress for more than a year. Upwards of five hundred had been added to the churches.

In 1822 the attention of the Assembly's Board of Missions began especially to be drawn toward this region. In that year Thomas Alexander was commissioned to labor for six months within the bounds of the State. In 1824, John S. Ball, Jesse Townsend, and William Dickson were sent out to this field, and John Matthews, already a veteran in pioneer labor, was to devote three months to the upper settlements within the Forks of the Mississippi and Missouri. He was succeeded in the following year by William Lacy, and, in conjunction with Mr. Ball, whose commission was renewed, was to visit the most inviting missionary fields and pay special attention to the infant churches. William Dickson, who was also reappointed by the Board, was to labor at Boon Lick settlement and Salt River.

In 1825 Ralls county contained two thousand four hundred and fifty-four inhabitants, without a clergyman except an uneducated Baptist who rarely attempted to preach. Pike county, with three thousand four hundred and thirty inhabitants, had a small Presbyterian church of twenty-seven members, but nc pastor. Lincoln county, with two thousand two hundred and forty-one inhabitants, had no Presbyterian church,—although it was thought two feeble ones might soon be organized. St. Charles county, with a population of three thousand nine hundred and sixty-four, had two churches, and several more might soon be gathered "if there were laborers,"—Mr. Robinson being the only clergyman of any denomination in the county. North of the Missouri, Montgomery county, with a population of two thousand three hundred and sixty-five, had no church; but congregations might easily be gathered. In Callaway county, numbering two thousand four hundred and fifty-five, the people were anxious for the formation of a church. Boone county, with a population of five thousand one hundred and fifty-seven, offered an inviting field, hitherto neglected, for missionaries. Howard county, population seven thousand four hundred and eighty-five, had a single church, but offered an extensive field for usefulness. Chariton county, with seventeen hundred and forty-seven inhabitants, was willing, and able in part, to support a pastor. Ray, Clay, Sillard, and Saline counties, with an aggregate population of six thousand two hundred and ninety-two, gave little promise of speedily forming churches. In Cooper county (four thousand three hundred and seventy-nine) two congregations might soon be gathered. In Cob, Gasconade, and Franklin (aggregate four thousand and one) the field was uninviting, and no prospect of churches being formed. In St. Louis county (eight thousand six hundred and fifty-two) one church had been organized, and several others might be gathered. In Jefferson (nineteen hundred and thirty-four) was one small church without a pastor; in St. Genevieve (two thousand and twenty-five) none. In Perry (two thousand three hundred and forty) one might soon be formed. In Washington (four thousand three hundred and three) was one church, under Thomas Donnell; and another, if a suitable man could be found, might be formed at Potosi. In St. François (sixteen hundred and seventy-one), Madison (sixteen hundred and forty-seven), Scott (nine hundred and ninety), New Madrid (fourteen hundred and forty-two), Wayne (two thousand five hundred and twenty-seven), and Cape Girardeau (five thousand seven hundred and twenty-six) was no church except in the last-named county. The population of the State amounted to eighty thousand six hundred and seventy-seven.[1]

At this time (1825) the Presbytery of Missouri consisted of only six ministers.[2] Thomas Donnell was still laboring at Bellevue, Salmon Giddings at St. Louis, Charles S. Robinson at St. Charles; while William S. Lacy, Jesse Townsend, and John Matthews, commissioned by the Assembly's Board and members of the Presbytery, were without pastoral charge. John S. Ball was connected with the Presbytery as a licentiate.

Meanwhile, several new churches had been formed. In January, 1821, Rev. E. Hollister, from the United Domestic Missionary Society of New York, and the Rev. William McFarland, from the General Assembly's Board, came to Missouri and proceeded into what was then called Boon's Lick county. While there they formed a church of twenty-three members at Old Franklin, opposite Boonville, the germ of the church at the latter place. They also organized the Chariton Church, of nine members, May 9, 1821. On the 21st of the same month Mr. Giddings organized the Apple Creek Church, of forty-one members.

The churches under the care of the Presbytery (1825) numbered eighteen; but of these about one-half were in Illinois. The churches at Concord, St. Louis, and St. Charles numbered each from thirty to forty members. The one at Bonhommie had but fourteen, and the one at Buffalo but twenty-seven.

---

[1] Report of United Domestic Missionary Society for 1825, p. 74.

[2] Mr. Robinson writes at this date that he "could not answer one-half of the calls for him if he was to preach every day for six months."

In 1830 the Presbytery of Missouri had but eight members. The churches numbered sixteen,[1] with a membership of about four hundred. The geographical position rather than size of the Presbytery led to its division; and, upon an increase of members, it was divided in 1831 to form the three Presbyteries of Missouri, St. Charles, and St. Joseph.

In 1837 the Presbytery of Missouri had seven ministers and ten churches; but of the ministers four were stated supplies and three were without charge. The Presbytery of St. Charles had seventeen ministers and eighteen churches; but five of its members, Messrs. Gallaher, Ely, Hays, Agnew, and Nassau, were connected with Marion College, four of the others were stated supplies, and several were without charge. There was not a settled pastor in the two bodies. The Presbytery of St. Louis had reported in 1833 five members,—Thomas Donnell, at Concord, John F. Cowan, at Apple Creek, William S. Potts, at St. Louis, Joseph M. Ladd, at Farmington, and E. F. Hatfield, stated supply of the Second Church at St. Louis. The first three were the only pastors within the State. Not far from forty churches had been gathered, and, including those who were engaged in the work of instruction, the ministers numbered about thirty.

In 1834 the Rev. Dr. Ely, of Philadelphia, conceived the plan of establishing a colony in Missouri, then a young and rapidly-growing State, and in connection with this colony to erect and found a college and theological seminary. In this enterprise he embarked with great zeal, investing in it his large fortune. The institution rose upon a foundation laid for it by David Nelson. Impressed with the importance of increasing the means of education in the far West, Dr. Nelson, relin-

---

[1] Those in Illinois were now in another connection.

quishing his pastoral charge at Danville, Ky., removed in 1830 to Marion county, Mo., and located himself about eighteen miles from the Mississippi and twelve miles from Palmyra. There he commenced the school which subsequently grew into Marion College, of which he became the first President. Upon the same ground upon which his school-house was built, other buildings, for dormitories, recitation-rooms, and boarding-houses, were from time to time erected. Pupils were called from a distance, teachers were procured, and in 1832 a charter was granted by the State. Dr. Nelson visited New York, New England, and other parts of the country, with a view to secure the requisite means to carry forward the enterprise. Dr. Ely, in common with many others, became its patron. It was to be conducted on the manual-labor system, then remarkably popular in some parts of the land, and quite a large number of students was drawn together. But an unwarrantable expenditure, in connection with extravagant, wild, and speculative notions, hastened the defeat of the whole project. In 1835, Dr. Nelson relinquished his post, and soon after removed to another State.

His successor in the Presidency was Dr. William S. Potts, pastor of the First Presbyterian Church of St. Louis, where he had succeeded the lamented Giddings. The four years during which he retained the post of President were to him years of intense and exhausting labor. During one season he travelled from Missouri to Maine in the prosecution of his efforts to collect funds in aid of the college.

But the times were unfavorable. The whole country was financially prostrate. The success of Dr. Potts did not equal his expectations; and in 1838 he felt it his duty to listen to the proposals of some of the members of his former charge to attempt the establishment of a new church in St. Louis. Resigning the Presidency in 1839, he was succeeded by Hiram P. Goodrich, a native of Massachusetts, who for several years had been a professor in Union Theological Seminary, Va., and subsequently for a single year had been Professor of Ancient Languages in Marion College. For four years more the institution continued in operation under President Goodrich; but by this time it had lost the confidence and prestige necessary to its success. The fortune of Dr. Ely, and large sums from other sources, had been absorbed in the enterprise, which was finally abandoned.

Although Detroit was visited as early as 1610 and a settlement effected and a fort erected in 1701, it was not till 1805 that a Territorial government was established in Michigan. Among its earliest settlers were emigrants sent out (1749) from France at the expense of the Government.[1] In 1801, when Mr. Badger, on his visit to the Indians, reached Detroit, he reported that "there was not one Christian to be found in all this region, except a black man who appeared pious." In 1804 it was spoken of as "a most abandoned place." At this time Dr. Bangs visited it as a Methodist missionary,[2] and the Congregational minister told him that he had preached in Detroit until none but a few children would come to hear him. "If you can succeed," he added,—"which I very much doubt,—I shall rejoice." He did not succeed, but "shook off the dust of his feet as a testimony against them, and took his departure." Barely a month elapsed after this significant expression of disappointed effort before the place was almost entirely destroyed by fire, a single house only remaining uninjured.

Till after the reorganization of the Territorial govern-

---

[1] Sketches of the City of Detroit, p. 3.

[2] Bangs's History of Methodism.

ment in the fall of 1813 and the close of the war, no effort was made to send missionaries into this region. The principal portion, indeed, of the white population consisted of soldiers resident at the military station.[1] For successive years—after 1817—the missionaries of the Assembly—one or more—were commissioned to labor for a portion of their time in connection with these stations. The first to enter this field was the Rev. John Monteith, whose commission was renewed in substantially the same form for several years.

Mr. Monteith, sent out by the Board of Missions, reached Detroit June 27, 1816. He met from the people so cordial a reception that it appeared to him unnecessary any longer to bear the character of a missionary. He commenced his labors as a stated minister, and found himself in the midst of "a wide field of usefulness." "The profaneness of the soldiers," he says, "exceeds any thing I ever imagined. There is no Sabbath in this country." Faithful in the discharge of his duty both in public and private, he was treated by all classes with the greatest respect, and not a word was uttered in opposition.

In this place he found himself two hundred miles distant from any Presbyterian minister, and almost crushed under the task imposed upon him. Amid prevailing ignorance and wickedness, there was scarcely an individual from whom he could derive assistance. The only Christian zeal perceptible was among the Methodists. The army was without a chaplain, and his work was greater than he felt able to perform. Yet one month of each year, with the consent of his people, was devoted to missionary excursions. He accordingly visited Raisin, the Rapids of the Miami, Sandusky,

[1] Although the oldest of the Western cities, Detroit had risen in one hundred and thirty-seven years only to a population, in 1820, of fourteen hundred and forty-two.—*Eighty Years' Progress*, i. 177.

Cleveland, and other places, and preached frequently. At Fort Meigs and Raisin he felt confident that congregations might be gathered.[1]

Doubtless in consequence of his report, the Assembly in 1818 directed that a missionary should be sent for six months to the settlements on the river Raisin; and this direction was repeated in the two following years.

In 1820 it was said of Mackinaw that "the Christian Sabbath had not got so far." It was, however, recognized in that year for the first time by the people, on occasion of the visit of the Rev. Dr. Jedediah Morse, who gathered the people of the place to listen to the preaching of the gospel. A year later, the Rev. Dr. Yates, of Union College, visited this place, and once again there was an external recognition of the claims of the Sabbath. In 1822 the Rev. Mr. Ferry came to Mackinaw as a missionary of the United Foreign Missionary Society; and, although he could not find in the place a single Christian brother with whom he could say, "Our Father," he did not despond. Cheerfully and patiently he toiled on; and in ten years the character of the place was reported to have become entirely changed.

In 1820, Mr. Monteith (afterward settled at Blissfield, Mich.) reported the results of his visits to the military stations in the Territory. The substance of it was discouraging, and even appalling.

"The general aspect of manners among the troops" gave "an idea of infernal spirits, rather than of human beings." Meanwhile, he had urgent calls from the surrounding territory to preach the gospel. In the same year Rev. Moses Hunter performed a mission of six months at Fort Meigs, on the river Raisin, and in other

---

[1] Christian Herald, iii. 320.

destitute settlements in that region. The places where he itinerated were important and growing. So acceptable were his labors that he was invited by the people to return and reside among them. There was but one Presbyterian minister in the region,—at River Raisin. At Fort Meigs a church had been organized, originally with but twelve members.

Mr. Monteith continued his labors in this region during the following year. At Monroe and Meigs, Presbyterian churches were now organized and were reported as in a flourishing condition. In the course of the few succeeding years, churches were gathered at Detroit, Ypsilanti, Monroe, Dexter, Farmington, Bloomfield, Pontiac, Mackinaw, Statesburg, Plymouth, Tecumseh, Dixborough, and Ann Arbor. The church of Pontiac was under the care of the Presbytery of Geneva for some years after 1824. The name of Ypsilanti indicates its date. It was formed in 1823, at the period when sympathy for Greece in her struggle for independence pervaded the land and was felt even in the Western forests.

In December, 1824, Isaiah W. Ruggles was sent to Michigan by the United Domestic Missionary Society, and commenced his labors at Pontiac, limiting his excursions mainly to Oakland county, yet having a large circuit in which he had no fellow-laborer.[1] In August, 1824, the church of Pontiac numbered fifty-five. During the month Mr. Ruggles organized a second church, in the southern part of the county, consisting of eight members, from which an application was forwarded for a minister. Mr. Ruggles soon after commenced his pastorate at Monroe. Noah M. Wells, after laboring in the summer of 1824 at Detroit, was settled there as pastor, and Stephen Frontis, As-

---

[1] Report of United Domestic Missionary Society for 1826.

sembly's missionary, was laboring at the same period with good success at the river Raisin. William Page was settled at Ann Arbor, Oct. 24, 1826; Ira Dunning at Farmington on the 10th of the same month. Eric Prince commenced his labors in Monroe and Oakland county in 1827; Alanson Darwin entered this field in September, and Isaac McIlvaine in October, of the same year.

The church at Mackinaw was organized and served by Rev. William M. Ferry, sent out in the latter part of 1823, by the United Foreign Missionary Society, as superintendent of the Indian mission at this important station. The same society had missionaries transferred to its charge from the Northern Missionary Society, laboring at Fort Gratiot, on the St. Clair, about a mile below the outlet of Lake Huron.

The Western Missionary Society of the Synod of Pittsburg was also engaged in this field. In 1823 it established a mission at the Falls of St. Mary. There were several French and English families already located here, and it was largely resorted to for fishing-purposes by the Indian tribes. As a military and trading post its position was regarded as of great importance, and all the fur-trade of the Northwest was compelled to pass through it. Here also was a United States military station, and here also Mr. Schoolcraft, the Indian agent, resided. The labors of the missionary, Rev. Robert M. Laird, were followed by signal success, especially among the soldiers of the garrison. Early in 1824, he writes that twenty-two persons had attended his inquiry-meetings. He was constantly engaged in preaching, distributing Bibles and other books, and in religious visitation. A timely donation of a box of books for his Sunday-school was forwarded to him by Rev. Thaddeus Osgood.

The Assembly's appointments for Michigan were, in

1822, Joshua L. Moore for six months at Detroit, or, in case this field was occupied, in destitute portions of the Territory; and in 1823 two missionaries were appointed, one of whom, Eldad W. Goodman, was to labor for six months, mainly in the vicinity of Monroe and Fort Meigs. In the following year Daniel Waterbury and Judah Ely were sent out by the Board to labor within the bounds of the State, and in 1825 Alvan Coe[1] was directed to spend three months at Sault de St. Marie, or Green Bay, while Stephen Frontis was to visit the infant churches of Fort Meigs, Monroe, Mount Clemens, and Pontiac, and, if Detroit was still unoccupied, pay particular attention to that place.

The Presbytery of Detroit was erected by the Assembly in 1827. It consisted of five ministers,—Noah M. Wells, Erie Prince, Isaac W. Ruggles, William M. Ferry, and William Page,—and of the five churches of Detroit, Farmington, Monroe, Pontiac, and Mackinaw Mr. Wells, the patriarch of the Presbytery, was at Detroit, Ruggles at Pontiac, Ferry at Mackinaw, Prince at Farmington, and Page at Monroe. The Presbytery stood connected with the Western Reserve Synod. In the course of the five succeeding years, Ira M. Weed, P. W. Warrener, C. G. Clark, G. Harnell, Luther Humphrey, Cutting Marsh, and others, entered the field. Churches were organized at Dexter, Bloomfield, Beardlie's Prairie, Statesburg, Plymouth, Tecumseh, Dixborough, and Ann Arbor: so that in 1832 the Presbytery could report thirteen ministers and fourteen churches.[2]

---

[1] From Granville, Mass.

[2] In 1831 the church at Saline, Mich., was established. It consisted of twelve members regularly organized at Newark, Wayne county, N.Y. In October they were visited by the Assembly's missionary, R. Sears, who remained with them four weeks and gathered in persons, previously members of Presbyterian churches, sufficient

In the following year the two new Presbyteries of St. Joseph's and of Monroe were formed out of that of Detroit,—the first embracing four and the last seven members. John P. Cleaveland succeeded Mr. Wells as pastor at Detroit, and was the leading member of the Presbytery which retained the old name. Three years later, the three Presbyteries numbered together thirty-two ministers and fifty-nine churches,—so rapidly had the new State been occupied by the tide of immigration.

CHAPTER XXXIX.

STATE AND PROGRESS OF THE CHURCH, 1830-1837.

The growth of the Presbyterian Church in this country has never been more rapid than during the first portion of the period which now comes under review. In the preceding five years there had been an advance till then unprecedented; but even this was exceeded by the results set forth in the Assembly's reports for some years subsequent to 1829.

At the close of that year there were in connection with the Assembly nineteen Synods, ninety-eight Presbyteries, fourteen hundred and ninety-one ministers, and two thousand one hundred and fifty-eight churches, with a membership of one hundred and seventy-three thousand three hundred and twenty-nine. In 1831 the additions to the churches on examination were fifteen

to increase the number of the new organization to about thirty. While there, Mr. Sears preached to a congregation of from forty to sixty in a wood-house at the rear of a tavern. Many of the people had their own houses yet to build; and they had not erected even a school-house.—*Miss. Reporter*, Nov. 1831.

thousand three hundred and fifty-seven; in 1832, thirty-four thousand one hundred and sixty; in 1833, twenty-three thousand five hundred and forty-six; in 1834, twenty thousand two hundred and ninety-six; in 1836[1] the number had fallen to eleven thousand five hundred and twelve; and in 1837 it was only eleven thousand five hundred and eighty. In the latter year the aggregate strength of the Church was twenty-three Synods, one hundred and thirty-five Presbyteries, two thousand one hundred and forty ministers, and two thousand eight hundred and sixty-five churches, with a membership of two hundred and twenty thousand five hundred and fifty-seven. The rapid increase during the earlier portion of the period was largely offset by an actual decrease of membership from 1834 to 1837.

The new Presbyteries erected previous to 1834 were Delaware, St. Louis, St. Charles, Tabor, Clinton (1831), Philadelphia Second, Philadelphia Third, Long Island Second, Montrose (1832), Schuyler, Palestine, Philadelphia Fourth (Synod's Second), Wilmington, Good Hope, Flint River, St. Joseph, and Monroe (1833). The membership of the churches had risen to two hundred and thirty-three thousand five hundred and eighty, or over thirteen thousand more than it was four years later, in 1837. In the reaction of some of the causes which had accelerated the growth of the Church, we may find an explanation in part of this unprecedented decline. To these and to other influences, which had already begun to operate, and which produced wide-spread agitation and excited grave apprehension, our attention must now be directed.

It was in the midst of the remarkable and unprecedented advance of the Church, not only in numbers but in enterprise, that the signs of approaching danger

---

[1] No report was published in 1835.

manifested themselves. The Assembly, unequal to the task devolved upon it, had itself given ready encouragement to local effort. It recommended to its Presbyteries and churches the various benevolent societies which aimed to supplement its own short-comings. In 1828, ministers and churches were urged to effort in seeking out fit young men as candidates for the ministry, and were directed to recommend them "to the Presbytery within whose bounds they are found, *or* to some Education Society." In the following year the Assembly declared they would "affectionately solicit the co-operation of its churches with its own Board of Missions." Yet, in view of the fact that many had united their efforts with the Home Missionary Society and the American Board, it was resolved as the sense of the Assembly "that the churches should be left entirely to their own unbiassed and deliberate choice of the particular channel" of their charities. In the following year similar language was employed with reference to the cause of education.

The resolution of 1829 on the subject of co-operation with the Home Missionary Society was warmly discussed, and some strenuous opposition to its passage was made by those who wished the Church in its organic capacity as an ecclesiastical body to make more earnest and effective effort in behalf of the missions of its own Board; but it was at length passed by an overwhelming majority. Up to this period a remarkable degree of harmony had characterized the meetings of the Assembly. The reports from the churches from 1826 to 1830 had been the subject of mutual congratulation and devout thanksgiving. "Never," says the editor of the "Christian Advocate," Dr. Green (June, 1830), "have we seen a General Assembly—and we have seen the most that have met—in which there was apparently so much brotherly love, so much mutual concession, and so little in the speeches that were made to give offence to opponents in argument."

But before the meeting of the next Assembly ominous clouds had begun to appear in the distant horizon. The conflict of theologies had begun in New England.[1] Indeed, for some years there had been a growing mutual distrust among the ministers and churches. The views and positions of Dr. Nathaniel W. Taylor, of New Haven, were attacked by Dr. Woods, of Andover, and by Dr. Tyler; while the "Christian Advocate" of Philadelphia, under the charge of Dr. Green, with more, if possible, than their own zeal, joined in the repudiation of the New Haven theology. It declared that the atonement, as a doctrine long held by the Protestant Church, was virtually and substantially rejected by Dr. Taylor.

Nor was this all. The Assembly's Board of Missions—reorganized in 1828 with a view to the more effective prosecution of its work—and its Board of Education were now in the field, pressing their peculiar claims with unprecedented urgency. In 1830 the "Missionary

---

[1] Something of the strength of theological prejudice which prevailed at this time (1833) in New England may be inferred from the statement given by Rev. (Dr.) Leverett Griggs, of North Haven, in his "Review of Twenty-Five Years' Ministry (1858)."

In October, 1833, he was ordained pastor of North Haven Church. "The excitement produced by what was called the 'New Haven Controversy' was at its height. It was manifested on almost all occasions when ecclesiastical bodies assembled. It was seldom that a young man was licensed or ordained without passing through a fiery ordeal." Having spent the last two years of his theological course at Andover, Mr. Griggs, although expecting a strict and careful examination, did not dream of the least difficulty about his ordination. To his surprise, he found that by a not small part of the Council he was regarded as a rank heretic. The examination continued from one o'clock P.M. till midnight; and the motion to ordain passed by the vote of a bare majority.

Reporter and Education Register" was published in their interest, and, by the vigorous efforts of the Secretary of the Board of Missions, not only was a large subscription-list secured for it, but numerous auxiliaries to the Board itself were formed. These auxiliaries consisted of Sessions, Churches, and Presbyteries, and were formed in such numbers in the course of 1830 that more than two hundred and forty were reported in a single month. The funds of the Board were correspondingly increased. In 1829, one hundred and one missionaries had been employed within the bounds of the Church, and the funds had amounted to seven thousand six hundred and sixty-five dollars. In the following year one hundred and ninety-eight were employed, more than three hundred churches were aided, and the receipts had risen to fourteen thousand four hundred and forty dollars. In 1831 the increase upon this, both in funds and missionaries employed, was between thirty and forty per cent.

These were cheering facts to those who favored action distinctively ecclesiastical. The number of these, from growing apprehensions or dissatisfaction with the Home Missionary Society, rapidly increased. They believed, and felt themselves justified by facts in believing, that the liberality of the Church could flow out in channels other than those constructed by voluntary societies.[1]

---

[1] In 1828, when the overture for the reorganization of the Board was before the Assembly, action upon it had been temporarily arrested by notice of a communication from the Executive Committee of the Home Missionary Society, who had appointed a committee to state their views upon the general subject to the Assembly. The committee were courteously heard, but the friends of the Board would not abandon it; and the result was that the whole subject was indefinitely postponed, a committee of conference having reported in favor of the full and independent authority of the Board as already constituted, and their report having been adopted by the Assembly.

There was now less disposition than before to yield up the mission-field almost exclusively to an irresponsible voluntary society, over which the Assembly had no control.

Thus the Assembly's Board and the Home Missionary Society were left to occupy the same field. An effort was made in 1830 to effect arrangements by which the missionary operations of both at the West should be conducted through a common Board of Agency. This measure was favored by a committee of which Dr. Green was chairman; but it was rejected by the Assembly. In 1831 the subject was again introduced by a memorial from the Presbytery of Madison. The grave question was now virtually raised, whether by the method of constituting the Board it should continue its operations. It was at first proposed "to reappoint the present Board." This was negatived. The committee appointed by the moderator, Dr. Beman, to nominate members of the Board, was regarded as hostile to its existence, and the persons nominated by them were considered equally hostile. A motion was made to lay the committee's report on the table; but the matter was finally compromised by a resolution, in which the General Assembly, "in view of existing evils resulting from the separate action" of the Board and the Society, recommended the Western Synods with their Presbyteries to correspond with each other and agree upon some plan of conducting missions, to be reported to the next Assembly. It was also understood that they were to "be left to their freedom to form any organization" which they might deem best to promote the cause of missions.

But at the West even more, if possible, than at the East, there was a divided sentiment in respect to the Home Missionary Society. Some, and a large number throughout the country, regarded it as sufficiently Presbyterian. Its origin—a transformation of the United Domestic Missionary Society—was Presbyterian. Its most efficient aid was derived from Presbyterian churches. Till 1833 more than half its funds came from New York State alone. Its officers were Presbyterians. Its Board of Directors in New York was exclusively Presbyterian. It was no more than natural, therefore, that it should be warmly cherished by those who saw the good which it was effecting, and who, while more anxious for the evangelization of the country than for any mere denominational success, might yet regard it as the especial ally of the Presbyterian Church.

But in the minds of others its very prosperity excited apprehension. The first year (1826–27) its receipts were but little more than eighteen thousand dollars. In 1833 it expended more than eighty thousand dollars. Its one hundred and sixty-nine missionaries and agents in 1827 had multiplied to six hundred and seventy-six in 1834. It had accomplished a great work. It had brought into co-operation with itself the New England and the Western Societies. It had scattered its missionaries throughout the bounds of the Presbyterian Church, from the Atlantic States to the field beyond the Missouri, from New York to New Orleans. From the necessity of the case, a large number of its missionaries were from New England. Some of them, educated under another system and imbibing their peculiar views from teachers whose theological soundness was in some cases suspected, would not have been the best men to secure confidence in the fields they were called to occupy.

The result was that, in the midst of the general prosperity, two parties were formed in the Presbyterian Church. It was comparatively easy to excite alarm among those who were already jealous of New England influence, and who had gathered their ideas of New England theology from the reports—diligently spread abroad—of the views presented in the "Quarterly Spectator," which just at this period became the organ of the New Haven Congregationalists. On the other hand, those whose thoughts were more especially directed to the great missionary field of the Church, and who had more regard to results than to the means by which they were attained, were drawn to the society the more strongly in consequence of what they considered the groundless jealousy and hostility of others. A division of sentiment was thus produced which was continually becoming more marked and irreconcilable. In 1831 it had in some quarters become largely developed. Before the meeting of the Assembly in that year, the Presbytery of Philadelphia declared it as their deliberate opinion that "it is the duty of the Presbyterian Church in these United States to conduct Christian missions, both foreign and domestic, in her distinctive character." Similar resolutions were passed by quite a number of the Western Presbyteries. Some of them unhesitatingly declared the "transaction of the missionary business appertaining to the Church in her distinctive character too sacred to be safely committed to any irresponsible and self-created body."[1]

In the Assembly it became a grave question whether the Board of Missions of 1830 should be reappointed. It was no less to the friends of the American Home Missionary Society than whether the spirit of jealousy, if not hostility, toward it, should be sanctioned or allowed to triumph. It had been proposed that a committee should be appointed to nominate the members of the Board for the ensuing year. On the motion to postpone this with a view to taking up a resolution re-

[1] Presbytery of Louisville; and others in almost the same words

appointing the old Board, warm discussion ensued, and the yeas and nays were called for. The vote stood—in favor of the motion eighty-seven, against it one hundred and nine. Yet a resolution was subsequently passed reappointing the old Board. Several members of it—whose names indicate their sympathies[1]—immediately resigned. Evidently they were unwilling to be the instruments of demanding for the Board the exclusive patronage of the churches, or acting in its behalf in the collisions with the Home Missionary Society which must almost necessarily ensue.

While such was the divided sentiment of leading members of the Church, the Western Convention was held. A large number of the Presbyteries were represented. The subject was fully and warmly discussed for several days. It was then found that the views of the Presbyteries were so discordant that no common plan could be adopted.[2] The project of a Western Board under the care of the Assembly was rejected, by a vote of forty-one to twenty-eight. Of the fifteen Presbyteries represented, one was in favor of the American Home Missionary Society. One favored both this and the Assembly's Board. Two preferred an independent Western Society. One was in favor of ecclesiastical supervision; and seven favored the Assembly's Board. No change, therefore, was recommended by the convention, and the two agencies were left each to pursue its independent course. It was only natural that the friends of the Board should extend a cold welcome, in a field which they claimed as their own, to a society which came into rivalry with it.

---

[1] Drs. McAuley, McDowell, and Skinner, and Messrs. Patterson, Barnes, James Moore, and G. W. Blight.

[2] The failure of the convention to harmonize was charged to the influence of the Synod of Pittsburg, whose presence had not been expected.

An overture was presented to the Assembly of 1831 on the subject of Foreign Missions, from Dr. John H. Rice. This venerable man was now approaching the close of his laborious and useful career. He had been from the first the steady and consistent friend of what in 1828 he termed "the union which happily subsists between our Church and the orthodox of New England." He had said, "Should the Presbyterian Church withdraw from others in this cause [united exertion for missions], we venture to predict her future history;" and that future he drew in the darkest colors. He declared himself (1829) "much grieved at the controversy about the American Education Society." The brethren on both sides he regarded as sincere; nor did he "think that the thing originated in sectarian jealousy." Yet, with these views, he felt that something should be done to enlist the sympathies of the Presbyterian Church more largely in the cause of missions. The theological discussions of the day were repugnant to him. "The evangelical men," he said, "are disputing, some for *old* orthodoxy and some for *new* metaphysics." He grieved over "the spirit of controversy" which prevailed, and preferred the exercise of Christian love and prudence to disputation. Yet he did not feel altogether satisfied with the New Haven theology. "I do not yet know," he wrote (1829) to Dr. Woods, "what our brother Taylor is driving at. I find it hard to understand him. Is the fault in me, or in him?"

Yet, with unabated attachment to members of both parties, and with a charity for others that knew no diminution, he perceived that something should be done to arouse the Presbyterian Church to a more active missionary spirit. He saw, or thought he saw, the kindling of a sectarian zeal. He felt that there was "a storm raging against Presbyterians." That Congregationalists and Presbyterians were "further apart than they were some years" previous, he considered "manifest." He thought he saw on his visit to Boston "a growth in the strength of New England feeling." Presbyterian feeling also was "considerably roused up." Yet "these denominations," he says, "have in every particular the same enemies, who are everlastingly attacking them."

In these circumstances, he declared himself in favor of some plan for promoting in the Presbyterian Church "the true spirit of missions," and not "the *Presbyterian* spirit," which in his view had been "so awakened up" that he began "to apprehend that no power of man will ever bring the whole body to unite under what is *thought* to be a Congregational Board." "I will never do any thing," he said, "to injure the wisest and best missionary society in the world,—the American Board. But can no ingenuity devise a scheme of a Presbyterian Branch,—co-ordinate,—sufficiently connected with the Assembly to satisfy scrupulous Presbyterians, yet in union with the original Board?"

Here was the germ of his overture,—one that does honor both to his head and heart. The draught came from his sick and, as it proved, his dying bed; but he felt that its spirit did not jar with the occasion. It called the attention of the Church to the subject of a modified co-operation with the American Board, yet with the principle distinctly embodied in it "that the Presbyterian Church in the United States is a missionary society, the object of which is to aid in the conversion of the world, and every member of the Church is a member for life of said society, and bound, in maintenance of his Christian character, to do all in his power for the accomplishment of the object."

The overture was presented, and a committee was appointed to confer with the American Board. It was considered by some as unwisely constituted;[1] and, in the apprehension that some arrangement would be made which would forestall ecclesiastical action in favor of a Foreign Board, the Synod of Pittsburg (1831) constituted itself a Foreign Missionary Society, composed of its ministers, Sessions, and churches, and styled itself *The Western Foreign Missionary Society of the United States.* It invited the co-operation of other Presbyterian churches or Synods. Thus, in a form which Dr. Rice had not anticipated, and which he had sought to guard against, the germ of distinctive Presbyterian effort for foreign missions was developed. The committee—as constituted—made no satisfactory arrangement with the American Board, and the Synod of Pittsburg had taken a step which it was impossible to retrace. The fraternal spirit which allowed free voluntary contributions on both sides was fast disappearing. Compromise was no longer possible. Dr. Rice, who might have acted as a mediator in the strife, had already passed from the scene.

At this juncture it was natural that those who were distinctively Presbyterian should feel a jealousy of the presence and influence in the Assembly of delegates from the Plan-of-Union churches. Constituted as the Assembly repeatedly was, so that a few votes would turn the scale on important questions, they felt it hard that a committee-man not an elder in the Church should be allowed such a measure of power. The question raised was a new one. It had never been agitated, it had never fairly been regarded as a question, before. In 1827, arrangements were made with general approval,

[1] That is, for attaining the object suggested in Dr. Rice's overture. Drs. McDowell, McAuley, and Richards were the committee. At the meeting of the Board, they composed three of a committee of six, who reported unanimously against making any change respecting the relations of the Board to the Presbyterian Church.

and by the consent of both parties, to abrogate that feature in the correspondence between the New England Associations and the Assembly by which the delegates from either body were allowed to vote in that to which they were sent. Massachusetts alone objected; but in 1830 her consent was secured. Thus, in an orderly manner and with harmony of feeling, this result was attained. But meanwhile the more scrupulous members of the Assembly had raised the question of the constitutionality of allowing not only congregational delegates, but committee-men from Plan-of-Union churches, the right to sit as full members of the Assembly. The first case that arose was in 1820; but the committee to whom it was referred reported in favor of the principle, established by the Plan of Union, that the rights of a committee-man were the same in regard to delegation as those of a ruling elder. In 1826 another case occurred, in which, however, the delegate was not even a committee-man, which was decided in the same manner. But the decision was met by a protest of forty-two members, some of them differing widely on other points. In reply, the Assembly said that every Presbytery was to judge of the qualifications of its own members, amenable to the Synod and not to the General Assembly, and that unauthenticated verbal testimony should not be allowed to set aside an authenticated written document.

In 1831 a similar case occurred. It was decided as before, and the decision was met by a similar yet more earnest and elaborate protest, signed by sixty-eight members. The substance of the reply to it on the part of the Assembly was that to deny the delegate a seat would be a violation of the Plan of Union, and that while the admission of the member might seem a violation of the *letter* it was not a violation of the spirit of the constitution. At a later stage of the proceedings, when the absence of some members had given the party of the protestants the majority, a resolution was passed discountenancing the election of committee-men, and declaring it to be "inexpedient and of questionable constitutionality."

Yet in 1832 there were committee-men among the delegates. They submitted their commissions, but finally withdrew them. A resolution was then passed that the Plan of Union, "truly construed, does not authorize any committee-man to sit and act in any case in any Synod or in the General Assembly."

To add to the feeling which was thus excited, reports were current that some of the Presbyteries in the Northern Synods had received ministers from Congregational churches without requiring their assent to the Confession of Faith and form of government.[1] As early as 1826 the zeal of the Synod of Pittsburg had been directed to this matter, and in an overture to the Assembly they expressed their "deep and growing concern" under the apprehension which they felt of the danger to which the "constitutional standards, ecclesiastical institutions, and doctrinal purity of the Church were exposed." In succeeding years this was a subject in regard to which increasing numbers professed to feel alarm.

The system, moreover, of conducting revivals in con-

---

[1] Dr. Green was one of the first to take and give the alarm. In July, 1831 ("Christian Advocate," p. 362), he said, "This Church, it is our solemn conviction, has reached a most important and, in our view, a very fearful crisis." Yet he says, again, "We have, indeed, heard a rumor—which we mention to say that we do not credit it—that there are Presbyteries in connection with the General Assembly in which the questions required in our constitution to be affirmatively answered by candidates for the gospel ministry at their licensure are not put to the candidates, or, at least, it is not held indispensable that they should be put "—p. 364.

nection with the labors of evangelists, was during the early part of this period carried to an extent altogether unprecedented, and for a while its popularity forbade any general resistance to it. Mr. Nettleton and Dr. Beecher, however, were conspicuous in opposition to what were termed the "New Measures," which had been largely introduced by Mr. Finney and his imitators in Western New York.[1] But they were thought to have exaggerated the evil which they condemned; and when, a few years later, it began to manifest itself more openly and justify the fears they had expressed, it was boldly and effectually resisted by the Presbyteries and ministers generally of Western New York. There were extravagances and questionable measures, indiscretions of men who hastily assumed the office of evangelists, and which only worked mischief; but the results, sad as they were in some respects, were by no means such as permanently to affect the integrity of the churches as a body.

Still, there were extravagances and disorders. Suspicion had materials to work upon. The report was spread, and impressions went abroad in some quarters, that Western New York was altogether unsound. Apprehension was felt and expressed in regard to the evils which might thence result to the Presbyterian Church at large.

In various quarters it was claimed, in behalf of those who expressed alarm, that dangerous errors were rife; that, through New England influence and candidates sent out as home missionaries from New England, these errors were finding their way into the Presbyterian Church. New Haven, indeed, was regarded as the fountain-head of heresy. The professors in the Theological Seminary had put forth speculations which had

---

[1] New York Observer, 1827-28: Correspondence of Nettleton, Beecher, Aikin, &c.

occasioned not only earnest discussion, but disturbance, and even alienation of feeling, in New England. Men like Dr. Woods, of Andover, Dr. Griffin, Dr. Tyler, and Mr. Nettleton made no secret of their apprehensions. The former wrote to Mr. Plumer (Feb. 8, 1836), "I believe what you say, that there is a perfect understanding among those in every part of our country who are opposed to Calvinism, and that they are acting in concert; that there is an alarming looseness among young preachers, and that there is a fixed determination to maintain a party holding loose opinions, and that there must be a battle fought here, and there, and everywhere." "The fact is that Dr. Porter, Mr. Evarts, and Dr. Cornelius were most deeply alarmed and distressed with the loose speculations which have come from the New Haven School and from Mr. Finney and others of that stamp. I know how they all felt, and what a full conviction they had that the notions which are peculiar to Dr. Taylor and Mr. Finney would undermine the fair fabric of our evangelical churches and spread a system far more unscriptural and pernicious than Wesleyan Methodism."

The views of Dr. Griffin were not dissimilar. Speaking of the New Haven speculations, he said, "I consider the honor of raising to spiritual life a world dead in trespasses and sins, as one of the brightest glories of the Godhead; and I have been grieved at my heart to see this honor taken away. This has been the severest cut of all."

Yet in some portions of the Presbyterian Church the effort was made to identify New Haven divinity with New England divinity,[1] and cover with odium all who

---

[1] "Great pains have been taken to make the impression that New Haven divinity is New England divinity, and in this way to awaken jealousy and prejudice in the Presbyterian Church against the

entered the Church from New England. A blind zeal refused to discriminate.[1] All were classed together. "Old School" men, if from New England, were still Congregationalists. The Third Presbytery of New York became subject to grave suspicions. In Philadelphia, men like Skinner and Patterson were accounted errorists, if not charged with heresy. The preaching which was full of the life and power of the gospel, and which took the form of direct aggression upon the power of darkness, was spoken of with contempt. The feeling which had been displayed by the Old Side at the time of the division nearly a century before, seemed still to linger about the scenes of its former triumph. The jealousy which had attempted to defeat the entrance of such men as Dr. Cox, and Dr. Howe of South Carolina, into the ministry, and had embarrassed Patterson in efforts for city evangelization worthy of a Chalmers, was reawakened, and a large portion of the Presbyterian Church, who scarcely knew the peculiarities of New Haven theology, or who would have repudiated all sympathy with them if they had known them, was held up to reproach and covered with odium.

In these circumstances, it is scarcely surprising that such results followed as those which history is called to note. Much might well be conceded to the vigilance which would guard against the silent and stealthy progress of doctrinal error. Much might well be said of the danger to be incurred by the indulgence of that fanaticism which resolved revivals into the enthusiastic employment and right management of spiritual machinery. But when the innocent were classed with the guilty, when an indiscriminate condemnation was meted

---

ministers and churches of New England generally."—*Letters on the Origin and Progress of the New Haven Theology*, p. 108.

[1] See, among other things, one of the pamphlets of Dr. Wilson, of Cincinnati, published about 1831.

out to those who reproved as well as to those who favored revival extravagances, and when garbled extracts of books and sermons were seized upon as the means of exciting suspicion against the orthodoxy of men whom time has proved as sound in faith as their accusers themselves, it is evident that unhallowed motives or unwise counsels had begun to operate.

The antagonism which rent asunder associations and even divided churches in New England was destined to a kindred development within the bounds of the Presbyterian Church. In 1829, Mr. Barnes was called from the church of Morristown to Philadelphia, and a sermon which he had published on the Way of Salvation—doubtless shaped somewhat by the controversy with Arminianism in which it originated, and containing expressions which some of his friends regretted—was made the basis of opposition to his reception and installation. In 1832, Mr. Duffield, of Carlisle, was put on trial for doctrines presented in a work from his pen on the subject of Regeneration. And in 1835 the case of Dr. Beecher, arraigned for doctrinal error, drew the attention of the whole country.

As to the case of Mr. (Dr. George) Duffield, his Presbytery, before taking any direct steps toward his prosecution, resolved to investigate the doctrinal positions laid down in the volume mentioned above. It had recently been published, and bore on the title page its author's name. Some of its teachings were regarded as dangerous and unsound. In April, 1832, the attention of the Presbytery of Carlisle was called to this book by Rev. James Williamson, a member of the Presbytery, who complained of it as containing doctrinal errors, and asked the appointment of a committee of Presbytery to examine and expose them. Mr. Duffield was absent at the time; and, at the suggestion of a member, the matter was postponed till he should be present. It was then demanded that some one should come forward as a responsible prosecutor; but no one was willing to appear. The method proposed was pronounced by Drs. McKnight and De Witt to be unconstitutional. Let the charge of heresy be made, they said, and sustained, if possible. But to this the majority would not accede. It was resolved to appoint an examining committee on the ground of "crying fame," although the obnoxious book had not yet been delivered to the subscribers. But attacks had already been directed against it in the columns of public journals, and two or three members, possibly, of the Presbytery had hastily perused it.

Dr. Duffield took no part in the proceedings till the committee had been appointed. He then objected to the measure as unconstitutional, complaining, moreover, that, notwithstanding their intimacy, the mover of the resolution for the appointment of the committee had never called to confer with him on the subject. Mr. Williamson was appointed chairman of the committee, which, with the least possible delay, brought forward its report, divided into twelve sections. Mr. Duffield proposed a friendly conference as to the doctrinal views of the members of Presbytery, and expressed his readiness to communicate freely his own sentiments, but objected emphatically to a judicial examination or decision concerning his book on the report of the committee. His objection was overruled, however, and the Presbytery proceeded to condemn the obnoxious positions pointed out in the committee's report.

Mr. Duffield disclaimed holding some of the views with which his book was charged, and complained that in their condemnation he had been virtually prejudged. His trial, however, followed. On the ground of common fame he was charged with maintaining and industriously propagating, both from the pulpit and through the press, doctrines or opinions absurd or at variance with vital truths and with doctrines taught in the standards of the Presbyterian Church. These were classified under ten counts. On all of these except two he was found guilty. Yet the Presbytery, on his alleging that his expressions had been misinterpreted,—that he did, in fact, hold all the doctrines of the Church, and desired in amity with his brethren to labor uninterruptedly for the glory of God and the salvation of souls,—declined further censure, only warning him to guard against dangerous speculations and study to maintain the unity of the Spirit in the bond of peace.[1]

It was while the state of feeling indicated by this trial and the opposition to Mr. Barnes was becoming rapidly developed, that Dr. Lyman Beecher was called (1832) from Boston to the charge of the Theological Professorship in Lane Seminary. The well-known opponent of Unitarian error and of the "new measures" of the Western revivals,—originally a Presbyterian pastor on Long Island, and repeatedly, as a delegate from New England, a member of the General Assembly, —he was regarded as pre-eminently the man to occupy the most responsible post within the bounds of the Mississippi Valley. The founder of the professorship had named him as the incumbent; but the condition of the endowment was not unacceptable to the prominent men in the Western field. His accession to their ranks was hailed with gratulation, and Dr. Nelson, of Danville, and Dr. Wilson,[2] of Cincinnati, as well as the pro-

---

[1] This action of the Presbytery was disapproved by the Synod; but it served to encourage disaffection in the church of Carlisle, and led ultimately to a secession and the organization of another church. In 1835, Dr. Duffield accepted a call to a church in Philadelphia, and was transferred to another Presbytery.

[2] Davidson's Kentucky, 365; Sprague's Annals. [Dr. Wilson convened the Board of Directors of the Seminary *at his tent at a*

fessors at Princeton, were consulted in the matter, and gave expression of their satisfaction with the arrangement.

Dr. Beecher accepted the appointment, and removed to Cincinnati (September, 1832). On his way he transferred his ecclesiastical relations to the Third Presbytery of New York, and by that body was dismissed to the Presbytery of Cincinnati. It was a step well calculated to excite distrust; and he had been only a short time at his post when his doctrinal views began to excite suspicion.[1] He was not a man to conceal his sentiments, and courted rather than shunned investigation. Dr. Wilson became his prosecutor. This, however, was only after a vain endeavor to institute process on the ground of common fame. Dr. Beecher was charged with holding and teaching Pelagian and Arminian doctrine in respect to Free Agency, Accountability, Original Sin, Total Depravity, Regeneration, and Christian Character, contrary to the Confession and the word of God.[2]

Presbyterian camp-meeting, at which meeting Dr. Beecher was elected professor.] F.

[1] In the case of Dr. Beecher the same method of reaching him without a trial, which had previously been attempted in the cases of Mr. Barnes and Mr. Duffield, was attempted. The Presbytery of Cincinnati was "called upon to appoint a committee to examine some of Dr. Beecher's sermons and report whether they contained doctrines at variance with the standards of our Church." This call was disregarded by the Presbytery, and complaint was made to the Synod; but they replied that the Presbytery could not be compelled to take up the charges without a responsible prosecutor. From this decision an appeal was taken to the General Assembly; but it was cast out by the Judicial Committee. Thus, the only course left was to present charges.—*Beecher's Trial*, p. 3. The language quoted above is Dr. Wilson's.

[2] The charges were based on a sermon of Dr. Beecher which Dr. Wilson prior to Dr. Beecher's election had said he believed to be sound. F.

With these charges were connected others, which bore upon his moral character. He was accused of slandering the Church, and attempting to bring odium upon all who sincerely received the standards of the body with which he was now connected. He was accused of "the sin of hypocrisy" or "dissimulation in important religious matters." He had declared his full acceptance of the Confession of Faith, while aware that his own views, as repeatedly advocated, were opposed to it. This he had done, in the opinion of Dr. Wilson, for popular effect.

The Presbytery met for the trial June 9, 1835. It was no ordinary occasion. Both the prosecutor and the accused were no common men. Dr. Wilson had been for nearly thirty years pastor of the First Church in Cincinnati. By his own almost unaided energy he had acquired an education, and from his first entrance upon the ministry had been a man of mark. For more than a quarter of a century he had been regarded as a leader and as one of the fathers of the Church. Intensely devoted to the body with which he had been so long identified, he regarded with avowed apprehension every measure which threatened to disturb its integrity. When the Home Missionary Society came into conflict with the Assembly's Board on the Western field, his sympathy with the latter was so strong as to forbid any thought of compromise. In his somewhat celebrated "Four Propositions" he endeavored to expose the ambitious designs of the Home Missionary Society. On nearly every point, after he had discovered his error in inviting Gallaher and Ross to assist him in the revival, he took the extreme ground of ecclesiastical conservatism and rigid subscription. No one could doubt his sincerity. Not a few regarded him as more partisan than judicious.

In nearly all that could render him a formidable opponent, Dr. Beecher was not inferior to his able prosecutor. In some respects he was vastly his superior. For the last few years—a guardian of orthodoxy against Unitarianism in the very heart of its strength—he had been a man of war, and with a vigor of thought and a force of utterance rarely equalled combined a fearless energy that threw a charm, even in the eyes of his opponents, over his manly bearing.

For several days the trial continued, with intense and unabated interest. But the vindication of Dr. Beecher was so complete that by a vote of nearly two to one it was resolved that the charges be not sustained. Dr. Wilson appealed to Synod. Here the case was gone over anew; and again he was defeated. From the decision of the Synod he appealed to the Assembly of 1836; but, on learning the facts in regard to another case which was to come before that body, in which the same principles were involved, he asked and obtained leave to withdraw his appeal.[1]

The case referred to was that of Rev. Albert Barnes, of the First Presbyterian Church in Philadelphia. In 1830 this church, with the hearty concurrence of Dr. J. P. Wilson, its pastor, had called him as colleague.

Of fifty-four votes cast by the congregation there was but one adverse to his settlement. The church, in due form, asked leave of the Presbytery of Philadelphia to prosecute the call. The motion was made

---

[1] The real fact was, some rogue on the boat in the Ohio River stole the doctor's coat, money, and papers in the case of Dr. Beecher; and he was glad of any excuse for dropping the matter. F.

Dr. Wilson himself, in explaining his course, stated that on arriving at the Assembly he was urgently besought by his own friends to drop the prosecution. They considered it inexpedient to incur the odium of attacking Dr. Beecher, and they flattered themselves, from things he had said and done, that he would come out right at last.

and seconded that leave be granted,—when Dr. Green arose and opposed it. The ground of his objection was a sermon recently preached by Mr. Barnes, entitled "The Way of Salvation." It contained, he asserted, fundamental errors. Unless explained to his satisfaction, he could not favor the motion.

He was called to order, on the ground that he was arraigning a member of another Presbytery in good standing without a proper form of trial. But the point was overruled, and the discussion proceeded. Several members declared their opposition to Mr. Barnes's views. Dr. Green was opposed to *innovation.* He maintained that those who did not hold the doctrines of himself and the brethren who, with him, opposed Mr. Barnes should withdraw.[1]

The discussion continued through four days. Strong testimony was borne to Mr. Barnes's fidelity as a devoted pastor by some who differed from him; while by those who favored the prosecution of the call the opposition was pronounced unfair and unkind. Let him be received by the Presbytery, they said, and he could then, if it was thought best, be put upon his trial. The vote was finally taken, and stood—twenty-one to twelve—in favor of the prosecution of the call.

This was on May 20. On the 18th of June, Mr. Barnes presented his certificate of dismission and recommendation from the Presbytery of Elizabethtown to the Presbytery of Philadelphia. But here, again, the opposition to his reception was vigorous and persistent. A protracted debate ensued; but finally, on the 22d of June, he was received by a vote of thirty to sixteen.

Charges were then presented against him for unsoundness in the faith, with a view[2] to arrest his instal-

---

[1] New York Observer, May 1, 1830. [2] Ibid. July 3.

lation. These were decided by the moderator to be out of order "at the present meeting called for a special purpose;" and the vote for his installation stood thirty-two to seventeen.

The dissatisfied minority complained to the Synod (Oct. 27, 1830). The ground of their complaint was the refusal of the majority to allow the examination of Mr. Barnes before he was received. The Synod sustained the ground of complaint by a vote of thirty to eight, and enjoined the Presbytery to hear and decide on the objections to the orthodoxy of Mr. Barnes's sermon.

In obedience to this injunction, the Presbytery met, November 30, for the express purpose of taking up the resolutions of Synod. Dr. Green read a minute of great length on the subject of the obnoxious sermon, which he wished the Presbytery to adopt. Dr. Ely objected to taking any steps till some person appeared as Mr. Barnes's accuser. This motion was ruled out of order; and it was moved and seconded that Dr. Green's motion be postponed with a view to hear objections against the sermon. At this stage of proceedings, Dr. Ely and others entered their protest against the decision rejecting his motion. He demanded that the charges that at a former meeting had been made against Mr. Barnes should now be produced. They had been read, and Presbytery had given no one leave to withdraw them from their files. The complaint of the minority had respect to these charges. They ought not to be left on the records without final adjudication. Till they were disposed of, the signers of them should be held as accusers, and especially as at a previous meeting the Presbytery had resolved to take them up and consider them.

Moreover, the vote of the Presbytery, allowing objections to be offered without responsible accusers, was contrary to the express directions of the Book of Discipline, and really commenced a process against Mr. Barnes in an unconstitutional way. Dr. Green's paper contained numerous impeachments of his orthodoxy, and proposed censures, while the method pursued allowed his accusers to be also his judges.

Such was the substance of the protest. Previous to the next meeting of Presbytery it was signed by twenty-five members, who declared that if the others were resolved to proceed in an unconstitutional manner they should withdraw from all participation in the matter and complain to the next General Assembly.

The motion to postpone in order to hear objections was then put, and carried by a vote of twenty-seven to twenty-one. Mr. Barnes gave notice that he appealed to the Assembly, and read a paper in which, on the ground of the unconstitutionality of the present proceedings, he requested to be put on trial before the Presbytery, either on the ground of common fame or by responsible accusers. This request was denied, and the members were allowed, one after another, to rise and state their objections to his sermon.

Dr. Green's paper was finally adopted, the first part by a vote of twenty-six, the second by a vote of twenty-five,—the exact number of the protestants. In behalf of himself and the protestants, Dr. Ely gave notice that he should complain to the next Assembly. As to Mr. Barnes's appeal, the Presbytery decided against his right thereto, on the ground that he had not then submitted to a trial. Yet, when he asked the privilege of a trial, it was refused.

A committee was appointed to confer with Mr. Barnes; but he declared that he considered the whole proceeding of the Presbytery unconstitutional, and must consequently decline to hear them on the subject. The entire case was then referred by the Presbytery to the Assembly, while by the minority it was brought before that body by way of complaint.[1]

The Assembly of 1831 had thus the whole case placed by both parties in its hands. Several points were made by the Presbytery in regard to which they desired a decision, and by means of which they skilfully entered an argument in their own vindication. With the consent of both parties, the case was submitted to the Assembly without argument, and by them referred to a select committee, of which Drs. Miller, Matthews, Lansing, Fisk, Spring, McDowell, and (Leonard) Bacon were members.

Their report, which was adopted by the Assembly, admitted the conscientious zeal of the Presbytery for the purity of the Church, and "a number of unguarded and objectionable passages" in Mr. Barnes's sermon, but decided that the Presbytery should suspend further proceedings in the case, and recommended a division of the body in such a way as to promote the peace of its ministers and churches. As to the points presented by the Presbytery, it was declared more advisable that they should be discussed and decided *in thesi* than in connection with the case of Mr. Barnes.[2]

---

[1] Quite a number of important documents bearing upon the case of Mr. Barnes will be found in the Presbyterian Historical Society Library, mainly in the Ely collection. I have not felt it necessary to specify them here.

[2] The action of the Assembly of 1831 gave great dissatisfaction in some quarters. Dr. Green, who complains that the party with which he sympathized had been, "in military phrase, completely outgeneralled and taken perfectly by surprise," confesses that "they had themselves made some exertions to secure a return of such members to the Assembly as they believed would favor their cause, and they did not doubt but that their opponents had done the same."—*Christian Advocate*, 1831, p. 413. He admits for those that acted with him that they "had taken more pains" to secure a majority "than they had ever used on any previous similar occasion."

These points were not decided by the Assembly of 1831; but the first of them came before the Assembly of the following year. It concerned the right of a Presbytery to examine a minister or licentiate coming by certificate from another Presbytery. The committee to whom it was referred could not agree. The majority and minority each presented a report, and the whole subject was indefinitely postponed.

Meanwhile, however, the Synod declined to divide the Presbytery of Philadelphia according to the direction of the Assembly of 1831. The friends of Mr. Barnes complained to the Assembly of the following year, and, after long and warm discussions, continued through several days, the complaint was sustained, although without censure of the Synod, and the prayer of the petitioners was granted. Fourteen ministers, with the churches connected with them, were set off from the Presbytery of Philadelphia, to form the Presbytery of Philadelphia Second. This was designed as a peace measure. The directions of the Assembly of 1831 had been disregarded, but the contumacy of the Synod was passed over as lightly as possible; while the newly-elected Presbytery embraced the aggrieved minority.

This measure, however, failed of the desired effect. The Synod, disregarding the action of the Assembly, created a Second Presbytery of its own, thus defeating the object which the Assembly had desired to attain.

The next year, 1833, was fruitful in remonstrances and complaints. The Synod of Philadelphia remonstrated against the proceedings of the previous Assembly. The Second Presbytery complained against the Synod. Several individual ministers presented their complaints to the Assembly against the same body. The whole subject was one of no little perplexity. The remonstrance and complaints were all referred to a committee, who were diligent in investigating the whole matter and in endeavoring to discover some satisfactory method of resolving the difficulty. After a free conference with the parties concerned, during which "the subject of the conference was treated with much tenderness and Christian affection," the committee reported, recommending a resolution to the effect that the complainants have leave to withdraw their complaints, and that the consideration of all the other papers relating to the Second Presbytery of Philadelphia be indefinitely postponed. The report was adopted; and, "from considerations of discretion and peace," no judgment was passed on a review of the Synod's records in the case of the Second Presbytery. With such satisfaction was this result viewed by the Assembly that they united in prayer, returning thanks to God for his goodness in bringing the affair to "such an amicable adjustment."

The matter, however, did not end here. The Synod took up the subject of a rearrangement of the Presbyteries, and, in opposition to the wishes of the members constituted by the Assembly as the Second Presbytery, made a new division by geographical lines. From this action an appeal was taken to the Assembly of 1834. The appeal was sustained, and the action of the Synod, so far as it was intended to unite the two Presbyteries, was declared void. Yet, as a peace measure, the integrity of the Presbytery erected by the Synod was not disturbed, only it was recommended that its name be changed. The Synod's Second Presbytery, however, was still known as the Synod's Second, and the Assembly's as the Assembly's Second, until 1836, when it was by the Assembly of that year entitled the Third Presbytery of Philadelphia.

Thirty-eight members of the Assembly (1834) protested against its action. They based their protest on the ground that the Assembly had invaded a jurisdiction exclusively secured to Synods, and condemned altogether the forming of Presbyteries on the principle of *elective affinity*. This principle, however, was not altogether new in the history of the Church. Four years after the union of the Synods in 1758, the wishes of the Old Side had been consulted in the formation of the Philadelphia Second Presbytery of 1762, afterward reconstructed under another name. The Third Presbytery of New York had been constituted by the Synod at the request of eight members to be set off in a new Presbytery, and the results which almost immediately followed, in developments of a new religious life in the churches, were thought to justify the measure. If it was unwise to allow the principle of *elective affinity* to determine the manner in which a Presbytery should be constituted, it was at least more unwise to offer it studious opposition. Its only effect could be to irritate and exasperate.

To remove the difficulty from the bounds of the Synod of Philadelphia, the new Synod of Delaware, consisting of the Presbyteries of Wilmington, Lewes, and Philadelphia Second, was constituted by the Assembly. The two first were in sympathy with the last: so that there was no longer any occasion for discord.

The Assembly of 1835 (at Pittsburg) was of a different character from its predecessors. It favored the Synod of Philadelphia, and pronounced emphatically against the principle of *elective affinity* in the constituting of Presbyteries and Synods. In consistency with its declarations, it proceeded to dissolve the Synod of Delaware "at and after the meeting of the Synod of Philadelphia" in October ensuing, uniting the Presbyteries connected with it with the Synod of Philadelphia. The

[1] This was disputed by some members of New York Presbytery in 1837.

Synod thus constituted was to take such order for the organization of its Presbyteries as might be deemed "expedient and constitutional."

By this act the members of the Third (Assembly's Second) Presbytery of Philadelphia were brought into connection with the Synod of Philadelphia, and thus became subject to its jurisdiction. Meanwhile, Mr. Barnes had been arraigned before his Presbytery on the charges of Dr. Junkin, and had been acquitted,—Dr. Junkin appealing to Synod from the decision of Presbytery.

The circumstances, briefly, were these. Soon after his arrival in Philadelphia, Mr. Barnes commenced the work of giving to the public, in a series of volumes, a popular commentary on the New Testament. In 1832 the Notes on the Gospel of Matthew was issued, and in 1835 the author had completed his volume on the Epistle to the Romans. Some of the views which it presented were regarded as especially objectionable by the party which had taken alarm on the subject of theological innovation. Dr. Junkin, President of La Fayette College, a member of another Presbytery and another Synod, became Mr. Barnes's accuser, and tabled charges against him as maintaining doctrines contrary to the standards of the Church. Carefully avoiding the term of *heresy*, as ambiguous and calculated to prejudice the prosecutor in public opinion, he drew up his accusation under ten specifications. Mr. Barnes was charged with holding—1. That sin consists in voluntary action. 2 That Adam (before and after his fall) was ignorant that the consequences of his sin should reach further than to natural death. 3. That unregenerate men are able to keep the commandments and convert themselves to God. 4. That faith is an act of the mind, and not a principle, and is itself imputed for righteousness. 5. Also, with denying the covenant with Adam; 6. the imputation of Adam's sin to his posterity; 7. that mankind are guilty, *i.e.* liable to punishment, on account of the sin of Adam; 8. that Christ suffered the proper penalty of the law as the vicarious substitute of his people, and thus took away legally their sins and purchased pardon; 9. the imputation of Christ's active righteousness; 10. that justification was other than simply pardon.

The decision of the Presbytery, after a patient hearing of the case, justified Mr. Barnes. He had not asserted that *all* sin consisted in voluntary action. He had not asserted that Adam was unacquainted with his moral relations, but only that there was no reason to suppose him so possessed of scientific knowledge as asserted by the Rabbins. He had not in his Notes taught one way or the other on the subject of man's ability or inability, nor was there any evidence whatever of his affirming that the unregenerate man could convert himself to God. He had affirmed, in accordance with Scripture, that saving faith is an influential act of the mind, but had not taught that faith is a justifying righteousness. Certain legal technicalities, as covenant of works, federal headship, representation, &c., he had preferred, for reasons assigned, not to use; yet the real truths contained in the Confession upon these points he had not denied. He had not taught that we have no more to do with the sins of Adam than with the sins of any other parents. He had not denied the penal consequences of the sin of Adam as an expression of the evil nature and tendency of apostasy, but objected to the use of the words guilt and punishment according to certain theological definitions which, by not implying personal criminality, were made to conflict with their use in common language. Instead of denying that Christ is the "vicarious substitute" of his people, or that he has "purchased pardon," Mr. Barnes had explicitly affirmed and taught these things. So far, moreover, from teaching that justification is simply pardon, he had taught the very reverse.

The evidence submitted by the prosecution to prove the charges was pronounced by the Presbytery to be that of "inferences drawn from Mr. Barnes's language" which were not legitimate, and, even if they were, could not, according to the decision of the Assembly of 1824, be used to convict of heresy or dangerous error, affecting the foundation of a sinner's hope or the Christian's title to eternal life.

The Presbytery judged, therefore, that the charges had not been sustained. Mr. Barnes was acquitted of having taught in his Notes on Romans "any dangerous errors or heresies contrary to the word of God and our standards." Yet the Christian spirit manifested by the prosecutor was allowed to shield him from the censure to which, on failing to support his charges, he was liable.

Dissatisfied with the decision, Dr. Junkin appealed to the Synod. But the records of the Presbytery previous to the present meeting of the Synod were not subject to its control.[1] The Presbytery refused to give them up. Previous to this refusal, Dr. Junkin and Mr. Barnes, being called on, answered that they were ready personally to proceed with the case. But, upon the refusal of the Presbytery to give up its records, Mr. Barnes put in a paper pleading to the jurisdiction of the Synod, and, declining the trial, withdrew. The Synod, however, would not allow this to be a bar to their proceeding. They decided that the Presbytery had acted disorderly in its refusal, and censured them therefor. The appellant, Dr. Junkin, was fully heard. Mr. Barnes

---

[1] They were subject only to the revision of the Synod of Delaware, which by act of Assembly had been dissolved.

was called, but, in accordance with the paper which he had submitted, could not, and did not, appear. The Presbytery was called on to explain their decision, but put in a formal refusal. The roll was then called, and the minute expressing the decision of the Synod was prepared.

This minute contained the argument of the Synod in defence of the regularity of its proceeding to issue the case, with resolutions sustaining the appeal, declaring Mr. Barnes convicted of holding fundamental errors, and suspending him from the ministry. Upon the question of its adoption a warm and at times tumultuous debate sprang up. The majority were not unanimous. Some preferred a reference of the whole subject to the Assembly, sustaining the appeal, but not pronouncing sentence. Some were in favor of sending it back to the Presbytery to review and correct their action, or, to make sure of the desired result, to put Mr. Barnes in connection with a Presbytery so constituted that it could "manage" him. Dr. Green would not listen to the first proposition. He said, "I freely confess that I dread a question of reference, as a burnt child dreads the fire." Robert J. Breckenridge took the opposite ground. He was not in favor of any action which might *seem* harsh and throw popular sympathy on the side of Mr. Barnes. He spoke freely of the "orthodox gentlemen" of Princeton and Philadelphia not acting together. He wished to ally them—as in the last Assembly—and so crush out heresy. Dr. Green—as well as Mr. McCalla—was more decided. He had said to "the Princeton gentlemen," "We will do you good against your will." And he had kept his word. "I did oppose them," he said, "and I shall oppose them again." By a very large majority the amendment of Mr. Breckenridge in favor of reference was voted down. By a still larger majority—one hundred and sixteen to thirty-one—Mr. Barnes was "suspended from the exercise of all the functions proper to the gospel ministry," until he should retract the errors condemned by Synod and "give satisfactory evidence of repentance."

Among those who voted with the majority were some who doubted the right of the Synod to take such action as this, and more who questioned its expediency. But distrust of the complexion which the next Assembly might assume, impelled to decisive action. Mr. Barnes gave notice of his appeal from the decision and his purpose to complain of the same to the next Assembly, meanwhile desisting from the exercise of his functions as a gospel minister.

The Synod then proceeded to reconstruct the Presbyteries. The censured Presbytery proposed for its boundaries geographical lines, and Dr. Duffield in its behalf declared, "We have no *elective affinity* principle for which we wish to contend." R. J. Breckenridge proposed its dissolution, and that its members within six months seek admission to the Presbyteries within whose bounds they were situated, or, in case they failed to do so, be declared *ipso facto* cut off from the communion of the Presbyterian Church. Dr. Cuyler declared that "the only true course was to extirpate" the offending Presbytery "root and branch." Mr. McCalla thought it better to keep them "together in one mass." To distribute them would be "like spreading poison." He was for letting them alone, leaving them to lay "their eggs in every nest." This, he believed, was the only way by which men would ever be got "to vote to put them out altogether." He would exclude the Presbytery from the watch and care of the Synod, and proposed resolutions to this effect. This, he thought, "would free us from wolves in sheep's clothing."

The plan of R. J. Breckenridge was postponed to take up Mr. McCalla's. Mr. Breckenridge opposed the proposed substitute. He distinctly declared that the members of the obnoxious Presbytery stood *recti in ecclesiâ*, and that the Synod had "no right to put it out of the Church without trying *its members* for irregularity of conduct." These members were not before Synod either on corporate or personal trial. Mr. McCalla's resolution was declared out of order, and the plan of Mr. Breckenridge was adopted.

The Presbytery which it was proposed thus summarily to dissolve, presented their appeal and complaint. The attempt of the Synod was a continued resistance to the authority of the Assemblies of former years. The dissolution "at the present time and by the Synod of Philadelphia" would be highly prejudicial to the best interests of religion. The manner of the dissolution was wholly unprecedented and unconstitutional. On these grounds they appealed to the next Assembly.

This Assembly (1836) met at Pittsburg, and numbered over two hundred and fifty members. A week was spent in hearing the case. The entire ground was carefully gone over, and resulted, by a vote of one hundred and thirty-four to ninety-six, in favor of sustaining the appeal of Mr. Barnes. By a still more decisive vote of one hundred and forty-five to seventy-eight, the decision of the Synod suspending him from all the functions of the gospel ministry was reversed. A resolution was immediately introduced by Dr. Miller, declaring it as the judgment of the Assembly that Mr. Barnes had published, in his Notes on Romans, opinions materially at variance with the Confession of Faith, and admonishing him to "again review the work and modify still further the statements which had grieved his brethren." On the vote upon this resolution, the Synod of Philadelphia, as a party, were excluded, and the resolution was rejected[1] by a vote of one hundred and twenty-two to one hundred and nine. It was met by a very decided protest on the part of the minority, which was signed by one hundred and one members. Sixteen members who held that Mr. Barnes's appeal should have been only in part sustained, and who admitted that the course of the Synod "was questionable and perhaps injudicious," and that it might be doubted whether the sentence of suspension should have been inflicted, entered their protest, in which they expressed their dissatisfaction that "a justly modified decision" was prevented by the differences between the opposite parties of which the Assembly was composed.

In their reply to these protests, the Assembly took occasion to review the charges, and to state the actual views of Mr. Barnes as brought out upon the trial. Many felt with him that the question which the Presbytery, Synod, and Assembly had been successively called to decide, was whether the views which had been presented in the Notes on Romans were any longer to be tolerated within the bounds of the Church; "whether a man who held them at the time of his licensure and ordination, who had held and preached them for ten years, and who held them in common with no small part of two thousand ministers in the same connection, was to be allowed peaceably to hold them still, and to labor under the influence of these views in endeavoring to save souls; or whether he was to be pronounced heretical and unsound, his character to be ruined, so far as a decision of his brethren could ruin it, himself to be harassed in his feelings, embarrassed in his preaching, and the large number of ministers, elders, and com-

---

[1] Although the motion was rejected, the spirit of Mr. Barnes was manifested in his voluntary revisal and correction of his Commentary on the Romans.

municants in the churches, who held the same views, declared unworthy an office, a name, and a place in the Church of God."

Upon this question the Assembly had now virtually pronounced. It was not ready to disown and reject men of the stamp of Dr. Beecher and Albert Barnes. Through a protracted period of six years the latter had borne himself in a meek and becoming manner, never using the tone of defiance, and never forgetful either of self-respect or of Christian principle. The processes against him had increased the number and strengthened the confidence of his friends, while they had contributed in no small degree to a more extended circulation of his works. In accordance with the decision of the Assembly,—who also sustained the appeal of the Presbytery from the decisions of the Synod,—he resumed his pastoral duties, to the discharge of which he was welcomed back by an affectionate people.

The prosecution and trial of Dr. Beecher and Mr. Barnes were but the more striking and public development of that antagonism of feeling which pervaded certain portions of the Church in regard to the theological questions which were agitated. The prominent position of these men concentrated public attention upon the issue of their case. Had *they* not been found obnoxious, there was no lack of those who might have been thus designated. Dr. Duffield's work on Regeneration was considered in many quarters as objectionable as Beecher's theology or Barnes's Notes. According to Mr. McCalla, and to use his own expression, Mr. (Dr. Thomas H.) Skinner was "the first man of this kidney." Although the only one in the Presbytery, "we could not manage him, but he soon found the way to manage us."

The great evil—according to those who were loudest in their complaints—came from New England. The laxness of Congregational usage and Taylorism were denounced almost in the same breath. As early as 1826 the Synod of Pittsburg had expressed its apprehensions. Notwithstanding the adoption and promulgation of rules designed to preserve the purity and order of the Church, and notwithstanding all the care taken and means employed for their correct application, yet, according to the Synod, these rules were evaded. Ordained ministers of other denominations were received by some of the Presbyteries without being required to assume the obligations of those ordained within the Church, and there was reason to apprehend that this practice was becoming more common. In 1829 an abortive attempt was made to secure uniformity of doctrinal instruction in the different seminaries; and in 1830 a rule was made by the Assembly—intended to meet the complaint of the Pittsburg Synod—by which licentiates and ordained ministers were required to give their assent to the questions proposed to the licentiates of the Presbyterian Church when about to be ordained.

Here the matter rested for a year or two. But the apprehension of danger was not removed.[1] Reports were rife—they were openly made in the public prints—that the Western Reserve Synod was especially delinquent. In the Assembly of 1832 a motion was made that the Synod be cited before the next Assembly; but, after considerable discussion, it was resolved to direct it to review and examine the state of its Presbyteries and churches and report to the next Assembly. In regard to the general subject of subscription, brought

---

[1] "We speak what we firmly believe when we say that unless in the passing year there is a general waking up of the *Old School* Presbyterians to a sense of their danger and their duty, their influence in the General Assembly will forever afterwards be subordinate and under control."—*Christian Advocate*, 1831, p. 366.

by overture before the Assembly, its action was unanimous. It decided that the Catechisms, as well as the Confession, are included in the standards of the Church, yet that the rules made by the Assembly of 1830 in regard to ministers coming from other bodies were sufficiently explicit. Further legislation on the subject was therefore pronounced unnecessary.

In the following year the Synod of the Western Reserve made their report to the Assembly. They had complied with the order to review and examine the state of the Presbyteries and churches under their care, and declared that they found no ground for the charge of delinquency in relation to the permission alleged in the first specification against them. Previous to the passage of the resolutions of the Assembly of 1830, there had been a difference of practice in the Presbyteries, some of them receiving members without a formal profession of adopting the Confession of Faith of the Presbyterian Church. But since that period no such practice had obtained. As to the licensing and ordaining of persons by the Presbyteries, they had no knowledge that this had ever been done without requiring an adoption of the Confession of Faith. As to ruling elders, they held that the constitution did not make the eldership essential to the existence of the church, and in some cases the number of members in communion was too small to admit the election of suitable persons for the office, while the fact of the intermingling of Congregationalists and Presbyterians in many churches was a sufficient reason for the non-existence of the eldership, according to the conditions of the Plan of Union. The report was accepted and ordered to be placed on the minutes of the Assembly; but no further action was taken, except to disclaim the views of the Synod in regard to the eldership.

But the subject was not yet put to rest. It was

brought forward, along with others, in 1834, in "The Western Memorial," addressed to the Assembly, and signed by eighteen ministers and ninety-nine elders.[1] It presented a most startling picture of the doctrinal error and defection which prevailed throughout the Church. It was not limited to complaints against the negligence of Presbyteries in requiring assent to the standards of the Church, but boldly reviewed the published writings of some of the most prominent ministers connected with the Assembly. It charged upon the policy that had characterized the proceedings of previous General Assemblies "an evasive character," an apparent intent "to avoid a prompt discharge of their constitutional duties," thus indicating "a widely-spread principle of evil operating in the Presbyterian Church, to the general change of its form of government and the character of its creed."

The memorial denounced the impolicy and unconstitutionality of the Plan of Union, pointing out its mischievous workings. It asserted "the existence of a sentiment now avowed by numbers who bear the Presbyterian name," that in the adoption of the standards every man might put upon them his own construction. It complained of the frequent ordination of licentiates from Congregational bodies *sine titulo*, thus "suddenly, nominally, and geographically converting them into Presbyterian ministers before they could know what Presbyterianism was." In this connection it specified the ordination of eight young men by the Newbury-port Presbytery, and ten by the Third Presbytery of New York, for the service of the American Home Missionary Society, although for the most part destined to fields where Presbyteries were already in existence.

---

[1] This memorial was probably drawn up through the influence of Dr. Wilson, of Cincinnati. It is spoken of as the "Cincinnati Memorial." Baird's Digest, 877.

Another grievance, ascribed "to the principles of Independency," was "the departure of the General Assembly from the due discharge of its own constitutional duties in conniving at an irresponsible voluntary association,"[1] which assumed to a great extent the management of domestic missions within the Presbyterian Church. The "patronage" of the Home Missionary Society—actually encouraged by a recommendation of the Assembly of 1829—was declared to be detrimental to the interests and subversive of the system of the Presbyterian Church. The missionaries and agents of this society had almost uniformly voted, in the supreme judicature of the Church, on the side of innovation.

To these evils were to be traced the lamentable declensions of the Assembly of 1831, on the first trial of Mr. Barnes. Here "a decision of the question on its doctrinal merits was evaded," and "the claims of truth were smothered in their well-known compromise." Thus in the Assembly and in other church courts a course of procedure was pursued which rendered the principles of the constitution nugatory and reduced the government of the Church to spiritual anarchy. Against these perversions the memorialists testified.

The memorialists then proceeded to point out the specific errors which they declared to be held and taught within the Presbyterian Church. These were substantially the same as had been charged against Mr

[1] A large proportion of the leading ministers of the Church had, previous to this period, manifested a friendly spirit to various voluntary societies, though operating within the bounds of the Church. It is not strange that Dr. Green, as charged by Dr. Peters, should have exerted himself to secure the establishment of a Pennsylvania Home Missionary Society which might take charge of a field with which the managers of the A. H. M. S. were comparatively strangers. He might do this, even while using more strictly ecclesiastical methods, if he found the latter impracticable in the case.

Barnes. They were selected from the writings of Barnes, Duffield, Beecher, and Beman. After reviewing the history of the Church to show the light in which subscriptions to the standards had been regarded, they earnestly requested of the Assembly the abrogation of the Plan of Union, measures to prevent Presbyteries from receiving and dismissing ministers to be sent into the bounds of other Presbyteries to their annoyance, the resumption by the Assembly of the full exercise of its own functions in conducting missionary operations, and a testimony on its part against the errors taught and circulated within the bounds of the Church.

They closed by presenting for the opinion of the Assembly some of the points which had been previously brought up by the Synod of Philadelphia for its decision. They wished to know whether a member in one Presbytery in good standing might claim, on dismission and recommendation, to be received without examination into another; whether any Presbytery might take up, examine, and pronounce upon a publication which they found to be erroneous and dangerous, or whether they must first prosecute its author; and whether, in the adoption of the standards, a candidate or minister from a foreign body might give to them his own construction. If no remedy was afforded for the evils complained of, the memorialists professed to tremble for the consequences. Such was the document presented to the Assembly.

But the Assembly refused to sanction the strictures of the memorial upon preceding Assemblies. They declared it inexpedient and undesirable to abrogate the Plan of Union. They declared that on the subject of ordination the rules already made were deemed sufficient; that the work of licensing and ordaining men belonged to the Presbyteries; that publishing to the world, as heretical and dangerous, ministers in good standing who had not been constitutionally tried and condemned, was to be discountenanced; that the Assembly had no authority to establish any exclusive mode of conducting missions; that ministers in good standing in one Presbytery when dismissed to another should be received on the credit of their constitutional testimonials; that to take up, try, and condemn printed publications as heretical and dangerous was equivalent to condemning the author as heretical; that those who adopted the standards of the Church should be presumed, without opposing evidence, to adopt them according to their obvious, known, and established meaning; and that Presbyteries and Synods should strive in charity and forbearance to settle, as far as practicable, all their matters of grievance and disquietude, without bringing them before the General Assembly and the world.

Such was the result reached after a long and thorough discussion of the several points contained in the memorial. It could not, in the circumstances, have been expected that it should be received with equanimity by those whose action it condemned. Dr. Green, especially, must have felt that certain portions of it bore severely upon the course pursued by the Presbytery of Philadelphia; and he was the first to sign a protest against it which received, beside his own, thirty-five signatures.

The dissatisfied minority now offered a resolution, which proposed to condemn in the abstract the errors charged upon Mr. Barnes's sermon. This was indefinitely postponed for another, which declared the unabated attachment of the Assembly to the system of doctrines contained in the standards, and enjoined the study of them upon all the members of the Church, and their firm support by all scriptural and constitutional methods.

The yeas and nays were called upon the question of postponement; but the call was withdrawn with a view to substituting a protest in its place. This protest was signed by thirty members. It spoke strongly of the action of the Assembly in its vote of postponement, as "a refusal to discharge a solemn duty enjoined by the Confession of Faith and loudly and imperiously called for by the circumstances of the Church." A more temperate protest might have been received; but this was refused a record, by a vote of fifty-six to forty-two.

In these circumstances, the minority resorted to an extraordinary measure. They met, and drew up a paper, which they styled "The Act and Testimony." In this they re-echoed in still more startling tones the statements of the memorial. They declared their dissatisfaction that for several years the highest judicatory of the Church had failed to redress their grievances, and had only aggravated the evils of which they complained. They spoke of the "unchristian subterfuge to which some have recourse" in avowing adherence to the standards but holding doctrines at complete variance with the system.[1] After reciting the errors charged upon the party which they opposed, they dwelt upon the agitation and division of the churches and ecclesiastical bodies consequent upon the propagation of "these and similar errors;" they declared that "our people are no longer one body of Christians;" that "Presbyteries were convulsed by collisions;" that the Synods and Assembly were "made theatres for the open display of humiliating scenes of human passion and weakness." They asserted that their hope that the dignified and impartial course of justice would

[1] There was doubtless some ground for this complaint. Evidence of the fact that might satisfy many would not suffice to establish it in an ecclesiastical court.

flow steadily, had expired. They complained that the "memorial" had been "sternly frowned upon" by the Assembly, while they who had "corrupted our doctrines" sought "to give permanent security to error and to themselves by raising an outcry in the churches against all who love the truth well enough to contend for it."

In regard to church order, the gravest apprehensions were expressed. They declared their increasing alarm at "a fixed design to organize new tribunals upon principles repugnant to our system and directly subversive of it, for the obvious purpose of establishing and propagating the heresies already recounted."

In conclusion, they recommended to all who loved the Church and desired to restore it from its abuse and corruption to give no countenance to teachers or preachers who held "the preceding or similar *heresies*," to strive rather to subject them to discipline, to labor to restore the tribunals of the Church to their original purity, and that all ministers, elders, church-sessions, Presbyteries, and Synods, who approved it, give their public adherence to this Act and Testimony.

A convention, composed of members from each Presbytery or minority of Presbytery favorable to the measure, was invited to meet in Pittsburg previous to the meeting of the Assembly, in May, 1835, to deliberate and adopt such measures as should be "best suited to restore the prostrated standards."

The document was signed by thirty-seven ministers and twenty-seven elders. Among the names of the former were R. J. Breckenridge, Joshua L. Wilson, George Junkin, Dr. Green, and James Latta. It was the first step as yet taken by either party toward marshalling and disciplining its forces. It had the distinct aspect of providing for ulterior and decisive measures. As such it could not fail to be regarded.

Strong opposition to the "Act and Testimony" was manifested by the conductors of the "Princeton Review." Their view of the document was that all who did not accept it—from whatever reasons—subjected themselves to the suspicions of those who did. An alternative was offered them on the authority of a body self-constituted, which nobody, not even the Assembly itself, had any right to impose. The "Princeton Review" therefore characterized it as "an act of gross injustice to multitudes of our soundest and best men." The "Princeton gentlemen" declared the recommendations of the document, recommendations "to renounce allegiance to the Church." They were "extra-constitutional and revolutionary, and to be opposed." They denied the facts which the document assumed. They exculpated the Assembly for not passing the resolutions on heresies and errors which the minority urged. "Is it to be expected," they asked, "that at this time of the day the Assembly would condemn all who do not hold the doctrine of a limited atonement?" They distinctly declared that "had the ingenuity of man been taxed for a plan to divide and weaken the friends of truth and order in our Church, we question whether a happier or more effectual expedient could have been devised." "Division is the end to which this enterprise leads, and to which, we doubt not, it aims." To request and urge the signing of the Act and Testimony was characterized as "an unauthorized assumption," as "fraught with injustice, discord, and division." It made one a heretic for being "unable to adopt an extended document" containing a multitude of statements and counsels, many of them questionable, and some of them unwarranted and unwise. "We have not the least idea," they add, "that one-tenth of the ministers of the Presbyterian Church would deliberately countenance and sustain the errors specified."

Such was the view taken by a large minority in the church. They could not accept the statements of the "Act and Testimony" as correct in matter of fact. To them the alarm excited appeared groundless. Within the sphere of their own observation they discerned nothing to warrant the extraordinary measures that had been adopted. Firm in their own views of truth, and associating in their own spheres with men kindred in spirit and doctrine, they knew only by vague report of the actual condition of things in other, and perhaps distant, portions of the church. The "Western Luminary" declared that not one of the ministers or elders in its own region, so far as known, held the errors alleged. The representations therefore of the "Act and Testimony" were regarded with suspicion by many who were by no means friendly to the operation of the "Plan of Union," or to the disorders in discipline and errors in doctrine which it was charged with introducing into the church. Some regarded its authors as inconsistent in condemning the neglect of the tribunals of the church, while they assumed for themselves something of the authority of a tribunal.

The Act and Testimony convention met, according to appointment, at Pittsburg, previous to the meeting of the Assembly, in May, 1835. Forty-one Presbyteries and thirteen minorities of Presbyteries were represented. By this body a list of grievances was drawn up to be presented to the Assembly, with an earnest demand for redress. These grievances were for the most part already familiar,—the points presented by the Philadelphia Presbytery to the Assembly and re-echoed in the memorial. Besides these, it denounced the Plan of Union, and presented the "alarming features of the condition of the Church." As to the Plan of Union, its language was somewhat guarded. While tracing to it "not a small proportion of the evils" that disturbed the peace of the Church, it added, "We say nothing here of the wisdom of the measure at the time, nor of its constitutionality. We know it was the work of wise and good men. But we must be allowed to express the opinion that now it leads to alienation, contentions and disorders." On these grounds, and for the additional reason "that the terms of compact are not complied with by our Congregational brethren," the Assembly were besought to annul the act by which the Plan of Union had been adopted.

The Assembly, to the gratification of the memorialists, contained a majority who sympathized with them. The grievances were taken up, and the action of the Assembly substantially reversed the proceedings of the Assembly of the previous year. Yet it did not fully come up to the standard of the memorialists. It justified Presbyteries who examined members in good standing coming to them with certificates. It allowed any judicatory to pronounce judgment upon any printed publication which might be regarded as inculcating injurious opinions, even though its author, untried, was still a member of the same body. It condemned the principle of *elective affinity* in the constituting of church courts. It consequently dissolved the Synod of Delaware. It pronounced against the desirableness of a longer continuance of the Plan of Union. It substantially endorsed the complaint of the memorialists that the extensive spread of doctrinal errors was by no means unfounded. But here it stopped. It was not prepared to break off the correspondence with the New England churches, and, while acknowledging the "painful evils" resulting from the divided sentiment of the Church in regard to the method of conducting domestic missions, it declared its persuasion that it was inexpedient to attempt to prohibit the operation of the Home Missionary, the Education, or any other voluntary society, not subject to the Assembly's control, within the bounds of the Church.

With such endorsement the memorialists had good reason to be satisfied; and the Synod of Philadelphia followed up such action by the prosecution, trial, and suspension of Mr. Barnes. But in the following year (1836) the party in sympathy with them were in a minority in the Assembly. The appeal of Mr. Barnes and the aggrieved Presbytery against the Synod of Philadelphia were triumphantly sustained.

This gave new cause of alarm to the defeated party. Again they met, and, encouraged by their previous experiment, summoned a convention to meet in Philadelphia a few days previous to the meeting of the Assembly of 1837. They had now gone too far to recede, and felt the necessity of prompt action in order to maintain the position they had so boldly taken.

Meanwhile, however, a new grievance had been added to the list. All along, theological and ecclesiastical questions had been intermingled; but the ecclesiastical were now to rise into greater prominence. In 1831 the Pittsburg Synod—anticipating the report, whatever it might be, of the commission which, in consequence of Dr. Rice's overture, had been appointed to confer with the American Board—had formed itself into a Foreign Missionary Society, and invited the co-operation of the Church at large. This they could do without asking the sanction of the Assembly, and none could question their right to do it. The Assembly did not molest them, nor interfere in any way with their proceedings. But in 1835 the memorialist party was in the ascendant, and it became a natural inquiry for them, what was the speediest and most efficient method of committing the Church at large, by means of the Assembly, to distinctly ecclesiastical action on the subject of foreign missions. With the Western Missionary Society of the Synod of Pittsburg—which already had not only invited, but to some extent received, the co-operation and contributions of other portions of the Church—already in the field, it was not difficult to find an answer. On the afternoon of the last day of the sessions of the Assembly, when less than one-third of its members were present, the Committee on Foreign Missions made their report. Previous to this, however, a committee had been appointed to confer with the Synod of Pittsburg on a transfer of the Western Missionary Society to the Assembly, to ascertain the terms of such transfer, and to digest a plan of conducting foreign missions under the direction of the Assembly; and this committee were to report the following year. But this measure was regarded as too dilatory and too uncertain in its issue. It was, therefore, resolved that the committee of conference be authorized, in case they should approve the transfer, to ratify and confirm the same and report to the next Assembly.

The Pittsburg Synod had no selfish ambition. It was comparatively easy to fix upon terms of agreement, where the views of both parties were directed toward the speedy accomplishment of the same result. The plan of transfer was perfected, and the Assembly's committee and the Synod of Pittsburg proceeded jointly to construct a plan and constitution for a Board of Foreign Missions for the General Assembly. To make this measure final and conclusive, and to put it out of the power of the Assembly to lay aside the burden and duty thus imposed upon it, it was expressly stipulated that the Assembly "will never hereafter alienate or transfer to any other judicatory or board whatever the direct supervision and management" of the missions thus transferred to its hands.

Had the Assembly of 1836 been of the same type with that of 1835,—as was perhaps anticipated,—the nature of this strange proceeding—delegating the power of not only one but all succeeding Assemblies to a small committee, in regard to a matter vital to the interests of the Church—would, doubtless, have been overlooked.

But the Assembly of 1836 was not disposed to endorse a measure which the majority of its members regarded as not merely questionable in policy, but as stealthily thrust upon the Church,—a measure which, if adopted, should first have been submitted to the Presbyteries. The committee on the transfer reported what they had done. The Assembly was placed in a difficult position. There was much to be said on both sides, and much was said. But the report of a minority committee pronouncing against the ratification of the terms of agreement was approved; and thus this project, which could have committed the Assembly to a Foreign Board, as to the policy of which the Church at large was perhaps nearly equally divided, was defeated.[1]

This was a grievance not less sore and sad than that of imputed theological errors. The acquittal of Mr.

[1] It may well be doubted whether the majority of the Assembly of 1836, in rejecting the proposed transfer of the Western Foreign Missionary Society, and thereby cancelling the arrangements—really obnoxious as they were in several respects—which had been made for transforming it into one of the boards of the Church, did justice to the real sentiment of the great mass of ministers and members at the West and South. Seven years had wrought a great change in public sentiment. Dr. Peters speaks somewhat caustically of the sudden change in Dr. Miller's views between 1833, when he was opposed to a Board of Foreign Missions, and 1835, when he was won over to its support. But the success of the Board of Domestic Missions must have surprised its friends, and satisfied many—hitherto inclined to doubt—that ecclesiastical boards as well as voluntary societies could draw out the charities and enlist the confidence of the churches. Dr. Miller was not a man to overlook the importance of such a fact. Considering the method employed to fasten a Board of Foreign Missions on the Assembly,—a method the objectionable features of which are fully exposed in the "Plea for Voluntary Societies,"—it would have required great patience on the part of the majority not to have resented it, while there can, I think, be little doubt that the exasperation produced by the rejection of the proposed transfer contributed not a little to the final result of division.

Barnes, and, by implication, of Dr. Beecher, the repudiation of the positions taken in the memorial, and the refusal of the Assembly to commit itself to exclusively ecclesiastical action, all combined to exasperate the memorialists. They had exerted themselves for years, had consulted and combined, seeking to call public attention to what they believed to be a most alarming state of things. They had pointed out specifically the errors which excited their apprehension, and which they believed to be dangerously rife in many quarters. They had exposed themselves to criticism, and even reproach; by their firmness and persistence they had given undoubted evidence of the strength and sincerity of their convictions. They had encouraged themselves with the hope that their measures must bear the anticipated fruits, and their own conclusions be adopted by the authoritative voice of the Church, and hence with sore disappointment and strong indignation they saw their whole work undone by the Assembly of 1836.

It was in these circumstances that the memorable convention of 1837 was called, not, however, on the Pittsburg plan. That was too open. This was to be more cautious. It met in Philadelphia a few days before the Assembly convened. No means had been spared to promote the objects which it had in view. A confidential committee of correspondence had been appointed to write to such ministers and elders as were known to be in sympathy with them, to secure their influence in the appointment to the next Assembly of commissioners who could be depended on. The correspondence was carefully to be kept out of the public prints. The precaution, however, proved vain.

A pamphlet was issued by the *confidential committee*, but preceded by a secret circular, addressed in a confidential way to persons of influence supposed to be aggrieved by the proceeding of the Assembly of 1836. It asked replies to certain specified questions, and held up distinctly the probability of a division of the Church. It subsequently declared, "*We cannot continue in the same body.*" "In some way or other, *these men must* be separated from us."[1]

Such was the method of preparing the minds of the ministers of the Church and the members of Assembly for decisive measures. The convention labored in the same direction. More than one hundred members were in attendance, nearly if not quite all of them commissioners to the Assembly. The question was agitated as to the course to be pursued. It was yet uncertain which party would be in the majority. This alone occasioned doubt, apprehension, and hesitation. The

---

[1] With historical documents before us, and with the accounts we have received of the conference of the party of the memorialists held on the afternoon of the day on which the Assembly of 1836 adjourned, it is evident that the policy of separation, or of division in some form, was resolved upon before the members of the Assembly dispersed. The "Princeton Review" of July of that year still pleaded for union. It declared, "We cannot see how any set of men can, with a good conscience, desire to effect the division of the Church, until they are called upon to profess what they do not believe, or required to do what they cannot approve." In their view, no good could result from division. Discord would only be increased, error promoted, and the influence of Presbyterianism destroyed.

But the "Princeton Review" pleaded in vain the cause of peace and union. After the conference held, as above stated, the moderator of the Assembly (Witherspoon) remarked to a friend, "The die is cast: the Church is to be divided." The confidential committee, while the "Review" was yet fresh in the hands of its readers, had written—doubtless after careful deliberation—the language noted above.

The publication of the circular of the committee brought matters to a crisis. Only a few weeks after the "Review" had denounced division, New Brunswick Presbytery *unanimously* declared themselves unable to see any prospect of good in the continued union of the discordant parts of the Church. "The die" was indeed cast. Division was a foregone conclusion.

convention was at a loss what to do. If a minority, should they secede and constitute a new Assembly, or declare themselves *the* Assembly? If a majority, should they move to cite the Synods regarded as obnoxious? Delay was out of the question. Some decisive step must be taken at once. But the convention was irresolute and divided in sentiment. Dr. Blythe favored citation. It would gain a double object: it put out those who made the trouble, and strengthened the party who were to give judgment. R. J. Breckenridge denied that there was power anywhere to exclude the persons at whom the speeches and memorials were aimed. Dr. Baxter was opposed to setting aside and excommunicating Synods. Dr. Junkin declared, "We must be ready for amputation." Dr. Wilson was in favor of "ulterior and decisive measures;" but this was too indefinite. It was proposed to separate the Pelagian and anti-Presbyterian party from the Presbyterian Church, but he disavowed any knowledge of Pelagianism in the Church. He had never accused any man of it. There was a great deal of semi-Pelagianism and Arminianism. But this was the last convention he should ever attend, if he lived to fourscore.

There was some reason for his dissatisfaction. The convention was strongly enough resolved upon decisive measures if possible;[1] but no man could tell, till the Assembly was constituted, whether or how it could be done. The voluntary societies were largely dis-

---

[1] Dr. Junkin said, "It was not to be endured that in the General Assembly there should be fourteen men who represented but two Presbyterian churches." Dr. Musgrave said, "No! they never could agree. They must get apart; they must separate somehow." Dr. Blythe, speaking of the American Home Missionary Society, said, "He knew the man well who guided that piratical ship. He knew Absalom Peters, and nothing would satisfy that man but the whole carcase."

cussed. Language was employed which was avowedly an indictment of the American Board. But Dr. Smyth declared that the Western Missionary Society was equally obnoxious through its agents. Others asserted that the Home Missionary Society was scarcely more culpable than the Tract or Sunday-School Union Societies. Yet a memorial to the Assembly was at last agreed upon. It proceeded, somewhat after the manner of preceding memorials, to specify the doctrinal errors that were alarmingly rife, and which struck "at the foundation of the system of gospel grace." It declared it the duty of the Church to bear public and open testimony against them. As to church order, it minutely specified the several ways in which it had been violated: as, the formation of Presbyteries on the *elective affinity* principle; the refusal of Presbyteries to examine applicants with regular certificates of dismission from other Presbyteries; licensing men who merely adopted the Confession for "substance of doctrine;" the formation of many and various creeds for individual churches; the needless ordination of men as evangelists, thus multiplying spurious excitements and bringing the ministry into contempt; the disuse of ruling elders, or their election for a limited time; a progressive change in the system of Presbyterial representation; the unlimited and irresponsible power of voluntary associations over Presbyteries; and the unconstitutional decisions and violent proceedings of several General Assemblies.

It complained also of a neglect of discipline, mainly with direct reference to the decisions in the case of Mr. Barnes; and the license and countenance given to error preached and published in sermons, newspapers, pamphlets, &c. the influence of which was subversive of "our system of truth and order," but could not be reached by discipline.

As to the method of reform, it declared, in behalf of the convention, "We cannot consent to meet any longer on the floors of our several judicatories to contend against the visible inroads of a system which, whether so designed or not, is crippling our energies and menacing our very existence." It demanded the abrogation of the Plan of Union, as unconstitutional; the discountenancing of the Home Missionary and Education Societies, and the prevention of their operation, as far as possible, within the bounds of the Church; the dissolution or exclusion of every church, Presbytery, or Synod nominally connected with the Assembly, which was not organized on Presbyterian principles; the examination by Presbyteries of every member received, no matter what his standing in another Presbytery; the citation and trial of errorists, and an admonition of the Assembly to the national societies to be cautious in the selection of their agents, so as not to interfere with the order or interest of the Church.

From 1833 to 1837, while the membership of the Church had absolutely decreased, the Presbyteries had increased from one hundred and eleven to one hundred and thirty-five, the churches from two thousand five hundred to two thousand eight hundred and sixty-five, the ministers from eighteen hundred and fifty-five to two thousand one hundred and forty. But, instead of a corresponding advance in the membership of the churches, there had been not only a relative but an actual decrease. The number reported in the minutes of Assembly for 1833 was two hundred and thirty-three thousand five hundred and eighty, or an increase of about sixty thousand during the three years that had intervened since 1830. But in 1837 the entire membership of the Church was reported as only two hundred and twenty thousand five hundred and fifty-seven.

The decrease had been most marked in some of the Northern Presbyteries, especially within the bounds of the Synods of Albany and Geneva. Londonderry had lost about four hundred, Champlain nearly one thousand, Troy over two thousand, Albany over two thousand, Columbia about eight hundred. This was the case in other parts of the Church, although to a less extent. The Presbytery of Elizabethtown had lost over two hundred, New Brunswick over five hundred, and in Philadelphia there had been a marked decrease. New York Third, Bedford, Newark, Newton, and Montrose had advanced, the first of these having gained nearly one thousand members. In quite a number of the Western and Southern Presbyteries there had been a marked decrease, accounted for in some instances by the erection of new Presbyteries.

In 1834 the Presbyteries of Ottawa, Nashville, Arkansas, Tuscaloosa, and Wooster were erected; in 1835, those of Marion, Logansport, Roanoke, Morgantown, Amity, and Louisiana; in 1836, those of Chemung, Maumee, Loraine, Medina, Sidney, Peoria, and Alton; and in 1837, that of Greenbrier. Two Synods, moreover, had been formed from that of Alabama and Mississippi, while the Synod of Michigan had been erected and that of Chesapeake had been dissolved: so that the number of Synods in 1837 (twenty-three) was but one more than in 1833.

As to the decrease of membership, it is to be accounted for through the influence of several causes. The controversies of the Church were not without their influence. Attention was diverted by them from the proper work of the Church. Religion languished, and a much smaller number than in preceding years united with the churches. There was, moreover, a reaction from the fervor and enthusiasm of what had been regarded as the Revival period; and this reaction was most marked, as we have seen, in some of the Northern Presbyteries, where the "new measures" had been most extensively adopted. It is probable, moreover, that already some of the Congregational churches under the care of Presbyteries had begun to withdraw and had ceased to be reported. Nor could the religious decline be dissociated from the wild spirit of speculation which began just at this period to spring up, and which culminated in the disastrous financial crisis of 1837.

Taking all these things into consideration, it is scarcely surprising that the Church in 1837 should report a membership of less than three thousand in advance of what it might claim in 1832. Its absolute advance had been almost entirely checked, while it was forced to await the effects of the reaction of the preceding period.

Yet it was at this time that the project for the establishment of the Union Theological Seminary at New York was conceived and executed. It was justly felt that a large city afforded some peculiar advantages for the establishment of such an institution; and experience has justified the anticipation.

It was felt, moreover, that, sustained by the patronage and confidence of the pastors and churches of the city of New York, and those who sympathized with them throughout the Church, the proposed institution might be competently endowed, ably officered, and well sustained. It would, at least, in the hands of directors independent of the Assembly, remain under the control of men who would promote its interests without reference to an accidental majority in the Assembly. It was consequently established, and placed under the care of a Board of Directors appointed by its friends and founders.

The institution was projected in 1835. In October

of that year nine persons—four ministers, of whom Erskine Mason was one and Dr. Thomas McAuley and Henry White, probably, two of the others, and five laymen—met at a private house to consult in regard to the project.[1] The original faculty[2] were Dr. Thomas McAuley, President, and Professor of Pastoral Theology and Church Government, Henry White, Professor of Theology, Dr. Edward Robinson, Professor of Oriental and Biblical Literature, Dr. Thomas H. Skinner, Professor of Sacred Rhetoric, Dr. I. S. Spencer, Professor of Biblical History and its connections, and Erskine Mason, Professor of Ecclesiastical History. George Bush was temporarily engaged to supply the place of Dr. Robinson.[3]

The institution was founded in January, 1836, and went into operation before the close of the year. It was opened for instruction December 5, 1836, and by its almost immediate success vindicated the wisdom of its founders. The first class of graduates (1839) numbered six; the second, twenty-one,—since which period there has been a steady and healthful advance, until the institution takes rank in character, as well as the number and standing of its graduates, with similar institutions its seniors in age. Its endowment has been increased until it stands upon a firm and permanent basis.

---

[1] Sprague, iv. 709.

[2] A very strenuous effort was made to secure the services of Professor Addison Alexander, of Princeton.

[3] American Quarterly Register.

CHAPTER XL.

THE GENERAL ASSEMBLIES OF 1837 AND 1838.

THE General Assembly of 1837 met in the Central Presbyterian Church in Philadelphia, on the 18th of May, and was opened with a sermon by the Rev. Dr. John Witherspoon from the words (1 Cor. i. 10, 11), "Now, I beseech you, brethren, by the name of our Lord Jesus Christ, that ye all speak the same thing, and that there be no divisions among you; but that ye be perfectly joined together in the same mind, and in the same judgment. For it hath been declared to me of you, my brethren, by them which are of the house of Chloe, that there are contentions among you."

The parties into which the Assembly was divided were ably represented. On one side were Rev. Messrs. Breckenridge, Plumer, Murray, and Drs. Green, Elliott, Alexander, Junkin, Baxter, Cuyler, Graham, and Witherspoon. On the other were Drs. Beman, Porter, of Catskill, McAuley, Peters, and Cleland, and Rev. Messrs. Duffield, Gilbert, Cleaveland, Dickinson, and Judge Jessup. The respective strength of the parties was declared in the vote for moderator, the candidate of the former receiving one hundred and thirty-seven votes, while the other candidate, Baxter Dickinson, received but one hundred and six. Thus encouraged, the memorialists were confident that they should now be enabled to adopt decisive measures.

The Committee on Bills and Overtures consisted of Messrs. Witherspoon, Alexander, Beman, Cleland, Murray, Todd, and Latta, with four elders. To them, along with overtures from Presbyteries on the same subject, the memorial was referred. The report of the committee recommended the adoption of the testimony of the memorialists concerning doctrines, as the testimony of the Assembly. Objection was made. The list of errors noted was fifteen in number. Some members thought that others should be added. One member proposed four others. Dr. Beman thought the list already too long. Of some mentioned in it he had never before heard. It was finally resolved to postpone the question for the present, and to take up the portion of the report bearing upon the Plan of Union.

This subject came before the Assembly on the afternoon of Monday, May 22. It was resolved, first, that between the two branches of the Church concerned in the Plan of Union, sentiments of mutual respect and esteem ought to be maintained, and that no reasonable effort should be spared to preserve a perfectly good understanding between them; secondly, that it was expedient to continue the plan of friendly intercourse between them as it then existed; but, thirdly, that as the Plan of Union adopted for the new settlements in 1801 was originally an unconstitutional act on the part of the Assembly,—these important rules having never been submitted to the Presbyteries,—and as they were totally destitute of authority as proceeding from the General Association of Connecticut, which is vested with no power to legislate in such cases, and especially to enact laws to regulate churches not within her limits, and as much confusion and irregularity have arisen from this unnatural and unconstitutional system of union, therefore it is resolved that "the act of the Assembly of 1801, entitled a 'Plan of Union,' be, and the same is hereby, abrogated." The vote upon this important measure, which tested the relative strength of the parties in the Assembly, stood one hundred and forty-three to one hundred and ten.

Thus was the Plan of Union abrogated as "unnatural and unconstitutional." Its friends naturally felt aggrieved. It had been, they said, universally approved and unquestioned for a quarter of a century. Its character —as by practice and continued recognition the common law of the Church — was disregarded, while its results in building up churches and preserving harmony in the frontier settlements procured for it scarcely a kindly word from the party of the memorialists. The assent of the other contracting party—the General Association of Connecticut — was not even asked, or proposed to be sought. The abrogation, therefore, it was argued, bore the aspect of a breach of faith, and as such might justly be regarded as void and of no effect. It was, moreover, in substance, recommended by the memorial of a body unknown to the Presbyterian Church and unrecognized in its constitution, members of which formed a majority of the committee who reported in its favor. These and other objections were embodied in a protest which received the signature of one hundred and three members of the Assembly.

From the first, none could doubt that the fate of "The Plan" was sealed. Its abrogation had been resolved upon, and there was to be no unnecessary delay. By postponement for the action of another Assembly, the favorable moment for carrying out the views of the memorialists might be lost, and lost forever. Dr. Green said the plan was well designed, but had done all the good it ever would, and was not working well. Dr. Alexander declared that it had been originally adopted as a temporary expedient, but it was working ill and ought no longer to be tolerated. Dr. Junkin expressed his apprehension of the foreign and un-Presbyterian element which it introduced into the judicatories of the Church. On the other hand, some voices were heard in its favor. Dr. McAuley said that he had been a missionary as early as 1799, and had seen the operation of the plan in the new settlements. Its influence had been good; and he could not call it unwise or unnatural, for it had sprung from the necessities of the times. He should not be so much opposed to the resolution for its abrogation if time (say three years) was given to the churches to change their forms. Others, who admitted that the plan was extra-constitutional, pleaded in its favor and expressed apprehension of the results of its abrogation. It was pronounced a virtual division of the Church and as such to have been designed. The principal speakers on opposite sides were Rev. William S. Plumer and Dr. Absalom Peters; and the discussion was continued with much ability till Tuesday afternoon.

Meanwhile, the other portion of the report of the committee, presenting the list of doctrinal errors to be condemned, was from time to time postponed. Those who favored its adoption were apprehensive lest, in the course of discussion, it should be overladen with amendments, and the list become so enlarged as to lose all point or pertinency. By their own votes, therefore, it was still kept back. Other measures were to be first tried.

On Thursday afternoon, resolutions were offered by Mr. Plumer to the effect that "such inferior judicatories as are charged by common fame with irregularities" be cited to the bar of the next Assembly; that a special committee be appointed to ascertain these and digest a suitable plan of procedure; and that the report of this committee be made "as soon as practicable." A third resolution, on the ground that such citation was the commencement of process, proposed that the members of the aforesaid judicatories be excluded from a seat in the next Assembly till their case should be decided.

The discussion of the resolutions continued to the

close of Thursday and through the greater part of the following day. After Mr. Plumer had closed his argument in their support, he was answered by Judge Jessup, who opposed the resolutions as unconstitutional. The right to arraign belonged to the judicatory next above the body charged. R. J. Breckenridge claimed this as an admission that Synods might be arraigned, and, of course, disciplined; and on whom could the effect fall but on Presbyteries and churches? The Assembly might appoint committees to visit every Presbytery, arraign unsound members, and on appeal bring them to its bar. The process might be difficult, indeed; but the straight way was the safe way. Rev. Elipha White did not concede the right of the Assembly to cite a Synod. It could have power over ministers only in cases regularly brought before it by appeal. The resolutions tended to consolidation in the General Assembly, robbing Synods and Presbyteries of their rights.

Dr. Beman spoke of the impracticability of carrying out the resolutions. It would be impossible, according to the book of discipline, and if attempted would excite strong resistance in Presbyteries and churches. Dr. Baxter favored the resolutions as a basis for subsequent action. Presbyterians and Congregationalists could not live together in peace, and they ought to separate. Each denomination would thus be more efficient. Mr. Dickinson objected to the indefiniteness of the resolutions. The Assembly had not the facts on which to base its action. The plan proposed was unconstitutional. The severest discipline was proposed before taking the preliminary steps, and odium was cast on one-half of the Presbyterian Church. Mr. Plumer and Dr. McAuley, on opposite sides, closed the discussion, and the vote on the resolutions showed a wavering in the hitherto firm phalanx of the majority. It stood one hundred and twenty-eight ayes to one hundred and twenty-two nays. It was a critical moment. The victory had been gained, but with a relative loss which showed that scrupulous consciences could not be bound by the policy of the already-reduced majority. It was natural that apprehension should be felt of the issue. As soon as the debate had closed, Mr. Breckenridge gave notice that he should bring in a resolution for the voluntary division of the Church. He is said to have done it in consequence of a proposition submitted to him by Dr. Peters.

It was, indeed, evident to both parties that the prospect of continued harmony in the same body had entirely vanished, and it was not unnatural that the minority—with the resolutions just passed, held *in terrorem* over their heads, and with the prospective triumph which would thus be assured to their opponents in the next Assembly—should be far from indisposed to take into consideration the plan of a voluntary division, offered them by a half-dismayed majority. On Saturday morning the resolution of Mr. Breckenridge was adopted, and a committee of ten—five members from each side of the house—was appointed to consider it and digest a plan for carrying it out. The committee consisted of Messrs. Breckenridge, Alexander, Cuyler, Witherspoon, and Ewing on one side, and Messrs. Beman, McAuley, Peters, Dickinson, and Jessup on the other. This committee met for consultation from time to time until Tuesday morning (May 30), when their chairman reported that they were unable to agree and asked to be discharged. Each portion of the committee, however, made a separate report, accompanied by the papers containing the propositions which had been mutually exchanged.

In these papers the insurmountable difficulties of a voluntary division are distinctly brought out. The questions of the true succession of the General Assembly, the power of the Assembly to take the initiatory steps as proposed, and the propriety of submitting the matter to the Presbyteries, presented points on which agreement was impossible; while the report of the committee representing the minority of the Assembly expressed the conviction that the members of *this* Assembly, uninstructed by the Presbyteries, had neither a constitutional nor moral right to adopt a plan for the division of the Church,—a plan which might result in evils greater than those it proposed to remove.

In these circumstances, it only remained that the committee be discharged. This was accordingly done, and the whole subject was laid upon the table by a vote of one hundred and thirty-eight ayes to one hundred and seven nays. But the purpose to effect a division of the Church, although the committee had not been able to agree, was not abandoned by the majority. They reaffirmed the action of the Assembly of 1835, asserting the constitutional right of every Presbytery to examine all seeking a connection with them, and, moreover, enjoined such examination. Meanwhile, the difficulties of the method proposed for the citation of inferior judicatories—as eloquently set forth by Dr. Beman—had produced a profound impression. Dr. Baxter was astounded and distressed. He saw more distinctly than many others the inextricable confusion in which the next Assembly would be sure to be involved. If a Presbytery was cited, it would be sustained by its Synod; if a Synod, it would be defended by its Presbyteries. The Gordian knot could not be untied. It must be cut. The sagacity of Dr. Baxter enabled him to perceive this, and he was led to seek for some principle which would render plausible, if not justifiable, a more summary method. This principle he persuaded himself he had discovered in the proposition that "an unconstitutional law involves the unconstitutionality of all that is done under it."[1] It was the principle which, in the political history of the country, involved the repeal of the Missouri Compromise and its inferential results. Dr. Baxter blinded himself to its remote consequences. He failed to perceive that it reached—if applicable at all—far beyond the bodies which he sought to arraign or exclude from the Church; or perhaps he was content to apply it just so far as might appear expedient.

The principle was endorsed by Mr. Plumer and adopted as his own. As such he embodied it in a resolution which he offered (Tuesday morning, May 30) to the

---

[1] The reference to the Yazoo claims, made in this connection, was a most unfortunate one. It was found in the course of the discussion that their history furnished no proper analogy to the case in hand, except on a single point, in which it went directly against those who cited it. The innocent parties, who had obtained possession second-hand, were left unmolested. The point, moreover, on which Dr. Baxter relied—that if a law was unconstitutional, all that was done under it was likewise unconstitutional—was replied to by Dr. Peters. Without referring to civil parallels, like the Missouri Compromise, for instance, under which State after State was received into the Union, and not ejected on its repeal, it suffices to note the positions taken in the Yazoo case by Chief-Justice Marshall, as cited by Dr. Peters. The Chief-Justice said, "The question whether a law be void for its repugnancy to the Constitution is, at all times, a question of much delicacy, which ought seldom, if ever, to be decided in the affirmative in a doubtful case. . . . For a party to pronounce its own deed invalid, *whatever cause* may be assigned for its invalidity, must be considered as a mere act of power, which must find its vindication in a train of reasoning not often heard in courts of justice. . . . If an act be done under a law, a succeeding Legislature cannot undo it. The past cannot be recalled by the most absolute power. . . . Where a law is in its nature a contract, where absolute rights have vested under that contract, a repeal of the law cannot divest these rights; and the act of annulling them, if legitimate, is rendered so by a power applicable to the case of every individual in the community."

Assembly immediately after the Committee on Division had been discharged. This resolution was to the effect "that, by the operation of the abrogation of the Plan of Union of 1801, the Synod of the Western Reserve is, and is hereby declared to be, no longer a part of the Presbyterian Church of the United States of America." This was the position to which the majority had at last been driven. If this could be maintained, if the majority could be rallied unitedly to its support, their triumph was sure.

But the resolution was not offered unadvisedly or without precautions. On the night preceding the day on which the resolution was offered, the members of the convention met. Propositions were made and silent votes were given; but no speeches were made. The feeling and interest of the occasion were intense. It was resolved, in order to prevent confusion or the risk of disagreement or surprise, that the subjects to be brought before the Assembly should first be agreed upon in convention,—that the propositions agreed upon should be presented by some one known to all. The principle set forth by Dr. Baxter was accepted and endorsed. Five persons were named, one of whom should bring it in a practical form before the Assembly. It was resolved that, in case the Committee on Division could not agree on some acceptable proposition, the principle should be applied in the first instance to the Western Reserve Synod.

The way having thus been prepared, the resolution was offered. Dr. Baxter rose to defend the principle it involved, although few perhaps knew that it was the product of his own subtle brain. He cited the Yazoo claims in Georgia in illustration of it,—unaware, probably, of the real facts of the case or the principles laid down by Chief-Justice Marshall. He applied it to the case of the Western Reserve Synod. His logic left all the churches exposed indiscriminately to the sure doom of excision. They all had but "one neck." As he proceeded, he revealed the fact that his reasonings derived their force from the apprehended necessity of a separation.

He was followed by Judge Jessup, who denied the power of the Assembly to cut off the Synod. Such a measure was to be deprecated, as unconstitutional and, moreover, unnecessary. Dr. McAuley continued the discussion, portraying with deep feeling and at times with much pathos the lamentable bearings of such a measure as the one proposed. The act, he said, was an attempt at dissolving churches, and unclothing ministers blessed of God. Other remedies for the evils complained of might surely be devised, and remedies more accordant with justice and prudence. Mr. Plumer replied, denying that the churches were dissolved or the office of the ministry interfered with. If there were true Presbyterian churches in the region, they would come out and unite with the Presbyterian Church on the true principle, while others would follow their predilections.

Mr. Cleaveland followed. His earnest desire, he said, was for peace. Retaining the floor upon the adjournment of the Assembly, he concluded his speech on the following morning, closing with a motion to postpone the resolution in order to take up the question of separation in a constitutional and amicable way. Dr. Junkin opposed postponement, and advocated speedy separation. The overwhelming majority of the churches in the obnoxious Synod, he declared, were not Presbyterian. This was disputed by members of the Synod. The discussion was continued by Dr. Peters, and on the following day by Judge Jessup, S. C. Anderson, and Mr. Ewing. A general call was at length made for the previous question, when the motion to postpone was lost and the main question was put. By a vote of one hundred and thirty-two ayes to one hundred and five nays, the Western Reserve Synod was declared not to be a part of the Presbyterian Church in the United States.[1]

The Rubicon was now crossed. The decisive principle had been adopted, and all that remained was simply a matter of detail. The majority were sure of their ground. They proceeded to perfect their work with coolness and deliberation. On Friday afternoon a resolution was passed "affirming that the organization and operations of the so-called American Home Missionary Society and American Education Society, and its branches of whatever name, are exceedingly injurious to the peace and purity of the Presbyterian Church. We recommend, therefore, that they cease to operate within any of our churches." Upon this resolution the vote stood one hundred and twenty-four yeas to eighty-six nays.

On Saturday morning, the resolution proposing to exscind the Synods of Utica, Geneva, and Genesee in the same manner as the Western Reserve Synod had been exscinded, was brought forward. Judge Jessup proposed a substitute requiring investigation and citation. Discussion arose; and it was not till Monday afternoon that the question could be taken. It was then determined by a vote of one hundred and fifteen ayes to eighty-eight nays, and the obnoxious Synods were "declared to be out of the ecclesiastical connection of the Presbyterian Church" and "not in form or in fact an integral portion of said Church." Further resolutions were adopted, declaring "the gross disorders" that had prevailed in the Synods, disclaiming any dis-

[1] The "Princeton Review," while asserting the *right* of the Assembly to take such action, very significantly adds, "Whether wisely or unwisely, it is not for us to say."

position to disturb the harmony of churches and the standing of ministers, and directing churches and ministers Presbyterian in doctrine and order to apply for admission to Presbyteries most conveniently located.

Little now remained to complete—so far as the occasion would allow—the task which the majority had resolved to accomplish. The Third Presbytery of Philadelphia, of which Mr. Barnes was a member, was regarded as especially obnoxious; and with this the Presbytery of Wilmington was also classed. On the afternoon of Tuesday (June 7) a resolution was offered by R. J. Breckinridge that these two Presbyteries be dissolved,—the constituent members and churches to apply to neighboring bodies to be received, as in the case of ministers and churches in the exscinded Synods. Wilmington Presbytery was finally omitted from the resolution; but in the case of Philadelphia Third there was no hesitation or scruple as to the course to be pursued. It was declared to be dissolved, and it was left for its members to seek connection with some other body. Some of them had been born and educated in the Presbyterian Church, and regarded the act by which they seemed to be disinherited, as one of peculiar hardship. But in the judgment of the Assembly, the continued existence of the Presbytery to which they belonged was inconsistent with the peace of the Church. It ceased of course to be any longer represented in the Assembly.

No further obstruction now remained to the perfecting of those measures which had been so strenuously opposed by the party represented by the minority of the Assembly. The Board of Foreign Missions was established, almost without discussion. The Presbyteries were enjoined strictness in exercising discipline, and the errors in doctrine and practice, as drawn up by the memorialists, were condemned. Meanwhile, the various parties affected by the action of the Assembly prepared and presented protests against the proceedings. In these protests the injustice of the measures adopted was set forth, as well as the consequences to which they would legitimately lead. The Assembly was declared to have been dismembered by its own act. Members, without citation, trial, or any notice to the Presbyteries which they represented, were summarily excluded from the Assembly. This was the case not only with those who came from Presbyteries representing churches formed on the *accommodation* plan, but from bodies organized by the Synod of Pittsburg and as sound as that Synod itself. Nearly the whole Assembly might have been unseated by a consistent and thorough application of the principles it had adopted. It was utterly impossible to say how far the imputed mischief had spread. It was impossible to say how far the legislation and the very constitution of successive Assemblies had been vitiated by a plan "projected and brought into operation by some of the wisest and best men the Presbyterian Church has ever known." The poison—if such it was—had for thirty-six years been rankling through the frame; and it was difficult to say where that drop of blood was to be found which had not something of the virus in it. In the shape of ecclesiastical legislation it pervaded the minutes of the Assembly and the records of Presbyteries and Synods. In the form of wealth largely and freely given it was to be met in the endowments and scholarships of colleges and theological seminaries. It was in Princeton, in Alleghany, in Union, and beyond the mountains, in Tennessee. It had been assimilated, as food to the body, through the whole system. Even the brick and mortar of many a sacred edifice might have almost cried out with remonstrance against that tone of intolerance which found expression within its walls. To attempt to discriminate that which in the view of the majority was unsound, and that also which must therefore be admitted to be vitiated by such unsoundness, was like proposing to determine what parts of the head, heart, members, and vital currents, and even bones and sinews, should be dispensed with.

Such an attempt was possible indeed only, when the action was based no longer on doctrinal heresies, but simply on the unconstitutionality of the Plan of Union. No wonder the Assembly should find it "painful," as they confess, "to declare bodies in which were brethren whose piety we cannot question, and whose activity in extending the visible Church we must regard with approbation, to be no longer connected with the body." "We could not hope they would walk together in peace with us," was the apology offered,—an apology that must be judged in view of the necessity that called it forth.

The task of the Assembly was completed by the adoption, in substance, of the memorial of the convention above mentioned. The resolutions condemning doctrinal errors were passed by an overwhelming majority. With slight modifications, they would have received nearly, if not quite, unanimous support. A protest, headed by the name of George Duffield and signed by fourteen others, was offered, in which the objectionable features of the resolutions were reviewed, and the "error" and the "true doctrine" were placed side by side, while other doctrinal errors were specified against which the Assembly had *not* borne testimony. The utter impropriety of asserting in the resolutions that the doctrinal errors specified were rife throughout the Church was pointed out; and the injustice of imputing them to the minority as a body was inferred from the fact that the "gentlemen of Princeton" had distinctly declared their conviction that they were not held by one-tenth part of the ministers of the Church.

But the "gentlemen of Princeton" were no longer

undecided. They remained and acted with the Assembly. They had done what was in their power to allay the agitation of the Church. They had, as we have seen, opposed the representations sent abroad to excite suspicion of doctrinal unsoundness when such unsoundness did not exist. They had brought down upon themselves the censure of those into whose counsels they could not enter. They had forced Dr. Green to say he "would do them good against their will." But they could neither arrest the action of the Assembly nor stay the division that had become inevitable. They found themselves forced to accept the situation, and by their votes the decisive measures of the majority were sustained.

The exscinding act took a larger portion of the Church by surprise. The result was such as few could have anticipated. The very statement of it was startling. Four Synods and nearly thirty Presbyteries, with a church membership far greater than that of the entire Church at the time the Plan of Union was formed, were declared no longer a part of the Presbyterian Church. A provision almost coeval with the Constitution, and indeed by many regarded as equally sacred, that had been recognized as the law of the Church for more than a generation, and to which hundreds of churches had looked as their charter of right, was summarily set aside. All this was obvious enough.[1] It was not equally obvious how incongruous the Plan of Union was with the Presbyterian system, and what infelicities of organization and representation, as well as conflicts of policy, its continued operation was sure to engender.

---

[1] The impression made by the acts of the Assembly upon the minds of not a few who were theologically in sympathy with Princeton and with the majority, may be inferred from the language of the venerable Dr. Woods, of Andover. He said: "When I heard of them, I was grieved and astonished, and constrained to ask whether there is any thing in the Bible, or in the Constitution of the Presbyterian Church, or in the laws of any Protestant nation,

Those opposed to the action of the Assembly insisted that it contravened the spirit of the Constitution. They could discover that spirit in the representations made to Suffolk Presbytery to overcome its reluctance to unite with the Assembly. There was an express understanding that no rigid ecclesiasticism was to be introduced or predominate. The adhesion of other bodies was based on the same understanding.

On the other hand, there can be no question that a strict construction of the Constitution was inconsistent with the Plan of Union. This was one of the strong points maintained by the majority of the Assembly. The Constitution, as such, knew nothing of committee-men or churches constituted without elders or session. Their introduction had, to a certain extent, vitiated the practical working of the Constitution. It had made the Presbyterian Church a mongrel body. It had introduced foreign and incongruous elements, and the ascendency of these elements tended to revolutionize the Church. This difficulty was not easily to be overcome. Indeed, to meet it, there seemed to many to be no alternative short of a counter-revolution, and the exscinding measures were consequently justified on the ground of necessity.

But, on the other hand, when these measures were adopted, and synods, churches and ministers were cut off from the Church without legal process or trial, and simply by a sum-

---

which can warrant such proceedings." He thought the majority when they came to reflect upon their course would regret it; "for they had neglected the New Testament rule, which requires ministers and Christians to do to others as they would that others should do to them, and to conduct themselves with all meekness and gentleness, forbearing one another, and doing all things with love." This language is historically significant as indicating the views of many New England Congregationalists. Dr. Woods was the intimate friend of the professors at Princeton, and of several others who were prominent leaders in urging forward the excision.

mary act, the question was raised, What constitutional security for the future could the Synods that as yet were spared continue to claim? Five of these—Albany, New Jersey, Michigan, Cincinnati and Illinois—had been directed by the Assembly to take like special order on the subject of errors in doctrine and church order, and report in writing to the next Assembly. Why might not these be subjected to the same fate as the four that already had been cut off? If the Assembly might continue the exercise of such powers as it had already assumed, if it might declare whole Synods no longer in connection with the Church; where was this to end? On these grounds the minority regarded the policy now initiated as unconstitutional and revolutionary. Such was the relative position, and such the views, of the two parties in the Assembly, now that division had been precipitated. Neither could surrender its convictions or recede from its claims.

---

[1] Those who asserted the unconstitutionality of the exscinding acts supported their views by reference to the decision of Chief Justice Marshall in the case of the Yazoo claims, already referred to, and also by the opinions of such men as Hon. George Wood, who stood for years at the head of the New York bar, Hon. S. M. Hopkins, eminent alike as a lawyer and a judge, and Chancellor Kent. It may not be out of place to note some of the positions taken by Mr. Wood, representing as they did the views of many.

Mr. Wood says, "I see nothing in the Constitution which prohibits a union with other denominations of Christians in a modified form." It might be said the Plan of Union should have been submitted to the Presbyteries; but "long-established usage must be considered as settling that question." Yet the revision of the Constitution in 1821 left the Plan of Union untouched, and so it had remained; for it could not be supposed that the guardians of the Constitution "could have sunk into a profound sleep for six-and-thirty years." "Upon the whole, I consider these proceedings as inoperative and void, and I think they will be so declared, if any question about property or right should arise out of them, by our legal tribunals."

Judge Hopkins held that the argument for the exscinding mea-

With the causes which conspired to bring things into the shape which they had now assumed, and which have been already enumerated, there are some others which deserve our notice. It had for some time been felt that the General Assembly had become too large and unwieldy for wise deliberation. A plan for a geographical division of the Church so as to form two Assemblies had, some years previously, been agitated at the West. It had been overtured to the Assembly, but by them rejected. In other forms the project for reducing the numbers of the Assembly was entertained. In 1831 a proposition was submitted, and discussed at considerable length, that the opinion of

---

sures proved too much. "If the votes of unconstitutional delegates vitiate the proceedings of Synods and Presbyteries, they would on the same ground vitiate those of the Assembly itself. I believe that it has even been alleged that such delegates have had seats in the Assembly; and in this case, and upon this ground, the Assembly itself would thenceforward have become illegal, possessing no higher rightful existence than it has allowed to the exscinded judicatories."

But "the Synods of Genesee and Geneva were constituent parts of the Presbyterian Church" when the Constitution was revised. They were represented in the Assembly of that year. This it was inferred would give them legal status in the Church.

Judge Kent held that "the contracting parties [in the Plan of 1801] were competent to make it," that no clause in the Constitution prohibited the General Assembly from doing what they did; that acquiescence in the Plan sanctioned it, on the principle, *Qui tacet, consentire videtur; qui potest et debet vetare, et non vetat, jubet;* that the abrogation of the Plan "could not affect in any degree the rights and privileges of the churches, Presbyteries, and Synods formed, organized, and governed more or less under that compact;" that "the repeal of a grant or the recall of a power will not and cannot invalidate acts done and rights acquired under it, provided the grant or power did not originate in fraud;" that nothing "could be more mischievous than the principle assumed in the exscinding resolution, if carried out to its practical consequences;" and that the resolution itself "was irregular, illegal, and void."

the Presbyteries should be taken on the expediency of changing the constitutional plan of electing commissioners to the General Assembly,—transferring the choice of commissioners from the Presbyteries to the Synods. The proposition was rejected by the majority; but the large number of commissioners was felt by the party then in the minority to be a great evil.[1]

The proceedings of the Assembly, in the divided

[1] In justice to many of those who urged forward the exscinding measures, it should be stated that they were not without some grave occasions for complaint. The refusal of the Assembly of 1836 to endorse the action of the committee of the previous year, by whom the Foreign Missionary Society of the Pittsburg Synod had been transferred to the Assembly, was a sore provocation, not only to those directly concerned, but to many who saw in it an attempt, as they believed, to place the policy of the Church under the control of voluntary societies which no organized or responsible body could call to account. In the light of history, it seems not improbable that a fair representation of the entire Church might have given a majority in favor of the transfer. But a full representation, especially of the Western churches, could not be secured at any meeting held at Philadelphia. The Synod of Pittsburg felt deeply aggrieved on this account. In their minutes (1831) will be found statistics which are quite significant. Dividing the Church by a line bounding the Synod of Philadelphia on the south, and running directly north of its western extremity, it was found that the twenty-seven Presbyteries of the East and North had in the Assembly of 1821 twenty-eight elders, while the remaining thirty-five had but three. In 1825 the former had thirty-eight Presbyteries and thirty-five elders, the latter forty-three Presbyteries and one elder. In 1828 the first had forty Presbyteries and thirty-four elders, the latter fifty Presbyteries and four elders. In 1831 the first had forty-four Presbyteries and fifty-one elders, the latter sixty Presbyteries and fifteen elders.

It will readily be perceived that where from thirty to forty members of the Assembly were drawn annually from that portion of the Church most in sympathy with voluntary societies, while the other portion was but half represented, the proceedings of the majority would naturally be regarded in many cases as oppressive, and in some as intolerable.

state of parties, led many good men to fear and question the character of the influence exerted by it upon the Church at large. Quite a number, as a prudential measure alone, leaned toward a division.

But at this juncture the subject of slavery had assumed an unprecedented importance. The agitation of it had not, indeed, originated with the North. Several of the Ohio ministers had removed from Carolina to that State on account of slavery; and the most earnest discussions of the matter for several years had been south of Mason and Dixon's line.

In Kentucky especially, a decided anti-slavery sentiment had from an early period manifested itself in connection with the Presbyterian Church. "Father" Rice, while a member of the convention that framed the State Constitution, endeavored to secure the insertion of some provision for the ultimate emancipation of slaves, and, in a pamphlet on the subject which issued from his pen —embodying his speech in the convention—in 1792, undertook to answer objections, especially those drawn from the supposed sanction of the Scriptures and the silence of the apostles. In 1794 the Presbytery of Transylvania passed resolutions to the effect that slaves should be taught to read the Scriptures and be prepared for freedom. In 1796 their views on the general subject were again freely expressed. In the following years attention was still largely directed to questions bearing upon the character of slavery; and in 1800 the West Lexington Presbytery, in their letter to the Synod of Virginia, speak of slavery as "a subject likely to occasion much trouble and division in the churches in this country." In 1823 the claims of the Colonization Society were favorably entertained, and in 1825 the Synod directed ministers to pay more attention to the religious instruction of slaves.

At this latter period the question of slavery attracted

more attention at the South than at the North. In 1826, of the one hundred and one anti-slavery societies in the country, less than one-fourth were in the Northern States. There were forty-one in North Carolina, twenty-three in Tennessee, six in Kentucky, and many in Virginia. More than forty of these organizations had been established at the South within the two preceding years.[1]

In 1833 the Synod of Kentucky discussed for two days, with much spirit, an overture which declared slavery, as existing within its bounds, a great moral evil and inconsistent with the word of God. The Synod were much divided upon the question, and the whole subject was indefinitely postponed; and, when it was postponed, R. J. Breckinridge left the house, saying, "Since God has forsaken the Synod of Kentucky, Robert J Breckinridge will forsake it too."[2] In the following year it was again introduced. By an overwhelming majority of fifty-six to eight, a committee of ten was appointed to prepare a plan for the instruction and future emancipation of slaves. Of this committee, Judge Green, President Young, Drs. Cunningham, Stuart, Hall, and W. L. Breckinridge were members. The proposed plan was published by the committee in the following year, and took strong ground in favor of gradual emancipation. "It fearlessly recounted the evils of slavery: its degrading influence; its dooming thousands to helpless ignorance; its depriving them, in a great measure, of the privileges of the gospel; its licensing cruelty; its producing licentiousness among the slaves; its demoralizing effect upon whites as well as blacks; and its drawing down the vengeance of Heaven."[3]

No formal action upon the plan was taken by the

---

[1] Christian Advocate, 1826, p. 93.

[2] Testimony of a member of Synod.

[3] Davidson's Kentucky, p. 339.

Synod. The propositions of the committee were in advance of public sentiment. In connection with the exasperation produced by "Northern aggressions," loading the mails with publications styled "inflammatory," a reaction was inevitable. The prospect of emancipation became less hopeful. Slave laws were made more stringent. The religious meetings of the blacks were broken up or interrupted, and their Sabbath-schools dispersed.[1]

But already the agitation had commenced at the North. Here, too, societies were formed, less discreet perhaps than they should have been. For several successive years the subject had been brought before the Assembly, and not a little warmth of feeling had been elicited by the discussions. Although the strong anti-slavery feeling of the Northern members was not limited to either party, it was most deeply shared by those who were classed as hostile to a rigid ecclesiastical system and in favor of voluntary boards. This at least was the full belief of many of the leading minds in the Southern churches, as manifested in word and act. From that direction the demand was loud for division, especially after the discussions in the Assembly of 1836.[2] A cor-

[1] In 1837 the question of a convention to amend the Constitution so as to provide for gradual emancipation, before the people, was defeated, in consequence of excitement produced by abolition publications scattered through the State, as was supposed by J. G. Birney, a Kentuckian then residing in New York and connected with an abolition paper.—F.

[2] The subject of slavery was brought to the attention of the Assembly of 1836 by the report of a committee—Drs. Miller, Beman, and Hays, and Rev. Messrs. James H. Dickey and J. Witherspoon—appointed for the purpose by the Assembly of the preceding year on an overture based on memorials and petitions from individuals and two Presbyteries. The majority report was brief, and, in substance, declined any action on the subject. The minority report, by Mr. Dickey, was quite extended, and proposed certain resolutions

respondent of the "Southern Religious Telegraph," a few days after the adjournment of the body,—of which he had been a member,—wrote, "I hope that such another Assembly will never meet but once again, and then only with full and delegated powers amicably to separate." The comment of the editor was, "A crisis has come: if there can be no compromise, division must be tried." The Presbytery of Concord, N.C., said, "Rather than surrender the truth, or perpetuate the present distracting agitation, we shall feel bound to submit to a division of the Church." The Presbytery of South Carolina resolved, "The parties ought to separate." The Synod of Virginia declared, "One thing which presses with peculiar force on the Presbyterian Church in the South is the spirit of *abolition*." It declared that the attempt then making on the subject was "changing the Constitution of our Church."

By Charleston Union Presbytery the position was taken (November, 1836), and it was subsequently endorsed in substance by the Synod, "that as the relation of master and slave is a civil institution, it is one on

---

strongly opposed to slavery. Pending the earnest discussion which ensued, a substitute was offered which, on the ground that slavery was recognized in the Old and New Testament, proposed a resolution to the effect that "the Assembly have no authority to assume or exercise jurisdiction in regard to the existence of slavery." This was superseded—after some discussion—by a motion of indefinite postponement, based on the fact that no church judicatory had any right by its own authority to make laws to bind the conscience, and on the fact that the limited time of the Assembly would not allow of the deliberation necessary to a judicious decision. The motion for postponement was by Dr. Hays, of Virginia, and was carried by one hundred and fifty-six yeas to eighty-seven nays. Twenty-eight members protested against the decision.

In the course of the convention-discussions of 1837, R. J. Breckinridge, referring to slavery, remarked that it was the opinion of many brethren that the testimony of 1818 went too far.

which the Church has no power to legislate."[1] As a general thing, the Southern churches gave their preference to Ecclesiastical Boards, and in the case of Mr. Barnes a respectable minority might be regarded as in sympathy with him. But on the subject of slavery there was but one sentiment. The project was subsequently agitated, especially in the South Carolina Synod, of forming an independent Southern General Assembly and withdrawing altogether from connection with the North. This was strenuously and successfully opposed by those who sympathized with Ecclesiastical Boards and the prosecution against Dr. Beecher and Mr. Barnes. On the subject of slavery they felt that the party represented by the memorialists might be trusted. It was not till the obnoxious Synods were exscinded in 1837 that the South became really divided within itself. It was then seen that some who were most strenuous and outspoken in their condemnation of the exscinding acts were foremost in repudiating and condemning the anti-slavery agitation. On the other hand the importance of anti-slavery manifestos was, in the view of the memorialists and their friends, entirely overshadowed by that of the question of the doctrinal soundness of the Church. Toward the close of the sessions of the convention (1837), Dr. Wilson, of Cincinnati, was asked if he was not going to bring up the subject of slavery. He hesitated in reply. Something of the kind, he was told, was expected of him from his previous declarations and expressed opinions. "I believe," he answered, "that I shall let the Southern brethren manage their own concerns in their own way: they will probably take care of them the best."[2] The most zealous anti-

[1] The Late Charleston Union Presbytery. The Occasion of its Division fairly stated, and the Action of the Presbytery fully justified. By the Rev. Thomas Smyth.

[2] Foote's Sketches of Virginia, Second Series, 520.

slavery men of the North felt, like Dr. Wilson, that in order to secure the triumph of the memorialists a compromise, understood if not expressed, must be made. It was not an agreeable thing, indeed, but it had become a necessity. It is idle, perhaps, to speculate upon the results that would have followed the attempt to introduce into the memorial the views of Northern members of the convention. Undoubtedly it would have rent the convention in sunder, and not improbably might have led to the organization of a Southern Assembly. But in such a case the memorialists of the North would have lost Southern sympathy and the Southern alliance. They would, doubtless, have been left in a hopeless minority, and have been compelled to withdraw and organize by themselves. The terms of their final triumph were defined by the necessity of the case. The South held in its hands the casting vote. To secure this, it was clearly understood that the slavery question was no longer to be allowed to disturb the Assembly. In justice, however, to a very large portion of the Church at the North, it should be said that, repelled by the fanatical zeal of "abolitionism," and the violent utterances of its representatives, they discountenanced what they regarded as a pernicious agitation in the ecclesiastical as well as civil sphere.[1]

---

[1] The Pastoral and the Circular Letter of the Assembly of 1837 are mainly devoted to a vindication of the exscinding acts. It is admitted that the "Plan of Union" was brought into operation by some of the wisest and best men the Presbyterian Church has ever known. Yet it is pronounced "most unnatural," unconstitutional, and "deeply injurious." It is declared that when the Assembly met it was "manifest that a division of the Church was the most desirable object that could be effected;" that till "the parties are separated and formed into different denominations," there was no ground to hope that contention would cease.

Yet "narrow party zeal" was disclaimed, and it was confessed "a

The Assembly of 1838 met in the Seventh Presbyterian Church in the city of Philadelphia, on the 17th of May. The first question before it was the manner in which it should be constituted. Were the exscinding acts of the previous year, which denied the right of representation to nearly thirty Presbyteries, to be considered constitutional and valid? Was the roll to be made up in accordance with these acts? Each party, of course, was tenacious of its own views, but a practical answer was demanded, and could no longer be deferred.

The moderator, at the close of the preliminary exercises, called upon the permanent clerk to report the roll. Rev. Dr. William Patton, of the Third Presbytery of New York, rose and asked leave to offer certain resolutions which he held in his hand. The moderator declared the request as out of order at this time, and Dr. Patton appealed from the decision. The appeal was declared out of order. Dr. Patton stated that the resolutions related to the formation of the roll, and began to read them, but was called to order, and took his seat.

The permanent clerk, from the standing Committee

---

painful duty" to cut off the Synods. The spirit of the Assembly is manifest in its denunciation of the "ever restless spirit of radicalism manifest both in the Church and the State." This fanaticism had been displayed in connection with "revivals of religion, temperance, and the rights of man."

These revivals had prevailed largely in the region of the obnoxious Synods, and the danger of their rapidly-growing influence impelled to prompt action on the part of the majority. They confessed that if action was longer delayed their case was hopeless. The "fanaticism" in connection with the temperance cause which the Assembly denounced was scarcely worthy of mention, except as an introduction to fanaticism concerning "the rights of man." By a vote of ninety-three to twenty-eight, the subject of slavery, which had again been brought up, was laid upon the table. This disposed of several overtures, and was not without effect in securing the sympathies of the Southern churches.

of Commissions, reported the roll. It was made out in accordance with the exscinding acts of the last Assembly. The moderator then rose, and stated that if there were any commissioners present from the Presbyteries belonging to the Presbyterian Church in the United States of America, whose names had not been enrolled, then was the time for presenting their commissions.

Dr. Erskine Mason, of the Third Presbytery of New York, rose to offer a resolution "to complete the roll" by adding the names of certain commissioners who had offered their commissions to the clerks, which the latter had refused to receive. The moderator inquired if they were from Presbyteries belonging to the Assembly at the close of the sessions of last year. Dr. Mason replied that they were from Presbyteries belonging to the Synods of Utica, Geneva, Genesee, and the Western Reserve. The moderator stated the motion to be out of order at this time. Dr. Mason respectfully appealed from the decision, and the moderator declared the appeal out of order, repeating at the same time his call for commissions from Presbyteries in connection with the Assembly.

The Rev. Miles P. Squier, a member of the Presbytery of Geneva, then rose, and stated that he had a commission from the Presbytery of Geneva which had been presented to the clerks, who refused to receive it, and that he now offered it to the Assembly and claimed his right to his seat. The moderator inquired if the Presbytery of Geneva was within the bounds of the Synod of Geneva. Mr. Squier answered that it was. "Then we do not know you, sir," replied the moderator, and declared the application out of order.

Upon this Mr. John P. Cleaveland of the Presbytery of Detroit, rose, and, amid much interruption and many calls to order, proceeded to read a paper which he held in his hand. The contents of it were, substantially, that whereas the rights of certain commissioners have been violated in their being refused their seats as members of the General Assembly, and the moderator has refused to do his duty, it therefore becomes necessary to organize this General Assembly at this time and in this place in the most prompt manner, and with the least interruption practicable. To this they had been advised by counsel learned in the law, as a measure necessary to retain their rights in the Presbyterian Church.

He then moved that Dr. Beman, moderator of a previous Assembly, take the chair till another moderator should be chosen. The motion was carried by "a very loud *aye*." Dr. Beman took his station in the aisle of the church, and a motion was made that E. Mason and E. W. Gilbert be the clerks, which was agreed to. Dr. S. Fisher was in like manner elected moderator. The questions were moved and taken both affirmatively and negatively, with but few negative voices. It was then moved that the Assembly, as thus constituted, adjourn to the First Presbyterian Church. The motion was carried.

The members of the body then withdrew from the house. It was announced in a loud voice at the doors and in the body of the house that the Assembly had adjourned to the First Presbyterian (Mr. Barnes's) Church. In the judgment of those who had good opportunities of information, if the commissioners from the four exscinded Synods had voted in the Assembly previous to the adjournment, there would have been a majority of all the commissioners in favor of Dr. Mason's motion and opposed to the exscinding acts. Dr. Fisher estimated the relative strength of the two parties in such a case as one hundred and forty to one hundred and thirty-six.

The appeal from the moderator's decision was based on the unconstitutionality and injustice of the exscinding acts, and the right of the representatives of the exscinded Presbyteries to a seat on the floor of the Assembly. Here was the distinct issue.[1]

---

[1] A parallel to the manner in which the (N. S.) General Assembly of 1838 was organized was sought in the proceedings of the Twenty-Sixth Congress, which met Dec. 2, 1839. According to established usage, the clerk of the House of Representatives takes the chair till the organization of the body is completed. In accordance with this usage, the clerk commenced calling the roll, and proceeded with the States till he came to New Jersey, which he proposed to omit, as the seats of its members were contested, and by passing by whom the clerk's party would be left in the majority and would hold the balance of power in the organization. Here business came to a stand. The clerk would proceed only in his own way. On the fourth day John Q. Adams arose and stated the circumstances of the House. The action of the clerk barred all progress, and placed the House under his control. "But," said he, "we must organize." He referred to the report given by Mr. Jefferson of what was done by the Virginia Legislature when dissolved by Lord Dunmore. They adjourned to a tavern, constituted themselves a convention, and acted as the Legislature of the State or Colony. Thus, in another place than that from which they had been excluded, they formed themselves into a convention and acted in the name of the State. "I call upon you in the name of the people to organize. I call upon the House to set aside entirely his [the clerk's] decisions and act for themselves. I have no doubt of their power to do it." He proposed that the House choose itself a temporary clerk. He was asked by members, "How shall the question be put?" Raising his voice above the tumult, he replied, "I intend to put the question myself." The result was that the House was organized.

CHAPTER XLI.

RESULTS OF THE DIVISION.

THE course pursued by those who sympathized with the exscinded Synods in organizing the Assembly of 1838 had been a subject of careful deliberation. Shortly after the adjournment of the Assembly of the previous year a convention had been called to meet at Auburn (Aug. 17, 1837). It was numerously attended. Nearly one hundred and seventy persons, most of them commissioned as clerical or lay delegates from more than thirty Presbyteries, met to consider the circumstances of the Church and the policy to be adopted. Drs. Richards, Halsey, Hillyer, McAuley, Beecher, Cox, and others, were present. The convention were unanimous in declaring the exscinding acts unconstitutional, and in recommending the Synods and Presbyteries to retain their present organization. A committee of correspondence was appointed to confer on the state of the Church, and take measures to secure the objects for which the convention had been called.

Other committees were appointed,—one to draw up a statement of the reasons for the action of the convention, one to draft a letter to the judicatories and ministers of the Church in regard to its present unhappy condition, one on the rights of membership in the Presbyterian Church and the manner in which they are guaranteed or forfeited, one on a statement of facts in regard to the formation and character of the churches within the bounds of the Synods declared to be exscinded, and one on a summary of doctrine as believed and maintained by this portion of the Church.

The report of this last committee exhibits the state of doctrinal sentiment which prevailed among the churches against whom charges of grievous departures from the faith were most rife. It presents in itself the evidence upon which the charges were denied,—distinguishing and vindicating the true doctrine from its correspondent error, and, with a firm conviction of its scriptural consistency and sound orthodoxy, it was given to the world.

The recommendations of the convention to the Presbyteries and Synods were generally complied with. Only a small number of churches withdrew from their connection with them in consequence of the exscinding acts.[1] The very sharpness and summary severity of the measures adopted by the last Assembly served but the more effectually to bind together those who felt it a duty to resist them. They expressed apprehension that, if no decided steps were taken to arrest the progress of unconstitutional measures, the whole of the obnoxious portion of the Church would be cut off in detail, and thus be denied not only their title to any share in the funds and institutions of the Church, to which they had largely contributed, but all their rights as members of the common body.

To guard against this result, counsel was taken as to the course to be pursued. It was resolved that the commissions of the delegates from the Synods declared to be exscinded should be offered immediately after the opening of the next Assembly, and in case of their refusal, or the refusal of the moderator to put the question, the Assembly should be constituted forthwith by the choice of a new moderator.

The organization was effected as narrated above, and

[1] "As far as we know, not a single Presbytery within the four Synods has consented to withdraw from their Congregational churches."—*Princeton Review*, 1838.

the Assembly adjourned to meet in the lecture-room of the First Presbyterian Church. It observed the order and the forms of previous Assemblies, even to the calling for the reports of committees that did not appear, and the election of trustees of the seminary at Princeton. The obnoxious acts of the previous Assembly were repealed. The resolutions discountenancing the operations of the American Education Society and the Home Missionary Society were rescinded, and these institutions were cordially commended to the continued confidence and increasing patronage of the churches. The action by which the four Synods were declared to be out of the ecclesiastical connection of the Presbyterian Church, and the Third Presbytery of Philadelphia to be dissolved, was pronounced "utterly at variance with the Constitution of the Presbyterian Church in the United States of America, and therefore *inoperative and void.*"[1] The rules of the previous Assembly excluding commissioners from newly-formed Presbyteries till after the organization of the Assembly, "not having been submitted to the Presbyteries, and being contrary to the established usage," were declared "not binding on this or any future Assembly." The inherent right of Presbyteries to expound and apply constitutional rules touching the qualifications of their own members was asserted, and the action of the last

[1] Dr. Green had said, in the columns of the "Christian Advocate," in 1831, "The General Assembly is as much the creature of the Constitution as the church session, and has no better claim than the church session to go beyond its appropriate powers and duties." A few months after, he says, again, "The proceedings of the General Assembly are not reviewed by a higher court; but that body has no more right or power to violate the Constitution than any church session in the Presbyterian community; and, when such violation takes place, the violating act is a nullity." The last was said to invalidate the Assembly's proceedings in the case of Mr. Barnes.

Assembly making examination of applicants from other Presbyteries *imperative*, was pronounced *null* and *void*.

No steps were taken with reference to any rearrangement of Presbyteries and Synods, except such as the circumstances rendered absolutely necessary. The relations of the Third Presbytery of Philadelphia, declared by the previous Assembly to be dissolved, were such, however, as to require some change by which it might be brought into synodical connection. A new Synod, therefore, entitled the Synod of Pennsylvania, was erected, embracing the ministers and congregations of the Presbyteries of Wilmington, Lewes, Philadelphia Second, Philadelphia Third, Carlisle, Huntingdon, and Northumberland.[1] In view, moreover, of the peculiar condition of the Church and the necessity of a vindication of its legal rights, a committee of twelve was appointed with power to advise and direct in respect to any legal questions and pecuniary interests that might require attention during the ensuing year.

Still, no disposition was evinced to obtain the exclusive control of the funds and institutions of the Church. Propositions were made to the other Assembly looking toward a reunion; but the answer given implied the endorsement as constitutional of the exscinding acts, and could not be entertained. Yet the Assembly placed it upon their records as unanimously resolved, "that this body are willing to agree to any reasonable measures tending to an amicable adjustment of the difficulties existing in the Presbyterian Church, and will receive and respectfully consider any propositions which may be made for that purpose."

Unless the Assembly was prepared to relinquish all right to its funds and property, nothing now remained but to bring the question to a legal adjustment. The

---

[1] Digest, p. 149.

most appropriate method of doing this was to test the rights of those whom it had elected as trustees to a seat in the Board. To have consented to throw themselves upon the *generosity* of the other Assembly, or the offers made by them, of giving back a fair proportion of the funds, would have been to forego much to which the Assembly felt that they had a rightful claim, and to sink their own character, as an Assembly still entitled to the benefits of the Act of Incorporation of 1799, into that of a body which could have no legal recognition whatever.

In these circumstances, the case was brought in the first instance before the Supreme Court for the Eastern District of Pennsylvania. The trial commenced before Judge Rogers at *Nisi Prius* and a special jury, March 4, 1839, and occupied twenty days. Both sides were heard at length, and the history of the facts of the case was embodied in the charge to the jury. The Plan of Union was elaborately vindicated as not only constitutional and a measure which the Assembly had power to make, but one "well calculated to promote the best interests of religion." The exscinding acts were pronounced "a judicial proceeding to all intents and purposes," and as such "not only contrary to the eternal principles of justice, the principles of the common law, but at variance with the Constitution of the Church." The jury brought in their verdict "that they find the defendants guilty."

The latter applied to the Supreme Court in Banc for a new trial, March 29, 1839. The exceptions to the rulings and charge of Judge Rogers were ably argued. On May 8, Chief Justice Gibson delivered the opinion of the court, granting a new trial, and presenting views in conflict with those of Judge Rogers. As to the exscinding acts, he denied that they were to be regarded in the light of a judicial process. The measure was "a legislative act." As such he said, "it may have been a hard one, though certainly constitutional and strictly just.

Nor was there anything in the course pursued by the moderator of the "Old School" Assembly which warranted the "irregularities" of his deposition. Hence the rule for a new trial must be made absolute. Here the matter was suffered to rest. Each party retained the control of the property which it actually held.

No further prospect now remained of the reunion of the Church. The portion represented by the Assembly pronounced by the civil court in the first instance to be the constitutional body, embraced in 1840—so soon as any proper estimate could be formed of its strength —about one hundred and two thousand members in thirteen hundred and seventy-five churches.[1] A large number of these churches, however, were in a feeble state, and were receiving missionary aid. Their real strength was far less than their numbers would seem to imply. Many whose sympathies had been in favor of the body remained in connection with the other Assembly, from an indisposition to disturb the peace and harmony of the Presbyteries and Synods in which they were in the decided minority.

This was the case especially within the bounds of the Synod of Kentucky. By a large majority of its members the action of the Assembly of 1836 had been strongly disapproved. The motion of W. L. Breckinridge, condemning the Notes of Mr. Barnes on Romans, had been carried by a vote which stood thirty-four to nine, with five *non liquets*. By a still stronger vote, the refusal of the Assembly to take distinctive action on the subject of Foreign Missions was deplored. The further operation of the Home Missionary and Education Societies within the bounds of the Synod was declared, by a

---

[1] This includes a large number of churches that finally adhered to the other body.

vote of nearly four to one, to be against their wishes and consent. The request that they would withdraw and make no further collections or appointments within the Synod's geographical limits was less decidedly sustained, the vote standing thirty-four to fourteen, with three *non liquets*. Eleven members, seven of whom were ministers, signed a protest against these resolutions.

In the fall of 1838,[1] when the division had taken place, the Synod, in consequence of a previous conference and understanding on the part of members, resolved unanimously to adhere to "the General Assembly which organized and continued to hold its sessions in the Seventh Presbyterian Church in Philadelphia" as "the *only true* General Assembly." Eleven ministers, however, and seven elders, while declaring their adherence to said Assembly, distinctly declared that they withheld their approbation of the "Reform" measures of the Assemblies of 1837 and 1838; and this paper was placed on the records of the Synod.

But the matter was not suffered thus to rest. In the "Protestant and Herald," a journal recommended by the Synod to the churches, articles appeared on the subject of the two Assemblies, from the pen of Dr. Nathan L. Rice, which gave great offence. In the editorial columns these views were virtually endorsed by Dr. Breckinridge. The members of the section of the Synod which had consented to a compromise of silence on the subject for the sake of peace, felt themselves aggrieved, and, at an interlocutory meeting with closed doors, gave expression to their dissatisfaction. They had trusted that the compromise—as they understood it—would have been kept inviolate, and that mutual silence on controverted points would have been preserved.

---

[1] Davidson's Kentucky.

The complaint of Messrs. Thomas Cleland and Joseph C. Stiles brought out Messrs. Rice and Breckinridge in their own vindication. Considerable warmth of feeling was manifested. Some unkind words were uttered, and, in consequence of the dissatisfied members requesting leave of absence, for private reasons, the interlocutory meeting was abruptly terminated. No action was taken, and the aggrieved members received no satisfaction.

Meanwhile, the Bowling Green Church had called Rev. Archer C. Dickerson to be their pastor, and, when the Synod interfered with what the church considered their just rights, took an independent stand, and published to the world the reasons for their course.

Rev. (Dr.) Stiles, feeling himself absolved from the obligation of silence by the action of the other party in the Synod, gave public expression to his convictions. In two sermons, preached at Versailles in January, 1840, he vindicated his own views and those of the brethren who sympathized with him. For this he was called to account by the West Lexington Presbytery, and cautioned to be more careful in his future course and statements.

Had the Synod pursued a like course with Drs. Hall and Breckinridge, peace might have been preserved and the Synod have remained undivided. But silence on one side, while the other was left at liberty, was impossible. Before the spring of 1840 a manifesto appeared, signed by Messrs. Stiles, Cleland, Winston, and Maccoun. It denounced the "Reform measures" as erecting a new basis, and invited a convention of those who sympathized with the signers, to meet at Versailles.

The convention met March 17. Nine ministers and twenty elders were present, and an address was issued to set forth the views of the convention.

The discussion had now commenced; and it was vigorously carried forward. The subject was introduced into meetings of Presbytery, and matters were brought to a crisis by a remonstrance of a minority of the Versailles congregation against the settlement of Rev. (Dr.) Stiles. The sympathies of the Presbytery were with the minority, and they acceded to their request. Upon this the Versailles session undertook to discipline the memorialists, among whom was one whom they had suspended. The latter appealed to the Presbytery, and the decision was reversed and the session deposed. These now appealed to the Synod; but the decision of the Presbytery was sustained.

The difficulty was aggravated by mutual charges against each other of Messrs. Stiles and Price, members of the Presbytery. By the intervention of friends, mutual concessions were made, and private charges were withdrawn. But Dr. Stiles insisted on a trial. He was tried, and sentence was pronounced that he be admonished by the moderator, and be requested to subscribe an acknowledgment of the evil of his course, with an engagement hereafter to "abstain from all such measures as tend to divide and distract the Church." Upon his refusal to do this he was to be suspended for contumacy.

As might have been expected, he refused, and the sentence of suspension was pronounced. He rose and left the house, followed by large numbers whose sympathies were on his side. As he continued to preach in disregard of the sentence of suspension, the Presbytery deposed him from the ministry. The sentence, however, was a mere *brutum fulmen*. The Synod themselves disregarded it, and its prominent members freely invited him to their pulpits.

There was now an open rupture. The convention which had met at Versailles was again called together, and it resolved itself into a Synod, consisting of three

Presbyteries. One of its first acts was to restore Dr. Stiles. At first the body had but ten ministers and a single church; but it soon connected itself with the "Constitutional" General Assembly, and in 1842 could boast of eleven ministers and fourteen churches. In 1846, notwithstanding the removal of Dr. Stiles to Richmond, the Synod of Kentucky—embracing the Presbyteries of Harmony, Providence, and Green River—contained fourteen ministers, twenty-one churches, and nearly a thousand communicants.

In Missouri, the Presbytery of St. Charles alone had taken part, through its commissioner, in the organization of the "Constitutional" Assembly of 1838. In the following year, however, it was represented in the other Assembly, and for a time there was faint prospect of any division within the bounds of the Synod. Still, there was grave dissatisfaction with the "Reform measures" of the Assembly of 1837; and in the fall of 1841 a convention of Presbyterian ministers and elders in Missouri was called to meet at Hannibal, and the result was the formation of an independent Synod, to which the First Church of St. Louis and its pastor adhered. After acting in an independent capacity for two or three years, the Synod connected itself with the "Constitutional" Assembly.

As the Synods of Michigan and Tennessee adhered to the "Constitutional" Assembly, they were pronounced by the other Assembly dissolved, and the minority of the ministers and churches of the former Synod were declared (1839) attached to the Synod of Cincinnati, although they were subsequently (1840), at their own request, attached to the Synod of Indiana; while the minority of the Synod of Tennessee—likewise declared dissolved—was attached to the Presbytery of Holston, which was by the extension of the Synod of West Tennessee brought within its limits. The Presbyteries of Union and French Broad adhered by large majorities to the "Constitutional" Assembly.

The meeting of the Synod of Illinois in the fall of 1838 was held at Peoria, and the attendance was unusually large. The members opposed to the exscinding acts of 1837 were greatly in the majority. The minority, after consultation, decided to introduce a series of resolutions covering the whole case, and take issue on their reception or rejection. The house in which the Synod met was crowded to its full capacity. The election of the moderator, Rev. J. Blatchford, was carried by those in sympathy with the exscinded Synods, and the vote stood about two to one.

The minority "sought every opportunity to introduce" their "decisive measures."[1] But they were foiled by the promptness and tact of the moderator, who was well versed in parliamentary usage and ecclesiastical law. At length, with some demur, he admitted "a declaration and protest" to be read as an argument in a case before the house, although its friends did not pretend that it was specially relevant to the matter in hand. "We took," said they, "parliamentary liberty in the debate, and ignored its exact relevancy to the point then before the body." Handing a copy of the declaration to the moderator, which he refused to receive, and then laying it on the table, the minority felt that they had accomplished all that was possible in the circumstances, and, on the adjournment, withdrew to hold their sessions in the First Presbyterian Church.

The Synod of Indiana was divided without difficulty, on the principle of elective affinity. The two parties met separately: those opposed to the exscinding measures, in the court-house (New Albany?), where Rev. John Dickey preached the opening sermon; the other

---

[1] St. Louis Presbyterian, March 15, 1860.

in the church, where Rev. Alexander Williamson presided. Each party was organized as the Synod.

The Synod of Ohio consisted in 1838 of six Presbyteries,—Columbus, Richland, Lancaster, Wooster, Athens, and Marion. Of these the four first had, previous to the meeting of Synod, declared by majorities in favor of the measures of the Assemblies of 1837 and 1838. When the Synod had convened, Dr. Hoge moved that a recess of five minutes be taken, and that the two parties of the Synod act according to their views of duty,—the "Old School" to occupy the upper part of the house, and the "New School" the basement of the building in which the Synod was then assembled. A substitute for this motion was offered, but rejected. The vote on the motion of Dr. Hoge stood fifty-five ayes to forty-three nays, with eleven *non liquets*. The records of the Synod (New School) state that "the fifty-five then left the Synod, and have not returned."

The Synod of Cincinnati was divided on the motion that Dr. Beecher, T. J. Briggs, B. Dickinson, and others, on the ground of having sustained the measures for organizing the so-called Assembly that met in the First Presbyterian Church of Philadelphia, cannot longer be considered in connection with the Presbyterian Church or members of this Synod, and that Dr. J. L. Wilson and others who were specified be recognized as the Presbytery of Cincinnati. The vote on the motion was carried by sixty-two ayes to forty-four nays, while eight or ten were excused from voting.

The Synod of Albany met at Hudson, Oct. 9, 1838. When the roll had been called, a resolution was submitted by President Nott, of Union College, to the effect that, "Whereas a diversity of opinion is known to exist among the members of this Synod in relation to certain acts of the General Assemblies of 1837 and 1838, therefore—without deciding at this time upon the character of these acts—Resolved, That this Synod be and continue a constituent part of the Presbyterian Church represented in the Assembly which held their session in the Seventh Presbyterian Church in the city of Philadelphia." This motion was laid upon the table by a vote of seventy-five to nineteen, with thirteen *non liquets*. Upon this Dr. Nott requested those who were prepared to adhere to the Assembly approved by his resolution, to withdraw to an adjoining room. Thirty-five members thereupon left the Synod, and did not afterward answer to their names at the calling of the roll. Among these thirty-five were those who represented the majority of Albany Presbytery. The minority who did not withdraw, and those of the Presbytery who sympathized with them, were thenceforth recognized by the Synod as the Presbytery of Albany. The members who withdrew also assumed the title of the Synod of Albany.

The Synod of New York, embracing eight Presbyteries, met at Newburgh, Oct. 16, 1838,—one hundred and eighty-one members answering to their names, and the number of ministers exceeding that of elders by only eleven. After the calling of the roll, resolutions were submitted to the effect that a division of the body appeared inevitable, that it should be amicably effected, and that certain proposed steps should be taken to secure the object. The vote in favor of these resolutions stood one hundred and three to sixty-four. The roll was then called in accordance with the plan proposed in one of the resolutions, and forty-six ministers and forty-one elders declared their adherence to the Assembly that met in the Seventh Presbyterian Church; thirty-five, including twenty ministers and fifteen elders, declared their adherence to the Assembly that met in the First Presbyterian Church; while forty-nine members, of whom twenty-two were ministers, refused to answer, regarding the whole proceeding purporting to divide the Synod as unconstitutional, null, and void.

Taking this view of the case, fifty-six members of the Synod entered their protest against the resolutions that had been adopted. They claimed that the Synod had no power to divide itself; that it would be eminently a violation of the Constitution of the Church for the Synod to divide itself in such a way that either portion would virtually put the other without the pale of the Presbyterian Church; that there was no sufficient ground for any division whatever; that the proceedings in accordance with the resolutions, while subversive of the Constitution, were likewise inconsistent with the ordination vow to study the peace, *unity*, and purity of the Church; and that there was no evidence that the division of the Church was either inevitable, necessary, or reasonable at the present time.

While it was agreed that the majority in favor of the resolutions should meet in the church-edifice, and the minority in the lecture-room, the protestants, claiming to represent the undivided Synod, met at the High School and constituted themselves as the Synod. The minority who voted for the divisory resolutions, declaring that they had voted as they had simply on the grounds of expediency, and expressing their willingness to waive their opinions in favor of the scruples of their brethren, were received by the latter, and thus assisted to constitute the body which adhered to the Assembly that met in the First Presbyterian Church.

When the Synod of New Jersey met in the fall of 1838, the first question that tested the relative strength of parties was taken on the motion that the Presbytery of Newark take order on the course of its commissioners, and that, if its commissioners for the ensuing year act with the body succeeding that which met in the First Presbyterian Church, it shall be no longer considered as belonging to the Synod. The vote stood eighty-one ayes to eighty-one nays, and the motion was carried by the casting vote of the moderator. The minority of the Synod, consisting of the Presbyteries of Newark, Rockaway, and Montrose, was constituted by the (N. S.) Assembly of 1839[1] the Synod of Newark. But in the following year the two Synods, of New York and Newark were united by the Assembly in a single body, to be known by the name—which it has since retained—of the Synod of New York and New Jersey.

In Eastern Pennsylvania and Delaware the lines of division were already quite distinctly drawn. The Synod of Delaware, erected by the Assembly of 1834 and dissolved by that of the following year, represented in the main the portion of the Church in this region opposed to the exscinding measures.

The "Constitutional" Assembly of 1838, on the petition of members of several of the interested Presbyteries, erected the Synod of Pennsylvania,—which was to consist of the Presbyteries of Wilmington, Lewes, Philadelphia Second, Philadelphia Third, Carlisle, Huntingdon, and Northumberland. The churches and ministers of Western Pennsylvania opposed to the excision, who constituted a decided minority of the Synod of Pittsburg, were in 1843 constituted the Synod of West Pennsylvania, and consisted of the Presbyteries of Erie, Meadville, and Pittsburg; while the minority of the Presbyteries of Northumberland, Huntingdon, and Carlisle were erected into the Presbytery of Harrisburg. The name of Philadelphia Second was changed to that of Philadelphia Fourth, to distinguish it from the Presbytery of the same name adhering to the exscinding Assembly.

[1] Rockaway Presbytery was formed at this juncture by a division of Newark. See Digest, 150.

In Virginia the majority of the Synod sustained the action of the Assembly of 1837. Dr. Baxter had taken an active part in devising them and giving them shape, and his influence was powerful among the churches of his native State. His associate instructors in the seminary and the President of the college disapproved his course, although it was approved by Rev. B. F. Stanton, the pastor of the church. The Southern "Religious Telegraph" opposed the obnoxious acts. Dr. Carroll published his strictures in pamphlet form. Dr. Baxter explained and defended his course. Comments and replies followed. The venerable Dr. Hill, feeling that the Constitution of the Church had been violated, took up his pen vigorously in its defence. In the midst of this discussion, "The Watchman of the South," under the editorship of Rev. Dr. Plumer, made its appearance at Richmond. It became the organ of those who sustained the acts of the Assembly of 1837, and its energetic utterances produced a deep impression.

In these circumstances, the Presbyteries met for their autumn sessions. In Winchester Presbytery the acts of the Assembly were sustained by a small majority. In Lexington, where the influence of Dr. Baxter was paramount, the unanimity in their favor was almost entire. In the other Presbyteries the minorities opposed to them were large. The Synod met in October at Lexington. The subject was ably discussed; and, though a majority was found to sustain the acts of the Assembly, the minority was numerous and able. Few, however, as yet apprehended a division of the Synod.

A few months later, the Board of the Seminary felt it necessary to request the resignation of Messrs. Goodrich and Taylor, Dr. Baxter's associates. They could not agree with the majority of the Synod; and this fact they did not disguise. They disapproved of Dr. Baxter's course and of the acts of the Assembly, and, in accordance with the request of the Board, resigned their positions. The minority could now perceive that the lines were to be closely drawn, and that approval of the acts of the Assembly was to be made a test of office. With the organization of two General Assemblies in 1838, it was manifest that their choice could not longer be delayed. The project was, indeed, agitated of forming a Southern Assembly; but the majority felt that even with reference to the vexed question of slavery it was better to leave it in the hands of their Northern sympathizers. In these circumstances, the commissioners for 1838 were elected. The effort made to effect a compromise between the parties proved ineffectual, and the commissioners were left to take their places in the Assemblies to which they or their Presbyteries respectively adhered. Division was now inevitable. It began in the Presbytery of the District of Columbia. Their commissioners, in accordance with the known sentiments of the body, had taken their seats in the "Constitutional" Assembly of 1838. A minority of four withdrew, and were constituted, by the Synod in sympathy with them, the Presbytery of the District,—two bodies of the same name thus occupying the field.

In the Presbytery of Abingdon, a Committee on the State of the Church made a report embracing resolutions in favor of the "Constitutional" Assembly, and disapproving of the course of their commissioner in attending the other. These, however, were voted down, and at the close of the sessions the minority withdrew to form themselves into a distinct body. In Lexington Presbytery, the single church of Cook's Creek and Harrisonburg, out of adherence to the "Constitutional" Assembly, withdrew. In Winchester Presbytery, a resolution to adhere to the "Constitutional" Assembly was voted down, ayes thirteen, nays sixteen. The minority withdrew to the court-house in Charleston (where the

Presbytery met) and formed themselves into a Presbytery, retaining the old name. Five ordained ministers and eight churches composed the strength of the secession, while ten ministers and twenty-four churches adhered to the Assembly which met in the Seventh Church.

In the Presbyteries of East and West Hanover no formal division took place, but a strong opposition to the acts of the Assembly of 1837 was felt and manifested. Dr. Plumer's church was divided, and a portion withdrew to form a new organization, which was soon merged in that of Shockoe Hill, the latter having been depleted to strengthen that of Dr. Plumer, by members who sympathized with him in his course. In Petersburg, the minority—opposed to the action of the Assembly of 1837—withdrew and formed a new church. In Hanover this was likewise the case with a minority of opposite sympathies. Three ministers and four elders from the Presbytery of Hanover, and some likewise from West Hanover, withdrew to form the Presbytery of Hanover in connection with the "Constitutional" General Assembly.

From the several Presbyteries thus formed and the Presbytery of the District of Columbia, the Synod of Virginia in connection with the "Constitutional" Assembly was constituted. In the separations incident to the division, kindness and courtesy, for the most part, prevailed. But old friendships were severed, and many who for the best part of a generation had stood together shoulder to shoulder were thenceforth separated and brought into new or distinct associations.

The other Southern Synods by decided majorities sustained the acts of the Assembly of 1837. This was the case especially with North Carolina. In South Carolina, the Charleston Union Presbytery at first seemed not far from equally divided, its commissioner meeting at different times with both Assemblies. But the friends of the "Constitutional" Assembly, composing a decided majority, retained the name and organization, while refusing to comply with the direction given by the Synod that each Presbytery should express approval of the Assembly of 1837 so far as to adhere to the new basis. Dr. Smyth, of Charleston, and some few others who sympathized with him, withdrew, claiming, although a minority, the name and rights of the original Presbytery.

In Eastern Tennessee there was strong opposition to the action of the Assembly of 1837, and a very large proportion of the churches remained in sympathy with, and adhered to, the Constitutional Assembly. In Western Tennessee the case was reversed, as it was generally among the churches of Georgia, Alabama, and Louisiana.

In the great majority of cases, the Presbyteries, including the dissatisfied minority, remained united in their adherence to the Assembly to which each several body attached itself. Some, like that of Newburyport, which was declared by the "Old School" Assembly of 1840 to have "virtually separated itself,"[1] hesitated to take decisive steps to declare its adherence. Of those whose commissioners were present in the Constitutional Assembly of 1838, several adhered in part to the other Assembly. These were, in 1839, Troy, North River, Erie, Marion, Cincinnati, Crawfordsville, St. Charles, Holston, Clinton, and District of Columbia. All, or nearly all, of these were rent in sunder, and each fragment of the Presbytery retained the old name and was represented in the Assembly to which it adhered. A single new Presbytery, that of Caledonia, connected with the Synod of New Jersey, was formed by secces-

---

[1] It was afterward received.

sions from the exscinded Synods of New York. In 1840 it numbered but six churches, the aggregate membership of which was less than four hundred.

In a large number of instances, ministers and churches who regarded the acts of the Assembly of 1837 as un. constitutional saw no sufficient reason for a change of ecclesiastical relations. In some cases they contented themselves with simply expressing their disapproval, and in others—as in the case of the Brick Church of New York and its pastor[1]—with a solemn protest against their constitutionality. This course was taken in order to prevent churches from being rent in sunder, and with the desire of promoting peace. The division, as it actually took place, by no means represented the real sentiment of the churches as a body with regard to the action which had occasioned the division. Many individuals, and even churches, who did not connect themselves with the "Constitutional" Assembly, felt aggrieved at the unconstitutional course, as they considered it, which had been the occasion of its existence.

Indeed, so manifest was the disapproval with which they were regarded by some who adhered to the "Old School" Assembly, that express stipulations were made, as in Albany Presbytery, that the views of members on that subject should not be called in question. The General Assembly itself, while forced to take exception (1839) to the records of the Synod of Cincinnati, which declared the four Synods to be still constitutional branches of the Presbyterian Church, was compelled subsequently to provide that a disapproval of the ex-

[1] Rev. Dr. Spencer, of Brooklyn, N.Y., united with Dr. Spring in the protest, though he also adhered to the Presbytery. "With that fearlessness and emphasis which characterized him," he condemned the measures of the Assembly of 1837, and deplored their evil effects.—*Life of Spencer*, p. 46.

scinding acts should be no bar to ministerial fellowship or Presbyterial standing.

In numerous instances, the results of the division were lamentable. New and feeble organizations were formed by seceders from old churches. Organizations once strong and flourishing were rent asunder. Lawsuits were instituted to determine the title to church property. Old friendships were broken up, and bitter and lasting alienations were produced. The strength that should have been concentrated for aggressive efforts was frittered away in mutual strife and exasperation. In some instances the animosity was such as could scarcely fail to be transmitted to another generation.

In the Western field, some of the results of the division were specially disastrous. A sad check was given to the spirit of Christian and missionary enterprise. A prejudice was excited against the Presbyterian system; and thousands who could distinctly apprehend the injustice of the exscinding acts were far from disposed to interpret them as the result of the violation and not of the consistent application of the principles of the Constitution. There were not wanting those, moreover, who were disposed and able to extend and confirm this prejudice, and thus cover with odium whatever bore the Presbyterian name. It was thus that serious and embarrassing obstacles were thrown in the way of aggressive effort, and a kind of Independency, often allied with error, which the New England churches were constrained to disown, was introduced. Those who had entered the Western field with hopes inspired by the previous history of the Church were in some instances disheartened, and constrained to abandon the field. Not a little energy which might have been wisely and profitably employed was wasted in the mutual rivalries and antagonisms which the division produced.

CHAPTER XLII.

THE TWO ASSEMBLIES—CONCLUSION.

THE division of the Presbyterian Church resulted in the establishment, virtually, of two denominations, each claiming the same title, adopting the same standards, and, to a considerable extent, occupying the same field, and represented by its General Assembly. The constituent elements of the two bodies, however, were somewhat diverse. Those which adhered to the "Constitutional" General Assembly were far from homogeneous. They were united mainly by their aversion to a rigid ecclesiasticism, their conviction of the injustice of the exscinding acts, their sympathy with those who had thereby been denied their rights by the Assembly of 1837, as well as by a tolerance of minor diversities of belief which did not affect the intelligent and sincere adoption of the standards of the Church. They readily accepted, if they did not prefer, the voluntary system of conducting missionary operations; for experience had not yet taught them the lessons which they were to learn when called to provide for the necessities of those of their own household.

But these men, seeking to perpetuate rather than introduce the co-operative system which for more than the lifetime of a generation had been encouraged by the General Assembly, were many of them possessed of more zeal than prudence. Some of them, with Congregational education and predilections, were Presbyterians simply from the force of circumstances, or the influence of locality or association. These, especially under the pressure of revived denominational zeal which found them predisposed to lax views of church order, were ere long to fall back, by elective affinity, into those associations to which they more properly belonged. Others still, while Presbyterian by intelligent preference and conviction, had been repelled by the course and conduct of those whose policy they opposed, and were prepared to dispense with those features of the Presbyterian system which appeared to them non-essential, and which—like the plan of *annual* Assemblies, or of final appeal to the General Assembly—appeared to them a kind of superfluous ecclesiastical machinery. Among these were to be found men little qualified for leadership, and better fitted to expose the injustice that denied them their rights than conciliate the confidence that would respect their counsels.

But there was yet an element belonging to this body, composed of as true friends as any which the Church has been privileged to boast, men like Richards, Fisher, Hillyer, McAuley, Cathcart, and scores of others, of whose soundness in the faith and of whose attachment to the Presbyterian Church no whisper of doubt had been ever breathed, and who regarded the progress of the ploughshare of division with the undissembled grief of the true parent at the sundering of the living child. And in full sympathy with these, though reproached or molested on account of the peculiarities of doctrine or practice charged upon them, were men like Skinner, Patterson, Barnes, Beman, Beecher, and Duffield, could not abandon the name and faith which had been bequeathed to them from the fathers.

As to the past, these various elements were a unit. But as to questions of future policy they were divided among themselves. Unfortunate in their leaders, some of whom lacked experience, if not prudence, they allowed the project of modifying the Constitution of the Church to pass without marked opposition, only a few years later to repudiate, by a prompt restoration of "the book" to its original integrity, their inconsiderate mistake. They ignored to the last moment the rising spirit of denominational zeal which was ere long to render the former co-operation of Presbyterians and Congregationalists in education and home missions impossible, and which, receiving a new impulse from the repudiation of the Plan of Union by the (Congregational) Albany Convention of 1852, culminated in that subservience of the Home Missionary Society to the policy of Western Congregationalists which forced upon Presbyterians, against both their preferences and their prejudices, the care of their own churches.

On the subject of slavery the Assembly was also divided. Year after year, memorials and overtures were presented, which repeatedly elicited warm and extended discussions, and resulted in action which frequently failed to satisfy the more zealous anti-slavery men of the North, while it excited dissatisfaction at the South. Yet the preponderating sentiment of the Church was decidedly anti-slavery, and the utterances of the Assembly from year to year showed that it fully responded to that sentiment. Still the continued agitation of the subject, and the mutual alienation of feeling thus produced, diverted the attention of the Assembly more or less from its appropriate work, while the opportunity was afforded, and in some cases was eagerly improved, of misrepresenting its position both at the North and South, and repelling from its communion both the radical reformer and the apologist of "Southern institutions."

In such circumstances as these, the growth of the Church was greatly retarded. Before it could be fully prepared to occupy its true position, it was essential that it should be brought into harmony within itself.

The Albany Convention of 1852, which gave expression to that zeal for Congregational usage which for several years had been steadily increasing, resulted—as statistics show—in detaching from the Church, to a considerable extent, certain elements which had hitherto but loosely adhered to it; while its action discountenancing the Plan of Union seemed to indicate that co-operative sympathy, so essential to the prosecution of common efforts in Education and Home Missions, had experienced a marked decline. The Church was thus forced—while in a fraternal spirit refusing to disturb the Plan of Union, and while cherishing still the hope of co-operation in voluntary societies—to consider more seriously than heretofore the policy which duty to its own interests, to the country at large, and to the cause of Christ required it to adopt. The pressure of this necessity was, from year to year, more and more deeply felt; while the voluntary withdrawal of those who were not in sympathy with the policy of the Church left the Assembly more free to adopt the measures which the emergency required.

As early as 1853 it was evident that in some way the Church must come into unity with itself on the vexed question of slavery, if it was ever to make progress in the direction of homogeneous and healthy growth. The Assembly of that year, in a fraternal spirit, and in response to overtures both from the North and South, proposed that the facts that concerned the actual relation of the Southern churches to slavery should be reported to the Assembly of the following year. The measure was denounced as an inquisitorial proceeding; and the response of 1854 showed that a solution of the question was still prospectively as distant as ever. In 1855 a committee was appointed to report the next year on the constitutional power of the General Assembly over the subject of slaveholding in the churches under their care; but a prolonged discussion followed the presentation of this report, which, though adopted by the Assembly, was so unacceptable to Southern members that a minority report was presented by the portion of the committee in sympathy with them. Southern ministers and churches complained of these protracted discussions and frequent resolutions on the subject of slavery; and in 1857 the Presbytery of Lexington, South, gave the Assembly official notice that many members of its churches, as well as a number of its ministers and elders, held slaves "from principle" and "of choice," believing it to be right according to the Bible, and that the Presbytery itself sustained them in their position.

Even had the Assembly desired, it was no longer possible for it to evade the issue which was thus presented. By a vote of one hundred and sixty-nine yeas to twenty-six nays, a report was adopted which presented a summary history of the action of successive Assemblies on the subject of slavery, and which "disapproved and earnestly condemned" the position of the Presbytery of Lexington, South, as opposed to the established convictions of the Church, and tending necessarily to mar its peace, seriously hinder its prosperity, and bring reproach on our holy religion. The Presbytery were called upon to review and rectify their position, while "such doctrines and practice," it was declared, could not "be permanently tolerated in the Presbyterian Church."

This action of the Assembly was met by a protest of twenty-two members, representing the Southern churches, and identifying their own case with that of the Presbytery of Lexington, South. They protested that this action "degraded the whole Southern Church;" that it was "the virtual exscinding of the South," "unrighteous, oppressive, uncalled for, the exercise of usurped power, destructive of the unity of our branch of the Church, hurtful to the North and the South, and adding to the peril of the union of these United States." The Assembly replied by declaring the assumption that its action was an "indirect excision" of the South to be groundless, and that the allegations respecting that action were, consequently, unwarranted.

But the protestants had taken their stand, and upon their return to their homes they were sustained by their Presbyteries with great unanimity in the position they had assumed. The result was the voluntary withdrawal of the Southern churches under the care of the Assembly, almost in solid column, and the formation April 1, 1858, of the "United Synod of the Presbyterian Church." Thus, before political convulsions had occurred to rend the Church *through the State*, the body represented by the "Constitutional" General Assembly had defined its position, had attained internal harmony, and had thrown off an incubus which for years had oppressed it and crippled its energies.

But, while the causes were at work which were destined finally to unite the Church within itself, and enable it to put forth, with intelligent consciousness of duty and discernment of its true policy, the efforts necessary to its progress, those measures were inaugurated which were at length to express that duty and shape that policy. In 1853 the wants of feeble congregations, compelled repeatedly to apply, at great inconvenience and considerable expense, as well as with uncertain prospects of success, to Eastern churches for aid in erecting houses of worship, were brought to the attention of the General Assembly; and it was resolved, with great unanimity and no little enthusiasm, that an effort should be made to raise a permanent fund of one hundred thousand dollars, which should be available for the relief of applicants entitled to aid. In this effort the churches generally participated, and it was at length crowned with complete success. It thus not only gave new hope to feeble congregations, and inspired them to the exertions necessary on their part to meet the terms on which aid might be secured, but it reacted upon the Church itself, arousing it to a consciousness of its ability and to a sense of its obligations, and preparing it for still further steps in the same direction. Each successive Assembly afforded increasing evidence that the problem of what the denomination owed to itself and to the cause of Christ throughout the land was becoming better understood, and that it was rapidly preparing itself to discharge the task which had been assigned it in the providence of God.

For several years after the division, the churches under the care of the Assembly cordially co-operated with the American Home Missionary Society. By the Assembly of 1838, not only this, but the American Board of Commissioners for Foreign Missions and the American Education Society, were recommended to all its churches as suitable channels for dispensing their charities. In 1840 the recommendation was renewed, and these societies were pronounced "every way worthy of patronage and support."

But previous to 1847 it was found that the American Home Missionary Society, governed by its rules respecting co-operation, and without the local knowledge possessed by the Presbyteries, failed in repeated instances to extend the aid to feeble enterprises, or to the mission-fields of Presbyteries, which the emergency demanded. A Committee on Home Missions was appointed, and their report made to the next Assembly (1849) had respect mainly to the methods necessary to promote the efficiency of Presbyteries in mission-work, supplying destitute churches, promoting Sabbath-schools, and securing the erection of suitable houses of worship.

Still, there were fields from which the Presbyterian Church was virtually excluded by the rules of the Society. The Congregational churches in similar cases could apply to the American Missionary Association. The Presbyterian Church had no such supplementary agency; for in good faith it had poured its undivided funds into the treasury of the Society. In successive years (1852, 1853, 1857, 1858) committees of conference with the Society were appointed, having in view some arrangement by which feeble churches hitherto denied aid by its rules might be provided for. If the Church was to sustain itself and extend its domain, it could not cast off these organizations which appealed to it for aid, while Congregational churches in a like condition could receive assistance from another source.

Meanwhile, Presbyteries were recommended to take measures, either by themselves or by the aid of the Society, for the organization of new churches and the stated preaching of the gospel to destitute churches whenever the circumstances of the case required (1850), and to elect standing committees on church extension annually, whose duty it should be to see that the claims of Home Missions were presented to the churches, and to recommend the applications made for aid. It was resolved (1852) that, with the other standing committees, one on Home Missions should be annually appointed by the Assembly, to be known by the name of the Church Extension Committee. In 1855 the number of the committee was fixed at fifteen, and it was empowered to fill its own vacancies when the Assembly was not in session. In 1857 the committee was allowed to exercise its discretion in regard to the aid extended, irrespective of the restrictions by which it had been hitherto bound. The wisdom of granting this privilege was soon justified by the refusal of the American Home Missionary Society to extend aid to the churches of Missouri, and by its declining to recognize the claims of the Missouri Home Missionary Society as an auxiliary.

But, with the denominational zeal that had already been aroused at the West, it was inevitable that cases should occur in which the jealousy of Congregational churches on the ground would take offence at the extending of that aid from the Society which Presbyterian churches had been accustomed to receive, and which they felt that they had a right to claim. The Society was forced by the pressure of circumstances to adhere to its rule, that *all* the home-mission funds of Presbyteries whose churches received aid should be poured into its treasury; and offence was taken when extra collections for the special aid of feeble churches were made by Presbyterian churches, even while their annual contributions to the Society were not diminished. Unless it would refuse to aid the churches of Presbyteries in which such an instance occurred, it was publicly threatened by the organ of Western Congregationalists with having the funds which it derived from New England diverted from its treasury and applied directly by Congregationalists at the West. Alton Presbytery, with its extended mission-field, for which an exploring missionary had for many years been annually appointed, was one of the first to complain of the application of a rule that virtually forbade it to cultivate its own field. Yet to abandon it in its extremity would be virtually to abandon all feeble Presbyteries and struggling churches which the Society refused to aid. Such a policy was inadmissible, suicidal; and the Assembly felt itself constrained not only by principles of expediency, but the obligations of duty, to reject it. The claims of the Church Extension Committee were presented by the Assembly to the churches, and were met by an enlarged sympathy throughout the bounds of the Church.

The affection long directed toward the American Home Missionary Society was shaken only by the conviction that it could no longer, in consistency with the rules it had adopted and the circumstances in which it was placed, do justice to the claims of the Presbyterian churches. So late as 1862, the Society acknowledged the receipt of nearly forty thousand dollars for the previous year from persons known to be Presbyterians, or from churches connected with Presbyteries, or places where there was known to be only a Presbyterian church. Yet from this sum, or from any considerable portion of it, Presbyterian churches could derive no aid.

But already (1861) the General Assembly, "in accordance with the obvious indications of Divine Providence, and agreeably to the Constitution of the Church," had assumed "the responsibility of conducting the work of Home Missions within its bounds." A permanent committee, known as the Presbyterian Committee of Home Missions, to be located in New York, was appointed by the Assembly; and from November, 1861, when the committee commenced operations, to the time of the meeting of the General Assembly in the following year, more than twenty thousand dollars, in addition to seven thousand dollars secured during the preceding six months, were raised to enable it to extend its efforts. In 1863 the amount contributed by the churches to be dispensed through the same channel was nearly fifty-two thousand dollars; and in 1864 it had risen to over seventy thousand dollars.

The measures of the Assembly resulting in the establishment of a permanent Committee on Ministerial Education date from 1854. In respect to this department of Christian effort there was at that time a growing conviction, owing to the apparent failure of the co-operative plan, and the lack of system in the operations of Presbyteries and Synods, that something should be done to harmonize the plans and concentrate the energies of the Church. In 1856 the committee was appointed, and located at New York. In 1858 an act of incorporation was secured; and since that period the Presbyteries and Synods have largely co-operated with the committee in their work. The receipts of the committee for 1864 were nearly fifteen thousand dollars.

In 1846 an overture on the subject of doctrinal tracts was presented to the Assembly. The object which it had in view was favorably regarded; but, although it was considered by several successive Assemblies, it was not till 1852 that a standing Committee of Publication was appointed. In 1853 the number of the committee was enlarged, and measures were taken to secure funds for the erection of a house of publication. In 1854 the number was again enlarged, so as to consist of fifteen persons; and in 1855 the name of the committee was changed from that of Doctrinal Tract Committee to The Presbyterian Publication Committee. In 1857 they were encouraged by the Assembly to publish "such works of an evangelical character as may be profitable to the Church at large." Meanwhile, mainly through the liberality of a member of the Church residing in Philadelphia,[1] a house of publication had been secured, and the publication of the Church Psalmist—authorized by the Assembly for the use of the churches—had passed into the hands of the committee. In 1860 the Assembly recommenced an effort to secure a working capital for the business of publication, and authorized the committee to employ an agent for the purpose. No marked progress was made till 1863, when the effort was made to secure a fund of fifty thousand dollars. Nearly three-fifths of this amount was collected before April,

[1] John A. Brown, Esq.

1864; and by the Assembly of that year it was resolved to prosecute the effort to secure the whole amount. The importance of the cause was more generally appreciated than ever before, while the publications of the committee enforced its claims upon the patronage of the churches.

The actual increase of the aggregate membership of the Church at large during the period that has elapsed since the division has by no means been proportioned to the real progress of the Church. The causes which operated to reduce its numbers—viz., the revived zeal for Congregationalism, which drew off no inconsiderable element, as well as the Southern secession, which resulted in the withdrawal, in 1858, of the Synods of Missouri, Virginia, Kentucky, Tennessee, West Tennessee, and Mississippi, embracing twenty-one Presbyteries and over fifteen thousand members—have been already noticed. But, notwithstanding these adverse influences, the advance from 1840 till 1864, according to the reports for those years respectively, was—of Presbyteries, from eighty-nine to one hundred and five; of ministers, from twelve hundred and sixty to sixteen hundred and forty-four; of churches, from thirteen hundred and seventy-five to fourteen hundred and forty-two; and of members, from one hundred and two thousand and sixty to one hundred and thirty-eight thousand and seventy-four; while the efficiency and unity of the Church as a body had been vastly increased.

Its growth in the Western States for a considerable period was greatly checked in consequence of the violent manner in which the division of the Church had been effected. A prejudice was created against the Presbyterian system, and the uncertainty of the future policy of the denomination inspired distrust on the part of some who might otherwise have labored cordially and zealously in connection with it. Missionaries in the new States found their position so unfavorble that in some cases they felt constrained to abandon the field. It was occupied in repeated instances by men who, without the sympathy of the New England churches, sought to build up religious institutions in which the friends of sound doctrine and order could repose but feeble confidence. In spite of all obstacles, however, new churches were formed and Presbyteries erected at an early period in the new States of Wisconsin, Iowa, Minnesota, and Kansas, as well as in California.[1]

In 1861, the long-continued agitation of the slavery question in political circles culminated in the secession of State after State from the Federal Union, and the inauguration of a "Confederate" Government, based avowedly on slavery as its corner-stone. The General Assembly of that year met at the very time when the first actual conflicts of the desolating war that has followed had taken place. Resolutions were passed appropriate to the occasion, and a day was appointed to be observed as a day of fasting, humiliation, and prayer. In 1862 the action of the Assembly evinced its steadfast and devoted loyalty, and its conviction that the entire insurrectionary movement "can be traced to one primordial root, and one only,—African slavery, the love of it, and a determination to make it perpetual." A copy of the resolutions passed by the Assembly, and accompanied by a respectful letter, was forwarded to the President of the United States, and met with an appropriate and gratifying response. In 1863 the Assembly, "true to its traditions," showed itself enthusiastically loyal and patriotic, and reiterated the testimony it had so long and earnestly borne in respect to

---

[1] More detailed accounts of early missionary labor in these States have been omitted, from the necessary limits of these volumes.

the evils of slavery, and in vindication of the principles which it had so often avowed. In 1864 the Assembly reaffirmed the principles and renewed the declarations of previous General Assemblies, so far as applicable to the state of public affairs. It recognized the hand of God in the disappointments and delays of the war, by which "the complete destruction of the vile system of human bondage" was rendered more sure. It made acknowledgment of national sins, and exhorted the churches to prayer for the deliverance of the land and the prosperity of Christ's kingdom through the blessings of national peace and fraternity. It expressed its cordial sympathy with the Government in its efforts to suppress the rebellion, and directed that a copy of its resolutions, duly authenticated, should be transmitted to the President of the United States.

The terrible crisis of civil war has proved a trying one to the Church; but it was a crisis for which, in the providence of God, it had been wisely prepared. Its record was one at which it had no occasion to blush. It had allowed in its annual Assemblies full and free discussion. Of the resolutions it had passed, there was not one line which it could wish to blot. Not a single step had been taken which it needed to retrace. While the war had drawn off large numbers of its membership to the scenes of actual conflict, and deprived the churches, in many cases weak and impoverished, of their presence and their aid,—while not a few of its most efficient and devoted friends had fallen in battle, and large numbers of its ministers had served as chaplains in the army,—it not only maintained its position, but made actual advance in membership, as well as a large increase in the measure of its charitable contributions.

A fraternal spirit toward the other branch of the Presbyterian Church has likewise been evinced on all suitable occasions. In 1838 the Assembly declared their willingness to "agree to any reasonable measures tending to an amicable adjustment of the difficulties existing in the Presbyterian Church." In 1839, to avert all unpleasant controversy and prevent all unhappy litigation, they proposed a plan of amicable settlement, which, while securing their own privileges as Presbyterians, relinquished to the other branch of the Church "all chartered rights, institutions, and funds."[1]

In 1846 the desire for union was expressed, and the proposal of a mutual recognition of each other as brethren was made by the Assembly to the members of the other Assembly, by uniting together in the communion of the Lord's Supper. The rejection of this proposal produced grief rather than alienation; and when the crisis of civil war arrived and the Southern churches withdrew from their connection with the other Assembly, the prospect of reunion appeared more favorable. Slavery no longer presented a bar to mutual sympathy; both Assemblies had been brought to stand substantially on the same platform of ecclesiastical missionary policy; while from the first they had adhered to the same standards.

The other branch of the Church was left at the time of the division in the full possession and in the energetic employment of all the machinery necessary to its equipment for its proper work as a distinct denomination. It embraced, indeed, some elements not in entire sympathy with it. Quite a number of its ministers and members were dissatisfied with the exscinding measures of 1837; and some—like Dr. Spring,[2] of New

[1] Digest, p. 562.

[2] Dr. McDowell's views were similar to those of Dr. Spring.

York, and Dr. Spencer, of Brooklyn—entered against them their strong and decided protest. A considerable number rather accepted than approved them, and in silent acquiescence adhered to a body whose acts they would not endorse. The unprecedented methods adopted by those who chose to secure their legal rights by interrupting the proceedings at the opening of the Assembly of 1838 repelled them from connection with the body to which they properly belonged, and induced them finally to co-operate more or less heartily with those with whom they were still ecclesiastically connected. A decided anti-slavery sentiment, moreover, prevailed in certain portions of the body; but its disturbing influence was restrained by the overwhelming preponderance of the party which contended, in behalf of their Southern brethren, that the subject of slavery, after the already sufficient utterances of the General Assembly on the subject, should be left in their hands.

In these circumstances, the Church proceeded energetically in the prosecution of its work. Its methods of operation inspired confidence, and to its missionary enterprise the whole Southern field was open. In the new States of Arkansas and Texas,[1] as well as in Missouri, Louisiana, Mississippi, Alabama, and Georgia, its progress was steady, and in some cases rapid; while at the North and West its attitude was also aggressive. Its missions to foreign lands were carried on with vigor and success through its "Board of Foreign Missions;" its educational efforts and its work of publication made steady progress; and aid to feeble congregations, in the erection of houses of worship, was bestowed through its Board of Church Extension. Its membership, which in 1840 had been only about

---

[1] Details of early missionary labor in Arkansas and Texas have been omitted, on account of the limits of the work.

one hundred and twenty-six thousand, had risen in 1860 to two hundred and ninety-two thousand nine hundred and twenty-seven; while its Presbyteries had increased from ninety-five to one hundred and seventy-one, its ministers from thirteen hundred and four to two thousand six hundred and fifty-six, and its churches from nineteen hundred and eleven to three thousand five hundred and thirty-one.

But, unfortunately, a very considerable portion of its strength was within the limits of those States which in 1861 seceded from the Federal Union; and upon the Assembly of that year the long-deferred question of slavery pressed with the weight of an avalanche. The General Assembly could not evade the issue. It might, indeed, decline to recognize loyalty to established government as a Christian virtue; but, if it did so, its course would be repudiated by the great mass of its Northern constituents. No longer blinded by zeal to maintain its Southern alliance,—the prospects and advantages of the continuance of which were more than questionable,—the Assembly vindicated its loyalty, and manifested its repugnance to a rebellion initiated in the interests of slavery, by appropriate resolutions, which were passed by a vote of one hundred and fifty-six yeas to sixty-six nays.

The result of this action was the secession of the Southern churches and Presbyteries almost in a body, and the formation of a Southern General Assembly. The membership of the residuary portion of the Church was thus greatly reduced; and in 1863, according to the report of that year, the Church numbered only one hundred and twenty-seven Presbyteries and two hundred and twenty-seven thousand five hundred and seventy-five members.

In these circumstances, the disposition in favor of a reunion of the two branches of the Church naturally received a new impulse. Two great causes of alienation had been removed,—the desire to favor the South by silence on the subject of slavery, on one side, and hostility to *ecclesiastical* missionary organizations, on the other. The Assembly of 1863 evinced its loyalty to the General Government and its fidelity to the cause of freedom by appropriate resolutions, and, while expressing their judgment against the expediency of any decided action on the subject of reunion, recognized the fraternal correspondence which had been opened with the "Constitutional" General Assembly as "initiative," and as instrumental in promoting the mutual charity and clearer views which might serve to prepare the way for a beneficent union.

The Assemblies of 1864 both evinced a fraternal spirit, and were alike outspoken on the subjects of slavery and of loyalty to the National Government. The delegates of each to the other were courteously and kindly received, and it was felt by many members of both that the era of reunion could not be far distant. For the present, however, neither body was prepared to recommend the adoption of any immediate action, but was rather disposed to leave the policy of the future to be shaped by the growing spirit of mutual Christian charity and the wisdom which further experience might afford.

For years to come, the influence of the sympathies and prejudices which date from the era of the division will in certain quarters continue to be felt. But already a new generation has entered upon the stage, and the passions of the past are yielding to the cooler judgment of the present. Men are no longer identified in our estimate with the measures to which, under the pressure of circumstances, they lent their sanction. We can discern errors and mistakes of which their authors were unconscious, and we can make due allowance for men who, acting as they believed from principle, were yet so warped in their views as to diverge from the line of policy which the ethics of the gospel would have required them to follow. Adopting the same standards, aiming at the same ends, studying the same lesson, reverencing the same founders, reading the same history, the members of both branches of the Church must unconsciously approximate, till the line of separation between them becomes, except in ecclesiastical organization, ideal and intangible, and the difficulties in the way of reunion become simply those of convenient and effective organization. Hand in hand they will pursue together the common object of hastening forward by evangelical and missionary effort that blessed period when the words of prophecy shall have been fulfilled, and the kingdoms of this world shall have become the kingdoms of our Lord and of his Christ, and he shall reign for ever and ever.

We have thus traced from feeble beginnings the rise and progress in this country of a Christian denomination which has attained a position second to that of no other in social influence, intellectual cultivation, and the means of extended usefulness. Its history is largely identified with that of the nation. It has planted far and wide religious as well as literary institutions, under which millions have been trained. It has evinced its unswerving patriotism and loyalty during the most trying periods of our national existence. It has sent forth to take their places at the bar, in the senate, or in the pulpit, men whom it has educated, of whom the nation may well be proud, and whose names it will not willingly let die. Its annals are enriched with the frequent records of that heroism which has characterized the efforts of pioneer missionaries and self-denying pastors to evangelize the land and speak in the ears of heedless men the words of eternal life. Throughout the Middle,

Western, and Southern States there is scarcely a nook or corner to which the representatives of its faith and order have not penetrated, bearing with them, wherever they have gone, the principles of sound morality and the intelligence of a large-hearted Christian manhood.

From the earliest period the Church has been the tried and consistent friend of civil and religious freedom. Suffering for a time, in certain portions of the land, from the intolerance that pursued her across the ocean, she learned, almost in her cradle, to detest and rebuke the iniquity that would thrust her beneath the blighting shadow of a State-Church establishment. In the Revolutionary struggle she could boast her Witherspoon, Rodgers, Caldwell, Read, and Duffield, representatives of scores of others true as steel to their country's cause. Liberal in spirit, and not unfrequently—especially in the early part of the present century—open to the charge of laxness in ecclesiastical order, she has combined in an admirable measure attachment to sound doctrine with a generous recognition of other branches of the Church, and a hearty co-operation, so far as circumstances would warrant, in plans of charitable and missionary effort in behalf of a perishing world. And now, embracing in her communion (under both Assemblies) a membership of nearly four hundred thousand, with a full equipment of schools, colleges, seminaries, and missionary and charitable organizations at her command, she is manifestly better prepared than ever before for the great work to which the providence of God has called her, and the future destinies of the country cannot fail to feel the impress of her shaping hand.

It is not to be disguised that some mistakes have been committed,—that there are passages in the history of the Church which we peruse with saddened hearts and with feelings of regret. But even these may yield us their lessons, and afford richer contributions for future guidance than more inviting portions of the record. I have endeavored to present them with impartial fidelity; yet the conclusions of the historian most unbiassed are ever based, from the necessities of the case, on a partial acquaintance with all the facts that are important to the formation of a correct judgment; and history itself is ever only a nearer or more remote approximation to the truth.

It is well that the Presbyterian Church, moving manifestly on to a more wonderful future, should be made familiar with its past career. It needs the lights of experience to guide its steps. With these shining upon its path, and with the providence of God leading it on and still onward to more extended usefulness and to enlarged plans of effort, its future can scarcely fail to furnish even more inviting and wonderful records than its past. Our nation is still in its youth. In its present gigantic conflict it reminds us of a Hercules strangling the serpent even in his cradle; and it is not a mere fond fancy that our Church is destined also to grow with its growth and strengthen with its strength. And when this broad continent, restored to peace and a unity secured and perpetuated by just government, shall be overspread from ocean to ocean with the institutions of civilization, learning, and religion, when our rapidly-multiplying millions, swelled by accessions from foreign lands, shall cover hill and valley, shore and sea, with the testimonials and triumphs of their enterprise, the Christian patriot can invoke for its lasting prosperity no pledge more fitting to inspire hope and confidence than the prevalence of those principles of which the Presbyterian Church in this land has shown itself to be a worthy representative and a faithful guardian.

Ten years have elapsed since the preceding paragraphs of this concluding chapter of the history were written. The anticipation of the reunion of the two branches of the Church, which was expressed in them, has been accomplished. By an evident preconcert on the part of leading minds on both sides, St. Louis was selected as the place of meeting for the two Assemblies of 1866. Steps were then taken which led to the appointment of a joint-committee representing the two bodies, to which the subject of reunion was given in charge. Year by year progress was made in overcoming the difficulties that stood in the way of reunion, until, in 1869, the two Assemblies, acting in concert, met alike in the city of New York, and adopted such measures as were necessary to perfect the work. In 1870, a single General Assembly at Philadelphia represented the united Church, in which were now combined long-separated elements, no longer estranged, but

"Like kindred drops commingled into one."

The narrative of the reunion, with the enthusiasm it excited and the liberality it called forth, adds another, and by no means the least interesting, chapter to the history of the Church, but it belongs to the annalist of the future to present in their proper bearings and relations the facts of whose full significance, by reason of our nearness to them, we are incapacitated to judge.

INDEX.

CPSIA information can be obtained
at www.ICGtesting.com
Printed in the USA
LVHW101921170422
716440LV00004BA/251

9 783752 592160